Praise for Book 1: *A Little Knowledge*

"Richard Hawley, one of my favorite writers, offers a rare, dazzling view of an original boy's inner life."
—Hilma Wolitzer, author of *Hearts*

"Richard Hawley explores the numinous life force we can only sense, sometimes glimpse from the corner of our eye…It is vital to our lives, and Hawley illuminates this other world in this lovely volume."
—Mike Ruhlman, author of *Boys Themselves*

"Explores, with eloquence and sensitivity, the secret life of children and the unexpected moments that linger in memory and give shape to our souls."
—Blake Bailey, author of *Cheever: A Life*

Praise for Book 2: *Knowing It All*

"In Richard Hawley's absorbing *Knowing It All*, Jonathan Force, a successful and culturally influential man, examines the arc of his charmed life and is shaken by what he discovers. As the ironic title Knowing It All signals, Force does not know it all. As he reviews his path from boy to man, from lover to husband, from student to public intellectual, his introspection is suffused with memories and longings unmet. What is the measure of a life? How can everything that appears to be right feel so irrelevant? What is real and what is a sham? Writing with crystalline prose and profound insight into the interior life, Hawley entwines a singular man's story with an inquiry into what makes a life meaningful. A gripping, powerful and deeply felt novel."
—Lynn Sloan, author of *Principles of Navigation*

BOOKS BY RICHARD HAWLEY

FICTION
The Three Lives Of Jonathan Force
Greeves Passing
The Source Of Longing
The Other World
The Guru
Paul And Juliana
The Headmaster's Wife
The Headmaster's Papers

NON-FICTION
Forward and No Retreat: A History of the Linsly School
I Can Learn From You: Boys as Relational Learners
Souls in Boxes
For Whom the Boy Toils
Kiski: The Story of a Boys' School
Reaching Boys/Teaching Boys
Beyond the Icarus Factor
Hard Lessons and Other Talks to the School
Papers From the Headmaster
Hail University! A Century of University School Life
In Praise of the Teaching Life
Seeing Things: A Chronicle of Surprises
Building Drug Free Schools
The Purposes of Pleasure
A School Answers Back
Coming Through School (Editor)

POETRY
Twenty-One Visits with a Darkly Sun-Tanned Angel
The Headmaster's Poems
St. Julian
With Love to my Survivors
Aspects of Vision

The Three Lives of Jonathan Force

Richard Hawley

*For Keith,
Patient reader, with
gratitude for his
friendship,*

R

Fomite
Burlington, VT

Copyright © 2016 Richard Hawley
Author photo: M.S. Watson

All rights reserved. No part of this book may be reproduced in any form or by any means without the prior written consent of the publisher, except in the case of brief quotations used in reviews and certain other noncommercial uses permitted by copyright law.

This is a work of fiction. Any resemblance between the characters of this novel and real people, living or dead, is merely coincidental.

ISBN-13: 978-1-942515-17-3
Library of Congress Control Number: 2015960524

Fomite
58 Peru Street
Burlington, VT 05401
www.fomitepress.com

Cover art — © Mary Hawley

For Karl, Gary and Peter

Grateful acknowledgement is made to Tim Johnston and to Short Story America Press for permission to "novelize" the cycle of stories originally published as *The Other World*. Three of the stories in that volume--"The End of Baseball," "The Ottawanna Way," and "For Love"-- were also published, successively, in volumes I, II, and III of the Short Story America anthologies. This material composes the heart of A Little Knowledge, the first "life" of Jonathan Force.

Book I

A Little Knowledge

Not in entire forgetfulness,
Not in utter nakedness,
But trailing clouds of glory do we come...
Shades of the prison house begin to close
Upon the growing boy...

—Wordsworth, "Ode on Intimations of Immortality from Recollections of Early Childhood"

Chapter One

I WAS BORN INTO Christmas. It's true, and I can tell you everything about it. I must have been about one. I was lying there, curled into the damp, sweet, lovely warmth of my own sleep when I opened my eyes to it. There was that milky winter light that lets you see the air, and the gray and pink swirls of the wallpaper were moving a little in the light, and through the dark wooden archway of the open door I could see the spangles and flashing jewels on the evergreen boughs in the living room. The plastic kitchen radio was playing Joy to the World, which I did not know as words then, but I knew it, and it grew in me, swelled up in me until, just as I knew she would, my mother's beautiful dark figure filled the doorway arch, and for a moment all I knew was the shape of her red mouth, which said, "Merry Christmas, Jonathan Force."

Then there was laughter, mother's and mine, fused together, and I was lifted wonderfully, still wet and warm, up into her arms, and over her shoulder the tree with its sparkles and pine sweet smell was no longer striped by the slats of my crib, and I was carried from a happiness to a still greater happiness so fine and so full I did not believe I could bear it.

And that is the way Christmas has always been in my life—being picked up and carried into an aching beauty, a beauty that opens and opens. Christmas was the first thing I really knew, and since that time the other necessary and important things have gathered themselves to that first knowing. Of course the family gathered, in the morning my mother and father and sister, later in the day my grandparents Nana and Papa and their son, my uncle Desmond. There were presents, mounds of brightly wrapped and bowed presents under the tree, then as guests arrived, box loads and bag loads of more presents. There were presents stacked on the lamp tables, heaped on the piano, and so many of them opened and unopened on the floor that we waded through wrappings and tissue and swizzles of ribbon in order to cross the room. From the midday arrival of guests until their departure late that night there would be a fire in the fireplace, a strong crackling blaze when first lit, then quieting to a radiant mound of lavender, blue and buttery gold. The scent of the burning hardwood met the blood-rich cooking smells of the roasting turkey, the sage dressing, creamed onions, apple pies and pumpkin pies. As the dinner was readied, drinks were prepared, amber cocktails in martini glasses with delicate stems. Secure in the vee of each glass was the scarlet orb of a candied cherry. In time it was understood that these were to be saved for me, The ritual of handing them over became to me a kind of sacrament, token after token of pulpy cherry sweetness, of Christmas itself, held between tongue and palate for as long as I could stand it.

In the course of what must have been many years, Christmas came to include the out doors. I always felt that the secret of the day, the secret of winter itself, was the lively tension between outdoors and in, between shallow breathed ventures out into the cold and blessed relief inside. From my first winter swaddling at the hands of others, I was taken with the elaborate and rather formal ritual of girding for the cold: knitted caps, long heavy coats the arms of which grew stiff in the freezing air, woolen scarves sealing the neck, mittens which within minutes of true cold reduced the fingered hand to a numbed club, high black rubber boots fastened tight with complicated metal clasps. To be outdoors in winter cold was stolen time. I was out where seemingly no one was supposed to be. The cold clarified everything. It seemed to want silence. The easiest thing became effortful in the cold, but marvelous for that. Then snow came into the picture, the whirl and blur of it in the air, thrilling the first time, thrilling always. Snow was specks and clumps of lively light against the gray of winter afternoons. Snow at night, silent snow, whitening the void.

I cannot tell you where I got this picture, although it is a fixture in my Christmas memory. The impression is so cold and fresh that I could be there now. It is deep winter, and I am stopped still in a sloping field of cedar trees. It is late afternoon, and the sun is about to set. The sky is clear, and as I look out toward the horizon, the cold glass blue overhead passes into vivid rose and peach and shimmering gold as it meets the sinking sun on the horizon line. I am fascinated by the look of the snow resting on the branches of the cedars, how the snow holds rose and smoky blue afternoon light, and all of it is saying "afterward," as if beauty itself was explaining the end of beauty.

Somehow the snow on the cedar bows in the declining afternoon and the cedar boughs sparkling with lights and ornaments beyond my crib on that first Christmas morning form a single picture, and it is all Christmas, and it is forever about to begin and yet has always been over.

A few years after my mother gathered me up and walked me under the archway into Christmas, I was taken to church one winter night and beheld Jesus in the manger. I recall that it was a Lutheran church, not that we were Lutherans or that the idea of Lutheran would have meant anything to me at the time. But my mother had said it was the Lutheran church, and that became important to me. The sanctuary was darkened for a Christmas service of some kind, and it smelled of the musty hymnals and of the slightly sweet, slightly sour smell of flowers standing out too long. A bright light from high up in the apse beamed down on the manger where colorfully robed shepherds knelt and little goats and lambs looked on. The light shone directly on the baby's face in his crib.

This was the holy child. I don't know if mother told me or I heard it in the carols or if I just knew it. But everything that evening was about the holy child, how long the world had waited and now here he was. The world had been waiting for a baby. I had only to hear that to realize I had always known it. Of course it was a holy child. Wasn't I?

Everything about that Lutheran service for the holy child was serious, gentle, and strangely sad. The baby Jesus had always been coming.

And it came to pass in those days, that there went out a decree from Caesar Augustus that all the world should be taxed...

It was important to kings, it was important to wise men. Angels and shepherds were waiting for it. The waiting was unbearable and very beautiful. It was like waiting for Christmas to come. Silent night, holy night. Then the announcement, the arrival—even more beautiful, but cheerful and loud. Hark the herald, joy to the world. It came upon a midnight clear in the sanctuary of the Lutheran church.

Chapter Two

So that was the first of the Three Great Things, the coming of the holy child, and just as it was in my case, the coming involved Christmas. But there was the other story about my coming. In the course of my growing up I heard it again and again, and when I knew enough to ask, I would check on the facts and details. The other story is not a very good one, far from beautiful and even farther from Christmas.

I was born during the war, World War II, near the end. Later in school I was confused about the war because I felt I had long known the enemies. I had lived with them, and they were good, kind people—my family. That is, my mother's parents, Nana and Papa, were English and German. They had fallen in love and gotten married after the previous war, World War I, in which my German grandfather who had become an American and was fighting for the Americans got shot in the leg and was shipped to England where my English grandmother met him, nursed him and fell in love with him. She followed him back to Chicago where they married and had my mother and my uncle. They were such kind, beautiful people, and they made such a beautiful house.

England was married to Germany in that house, and when my father got drafted into the Navy, he had to leave his job as a trumpet player in the dance band and board a battleship in the Pacific. My mother worked as a secretary in an office, but when she got pregnant with me and then very sick she had to quit work and move in with her parents. There wasn't much money then, she told me. The Navy pay wasn't very much, and so she could no longer afford her own place which, she told me when I was much older, made her feel like a girl again and not a woman, and this made her feel worthless and small. Then she got sick and almost died. The good doctors, people told her later, were all in the service, and she had a bad one who didn't understand what was wrong with her. We know what was wrong now, a condition called *edema*. Edema made my mother swell up to almost twice her size. Her legs and arms filled with fluid, and her joints—elbows, knees, ankles—felt as if they were about to burst open. My mother told me about sitting in a chair and watching in helpless tears as her legs filled with fluid and her ankles swelled enormously so that the flesh of her legs spilled out over the sides of her shoes. I cannot bear picturing my mother picturing this. She had been such a beautiful woman. The edema, doctors told her later, could have killed her. Moreover, there were simple medicines that could have helped, but mother's doctor didn't know about them, and she suffered. Possibly, I had edema too, although no one has ever told me that. It cannot have been good, my mother so unhappy, feeling no longer a grown woman but a little girl back in her childhood room in her parents' house, her husband far away on a battle ship in the Pacific where, he wrote, the Japanese suicide planes dive-bombed the ship, the U.S.S. West Virginia, as often as they could. What could she do but sit there waiting for the swelling to subside, wondering if my father would ever come home, wondering if she would ever have her exquisite woman's body again?

Whether or not the edema was to blame, I was cut out of my mother by a Caesarean section, which further weakened her, and I came into the world early, undersized, and quite ill. I had pneumonia, of which I have no recollection, except in a kind of bodily awareness that has inclined me to bronchial troubles all my life.

I had to stay in the hospital two weeks after my mother was able to go home. I wish I could remember what that was like, or maybe I don't. I'm sure my mother came to see me, or somebody, probably Nana, did. They had to have started feeding me, formula in a bottle, not my mother's breast. It feels funny to have only a voided impression of all of that, to have no feeling or recollection of any kind until the Christmas story. By then my father was back from the war. I can't remember anything about that either. Sometimes I think I do, but it's just the memory of a photograph we have of my father, still in his navy uniform, the old fashioned dark blue wool kind with the white stripes around the open neck on the jersey and the square flap at the back. My father is standing in our back yard in that uniform, looking pleased and kind of jaunty. With one arm he is holding me to his chest in a blanket, and his other hand is gripping his trumpet under the valves, as if he has just played a riff. He doesn't look quite related to me in the picture. He looks like a boy.

As hard as my mother's life was while my father was away in the Pacific, she said it didn't get much better after he returned. My father had to get work and save some money before they could move out of my grandparents' house and live on their own again. My mother didn't like this at all, and one day my father made a big mistake that made him feel uncomfortable for years. It happened one morning when he came back into the house after doing an errand. He went upstairs to the bedroom to look for mother. He said he had a sense of her in the room as he entered. She was leaning over the bed, making it up, and my father reached out and, he said, gave her bottom a good squeeze. But it wasn't my mother; it was Nana. She was startled and then quite angry. My father was so surprised and embarrassed he couldn't say anything. He tried to explain and to apologize, but Nana was too flustered to hear him, and she bolted from the room. Once, not too many years before he died, my father tried to tell the story as a funny story, but even then I could feel the misery in it. But I think that goosing of Nana accelerated my mother and father's departure plans and their eventual independence.

There are plenty of stories like that from that period in my waking up to the world—stories that I will never forget, stories that trouble me or that for some reason won't subside into oblivion, but they are not good, not holy and alive like the Christmas story. For a long stretch there I felt not only far from a holy child, I felt that the child I was and the things that kept happening to me were a teasing mockery of what I sensed should have been a much, much better world. There was only one miracle that I remember from that time. It involved the biggest turtle I have ever seen.

One cool gray spring morning my mother let me out into our small fenced in back yard to play. There was not much to do in the yard. There was no swing or sand box, just a narrow concrete walkway to a back gate that opened up onto a narrow alley of cinders. I was shuffling along this walk toward the alley, where it was possible to get a glimpse sometimes of the trash man's blinkered horse or of a stray cat out on a rove or possibly rats, which were known to slither about the trash cans set out in the alley. About half way down the walk I saw something amazing, the large, oily looking black shell of a turtle. It was enormous, half as big as I was, its girth wider than the walkway. I didn't think turtle at first, because all I could see was the great heavy looking shell, but then its black scaly head came out a little and looked around, and I knew. I could not have seen a real turtle before, but I knew this was one, and I my heart flew up, and I jumped back a little because I was afraid it might bite me. I wanted it to move, so I stamped my feet on the concrete, but all it did was draw in its head. I just stood there, bent at the waist, looking hard at the shell, I think for quite a while. I was certain this was an agent from the other world. Then it moved a little, and I was startled again. It occurred to me that mother must see this. I felt it would amaze her to see it, amaze her that I had found it. Inside, mother was doing dishes, and it took her a long time to make sense of what I was telling her and even longer before she would come outside into the yard to look. When we got to the spot, the turtle was gone. I ran to the back fence hoping to catch sight of it, but it was gone. I assured my mother it had been there, indicating its size with my arms. My mother smiled in an odd way, which let me know she didn't believe me. Where would a turtle live around here, she asked. We lived in a densely packed neighborhood of wooden clapboard houses, close to the elevated train, far from any open land or rivers or streams. A huge black turtle was as likely to show up in our yard as a puma or an ostrich. Mother went back into the house, and I remember standing for some time in the empty yard, thinking. The turtle, for some reason, had appeared, and I understood that I must bear the burden of this kind of knowledge alone.

Blackie, our duck, was not quite a miracle, but I will never forget him. I was four by then, my sister Annabel was six, and we had moved to a fresh, raw housing development on the prairie edge of Chicago's northwest side. My father worked for a big bank now in the city, and the bank staff was invited to a summer outing in a state park. There was a picnic, boat rides, and races and games and contests for the kids. There were contests for the grownups, too, and one of them, which fascinated me, was to ring a duck. The rings were wooden hoops about the circumference of a small pie. For a quarter you got three hoops and tried to toss them around the neck of one of the ducks huddled in a little pen about ten yards behind the throwing counter. I stood a long time watching, and nobody succeeded in landing a hoop around a duck's neck. The exercise was actually kind of upsetting. The tossed hoops grazed the ducks' heads and flanks and sent them scuttling and quacking into each other. My father appeared and bought three hoops. I was barely paying attention, and then there was a tremendous shriek of surprise and laughter, because my father's toss had fallen around the neck of a black duck. That meant we had won him; he was ours. Annabel was so surprised and happy she started to cry. She loved animals of all kinds. She cut out pictures of especially cute ones and taped them to the top of her dresser. The man selling the rings said the ducks' wings were "clipped" so that they couldn't fly away. My dad held the duck in the crook of his elbow and exchanged jokes and cracks with the people standing around, and then he handed the duck down to Annabel, who was so transported with pleasure she could not speak.

As we drove home in the car afterward, Annabel still clutching and petting the duck, my mother and father talked about what we would do with it. There was the terrifying suggestion in the air that we would have to "get rid" of it. I felt Annabel tense up at the words, her eyes welling with tears. From the back seat I shouted out, "We're keeping it! We're keeping it!" to make Annabel feel better. When we got home, my father went down into the basement and reworked a big cardboard box our washing machine had come in, and put the duck inside. Mother and Annabel brought down a little bowl of water and some cut up vegetables for the duck then left us alone with it. For a long time we just watched it, and Annabel decided to name it Blackie, as it was a black duck. I was now as mesmerized and in love with Blackie as Annabel was. This was partly because the force of her feeling was so overwhelming I felt drawn up into it. But there was something about the duck itself that was impossible to resist. It was just so beautiful, if that is the word, or cute. Something about it was more vivid and wonderful than we were. I could not stop looking at it. The perfectly rounded top of its shiny black head somehow matched the beautiful curve of its breast, and its bright black eyes flashed a fiery fleck of gold in the basement light.

It was not easy to pick Blackie up and hold him, because he would get excited and push away with surprising force with his little legs and duck feet. But every few minutes we could not bear not to pick him up again and hold him close, so we took turns grabbing him up out of the box until in one clumsy attempt he got away from us and disappeared between the furnace and the basement wall. Even my father with the aid of a broom handle could not dislodge Blackie from behind the furnace, so Annabel and I had to bathe and go to bed in agonizing uncertainty.

In the bright morning, my father was able to retrieve Blackie, and all was well again. Annabel decided to take Blackie's box outside, so that he could breathe the air and get some sun. We also were eager to show him to the Weisblatts, our neighbors. Not wanting to lose him again, Annabel took special care lifting Blackie out of the box, but as she held him quietly in her arms, something—a shout or a car door slamming—startled him and he erupted out my sister's grasp and onto the sidewalk down which he scooted with phenomenal speed, trailed by me, my sister, and the shrieking Weisblatts. I remember a warm, smiling feeling in my heart because this was an adventure and Blackie's wings were "clipped," which meant he could not really escape us—but then he did. After a run of perhaps a quarter of a block, Blackie arose. Powerful and sure in flight he ascended up over the power lines, then the treetops and in a minute or two disappeared into the sunny blue sky. Blackie's escape was so sudden and so sure that it seemed to me, and I suspect Annabel too, natural and right. The loss was stunning, but something about Blackie had seemed from the outset too good to be true. Blackie, I decided, was a clue, but far from the whole story.

Chapter Three

Of course I had no idea then how far away I was from anything like the whole story. It took a long time for me to realize that something in the world *doesn't want* us to see the whole story. Something wants to overwhelm us with the ordinary, usually bad stories that carry us away from, not into, the better world. Some kind of force—including plenty of people—won't let us see or even talk about the golden side of things, as if they cannot bear so much unspoiled possibility, such gladness. Sometimes for days and weeks on end I felt as if the holy child were being slapped out of me. These were the times when seemingly everybody, but especially my father, was telling me I couldn't do anything right. My father liked to joke about me, "Jonathan, you get dumber every day," but it was no joke to me. Some days I knew I was dumber, and I remember feeling that there was no end to how dumb I could get, and I began to think up ways to conceal from others how dumb I was, a dumbness at my very core of which I was so ashamed I could barely breathe.

When I say I thought the holy child was being slapped out of me, I don't mean slaps or punches right in the face. My slaps were what my father called "cracks in the head." Every now and then my father would look at me or at something I had done or just hear about something I had done and then give me a crack in the head. These cracks in the head were jarring, upward clouts against the back of my skull. If the annoyance was minor, if I just said something that irritated him, he might just crack me with the first two fingers of his right hand. But if he was really mad, I'd get the full force of his open palm against the back of my head. I hated getting cracks in the head. I never got used to them, and the worst were the ones that I did not see coming, which, because they came up from behind me, was a lot of the time. My father wasn't always angry with me, and when he was in a good mood, he liked to make jokes about cracking me in the head, so that I'd see the funny side of it, but I could not see it. When I got a sudden, full handed crack in the head, I'd see a terrible white light and feel as if my existence had stopped altogether for a second. A crack in the head, even the two finger, always surprised me and scared me. Cracks in the head also made me cry, which made me feel babyish and ashamed, not ashamed of whatever I had done, which sometimes I didn't really know, but that I had been cracked in the head and that I was crying. Once, after several years of being cracked in the head, I looked up at my father after a really rotten crack and even though I was crying and afraid, said to him, "What am I, a dog?" A jolt, white light—another terrific crack in the head.

I don't think my skull or my brain was ever in any danger from all the cracks in the head, but they had a terrible effect on me in another way. I started to lose confidence. I started to lose my connection to the bright world, the Christmas world, and to the clues and signs that had once made me so excited and happy. Even worse, I could not seem to forget being cracked in the head. I felt as if I were carrying them around with me. After the first one, I wondered if I might die.

Just before I got that crack, I thought I was doing a good thing. I had figured out how to move my chair around the kitchen to get up to things I was interested in, like the crackers and the cookies on the counter. I could pull the chair across the kitchen floor to the table and get up there too, to see what was going on. I was actually quite excited about this new range of operations. Between meals my chair was placed in a little nook between the side of the ice box and a counter near the back door of the kitchen. It wasn't a baby's high chair with a tray, but it was higher than a regular chair and it had a kind of step in front that enabled me to climb up onto it by myself. I liked the feeling of moving the chair around the floor. I think mother liked it that at mealtimes I would drag it out of its nook across the linoleum to the table without even having to be asked.

One winter evening I was in the bright kitchen with my mother while she prepared dinner. She had just finished stirring up a huge white bowl of cake frosting and had let me lick the spoon. She took off her apron and left the kitchen to change clothes before my father got home. I spotted the bowl of frosting up on the counter and realized I could get to it by moving my chair over there. But when I gave the chair legs the usual yank to get it out of its spot, something terrible happened. The cord that plugged in the radio must have gotten in front of one of the chair legs, because the purple plastic Zenith slid off the counter and smashed onto the linoleum. It made a loud, terrible crash, and it was all broken. There were sharp shards of purple plastic, and the metal chassis and broken glass tubes were exposed. Still plugged in, the radio made an angry, urgent hum. Mother appeared in the kitchen tying the sash of her dress behind her. "Jonathan, *what did you do?*" I didn't know what I did. I said, " The radio fell down." I was still holding onto the legs of my chair. My father had entered the front of the house and was calling out a greeting. Then he was in the kitchen, standing next to my mother, staring at the shattered mess of the radio and at me. "Jonathan," mother said in a voice I had not heard from her before, "look what you've done." She looked as though she were about to cry. "Now we don't have a radio." The kitchen seemed to grow brighter and brighter. Then my father sprang toward me like an animal. He tore the chair out of my hands. He gripped the back of my neck and turned my head painfully in the direction of the mess on the floor. "Look what the hell you've done!" Jolt, white light—the crack. Then I was up under one his arms, feet off the ground, as he hauled me through the dark house to my bedroom where he dropped me onto the bed and shut the door. I was left in complete blackness, and the blackness was inside me too. I had broken something of enormous importance from the world of my mother and father, something that could not, I believed, ever be restored. I had been cracked in the head and was now banished to the dark, and the only thing I could think to do was to complete the process, find an even greater darkness and stay in it forever. The darkest abyss I could devise was my closet, and I made my way to it in the dark, pulled the shoes and boxes away from the back wall, shut the closet door and curled into a ball. The misery I felt was like a sickening electric current. It soured what was in my stomach and made me retch. I held myself in the ball and tried to darken the darkness by shutting my eyes tight. I don't know if I slept, but I remember suddenly blinking into the light of the closet, staring up into the enormous standing figures of my mother and father. Mother reached down to pull me up. My father said, "Half wit."

After a few more cracks in the head, I began to wake up in the morning with a different feeling. I did not feel the glad surge that had made me tear the covers away and race out of my room to mother, breakfast, and bright day. Now I needed to lie there in the warmth. I remember feeling that as long as I could stay there under the covers I was safe, not just safe from cracks in the head, but from doing the things that brought them on. I would not have found the words for it then, but until my loss of confidence, I believed I had a knack for making myself happy. I didn't have to make an effort for interesting things to happen, they just happened, like the appearance of the turtle or of Blackie or Papa walking me down into the basement of my grandparents' house and opening up the old wooden chest and taking out the velvet lined case where he kept his pearl handled pistols, real pistols, pistols that, if they were loaded, would shoot. The stubby silver barrels and the embossed trigger housings were a little dull with oil and were surprisingly heavy in my hands. I could not get those pistols out of my mind, or their velvet case or the trunk. There were many other treasures in that trunk, treasures from Germany and England, and I was sure that in time Papa would show them to me.

That was just one kind of sign. Nearly any encounter with an animal excited me, but there was no greater happiness than the parties in our living room or at Nana's and Papa's, parties where my mother would wear her sparkly green dress and there would be amber cocktails with sweet cherries for me and delicious cream-filled desserts and always music, music from the R.C.A. Victor or music around the piano. My uncles would remove the shiny black Gilbert and Sullivan recordings from their brown paper sleeves, and I could not stop watching the gorgeously scripted green record labels as they circled the Victrola spindle. Papa could play some of the airs from "The Merry Widow" on the piano, and my father would fill in harmonies on his trumpet. My mother's brother, Uncle Desmond, could sing all the words to "I am the Very Model of a Modern Major General." Mother was shy, but she could sometimes be coaxed to sing "You Made Me Love You," and when she finished, Annabel and I would always beg her to sing it again. I remember the buttery lamplight of those parties, the excited talk and shrieks of women's laughter. I can see slivers of light on the cocktail glasses and wine glasses, the amber and reds like jewels in the faceted glassware. I remember my father and his jokes and how his handsome face seemed to shine and that he was always at the center of the music and the laughter.

But after I started getting cracked in the head, all of this seemed spoiled and out of reach. For months and even years, for what seems now like a separate lifetime, there was no gladness at all. I got dumber every day. I had only to take something delicate into my hands, and I would drop it and break it. I spilled my milk, and it slopped down onto my lap, into my socks, down onto the floor. Flash—crack. I could not manage my knife and fork. Big bits of meat would slide over the side of my plate onto the clean tablecloth or onto the floor. Annabel could cut up her food— my father would ask: *what the hell was wrong with me?* Crack. Sometimes, especially at supper, I could not eat, even though I was told I could not leave the table until I cleaned my plate. Gray mounds of meat pooled in dark juice, hard potatoes yellowed with butter and parsley, cooked carrots and sour florets of steamed broccoli loomed horribly before me. "What's the matter," my father would say, "you fill up on a lot of candy and crap?" *Crap.* I could see steaming messes of dog excrement on the pavement. *Filling up on crap.* My stomach clenched like a fist. I repeated the word: crap. Flash—crack. I could taste the sour acidy spit that arose before I threw up. I could not look at my plate. I could not look up at my father's awful face. Annabel was crying. My mother said, "Frank, don't." I wanted dark, I wanted night.

It seemed, especially around adults, I could only say the wrong thing.

Uncle Dennis, my father's brother, and Aunt Betty were visiting from St. Louis. I loved Uncle Dennis because he liked to talk to me and play with me. He would get right down on the floor with me and do what I was doing. His voice was soft, and he made a lot of jokes, and I remember wanting him to keep talking to me and never to go home. One morning he taught me how to thumb wrestle, a game in which we would lace our fingers together and each of us would try to pin the other's thumb down with our own. It was an awkward, silly game, and for some reason it made me laugh uncontrollably, which made Uncle Dennis laugh so hard tears came down out of the corners of his eyes, and then when he wasn't paying attention I would clamp my thumb down over his huge bony thumb and win. Uncle Dennis seemed to have all the time in the world to sit on the floor with me, thumb wrestling or just fooling around. Once in that very position I looked into Uncle Dennis's open smile and said, "Why are your teeth like that?" He gave me a funny, questioning look and said, "Like what? They're just teeth," and I said, "They're all yellow and brown." White flash—crack. I didn't even know my father was in the room.

Teddy Weisblatt and I were playing outside in his yard one late cold autumn afternoon. Mother and father had some kind of engagement in the city and would not be home until after supper, so the Weisblatts were watching me until they came home. Annabel had gone to Nana and Papa's. Teddy and I were digging in an untended patch of dirt behind his garage, but the clay was cold and hard to penetrate, and our hands were getting raw and stiff as we took turns with Mr. Weisblatt's big spade. Then I realized I really had to go the bathroom. Number two. I told Teddy and we left the spade and went to his back door, but it was locked. Mrs. Weisblatt had run out to the store to get something she needed for dinner. She told us she would be right back, but we didn't know the door would be locked. I really had to go, so we ran around to the front of the house, but those doors were locked too. Teddy told me I'd better hold it, but I knew I couldn't. Something was already happening in my butt. I made my way back to our house, trying as hard as I could not to poop, but the doors were locked there too. I needed to go. I wished Teddy would disappear and leave me alone, but he was right there at my side. "Go away for awhile," I told him, as I waddled back toward his garage. I decided I would go there, someplace behind the garage where no one could see. I barely got around the corner of the garage before I had to unbuckle my belt and unzip my pants and pull them down around my ankles. I pulled my jacket up above my waist so I wouldn't poop on it, squatted down and started to go. It was a big, difficult poop, and it took a long time, because there would be a big plop and then those intervals when nothing more would come out, but I could tell I wasn't done at all. It took forever, and I was cold, and my legs ached from squatting. Teddy had followed me around to the back of the garage, even though I shouted at him not to. "You shouldn't do that here," I heard him saying, "My dad is going to be really mad." But I was already pooping hard. I thought Teddy might have wandered off. I had forgotten about him when, a few minutes later, I heard his voice behind me saying, "Oh boy, this is really terrible. When are you going to be finished?" I was in a not-done-yet interval, and I didn't know when I would be finished. It seemed like I would never be finished. I wasn't really finished when I finally stood up and pulled up my pants. Teddy saw his mother's car pulling into the drive, and said, "Here's my mom!" and that was enough for me.

Before I could ask him not to, he ran to the car and told his mother, "Jonathan just made a B.M. in the yard." After that, everything seemed as if it were happening very far away from me, as if I were under dark soupy water. I can't even tell if I remember what happened or whether I have just filled in with pictures from the way my mother and father told the story for years afterward. I do know that Mrs. Weisblatt used the key my mother had left her and unlocked our house. She turned on the lights and told me I had better go into the bathroom and take a bath. She didn't run the water or help me. She went home to make supper, and I sat in the bathroom by myself for a long time, until mother and father came home. I may have told them, or tried to tell them, what happened, but I cannot remember succeeding. Mrs. Weisblatt came over later and told my parents what I had done. I remember my mother saying the words, "sick with embarrassment." *Sick with*. My father never got tired of telling the story, which included his cracking me in the head. He always concluded with an account of shoveling up and burying the mess with the Weisblatts' spade. "It must have taken me a half hour," he would say. "It was like something you'd expect from a hippopotamus." Much later, when I was grown up, he would add, "and this is from a man with two college degrees!"

Chapter Four

I WAS NOT QUITE ten when I realized that certain things you felt like doing could, if you actually went ahead and did them, carry me out of the ordinary world altogether. And it wasn't just me. Certain books give you that feeling, too, books about adventures.

I first got the adventure feeling by discovering things. There were indoor discoveries, and there were outdoor discoveries. Each kind was thrilling. My first indoor adventures were in attics and cellars. I can still feel it today. There is something about entering the forgotten, underdeveloped parts of a building that breaks your connection to the ordinary and the expected. True basements carry the dark and damp of the building before it was a building. A true basement can feel as much outdoors and indoors, especially if there is only stone and earth. But even concrete, provided it is not covered over with upstairs finishes and furnishings, can create an earthy effect. People leave their oldest stuff in basements, hardware and machines and tools and gadgets from another time. I loved basements with surprising bins and recesses and dark crawl spaces. In some old houses I played in as a boy there were coal rooms with coal chutes and cold storage cellars timbered like mine shafts right into the earth. A really great basement captures the feeling of a cave. Attics, although they have a different kind of light and an airless, almost unbreathable atmosphere, can carry the same wonderful sense of a house beyond what anyone living in the house is thinking about. I like attics best that have multiple partitions and tight, complicated crawlways under the eaves. I like attics that are loaded with boxes and chests filled with pictures and treasure somebody wanted to save but forgot about. I like attics and cellars that have trunks in them like my grandfather Papa's basement trunk that had beautiful cloths wrapped around polished wooden boxes lined with green velvet holding old, real pistols. Going down into Nana and Papa's cellar with Papa to look at his heavy, dully gleaming pistols and to handle them was one of the holiest times of my life.

Those first discoveries create a tremendous longing for adventures, and some of my very best were in the basement of Cyrus Best's house. I met Cyrus when he entered mid year into the second grade of my primary school, Palatine South, in Palatine, Illinois where we lived after we moved out of Chicago. Cyrus, everyone could tell right away, was a different kind of boy. He had a massive block of a head, and his hair was cut very short. There was a dark thatch on top, but the sides and back were shaved nearly bald. He told me, when I got to know him later, that his brother Len cut his hair. His brother Len and two other older brothers, Cal and Jessie, were teenagers. Len was a big boy at Palatine High School and Cal and Jessie had dropped out and were working. They looked like men to me, bigger and rougher and older than my Uncle Desmond who was out of college and out of the army and worked for a magazine. Cyrus's brothers had haircuts like Cyrus's.

Cyrus stood out in school. Seated midway down his row of boys and girls, he gave off a kind of vibration. With his huge head and his washed out flannel shirt buttoned up tight around his throat, he seemed to be beaming out a desperate message from his little blond desk. Part of it, I suppose, was discomfort, as he was always tense and miserable at school. It didn't take long for it to become clear that Cyrus could not read yet. He could not read at all, even "the" or "of." He told me he had been to a different kind of school, a school kept by his church where he used to live which, he told me, was "down state." I actually made a picture of Illinois's arrowhead shape and imagined Cyrus and his people down by the pointed end. He told me he and his people—he didn't say "family"—lived "by the river." That helped explain Cyrus's difference and his special force.

He came from another kind of people, downstate river people with small dark eyes set deep behind their big bony foreheads. Cyrus could not read, and I think he was unbearably ashamed that he couldn't. I would ask him about it sometimes, in a nice way. I would say, "Can you really not read?" I thought maybe he could but he was just afraid to do it out loud in class. He just looked at me hard and hunched his neck down into his shoulders and said, "I cain't." He—and his people, when I met them—said "cain't" and "ain't."

I was fascinated that Cyrus could not, or at least would not, read. He didn't even try or stumble when Mrs. Packworth asked him to read a passage in class. He would just hunch his neck into his shoulders and freeze. His small gray eyes seemed to recede even further behind his brow. "Cyrus," Mrs. Packworth would say, "Try sounding it out: wuh-wuh, wih-wih, with-*with*—" Cyrus could have been in another town. He did not look up at Mrs. Packworth or respond to her words. He waited, frozen, until she moved on. Once I took Cyrus aside when a group of us were standing around a big table molding bits of clay for what was supposed to be a colonial fort. "See this," I said to him and drew a large 'A' on a piece of construction paper. I asked him what it was. A look of suspicion flashed across his big face. "You know what it is," I told him. "It's 'A'." He looked hard into my eyes. "A," he said. I was excited. I asked him, "OK, what does that spell?" Cyrus froze. His eyes retreated into his head. He would not read, not even read "A." His refusal was total, and in it there was a force I had not encountered before, a force that I fell under like a spell.

It took me a while to realize that Cyrus, while a special presence in school, was not really himself there. Seated in his assigned row, silent, inert, neck hunched into his shoulders, he was like a photographic negative of his real self. Outside or in his room or in his basement he had a lot to say. He knew about Jesus and hell and sinning. When he and his people lived downstate, he had been baptized in the river with all his clothes on. He told me his preacher had held him down under the brown water for a long time. He said, "I almost drown't." Now he was saved. I never asked him what saved meant, but I kind of knew. Cyrus carried that saved quality with him into our classroom from the first day. He carried it with him everywhere he went. I don't remember him ever laughing or thinking anything was funny. He was always pretty serious, even worried. Once when we turned the corner of his street he pointed up in the direction of the Miller's big stone house and told me the Millers were going to hell. His mother worked for the Millers, and he told me they went around naked there, that it was a "sex house." I didn't know exactly what he meant, but his words carried an electric charge. After that I could never pass the Millers' house or see Freddy Miller at school or see Mrs. Miller at the A&P without picturing them naked, walking around their house naked, walking around in the unbearably charged atmosphere of a sex house.

Cyrus told me about other sins his people knew about. Playing cards and dancing were sins, but knowing this made me feel uneasy because my mother and father went out dancing. On our piano we had a framed picture of them dressed up and dancing. My mother was smiling beautifully in the picture, and it scared me to think of this as being part of a sin that could send her to hell. I could not even imagine my mother in hell. I was sure she was saved. Sometimes in bed at night I would think about playing cards and how that could be a sin. Playing cards seemed to carry none of the tension of being naked in a sex house. Nana and Papa and Uncle Desmond played cards. They played pinochle and cribbage and kept a running score in a leather notebook. Annabel and I played cards sometimes. We played war and crazy eights. Even when I tried to feel bad about the sin of cards, I couldn't. There was no special feeling in it.

Chapter Five

It was more fun to talk to Cyrus about hunting and about guns, especially after we started hunting, with real guns, in his basement. Cyrus had a true basement with a dirt floor and walls of piled stone. A few bulbs on looping wires were suspended from the floor joists overhead, creating a complex impression of islands of light and dark shadowy caverns. The full basement didn't go under all the rooms of the house, but there were crawl spaces of two or three feet under the other rooms, and Cyrus and I were able to wriggle into these through manhole-sized openings in the foundation walls. It was not really like a basement of a house at all. It was a subterranean world. In the winter we could hear the whoosh of the furnace kicking in and water glugging through the overhead pipes, and these sudden, purposeful sounds seemed proof of the secret separateness of the place. The basement, Cyrus warned me, was full of spiders, and we saw quite a few, but even when our faces and hair were filmy with webs, the spiders seemed less dreadful down in this realm where spiders rightly belonged than they did when a frenzied brown centipede would appear in the tub as mother ran my bath water or when a black spider of any size stood out in stark relief against the white paint of the ceiling above my bed. What was a little frightening, but also alluring, was the prospect of animals in the cellar. Like what, I remember asking Cyrus, when he told me "we got critters." Mice and rats, he said, maybe sometimes a chuck or a possum.

Cyrus's older brothers all hunted and had guns—shotguns, twenty-twos, and pellet rifles—and they had taught Cyrus how to load them and how to shoot. You loaded the twenty-two by pulling back a metal cylinder, slipping in a brass shell, then sliding the cylinder back in place. The pellet rifle had a kind of pump running beneath the length of the barrel. After you loaded a pellet into the chamber, you had to slide back the pump to build up enough compressed air to shoot the pellet. The pump was hard for me to operate. Holding the rifle stock against my shoulder, I wasn't strong enough to pump the rifle with my left arm. Cyrus could do it, but I couldn't. This was a problem because his brother Len would only allow Cyrus to shoot his twenty-two. That meant I got the pellet rifle, which Cyrus's brothers thought of as a kid's toy, but I wasn't strong enough to work it.

Feeling too weak started to spoil the whole basement adventure. I felt as if I had at last been granted access to a place of limitless adventure, a place Cyrus and I could feel that electric feeling of being armed and on the loose-- but I was too weak to do it. What was wrong with my skinny arms? I could see they were only sticks compared to Cyrus's. I couldn't stand asking Cyrus to help me pump my rifle every time I wanted to shoot. That would mean that he belonged in the adventure, but I did not. I could feel myself starting to lose confidence, the feeling dangerously close to the can't-do-anything feeling that led to cracks in the head I got from my father when I disappointed him. Not being able to pump the rifle was like not being able to hammer a nail straight into the board after my father had shown me how so many times that he started to get mad. It was like the time he asked me to help him wash the windows on the storm doors. He was outside with his ammonia and rags, and I was on the inside with mine. He would wash a square from the outside, and then tap the glass so that I would do my side. When we were both finished, there would still be filmy swirls and streaks. He would swipe at them from his side, but they wouldn't disappear, because they were on my side, and the more I sprayed and wiped, the cloudier it got. It was a curse. I would apply the spray, then pull my rag as evenly and as hard as I could over the glass, and then, just for an instant it would look clear, and then the cloudy swirls would reform. "For Christ sake," my father finally said. He came inside and tore the rag out of my hand and gave me a little shove away from the door. "Get lost. Find something to do. I'll do this myself."

That's what it felt like as I loaded the pellet into the chamber and stood there on the damp floor of the basement unable to slide back the pump of the rifle. Then in a rage that made a bright flash behind my eyes, I knew what to do. I set the heel of the rifle stock against the basement floor, bent down over the barrel and grabbed the pump with both hands. I pressed down with all my strength and all my weight. Then the pump gave way, and I heard a gassy *poof* and then a metallic *ping*. The light bulb over our heads shattered and went dark. "Dang it," Cyrus said. "You shot the light out." It took me a minute to figure out what he meant. Then I realized the rifle had fired. It had gone straight up and broken the light bulb. "Come here," Cyrus said, pulling me by the wrist until we were standing under another light bulb. "Know what else," he said, "You shot yourself in the ear." The tip of my ear was cold. It started to sting. I reached up to touch it, and there was new red blood on my grimy fingers. "Let's go and get you cleaned up," Cyrus said. I didn't know if he was mad or disappointed. We were just getting ready to hunt in one of the crawl spaces. We had shells and pellets in our pockets and a flashlight with new batteries. Upstairs at Cyrus's kitchen sink I washed off my ear with a dishcloth, and Cyrus brought me a bandage. At the door as I was leaving, he said, "You coulda shot yourself in the head and killed yourself."

I thought about that, about having shot myself accidentally in the head or through the eye and being finished with the world at nine years old. Obviously it wasn't to be, but it was a warning of some kind, a message. If it was a message about guns and hunting, I missed it completely, because Cyrus and I went at it every chance we could. We spent many long afternoons after school reclining back against the stone foundation walls of his basement, rifles cocked, a sharp eye out for possum or rat. Or, more uncomfortably, we would lie prone in the damp, buggy earthen floor of one of the crawl spaces, a flashlight beaming a funnel of light through the murk. No critter ever entered those funnels of light, but I spent many wide-eyed nights in my bed at home picturing exactly how it would be.

Cyrus and I would be huddled shoulder to shoulder in the dirt, our eyes following the shaft of light, our rifles before us, cocked and ready. Then it would happen. The picture grows larger, the flashlight beam brilliant as a flashbulb as into the white circle of light slithers the ugliest, most menacing creature I had ever seen, yet exactly the kind of creature I imagined when Cyrus had told me we might expect a rat, or maybe a possum. The rat-possum was about the size of a largish, low-slung cat. Its wet fur was silver and black. Its long bald tail was obscenely pink. Spotlighted against a far wall, it turned to us. A circle of green and gold glowed in its black eyes. Looking directly into the light, it bared a line of crooked yellow teeth. It is the time, the exact moment for us to fire. And I am caught there, holding that picture before my mind's eye. I can see it now.

Later, when we got our axes and spears, we took the adventure and the hunt outdoors, which was even better. It may have been a blessing, although it didn't seem like it at the time, that Cyrus's brother Len met us on the basement stairs as we were coming up from a hunt. Cyrus had the pellet rifle, and I had Len's twenty-two, which Cyrus wasn't supposed to let me use, but he did because I couldn't pump the pellet rifle. I loved the twenty-two. I loved that it was the more powerful rifle, a man's rifle, a rifle that, as Cyrus told me, "could kill a man." I loved it so much I would forget that it wasn't mine. It felt like mine. I loved the clean feel of firing it, the little tug I felt through the stock under my arm when I fired. I loved the startling flash of sparks where the bullet met the stones of the foundation wall. I loved the sweet char of gunpowder that hovered around the spent copper colored shell casings. But Len startled us. Even before he spoke, the adventure was over. He was really mad. What did we think we were doing with those guns in the cellar? What was I doing with his twenty-two? He told us we better not have taken any of his pellets and cartridges. He looked at Cyrus with the same kind of steady, unbearable look Cyrus gave me when he was upset about something. It felt dangerous to be standing on that little wooden stairway. I didn't know what Len was going to do, but I could imagine him doing something terrible. I could imagine him stabbing us or shooting us, and my ears began to ring. He did not look at me, only at Cyrus, and Cyrus's neck was hunched all the way into his shoulders. Len reached down and pulled the twenty-two out of my hands, and then he took the pellet rifle away from Cyrus. "All right, boy, now I know." He took hold of Cyrus's chin and made him look up into his eyes. "I cain't trust you. Now git." After that we had our adventures outside.

There were a lot of things eight and nine-year-old kids aren't allowed to buy in the hardware store. For instance, Cyrus and I couldn't buy guns, even the Daisy air rifles that other kids in town owned. I wanted a Daisy BB gun, the deluxe model that pumped air into the barrel by cocking a lever beneath the trigger. The Rudd brothers had that gun, and they used to take it out into the fields behind Our Lady of the Wayside school and shoot cans and bottles and birds. Freddy and Eddy Rudd were eleven and thirteen, and their father didn't care if they had guns. Eddy said his father bought him the Daisy deluxe when he was eight. I asked my father if I could ever have a BB gun, and he said, with frightening force, "Never. Absolutely not." The more he thought about it the madder he got. "What would you like to do," he said, "put somebody's eye out?" I told him I would be completely careful, and that I would never shoot it around people or around the house, only way out in the fields, at cans and bottles and maybe birds. I said Freddy and Eddy Rudd had a Daisy and their father got it for them when they were eight. "Then you stay the hell away from them," my father said. "Do you hear me? I *mean* it." I knew he meant it. I thought he was going to crack me in the head.

Even if my father wasn't so against BB guns, I don't think he would have bought me one. I didn't seem to get big presents like that, especially if it wasn't Christmas or my birthday. Even if I had some of my own money stashed away— my sister Annabel had about fifteen dollar bills rolled up in her jewelry box-- I could not have bought a BB gun at the hardware store. Once of the men who worked there saw me looking up at the rack of Daisys on the wall behind the counter, and he asked me if I wanted to hold one. I said yes, I wanted to hold the deluxe. He took it down and handed it to me and showed me how to pull back the spring-coiled slot where you loaded the BBs and how to cock the rifle. He let me try it, and it wasn't too hard. I could feel the air caught in the chamber

31

behind the barrel. The man said go ahead, pull the trigger. I did, and there was a metallic *pfft*. It was a great feeling, a perfect feeling. The Daisy had the look of some of the twenty-twos and shotguns on display, and it was just the right size. It smelled new. The man asked if I was thinking about getting a Daisy one of these days, and I told him yes, definitely, but I knew I would just picture it and picture it, as I pictured certain other things or places that seemed to shine and beckon from a real world not quite connected to mine.

But for some reason there were no rules against the hardware store selling Cyrus and me little hatchets. Cyrus noticed them first. They were in a bin next to the long handled axes and sledgehammers. The shaft of the little hatchets was not much longer than the one on my father's hammer, but they had a real axe heads, painted blue at the fat end, then becoming shiny gray steel as the blade narrowed to a sharp edge. I couldn't believe it. I asked a man who worked there how much the little hatchets cost. He walked over to look and told us, two dollars and ninety-eight cents. That didn't seem like too much. The man didn't say: these aren't for kids. I had two dollars at home in my bank. Cyrus said he had had five dollars saved. We could buy two of those axes, and we did.

I don't know what Cyrus did with his, but I hid mine in the garage behind some old coffee cans filled with rusty nails and screws. I knew my mother and father wouldn't like me having a hatchet of my own, and my father would get mad at me for going out and buying it without telling him. So it was a secret, but I pictured it behind the coffee cans in the garage all day long at school, and I pictured it there at night in my bed.

It was fall then. As soon as school let out, Cyrus and I would race back to our houses, put our books inside, grab our hatchets and head for the fields. There was still red and orange in the trees, and out in the fields the tall grasses and corn stalks had dried to the color of khaki. It would get cold enough as the sun started to set that our fingers would get stiff, and we knew we would have to hurry home for supper or we would be in trouble.

Maybe everything we did with those hatchets took place in a single fall, but it felt to me like a whole season of my life. As soon as we turned off the paved street onto the double-rutted tractor path of the fields we entered the other world. The cool air seemed to go deeper into my lungs. I could smell sweet rot behind the hedgerows and musk from the barns and ruined sheds we passed by or foraged through. The spent grasses were alive with rabbits and the sudden heart-stopping ascent of pheasants. Uncle Desmond had bought me a suede leather cowboy jacket with a row of rawhide fringe along the shoulder line, and this was my fields jacket. It enabled me to conceal my hatchet when I emerged from the garage, but when I met Cyrus and we were nearing the tractor path, I would take it out and slide the shaft into the holster of what had been my cap pistol. Cyrus didn't have a holster, but he would stuff the handle of his hatchet under his belt. We would begin each hunt or adventure by snapping down a branch of one of the bushes that lined the path, hacking it free with our hatchets, then whittling one end to a point with our pearl handled pocket knives. These would be our spears, and although we never came even close to doing it, our hope was to spear some kind of animal that we might scare up out of the bramble. It felt good, it felt just right, to be walking through the empty fields in the autumn chill, the pleasing heft of a spear in one hand, the holstered weight of my hatchet against my thigh, and my knife deep in the pocket of my jeans.

It often felt like a good idea to make a shelter, which we called forts. These became more elaborate and even provided a kind of shelter once we were able to use our hatchets to cut the larger shoots away from the base of shrubs or to hack low lying branches from trees. One afternoon, it occurred to us that we might make something really substantial, a fort that would stand and last. We could do real Work. Maybe it would take days, maybe years. We could build a fort that we could live in. It would take tremendous effort, day after day, and it would take our hatchets. That afternoon and for many afternoons afterward we did nothing but work on that fort. At home I couldn't wait to get away from the table and go to my room where I could picture the fort and make new plans. At school I could only twist around in my chair and look at the big circular face of the clock and watch the agonizingly slow procession of minutes. The clocks were the same in every room in the school. There was a notch for each minute etched into the circumference of the face, and there was a fatter notch to indicate five minutes. When the minute hand was about to move a notch, there would be a cranking sound, and the hand would cock itself backwards a little and then click forward into the next minute. I tried to stop watching the clock and let some other thoughts carry me away so that time would just flow, but I couldn't do it. Every time I looked up it seemed like the clock was on the same minute, and I would keep looking at it until it cranked into the next one. I could not pay attention. I could not sit still. I could see the sun in the trees outside, and I wanted some force to lift me out of my chair and set me down in the fields with my hatchet.

Cyrus and I found a perfect place for our fort. It was down over a rise of a hill not far from an old barn. It was out of the wind and had a protected feeling about it. But the best thing about it was that there were lines of little trees, trees about six or seven feet high with trunks and branches we could, with effort, chop down. Cyrus knew how to cut down trees by hacking a triangular wedge into one side of the trunk, then, when you were almost through, chopping into the other side. Our building plan for the fort was to chop down as many lengths of trunks and branches as we could. Then we would sharpen one end of each pole, dig a little hole and stick them in so they would be standing upright. We would make two rows of these just a little ways apart and then fill in the space between with smaller branches, scrub and grass. These would be the walls. Over the top we'd lay longer branches with the leaves still on them to make a roof, leaving an open space in one corner to let the smoke rise from our fires. We would leave an opening at one end for a door, and maybe later we would get some blankets from our houses for the floor. This was my first real feeling of work, and it connected me to something vast and ancient and great. We chopped and hauled and stacked until we could hear each other panting, but I never wanted to stop or for the sun to get any lower. It seemed to me that the work stimulated ideas and new plans for the fort, and the ideas made me want to work. I remember looking back as we left for home one afternoon and seeing the neat lines of stumps we had left. We had chopped down almost half of that stand of perfect little trees.

Cyrus and I decided that if we were going to finish the fort and get any use out of it before winter we were going to have to find a way to spend Saturdays on the job. This was hard to arrange because of the things our families wanted us to do on Saturdays, but we finally managed to get together one Saturday. It was cold, and the sky was a solid gray as we made our way into the fields along the tractor path. It felt strange heading out at this different time on a Saturday. We passed Freddy and Eddy Rudd on the path. They had the Daisy with them, and they told us they had shot a bunch of birds but now they were cold. Eddy Rudd said he was "cold as shit." We didn't tell them where we were going. We heard other voices in the distance and the whine of engines as we walked along. After school we never heard anybody else. We were always completely by ourselves.

We reached the rise just above our fort and were heading down the hillside toward the trees when we heard the sputtering of a motor. We stopped for a minute. It didn't feel right. I decided to go to work anyway. I started chopping a wedge into the trunk of a tree, and the bad feeling opened up into a scream. Cyrus said, "Look *out*," and I looked behind me and saw a man on a tractor heading down the hill straight for us. The tractor motor was deafening, but I could hear some of the things the man was shouting. I could hear "*filthy little bastards*," and I could hear "*god damned sons of bitches*," and "*my fruit trees*."

Cyrus was running ahead of me, and I was right behind him, running in a way I had never run before. This was serious. I heard, "*blow your fuckin' brains out.*"

I don't think I turned back to look, but I remember the man's face. He was old. Stringy skin was hanging on his neck. I knew he wanted to catch us and kill us. We ran out of the clearing into the tall grass and scrub. I thought: go where his tractor can't go. I could still hear the motor behind us when we reached a cornfield and charged in between the stalks. Cyrus led the way as we zig-zagged through the corn, and when we got out, we were pretty far from the path, but we decided to keep to the high grass and as far from people as we could. It was cold, and it was hard going, hunched down low, finding our footing through the tall grass of the fields. Cyrus said, "He's going to be looking for us. They're going to want to arrest us." *Arrest.* The man had shouted, "my fruit trees." I had never thought of trees way out in the fields belonging to anybody. I thought they were part of nature. "They were his property," Cyrus said, and as he said it I knew, just as surely as I know now, the meaning of *property*.

WE ESCAPED FROM THE FIELDS without being arrested, but the closer I got to my house, the sicker I felt inside. I made it into the garage and slipped my hatchet behind the coffee cans. I had the feeling that as soon as I went inside the house everything about what I had done to the fruit trees would be known, and there would be terrible yelling and cracks in the head. Even when that did not happen, I felt it was coming. I waited for it, and it spoiled the days. Cyrus and I never went back to the fort, and then it was winter, and the fields filled up with snow.

Chapter Six

For a long time there was nothing close to that feeling of Work, of using our hatchets to make something that was all ours and that would last. But not too long after that something amazing started to happen, and it happened in school. We were leaving the lunch room on our way to the gym for free play when a partly crazy boy in our class, Donny Greener, was trying to get everybody to follow him because he wanted to show them something. The girls didn't even slow down to look at him, and the boys in front of me were laughing at him and saying, "Oh, yeah, Donny, sure, sure. You want us to go down into the basement. Oh, yeah, we really want to go down to the basement." They moved on, and when Cyrus and I got to him, he said, "You got to see this. I went into this little room next to the bathroom downstairs, and there was a tunnel!" When Donny said the word "tunnel," something jumped in my chest. "Where's it go?" Cyrus asked. Donny said he didn't know. He said a janitor came by and told him to get out of there. But he could see it, he said, see the tunnel, and it went on and on. I looked at Cyrus, and he was interested, so we went down the stairs to the basement. Donny shushed us, so the janitor wouldn't hear us, and we tiptoed as quietly as we could past the boys' bathroom. There was always a little time after lunch when you could go to the gym or, in nice weather, out to the playground, but you were supposed to be there or in the cafeteria, not wandering around the halls unless you had a pass. Donny led us down past the bathroom to a grimy metal door. He put his ear against it to listen. "It was open before," he whispered, "the janitor must have shut it. Wait till you see."

Donny pulled open the door. There was a low table with some canisters and bottles on it, and a line of mops was leaning against the wall. It was only a closet, I thought, but then I saw that it kept going to the left. We stepped inside and we could see that under a curved archway cut into the wall on the left was a dark passage of about twenty feet where a bare bulb lit up what looked like a turning to the right. I was absolutely sure that I shouldn't go into that tunnel and absolutely sure that I would. "Let's go," I said, and we ducked under the archway and started making our way over the damp cement floor. When I got to the light, the tunnel turned to the right, and again I felt a tremendous surge in my chest as I saw that it went on as far as I could see, with other light bulbs down the way indicating a complicated system of turns and intersections. My skull and all down my spine was alive with electric tingles. As usual I had no words for it, but it was one of those times something I suddenly saw flowed into something I had always known in a way that felt like a message. There was an elaborate world underneath the world. I heard a muted clank from somewhere in front of us, and then a cough. Then we were running back toward the closet door, and I knew the sound of our rubber sneaker soles slapping on the cement was making a lot of noise. We heard a "hey!" and then a louder "hey!" and then we were out in the hallway and up the stairs.

Cyrus was in a special class now, and I didn't get a chance to talk to him again until after school, but then it was clear. He had seen what I had seen, and we started making plans. Without either one of us having to say it, we made our way from the playground back into the school building, which always seemed to me abandoned and forbidding after school hours. We walked along the waxy smelling hallways without seeing anybody, but as we were going downstairs to the basement level, we met Lodi, the German janitor who was washing the floor in the boys' bathroom. Lodi had a huge meaty red face that always looked to me as if something terrible had just happened to him, but the kids at school thought he was nice because he liked to talk to us and knew our names. He had big square front teeth like pieces of Chicklets gum, and some kids thought he was funny and even friendly because of the way he looked, but I didn't think he was especially funny or friendly. I thought Lodi was somebody I should stay away from. He didn't look clean.

He asked us what we were looking for, and Cyrus said we needed to use the bathroom. Lodi said we should use the one upstairs because he was washing the floor. We went back upstairs but waited at the top until we saw him go back inside the bathroom with his pail. Then we sneaked back down and found our way to the metal door, opened it as quietly as we could and slipped inside. It was just as it had been, except now the closet was dark, and the only light I could see was from the bulb down the tunnel to the left. We crept under the arch and moved in the direction of the light. In a minute my eyes were used to the dark, and I could see fine. We reached the bulb where we had to turn back earlier and continued along the passage until we reached the next pool of light, which turned out to be an intersection. The tunnel continued as far as we could see in either direction. It was even better than I imagined. It went on and on. I was moving through the world under the world. We turned left again. The pipes and ducts overhead clicked and hummed which gave me the feeling that there was an order and a plan to all this. We came to another turn where there were iron rungs of a ladder leading up the cinder block wall. Looking up the ladder I could see a white circle of daylight. We decided to climb up, which turned out to be easy, and with the wall behind us so close, I felt like I couldn't really fall and hurt myself. I was ahead of Cyrus on the ladder, and when I got to the top, I could see the sky and treetops through a screened grate. I pushed out a little into the screening and the grate lifted up in my hand. I climbed up to the last rung and poked my head out of the opening. It was bright daylight, and we were on the flat roof over the cafeteria. I slid over to one side so Cyrus could get up there and see. We considered the perpendicular contours of the school from our perch over the roof. Cyrus said exactly what I was thinking: "This has been here the whole time and we never saw it."

We climbed back down the ladder, silent with the pleasure of knowing what we had discovered, that there was so much more to see, and that nobody but us had any idea of what we had found. It felt to me closer to being in a dream than being awake. I don't know if we discussed it or just felt it, but somehow while we were whispering in that tunnel, we determined that the pleasure of exploring further was exceeded by the greater pleasure of knowing that there were other passages still to be explored. We decided to head back. When we reached the turn that led to the closet, we saw something and stopped still. Lodi was in the closet. He was rinsing out his mop and banging around, making enough noise that he didn't notice us. We stepped back out of sight and waited until we heard the door shut and it was quiet. We peeked down the passage, but it was completely dark at the closet end. Lodi had turned off the lights. We inched our way, very slowly, in the direction of the closet until we could see stripes of light through a vent at the bottom of the door. But then we got a scare. We couldn't open the door. It was locked. We sat down on the cement floor, and I stared hard at the lines of light through the vent. I realized I was sweating. I didn't like the idea at all, but I said, "We could go back and go up the ladder to the roof." At least then we would be outside. "But then we'd be on the roof," Cyrus said. He was right. How could we get down from the roof? We would have to call out to somebody, and somebody would have to come rescue us, and then we would have to explain about everything, and later at home I would be cracked in the head. Even while I was worrying, I knew there was something right about being in the tunnels, something that felt good even on the floor in the dark. When I am in that kind of mood, the right thing usually happens. As I sat there, my eyes got used to the dark, and I could start to see things, the mops, the pails, the canisters and bottles on the shelves. There was a coat rack with brass hooks that gleamed a little, and on one of the hooks—I stood up to touch them—a ring of keys.

We didn't see anybody as we made our way through the darkening corridors of the empty school. When I said goodbye to Cyrus at the turn off to his street, I had a wonderful feeling, a feeling of almost unbearable expectation. We knew about the tunnels. They were really down there, and we had our own key.

From then on—it must have been for the whole rest of that school year—I lived for the tunnels. It felt the way my dreams felt, but the tunnels were really there, pulsing like a kind of energy all around and underneath the school. I don't remember anything at all from the regular school day, except for the cranking of minutes on the clock face and moving in packs as we headed to the playground or to the cafeteria or to the gym. There was that little bit of time after lunch when we knew we could go down to the boys' bathroom, then sneak over to the tunnel closet, but since somebody heard us and almost caught us the time we looked inside with Donny Greener, it seemed that either Lodi or the tall, meaner janitor was hanging around the closet during the lunch hour, on the lookout. Cyrus and I managed some very exciting and very satisfying expeditions after school, but we had to be watchful every second, because we realized that janitors and other workmen used the tunnels. Two different tunnels led into a big boiler room, which was brightly lit from high ceilings. There always seemed to be a janitor or workmen in there, but Cyrus and I would sneak through from time to time because the boiler room was a necessary short cut when we knew we had to get out of the tunnels in a hurry. Some of the tunnels dead-ended into storage spaces, one of them full of old science equipment, including scales and microscopes and chemicals and all kinds of specimen jars capped with cork. That was the room where we found the complicated gadget with brass globes representing the sun and the moon and the earth connected by gears and chains so that they could rotate around each other to show how it got dark and when you could see the moon. This was heavy on its wooden base, and it looked and felt like something valuable and old. It was something Cyrus and I both wanted to keep, but even though it was stashed down in the cement storage room with old jars so gritty with dirt you couldn't see what was inside, we were pretty sure it would be stealing. The piece was also fairly big, and we knew it would be hard to get it out of the tunnels and out of the school and home without anyone noticing. But, like Papa's miniature pistols, it was just one beckoning treasure in a cavernous room full of treasures. Another room was stacked high with old typewriters. Another had two upright pianos with the wires exposed. Our problem was time.

We had to be sure to get out of the tunnels before someone found us or before someone locked up the school. I suppose part of the elevated feeling was knowing that we had to be on the lookout every second. We could never talk in a regular voice. We could never just walk; we either had to creep along in tiny silent steps or else run as fast as we could. Over the course of our time in the tunnels we saw Lodi and the other, mean janitor quite a few times. We'd usually spot them first, and then freeze or hide until they went away. But sometimes they saw us or heard us, and we would run out of there as fast as we could. We were chased a few times, but no one ever caught up with us, and I don't think anybody got close enough to recognize us. But after a close call, Cyrus and I would stay out of the tunnels for a while.

For me staying out of the tunnels every now and then was a kind of pleasure in itself. Knowing I couldn't go down into them made thinking about it even more exciting. I made a few forays by myself, but usually we went in together, and I do not think there was a single excursion or even a single thing we saw or did down there that Cyrus and I did not talk over in exact detail. In my bed at night I pictured the tunnels, the dimly illuminated network opening up before me from where you stood at the turning under the first bare bulb. After a week or so we knew the underground layout well enough to draw a map, but I always felt that, despite how many times we crept through the same passages and saw the same things, there was always the possibility of finding another opening to what I believed could be network after network of new tunnels and chambers.

Maybe he saw our maps or maybe Cyrus said something to him, but some time that spring in the nice weather as school was about to let out for the summer, Donny Greener found out about our adventures in the tunnels. Cyrus and I liked to make new, revised maps and show them to each other at lunch and then make plans. That is all I can remember talking about. I know it's all I thought about. Still I didn't expect to hear Donny Greener telling everybody about our going down into the tunnels all the time, and I certainly didn't want to take Donny down into them with us. Maybe it was Donny's fault—he never stopped talking, never stopped bugging us to take him along—or maybe the janitors said something to the teachers, but one day after lunch the principal gave a talk to everyone in the cafeteria about staying out of the basement and the "maintenance facilities." She said it was dangerous and discourteous and that if anybody was caught down there our parents would be called and we would be sent home. The principal was saying all of this as Cyrus and I were sitting together leaning over our maps. And of course Donny, who really was partly crazy, stood up at his table and started to look around for Cyrus and me. I glanced up and saw that his face was bright red and he was pointing to us like an idiot, right while the principal was talking. After that it felt hopeless to attempt another trip down to the tunnels. Also, something about the term "maintenance facilities" seemed to cancel out the charged, exciting feeling about the tunnels. I didn't ever want to lose that, so I let the idea of bright summer crowd out everything else, and neither Cyrus nor I ever mentioned the tunnels again.

Chapter Seven

THAT SUMMER I started to climb. I got the idea and the feel of it from a Tarzan double feature Annabel and I saw while we were on vacation in Michigan. For a number of years in a row we would pack up and drive out of Palatine to what my father called the North Woods. We would rent our own cabin, which would be in a line of other cabins along the shore of a lake, and sometimes there was a lodge where the people who stayed in the cabins could get special meals or sit around a fire on rainy days or play cards or ping-pong. Each cabin had its own little dock and a rowboat, and you could fish all day or swim or do anything you wanted. Once or twice we would drive out to a little town and eat chicken-in-a-basket and maybe go to the drive-in. This is where I saw the Tarzan double feature, and after that the idea of climbing up and over things took hold of me the way the building our fort in the fields and hunting and the tunnels had done.

I was just about to say that the Tarzan movies entered right into my brain, but that isn't quite right. It felt more as if I entered the movie, as if somehow I rose up to the bright screen and passed right through into the jungle. Everything about Tarzan was exactly right. I felt as if I had been waiting for that world for a long time. He only had to wear a little leather bathing suit. On anybody else I had ever seen this would have made him look as if he were in his underwear, but Tarzan looked absolutely right and natural. Tarzan movies always had the effect of making me want to get naked outside, or at least almost naked. He was always around water, and he was a terrific swimmer, but it was his climbing that took hold of me. It was not just that he was so comfortable and quick getting up trees; it was that he seemed to belong in trees. He and Jane and a chimpanzee, who I always thought of as Tarzan and Jane's son, lived in a tree fort, and Tarzan would swing from tree to tree, then, when he needed to, down to the ground on a vine. Tarzan moved through the trees the way a person would walk down the road. Watching Tarzan swinging from tree to tree almost naked made me want to walk right out of the theatre and get into some trees myself.

Because we saw the movies at night, I had to wait until the next morning before I could go outside and get at it. But it was nice, driving home from the drive-in, to realize that Annabel had the same kind of reaction to the movie. I could tell she was carried away. She couldn't really explain it. Her feeling wasn't about swinging through the trees nearly naked or being free all day to do whatever you wanted in the jungle. I could tell by the way she talked and by the way she rearranged the stuff in her room that what mattered to her was Jane and how she made a kind of house for herself in the tree fort and how she was somewhere between a mother and a girlfriend to Tarzan. I didn't think about those things all that much, but I remember being glad Annabel had that good feeling about Jane and Tarzan and the jungle.

As it turned out, I was good at climbing. The thing I liked best about it was that I could do it by myself. When I climbed something with other kids, it always turned into a race or a competition—who could get to the top first or who could hang from their knees from a high branch. I don't really mind competition and dares, but they spoiled the climbing. What I liked was the figuring out period and then actually doing what I figured out. Climbing sometimes took me quite a long time, but I liked that too. I could talk to myself, out loud if I was alone, wondering what would happen if I reached out to hang on a certain branch or if I put all my weight on a dead one. After each advance farther up the tree, I could rest for as long as I felt like. This was very important when I made a mistake and had a close call. I would lose my footing sometimes or something I was holding onto would snap off, and I would fall a little ways before there was something strong enough to grab onto. When this would happen, my heart would feel as if was flying right out of my chest and I'd be sweating all over until I calmed down. As long as I was by myself, this wasn't too bad. I could just get myself in a comfortable position and talk to myself in a calm way until my heart was back to normal and I got my strength back. I think that climbing was very good for me, because it taught me the way I learn. It helped me understand that I could do practically anything as long as I could do it completely my own way and no one else was around.

I did so much climbing and thought about climbing so much that the second I saw a particular tree, I knew whether I could climb it or not. I could tell by the way the biggest branches came out of the trunk. I could tell in advance whether there would be something to hold onto when you got to the top, whether there would be a place where you could rest and figure things out. I kept my climbing pretty much to myself, and I don't think I talked about it much, but occasionally, if we were on a family trip or a picnic, Annabel or mother would notice. They'd see that I wasn't around and call out for me, and I would answer them from up in a tree, sometimes practically at the top. A few times mother was really worried. When she called for me to come down her voice trembled the way it did when she was about to cry. Most of the time, though, she seemed surprised and maybe impressed that I had gotten up there. She would say things like, "Now don't fall and break your neck." The plain, matter-of-fact way she said it let me know she didn't really think I would break my neck and that I could keep climbing.

The hardest thing to figure out about climbing trees was how to get up to the first level of branches when they started high off the ground, which I found was usually the case with the biggest trees. If a tree was right around the house and my father wasn't home, I could drag one of his ladders over to the trunk, but this didn't feel like real climbing. I didn't mind using the seat of my bike or a box or something to boost me up to the first branch, but a ladder seemed too easy. Anybody could climb a ladder up a tree. One time I watched a workman climb up a telephone pole by sliding a leather strap around the pole, then pulling himself up the that level, then sliding the strap up higher and pulling himself up to it until he reached the wires. He went straight up in less than a minute. It was like something Tarzan could do. It was also the kind of climbing I liked to imagine myself being able to do. I didn't have a leather strap like the workman's, but I knew that if I did, I couldn't climb the pole the way he did. I knew I wasn't strong enough, and I started to feel that bad, never-be-able-to-do-things-right feeling, the feeling I got when I couldn't pump the pellet rifle or clear the smudges off my side of the window glass. I remember watching the workman until he came down. I stood practically right underneath him, and then I saw how he did it. He had special spikes, like steel nails, strapped under his boots. I watched the spikes rip into the dark wood of the pole, and I could see how they gave him enough of a foothold to free his arms to slide the strap into the next position. It was good to know that I could do that if I wanted to.

But it wasn't tar-blackened telephone poles I wanted to climb. I wanted to be up in the leafy breezes of treetops. I wanted to rest in the safe bowered crook of trunk and limb, high up over the lawns and garage roofs, unknown and invisible to kids playing on the sidewalk and to mothers talking to each other over their fences while they pinned billowing sheets and pillow cases onto their clothes lines. I wanted to be able to think about things for as long as I wanted up there, to talk to myself out loud. Sometimes when I was up in a tree I knew really well, and I was having a good day, I could feel my climbing become so effortless and sure it didn't feel like climbing at all, but like floating. It was what Tarzan must have felt flying on his vines from tree to tree. When I would get that feeling, everything I did turned out right. I didn't have to grip anything tight with my hands or strain to hold myself in position while my feet found a place to rest. I could just let everything go loose, so that climbing down from a perch at the top of a tree was just like shinnying down a pole. I'd barely hold onto things as my body slid into place from higher branch to lower branch. My body just seemed to know what to do and where to go.

Once I got the knack of climbing, I started picturing practically everything I saw as climbable or not climbable, and the more time I had to talk to myself and figure things out, the fewer things seemed not climbable.

I would look at the way people's awnings were attached to their porches by poles and wonder how I could shinny up those poles and get on top of the porch. When I saw a garage roof or a house extension that had a flat roof with railings, I would immediately start to figure out how I could get up there. That turned out to be pretty easy, provided there was a window with a ledge underneath it. If there was, I just had to pull my bike below the window, stand on the seat, and get a foothold on the window ledge. Then, leaning into the side of the building just enough to keep my balance, I would feel overhead for the roofline or, if I could reach it, the bottom of the railing. When I got a decent handhold, I could pull myself bit by bit up to where I could really get hold of the railing, then hoist myself onto the roof. If the building had gutters with sturdy down spouts, I could use those as hand holds when I climbed down. The more I climbed the more everything turned out to be climbable.

On Christmas Eve and other special days my father would take Annabel and me with him on the train downtown to Chicago, and we would ride the elevator of his bank up to the top floor where his office was. Out the window I could see the roofs and top floors of the skyscrapers across the street, and it seemed obvious that once you got a story or two above the street, these buildings would be easy to climb. There were big, deep ledges beneath all the windows and lots of obvious handholds and footholds into the decorative tracery. Not only that, the highest buildings tapered to a point, which would make the climbing a lot easier as you started getting to the top. I found I couldn't get those Chicago skyscrapers out of my head. From the minute we got out of the train station and stepped out onto the windy street, my eyes would scan the walls of the Wrigley Building looking for a way to get up past the first floor, where the really good footholds started. I remember thinking that the builders must have had climbing in mind when they put in all the special ledges and extra stonework. Once I heard Nana, who didn't like downtown Chicago, say something about "the unearthly canyons" of LaSalle Street, where my father's bank was. I realized that the word was just right. *Canyons*. Those streets really were canyons, and they made you feel like climbing.

I knew that if I was ever going to able to do that kind of climbing,

I would need practice and confidence. There were heavy ceramic downspouts and good window ledges at my school, and I had many times worked my way up onto the ledges of the first floor windows. These were only about four feet off the ground, but they were really higher than that, because directly below each window was a concrete window well that went down three or our feet. I knew falling down into one of the window wells would be serious. There was good footing, though, on the ledges, and some of the down spouts were just the right distance from the window so that you could lean into the column of the spout and hold onto it while you worked your feet up along the window trim. One time I started going up a little ways toward the second floor, but it was mid-afternoon and I was on the front wall of the school, and somebody on the street saw me and shouted at me to get down. I realized that I could do it, though, and that felt good.

It turned out that Nana and Papa's house was a better place to practice. Their house in Palatine was bigger and more solid than ours. The walls were made of rough brown bricks, and I noticed that at the corners of the house, every other brick was slightly recessed into the wall. It was probably a decorative touch, but I could tell right away that the indentations might make handholds and footholds. As soon as I could, I tried climbing up the corner of the house. It almost worked, but the indentations were only about an inch deep, and it was hard to hold on for more than a few seconds. But around one of the corners there was a corrugated metal downspout running from the gutter line to the ground. The downspout was only a couple of feet from the corner bricks, and I could see that it would provide the extra handhold I needed. It was getting dark, and my parents were already in the car getting ready to drive home to our house, but I slipped around the corner and tried it. It worked perfectly, just as I had thought. I climbed up three or four feet, heard the car horn honk, and jumped down. As I ran to the car, I was already making plans. I pictured myself standing at the peak of Nana and Papa's roof. I was leaning back against the chimney, holding onto the T.V antenna with one hand for support. I lay awake in the dark of my room, picturing my climb. I could feel the rough little ridges of brick against the pads of my fingers and pressing up into the soles of my sneakers. I would start up the wall, but then I would be back on the ground where I would start up again. I never got to the top, or even most of the way. I just kept starting my climb, knowing that I could do it.

A few weekends later Annabel and I went to stay at Nana and Papa's house for the night. On Saturday afternoon when Nana and Papa went to the store and Annabel was playing inside the house, I had all the time I needed to figure things out and start my climb. The corner of the house with the good downspout was in a side yard surrounded by high hedges, so I didn't have to worry about neighbors or kids on the street bothering me. The first three or four feet went easily, just like before, but when I got up above the level of the first floor windows, it started to get hard. I think I was getting a little scared, but it was harder to calm down on the wall than up in a tree where you can usually find a comfortable place to stop and rest. In order to keep a firm hold on the downspout, I could only wedge a little bit of the sole of my sneaker into the indentation in the brick. When I stopped to rest, I could feel the sharp edge of the brick digging into the bottom of my foot. The longer I stood still, the more uncomfortable and more cramped my foot felt. If I took my foot away from the little ledge to shake out the cramps, I was pretty sure the other foot wouldn't hold me, and I'd fall. I tried taking a step down, but my sneaker slipped off the ledge, and the only way I kept from falling off was by hanging onto the downspout with all my weight until I could reposition my feet. When I did that, the metal column of the downspout moved a little in my hands, and I could hear something scraping above me at the gutter line. Sweat started pouring out of my head and neck. If I pulled the downspout off, I was going to fall for sure. This was bad. This was a lot worse than a tree. My foot was really starting to ache, so I decided in a flash that since I had almost fallen trying to step down, I'd just continue up, with no pauses, so I could maybe get up to the roof and rest. I knew I couldn't think about the downspout anymore. Either it was going to hold me, or it wasn't. I had to stop thinking about it.

I just climbed, one indentation after the next, until I was at the level of the bedroom windows on the second floor. I had to rest a minute because my feet and calves were aching with cramps. There were just a few more steps up to where I could reach the gutter and grab onto something that would let me pull myself onto the roof. It didn't make my legs feel any better to rest like that, so I stepped up until I could feel the rim of the gutter with my hand. I looked up and with a sickening feeling saw that the woodwork below the gutter actually jutted out away from the house. If I grabbed onto something up there and tried to pull myself up, my legs would have to come away from the wall, and I would be dangling by my fingers. This was the electric shock moment in a dream when you know you are going to wake up or you are going to die. But I couldn't make it be a dream. The sweat was cold in my hair and on my neck, and I know I was talking out loud. I must have been leaning with all my weight on the downspout because it made another scraping sound and slid a little way from the corner of the house.

Then I was yelling *Help me! Help me!* My voice didn't even sound like me. It sounded like some kind of gargling, and I realized it wasn't really loud enough. I would have to relax a little. I would have to tilt back my head and let my throat open up. Then I started yelling really loud. My legs were getting wobbly against the brick. I looked down and saw Annabel's beautiful little face looking up at me. I could tell that she knew just what I was feeling. She pushed her way through the base of the hedge and ran screaming for help.

A man in a white shirt appeared in the yard where Annabel had been standing. He was asking me questions, but I couldn't make sense of them. Then he was gone, and Papa was standing there, telling me to hold still. This I understood. It was a relief to have something I thought I could do: hold still. A few times while I was holding still the downspout scraped a little further away from the corner of the house. Pretty soon I was going to be spread out horizontally. If the downspout broke away from the wall, I was sure I would fall down headfirst. I wanted to fall feet first.

The man in the white shirt was back, and he was pulling a ladder into the yard. Then the ladder was next to me up against the brick, and I knew I was going to be all right. I wanted to laugh out loud. I wanted to sing. I tried to tell Papa not to worry, because I knew that if I let go of the downspout and got a grip on the ladder, I could easily swing my legs over to the rungs and climb down. I had done that kind of thing many times in trees. I was actually hoping to show Papa that I could do this, that I could manage something impressive as a climber. But he said *hold still!* in a voice so sharp I knew he meant it. Then he was up on the ladder right next to me. The man in the white shirt held the base of the ladder in place, and Papa looped one arm around my waist and told me to let go of the downspout. Holding me tight in the crook of his arm, he backed down the ladder and set me down on the ground.

I did not feel glad or relieved anymore, because I knew I had caused trouble. The air in the yard was charged with trouble. I almost never caused trouble at Nana and Papa's, only at home and at school. If I were home, my father would be cracking me in the head, and he would mean it. I knew that when Papa told my father what happened, he would crack me in the head. I was starting to feel sad and ashamed.

Papa finished talking to the man in the white shirt, and the man dragged his ladder out of the yard. Annabel had come back. She was standing just behind Papa, looking as if she might start crying. "*Jonathan,*" Papa said, "you come here." I approached him, and he took me by the shoulders and turned me away from him. I felt a firm loud whack on my bottom. Then he was stooped low in front of me looking into my eyes, and I started to cry. "That was very, very stupid what you did," he said. "That was unnecessary." Papa looked as though he might start to cry himself. "You could have been *kilt.*"

I KNEW WHAT PAPA MEANT. He meant he didn't want me to be killed, that it would make the family sad. But deep down I knew just the opposite, that I could not have been killed, that it just wasn't meant to turn out that way. I could have shot myself through the head with the pellet rifle in Cyrus's basement. I had lost my footing and started falling down from trees so many times I couldn't even remember them all. The man on the tractor said he wanted to blow my brains out. In the summers ahead I would not go for a week without some car or truck's breaks screaming as they approached an intersection where I had coasted through on my bike, thinking hard about other things, not paying attention. If I could have been killed, I would have been.

That bad time at the top of Nana's and Papa's house put me off the idea of climbing buildings, but the climbing urge rose up again whenever I saw a formation of rock out in nature. It started with the western shows I watched on TV in the afternoons, Hopalong Cassidy or The Cisco Kid or The Lone Ranger. There was usually a part of each episode when somebody was being chased on horseback along a dusty trail that cut through formations of rock. Sometimes the riders would dismount and climb up into the rocks and have a gunfight, the bullets of the missed shots singing and whistling off the stones. There were no places like that in Palatine, which was completely flat, but when we went up to the North Woods for our summer vacation, there were rock formations that carried me up to the other world. I remember hearing my mother say the word for them: bluffs. The word, like the bluffs themselves, seemed too charged with feeling to belong in the regular world. There were bluffs over Devil's Lake in Wisconsin, and there were bluffs overlooking Lake Superior in Michigan, and there were lots of high stone ridges that mother told me had been carved over many, many centuries by the clear rushing streams which in sunlight turned the rocky stream beds the color of honey. The bluffs and ledges were made of granite or limestone or sandstone, each with its special feel and its own kind of weight. When we drove up north, as soon as I would see an outcropping of rock along the side of the road through the car window, I would start making plans. I liked to think that most rock faces would be possible to climb. There had to be at least a little inward taper and some crevices or plants growing out of the rock for handholds and footholds. All I could think about was climbing rock ledges. I thought about it so much and made so many plans that I was able to label instantly every new rock formation I saw as Possible, Impossible, or Perfect.

One morning in the North Woods we took a day trip to a state park, and as soon as we settled our stuff in a picnic area along a rushing river, I saw a Perfect ledge. You had to cross the river over the dry tops of the stones to get to it, but after looking at it for a while, I figured out which stones would get me there. As soon as I could get free, I made my way to the opposite bank where the granite ledge rose up to a piney ridge overhead. I don't know exactly how high it went. It could have been five houses high, or maybe ten. I looked back across the river to our blankets and table and saw that my parents and Annabel had started on a hike. This was a relief, because I didn't want anybody watching me or calling for me to come down. The ledge was ridged and creased in such a perfect way I didn't have to stop and plan. The footholds and handholds were just there where I expected them to be, and as I made my way up along the warm stone, I could hear the river whooshing in my ears and feel the white force of the sun on my cheeks. The climb went fast, and when I paused to look down to the water, I saw that I was much higher up than I pictured I would be. I didn't want to think about getting scared, so I kept going, but leaning harder into the rock face. The good footholds continued, but the higher I got, the more I thought I should take smaller, slower steps. I don't know if it was because I was up so high, or whether there is just something about sound and rock, but the river seemed to get louder the higher I got, and for some reason it sounded like it was warning me. I was not far from the top, and I could feel no-energy tingles in my calf muscles, so I paused to rest. A bee was buzzing around my sweaty hair, so I raised up my arm to swat it away, but the motion of doing that upset my balance just a little, and I glanced down again at the river which now seemed tremendously far below the white rubber soles of my sneakers. The bee wouldn't let me alone, but I knew I had to let it do whatever it was going to do, because I needed to hold on. The next ten feet up would not be gradual. The narrow indented ridge I had been moving along came to an end, and I would have to step up to a series of parallel ridges above me. But at this height it did not feel good to lift either foot from the rock. And if I did lift a foot to step up to the next level, I would need a handhold, and I couldn't see one in the rock, only some green scrub growing out of cracks. Back, I thought. I would inch my way backwards and back down. But after a few little steps I realized it wouldn't work. I could not see where I was going, and the ledge was too narrow for me to turn my feet around. Then I knew. I was too high. I was in trouble again, the way

I was at the top of Nana and Papa's house, only this time there were no people, no safe yard, no ladder. The horrible feeling started and I was saying out loud: *this is really happening*, and then the sound of the river exploded in my ears.

At those moments when you can feel your pulse pounding along the side of your head and your heart is pumping so hard, you stop thinking and move. I was crying, but I was also shrieking. I was shrieking to myself to *go! Goddamnit, go! go! go!*

I don't really know what I did or how I did it. I remember stepping up onto each new ledge without stopping, even if there was only an inch or two to catch the sole of my shoe. The only thing I could see overhead was bits of green scrub, and I grabbed for it, and when it started to come away from the stone I grabbed the plant just above it, and I knew that I was not going to stop moving no matter what my legs felt like. I was snuffling and swearing out loud, and if there had been a living being in my way between me and the crest of that ledge, I would have killed it.

I jack-knifed my upper body over the lip of the last ridge and wriggled forward until my whole body was on flat ground. For a while I just lay there sweating and panting, my breath honking out of me in a way that burned my lungs. When my chest stopped heaving, I stood up. A family hiking on the trail along the crest stopped and stared at me. I could see their faces were full of questions, but I knew I could never explain. I sat down where I was, turned my back to them and looked over the river. When Papa carried me down the ladder from the top of his house, he told me that my climb had been unnecessary. But it was necessary. This ledge too was necessary, even more necessary. I was still shaking with it. I could tell that the family who watched me crawl over the top of the ledge was still looking at me, but I could not bear to turn around and face them. I knew they had no idea about the other world, and no idea about me.

Chapter Eight

My urge to climb never really left me, but there was another message I felt was trying to reach me, a message I was almost but not quite getting, although there was a clue. A phrase from a song on one of uncle Desmond's records would pop up in my thoughts before I would go to sleep at night, or I would find myself singing it out loud as I walked to school in the morning: *there's oh such a hungry yearning burning inside of me.* A man's voice sang this on uncle Desmond's record, and it sounded to me like he really had the feeling. I started to feel it, too, but I didn't realize what I had it for, until I heard Nana and Papa's recordings of "The Chocolate Soldier."

This happened in Nana and Papa's living room on a Sunday night in winter. It was snowing outside, and there was a fire in the fireplace. Nana and Papa were in their armchairs, mother and father were lying back together on the sofa, and Annabel, Uncle Desmond and I were reclined on the carpet in front of the fire. Papa suggested that we change the music and listen to "The Chocolate Soldier," which I had never heard before. I pictured a full-grown soldier made of chocolate, and I wanted to laugh, but the feeling was more than just funny. "The Chocolate Soldier" was a story, a whole operetta on three records, and I wanted to hear it. Papa showed me the illustration on the cover of the album. Against a chocolate brown background were the golden faces of a soldier and his bride. The soldier's golden hair flowed back from his forehead in waves, and the same kind of golden light shone in the hair and on the cheeks of the bride. The soldier held the tips of the bride's fingers in his hands, and they both looked out ahead of them with expressions showing that they were overwhelmed by something beyond them. These, I would learn later, were the faces of the singers Nelson Eddy and Rise Stephens, and though I had never seen them before, I recognized them immediately.

In a similar way the story of "The Chocolate Soldier" and the songs that told the story were wonderfully surprising to me and also deeply familiar. The Chocolate Soldier isn't really a soldier at all. He's a clown, and he doesn't think he's really strong or brave. But he meets the Lady, and he is completely in love with her. Many other soldiers love the Lady, and she wonders if she should really love such a foolish soldier, but as they tease and play with each other, she knows that he is her love. When the Chocolate Soldier thinks he has lost her, it is worse than if she had died. He sings that there isn't really a world, not even a night-world "while my lady sleeps." But she wakes up, and all the Chocolate Soldier's silliness and play have been good enough, and she realizes she does love him, and, finally, they both know it and sing, "Come, come, I love you dearly." The Lady sees that his clowning has been his secret way of making himself known to her, and that he is really a hero, and in the duet that ends the operetta, they sing together, "Come, come, I love you only, my hero, mine!" They have the hungry yearning burning feeling, and they will have it together forever.

This was the Third Great Thing, romantic love. I realized it had always been all around me, in the stories and in the songs. I think sometimes mother and father had it, even Nana and Papa, but at the heart of it there had to be a hero and a lady the hero loved and who loved the hero. I was small and thin and dark, and nothing at all like Nelson Eddy with his wavy blond hair and handsome man's jaw and the gold braid crossing the chest of his soldier's uniform, but when the romantic love feeling rose up in me, it was as if I swelled up inside Nelson Eddy and really was a hero. It made me different, braver and more serious. I pictured myself giving off a golden glow. It also made me sing. I used to sing a lot anyway, but now all I wanted to do was sing the love songs in "The Chocolate Soldier." But to really sing them the way I felt them, I had to sing them loud, which meant I had to be all by myself somewhere. To sing out the way I wanted to, I needed a lot of space.

As soon as I understood the romantic love feeling and started singing like a hero, I pictured myself singing to—"serenading" (another word I automatically knew)—my Lady. I knew that if I sang my "Chocolate Soldier" songs to the right girl in the right situation, she would feel what I felt and we would have romance. At first she would think I was just funny, just a clown, but she would secretly like that, and if I could get to certain songs, she would see me as a hero. In bed at night and whenever I could, I thought about how I would set up the love singing. It could only be outside, not in somebody's house. Most of the girls who lived on our street in Palatine were older than I was, some of them even teenagers. The littler ones that I knew did not seem to go out of their houses much. At least they didn't wander down around my house where I could see them. Sometimes on warm summer nights during Daylight Saving Time, a whole bunch of neighborhood kids would come together in somebody's yard, and we would play a chasing game like tag or capture the flag. It was very nice coming together in that way in the soft air. As it got darker and hazier, fireflies would come out, and just running around in that smoky light whooping and shrieking felt very close to the other world. I liked the way the kids were on those evenings. They were different than they were at school, wilder, happier. You could talk to anybody. You could grab somebody's wrist you didn't even know and twirl them around. Somebody might run up and knock you down for the fun of it, but not hurt you. You got to find out the people you liked. One night when it was almost dark I realized I liked Beth Bartell, who lived about a block and a half down our street and who was in Annabel's grade. Even though she was older than I was, Beth Bartell was very small and delicate and her brown hair went out from the sides of her head like a round bubble and tucked in somehow under her ears. She had a little nose and bright eyes, and she was cute the way a kitten or a puppy is cute. She was also very shy, and she never seemed to say anything or run very fast to get away during the games. I had a strong feeling that night when I went home that Beth Bartell could be my Lady. I started to have the hungry yearning burning feeling. I started planning how I would sing to her.

Beth Bartell was hard to find. I was allowed to go out and play on my own in the neighborhood, and I took to walking down the Bartell's end of our street. I got to be very familiar with their house, which was a ranch house, and how the bushes were arranged around the front windows and how easy it would be to climb up on their garage and walk around anywhere I wanted to on their roof. In my plans, Beth would wander outside by herself one Saturday morning. I would happen to be there, and I might have my axe in my holster or maybe my knife out while I was carving the end of a spear. I would be behind some hedges, or maybe completely hidden inside, and when she got close enough, I would start to sing.

> *I am just a Chocolate Soldier man*
> *For me you feel great pity*
> *Just a funny Chocolate Soldier man*
> *In a uniform so pretty*
> *A silly Chocolate Soldier Man*
> *Just made to tease the misses*
> *So sweet I'd melt*
> *If e'er I felt*
> *A full-grown maiden's kisses*

In my plans, if she heard me sing enough songs and got used to it, then it might be possible, although I was not completely clear about this, that she might sing back to me in a duet. I wanted this to happen very much, but I wasn't sure I could set it up. It was hard to picture Beth Bartell singing. I had hardly ever heard her talk. My feeling was that if it was going to work, she would first have to get used to me and my songs. Then maybe there could be the duet I was hoping for.

> *Jonathan: To tell the truth I never knew*
> *There were maidens such as you*
> *Beth Bartell: Do you mean that I am charming?*
> *Jonathan: In a manner most alarming*
> *Beth Bartell: Each time we meet you're someone new*
> *How can I be sure of you?*

Beth Bartell would not come out of her house. I watched her mother and father come and go. I watched her sister and her friends sun bathing on their lawn. Every now and then I would hear the old lady who lived in the house with the hedge I was hiding in tapping at her window and shaking her head at me. She wanted me to get out of there. I tried some other bushes, and then I sat on the curb for a long time, waiting.

Then one day I just decided to sing it. I was across the street and a little way down from the Bartells' house. I thought maybe she would hear me and come out. It actually felt good to let it out. I thought I sounded better than usual, very loud and very high.

I am—just a Chocolate Soldier Man
For me you feel great pity

Beth Bartell never did come out, and after a while I stopped thinking about her as my Lady. By this time school had started again, and there was a real Lady in my class, a new girl named Gwendolyn Bliss. The second I heard the teacher read her name and turned around to see who it was, I felt the hungry yearning burning.

Gwendolyn Bliss was the smallest girl in the class. She was so slender and delicate that she seemed almost breakable. She had blue watery eyes and frizzy blond hair that caught the sunlight like spun glass. When she was called on in class, she spoke so softly Mrs. Roederer had to ask her to speak up. "Gwendolyn," she would say, "you are *whispering*." But whispering was as loud as Gwendolyn could get. I knew this right away, and I knew Gwendolyn could not bear to be called on. I don't really know how I got to know her so well, but after a few days I felt I knew her completely. She didn't really talk, to me or to anybody else. But at recess I tried to be around her as much as I could, and she didn't mind. I did not have words for it then, but I knew something had happened to Gwendolyn that made going to school and reciting and talking to other kids almost impossible. When I could get her to look at me, her eyes seemed to be saying, "Don't you *know?*" I thought I did know, and I wanted to protect her. Somehow I knew that this is what a hero did, and I wanted Gwendolyn to be my Lady. She didn't say anything about it, but I think she wanted this too. She let me be around her. I could talk to her, but she didn't talk back. She didn't have to.

On our playground there were two jungle gyms, a new big one with complicated extensions and inner chambers and an old one, which was just a simple box with evenly spaced bars going up and down every few feet. The kids only wanted to play on the new one, and since Gwendolyn never wanted to be with the kids, especially at noisy, wild times like recess and lunch, she would stand way off to the side by the old one. Sometimes a boy from our class would approach Gwendolyn and start to tease her, and I would go over and give him a shove. Then maybe he and his friends would come over to me and start saying, "*Jonathan likes Gwendolyn, Jonathan likes Gwendolyn,*" but I would just stand there looking at them until they went away. I knew I was protecting Gwendolyn and that she was glad. It was working. It occurred to me that the old jungle gym was perfect for protection, so I led Gwendolyn inside, ducking under the bars, until she was right in the center where she could sit on the ground in the inmost square. From the outside it looked a little like she was in jail in there, but she was always willing to go inside and sit quietly until the bell rang and we had to go back to class. It felt lonely, but in a good way, to be standing guard next to the old jungle gym, not running around or playing with the other kids. Protecting Gwendolyn felt important. It felt like my job.

The more days I spent standing close to where Gwendolyn and guarding her, the more I felt the love feeling, even though she never talked. It seemed that every minute of the day, no matter where I was, I could see her just behind my eyes. I couldn't see her clearly, just an impression of her pale little knees and wrists, the delicate point of her chin, her wet, worried eyes, and the bright frizz of her hair. After school at home I couldn't get her out of my mind. I felt the hungry yearning burning feeling.

I was starting to want to sing my love songs to Gwendolyn, but it never felt right out there on the playground. I had barely been able to talk to her, and I was pretty sure it would frighten her if I started singing my songs, especially if it was loud. But at night in my dark room I could picture it. Gwendolyn would be squatting in the innermost square of the old jungle gym, and I would be guarding her. Something would have happened, and the other kids would have gone away somewhere, and I would sing.

Ah---sweet mystery of life at last I've found you

For---at last I know the secret of it all--

Then one day Gwendolyn was gone. For several days her chair was empty in her row in class, and one morning Mrs. Roederer told us that Gwendolyn had moved away. *Moved away.* It is hard to explain the kind of sadness I felt. It was as if someone had lifted something solid up out of my chest, leaving just a weak, airy space. Later I would understand how suddenly and completely you can lose a beloved person, but Gwendolyn, I realized, had been lost to me even when I thought I had her. That's what the hurt, worried look in her eyes had been saying. The worst thing had already happened to her. There was no protecting her. She could only keep moving away.

It must have been at about this time that I asked Annabel to marry me. I realized now that people you felt the love feeling for could move away, and it was at least possible that you could go the rest of your life without having that feeling with somebody else who had it at the same time. The idea of that made me really sad. Annabel was safe. She was my sister. I knew I could never feel too lonely with Annabel. She told me that brothers couldn't marry their sisters, which I kind of knew, but she understood what I meant. She told me she hoped she could marry Burt Lancaster or somebody just like him, but if, when we were grownups and if there was nobody else to marry, we could live together on a ranch.

The next year I had the love feeling for Linda Bluestone. It was very different from my feeling for Gwendolyn. It was much livelier. Linda Bluestone had been in my class since kindergarten, and she didn't live far from my street. I just hadn't paid very much attention to her before, but a few days into the new school year she was standing in front of our class giving a report, and I realized that she was beautiful. She was beautiful the way the stars on the covers of Annabel's movie magazines were beautiful. She had thick shiny black hair, which was braided into pigtails tied in bright bows. She was always happy, so happy that as soon as you even started to talk to her she would laugh, which crinkled up the corners of her eyes in a way that made you want to laugh too. Probably the reason I didn't love her before is that she was so happy she just went along with everything and blended in, or maybe she became beautiful all of a sudden.

I wanted to be around Linda Bluestone as much as possible. Whenever I could I would twist myself around at my desk to look at her or to whisper something funny. My teacher, Miss Rodd, told my mother I was being a problem, and when mother mentioned this at the table, I got a crack in the head. But I couldn't stop paying attention to Linda Bluestone. She liked me. She laughed at everything I said, and this made me want to be funnier than ever. I practiced making certain faces in the mirror at home, and I learned how to cross my eyes, which always made me feel a little carsick. At recess the boys played with the boys, and the girls played with the girls, but I couldn't stop myself from looking over every few seconds to see what she was doing. The girls mainly skipped rope on long, extra thick ropes the teachers handed out at recess. A girl would hold each end of the rope and swing it around in loops while another girl would step in and jump. They would jump in rhythm to chants they all knew, like "my boyfriend's name is Fatty, he lives in Cincinnati." It seemed like every time I looked over, it was Linda's turn to jump, and she would go on and on without stopping the rope. It looked to me as if she was barely lifting her shoes off the pavement, but she seemed to know exactly how and when to make a little hop. When Linda Bluestone was skipping rope, she looked like she was in a happy trance, and I wanted to be in a trance like that.

The best thing I could do was to make her laugh. She laughed at everything. The more serious she tried to be, the easier it was to crack her up. Sometimes Miss Rodd would have been mad at us in class, and there would be a hush in the room, with everybody keeping our heads down close to our desks while we did our work. This was always the time to catch Linda's attention. If I could just twist my head around and get low so she couldn't help seeing me from her seat, which was a couple places behind me in the next row, I had her. I could cross my eyes or put the eraser end of my pencil up my nose and she would erupt. I loved watching her try not to laugh. She would clamp her mouth shut tight and close her eyes so hard her nose crinkled, but then it would just come out of her, a sound like steam from a kettle at first, then her gasps and high giggles which got me and everyone around her going too. I knew I was being a problem, and it was getting worse, but there was nothing I could do.

63

I think Mrs. Bluestone drove Linda to school in the morning, because I never saw her on the way, even though I changed my route to go close to her house. But she and her friends walked home after school, and I got my chance to be as funny as I wanted. It felt so good making those plans. There were a bunch of trees between the school and her house that were perfect for climbing and hiding in. I liked to run out ahead of everybody after school and get up on a branch that went over the sidewalk where she and her friends would pass by. Just as they were going under me, I would let out one of my high hooting sounds. I might even make it say *Leeeeeeeeendaaa Bloooooooooostone*. This really worked, especially the first time. Linda and her friends stopped still on the walk. They looked behind them and all around, but no one looked up. I could hardly keep quiet watching them. After awhile they caught on, and I could see them looking up ahead into the trees as they walked. They would see where I was, and when they passed under me, they would say, "Hello, Jonathan. Up in the tree again, Jonathan? Har-dee-har-har-har." But I could tell from the way Linda acted at school that she like it and she liked me.

At night in my room I liked thinking up new plans for Linda Bluestone. One that I really wanted to try but couldn't figure out how to do was to fall down wounded, really hurt but not too bad, at her feet. I was pretty sure this would make her feel worried and want to take care of me. It would have to happen on the playground or on her way home from school. Somebody might have hit me in the forehead with a rock and made a gash, or maybe I fell out of a tree just as she was getting close. The problem was that in my plan, Linda would be by herself, but she was never by herself. She was always with two or three other girls, and I didn't want them in on taking care of me, so my idea of being wounded was just something I thought about a lot.

At school I wanted to be as funny as possible, but Miss Rodd was completely against it. I think she thought I wanted to make trouble just to bother her, but I didn't want that at all. I kind of liked Miss Rodd. She seemed young and nice for a teacher, although her clothes had a sour little smell when you got up close to her. Actually, I wished Miss Rodd thought I was funny. I wished she liked me. I just liked being funny.

Certain remarks and sayings came right out of me, without any planning. Of course the best feeling was to hear Linda Bluestone's high giggles from her desk behind me, but most of the time the whole class laughed when I got off a good one. Miss Rodd told me that my good ones were "unnecessary." She said it very slowly. She said that if I kept talking without raising my hand, "there would be trouble." Most of the kids thought trouble meant going to the principal, Mrs. Gilooley, which actually wasn't too bad, but I knew Miss Rodd could call my mother again, and I would end up getting cracked in the head.

Miss Rodd kept me after school one afternoon and told me I had to learn to keep my comments to myself. I knew I did, too, and most of the time I did, but that did not stop them from coming up into my mind. In fact, knowing I couldn't get off a good one out loud only made a lot more good ones come up. Having to be quiet made me funnier and funnier, and sometimes I had to duck my whole head under the lid of my desk because trying not to laugh at my good ones made me make faces and make me start to laugh in a way I knew would make Miss Rodd mad. The only thing that helped, finally, was imagining my glass booth.

Not only in Miss Rodd's class but for several years to come, I pictured a glassed in booth up toward the ceiling at the rear of the classroom. The booth was very realistic. You'd get up to it through a trap door over a wooden ladder built permanently into the wall. The booth was built specially for me, and I had the only key. The arrangement was that I could leave my seat whenever I felt like it and go up to the glass booth where nobody could see what I was doing, but I could see and hear what was going on in class, if I wanted to. Inside the booth was a chair where I could sit and look out over the class, and there was a microphone next to the chair. Anytime I was up there and came up with a good one, I could say it over the microphone, and everyone would hear it. It would not be making trouble, just a regular part of class. There was plenty of room in the booth for me to lie out on the floor when I wanted and to think about other things, or just rest.

It really helped, picturing the glass booth. I thought about being up there even when I was at home after school. If people had asked me about it then, I probably would have told them there really was a glass booth like that in my room at school. Most of the time it felt like there was.

I was going to have to wait a while before getting off good ones could be part of my regular personality. I needed to find other ways to express my love feeling to Linda Bluestone. It didn't take long to decide that she would probably like presents. I thought a lot about giving her presents and what kind of presents I wanted her to have. I don't think my first ones were very good. They were mainly old things that I used to like. I put a bunch of them—a sheriff's badge that would pin onto your shirt, some little metal army men from a whole huge set of army men Uncle Desmond gave me, and some loose sticks of gum, which I put into an envelope—into a shoe box, which I wanted to wrap with wrapping paper, but I couldn't find any. Something told me that this present wasn't going to be right, at least not right for a girl, so I went into Annabel's room and looked around for something. I knew I shouldn't take her stuff, especially her important stuff, but I thought maybe I could find something she didn't care about anymore. I decided that she might not care about a little china cardinal, which she probably got at the Ben Franklin in town. It was cute, but pretty small, and it wasn't on her main shelf. I felt bad about taking the cardinal, because Annabel was pretty careful about her things, but I needed something I thought a girl would like for the shoebox.

My plan was to give Linda Bluestone the presents first thing in the morning when she came into the room before school started. She would take her seat, and there I would be and I'd plunk the shoebox down in front of her, and she'd be surprised. But the more I thought about it while I was lying in my bed, the more it seemed the shoebox wasn't right. It was too big. The things inside didn't take up very much room. I could picture them sliding into a corner and not looking very good. I needed some tissue paper, the kind that filled up Christmas boxes. I could crumple up the tissue paper and separate the different presents and fill up the box. Early in the morning, before my father and mother got up, I went down to the pantry and looked for tissue paper, but there wasn't any. There were plenty of old newspapers, but they wouldn't be right for a present. It seemed to me there was not much difference between tissue paper and toilet paper, so I unrolled a lot of it from the bathroom and rearranged the shoebox. It looked a lot better. Just before I left the house after breakfast, I took a few packs of Kool-Aid from the cupboard and lay them in the box on top of the toilet paper. I don't even know what made me think of that. I just came up with it.

That morning at school it didn't work out the way I thought. Linda did not come into the room until class was just about to start. There was no time for me to visit with her by the coats or in front of her desk. Miss Rodd was already telling us to take our seats when Linda walked by my desk. "Hey," I said to her, "got you something," and I handed her the shoebox. I couldn't see her reaction because I had to pay attention. But as soon as I could, when we were doing silent reading, I looked back and caught her eye. She had a funny look, as if she wanted to ask me something. She was mouthing some words but not making any sound. She was mouthing "Kool-Aid" and "toilet paper." I could tell she didn't think of it as a present. She wanted it to be funny, and I saw right away that it wasn't really a present at all, at least not a good present, to a girl. After lunch the shoebox was on my desk with all the stuff in it. That felt really bad.

I needed to get the right kind of present. I wanted Linda to be surprised and amazed. Just by luck I got another good idea. My mother had two jewelry boxes, a little green leather one where she kept her rings and what she called her good jewelry and a big one full of what she called "costume jewelry." I always thought the big box was the good one, because the necklaces and bracelets and pins in it were bigger and shinier and more colorful. The glass stones were bright green and red and deep blue like the jewels in the strongboxes of a pirate movie. When you opened the top of the big jewelry box and saw the light flashing on all of it tangled up together, it looked like treasure. Mother used to let Annabel play with her costume jewelry. She and her friends would put it on when they played dress up. I knew it was all right for me to go into the big box, so I did, and I took out some things for Linda Bluestone. I took out two necklaces, a bracelet and a big pin. Each piece was a different color. One of the necklaces was ruby, the other one emerald, the bracelet was diamond, and the pin had orange stones, the color of apricots. I thought they looked beautiful lying next to each other, and even without them, the big jewelry box still looked full. That night when I pictured Linda looking at the sparkling jewelry, I got a very excited feeling.

I knew the shoebox was all wrong, so in the morning before I left for school, I tore a section of aluminum foil off the roll in the kitchen and wrapped up the jewelry. This time I waited for recess to give Linda the present. I wanted to give it to her when she was by herself, but she was never by herself, so I gave it to her while she was standing in a line of her friends waiting for her turn to skip rope. I just wanted to hand it to her and get out of there, but I had to say something, so I said, "here you go," and ran away. At lunchtime, Linda walked over to my table and said, "Are they for keeps?" I told her they were, and after lunch her friends followed me all over the playground singing, "Someone's got a girlfriend."

That didn't stop me from wanting to give Linda presents. Cyrus and I were out in the fields one bright afternoon, and we made our way down into a grove of overgrown sumac where there was sometimes standing water and frogs. I looked overhead and saw that there were puffy clusters of what looked like red velvet pouches attached to the sumac leaves. I picked one and saw that it was like a mitten, and with the sun shining on its red and purple folds, it was very beautiful. I could imagine seeing velvet like that in a pirate chest along with the jewels and coins. I knew right away I wanted Linda Bluestone to have these, so I picked a bunch of them and wedged them into my holster. I thought they might amaze her because they were not only beautiful, they were from nature.

In the morning I got a pillowcase out of the linen closet and folded the red velvet pouches inside of it and took them to school. I waited till after lunch, when she was at her desk and her friends weren't right there, but something had gone wrong with the package. There were dark red sticky stains all over the pillowcase, and when we looked inside, the fruits weren't puffy and velvety anymore. They were dark and wet. Linda stepped back when she looked inside the pillowcase. She said, "*Oooh,*" and I could see she was really scared. She said, "Are they *alive?*" I thought she was starting to cry. I grabbed the pillowcase up off her desk and stuffed it into the wastebasket next to Miss Rodd's desk. I couldn't stand even to think about the slimy red fruits stuck together like leeches. It also made me mad that my hands and arms and the front of my shirt were stained and sticky. It was one of those times when I knew that even more things were about to go wrong, and they did.

As soon as Miss Rodd came into the room, she asked if she could see me out in the hall. This was always bad. I was sure she was going to tell me I shouldn't have brought the spoiled sumac pouches to school, and that she was going to call home, and I would have to explain about the pillow case. But that was not it. She had just gotten a telephone call from Mrs. Bluestone who wanted to know about some jewelry that Linda had brought home from school. Miss Rodd said that Linda told her mother I had given her the jewelry. She asked me if this was true, and I said yes. The skin around Miss Rodd's mouth pulled in tight around her teeth. She asked me where I got the jewelry. I said I just had it, it was mine. I meant that I got it at home, out of the big box we were allowed to use and play with. "Jonathan," Miss Rodd said, "Did you *steal* that jewelry?" I said no, but I said it way too loud, and Miss Rodd said she didn't believe me, and she took me by the hand down to Mrs. Gilooley.

My mother usually didn't get really mad at me, just my father. But that afternoon she was really mad. I don't think it was that I had given her jewelry to Linda. She was mad and embarrassed that Mrs. Bluestone had to call the school about me. She told me Mrs. Bluestone had almost called the police. *The police.* My mother put her face down close to mine. She was angrier than I had ever seen her. Her chin was trembling. "Jonathan Force," she said, "why can't you behave?" When my father got home, he talked to mother and then he talked to me. He would ask me a question, I would answer him, and then he gave me a crack in the head. It went on and on, until mother was crying and made him stop.

After that it was harder to feel the love feeling for Linda Bluestone, and it went away. It didn't feel too bad, because I could see that she was always so happy. There just wasn't anything I could give her.

Chapter Nine

IT FELT LIKE I lost touch with the other world for quite a while. There was just school and the things our family did and, in the summer, Little League. My school started a program called Reading for Life, which meant that each year our teachers would put a big chart up on the wall with all our names listed on the left and a long row of numbered boxes to the right of our names. The idea was that you would go to the school library on Friday mornings and check out up to three books, and each time you finished one you told the teacher, and she would ask you a few questions about it, and then she would put up a little orange sticker of a book in one of the boxes across from your name. You could also get a sticker for books you read from your house or from the big library in town There were special announcements when someone read a lot of books, and a few times during the year Reading For Life Special Achievement Certificates were handed out after lunch to kids who had lots of stickers. I liked Reading for Life. I liked looking up in class and seeing the chart above the blackboard with the long orange line of stickers after JONATHAN FORCE. I usually had the longest line, and the only kids close to me were one or two girls, and sometimes they would read Golden Books, which were mostly pictures, and other really easy books just to get stickers.

I liked real books, like the Patriots Series, which were on a shelf right in the back of our homeroom. The Patriots Series were books about great Americans like Molly Pitcher, Sacajawea, Paul Revere, George

Washington, Nathan Hale, John Paul Jones, Andrew Jackson, Tecumseh, and Abraham Lincoln, who was from Illinois, downstate where Cyrus came from. The Patriot Series books could have been boring, but they weren't because they always started with an exciting episode and then backed up and explained. They also included a lot about the great person's childhood, which really interested me. There was a tremendous amount about Abraham Lincoln's childhood, which in a lot of ways reminded me of myself. Not just that he was from Illinois down around the region of Cyrus's people, but the way things would happen to him and how he got out of trouble. It was really hard for Abraham Lincoln to get books when he lived in cabins, but he got hold of every book he could and read it, like me. He had a lot of good moments, and the one I kept thinking about was when he was in a spelling bee at school and he was on the opposite side from a girl in his class he had the love feeling for. She was about to misspell a word by leaving out the letter "i" and Abraham Lincoln winked and got her attention and pointed to his eye, and she got the word right. That would have been cheating, except that he didn't do it for himself, and he also had the love feeling. Abraham Lincoln remembered practically everything he read in his books, and that helped him a lot when he grew up and started getting great. One time he read a book about a trial in ancient times where a witness lied that he saw a crime happen at night in the moonlight, but someone checked the records and found out there was no moon on that night, so the witness got in trouble. Abraham Lincoln was a lawyer for a while, and he was defending a man who was supposed to have committed a crime at night, and a witness said he saw him do it by the light of the moon. Abraham Lincoln remembered the book, and he checked the records, and just as in ancient times, there turned out to be no moon out the night of the crime.

The Patriot Series only went up to Woodrow Wilson, but there were plenty of other books I really wanted to read, and I did. Annabel loved the Oz books by Frank L Baum, and so I read those as fast as I could. Something about the way Frank L. Baum wrote about the Oz people made me pretty sure he knew about the other world. Annabel must have, too, because her other favorite book, *The Wind in the Willows*, was so much like the other world that I kept getting neck tingles when I read it. Then I went mad for sports books. The only sport that anyone ever played in my grade was baseball, but with underhand pitching by the teacher with a big softball coated with rubber. But my uncle Desmond had a whole shelf full of real sports books he liked when he was a boy. They had names like *Lou Gehrig, Pride of the Yankees* and *Touchdown Fever* and *The Big Play*. Most of them were about football in high school, and they were a little old fashioned in the way the players talked to each other, saying things like "Dearborn wasn't really a bad fellow" or "Come on, lads, it's now or never." But the books were still tremendously exciting. The stars of the teams didn't think about anything else except football and what was going to happen in the game coming up. I don't know if it was actually in the books or I just sensed it, but I could tell the stars went through the regular part of their days in school and at their houses in a kind of trance, remembering exciting plays and making plans. The sports books made me want to have a group of sports friends like the high school stars and hang around with them and talk about plays and games, but there was only recess softball, with Miss Rodd pitching underhand in her long brown coat. I started picturing some of my friends as teammates anyway, but when I would talk to them in my sports way, it didn't have the right effect. They hadn't read any of the books.

Real sports began the next summer with Little League. Thanks to uncle Desmond's books and to my father, I was kind of great in Little League. Because of the books, I was already in the mood, and because of my father, I could catch long flies and throw really long and really hard. Our back yard sloped down to some low bushes and high grass, and the other side rose up gradually to a flat place where new houses were going to go. My father used to play shortstop for his high school and after that for a team called Johnny Lynch's Tavern, and all his friends and Uncle Desmond said he had been a really good player, a star. My father still had his old glove, a big flat leather one with three fingers and a thumb. I couldn't use his glove because it was right-handed, and I was left-handed. It was also the old-fashioned kind with the fingers not tied together, so a ball could get through, but my father could catch with it anyway.

After we started playing catch a little in the yard, and he saw that I could catch and throw, he bought me my own mitt, an orange leather one with a black leather web and rawhide stitching around the pocket. My glove had ENOS SLAUGHTER written across the pocket in handwriting, because it was the kind of glove Enos Slaughter, a famous major league player, liked to use. The new glove had a great tangy smell, and I liked having it with me at all times. At first it was so stiff the ball would bounce right out of the pocket, but by flexing the fingers a little bit at a time from the inside, and by wrapping them around a ball and squeezing for a long time when the glove was off, I finally got it so it was floppy and loose, and I could open it up and snag balls that I never would have even been able to reach before. My father and I played catch as soon as he got home from work and changed his clothes, and we played some more after supper, if he wasn't too tired or didn't have orchestra rehearsal. At first we'd just toss the ball back and forth, standing pretty close together, but then he would back up, so it would take some effort to throw a good one. He would hold his glove in the middle of his chest and say, "hit the target," and whenever he didn't have to move his glove, he'd say "atta boy," and he meant it. I got so I could hit the target practically every time. It was as if something outside of me took over and locked my throwing motion in place in a certain way, so that I was lined up with the target. My bad throws were out of line in a way I could feel exactly, and that told me how to correct the next one and hit the target. Later on, when I got really good at the piano, I had the same feeling about right chords and wrong chords. If I ever missed a good chord transition, I always knew automatically how to adjust it to the right one. It was just like throwing balls—after a while the right way feels built in.

Besides just playing catch and teaching me to hit the target, my dad taught me how to catch all kinds of ground balls. He liked throwing me high pop ups, including really hard ones that made me run backwards and not just back pedal, and then suddenly he would throw me a hard grounder. Because the grass on our lawn was new and kind of patchy, the grounders could zigzag or bounce up suddenly in your face, but my father taught me the trick about that. He said, "keep your eye on the ball." He said people who miss grounders did it because they were afraid of the ball and looked away. He said if you keep watching the ball all the way into your glove, you'll never miss and you'll never get hurt. It was scary sometimes looking at a really hard grounder all the way until it was in your glove, but the trick almost always worked. A few times I watched one all the way to my glove and it still came up all of a sudden and hit me in the chin. But it was a good thing to know, keeping my eye on the ball, and it worked for even the hardest kind of catch, which is the short hop. Practically every kid I knew would lift his head up from a short hop, because he was afraid of the ball.

Hitting the target and fielding balls with my father after supper on nice warm nights felt so good that I would make imaginary bargains in my head that if we could just keep doing it and if it could keep not getting dark, I would do something really hard and good in the future, like give up my life for my troops. After a while my father taught me how to catch fly balls, the kind that came out to the outfield. Nobody my age could hit balls like that yet, but my father got a bat and sent me down over the slope of our yard, through the bushes and scrub and up over the far side onto the flat place. We were so far away from each other that I could barely hear what he was saying. He would toss the ball up with one hand and then hit it way up in the air out toward me. I didn't get it at all at first. I just stood there trying to track the black dot of the ball against the sky until it thudded down somewhere, and I would run and get it. I could hear my father shouting at me. He said, *"Get under it! Get under the ball!"* He was getting mad, but I saw what he meant. I got so I could get under where the ball was coming down, but I had a feeling that because it was coming from so high up and so far away, it would have a terrific force behind it, and it would shatter my hand inside the glove. When I got under one of the fly balls, I would offer up a stiff arm and make a tight face. I kept missing, and then I saw my father walking down the lawn toward me holding the bat. I started to feel the can't-do-anything feeling, and I thought I was going to get a crack in the head. But my father wasn't even mad. He talked to me in a slow, nice way. He said that catching a long fly ball was the same as catching a pop up. I just had to keep my eye on it, get under it and gather it in. When he said "gather it in," he showed me how to bring the glove down into my body as the ball fell into it. He showed me what I was doing with my stiff arm and how that didn't work. I had to gather the ball into the pocket and seal it with my other hand. He made it look slow and smooth and graceful. He said to imagine that it was a bird I was taking into my glove. I should take it in firmly enough to keep it, but not to hurt it. He threw me a couple of pop ups to let me get used to the bird idea, then he walked back over to our yard and started hitting me long flies. After one or two, I got it. I heard the pop of the bat against the ball and tracked the dark dot. I ran a few yards to my right, got under it, and gathered it into the pocket of my glove. The ball made just the right smack in the mitt, and it didn't feel any harder than a pop up. I heard "*Atta boy! Atta boy*"! and I couldn't stop the waves of neck tingles. I caught all of the next ones, and in a few minutes I couldn't wait for my father to hit the next ball. I was tracking and getting under everything, including a few that started going way over my head. My father shouted, "Wait a minute!" and went inside the house and got my mother. Then he was hitting me more balls, and I got under them and gathered them in. I knew where the ball was going the second I heard the crack of the bat. I was talking to God out loud, saying please don't let it get dark. It was the other world.

That summer when school let out I was old enough for Little League, the eight and nine-year old division where you had teams and games but only got to wear hats and tee shirts. The ten to twelve-year-olds got full uniforms, and their teams had the names of real Major League teams, like the Cubs and the Dodgers. In our division all the teams were named after birds. I was on the Wrens, and we had red hats and tee shirts. Our coach was a big blond guy named Wayne Stegner. We all knew him because he was a lifeguard in the town pool. He went to college. He talked very loud and liked to clown around, and the other kids said they liked him because he was so funny. I didn't think he was that funny. He got your attention by making faces, and he liked to talk in an exaggerated dumb guy voice, but I wished he wouldn't. I wished he would never talk and just hit us fly balls and ground balls and let us play. He decided right away that I should be a pitcher because he could see that I could throw hard. He put on a catcher's mitt and had me pitch to him from the mound in the middle of the infield. He made a target and said, "throw it right into my glove, Lefty." This kind of made me mad, because I already knew where to throw it, so I pitched to him as hard as I could. I knew he was going to be surprised, and he was. The pitches went right in the target, and there was a really loud crack when they hit the mitt. Wayne Stegner made some whooping sounds and his exaggerated dumb guy face. He looked around at the other kids, took off his mitt and shook his hand as if it was hurt, and said, *"did you guys see that?"* in his dumb guy's voice. I pitched to him some more, and I kept hitting the target, even when he crouched down low behind the plate like a regular catcher. After a while he got up and said, "I've gotta see something." He got a new ball out of a box, and he asked Freddy Fox, who was the tallest kid on the Wrens, to put on one of the plastic batting helmets and bat. Then Wayne Stegner put on a mask and a chest pad, which was way too small for him, and crouched down behind the plate. He told Freddy to swing away.

It was interesting seeing the target right there behind the plate but with Freddy leaning over it with his bat. This made it seem like there was less space to throw into, and the target would be harder to hit. But I figured it out automatically. I threw a pitch as hard as I could, and the new white ball slanted down past Freddy's elbows and smacked right into the target. Wayne Stegner whooped and yelled *"Strike!"* I threw another pitch and it was exactly the same. Wayne Stegner told Freddy they were good pitches, and Freddy looked out at me with a worried expression. I kept pitching as hard as I could. I knew just when to snap my wrist and just when to let go of the ball, and they were all right in the target. Freddy started swinging at the pitches, but the swings were weak. It looked to me like the ball passed right through the bat. When my father saw people swing like that, he'd say to me, "He's just waving at the ball." Wayne Stegner had a bunch of other kids put on their helmets and bat, but no one even ticked the ball. After a while Wayne Stegner stopped talking, and there was just the loud smack of the ball hitting the catcher's mitt.

When there was nobody left to bat, Wayne Stegner walked out to the mound with one of his exaggerated faces. I knew he was going to do something stupid, and he did. He said, "I just gotta see something." Then he pushed the sleeve of my tee shirt up over my shoulder and held by left arm out straight. I could tell what he was going to do. My arm was pretty skinny, and I was embarrassed about it. Most kids' arms got bigger and more muscular from the elbow upwards, but mine stayed about the same. A boy in my class, Jimmy Mahler, said my arms looked like sticks, and I knew what he meant. Wayne Stegner made a circle with his thumb and first finger and closed it around my upper arm. He made one of his faces and then held up his hand to show the size of the circle to the kids standing around the plate. He said, "What have you got in that arm, Lefty?" I knew, in a way, he was trying to tell me he thought I was a really good pitcher, but I also knew that he wanted me to feel as bad as possible. I've learned that people like Wayne Stegner, people who need to funny all the time, are usually the meanest people of all.

That summer it felt like there was nothing in the world but baseball. My father got me a tin tube of Neat's Foot Oil for my glove, and I oiled and massaged the mitt until it was the color of cooked meat. My mother told her friends that I slept with my baseball glove, because I kept it with me in my bed. I liked playing catch with my father and having him hit me fly balls, and I liked playing baseball with my friends on dewy mornings and hot dusty afternoons in the town park, but something about Little League wasn't quite right. It felt too important. When we all showed up for the games with our same color shirts and hats, and the parents were sitting in lawn chairs behind the backstop, and the game was getting ready to start, I could feel myself getting a little dizzy and my mouth going dry. The only way I could make myself feel better was to go into a kind of trance. I was the main pitcher for the Wrens. I would usually pitch the first three innings and then other kids would come in to pitch the other three innings, because everybody was supposed to get a chance to play. It was always exciting to feel the new white ball in my hands, but I stayed in my trance watching my pitches smack into the target, passing right through the bat if the batter swung. Usually everybody struck out, and it usually took only three pitches. Once I walked a batter, because I threw four pitches in a row in exactly the same place just outside to the left. Then I made a little adjustment in my mind, and all the pitches went back to the target. I only remember one boy ever hitting a pitch. It was against the Finches, the team with yellow shirts. I was in my trance, and a boy who didn't look like he would swing at a pitch suddenly did. There was a loud *bink* and the ball went skittering between first base and where the parents were standing. It was a foul.

After my three innings, there would be nothing to do but sit on the bench and watch until I could go home. Even during my innings, when we were up at bat, it would take so long before I got my turn that I wished I could just take my glove and go behind the stands and play catch with my father. One night during one of our last games before we were about to go up to the North Woods for our vacation, I remember looking out from the bench across the park to the far diamond where the ten-to-twelves were playing. There were lights on over that field which gave everything over there an exciting yellow glow. Every now and then I could hear a little roar from that game, which meant somebody had gotten a good hit or made a great catch. I started to feel sad that I was sitting in my red Wren's tee shirt far away from all that. I knew when I went back out on the field to pitch, no one would hit the ball, and if I hit the ball when I was up to bat, probably no one would catch it, or if they did, they would make a bad throw, and I would run around the bases, but not because I had done anything especially good. I didn't want Little League to be bad. I wanted to like it and to like being such a good pitcher, but Little League wasn't anything like the other world. It wasn't even like baseball.

When school started again and it was still nice out, I got the idea that I could get the good feeling back into baseball if I could play it with other world people like Cyrus. He was a grade behind me in school now, in a special class, but we still liked to see each other after school and go out into the fields. I asked him if he wanted to play some baseball instead, and he said, "I'm no good." I got him to come over to my yard and play with me anyway. He didn't have a glove, so I gave him my father's old-fashioned one with the big fingers not laced together. Cyrus didn't know it wasn't a good glove, and he didn't seem to care. He looked limp and unhappy standing across from me in the yard with his arms hanging down at his sides and my father's old glove practically falling off his wrist. I threw him the ball, and I could see that he had probably never played baseball before. He turned away a little as if he wanted to protect himself, and when the ball got to him, he kind of batted at it with his glove, and it rolled past him into mother's flowers. I tried to show him a few things like keeping your eye on the ball and gathering it in like a bird, but I could tell by the way he lowered his chin into his neck that this was going to be like reading. I tried standing just a few feet away from him and tossing the ball underhand, but he only batted at it with the mitt. I could see I was only making Cyrus sad. Parts of the world just didn't go together. I put the gloves and the ball back in the house, and we went down the street a little way and practiced throwing our knives so they would stick in a tree.

Chapter Ten

Then, for quite a while, my life got small and dim and hard to remember. Almost no pictures come up, except sitting at my desk in school, trying to develop a secret handwriting or trying to learn to write with my right hand, so that the work I handed in wasn't always smudged with pencil lead or ink from the heel of my left hand. That whole period seemed to be cold weather, and I was usually sick, either just getting bronchitis or getting over it, or having it so bad I had to stay home from school coughing up blood- streaked phlegm into the toilet or blowing it out my nose into tissues that turned hard overnight. I hated the honking sound of my coughing and the raw feeling it made in my chest. Diane Fuerst who, because of alphabetical order, always sat next to me, would get mad at me for coughing all the time. She told me it was "disgusting." I got mad at her right back and told her I couldn't help it, but I actually knew what she meant. Sometimes the stuff would shoot out of my nose and my mouth and I'd have it on my hands or it would get on my work. We sat side by side at tables that year, not desks, and Diane Fuerst would slide her chair as far away from me as she could get. Once she turned back to me and said, in the meanest way she could, "I bet you have T.B."

I wasn't going to explain to Diane Fuerst, who wasn't even nice, about having pneumonia when I was born and because of that always having bronchitis, but I really did want to stop coughing all the time in school. And although I didn't show it, when Diane Fuerst said she bet I had T.B., it really scared me. T.B. was on our minds because one of the P.E. teachers, Mr. Kiner, got T.B. that year and had to leave school and go away to a sanatorium. After he left and Mrs. Gilooley told us about it at lunch hour, we all had to get T.B. tests, which involved every kid in the school lining up, one class at a time in the main lobby, to get a shot on the inside of our arms. I hated this for two reasons. First, I couldn't stand the idea of shots. I'd rather just get a terrible cut all of a sudden by accident than sit there watching someone sticking a needle in very slowly on purpose. Second, Mrs. Gilooley told us what went into you from the shot was a tiny bit of tuberculosis called bacilli. The idea was that the tiny bit would cause our body's immune system to rise up and resist real tuberculosis. It made me sick to think about this. I couldn't stand picturing little brown drops of tuberculosis squirting into my blood. I could picture the theory not working and the bacilli taking over. This is one of the reasons I wanted to stop coughing so much, not to please Diane Fuerst. What I actually told her was, "Yeah I've got T.B., and now you've got it, too," and then maybe I coughed at her.

When I got to be ten, everything got better. I had always wanted to be ten, and now I was. That was the year of fifth grade, the best grade and the last one before Junior High. I had Mr. Click for homeroom and I loved Patsy Prentiss. I remember thinking that if there were ever a time I could go back into and stay forever, it would be ten.

I was so lucky to get Mr. Click, but maybe it wasn't luck. I had been waiting a long time to feel something from the other world again. Sometimes, like when I was sick, I wondered if I ever would. So when I got Mr. Click, it actually felt like it was planned. There were three sections of fifth grade, Mr. Click's, Mrs. Mellors', and Mrs. Goodroe's. People hated Mrs. Mellors because she was strict and had a really sour expression on her face all the time. Annabel had Mrs. Mellors and was so scared and unhappy that she would beg mother to let her stay home from school. I hated Mrs. Mellors for making Annabel feel like that, especially since Annabel usually loved her teachers and would write really nice private notes about them in her diary. I had already decided that if I got Mrs. Mellors, I was going to be a problem. Mrs. Goodroe was tall and tired looking. Her hair and skin were the same grayish color, and on one side of her face she had some kind of purple growth or stain that started from under her hair and went all across her cheek.

Mr. Click not only turned out to be just as much fun as everybody said, he really liked me. He didn't care if I got off a good one every now and then, and sometimes he would get off a good one about me. He was really tall and not too old. He had short curly black hair and wore glasses with thick black frames that kind of went with his hair. He didn't dress like a teacher. He wore loose old corduroy coats and pants, with usually a dark green or a black shirt and a tie with bright swirls. He had a bunch of different pairs of suede shoes with dark rubber soles, and there was something extra exciting about his wearing those shoes because Elvis Presley had a hit song called "Blue Suede Shoes," and something about Mr. Click just went with the feeling of Elvis Presley. Mr. Click had a yellow Pontiac convertible, and sometimes when we were driving somewhere in town, we'd see Mr. Click heading somewhere with his top down. Mother would say, "Look, there's your teacher," and almost laugh. When she talked about Mr. Click with her friends she called him "a real character."

Being in Mr. Click's class was just as relaxing as not being in school. We did the same kind of work that the other sections did, but there was nothing tense about it. He was a good explainer, especially in math, and he always knew when to stop when somebody couldn't do a problem on the board and ask the whole class questions until everybody, even the kid at the board, got the idea. I think Mr. Click liked literature and social studies best, because that's what we spent the most time on. He liked to give us funny composition assignments, like "What is the Stupidest Thing You Have Ever Done?" Or "Describe a Place That Couldn't Possibly Be." Sometimes he would just talk to us in a personal way and tell us stories about things that happened to him when he was young. Before he handed back our compositions, he would sit on the front of his desk and read parts that he liked out loud to the class. He wouldn't say whose composition it was until he was finished. The first time he did it, the first week of school, he read practically all of mine. The assignment was to write about the best thing we did over the summer, and I wrote about going into the woods behind our cabin in Michigan and trying to spot a bear. I actually did that, but it didn't work, because I'm sure bears didn't want to hang around close to resorts during the day, and also it was sticky and airless in the woods. There was no path, and I was getting a lot of mosquito bites, so I cut it pretty short. But I decided to make my composition funny, with a lot of exaggerations and some made up stuff thrown in. I wrote how I thought I would be protected if the bear attacked me because I had my pearl handled pocketknife with me. I really did think that at the time, but the way I wrote about it made me seem like a real dork, but in a funny way. When I wrote about doing really stupid things, I liked to use very intellectual expressions, like "and this turned out to be not a particularly good idea" or "you can imagine my mother's surprise" because it had a funny effect. Mr. Click always read my good parts to the class, and sometimes he would laugh out loud. From then on, no matter what the assignment was, I couldn't wait to get going on it and to come up with something that would make Mr. Click and everybody laugh.

You couldn't make Mr. Click lose his temper. He could get everybody to quiet down just by standing up and saying, "*People--?*" When a kid got mad at somebody and was doing mean teasing or got in a fight, Mr. Click would just lead him away to some place quiet and ask him what was wrong and what the kid could do to make it better. He had to talk to me once when I got mad at Scott Overman for smashing into me while we were playing dodge ball. I called Scott Overman a fat, stupid slob, and Mr. Click heard me, and he came over and led me away. He leaned forward in front of me, so he was looking right into my eyes, and he asked me how I thought it made Scott Overman feel to be called fat. Mr. Click was calm and nice, not mad. I told him I thought it would make Scott Overman mad. Mr. Click asked me what else Scott Overman might feel, and I actually started to picture it. I'm not sure if Mr. Click explained it or if I figured it out, but I started feeling really bad about what I said, because Scott Overman really was fat. His tee shirts would come up out of his pants when he was out on the playground, and his fat stomach hung out over his belt, and I know he felt bad about it. I wasn't one of the kids who called him Fatso everyday, but I could see that calling him a fat slob when

83

he smashed into me could really hurt his feelings. Mr. Click asked me what I thought I could do about that, and I went right over to Scott Overman and told him I didn't mean it. I told him I didn't think he was fat.

Mr. Click always had a sense of what we were up to, who our friends were and who we didn't like, even things we did outside of school. He knew about Patsy Prentiss and me, not just that we were boyfriend and girlfriend and that we were together all the time, but the exact way I felt about her. In a way, I was glad he did, because that made it seem important.

Patsy Prentiss was the first person I had the love feeling for who loved me back in exactly the same way. It wasn't anything like the way I felt about Beth Bartell or Gwendolyn Bliss or Linda Bluestone when I wanted them to be the Lady in a romance with me. Patsy Prentiss was a girl I really got to know. She entered our school in the fourth grade, but she was not in my section, so I barely knew who she was. At the end of the summer my mother told me we got an invitation to a barbecue picnic and pool party at the Prentiss's house. It was for all the kids and families who were going to be in Mr. Click's class. I didn't think very much about it, except that I liked hot dogs cooked on a grill. I didn't quite understand the part about its being a pool party. It didn't seem much like a party to eat in somebody's yard and then go over to the town pool and swim. I didn't realize until we got to their house that the Prentiss's had their own swimming pool. I didn't think anybody in Palatine had their own swimming pool. It was nice, too, a lot smaller than the town pool, but completely closed in with a high wooden fence. Patsy was already in her bathing suit when we got there. She stood there in the driveway with her parents saying hello and shaking everybody's hand as they arrived. I thought it was going to be embarrassing saying hello to her and shaking the hand of a girl in my own grade, but she was in such a good mood and so natural about it that it was fine.

Inside, the Prentiss's house was huge and ritzy. You couldn't even see all the rooms. You went into a big hallway with shiny wooden floors, and on each side there were fancy living rooms with white carpets and light blue chairs and couches. It took me a minute to realize the thing that was so different from other houses was that the ceilings were really high, like at school or the post office. Mrs. Prentiss took me to a bedroom with its own bathroom and told me I could change into my suit in there if I wanted. When I went in there and locked the door, I had to sit on the bed for a minute and think about being rich. But I also wanted to get outside and get in that pool.

I had a good feeling the second I saw Patsy in the driveway smiling and talking to everybody. Her hair was a mixture of brown and blond, messy but interesting to look at. It was cut almost as short as a boy's if he didn't get a haircut for a long time. Patsy must have been in her pool all summer, or else she just got outside a lot, because she was brown and shiny all over from the sun. She was so tan the skin between her fingers and toes was bright white. When I got out of the changing room and found my way to the door to the pool, Patsy was standing at the edge of the diving board talking to the kids who were treading water below her. I loved Patsy Prentiss's voice. It sounded a little hoarse, the way you get when you've been shouting for a long time or when you've got a certain kind of cold and everything sounds lower and scratchy, but in a lovable way. When she was really excited about something, Patsy's voice would break into croaks and squeaks.

She was really good at thinking up things to do and setting up games. "Come on," she said in her croaking voice to the kids in the pool, "let's have a contest to see who can make the biggest splash off the diving board." We all wanted to do that. Then she set up contests to see who could do the biggest belly flop and who could swim the farthest under water. The sparkly blue-green water of that pool was the best water I ever swam in. It would hold you up even without dog-paddling. When it started to get dark, lights went on underneath, and the pool glowed like a huge blue-green jewel. I never went out to the yard to get anything to eat, because I wanted to stay in that pool, as close to Patsy Prentiss as I could get.

IT WAS ONE OF THOSE great swimming nights when the water felt warmer than the air, making you want to stay in and keep fooling around. When it was time to get dressed and go home, Patsy and I and two or three other kids were still in the water. We were crouched in the shallow end up to our chins, and everybody had been in the water so long, our voices shivered when we talked. This made us laugh, but everything was making us laugh, and I got off some really good ones. When I got home, I couldn't stop telling Annabel about everything that happened, the Prentiss's ritzy house and the pool and how great it was that we were all going to be in Mr. Click's class for the whole year. I didn't even try to tell her about Patsy, because I actually had too much feeling to express, but I think it came out in what I was saying about everything else.

Because of her pool party, Patsy and I already knew each other when school started. On the first day when Mr. Click read off her name, Patricia Prentiss, I turned around to look at her, and she was already looking at me. She had the same great smiling expression she had when we were fooling around in her pool. It was an expression that said *let's go, let's do something,* and that's pretty much what we did. The second we got out after school, we headed off somewhere to try something Patsy or I happened to think up. Patsy always liked there to be a lot of kids, and she was nice about asking everybody, even kids nobody ever talked to or who were never allowed to do anything and never came along. A lot of the best things we did involved jumping and falling.

In the town park closest to her house they put in a really high new slide. It was so steep, especially up at the top, that a lot of kids, even big kids, wouldn't go down it. But we figured out every possible way to go down, on our stomachs, sideways with our legs over the sides, two people back-to-back, two people face-to-face, and lying down backwards. Going down the slide in a tricky position could be really dangerous because unless you knew how to slow down by making friction with your legs against the sides when the slide started to level off toward the bottom, you'd just shoot out onto the gravel in whatever position you were in. That happened to Larry Landis when he went down backwards, headfirst. I was just about to go up the ladder when I saw him do it. Going down backwards headfirst made it hard to get friction and slow down at the end. Larry Landis's legs were hanging over the rails of the slide, so he couldn't get any friction at all. When he got to the bottom, he flew through the air for a little way, and then his head and back hit the gravel really hard.

I ran over and wondered if he would be dead. His eyes were open and he looked confused, and then he started to cry really hard, like a much younger kid. His voice went up really high, and he lost his breath and started slobbering and choking. It was terrible looking at him. Patsy ran home and got her mother, who helped Larry sit up. The hair on the back of his head was all bloody, and some of the blood was drying and turning black. Mrs. Prentiss had a towel with her, and she wetted it in the drinking fountain and held it against the back of Larry's head. She helped him to get up and walked him over to her station wagon where he and Patsy got in, and Mrs. Prentiss drove to the doctor's. The next day Larry came to school with six stitches sown into the back of his head. You could see them perfectly, like a spongy black zipper against the white circle of his scalp where the doctor shaved his head.

After that we still liked trying things on the new slide, but Patsy decided to make it safer by having a bunch of us drag an old mattress from the back of her garage over to the park. We put it right at the bottom of the slide to break our falls. It felt really good landing on the mattress, no matter what position you were in. You didn't even have to make friction with your legs and slow down at the end. One time Patsy and I went down face-to-face, with her frontward and me backward. This meant we were looking right into each other's eyes the whole way down, which made both of us scream with laughter. The next thing I knew we were at the leveling off place at the bottom, and then I was falling over backward in a kind of somersault with Patsy smashed up into me. I landed on my bottom, and her forehead hit my upper lip really hard. When we got untangled on the mattress and I sat up, I had pins and needles in the space between my upper lip and my nose. Patsy looked confused and was feeling her forehead with her hand. There were two white dents above her eyebrows, and while I was staring at them, they filled up with bright red blood. Patsy said, "Look at you!" I knew there was something wrong because my upper lip felt numb the way it did when the dentist gave me Novocain. Something metallic tasting was pooling in my mouth, and when I wiped it with my hand, my hand was all bloody. Somebody ran off to get Patsy's mother, and I sat there holding my throbbing mouth, hoping Patty was going to be okay and that my teeth wouldn't come out. They were my second teeth.

Mrs. Prentiss took us to their doctor's office, and in different little rooms Patsy and I both got Novocain and stitches. Mine were inside my mouth between my gums and my teeth, and when I got home I couldn't eat anything except cold soup. When the Novocain wore off, I felt like the front of my mouth was on fire. The next morning when I got up and looked in the bathroom mirror, I looked like a clown. It hurt to talk, and my front lip was so puffed up it looked like I was making a duck face. I didn't want to go to school looking like that, but mother said I had to. One of my front teeth was a little loose, and mother said I was lucky it didn't get knocked out. She was mad at me for fooling around on the slide. Patsy came to school with just a regular bandage on her head, and she looked even prettier and livelier than usual. That made the love feeling swell up inside me, and I really wished I didn't look so bad. I wanted Patsy to look at me and feel what I felt when I looked at her.

We weren't always trying dangerous things and getting hurt. Some of the things we thought up were just fun. By fifth grade we were old enough to walk into town after school and, if we had any money, buy a coke or an ice cream or maybe Hostess Cupcakes at the Creamery soda fountain. It was always felt good to be sitting at the soda fountain, getting off good ones with Patsy and a lot of kids. Sometimes there would be ten or twelve of us at once, and it was hard to get that many empty stools, especially next to each other. The ladies who worked behind the counter at the Creamery were usually mad at us, because the whole time we were there we'd only spend one dime on a small coke or a small chocolate phosphate, the cheapest things you could order. They kept telling us to keep it down or to go outside. They thought we were too loud, which we probably were, but I couldn't help it. Doing things with Patsy and other kids after school always put me in a great mood, and I would get off good ones without even trying.

It was Patsy's idea to see if we could get all the way to the Creamery from school going only through people's back yards. It was about five or six blocks into town from school, but the first few times it took so long to get over all the fences that by the time we made it to the Creamery, it was time to go home for supper. But we modified the rules a little so it worked. We said that if there were two fenced in yards in a row, you could just do the first yard and then go along the fence to the sidewalk and skip the next house. If the next fenced in yard had a dog in it, you could go straight back and continue along the yards of the next street over. Only one or two kids stuck with Patsy and me in the back yards game, because it could get scary. Sometimes an old man or an old lady would look through their window and see us running through their yard, and they would bang on the glass and yell at us to get out of there. One old lady, who had a fence, always yelled the same thing, "You're *trespassing!*" That got to seem really funny to me, although I was scared the first time I heard her. When we were sitting around at the Creamery or at the lunch table at school and somebody would say something just right, like "can I come over to your house after school?" I would go into my high crackling voice and say, "No, you're *trespassing!*" One day in class when we were discussing the Dakota Indians and how setting up railroads and towns and fences made it impossible for the Indians to keep hunting buffaloes, Mr. Click asked the class how we would feel if we were the Dakota Indians and people started settling right in the places where we had always been able to hunt. I didn't even have to think, I just croaked out, "You're *trespassing!*" It got to be one of my main jokes.

    Patsy liked to lead the way when we'd go by back yards to the Creamery. She was good luck, too, and nothing bad ever seemed to happen when I was running along close to her. Once we were sneaking through a yard, and just when we got to the garage, a car pulled up and a man and woman got out with groceries. I thought the man was going to get mad, but Patsy said in a loud, friendly way, "Excuse me, sir, may we cut across your lawn?" They didn't mind at all, and we just kept going. I had never thought of getting permission. In spite of the scary times when somebody might be yelling at you or there were fences with barbs at the top or mean dogs, I really liked the back yards game. Besides the risks, there was something interesting about seeing a familiar street in a completely different way, seeing the kinds of things people kept in their yards or behind their garages, seeing that some of the back yards were still kind of wild, or that some had little barns or a cement pond with fish in it. In the winter it was dark by the time I left Patsy's house or the Creamery, and I would even go home through people's back yards. This was easier and less scary because I was alone and no one could see me in the dark, and I wasn't in any hurry. The better I got to know everybody's property, moving from yard to yard in the dark, the more I felt I knew the town better than anyone else ever could. It was like the town was now arranged inside me.

Two of the times I had with Patsy Prentiss that year were like nothing that had ever happened to me before. I saw Patsy for most of the time every day. I got to school early so I could fool around with her in the main lobby or at her desk. We always had lunch together, and after school everybody would go over to her house, which had a ping-pong table and an electronic bowling machine in a big paneled room in her basement, or we'd go to the Creamery, or just think something up. Mr. Click called us the Bobbsey Twins, and without anyone having to say it, all the kids linked us up as boyfriend and girlfriend.

The first great thing with Patsy happened the afternoon we went out to look at the new housing development site at the edge of the fields. All week huge tractors and bulldozers had been roaring through town, past the school and past our house. It felt a little as if some kind of army was passing through on the way to a war. At the edge of the fields, where the new houses were going to go, the earthmovers had already dug deep pits for the foundations, and the dirt was piled up in a line of connected little hills. The weather was starting to get cold, and I remember hoping the hills would still be there when it snowed, so we could go down them on our sleds. Patsy and I and a bunch of other kids made our way up to the top of the side of one of the hills and walked along the ridgeline. About half way down the slope of the last hill, the packed dirt leveled off a little to form a kind of landing and below that was a pile of straw. Patsy and I sidestepped down to the landing, and I was looking down into the straw when Patsy tapped me on the shoulder. Her eyes were wide, and she looked like she was trying to hold in a laugh, and then, still looking me in the eye, she stepped off the landing. I don't know how far down it really was, probably a few feet, but it seemed at that moment like a long way.

She landed on her heels and then, still looking up at me, let herself fall backwards into the straw. Then there was the rattle of her laughter, and she was saying, "Jonathan, *come on!*"

Then we were all jumping down into the straw. We were jumping into it the way we would jump into a pool, legs crossed, tucked into a ball, as if we would make a splash when we landed. It felt really comfortable when you hit the straw. I could just tell that I wasn't going to get hurt. I really wanted everybody to watch my jumps, and I couldn't help screaming as soon as I took off. I rolled out of the straw and raced up the side of the hill as fast as I could to get back up on top and jump again. The air felt cold in my lungs, and I was just about out of breath every second, but it felt so good I couldn't stop. The clear sky overhead was getting rosy and gold and was starting to lose its light, which made landing in the straw feel like sinking into smoky cushions. The other kids were beginning to leave for home, and I was getting the sad, desperate feeling of not wanting it to be over. When it was practically dark and Patsy and I were the only ones left, we decided to do one last jump, but together at the same time. We stood side by side at the lip of the landing, not looking at each other. I said, "One, two, three," and as I was saying it Patsy took my hand, and then we jumped. I shut my eyes and didn't open them until we landed in the crunch and crackle. We were partly buried in the straw, and I could see bits of it in the tousles of Patsy's hair, and I could feel it down the collar of my coat. We were kind of tangled up, and it was going to take some effort to get up and get out, but I didn't want to move. I just wanted to stay there tangled up with Patsy in the half dark. I was glad that she wasn't moving either. I realized what felt so good: the side of her skull was touching the side of my skull. Patsy said, "That was really fun."

That feeling was completely new, and I will never forget it. It was like a swelling inside my chest that kept opening and opening. You couldn't describe it in words. It was more like a kind of music, or the way certain colors grow out of each other in a sunset near the horizon. I walked Patsy all the way back to her house, then walked home in the dark. Supper was almost over, and I got yelled at and cracked in the head for being so late and for being so dirty and full of little bits of straw. For once, though, it didn't feel like the worst thing in the world to be in trouble, and even getting cracked in the head didn't bother me for more than a minute. I knew that as soon as I could be by myself in my room, I could get back to that feeling of being skull to skull with Patsy in the straw.

The second great thing with Patsy was even better. It was like the completion of the first thing, which let me know it was real and would always be a part of the world inside me. It happened at the end of Donna Madden's Shock Theater party. Shock Theater was a new TV show that came on late on Saturday night. It started at ten and went till about midnight. There was a host named The Creep who wore a monster wig and black eye makeup and lipstick, and he would introduce famous old horror movies like *Frankenstein* or *The Thing*. During the commercial breaks The Creep would tell jokes and set up little skits with people in the TV studio. We didn't watch Shock Theater in our house because Annabel got really scared of the movies, so scared that it made you feel terrible to watch her. She couldn't even watch The Creep. But kids started having Shock Theater parties on Saturday nights when the show was on. You'd usually go over to the kid's house and play whatever games they had in the basement, then come up for pizza or something and then sit around on the floor in the living room to watch Shock Theater. A lot of kids got tired and went to sleep before it was over, and some kids' parents picked them up early, but at Donna Madden's Patsy and I and maybe three other kids were still awake as the movie was ending up. The movie was *The Invisible Man*, which I didn't think was very interesting or very scary, but I was in a good mood because I was sitting with Patsy, and I was getting off good ones.

People always turned out the lights to watch Shock Theater in order to make it scarier. Patsy and I were sitting on the floor leaning back against the front of the sofa, and it seemed like we were sitting there for hours. As it got later, the bits from the movie got shorter, and The Creep and the commercials got longer. The other kids started to get up and call their parents to take them home. Even Donna Madden stood up and said she was going to bed. By the end of the movie Patsy and I were in the dark, flickering living room alone. Without the other kids around, I didn't feel like getting off good ones. At the exact second I realized that being by ourselves was what I was hoping would happen, Patsy leaned into me a little and rested the side of her head against mine. It was the same ringing pleasure as when we were tangled in the straw after our last jump. We were skull to skull, and it made a low ringing tone inside my head. Without even planning it, I wedged my arm out from between us and rested it over Patsy's shoulder. She made a beautiful little humming sound and scrunched a little closer into me, to get more comfortable. I knew I was feeling as much as I could possibly feel and that I needed to hold perfectly still. I could not talk or think or even move my eyes to look around. My body felt frozen, except for a pulsing line where Patsy's head and shoulder and side pressed in on mine. I was aware that the final frantic scenes of *The Invisible Man* were flashing in front of me in a grainy old-fashioned way, but it could have been anything. There was only the swelling feeling, opening and opening. It was happening again, and I knew there would be no end to it. Then the lights were on, and Mr. Madden was hooting and joking, yelling to his wife, "Hey, we got two left!" Mr. Madden was being very cheerful. He looked down at Patsy and me and said, "looks like somebody got mighty sleepy," and all I wanted was to go home, get into my bed, and start thinking about everything that had happened.

I WISH I COULD GO back into every one of those days and open them up the way you might take old photographs out of an envelope. Some of the moments, like jumping into the straw or the Shock Theater party, are as vivid and clear as they were at the actual time, but so much of the rest of that year is a blur. I can feel the mood of it, the skull-to-skull love feeling for Patsy, but the procession of days and all the things we did seem like a kind of floating, with a sweet, achy feeling in my chest. I do remember, though, that when it got warm again at the end of our fifth grade year, Patsy and I started going to the country club for lunch.

Chapter Eleven

Barrington Lakes Country Club was at the north end of town where the fields stopped. I never knew anything about it, except to see its green sign with gold letters when we would drive by it in the car. The Prentisses were members of the country club, and on the night of the Fifth Grade Easter Dance, Patsy invited me to have supper there with her parents. I wasn't nervous about it when she asked me, although I didn't know what sitting around eating supper with her parents would be like. But something about going to the country club made mother tense, and then I started to get nervous. Mother told me the country club would be "dressy," a term I had never heard before. It meant not only dressed up, but really dressed up. When I got dressed up for Sunday school, I would wear my checkered sports jacket, a white shirt, one of my father's ties, my gabardine pants, and my good shoes. Mother said she thought my checkered jacket wasn't dressy enough and that we needed to go shopping to get a new one. We went to Zimmerman's department store downtown, and I had to try on all the jackets that were around my size. Mother didn't like any of them, and neither did I. They either had stiff shoulders that stuck out past where mine were or they were made out of ugly cloth, and just about every one looked too big in the mirror. They went down too far over my legs, and the sleeves went down to where my fingers started. So we had to drive out to a bunch of big stores in Chicago, which took the whole afternoon, and we didn't get home until after supper.

Getting me a dressy outfit made mother tense. I got really tired going into the stores and waiting around until mother found somebody to help us, then trying on all the jackets, and going into the changing closets to try on pants that went with the jackets. Each time I went in I had to untie my shoes and take them off, put the new pants on, then put my shoes back on, tie them back up, and go out there for mother and the salesman to look. Finally, at the last store, mother decided to get a dark blue jacket, which she called a blazer. We also got a new pair of pants made out of scratchy gray wool, which mother said looked dressy with the blazer, and my own tie. The tie had slanted blue and red stripes going down it, which I really liked. Actually, except that the pants felt like they were too long, so that I had to buckle them way up on my chest, I liked the feeling of getting dressy. Looking into the long mirror on the closet door of mother and father's bedroom, I liked the way the dark wool of the blazer made my shirt look extra white, which made the stripes of the tie really bright. Mother told me that I should always button the middle button of the blazer, which covered up how high my pants were. I looked really different, almost like another person, a person who belonged in cities or catalogs, and I couldn't stop looking at myself.

The idea of getting dressy didn't make me nervous, but the other things mother started talking about did. She told me that dinner at the country club would probably be formal, which was another term I hadn't heard, and I thought it had a dark, unpleasant sound to it. I had pictured the country club as a big ritzy restaurant, but Mother thought it might be more formal. She told me I should remember to do certain things at the table and to practice them at supper. She told me not to say things like "pass the butter" or even "please pass the butter," but always to make it a question, "could you please pass the butter?" She told me to be sure not to start eating anything that came to me until Mrs. Prentiss started eating hers. She told me to pass things to the person next to me, not to skip a person or reach across the table. From there it started to feel like too much to remember. She told me when we got to the table to keep standing up until all the ladies and girls sat down. She said if there was a lady or girl next to me, to pull her chair out a little and then slide it in behind her legs. She made me practice this a few times on Annabel. She said the first thing I should do when I sat down was to unfold my napkin and put it on my lap. She told me not to put my elbows or arms on the table while I ate. There were a lot more things, but I couldn't keep track of them. She said not to cut up all my meat at once, just the bite I was going to eat. She told me that I should put my knife and fork down during each mouthful, not to hold onto them while I was chewing. She told me there might be a lot more pieces of silverware than I expected, what each piece was supposed to be used for, and how usually it was a good idea to move from the outside in. I started to lose my confidence. The idea of going to the country club with the Prentisses started to feel a little sickening, like having to go to the dentist.

The night I went, it wasn't as bad as I thought. When I got into the back seat of the Prentiss's car with Patsy, Mrs. Prentiss smiled at me and said, in a really nice way, "don't you look nice." The country club dining room was crowded and bright. The tables had thick white tablecloths and napkins and extra heavy plates and silverware. Mr. and Mrs. Prentiss were friendly and relaxed, and they joked around a lot, which made me less nervous. I was sitting next to Patsy and remembered to pull her chair out and slide it into the back of her legs, but that seemed to surprise her, and her mother laughed and told her just to sit down. There were, as mother told me, way more forks and spoons than I needed, but I just looked over every now and then and used the one Patsy was using. The only time I was really nervous was when it came time to order my food. I couldn't understand a lot of the things on the menu, and Mr. Prentiss asked me if I wanted to have a shrimp cocktail. I had never heard of that, but I had a feeling if I saw an actual shrimp on my plate and tried to eat it, it would be sickening. I said no thank you to the shrimp cocktail and to anything else I didn't understand. I listened to what Patsy ordered and then ordered that. I said I wanted a thousand islands dressing on my salad, and I was pretty nervous wondering what that would be. It was just friendly, regular talking until dessert, but then the waiter came back and said what they had and asked me what I would like. I might not have been listening very well, because I couldn't make a picture of any desserts from what he was saying. I kept waiting for something familiar, like "pie" or "cake," but there was nothing like that, so I said no thank you again. Mr. Prentiss said, "Not even a little ice cream, Jonathan?" and I said yes, please. When the ice cream came in a little glass dish, it was vanilla, which was fine, even though the Prentisses all got what looked to me like big delicious pieces of cake.

By the time we left the country club to get in the car and drive to the dance, I wasn't nervous at all. The only reason I even bring it up is that, after that night, Patsy and I started going to the country club all the time.

We never would have thought about going to the country club by ourselves if we hadn't already started going into town for lunch, and the reason we started doing that was the weather. After Easter and all through May was the softest, most beautiful weather I can ever remember. Even if it rained a little, the sun would come right back, and make everything pale green and a little steamy, and as you walked along the damp sidewalks, the air was sweet with lilacs and honeysuckle and the pink and white blossoms of the fruit trees. I remember deciding on one of those days that I was going to stay outside, even if I got in trouble. It was during lunch period at school, and Patsy and I were taking a walk around the edge of the playground before going in to eat. There wasn't a rule against this, but nobody ever did it because people were usually hungry and wanted to eat lunch before they went outside to play for the rest of the period. The air was so green and bright, and the wind was so soft, I realized I didn't want to go back inside, and before I could even say it, Patsy said, "I've got an idea."

Patsy's idea was to slip through the hedges and go into town and have lunch at a restaurant. I couldn't quite imagine it. I had never gone to a restaurant in town during the day. I was pretty sure it wasn't allowed, but Patsy said that kids who lived close to the school were allowed to walk home for lunch, so this was really no different from that. We were already walking toward town, and I wondered how long it would take to get to a restaurant, eat our stuff, and walk back. Lunch period was forty-five minutes, and we had already been out for a while. Patsy said not to worry, it would be fun. Then I thought about money. I felt in my pocket and remembered I had a quarter and a dime, which was probably enough for something in a restaurant, at least a toasted cheese. I told Patsy I had thirty-five cents, and she told me not to worry, she was loaded. Partly because we didn't know how much time we had, but mainly because we just felt like it, we ran the rest of the way into town as fast as we could.

We were winded but in a really good mood when we got downtown. We decided to go to June's, which was a long, thin place with wooden booths running along each wall. My father had taken me there for a hot dog after Little League games, and I liked it. It was pretty crowded and noisy when we walked in, and we had to wait for a few minutes to get a booth. I got nervous while we were waiting, because there were no other kids around, only grownups, people I recognized from the stores. I looked around for a clock and tried to figure out how much time we would have. It felt to me like we had already been gone a long time. Patsy didn't care. She was in a good mood and told me not to worry, we'd think up a good excuse. When we got into our booth it felt much better, like we belonged in there. You could see out onto the street and all the people walking by, and past them the green park in front of the train station. Patsy said I should order whatever I wanted and not to worry about spending just thirty-five cents, so I ordered a BLT with potato chips and a chocolate malt. Patsy ordered a whole bunch of things, including soup. Before our food came, the waitress brought us chilled glasses of water and a basket full of rolls and crackers and butter. By the time our food came, the whole tabletop was filled with dishes and bowls and glasses, and all of it looked really good. The waitress filled up my glass with chocolate malt and left the huge silver container next to my plate. I picked it up and saw that it was practically full of extra chocolate malt. I couldn't believe it. The bright sun outside and the people walking by and all the food made me feel like I was in a new, much bigger world. Patsy was probably used to places like June's, but she seemed excited too, so I started getting off good ones.

I could tell that the people in the other booths were looking at us, but I don't think we were making trouble. I think they probably thought we were cute. Our waitress was really friendly and called us honey. When she first came over, she said, "Call off school today?" and Patsy looked right up at her and said, "Parent conferences." Patsy could always do that, come up with tremendous fibs, and she was always in such a cheerful mood, she never ended up in trouble. By the time we finally finished our food and the rest of my chocolate malt, I knew it was way past lunch period at school. I knew we should hurry back as fast as we could, but I just couldn't force myself to do it in that soft breezy air. When you feel really good in a certain way, partly in a trance but still aware of what you are doing, you almost never get in trouble. That's what happened to Patsy and me when we got back to school. It turned out it was even later than I thought. It was almost two o'clock, which was only an hour before school was over, when we got back to the building and started walking down the empty corridor to Mr. Click's room. I opened the door without making any noise and looked inside. It was quiet, and the kids were reading by themselves. I looked around for Mr. Click, but he wasn't at his desk, and I couldn't see him. Patsy and I gave each other a look and walked over to our desks and sat down. I could hear Patsy's friends whispering, "Where *were* you?" and Patsy whispering back, "We had an *appointment*." After a while Mr. Click came back into the room. He stood at the doorway for a minute and looked around. I glanced up from my book, and he was looking at me, his eyes extra big behind the black frames of his glasses. He smiled a little and said, "So you're back."

I loved that time at June's, and because it was so exciting and because there was that sweet, soft air practically every day, Patsy and I never wanted to eat cooped up in the cafeteria. We went to June's a few more times, which was kind of fun, but we had to run all the way there and all the way back, and even when we ate as fast as we could, we were always at least a little bit late. We were also running out of things to tell the waitress about why we weren't at school, which is when Patsy thought of the country club. She said they had great lunches at the country club, and we wouldn't even have to pay, because they were members and she could charge it. It made me a little nervous to think about sitting around the country club dining room in my school clothes. The country club was also twice as far away as June's downtown. Patsy said we should bring our bikes, and it would actually be faster than June's. So the next day I rode my bike to school, and as soon as we got out for lunch period, we rode out to the country club really fast. It felt so good, riding hard like that in the middle of the day, with the warm breeze blowing past my face and through my hair.

Lunch at the country club turned out to be much more fun than I thought it would be. It wasn't in the big dining room inside. It was in a low, screened in building between a bunch of tennis courts and the swimming pool. There was a counter where you ordered your food, and then a man would bring it over to your table. Because it wasn't summer yet, there were hardly any other people in the snack bar, just a few ladies wearing short white tennis dresses that showed their bumpy legs. We would sit as far away from them as we could, at a table close to the pool. With the breezes coming through the screens and the white sun sparkling on the pool water, it was even better than June's. For one thing it was much quieter, and Patsy and I could really talk to each other. We talked about everything. I told her about going to the north woods in the summer and about hunting with Cyrus and about the tunnels and our fort, and Patsy told me about going to her family's cabin on its own island on Lake Superior. Patsy had a way of talking about the things she did that made you feel like you were there, and it always made me wish I had done all those things with her. In bed at night I stopped thinking about my own things and started picturing Patsy's island and how the water was so clear you could see the rocks and sand thirty feet below on the bottom. I could actually see that water and the bright sky and feel the wind off the lake, but I was also mixing it up with sitting with Patsy at the country club and the sunlight sparkling on the pool.

I can hardly remember anything about school that spring, except that I knew it was going to be sad to end the year and not have Mr. Click anymore. All I remember is sitting across the table from Patsy at the country club snack bar. The sun would come out from behind a cloud, and in a second the whole side of my face would be warm. I would have a BLT on toast and a chocolate malt, and Patsy would have a bowl of clam chowder and a mound of chicken salad on top of lettuce. We must have been thinking about having to get back to school, but I can only remember feeling that we had all the time we could ever want and that I had so much to tell her. But mostly I remember looking across at her face and at the way the messy waves of her straw-colored hair framed her beautiful brown cheeks and the white teeth of her smile when she leaned forward to tell me something special. That's the picture I would make at night in the dark of my room.

The last day of fifth grade was a half-day, and there was no lunch at school, which meant Patsy and I would have all the time we wanted to have lunch at the country club. That's the only thing I could think of all morning, and then Mr. Click was saying good-bye to us and that he had really enjoyed getting to know us, and I wished there was something I could have given him, like a present.

Then we were all outside in the blinding sun, and before I went over to the bike rack to get my bike, I took all the books and graded work and supplies from my desk and threw them into the trash bin. Then I met Patsy, and we rode our bikes across town to the country club. I had made a plan, and when I got to the path in front of the snack bar, I parked my bike and took the shopping bag out of my bike basket. That morning I had put my blue blazer in there. It wasn't too wrinkled, and I put it on. Patsy was waiting for me at the door. She was smiling so hard I thought she had a secret, and she did. She had a box from a store under her arm, and she said, "Wait a second," and went to the bathroom. When she came out, she had changed her clothes. She was wearing a stiff light pink dress with no sleeves. Her face was extra beautiful, and I noticed she had also put on a pink band to hold down her hair in the front. She had thought of the same thing I did, getting dressed up. That turned out to be our best lunch. We didn't have to hurry, and we could lean back in our chairs. After a while we were the only people left in the snack bar, and the breezes were blowing through the screens, and we could hear the plip plip of the water against the side of the swimming pool. I know I was paying attention to Patsy and what she was saying, but I was aware of something else at the same time. I was watching myself from some other place, and I realized that I wasn't ten years old, that I had somehow skipped ahead to someone I would be later, or maybe even into a completely different person. That happens sometimes in the other world.

Chapter Twelve

When you are a kid you never think about things suddenly changing. Maybe you do if someone like your mother dies or if you have to move to a different state, but usually you just expect things are going to stay the way they were when you went to bed. I couldn't believe how much things changed over the summer between fifth grade and Junior High. Even though I needed to be with Patsy as much as possible every day during school, I knew that everybody did different things in the summer, and that I wouldn't get back into my school mood until next fall. When I think about it now, I wonder how I could keep from feeling bad about not doing things with Patsy or even seeing her, but that's just the way it was then. In my room at night I still pictured her, but I never thought of her belonging in my summer places.

The first different thing about that summer was that I moved up to ten-to-twelves in Little League. This meant you got to play on the good diamond, which had lights at night. You also got full uniforms with white or gray jerseys and pants, long socks with a loop on the bottom that went under your other socks, and a hat which was just like the real hat of a major league team. There were try-outs for the ten-to-twelve teams, and the managers picked you. All the teams were supposed to be equal, but they really weren't. The Indians and the Cubs were the best teams every year, because Mr. Hightower and Mr. Spinks were the best managers, and they always knew who the kids were and who was good, and they always ended up with the best players. I wanted to get on a pretty good team, but I didn't care too much which one, except the Padres, which had the worst uniforms. I was one of the best players in the eight-and nines, but I was a pitcher and also one of the smallest kids, and the pitching mound in ten-to-twelves was ten feet farther away from the plate.

The tryouts were on a really hot Saturday morning. The managers got everybody signed up for their positions and then had each position group go out to a base or to the outfield somewhere and take turns fielding balls. I was with the pitchers and catchers, and after we warmed up for a while, I got in a line behind the pitcher's mound and waited for my turn to pitch to a catcher behind the plate. One of the dads stood in the batter's box, but he didn't swing. Mr. Hightower, the manager of the Indians, was in charge of the pitcher tryouts, and I was nervous waiting for my turn, because he had a voice like someone with laryngitis, and I thought he might turn out to be kind of mean. "Okay, Force," he said, when it was my turn. He already knew who I was. "I hear you're the strike out king. Let's see what you can do." The mound on the good diamond was built up on a little hill, so you actually looked down at the batter and the catcher. Something about it made the catcher's mitt look really far away, not just ten extra feet. I threw a pitch, and it was pretty good. It made the right kind of smack in the glove, and I started to feel better. Mr. Hightower said, "That's good, now see if you can bring that down a little bit, right at the knees." I was starting to like the way he talked, and I liked that he thought I knew how to throw my pitch a little lower. I threw the next pitch as hard as I could, and it was lower, but right over the plate. Mr. Hightower didn't say anything for a while, and I kept pitching to the target. Wayne Stegner, my coach on the Wrens, was standing behind the backstop, and he was shouting things like, "You're throwing smoke, Lefty, you're burning them in." I didn't look up at him, and I really wished he would go away. After I had thrown a bunch of pitches Mr. Hightower said, "Nice job," and asked me if I had any other pitches. I said I did. I had a curve, which my father taught me how to throw by putting my first two fingers right next to the seam, and then twisting my wrist as I let go of the ball. I thought my curve was amazing because it would go straight, but with a funny spin on it, until about ten feet before it got to the target. Then it would seem almost to stop in mid air and float over to the right. My father laughed when he caught my curves. He said I had "a big hook."

I actually wanted to show Mr. Hightower my curve, but I had never thrown one with a batter standing there. I wanted it to end up in the target, down the middle of the plate, but I didn't know where I should aim it on the batter. I decided that if I threw it toward his hip, it might end up over the plate. I tried it, and for a second I thought the ball might actually go behind the back of the dad standing at the plate, but it kind of hesitated, the way I hoped it would, and started floating over to the right. The extra distance from the new mound made it curve even more than usual, and the ball went from almost behind the batter's butt to the front of his pants and then over to the far side of the plate. The dad batting laughed and said something, and behind the backstop Wayne Stegner shouted, "Hey, Lefty, where'd *that* come from?" Mr. Hightower said, "That's a helluva hook," and let the next kid in line pitch.

That night after supper, some kids called me up and said they heard I made the Indians, which made me feel excited but also nervous, and then Mr. Hightower called up and told me I really was on the Indians and that I was going to be the only ten-year-old pitcher. I had a funny feeling about being picked for the Indians. I knew they were the best team and they had most of the best players, but when I pictured those kids in my mind, they were all big kids, and I didn't know them very well. I pictured the best pitcher on the Indians, Craig Cummerford. He was twelve and really big. The kids said he was five feet nine. His legs and arms were at least twice as big around as mine. I wasn't even five feet yet. Later, when practices started and I came up to bat against Craig Cummerford, his pitches would seem to hiss past me before I could even think about swinging. They cracked into the catcher's mitt with such force I felt jittery in my stomach. I couldn't stand to think about what it would feel like if one of Craig Cummerford's pitches hit me. My father would always tell me that the worst thing in baseball was to be afraid of the ball. When I stood up to bat and Craig Cummerford was going through his wind up, I tried to squint back at him and tighten my grip on the bat like I was ready to take a big swing, but I knew I wasn't going to do it. I wanted him to throw balls and walk me. The truth was that I didn't want to get hit. He was a really good pitcher, and he almost always threw strikes, so I knew I had to swing, but I also knew I could never hit a pitch from Craig Cummerford. From the dugout Mr. Hightower would say, "You're late, you're swinging late." From behind the backstop my father would call out, "You're waving at the ball," and I was.

The kids in my grade I played baseball with were kind of jealous that I got on the Indians, but for some reason I wasn't that glad about it. I was pretty excited before the first game, mainly because of the new uniform and the way INDIANS was written in orange and black letters across the chest of the jersey. Also, my father took me to the sporting goods store and bought me a pair of spikes and a leather pitching toe that screwed in over the front of my left shoe. The smallest pair of spikes they had were one size too big for me, but my father bought them anyway. He said I would grow into them and that we could stuff some cloth up into the toe area where the extra room was. I was glad they were too big, because they made my feet look bigger.

Even when we were warming up before the game, I could tell something was wrong. I didn't really know the other kids on the Indians very well, and the one kid I did know, Gary Spender, wasn't much fun to be around. He was also the worst player on the team, and the only reason he was on the Indians was because his dad was one of the managers with Mr. Hightower. Just before the game started, Mr. Hightower called us over and read out the starting line up. It was the opening game, and I knew Craig Cummerford was going to pitch and that I wasn't going to be playing any other position, but it still surprised me for some reason that my name wasn't called and I wasn't going to play. I felt like I might even cry, which would have been really embarrassing, so I started walking fast out toward the outfield.

Maybe my face looked funny, because Mr. Hightower called after me and said I was going to be his fireman. I asked him what that was, and he said fireman was a name for a relief pitcher, a pitcher who came in and put the fire out. I liked the idea of being a fireman for the Indians, but after the game got started, I realized that there wasn't going to be any fire. Craig Cummerford was striking out just about every batter, and the Indians were getting a lot of hits and scoring runs in every inning. The games were six innings long, and by the fifth inning the Indians were winning by about sixteen to nothing. There was no reason for Mr. Hightower to take out Craig Cummerford and put me in, but I wanted him to do it anyway. I started to make a plan to slip away behind the bench and go home, but I knew my father was somewhere in the stands watching the game and that I would really get it if I went home without him. When it got to be the last half of the sixth inning, Mr. Hightower decided to put in a lot of subs. I was sent out to play right field, and Gary Spender was put in center, which made it worse. It was practically dark, and I'm not sure I would have been able to see a ball if it came out to me, but I could see Craig Cummerford winding up and then hear the ball smacking into the catcher's mitt. When the inning was over, I hadn't even moved. As I ran back to the bench, I saw that our team was forming a big huddle. They started the cheer, "Two, four, six, eight, who do we appreciate..." and I ran right past them into the parking lot to look for our car. I felt really terrible, and I hoped my father wouldn't make me talk to him, because I didn't want to start to cry.

A few games after that, Mr. Hightower told me I was going to pitch against the Dodgers. It was going to be a Saturday afternoon game, which felt to me less important than a night game, because there wouldn't be the fuzzed, golden look of everything under the lights. The Dodgers were supposed to be a pretty crummy team, but I kind of liked them because of the bright blue color of their hats and letters. Also, some of my friends from school were on the Dodgers. As soon as Mr. Hightower told me I was going to pitch, I started making pictures of myself up on the mound against the Dodgers on a bright, hot Saturday afternoon, but I couldn't make the pictures seem any good. I knew when the time came I would probably go into my trance, but when I thought about the game in advance, it just seemed like a lot of effort to be throwing all those pitches. Even so, the night before the game, I did not sleep for one minute. All I could do was make pictures of myself going through my wind-up on the mound and throwing toward the target, but every time something was a little off. I wouldn't shift my weight forward enough, so I would be off balance when I let go of the ball, or I'd be so off balance at the end of my wind-up that I couldn't throw at all. I wondered for a while in the dark whether I might completely forget how to pitch. I pictured myself being completely wild, throwing the ball way behind the batters' backs and over the umpire's head into the backstop. As it was started to get light out, I could hear it begin to rain. At first there was the tapping and hissing of a drizzle, then the roar of the big drops. I really didn't want the game to be rained out. I wanted to be able to stop picturing bad things.

It stopped raining by the middle of the morning, but they sky did not clear up. When I went over to the park at noon to warm up, the light outside was so strange, it almost didn't seem like the regular world. The clouds overhead were black and purple, making the sky look more like night than day, but it wasn't dark at all on the field. In fact, everything kind of glowed. The dirt of the infield, which was usually just dusty and gray, was moist and black, and the wet grass beyond the infield was a sparkly green. The white in our uniforms really did glow in that light, and the color of the letters and numbers—bright blue, black and gold—flashed in your eye the way bluebirds and orioles look in the woods. I had thrown plenty of new baseballs before, but I had never seen anything whiter and redder than the leather and the stitched seams of the ball they gave me to warm up with. Warming up was nothing like my night pictures. My wind-up was fine, and each white pitch went right into the target exactly the same way. I wanted to relax into my trance, and I'm sure I would have, but Mr. Hightower and the other managers kept talking to the umpires about whether we should play. They thought there might be a storm, but finally, because there was no lightning or thunder, they decided we could play the game.

We were the home team, so the Dodgers batted first. Because of the dark sky and the glowing colors, I went into a different kind of trance than usual. I wasn't thinking or planning at all, and if somebody had spoken to me or asked me something, I'm pretty sure I wouldn't have been able to answer. My warm up pitches were just like the ones I had been throwing on the sidelines, right in the target, with a terrific *smack*. Then the first hitter came up, Russell Weeks, a kid from my class. He was tall but skinny like me. He stood up straight in the batter's box and looked out at me with an expression that let me know he was never going to hit the ball. I threw three identical strikes to him, and he struck out, swinging at the third one, actually just waving at it. The next two batters also struck out. Mr. Hightower said nice going, and I stayed in my trance while we batted, then I was up on the mound again under the dark sky in the glowing light. I knew most of the other Dodgers. They weren't that good, and they didn't look as if they thought they would hit the ball. This was probably because the first three kids struck out. The next two kids did too, and it felt a little like pitching in the eight-and-nines, except the sixth batter swung and hit a ball pretty hard which bounced chest-high into the glove of our first baseman who trotted over to his base for the out.

When we were up again, I got to bat and walked and then scored. We were winning, but it never occurred to me that we wouldn't be. Then, in what seemed like a second, everything changed. The swollen dark clouds moved on, and they sky was just gray. The color of everything faded back to normal, and when I got back up on the mound to pitch again, there was a wind blowing into my face. I know you can't blame something like the wind, but I remember getting mad at it, because now it seemed like there was something in the way between me and the target.

The first batter of the inning was a big fat kid named Stu Freyberg, another kid from Mr. Click's class. He acted big and tough, and some of the dads thought he was really good because of his size, but I knew he wasn't that good, at anything. He was making a fierce-looking face at me, and he twirled his bat in little circles as he waited for me to pitch. I felt myself getting mad at the expression on his face, and I was already mad at the wind. I threw a pretty good pitch, and Stu took a big swing and hit it really far down the third base line. It went foul, but his hitting it like that all of a sudden made everyone on the Dodgers' bench start yelling and cheering. This made me mad too. I wouldn't have minded throwing one right into Stu Freyberg's fat stomach, but that would have been bad sportsmanship, and I wanted him to strike out.

He hit the next pitch even harder, and this time it was fair, into left center field between the two outfielders, who had to chase after it. It was a triple, and it probably would have been a homer if Stu Freyberg wasn't so fat and slow. The kids on the Dodgers bench and now a lot of the dads were whooping it up, and I started to feel really bad, a combination of still being mad and being ashamed that a kid like Stu Freyberg got a triple off me. Then I walked a kid, and the people on the Dodgers side started yelling and jeering. The next kid up was left-handed, and I knew a left-handed kid would have a hard time hitting my curve ball. So I threw one, and it was perfect. It started off headed straight for his butt, then it did its little wiggle and started floating to the right. It ended up right in the middle of the target. The umpire called out, *"Ball!"* I felt an electric shock behind my eyes. It wasn't a ball. I walked toward the umpire and said, "That wasn't a ball," and our catcher, Steve Minz, was standing up saying the pitch was right in there. But the umpire shouted right back at me. He said the ball was inside when it passed the plate and only ended up in the target. I looked up at him in a way that I hoped would let him see how mad I was, and as I was walking back to the mound, he came out after me and grabbed my shoulder and said, "What did you say, young man?" I told him I didn't say anything. I did say "total jerk" to myself, but without making any sound. He said he heard me say something and that I should watch my mouth. Then he told me again how my curve was inside when it passed the plate.

Now there was just crazy yelling and the wind and names I was saying to myself inside my head. I threw another curve, which started off toward the kid's butt, which I wouldn't have minded hitting, but then it floated even farther to the right than the last one. Steve Minz had to move the target outside to catch it, but I was pretty sure it was a strike when it crossed the plate. The umpire said, *"Ball two!"* I said, *"What?"*--I didn't plan it, it just came out. The umpire said it was a ball, outside, and that I better watch my mouth or I could watch the game from the bench. Mr. Hightower came out to the mound and squeezed my shoulders with his hands. He said to cool off. He said to just throw strikes. I couldn't think. I decided to pitch as hard as I could and not say anything. I threw the next pitch at the left-handed kid's butt, but I forgot to make it a curve, and it hit him. I pretended to be really calm. I walked over to the kid I hit, who was sniffling a little, and I said I was sorry and that I didn't mean it. He was okay, and when he went down to first, all the Dodgers people cheered.

Now the bases were loaded, and Russell Weeks was up again. My first pitch missed the target, and then I threw two good strikes. The next pitch was going to be a strike too, but Russell swung and hit the ball over the shortstop's head into the outfield. The Dodgers were scoring runs, and I went back into my trance, but in a different way, because now I was secretly crying the whole time. I didn't say anything bad. I watched my mouth and threw pitches, but my trance didn't work anymore. The Dodgers kept getting hits off me, and Stu Freyberg got a hit every time. The kids coming up to bat, even quiet kids like Russell Weeks, weren't afraid of the ball. They looked like they wanted to hit it, and they did.

I pitched the whole game, and we lost, nine to four. I knew I wasn't going to be amazing on the Indians. Something final had happened when the field stopped glowing and the wind came up. After that, playing Little League felt like another thing I had to do, like piano lessons or going to Sunday School. Mr. Hightower said I could be his fireman again, but I only got to pitch when we were way ahead, usually for just one inning. He also let me play right field a few times, but I almost never had to make any plays. I just stood out there, remembering things, trying to picture something good.

Chapter Thirteen

I THINK MOTHER REALIZED I didn't like Little League anymore, that it was actually making me sad. That may have been the reason she decided to send me to Camp Ojibwa at the end of the summer. Camp Ojibwa was an overnight camp on a big lake in Wisconsin. Mother told me that when she was a girl she had wanted to go to Girl Scout Camp more than anything in the world, but Nana and Papa couldn't afford it. She told me Camp Ojibwa would be wonderful. I would sleep in a cabin, and there would be boating and swimming and camping out in tents. She said there would also be sports, including baseball, and that I could bring my glove. I really didn't want to go. I wanted to go on our regular vacation with everybody else up to our own cabin in the north woods. I could see that saying this was hurting mother's feelings, so I stopped, but I really did not want to go to that camp.

Mother found out another boy from my school, Patrick Dannehey, was also going to Camp Ojibwa. She told me about it to make me feel better about going. She said, "You'll have a friend." I knew Patrick Dannehey was not going to be my friend. He was a grade behind me, and he had white hair and pale skin, and he was really weak. Thinking about Patrick Dannehey trying to hang around me for three weeks made me feel terrible.

I was right about it, too. Camp Ojibwa was completely terrible. The bad feeling I had about it right away was just a tiny hint of how terrible it would get. Mother took me to the Palatine station on a Saturday morning where a special train just for the camp was going to take all the kids to Wisconsin. Mother said she thought it sounded like so much fun, but I didn't think it would be fun. The train started out in Chicago, and it was about half filled with kids by the time it got to Palatine. Patrick Dannehey and his mother and father were waiting on the platform when we got there. Mother went right over to them and started talking and laughing with Mr. and Mrs. Dannehey. She was always cheerful and polite with other people. I said hi to Patrick Dannehey, who looked weak and sick, and he started talking to me. He asked me if I had been to camp before and what I thought the kids would be like. I knew mother and the Danneheys were watching us, wanting us to get along and be friends. This made me not want to talk to Patrick at all. I didn't want to be mean to him, but I couldn't help feeling mean. I said no, I never went to the camp before and that I didn't know how the kids would be. I felt bad about not being nice, but when I looked at Patrick Dannehey's weak face and his soft white arms, I got even madder about having to go off to a camp I never wanted to go to and that nobody even asked me about before signing me up.

Two big boys from the camp who might have been in college or even men came up to us and told us which car to get into, and I realized that Patrick Dannehey was going to get on the same car with me and sit next to me in the double seat all the way up to Wisconsin. Mother helped me lift my suitcase, which was a huge blue plastic one of Nana's, up the steps of my car, and then she gave me a long hug and said goodbye. She was crying a little and being really nice, so I tried not to show her how mean I was feeling. I dragged my suitcase to the seat where Patrick was already sitting by the window. I lifted it up onto the seat so there could it be a wall between us, and then I sat back and got as mad as I could.

The train seemed to stop every three minutes to pick up more kids, and our car got noisier and noisier. Some of the kids who must have gone to the camp before were singing songs about Camp Ojibwa, which got me to hate those songs right away.

We welcome you to O-jib-way
On the sandy banks of Lake Hathaway,

Where hearty braves can swim and play
in the old O-jib-way way

The songs were supposed to sound like real Indian songs with a *boom-ba-boom*ba rhythm, but they mainly sounded corny, and most of the kids couldn't sing at all, so they just shouted. For as much of the trip as I could, I shut my eyes and tried to look like I was sleeping, so I wouldn't have to talk to Patrick Dannehey or do anything.

When the train finally got to the last stop, I opened my eyes and looked out the window, but there was no camp or lake, just a station platform and some stores of a little town. From the train we all had to get in old yellow buses, which smelled like gasoline and sour sweat and throw-up. The ride was bumpy and kind of sickening, which made people stop talking and singing. The bus turned off the paved road and went through the woods for a while down a rutted dirt lane that came to a big clearing with a line of log cabins and behind them a big, shimmering lake. Seeing the lake got the other kids excited again, and they started talking about camp things they knew and remembered from last year and the names of the cabins and the counselors. We were about the third bus in, and when it came time for us to get out, one of the counselors who helped get us onto the train stood on the bus steps and blew a loud whistle. He said his name really fast, but told us to call him either Kip or Mr. K. He told us we were all going to have a lot of fun, provided we did one thing, and that was to do what he told us to do, right away with no lip. He told us to get off the bus and form a circle around a log bench he pointed to. When we were all off the bus, standing around the bench with our suitcases, he looked at us for a long time and didn't say anything. Then he got up on the bench and turned slowly around, still not saying anything. He blew his whistle again, which was unbelievably loud, and said, "I hope we're not off to a bad start here. I hope we're not off to a bad start. Because it would be a very bad thing to get off to a bad start, because a bad start is a very bad thing." Somebody laughed, and Kip jumped down from the bench and went over in that direction. He looked mad. He was standing right in front of Patrick Dannehey. "Was that *you?*" he shouted at Patrick. "Did I say something *funny?*" I could see Patrick Dannehey say "no" but it didn't make any sound. "Well, I hope not," Kip said, and he clapped his hands down really hard on Patrick Dannehey's shoulders. "Because that would get us off to a bad start, and that would be a bad thing." I felt terrible looking at Patrick Dannehey's scared white face. I knew he wasn't the one who laughed, and that made me start to like him.

"We're off to a bad start," Kip said, "because you guys didn't listen to the one important thing I told you." I couldn't stand this. I wished I could turn completely invisible and pick up a rock and throw it at his head. "I told you to make a *circle* around this bench, and would anyone call this a *circle?*" He blew his whistle and clapped his hands, and kids started moving around trying to form a circle. Pretty soon everybody got the idea, and we were all standing in a pretty good circle. "Well what do you know,"

Kip said, "so it's true, chimpanzees really can learn." Some kids laughed, and Kip didn't mind. He looked like he was in a good mood now and told us the first thing we were going to do before we went to our cabins was to learn the Camp Ojibwa song.

Kip said, "Here's what we're going to do. I'm going to sing this song for you, one line at a time, and you are going to listen to it and remember it. Then I'm going to ask some *volunteers*"—he looked around the circle. "I'm going to ask some *volunteers* from last year to demonstrate how it goes, and then we're all going to sing. *Because*, my little monkey friends, nobody is going anywhere until we can sing Ojibwa Way by heart. Got that? No suppy, no beddy-bye until we sing it loud and clear. Okay!"

Kip said a line of the song in his talking voice, and then he sang it. When he was done, he sang the whole song through.

> *On the banks of great Lake Hathaway*
> *Where chief Black Wing once came to stay*
> *We will pitch our tent and stake our camp*
> *In the old O-jib-way way.*
> *At O-jib-way where we work and play*
> *The weak go home but the strong ones stay*
> *To greet the sun at the break of day*
> *In the old O-jib-way way.*

Undabunda dee, undabunda ray
Kowakumpa ree, kowakumpa kay
This is what the young braves say
In the old O-jib-way way.
And now you know our sacred song
And evermore can sing along
In joyful voices clear and strong
In the old O-jib-way way.

KIP SANG THE SONG IN a loud goofy voice that wasn't really like singing, more like making fun of singing, and while he was doing it, I realized who he kept reminding me of—Wayne Stegner. It seemed like there was a certain kind of person, like Wayne Stegner or Kip or Lodi the German janitor, who were in charge of kids or who worked around kids and everyone was supposed to like them because they wanted to be with kids. They all had that exaggerated way of acting and talking that kids were supposed to like but I never liked at all. Something, though, about that kind of person seemed to hypnotize a lot of kids, and they talked about people like Kip as if they were really funny or really great guys, even though they were actually pretty mean and sometimes got way too personal. Our Youth Outreach minister at church was like that too, Reverend Klug. He was still partly in college, and you could see practically his whole scalp under the long strands of his hair, which made me wish he was just bald. Reverend Klug told all the kids in Youth Outreach that he believed God called him to work with us. He told Youth Outreach that we could tell him anything at any time and he would keep it to himself. Sometimes he was kind of interesting, like when he would tell us things he did when he was a kid in Duluth, Minnesota, but he wasn't very good at organizing us to do things or getting us to be quiet. It seemed like the main thing he wanted to do was talk to us while we sat and listened to him. Everything took him forever to explain before we could get up and actually do anything. Also, I didn't like looking directly in his face because he had some kind of extra lip behind his upper lip, and it would show a little when he said certain words. He wasn't very good at keeping us quiet, either. We would be fooling around, talking to each other while he was explaining something, and he would just stop talking and stare out at us, looking sad. I remember wondering what it felt like for him to be called by God to work with us in Youth Outreach. It was hard for me to picture, but it seemed to go with a lot of other church things like Sunday picnics and pancake breakfasts, which we went to but were never any fun. Almost everything about Reverend Klug made me want to get out of Youth Outreach as soon as I could.

We stayed in the circle and practiced singing Ojibwa Way about fifty times. Even after we knew it, Kip said it wasn't loud enough. He made us count off in threes, and had the ones and twos and threes sing it separately to see who could do it the loudest. By the end, everybody was practically screaming the words, so there was hardly any tune to it. Finally we were loud enough, and Kip led us over to our cabins so we could unpack and wash up before supper in Black Wing Lodge. My cabin was Laughing Bear, and there were twelve kids in it and six bunk beds. A big kid named Warren Keener was in charge of our cabin and had his own bed. Warren Keener was thirteen, and he got to be junior counselor by going to Camp Ojibwa for three years in a row and winning a bunch of Achievement Awards at the final Pow-Wow. Kip was in charge of Warren and the other junior counselors, but you could tell they were extra friendly and that he wouldn't make Warren do the kinds of things he would make the regular kids do. Kip told us Warren was our "lord and master" when we were in the cabin, and that if any of us of gave him trouble, we would be spending time, he said, "with Mr. K.," and that we wouldn't enjoy it very much. Then he went away to the next cabin and left us with Warren Keener, who told us to form pairs and choose a bunk and decide who was on top and who was on the bottom. He said we had to keep our suitcases under the bed and out of sight and to keep our bed made all day and to leave the bathroom neat and clean. He said it should be "spotless." He said there were cabin inspections every now and then, and he wanted Laughing Bear to get a lot of Achievement Points, so we could win the special banquet, which was steak, on the last day of camp.

Warren Keener was tall and bony. His chest was caved in a little, and he slouched forward while he talked to us. He had dark hair in a short crew cut with a funny dent in the front. He didn't seem like a nice kid at all, even though he got chosen to be a junior counselor. He liked using dirty words like "piss" for peeing and "crapper" for the toilet. He told us things like, "We'll get along great if you don't give me any shit."

He told us to let him know if kids from the other cabins gave us any shit. He said sometimes there were midnight raids on the cabin from kids in other cabins. The purpose was to mess up your cabin and get away before anybody got caught. The other thing he said kids from other cabins might do is pants you when you were walking back to the cabin after Camp Fire or some other time when they could get away with it. Somebody asked what pantsing was, and Warren Keener said it was a kid holding you from behind while another kid pulled your pants down or even off. He said sometimes when you got pantsed they might goose your balls, sometimes not. He said most of the pantsing was for fun, and it helped keep up the competition between the cabins. He said the best way not to get pantsed was to stick together.

A big blond kid named Wally Kanicky said he would share a bunk with me and that he wanted the bottom. I said fine. We were supposed to take the things we needed from our suitcases, like our toothbrushes and toothpaste, and put them under our pillows, then to stow our suitcases under the bottom bunk so they wouldn't show during inspection. Nana's big blue suitcase was too big to fit under the bunk, so I asked Warren Keener what to do. He said "Fuckin A," and gave me a mean look. I had to keep looking at him, because I didn't know what to do with the suitcase. Finally he said, "Why'd you bring such a big suitcase?" and told me he didn't care what I did with it, just to put it somewhere.

That turned out to be the way everything was at Camp Ojibwa. Everything was supposed to be all set up on a schedule, which was out to the flagpole in the morning when the bugle went off, breakfast at the lodge, getting into our bathing suits and going to the lake for swimming practice and races, changing back into our clothes for field sports, then lunch, then back to the lake for sailing or kayaking lessons, then cabin hour, then to the ball fields for volley ball or softball, then supper, then

Campfire, then either back to the cabin to bed or go somewhere for an overnight in a tent. After a day or two, I realized that each thing we did was terrible, and it wasn't going to get any better. The system was to make everything a little too hard or too rushed. For instance, when the bugle blew out at the flagpole in the morning, each cabin had to have every kid there in formation in ten minutes. This never worked, because some kids were so sound asleep they couldn't get moving even when someone pulled them out of their bunk onto the floor. Also there were only two toilet seats and two sinks in the bathroom, and everybody had to go and most kids wanted to brush their teeth, and there was no room, so most kids, including me, would go out and pee behind the cabin. I hated having to run out to the flagpole in my wrinkly clothes when the grass was still so wet my sneakers would get soaked through. Some kids were always late, and Kip would make them and sometimes their whole cabins do push-ups in the wet grass while everybody watched. Kids who made their cabins get push-ups would usually get pantsed on the way to breakfast.

The counselors worked it so that nothing could be fun or relaxing. The meals were terrible, especially breakfast, which was always the same, sour juice, cold toast, and eggs which were between scrambled and fried with streaky brown marks on them from the grill. They turned cold in your mouth, and there was no salt or pepper because when they used to have it, kids would unscrew the tops of the shakers so that the whole thing would come out on your food. I hated swimming the most, because it was right after breakfast when it wasn't really warm yet, and when it wasn't sunny, I would get so cold in the water my jaw would start shaking on its own, so I couldn't even talk. We'd have to start out swimming laps doing the crawl, breaststroke and backstroke, and then we'd have races against the other cabins, keeping score. There was a lot of screaming during the races, and if you didn't win your laps or fell behind during your lap of a relay, Warren Keener, who always had on dry clothes and a sweatshirt, would stand over you on the dock and say something like, "Thanks a lot, now we're in fourth" or "great speed." Some kids, like Wally Kanicky, could barely swim at all and were in a special beginners group during laps, but when races started everybody was supposed to swim for the cabin. Warren Keener would cheat every now and then by skipping Wally Kanicky and having some good swimmer go twice, but sometimes Wally had to swim, and Warren Keener would say something like, "Great, now we're in last," before Wally even started.

ONE OF THE MAIN COUNSELORS, Mort Emerson, was in charge of all the boats, and when Kip introduced him the first day, he said Mort Emerson had been on a boat racing team in the Olympics. Mort Emerson was pretty serious and quiet, and he didn't seem to like teaching kids about sailing and kayaking. He talked in a quiet voice and kept the same expression on his face. He didn't seem actually mad, but you could tell he didn't really want to be around a bunch of kids, especially on the camp's big sailboat, The Ojibwa. Mort Emerson was really strict, and he meant it. He wouldn't let any kid sail by himself, even in one of the dinghies, until he could pass a test of boating terms and then prove he could tack, jibe, and land a boat without smashing the bow into the dock. This was actually pretty hard, so only about four kids got Sailing Privileges the whole time we were there. There was also kayaking, which seemed to me like it should have been simple, but Mort Emerson told us it was really dangerous, and that we had to learn safety techniques like rolling completely over underwater before we could take out a kayak by ourselves. In order to roll the kayak, we had to be strapped inside in a very complicated way, which I couldn't keep track of, and most of the kayaks were missing some strap or buckle or something, so almost no one got certified to kayak by himself. That actually disappointed me, because I liked the feeling of paddling the kayak through the water and it would have been nice to be able to take off somewhere by myself.

The big treat in the boating program was supposed to be the day you got to sail out on Lake Hathaway in The Ojibwa. Starting the last few days of camp, each cabin got a turn, and even though I should have known better, I was kind of excited when it was time for Laughing Bear to go out. For one thing, The Ojibwa had a downstairs cabin with beds and sinks and cabinets and instruments built into the walls, and kids got to go "below" to see it. What I always liked best about ships in the pirate movies was that down inside they had big rooms with heavy dark furniture, like a house. The cabin of the Ojibwa was a little like that. All the woodwork and brass were polished and shiny, and it would have been nice staying down there, but something about being down out of the air while the boat was moving up and down made you automatically feel a little sick. Even if it didn't, we weren't allowed to stay down there or to do anything, just to look around. We were all supposed to do certain jobs on deck, things we practiced during boating instruction, like trimming the main sheet or raising the jib or setting the spinnaker. The afternoon of our sail was pretty windy, and none of us was strong enough to pull in the ropes that adjusted the sails by ourselves, so Mort Emerson had to step in and do practically everything. I mainly just stood there, holding onto a rope, feeling the boat dip down into a pocket then rising up to meet the wall of a wave, spraying me with cold water. As I stood there holding on and squinting at the shore, I kept thinking that if you took a picture of me and the other kids out on the lake sailing The Ojibwa, it would look exactly the way my mother pictured it when she decided to send me to camp, but thinking about mother only made me feel sad.

I don't think mother even believed in people like Warren Keener, people that mean. He wasn't mean every now and then or mean just to some kids. He was the kind of kid who tried to make you feel as bad as possible, no matter what it was about. If a kid got homesick and started to cry during cabin hour when the mail came, Warren Keener would go over to the kid's bunk and tease him. He'd say, "What's the matter? You miss mommy and daddy?" He'd keep going until the kid was really crying, until maybe the kid would start yelling swear words and swinging at him, and then he would jerk the kid around by the front of his shirt and tell him he was in big trouble. If Warren Keener was making fun of a kid, he tried to get other kids in on it, and some kids would join in, to get in good with Warren Keener for a while. Most kids, though, tried to stay away from him as much as possible. You just didn't want him to notice you, which was hard when he was with our cabin for most of the day.

You were supposed to be really excited and try really hard to get a lot of Achievement Points in everything, including inspections, swimming, boating skills, and crafts. The junior counselors reported each cabin's total Achievement Points at morning flagpole, but because Warren Keener was our junior counselor and got to give Laughing Bear's report, we pretty much stopped trying to get a lot of Achievement Points, which made Warren Keener start calling us "losers" when he talked to us after Lights Out.

Lights Out was really unfair, because the campers weren't supposed to be allowed to talk, only the junior counselor. But Warren Keener would get kids to talk by teasing them or by asking questions, and then, whenever he felt like it, he'd get mad at them and tell them he was reporting them to Kip. Sometimes he did report them, and they'd have to do push-ups or laps at morning flagpole, and sometimes he didn't. You never knew. Sometimes everybody was talking and laughing and screwing around after Lights Out, and Warren Keener wouldn't care. He would use really dirty words and let other kids use them, and this would get kids laughing, and it would get louder and dirtier until I had to go into a certain kind of trance. I hated talking and screwing around during Lights Out more than I hated anything else at the camp. At night in my bunk was the one time I had to make my pictures and tell my stories, but I couldn't do it with everyone making farting noises and Warren Keener saying "your mother's cunt" and "cocksucker" and getting kids to laugh at him. Whenever he felt like it Warren Keener could tell everybody to shut up and if they didn't, he said he would make sure something would happen to them on our next tent overnight.

Tent overnights were supposed to be where we learned camping and wilderness survival, but there was an old tradition where kids from a certain cabin were allowed to go out after Lights Out with their junior counselor and ransack the tents and scare the kids from the cabin that was camping out. Kip and the main counselors were in on it, and it was supposed to be fun because it was a tradition, but on our cabin's tent nights, some kids got into real fights. Weak kids got pantsed and tied up to trees, and some kids got their sleeping bags peed on. I think something bad happened to Patrick Dannehey on his cabin's first tent night, because a kid told me his parents drove up and took him home.

121

The final two days of camp were supposed to be the most fun. In the morning, instead of races and relays, there was free swimming. Kids who got certified in boating were allowed to take the sailing dinghies and kayaks out by themselves. Before supper on the second-to-last night was the Radio Show, which was supposed to be an actual program that went out over the radio in Wisconsin. Some of the cabins worked up skits, and kids who could play instruments or sing or do imitations performed at a big microphone in front of the whole camp. Before the show started, the kids in the audience had to practice clapping and laughing when the counselors held up a sign saying APPLAUSE or LAUGH. Almost from the time we sat down, kids started leaning over to other kids and saying it wasn't real, because the big microphone looked fake, and the headphones Kip was wearing didn't have wires connected to anything, but the kids went along with it, laughing and clapping when the signs went up. I couldn't understand what anybody was saying during the skits, and most of the kids who sang or played their instruments weren't as good as the kids at school. One kid was really good, though. He played a boogie-woogie on the piano, which was as good as an actual record. Toward the end of it, Kip stood up in front and made a big face and started clapping in rhythm to the boogie-woogie beat. Everybody joined in, but in my opinion it spoiled the song.

That night they put paper tablecloths on the tables for supper, and we got fried chicken. For the next-to-last Campfire everybody got marshmallows to toast in the fire, but the final Campfire was supposed to be the biggest tradition in the camp and people said that it made some kids cry. As I walked over to the fire pit from Black Wing, I wondered if they could actually do anything that would make me cry in a good way, but nothing like that happened. There were mainly a bunch of awards. You got a certificate for everything you did, for swimming, for boating, for softball, even if you didn't advance to a higher level. Kids got special awards for being the best in each thing. I had a feeling I might get the softball award, because I was one of the best players and was one of the captains, but I didn't get it. It went on and on, and even though you got up about every two minutes to get another certificate with your group, it was hard to keep paying attention and to keep clapping for everybody. When it was almost over, Kip gave special certificates and hunting knives to the junior counselors. Warren Keener went up to get his knife just like everyone else, and when he shook hands with Kip, he smiled and looked glad, just like a regular nice kid. It was like another awful thing he knew how to do. I knew that in a little while he would be lying close by in the dark after Lights Out talking about people's cocks and cunts.

Usually after Camp Fire the kids lined up behind their junior counselor, and he would turn on his flashlight and lead them back to the cabin. But the tradition for Last Camp Fire was for each kid to get his own candle, and Kip would light the junior counselor's candle, and the junior counselor would light the candle of the first kid in his line, and that kid would light the next kid's until everybody's candle was lit. Then they would walk single file through the trees singing *Fair Ojibwa*.

> *Though in the years to come*
> *Our paths will surely stray*
> *The sons of noble Dark Wing*
> *Will softly make their way*
> *Yes softly make their way*
> *To our fair O-jib-way.*

I held my candle out in front of me so I could see the path, and I tried to hear if anybody was crying. I hoped they weren't. I hoped that when I got back to the cabin and everybody was finally quiet, I could start thinking up things I could tell mother about the camp that wouldn't make her feel bad.

Chapter Fourteen

Going to Camp Ojibwa gave me a sad, sickening feeling that didn't go away even when school started. At the beginning of the summer I thought going to Junior High would be really exciting. We were going across town to a new, bigger building, and the whole set up was different. You didn't have your own homeroom with your own teacher and the same kids for most of the day. You went to a different class with a different teacher each period. You got a locker, and you had periods that were just study halls when you didn't have to do anything. When I was in Mr. Click's class with Patsy and all my friends, I liked picturing Junior High and all the new arrangements. I already had some good pictures in my mind from the times I would go to the Junior High with mother to pick up Annabel after school or to see one of her choir concerts. I liked the way the seventh and eighth graders looked. Some of the boys were really tall and dressed like high school boys with white buck shoes and khaki pants and crew neck sweaters. Those big kids laughing and horsing around in the lobby or shooting baskets on the paved courts outside seemed like they had their own secret world, and it made me start hoping really hard that I would get taller.

The week before I went to camp, mother took me to Zimmerman's department store to buy me school clothes for Junior High. I was secretly hoping she would get me khaki pants and crew neck sweaters, but I didn't see any in the part of the store that had my size, and I didn't really know the names of what to ask for, so I ended up getting some new jeans and corduroys and more plaid flannel shirts like my old ones. I did ask mother if I could get white buck shoes, but she didn't think I was serious. She said white buck shoes got dirty and ratty looking after a while and that mine would get dirty right away.

In Junior High there was no recess, but a separate class called Gym, and boys had to have their own gym shorts, gym shirt and sweat suit. The shorts and shirts and sweat suits said PALATINE PHYSICAL EDUCATION on them, and there was a box below the letters for your name. The gym uniforms stayed the same all the way through high school. I had seen lots of Palatine gym shorts and sweat suits because big kids wore them all the time in the summer when they played basketball under the lights at the parks. Zimmerman's had a special room just for school gym uniforms, and there were high stacks of new-smelling tee shirts and shorts and gray sweat suits on the tables. The sizes were Small, Medium, and Large, and mother thought even the Smalls looked like they would be too big for me. She held up a pair of size Small gym shorts and tried to figure out if the waist was too big. She told me to go into one of the changing closets and try them on. I knew I could figure out a way to wear them no matter how big the waist was, but I tried them on anyway, and they were fine because there was an elastic band puckered into the cloth that held them up over my hips.

The first thing I did when I got back to my room was to try on my whole gym uniform, starting with my athletic supporter, which had the effect of making me feel kind of nude. Then I put on the shorts and the tee shirt, which was so long it came down lower than the shorts. I decided to put on my sneakers too, so I could see what I would actually look like for Gym. I went into mother and father's room to look at myself in the long mirror. It wasn't good. The shirt was way too big, and the tops of my arms coming out the sleeve holes looked smaller and bonier than usual. The shirt came down so far it looked like a dress, and even when I tucked it in, the white cloth came down and showed below the bottom of the shorts. Finally I got the shirt not to show by wedging a lot of it inside the elastic of my athletic supporter. It still didn't look good, though. The shorts seemed too stiff and new. I wanted them just to hang down straight along the tops of my legs, but they flared out on each side, which made my legs look extra small.

My mother called up from downstairs and asked me what I was doing, and I shouted down that I was trying on my gym suit. I heard her move to the bottom of the stairs. She said, "Let's see." So I went over to the top of the stairs and stood there. I knew the gym suit wasn't right and that I felt skinny wearing it, but I didn't know mother was going to laugh. She wasn't mean at all and never tried to hurt my feelings on purpose, but she couldn't help it. She looked up at me and started laughing. She had to bend over at the waist and was kind of snorting trying to make herself stop, but that made her laugh even harder. I couldn't move or say anything. I just stood there, feeling cold and tingly, feeling the air blowing right up through the huge leg holes of the gym shorts. Mother caught her breath and tried to make me feel better. She said she was sorry. "It's just those… enormous shorts and your little knees." She was still laughing. She couldn't stop.

I wished she hadn't seen me, because even if I disappeared forever that second, it had already happened. She saw me and knew how skinny and ridiculous I looked, which was something I knew I couldn't fix. It was the way I really was, and it felt terrible. I had a feeling that from now on everything that happened was going to be terrible, like camp.

A FEW DAYS BEFORE SCHOOL was supposed to begin, I started praying, in a new way I came up with, that I wouldn't have to go to Junior High. In my method I would shut my eyes and make a picture of some sunny place in nature, like the fields or the north woods around one of our cabins. I'd hold the picture still for as long as I could, and then I'd make my mind as tense as possible and say to myself PLEASE GOD KEEP THIS. Then I'd open my eyes. The idea was that maybe I would be pulled up into the bright picture and stay there. It was a little like waking up on certain Saturday mornings and realizing the dream I just woke up from was so good I wanted to go right back to sleep to keep it going. I never figured out how to do it, but I wanted to so much. I knew that if my prayer method ever worked, I'd be gone from the regular world, and that would upset my mother and probably Annabel, but it would be worth it to be back in nature forever and not have to go to Junior High and come out from the locker room and show up in the gymnasium in front of everybody with my little stick arms and legs coming out of my gym uniform.

I don't think it was because of my praying method, but on the Saturday afternoon before school started, I did get pulled up into the other world. Nana and Papa invited me to spend the day and sleep over at their house, and then Annabel would get to do it on Sunday. I always liked sleeping overnight at Nana and Papa's because it took me completely out of my regular life and reminded me of the best things from when I was little. There were a lot of great things to look at in their house, like painted scenes of German towns Papa had wood-burned into a piece of wood, then painted and varnished. Nana had glassed in cabinets full of fancy china plates with scenes on them, and in Papa's study upstairs there was a shelf full of old-looking beer steins with painted scenes around the sides and pointed metal lids. He also had a rack of carved pipes on his desk and a huge dagger in a green leather sheath that he used as a letter opener. There was one whole bookcase full of big leather volumes of his stamp collections, which I was allowed to look at if he was there with me. Sometimes when he got a new packet of stamps in the mail, he would turn on a special lamp on his desk and let me stand next to him while he took the new stamps out of their little onionskin holders and set them into the albums next to the other stamps from that country. I never got tired of looking at the colored inks and the engraved letters and the little heads of the kings and the queens on the stamps, especially when there was a whole page of them lined up together.

Everything at Nana's and Papa's was like that. You just wanted to look around at the things they had. The big sofa and chairs in their living room were extra comfortable, and Nana always cooked the things she knew were your favorites. There was a bowl of M&Ms on the kitchen table, and I could have as many as I felt like. Maybe the best thing about being over at Nana and Papa's was that you were always allowed to do what you wanted, and there was always enough time. Nana would play Monopoly or cards or Chinese checkers if I asked her to, and she was always in a calm mood about it, kind of pretending to be mad or glad about how she was doing, but she really wasn't. If I felt like playing by myself, Nana would give me a pad of paper and pencils and crayons to draw with and let me alone. She seemed to know in advance the things I wanted to do.

The Saturday before school started was really hot and muggy. I was drawing by myself on the screened in porch, and Nana came out and asked me if I wanted to go upstairs and change into some cooler clothes, like my shorts and sandals. I actually did feel pretty sticky, so I went up to change. The only pair of shorts I had with me was a too-big pair that we got from my cousin Gordon in a package of hand-me-downs. I knew they looked terrible, and I never would have worn them at home or around other kids, but I knew no one would see me and that Nana and Papa wouldn't care what I put on, so I changed into the shorts My underpants were sweaty and were sticking to my skin, so I decided to take them off and not wear any. Gordon's old shorts were so baggy and loose, I could feel the air moving around the tops of my legs all the way up to my thing. This felt uncomfortable but also good at the same time, and all of a sudden I wanted to get outside, to get into nature, to get past the houses and into the fields right away. It was very a strong feeling, nervous and exciting all at once. It would be a long time until supper, and I decided not to tell Nana I was going out. I just left and started walking.

The fields were only about three streets away from Nana and Papa's house. The road going in was paved with gravel, and there were some houses along the way before the road changed to a dirt path and the actual fields began. Sometimes Nana and I would take a hike down this path, but it wouldn't last very long, because the path came to an end in high grass that sloped down to a swampy place. Nana didn't like hiking off the path, so we'd turn around and head back. Today I wasn't even thinking about what was along the path. I just needed to get past the houses and be by myself in the hot fields. By the time I got to the dirt path, I was really hot. I had to keep swatting at bugs buzzing around the back of my head, and my face got so sweaty I had to stop every now and then and wipe my eyes. It was the kind of hot day that made everything in the fields come to life. Big grasshoppers were making rattling arcs across the path, and crickets and peepers were screeching in a way that seemed to be coming from inside my own skull. There was no breeze at all, just the hot, heavy air. The excited feeling I got when I first put on the shorts kept building and building. I could feel the cloth brushing against my thing, and I not only didn't mind, it made me feel even more excited. I started to feel like getting naked somewhere all by myself. I had never felt anything like this before, and I knew that something even greater was coming. I took off my sweaty tee shirt and stuffed it into the pocket of my shorts, which made them slide down further on my hips. My thing started to rise up and in a minute it felt as hard as a bone. When I got to the end of the path, the waves of screeching from the fields and the pulsing in my chest felt like they were the same thing. It felt like the sticky air wasn't outside my skin anymore, as if I had somehow spilled out of myself and was all mixed up in everything. I just kept moving into the high grass and didn't care about it tickling against my bare arms and legs and belly. I was too excited to make a picture of where I was going or even to think. I just forced my way through the heavy grass until I was under the dark branches of sumac trees. I felt my feet sink down into something cold and both sneakers filled up with water.

I had reached the edge of a still black pool. Sumac and other trees with long slender trunks grew up out of the water, and the branches overhead made a dark leafy dome that only let in a few patches of sunlight. It was airless and a little cooler under the cover of the dome. I was aware of the hot white light outside, and I could still hear the waves of screeching from the fields, but, except for the plop and croak of a frog every now and then, it was a dark and quiet place, and it had called me there. I knew I was in another time in another world, the world before the regular world, and even though I knew in my mind it was afternoon, it was somehow also twilight. I untied my sneakers and took them off. Then I unbuttoned my shorts and let them slide down around my ankles. The back of my neck and skull and all down my spine started tingling, and then the tingling took over my whole body. I didn't know if I was dead or already in heaven. All I could do was stand still and feel everything, feel each wave of tingling give way to a stronger one until I was held in a spiral of all of them at once. Then the pleasure erupted. It came throbbing out of my thing, and then everywhere. It was everything I could feel, everything there was. It rose and fell, rose and fell, until it was gone.

The first thing I thought was that I did not ever want to leave. I wanted it to happen again, but the longer I stood there, the more I knew I was just standing in muck with my shorts down around my ankles. I knew I had been taken up into the other world and that I had felt everything there was, but I also knew that even now, even right afterward, I couldn't connect what happened to the regular world. There was no way to talk about it and nobody I could tell. By the time I was dressed and sloshing along the path in my mucky sneakers, I was so far back in the regular world that I couldn't even tell myself what had just happened to me.

Chapter Fifteen

THE FARTHEST YOU can get from the other world is school. Even the first days, which used to be the best days, I could see that something was wrong with Junior High. Almost nobody from Mr. Click's section was in any of my classes, and I could go practically all day without really talking to anybody. Every fifty-two minutes we went to a different room for a different subject, and we were supposed to have a different section of our notebook for each subject. Math was just a lot of problems, and in most of the other classes the teachers taught us how to take notes and make outlines, because we were going to have to make a lot of outlines of big topics like lumber and transportation and then do reports on them, along with maps and articles you cut out of newspapers and certain other things you could do for extra credit. At the end of the unit, you handed everything in to the teacher in a colored folder and then got a grade on the whole thing. I knew all about it from Annabel, who kept all her old units in her desk drawer. Annabel had beautiful, perfect handwriting, and she copied over all her written work in ink. She was right handed, so she didn't make a smeary mess of everything with the edge of her hand. Also, her extra credit drawings, especially in the Birds of the Americas unit, were really beautiful, as good as books, but in crayon. Annabel did her extra credit and her other work in her room by herself. She hardly ever talked about her units or about school. In Junior High you got graded on everything, and three times a year you got report cards with a list of your grades in each subject, along with a 1, 2, or 3 in effort and conduct, 1 being excellent, 2 being satisfactory, and 3 being unsatisfactory. Annabel got Bs on all her units, and underneath the B her teacher would maybe write "Good" or "Good Work." I asked her if B was pretty good, and she said it was okay, that it was average. Annabel was always quiet, but she got really quiet in junior high. She did her work at night, and she got Bs on her units, and when her report card came, she and mother would go over it, and mother would ask me to leave the table so they could have some privacy, because Annabel was getting Ds and Fs in math.

I had always been one of the smallest kids, but in Junior High I also started to feel small. Gym didn't turn out to be as bad as I thought, though. I didn't know most of the kids in my section, and because I was one of the kids who was really good at sports, nobody made any bad comments. I also noticed that some of the kids wore kneepads in Gym, and I thought the kneepads would make my legs look bigger. What bothered me the most was that my lower leg looked so small and skinny below my knee. Most kids' legs just tapered down gradually down to their ankles, and there would be a kind of bulge of muscle in the calf, but below my knee there was a big indentation and then just my skinny shin bone. It looked really terrible in the mirror, like the legs of starving kids in Africa. I knew the kneepads would sort of fill in the indentation, so I told mother they were required, and we got a pair at the sporting goods store. After that, I started to be able to relax in Gym.

Sixth grade was supposed to be the first grade of Junior High, but in a way it was separate. Palatine Central Junior High had sports teams with uniforms and played games across town with Palatine South and Palatine North and other places, but only seventh and eighth graders could be on the teams. Sixth graders just had Gym teams. Some sixth graders could be on Student Council if they got nominated and the whole class voted on them, but there were mostly new kids from the other elementary schools in my classes, so nobody nominated me, even though I secretly wanted them to, because in Mr. Click's class I got to be president and captain of just about everything. I didn't tell anyone, but it made me sad not to be one of the sixth graders on Student Council, because I could see that in seventh and eighth grade, the kids who got nominated and elected were the kids who got elected in sixth grade because they were the kids everybody knew, so I would never be on Student Council. That whole feeling of being elected and sitting up in front of everybody wasn't going to happen anymore.

But a much worse thing than that happened a few weeks later. It gave me the worst, most miserable feeling I ever felt, and it never really went away.

After lunch in the cafeteria you could buy candy bars at a special Student Council table. Members of the Student Council got to collect the money, which went for things like dances and foster children. Anybody with any money always got in line after lunch and bought candy bars. One day as I was about to stack up my tray and get in line, I looked up in front of me to where the Student Council kids were standing around, and I saw the back of Patsy Prentiss's head. I actually felt a kind of clout in my chest even before I recognized her. There was the crinkly swirl of blonde and brown hair, and then she turned around a little, and I could see her sunburned cheeks. She was talking to a bunch of seventh and eighth grade Student Council kids who were sitting on the edge of the candy table. I could see her start to laugh, and I remembered the sound of it, the helpless machine-gun rattle that came out of her. I remembered her husky voice and how it felt to be around her, the way she was always just about to do something I didn't expect.

Patsy. How could I have forgotten her? Then everything came back in a rush, running through people's back yards in the cold fall air, lying tangled in the straw, looking up into the darkening sky and feeling her skull against mine, sitting back in the breezy snack bar of the Country Club, seeing the crinkles in the corners of her eyes as she was telling me something funny. There were a lot of kids in line between me and where Patsy was standing. I kept watching her as I moved up, and the closer I got the worse I felt. It would take me a long time before I could understand it or explain it in words, but before I even got close enough to her to wave and say hi, I knew I wasn't going to be important enough. I was going to be too small, and I wouldn't know enough, and there was going to be something that wasn't right about my clothes. Maybe Patsy grew a lot over the summer, or maybe it just seemed like she did, but by the time I got up to her, she seemed not only much bigger, but a completely different kind of person, almost not even a kid.

She had on different clothes than I had ever seen her wear. She was wearing a gray skirt and a soft gray sweater under another sweater just like it but with buttons up the front. She had on white buck shoes and new white sweat socks, which made the skin on her calves look extra brown and shiny. Her calves were just the right size and looked really nice. I bought a candy bar and walked up next to her. She was telling a story and had just said, "We all practically broke out necks," when she noticed me. She said, "*Hey*, Jonathan!" She was being really nice. "Hey, this is Jonathan Force, my old bud." *Old bud.* The seventh and eighth graders looked at me, and then Patsy finished her story. It felt all wrong to be standing there. I was the smallest kid by a lot. I just had on my regular clothes, and the seventh and eighth graders had on khaki pants and nice shirts with button down collars and white bucks. They were supposed to be around the candy table, and I wasn't.

All that fall I would lie in the dark at night and try to understand what had happened, how Patsy could have changed into a new kind of person, a person I knew I didn't even belong with but still wanted to be with. I wanted to get back that feeling when we were running somewhere side by side. I wanted the skull-to-skull feeling, and the thought that it was gone and I'd never have it again made me too sad to cry. Before that day in the candy line I wasn't thinking about her at all. I had forgotten her. After that, I couldn't get her out of my head for a second. I figured out where each of her classes was and knew where she was every minute of the school day. Two or three times every day I would pass her in the corridor between classes or going up the stairs while she was coming down. For a while I tried hanging around where she was standing after lunch or on the playground, but that only made me feel worse, because she was always with a bunch of bigger kids I didn't know, and some of the boys were the tallest kids in the school.

A few days after I saw her in the candy line, I called her on the telephone. I didn't really know what I wanted to say, but I ended up asking her if I could come over to her house after school and do something. She said sure, but even though she was nice, I could tell that she didn't think my coming over was going to be anything special, probably because I didn't think it would be either. I knew I was too small. But I still loved to think about her. Even though she was bigger and was starting to have that teenager look, I couldn't wait to catch sight of her in the corridor, to see the way her hair bounced around her head when she walked, the brown and peach color of her cheeks. There are some people, and Patsy was one of them, who just cause your cells to change when you get near them.

The afternoon I went to Patsy's house after school wasn't much of anything. She met me on her front stoop, and we sat down and talked about school and the teachers we had. She said she liked Junior High so far but really missed the kids she was with over the summer on their island. She asked me about camp, and I said it was slightly crummy but okay. We played the bowling game in her basement for a while, and even though I kept feeling I wanted to talk to her more than anything and figure out a way that she would only want to be with me after school so we could do everything together like last year, I couldn't do it. Everything I thought of to say was boring, even to me. I couldn't even imagine getting off a good one. We talked a little more on her front stoop, and then I walked home and let the sadness take over.

IN SOME WAYS JUNIOR HIGH was even more terrible than camp. There was nobody who wanted to hurt you all the time or who was as dirty-minded as Warren Keener, but the days were organized pretty much the same way. You went to a new class every period, and you handed in homework from the day before for a check mark, and then the teacher explained something new, and then you had homework about that. Most of the teachers seemed to be in a hurry, and they acted like we were already behind in whatever we were supposed to be doing. The main classes like English and math and science were grouped by ability, Accelerated, Fast, and Average. In Art and Music and Gym ability didn't matter, and anybody could be in your section. I was in Accelerated everything except math, where I was in Fast. We got put in ability-grouped classes based on how we did on tests we took in fifth grade, the Iowa Standard Achievements. I couldn't remember taking the tests and wondered if I was even there on those days. I especially wondered how they figured out I was only Fast in math. I always thought I was one of the smartest kids in math, one of the kids who figured everything out right away and got problems right on the board and on tests. Somebody must have known something, though, because when we got into algebra later, I started getting things wrong even in Fast.

It was fine to be in Fast classes, but nobody wanted to be in Average. You weren't supposed to look down on kids who had all Average classes, but you couldn't help thinking about them in a different way and feeling sorry for them. Sometimes a kid would drop out of an Accelerated class into Fast or a smart Fast kid would go up to Accelerated, but no Average kids ever got moved up. They pretty much stayed in their own groups, and then in high school you would almost never see them because they would be in Vocational Ed, which prepared you for life in minor jobs.

Except for algebra later, I didn't think any of the work in Junior High was very hard, but there was always something you had to do. There were books and printed articles we had to read and outline for Social Studies, and the outlines would be part of our units. There was no Reading for Life competition anymore. Everybody in Accelerated English read the same books, books Junior High kids had always read, such as *Johnny Tremain*, *Julius Caesar*, and *The Diary of Anne Frank*. I got all of them from Annabel, and I had read most of them already. I ended up reading *Diary of Anne Frank* a bunch of times. I read it the first time because when Annabel read it, she was so upset she cried really hard and had to be alone with mother. After that she had nightmares. When I read it, I saw why she had that reaction. A story like that is too mean for a girl like Annabel, not that Anne Frank herself was mean in any way. She was actually tremendous and the kind of person I know I would have had the love feeling for if I ever met her, but knowing that the Nazis crashed into their family's upstairs hiding place and took them away to the concentration camps where they died was something Annabel couldn't stand to picture.

I didn't read *Julius Caesar* in advance, because when I started to read it, I couldn't understand a single thing. Not only could I not understand the way the words went together, I couldn't figure out who the people were whose names kept being mentioned. *Julius Caesar* was the kind of book the teacher had to tell you everything about in advance, and even then you weren't sure you were getting anything out of the actual words. It felt important to be reading something by William Shakespeare, and I could never get some of the phrases out of my head, like "yon Cassius has a lean and hungry look" or "lend me your ears," but for a play that was supposed to be about stabbing and battles, it never felt, when you were actually reading it, that anything was happening.

I did okay in Junior High and toward the end got straight A's a few times because I decided to make it a project, but I never got the feeling back I had with Mr. Click, the feeling that nobody could come up with the kind of things I could. I think Mr. Click thought I was kind of amazing, and that got me in a really good mood. I doubt that anybody thought I was amazing in Junior High. I know I didn't.

When I think back, the main thing I did in Junior High was try not to feel too bad. I didn't want to get into that nervous, black feeling I could get into in my bed at night where I'd think about some terrible thing about my body or that somebody had said to me, then circle back to it again and again until it connected to something that was even worse, so it felt like I was caught in a spiral of awfulness that was taking me down and down into a complete darkness that, if I went down into it all the way, was going to be the worst thing there was.

Sometimes I thought I could stay out of the spiral if I just kept doing things, even stupid little things, anything that would keep me up on the surface. For instance, I got really good at writing with my right hand, and with my left hand I learned how to do about six absolutely different kinds of handwriting, so I always had something to do in class that looked like I was working. I started buying baseball cards and trading them with other kids and building up my collection. It wasn't too interesting, but it was just interesting enough to keep me doing it. I liked knowing the players' names—Ted Kluzewski, Dee Fondi, Minny Minoso, Robin Roberts, Jesus McFarland, Nelly Foxx—just by the look of their big meaty faces. I liked the colors of their hats and the idea that their whole lives could be boxed into the little paragraph about them on the back of the card, along with their batting averages and pitching records. There was also something a little sad about baseball cards, because after you had a bunch of them, you realized that most of the players weren't that good and were never going to become famous stars. Most of them had batting averages of around .230 and had been in the Minors and were probably going to be in the Minors again. After awhile I had a whole shoe box full of baseball cards, and it gave me the feeling that I actually had all those guys captured in there, their lives shrunk down to cards.

I also started collecting comic books, which gave me the same kind of feeling the baseball cards did. Comics seemed to have a kind of thin life of their own. The people, like Archie and Veronica and Little Lulu and Superman, were just drawn outlines filled in with colored ink, but you could still go into their little worlds right away and stay there for a while. Sometimes I would go over to a kid's house who had a whole stack of comics I had never seen, and I would just sit down somewhere and read all of them, without even having to talk or to think. It wasn't like seeing a movie, because you never felt much about anything in the comics; comics just held you there in that thin world. I remember whole mornings and whole afternoons just lying around reading comics and then feeling that the only good thing was that time had passed.

By then we had a TV and just about everybody else had a TV, but I didn't like to watch it too much. First of all, I can't stand anything that keeps repeating, and the commercials, with the same people saying the same obvious things and the same pictures coming up in the same order, always made me want to go out of the room. Also, just about all the shows were terrible. You knew what was going to happen right away, and then it happened. I don't know who thought up there having to be laughter after just about anything anybody said, but it never sounded right and made me picture a terrible kind of world where people really did laugh at things like that. The whole effect was to make me hope that I would never know people like Lucy and Mr. Peepers and Our Miss Brooks or live in the kinds of places they lived.

Maybe it was my fault, but everything about life then, whether it was TV or comics or Junior High, seemed designed to bring you up to a busy but annoying surface where you had to pretend things were important that you knew you could never care about. I can't remember any miracles in Junior High or ever feeling like I was close to the other world. I didn't know how to get into that mood. All I could think about was figuring out something to keep me interested enough, something like working on a new handwriting or inventing my own language, to keep from getting caught in the spiral of terrible thoughts.

The spiral would usually start when I saw some kids at school who were pretty tall and looked good in their clothes and were obviously having a good time shooting baskets on the outdoor courts or goofing around the student council candy table. I would start to compare myself to them in the worst way, picturing myself as even smaller and skinnier than I was. I would see a kid's crew cut that looked dry and clean with perfect square edges, and then I'd go into the boys' lavatory and look at my crew cut and it would look all smashed down and ratty, probably because my father gave me the haircut with the new shears he bought. He said he knew all about giving crew cuts, that they were the easiest haircuts to give, but mine never looked anything like the dry, square-edged ones the kids had who got to go to the barber's. When I was in that kind of mood, I looked really terrible in the mirror. Besides my mashed down, shiny hair, my head looked way too big for my neck, and if I looked long enough, my nose, and especially my nostrils, started to look huge. I would go away picturing my face like some kind of monster skull with horrible dark nostril holes. That could really get the spiral going, or catching a glimpse of the tops of my skinny arms coming out of a short-sleeved shirt, or just seeing some kid's nice sized arms, or really anything.

The thing I felt the most terrible about was Patsy Prentiss. I couldn't do anything to make those feelings go away. I wasn't her friend anymore. I didn't even feel like I was the same kind of kid as she was. She had gotten pretty tall and had a figure now. She always looked comfortable in her clothes, and she was always wearing something, like a bright yellow sweater or a pleated plaid skirt or new saddle shoes, that made you want to keep looking at how she was dressed. Kids wanted to be around her, and the seventh and eighth graders let her into their group, and whenever I saw her standing around somewhere, she was with tall kids from the student council and the teams. She seemed to belong naturally around a bigger kind of kid than I was, which I couldn't blame her for, but I couldn't stand it.

I KEPT PICTURING HER BROWN cheeks and pretty teeth and the croaky way she talked and laughed. I could feel being skull to skull with her and how she felt leaning into me in the dark at the end of the Shock Theater party. I don't think I forgot anything we ever did, but I hated knowing it was over, that something had carried her up to a higher level where I wasn't included, which must have been because I was so small.

I also knew there was something not right about my clothes, but I couldn't figure out what. All I know is that it felt really terrible to have the love feeling for Patsy all by myself. It made me cry. It made me think that the only reason I got the love feeling in the first place was so that I would know how terrible I could feel. That is what the spiral was like. You got the feeling there was a big plan to hurt you and surprise you and disappoint you in more and more terrible ways. It made you wish you were never born and that it would be better to be dead than to go down the spiral all the way.

The only real things that happened during Junior High, the only things that took me up out of the blur, were sex and music. After that Saturday when I went into the other world at the edge of the black pond, I had a sense that my life in the regular world was never going to be the same. I knew that the every-thing-there-is feeling could take over my body, that it had really happened. I could feel it trying to start up again. I would feel it in my thing, which would get hard again, and then I'd wait to get carried away. But it never happened like that again. I would be in the bathtub or lying in bed in the morning, and a little bit of the feeling would start to come, but it would just stay there in my hard thing. By rubbing it or pulling on it for a while, it would finally let go, and there would be a big pleasure feeling, but only for a second or two, like a miniature, miniature reminder of what had happened to me at the black pond.

Chapter Sixteen

I DON'T KNOW IF it happened naturally or because I heard so many thousands of sex jokes and stories from kids like Warren Keener and other kids in Junior High, but starting about then I linked my sex feeling to the jokes and the stories. Almost all the girls now had boobs you could at least see. They started out like little buds, not much bigger than mine, but sticking out a little in their sweaters. After a while they got to be about the size of eggs and started to look really nice, and people got bras. Some of the fat girls' boobs were as big and full and droopy as women's, even in sixth grade, and the kids who talked about sex all the time in Gym and at lunch talked about the fat girls' boobs as if they were the sexiest thing. Those kids also used the word "tits" for boobs, which made them sound dirty. They would say things like, "How'd you like to get your hands on Barb Frolich's tits," and you were supposed to act like that would be really amazing, even though no one even wanted to sit next to Barb Frolich on the bus or talk to her at lunch. I never for a second wanted to get my hands on Barb Frolich's boobs, but I was aware that my sex feeling was starting to be connected to that kind of talk and those kinds of pictures.

I started to get interested in pictures of women in magazine advertisements. Mostly they were just pictures of big, smiling women holding a box of detergent or walking down a city street in shiny stockings and high heeled shoes, but I was starting to see something sexy in them, and that would get the little tickle of the sex feeling going. About twice a year we'd get Sears Roebuck and Montgomery Ward catalogs in the mail, and if I was by myself, I would look at the brassieres section, which went on for about twenty pages, showing hundreds of little boxes of women's necks and shoulders and breasts with brassieres on. It would only take me about two pages to get the sex feeling, and I would have to close the catalog.

Annabel was a freshman in the high school, and even though she was just starting to get a figure herself, she never talked about it, or about her body or boys or anything like that. The summer I went to camp, I got the idea that something terrible had happened to her, because when I got home mother took me into the living room by myself and told me that Annabel had had her period. I had no idea what that was, and when my mother told be it was about Annabel's female eggs coming into their place and getting washed out in blood through her thing for a few days every month, I really wanted her to stop talking about it. Mother said it was completely natural and healthy and that every girl had periods, but it sounded serious and disgusting to me. Maybe every girl does get periods, but I don't think Annabel thought that hers were completely natural and healthy. I tried to ask her about it in a nice way, but she gave me a sad, scared look, and I could tell she never wanted me to know things like that about her. I think Annabel hated having periods, and even though we never talked about it, I'm sure she would have hated the sex feeling. It's too bad that certain people like Annabel have to go through sex, which only scares them and hurts their feelings. I think now that if Annabel didn't have to go through sex, she would have been able have a regular life, quiet maybe, but doing really nice things for people, because that is the way she was. But as it turned out, having her period and having to go through sex was worse for Annabel than knowing what happened to Anne Frank.

I loved Annabel and never would have tried to hurt her feelings by talking about sex, but I did get the sex feeling sometimes when she had certain friends over to the house. Annabel was actually really pretty herself. Natalie Wood was her favorite movie star, and she had a way of making herself look like Natalie Wood, a look that made you feel like taking care of her. The friends in her grade, though, looked a lot older and bigger. I remember the house seeming to fill up with a lively, exciting feeling when they would come over and start giggling and shrieking in Annabel's room, trying on clothes and putting Rock and Roll records on Annabel's little portable record player. Annabel's friends had complete figures, like thin women, and they gave off a feeling that they could barely hold all their energy in, so that it came bubbling out in extra fast talking and giggling. They all said I was "cute," but that was not what gave me the sex feeling. I got it because I could just tell that these girls were glad about their periods and going through sex, and that made me kind of glad too.

Because of alphabetical order, I sat next to Barb Frolich in a lot of my classes. By seventh grade, any time anybody started talking about boobs, they'd get onto Barb Frolich's. One of my friends, Gary Wade, called them "jugs," and at least that sort of described them. "Tits" made me picture little, flitty things, like paper airplanes or swallows, and something about calling somebody's boobs "tits" seemed a little mean. Barb Frolich was actually nice enough. She was pretty fat, though, and she had puffy little pouches under her eyes, which made her look like she had been crying or was really tired. Maybe she was. I know it really hurt her feelings to have everybody teasing her about her big boobs. People had been doing it for almost two years, and you can really get to hate that kind of thing. I was pretty nice to her, but we didn't have any of the same friends or talk much. I think she thought I was in with the group that was always talking about her boobs, but I wasn't the one who would ever bring them up. Actually her boobs, which were right there next to me, about three inches away when we were in classes that sat around tables, made me kind of sad. She used to wear sweaters made out of a slinky looking cloth called Banlon. You could tell what everything looked like under the Banlon, so I could see the extra pouch of fat she had between her shoulder and her armpit, and I could see the straps and stitches of her bra. Barb Frolich used to cross her arms under her boobs, which probably helped hold them up. She also carried her books under them to make a kind of shelf when she was going somewhere. We had so many classes together I ended up looking at her boobs a lot without meaning to. They never gave me the sex feeling, because something about the sad, heavy way Barb Frolich sat in her chair made any kind of sex feeling impossible, although I did wonder sometimes what it would be like to have big heavy boobs like that growing out of your chest and what it would feel like to run or jump.

Barb Frolich wore a big silver heart on a chain around her neck. Sometimes it would be tucked under the Banlon, and sometimes it would be on the outside hanging down in the ridge where her boobs came together. Gary Wade got the idea that it would be really funny for me to try to touch her boobs. He told me I should pretend I wanted to look at her silver heart, and while I was grabbing for it with my hand, give her boobs a feel. He thought the idea of doing something like that in class was extra funny. I didn't want to at all, even though I was sure I'd probably get away with it. Every chance he could, Gary Wade, who was a really goofy looking kid, would be looking over at me from his side of the room, doing fake coughing and gesturing, trying to get my attention, so I would go for Barb Frolich's necklace. It got annoying, but I also saw that I could fool Gary Wade. So after almost a whole class where he was mouthing things to me, like "*Do* it," I nodded to him and then leaned in close to Barb Frolich and pretended I was writing something in her notebook, which she bent over to see. Then I turned back to look at Gary Wade, who was so excited he was standing up at his place. He was mouthing, "*Did* you?" and I nodded that I did. He made a high shriek, which he probably couldn't help, and said out loud, "Oh, *man!*" which got him sent out of class. After that all Gary Wade could do was go on and on about how "Force got a piece of Frolich's jugs." I didn't care what he said, but I hoped that Barb Frolich wouldn't hear about it, because she certainly didn't need to feel any worse.

It was really pretty strange, going all through Junior High with the sex feeling. If it wasn't down there in my thing, it was hovering all around me like I was wrapped in a huge bubble of it. It mainly felt like one of those permanent diseases like asthma or diabetes, which you always have but only rise up every now and then. But walking around in that new bubble could make certain times unbearable. For instance, any time I even caught a glimpse of Patsy Prentiss, I would get so excited and confused it almost made me sick. By seventh grade, she hardly even remembered me, and if I hadn't known her so well and loved her so much in fifth grade, I would probably not even have recognized her. She got really tall and had a complete figure. She wore lipstick, and her hair was in an actual hair-do that flared out in great way. She was one of the popular kids, but not with the kids in our grade. Practically all her friends were in the older grades, and she always had a boyfriend who was really popular and on the teams. By the time we were all in eighth grade, her friends and boyfriends were in high school, and she was going to dances and out on dates in cars, with kids driving.

It is hard to describe the effect Patsy Prentiss had on me. The thing that made me sad and almost sick was that my original love feeling, the skull-to-skull feeling in fifth grade, had not gone away. I still had it and felt it, and it ached. It seemed completely wrong and unfair that anything like that could be taken away. But at the same time, I could see her now, with her height and her figure and her hair-do, and know that she had grown out of me into something else. But she was still beautiful to me. I could still see her old face in her new face, and because of that her new face seemed even more beautiful. When I was by myself, I pictured it every second I could, but I couldn't make a picture of her with me in it. Picturing her kind of gave me a sexual feeling, and it kind of didn't. It was a little vague. I remember thinking that when it came time to have actual sex, like feeling bare boobs, then feeling inside their pants, and then sticking it inside to have intercourse, I wanted it to be with Patsy Prentiss, but when I actually saw her, I never felt like doing any of that. I couldn't picture it at all.

Looking back on it, going through sex and going through Junior High mainly made me duller and stupider than I really was. I did all those surface things to keep busy, but there were long stretches where I can't remember caring much about anything. When I'm in that kind of mood, that's when I usually get sick, and for practically the whole winter all through sixth and seventh and eighth grade, I was either getting the scratchy burning feeling in my chest that told me bronchitis was coming, or I had it with all the fevers and crud in my chest, or I was getting over it, back in school, but still hacking away and trying to keep my nose from running. We had a lot of photographs around the house, which are now arranged in albums, but there are almost none of me when I was in Junior High, and I'm glad, because when I look at an old picture of me then, all I see is a too big head with dark eyes, a big nose and, if the body is showing, everything too skinny.

THANK GOD FOR MUSIC. Music was the one thing I could do while I was in Junior High that was completely good. Nana and Papa had a Baldwin grand piano in their living room, and from the time Annabel and I were old enough to stay overnight at their house by ourselves, we would take turns playing it. We couldn't really play anything when we were little, just little trick songs where you rolled your knuckles over the three black keys that were in a row, then plunked the next one up. It made a little tune, but it wasn't very interesting. We also learned to play chopsticks, which was even less interesting, except when Papa sat down with me and played low, beautiful chords that made it sound like a great song. It started to irritate me that I couldn't play anything that I really wanted to hear. I tried a lot of experiments, but it didn't sound all that great. One thing I could do was pick out notes one at a time that would play the melody of a song I liked, and after I repeated it a few times, it would sound just like the song. Papa said that I had "a good ear" and told mother that I should take piano lessons, but I never did, because we didn't have a piano at home to practice on. But I kept fooling around on Nana And Papa's piano, trying to work out a system, and then in Junior High, I got it.

In Junior High I was allowed to stay over at Nana and Papa's practically every weekend, sometimes for both nights, so there was a lot of time to work on the piano, especially when my chest was full of bronchitis, and I couldn't go out. Two things happened that made me able to start making real music on the piano. The first was learning how to play "Heart and Soul," and the second was watching Liberace on TV. There was an old upright piano at the back of the lunchroom at school, and a bunch of kids knew how to play "Heart and Soul." Usually two kids would play it as a duet, with one kid playing the melody notes up high and the other kid making chords down low. Even though the kids playing were usually not musical at all, if they knew the pattern of the chords and the simple

147

melody line, they could make it sound pretty good, even though they were just banging on the keys. I had a kid show me how to do the chords, and it was easy. Then at Nana and Papa's I showed Annabel how to play the melody, and we got to be really good at "Heart and Soul." Sometimes Papa would lean over me and play extra chords below mine, and that really sounded good. For a long time I couldn't get "Heart and Soul" to stop repeating in my head.

ONE SUNDAY AFTERNOON AT NANA and Papa's when I was playing the piano by myself, it hit me that the "Heart and Soul" chords went with a lot of other songs, and I started trying that idea out, and it worked perfectly. I couldn't believe it. Pretty soon I was playing "Blue Moon," "The Way You Look Tonight," and about sixty Rock and Roll songs, just using the "Heart and Soul" chords. That night when my parents showed up at Nana and Papa's for dinner, I showed them all the songs I could play, and they seemed pretty impressed, but after a while they wanted to eat. I had to eat, too, which was frustrating because all I wanted to do was keep figuring things out on the piano. After supper on Sunday nights everybody always watched The Ed Sullivan Show and Fred Waring on Nana and Papa's TV, which I usually liked, except the TV was in the living room, which meant I couldn't play the piano. I could hardly stand to look at the screen. All I could do was imagine my fingers forming chords and silently pressing down the keys.

Every now and then I got to go over to Nana and Papa's on a weekday after school and play the piano, but usually I had to wait till Saturday or Sunday. Playing the piano kept getting better and better because Papa started showing me things, including a lot of chords that were not in "Heart and Soul" and a bunch of minor chords which had a feel of their own. He also showed me all the different keys you could play in. Everybody played "Heart and Soul" on the white keys, which is the key of C, but you can play it in lots of other keys just by shifting it up or down and learning which black keys you have to use instead of white ones. This actually took a few days to figure out, but I loved working on it. Nana would come into the living room every now and then and say, "You *can't* still be playing the piano!" but I always was. I went into the living room right after breakfast and worked on it until Nana called me for lunch. After lunch I would go right back and work on things until the room got dark and we would have to eat again.

I started to realize that I could play anything, which gave me the chills. When I heard a song on the radio or on a record, I could always keep it in my head, and after I started playing the piano for a while, I could play the melody of the song right away with my right hand. Getting good chords with my left hand was a lot harder. Sometimes I had to try a lot of chords or change around one of the ones I knew to get it to sound right, and this could take a long time if the song was complicated, like "Smoke Gets in Your Eyes" or "Some Enchanted Evening." Sometimes I had to wait until Papa was around to help me figure out a chord, but he didn't always know. If I got too frustrated, I'd play something like "Mac The Knife" or Rock and Roll songs, which were so easy they just went automatically and my mind could rest.

In seventh grade, on Christmas Eve, we got our own piano, a black upright. I wasn't expecting it, and it took a while to believe that we really had it, that I was going to be able to play the piano as much as I wanted, any day of the week. I liked our piano, especially the easy way the keys went down. Our piano sounded clinkier and brighter than Nana and Papa's Baldwin, but once I learned a new song I really liked, I couldn't wait to play it on the Baldwin, because it made everything sound fuller and deeper and more important.

I started to get a little conceited about how well I could play the piano, and this was partly because Annabel liked it so much. She would sit down next to me on the piano bench just watching my hands and not saying anything. When she had a new favorite song, she would ask me if I would learn it, and as soon as I did, she would sit next to me and listen to it over and over. She was always really nice about telling me how good I was, and after I played a song she liked, she would say, "I wish I could play the piano." I taught her how to play a few songs, which she learned pretty well, but she didn't know how to store things up in her head.

I could tell my mother and father thought my piano playing was kind

149

of amazing by the way they talked about it to their friends. When I started to get good, my father would take out his trumpet and play along with me. He knew just about every song there was by heart, and he would play harmonies to the melody line and also sneak in little extra notes between the ones I was playing in a way that almost made me laugh. One thing I didn't like, though, was when he would ask me to play something I didn't really like that much when certain friends came over. That was just about the only time playing the piano wasn't any fun. It felt like I was being ordered around, and a few times I could feel myself not playing very well almost on purpose, and I could tell that made my father mad.

Once when I was fooling around by myself, I tried playing a song in the key of F, which is all white keys except for one, with my right hand while my left hand was playing in the key of F-sharp, which is mostly black keys. It was a little confusing to do at first, but then I got the hang of it. I couldn't believe how completely terrible it sounded, and I knew it would be a great joke if I could figure out how to use it.

I don't know how I ever got the nerve to try it out when we had company, some of my father's friends from work. Something bothered me about the way he asked me to play for them. It was like he had a special trick he wanted to show them, and I was the trick. That's not explaining it very well. Something about the way my father asked me to play for people made it seem like whatever I did was all because of him. Anyway, the smart part of myself just shut off, and I started playing the song my father asked me to play, "Melody of Love," in F with my right hand and F-sharp with my left hand. I tried to look extra formal and serious to make it funny, but it didn't work. I heard my mother saying, "What on *earth*—" and then my father said, "*That's enough!*" I would have been willing to play it the right way, but I could tell he just wanted me to get out of there. I went out to the kitchen feeling pretty nervous, and in a minute my father came in, shut the door, and gave me a tremendous crack in the head.

The other great thing that happened to my piano playing was watching Liberace on television. I'd never seen a show like that on TV. It was on Monday nights, and it was a half-hour long, but it always seemed to me like it barely lasted a minute. Liberace was the first amazing piano player

I ever heard, and he was a very unusual person. He had kind of a plump woman's face, but really friendly. His hair went way up in front and then was slicked back around the sides like Elvis Presley's. He always wore a tuxedo with long tails, which he flicked out behind him just before he sat down at the piano bench. He had a great sounding piano, and the chords he played made me see crystal formations behind my eyes. It was also a great looking piano, and the panel at the back of the keyboard was shiny as a mirror, so you could see his hands working the keys in the reflection. I couldn't take my eyes off his hands while he was playing. He played some tremendous classical songs by Chopin and Liszt and Tchaikovsky, which I seemed to know already, but there was something about the way Liberace played them that told you this was exactly the way they should sound. He also played a lot of popular songs, which were just as good. In fact, he could make an ordinary song on the radio, like "Unchained Melody," sound like Chopin wrote it. He could play anything, including boogie-woogie and the fastest, hardest songs I ever heard, songs like "Bumble Boogie," Tiger Rag," and "Dizzy Fingers." A lot of times his fingers were going so fast up and down the keyboard they were just a blur, but you could hear every little note, and he never made a mistake. Liberace had a way of making his face look like a cat, and when he got to an especially hard and fast part of a song, he'd get a little secret smile on his face. The room he played in on TV was really nice, too, with flowers all around and a big candelabra on the piano. His brother George, who looked pretty regular, played the violin, and sometimes Liberace played a duet with him. He was always really nice to his brother George on the show, but I always wanted to get right back to Liberace.

Liberace really changed the way I played. Every now and then my parents weren't home on Monday night, and I got to watch Liberace all by myself. On those nights, as soon as the show was over, I'd turn off the TV and go right over to the piano and start playing. There was usually a song or part of a song I had stored up during the show, and I would try to play it while it was still fresh in my mind. One night when I was playing a song, "Night and Day," that Liberace had just played on TV, I realized there was something about my playing I didn't like any more. Just playing the melody and the chords of the song, even though I was playing them right, sounded completely uninteresting compared to Liberace. I finally got mad at myself and smashed my fist down on the keys, mainly because I couldn't figure out what he did to make his songs so jumpy and lively and complicated-sounding.

The next Monday night when I was by myself, I watched the whole Liberace show just concentrating on one thing, how he got his complicated sound. He had a theme song, "I'll Be Seeing You," which he played and sang at the end of each show, and since I knew how to play it, I tried to see what he did that I wasn't doing. It turned out to be pretty simple. He wasn't really playing the melody at all. Even though you could hear the melody and it sounded great, the actual notes of the melody where wedged in between hundreds of other notes. The notes of the melody just happened to be on the way to where Liberace was going in a zigzagging chain of notes. Realizing this also helped me to see how Liberace could sometimes seem to be playing really fast while the song came out slow. The trick was all the extra notes holding the melody in place. So there were two things I had to learn—how to play the zigzagging chains and how to work it out so the melody note you needed came up at exactly the right time.

This might sound easy, but it practically drove me crazy. Once when I was trying some Liberace zigzags on the old upright piano at the back of the lunchroom, Mr. Larson, the band teacher, came up behind me and listened for a while. "I see you are practicing arpeggios and glissandos," he said. I couldn't understand what he was saying. He showed me that you made a glissando by turning the back of your thumbnail or fingernail against the side edge of a key, and then sliding it up or down the keyboard as far as you wanted it to go.

Most people thought Mr. Larson was really dorky because he had dark hairs growing out of his nose, and he wore his pants really high, but I thought the glissando sounded amazing. It plays every single key along the line in a second, but so fast you can't hear any particular note, just all of them together in a really exciting *zshiiiiiiiiiiiiing!* Then he showed me an arpeggio, which turned out to be a little pattern of three or four notes you played together really fast then skipped up or down to the next group of the same notes and kept going. This was a big relief to me, because I thought Liberace was using all kinds of different notes in his zigzags, but there were only three or four played over and over all up and down the piano. Mr. Larson showed me three different kinds of arpeggios, which sounded great when he played them and definitely had the Liberace sound. I couldn't play them right on the spot, but once I figured out the fingerings at home and practiced them about thirty thousand times, they started sounding amazing. The trick is getting the fingering so automatic you don't even think about what your fingers are doing. Your mind just says something like "arpeggio—now *go*" and suddenly your hands are making blurry little loops up and down the keyboard like Liberace.

It ended up taking quite a while to work all the arpeggios and glissandos I needed into my songs, but it felt wonderful to work on it, even when I had to slow way down and repeat certain passages for a whole afternoon. One great thing about being able to play songs that sounded like Liberace is that once you could do it, you could also stop doing it at certain places in the song, so all of a sudden the melody would be really simple and stand out in a beautiful way. Papa told me he liked the way I would go back into my simply style. For some reason, he didn't like Liberace at all. He said Liberace was "all schmaltz."

I wasn't in Stage Band, because I couldn't stand the kind of songs they played, and also their concerts sounded really sour and terrible, but whenever there was a school concert, Mr. Larson would ask me if I wanted to play a solo. My first thought was a big no, because I didn't want people to think I was like anybody in Stage Band, but after I thought about it, I started to like the idea of playing something pretty great in front of the whole school.

The first time I did it, I was so nervous just before it was my turn that my mouth went completely dry, and I had to keep sucking on my tongue to get any juice back. I decided I would play my Liberace version of "Twelfth Street Rag" because it was really fast and had some great tricky sections that you wouldn't think a kid would be able to play. For a minute or two while I was backstage, I couldn't picture the first notes

I was supposed to play, but after a minute of feeling terrible, I got into a little trance and walked out there and played "Twelfth Street Rag" as fast as I could. It was completely automatic. When I was almost done, I knew the only way I could wreck it was by starting to think about what I was doing. Then I played the final chord and made a glissando from the bottom note of the piano all the way to the top. The kids made a huge roar and kept on clapping. When I stood up to look out into the audience, I could only see a milky blur. The rhythm of the clapping seemed to be shaking up the air in the room. I was still pretty much in my trance, but I liked the feeling of that applause.

Kids in Junior High thinking you're an amazing piano player is okay, but it's not like being a star on the teams or an officer of Student Council. I actually played quite a lot of concert solos by the time I finished Junior High, but I never got as excited again as I did when the kids were roaring after "Twelfth Street Rag." Even when teachers and kids said how great it was after I played something, I would start to get that irritated feeling I got when my father made me play for guests at home. I loved to play the piano, and I loved to figure new things out, but there was something I couldn't stand about being thought of as "the kid who can play the piano." People who said things like that probably thought they knew the kind of kid I really was, but they didn't know anything—and I didn't want them to.

I like playing the piano the most when I'm by myself somewhere, and the very best times are when it's late in the afternoon, and as I'm playing, the room keeps getting and darker, and I just let it. When I'm by myself I can play the piano for five hours straight, and it will feel like about ten minutes. My mind goes completely blank except for crazy little imaginary scenes where there's a meeting of world leaders like Stalin and Churchill and Roosevelt, and they set up a system that says if somebody in some country around the world is picked at random and can come up to the stage and play "Stairway to the Stars" perfectly, some big war will end. They pick me, thinking I'm just a regular person, and I play it perfectly, and as I am picturing this, I am actually playing the song in our living room in the dark.

Another scene I liked to imagine was playing in a big required-attendance school concert, and Patsy Prentiss is sitting somewhere in the middle of the audience with her friends, but I can't see her. I finish playing a tremendous song, like "Dizzy Fingers," and she thinks it's so amazing she can't believe it. She just sits there in her chair after everybody leaves the auditorium. She is remembering me, and she is figuring out a way to get to know me again. In Junior High I spent hundreds and hundreds of hours like that, playing the piano in empty rooms.

Chapter Seventeen

There's no way I could describe what happened to me in High school. It wasn't just that it was such a huge jumble; it was more that I stopped being able to picture things the way I used to. Even in Junior High, no matter what kinds of things were going on around me and no matter how crummy any of it was, I still thought of myself as being in a secret story that was going to come out in some amazing way. But in High School everything seemed so huge and set up in advance, the only thing you could do was get into the stream of things and see what happened.

It actually was like being in a stream, a stream you could never get out of. If there's one single thing I remember about Palatine Township High School, it's moving through the corridors. The red brick building was enormous, dark and heavy looking from the outside. It was the biggest building in town, and something about the way the stone blocks were set around the main entrances and along the roofline made it look like a fort. You never really had to do it, but it would take at least ten or fifteen minutes to walk from one end of it all the way to the gym at the other end. Your freshman year classes would be in one part of the second floor, and when you got to be a sophomore with classes on the first floor somewhere else in the building, it was like you were in a completely new place. Moving from class to class or to Gym or to lunch made me feel like I was in one of those newsreel scenes of someplace like Singapore or New Delhi, places where there was barely room on the streets for all the people. The rule at Palatine was that you had to stay to the right side of the corridor in the direction you were going, so you wouldn't smash into the people coming the other way. You were wedged in so close to the other people and all their books that you could feel them against your arms and shoulders and bumping into your back while you were walking. If you ever forgot something and had to go back the other way, you almost couldn't do it.

In High School I completely forgot the other world. If somebody had tried to tell me about it, I would not have known what they were talking about. I still thought about myself and pictured myself all the time, but in a different way. It was if the kind of kid I was before, being able to come up with things nobody else could come up with, being able to do certain things in sports, being able to play the piano like Liberace, was all erased, and the only thing I was at the High School was what I looked like and the clothes I had on. That's the way I thought about myself. When I got home from school and started thinking about the next day, all I could picture was what I'd wear and what I'd probably look like.

I can't remember one really funny thing about High School, but a few things were a little funny, like Morning Announcements. At the beginning of first period everyday, the teacher would turn on the public address speakers that were hung over the blackboard at the front of every room. Morning Announcements were only supposed to take two or three minutes, but the farther you were into the year, the longer they got. The funny part was that somebody like Mr. Gladhead, the Dean of Behavior, would say something that was supposed to be really strict and serious about vandalism or stealing and then the next voice would be some giggling girl trying to get kids to go to the Diaper Dance that weekend.

Morning Announcements had the effect of making the whole school seem confused and kind of crazy. I used to have to dig my thumbnail into my palm as hard as I could to keep from laughing out loud at certain times, like when the faculty advisor of Student Council would read the thank you letters from We Pin, our Indonesian foster child. Maybe there was something wrong with me, because her letters weren't all that funny, but there was just something funny about sitting there listening to a kind of radio show with nothing but people like Mr. Gladhead warning us not to write obscene words on people's lockers, followed by a girl with a high screamy voice telling people about cheerleader tryouts, followed by a tired sounding teacher telling you how to sign up for the field trip to the stock yards. But it was especially funny when out of the blue you'd get the letter from We Pin, thanking us for her new underwear, socks, stationery, and Kleenex.

Maybe it wasn't that funny. Maybe it was just a little relief before the rush of classes and everything else you had to do. On the first day we were handed out cards with our class schedules on them for the year. You taped them onto your notebook, but after a few days you knew where to go automatically, you knew who sat around you, what the particular smell and look of each room was, the different ways the teachers dressed and how they talked. The classes in high School were forty-six minutes long, but I remember feeling in the middle of the morning and the last period in the afternoon that time had somehow stalled completely. You got a lot of little grades for homework and daily quizzes, and about every two weeks you got a big grade on a test or a composition you had written at home. The kids talked about how much there was to do and how hard it was in High School, but it didn't seem to me harder than Junior High. There was just more of everything, and it all counted. There were Mid-Semester Report Cards, Semester Report Cards, and Year Report Cards, and your report card grade average qualified you for the Honor Roll. It took mostly A's and B's to make the Honor Roll, which wasn't that hard if you were in Accelerated or Fast classes, because those teachers were supposed to give A's and B's.

I always did fine, except for math, which got away from me completely when I got to advanced algebra and trigonometry. Mother always said I could do better than I did. She said I was relying on my natural ability and that I was slapdash and that I did my big assignments and projects at the last minute. She was right. I tried to change my system a few times, but I couldn't stick to it. I always got back to the feeling that if I could just clear out as much time as possible before I had to start working on some school thing, I might get some relief.

One really stupid thing I remember doing when I was getting used to High School was making charts to keep track of my grades and averages. I actually spent a lot of time doing this at home in my room and during study hall at school. I'd use a ruler to make a rectangle with all my classes listed inside on the left with a line of little boxes going off to the right. Each little box had a diagonal line cutting it in half, and on the left side of the diagonal line I'd write in my most recent grade, and on the right side I would put down what my new average was in that subject. I spent a lot of time on these charts. I would do them first very lightly in pencil, and when I had it right, I'd go over the lines in dark ink. It took a while to figure out all the new averages everyday, and I'm sure my mother thought I was working on my actual schoolwork. Later that year when we started working on graphs in algebra, I made up a little graph to go along with each of my classes. Even though I always knew exactly how I was doing without the charts, it still gave me a great feeling to see the complicated-looking tables of neatly written entries and the peaks and dips of the graphs.

I remember one time going into such a slide in algebra I was actually starting to worry about it. We were supposed to be solving equations with two unknowns, and I couldn't even follow the really easy sample problem that was in the orange box on the front page of the chapter. Our teacher was Miss Stein, a bony little woman with red runny eyes. She didn't like the boys in our section, because she thought we were always fooling around. There was a little fooling around, but some of the kids she thought were doing it were actually just complaining because they couldn't figure out the problems. She'd go up to the board and do them, and she'd even do some of them two or three times, but she couldn't explain how she went from one step to the next. She'd just do the problem, and it would come out right. Even when I copied every step she put on the board, I couldn't figure out how things were getting factored out and how the letters got down to just one equaling the right answer. I decided I might be able to come up with my own system, which had sometimes worked for me in the past. I factored and reduced and cross multiplied things the way I thought you were supposed to, but my solutions would go on and on down the page, and the second unknown would keep being a letter I couldn't get rid of. I started to get some really terrible math grades, but I didn't feel too bad about it as long as I could enter them and my new average and the new extension of the graph line in my notebook. I probably should have been getting worried, but instead I felt extra calm, as if I were studying myself like a scientist.

Stepping back like that and not even being inside myself for most of the day was the only way I could stand being in High School. I still did everything, and I even tried out for new things like Cross Country and Chorus and Winter Play, but freshmen and sophomores barely made it into anything and when you did, you just followed along doing what they said until somebody noticed you were any good.

The main effect of trying out for everything and being in activities and on teams was that nothing felt like after school anymore. All the way through Junior High I used to love after school. After school gave me a great feeling every single day. It even made me kind of like school, because I knew that as the day went along, no matter how terrible anything was, I was getting closer to after school. It's like liking the days before Christmas because Christmas is coming. But in High School there was only about ten minutes between the last class and having to go down to Boys' Lockers to change into my gym suit and sweat suit, rub tangy analgesic grease into my legs, then go out and run quarter mile laps, walk a lap, then run again until my lungs hurt and my leg muscles were burning in a sickening way. By the time I took a shower and changed back into my clothes and got all my books together, it would be starting to get dark.

A BIG PART OF THE reason I felt I was starting to disappear that first year of high school was that Annabel really did disappear. I know if I had been smarter then and way nicer, I would have seen that something was wrong, but I didn't see anything. To me Annabel almost wasn't like a separate person. When I was just born and still in my crib, one of the first things I figured out was that Annabel was always around, like a shadowy extra self. Even after I was allowed to get out of the house and to start doing things, when I came back inside, it was like coming back into my Annabel self. Annabel is the only person I ever knew who completely liked me, no matter what, even though I did some rotten things to her every now and then, like taking some of her stuff or scaring her on purpose by mentioning things, like poisonous spiders and dogs getting hit by cars, she absolutely couldn't stand.

Most of the time I was pretty nice to Annabel, because how could you not be. She was so quiet and careful, and she never bothered anybody. Nobody knew it, because she was so shy and got put in the Vocational Ed track, but she was really good at a lot of things. She was an amazingly good artist and could draw the heads of wild animals and good-looking dogs like collies as well as people did in magazines and books. She could also draw the faces and bodies of movie stars, and the ones she liked best, like Natalie Wood and Audrey Hepburn, she could draw without even looking at their picture. She was also a great singer, but she would only sing when I played the piano or when just my mother and father and Nana and Papa were around. Mother told her she had a beautiful voice and should try out for Chorus at school, but Annabel just looked at her and didn't say anything, and I knew what she meant. Actually, Annabel was tremendous, but everything about her seemed a little bit off, a little bit too delicate for the regular world, especially High School.

Maybe it was just because she was my sister, but I really thought she was beautiful. She was beautiful in that almost too-perfect way the movie stars looked in Annabel's *Hollywood Glamour* and *Teen Screen* magazines. She was also really small, even smaller than me. She weighted ninety-five pounds, which was perfect for her and not skinny at all, but nobody could ever believe she was a junior in high school. She had dark shiny hair that was kind of long, down to about her shoulders and curled under in a style she called a pageboy. She spent a lot of time getting her hair like that, and she went to bed with curlers on and a kind of bag over the whole thing so she could set up her pageboy in the morning. She wore lipstick now and a dark little line around the rims of here eyes. I used to like to watch her sitting in front of her mirror, very slowly and carefully drawing that bluish black line, without blinking or changing her expression. Everything she did was extremely careful like that. Her room was always perfectly neat and cleaned up, and her china animal statues and special souvenirs were set up in order on her shelves. Her jewelry box and mirrors and colored bottles of perfumes and creams were arranged on the top of her dresser in a design. It was actually really nice in her room, her own little world.

In Junior High and at the beginning of High School Annabel seemed to have regular friends. She would sometimes go over to other girls' houses or girls would come over to our house after school or sometimes for a sleepover. They seemed really nice and lively, and I always thought Annabel was having a pretty good time. But by sophomore year nobody would come over, and Annabel said she didn't care. She just wanted to stay in her room and draw and listen to her records. A few boys would call on the telephone, and my father would call them her "boyfriends," which was a mistake because I could tell it made Annabel feel ashamed. I actually saw who some of them were at school, and I was really glad Annabel didn't like them, because you could tell right away there was something wrong with them, something you could never get used to, like big flakes of dandruff coming out of the part in their hair or having practically no chin or being maybe not really fat, but having the kind of body that if you took your shirt off, it would be really terrible.

I'm sure it was because I was only thinking about myself, but I didn't know Annabel was getting mentally ill. I say "mentally ill," because that's what mother said and what she told me to say when somebody asked me about it—that, or just "sick." To me mentally ill meant people going nuts and thinking they were other people and shrieking and flailing around for no reason. That's not what happened to Annabel. She just got quieter and quieter. She was so quiet anyway, I didn't even notice.

One night at supper mother asked her something, and she didn't answer. Mother kept asking her, and Annabel didn't even look at her or change her expression. That got mother really scared. She got up from the table and walked Annabel upstairs to her room and stayed up with her until it was late. When she finally came out, I met her in the hall and asked what was wrong. She told me it was nothing, Annabel would be fine, but I could see mother looked really tense, which made me start to get really tense. I tried to get her to tell me more, but she said she had to talk to my father. I asked her if I could go in and talk to Annabel, but she said no,

Annabel needed to rest, and I should go to bed.

The second I woke up in the morning, I knew something really bad was happening. My parents were already up. Mother was on the telephone, and her voice sounded sharp and scared. When I got downstairs, Annabel was in the car with my father, and mother had her coat on and was about to go out. There was no breakfast or anything on the table. Mother was flying around the kitchen looking for her purse, stopping to write things down. She looked at me as if she was surprised I was there. She slapped some money down on the kitchen counter, and told me it was for lunch and if I needed anything when I got home from school and they weren't there. She said Annabel was sick, and they were worried about her. Then she went out to the car, and they drove away.

I didn't know what to do. I knew I should do something, like go upstairs and get my books ready for school or go over to the kitchen table and sit down, but I couldn't make myself move. School was going to be starting in a few minutes, and it didn't seem to matter, but after a while I went anyway, because it was the only thing I could think of. I didn't pay attention to anything in any of my classes, and if somebody called on me, I said I didn't know. I didn't care if I got in trouble. I remember thinking that if anybody gave me a bad time or tried to make me do anything I didn't feel like doing, I was going to stop talking completely. It felt like that was a way I could hate them, and it made me feel like Annabel.

Annabel never came back home, at least not to live. For a while she stayed in a psychiatric hospital in Chicago, where I visited her two times, but then mother told me she was having bad reactions and had to be put on a special ward where she couldn't have visitors. Mother said that would only be temporary, but it lasted for a long time, all the way through freshman year. I know I asked mother what was wrong with Annabel, and she must have told me, but something inside me just shut off and cancelled out whatever she said. Mother visited Annabel every day she was allowed to, and when she wasn't allowed to, she went to see the doctors or talked to people on the phone. If I listened to things my mother told people over the phone I could take it in, but whenever she tried to sit down with me by myself and tell me something about Annabel, I would freeze.

THE FIRST THING MOTHER TOLD her friends was that Annabel had a major depression. Later, when Annabel was on the special ward and couldn't have visitors, mother told people she was catatonic. That summer when Annabel was moved to the Residential Center in Elgin, mother would tell people things the psychiatrists said. One time I heard her tell somebody that the psychiatrist told her Annabel was "very angry." I tried to picture Annabel being angry, but I couldn't do it. I also didn't believe it, and I'm pretty sure I'm right. First of all, I'd like to see what they call angry. If anything, Annabel was too nice and too gentle. I couldn't picture her angry with anybody or anything. She just felt too small and left out. It made me want to go back to when we were little and start being really nice to her and doing a lot more things with her instead of with my friends. The truth is, I was the one who was angry. It made me feel like finding anyone who hurt her feelings and belting them.

AT THE END OF THAT summer, Annabel came home for two weeks, and she did that every few months for as long as I was home. I would always get really excited to see her, but after a day or so I could tell that it wasn't going to be anything special. She didn't talk at all except sometimes to make an *mmm* sound in the back of her throat, which meant yes. The skin on her face was a bad color. Mother said it was because of her illness and the medicines she had to take, but I think it was because she never went outside and did anything. She hardly had any energy when she was home, but she sat in the same room with us when we ate. At first I talked to her a lot. I don't think she wanted me to, but she didn't mind me being around her. She wouldn't look directly at me, but every once in a while I would catch her eye and get the feeling that she still knew we knew each other better than anyone else.

Chapter Eighteen

As soon as I realized that Annabel was never really going to come back and live with us, our house started to feel different. When I was on my way home from somewhere and knew that nobody was going to be in the house, I got almost afraid of it, of being in the rooms by myself, even though nothing bad ever happened. We still had our meals and certain routines like TV shows everybody would watch, but it felt like we were just staying there, not living there. Mother had to be away a lot to see Annabel, and I couldn't blame her, but it made me kind of sad to be in the empty house so much. My father must have been home at the regular time at night, but I can't even remember him being around. It even made me sad to know that I could sneak out and do just about anything I wanted on a school night and no one would catch me, but I didn't feel like it. The only thing to do was school, and the only way I could think of to make it interesting at all was to picture myself being tremendously popular and a huge success.

I know I sound really conceited saying it, but by the time I was a senior at Palatine, I actually was tremendously popular and a huge success. You could look at the yearbook. All I had to do was give up my own story and my own pictures and keep joining things.

The summer between my freshman and sophomore year I started playing American Legion League baseball with a lot of good players from the high school and even from the next town over, Barrington. For some reason this made me feel completely like a man, because there were hardly any practices, and the coaches just showed up at the park about when we did. They were usually college kids or old guys from town who still liked baseball, and all they would do is make up our line-ups, coach third base, and sit there and watch. They didn't talk to us like we were kids or treat us like kids. We were just supposed to show up and play. It seemed like we had a game just about every night, and I got to like that. I also got to like the other guys a lot, because I didn't know them except as players, and they didn't know me or about Annabel or anything about my life.

I was pretty good too, not great all the time, but I pitched some good innings and got some hits. When I was in the outfield, I had a lot of fun fooling around with the kid who was in the field next to me. We'd have ridiculous contests to see who could say some horrible word the loudest without people really hearing it. It would start out in almost a whisper, but loud enough so the other guy could hear it, and then the next guy would have to say it louder, and so on. Sometimes it was FUCK and sometimes it was COCKSUCKER, and it used to get me laughing so hard I thought I would choke. One of the best ways to do it was to start it out with a cough or a fake sneeze and finish up with the word. That way if somebody heard you, they'd think you just coughed or something. The other way was to barely say the first letter and shout the rest, so when people heard it, it would mainly sound like ...UCK or ...OCKUCKER. Maybe nobody even heard us. We didn't care. We weren't trying to offend anybody, we just wanted to be as crazy as possible in the outfield when there was nothing else to do on those warm summer nights.

That summer I also had an indoor job during the day at the bank. My job was to run mail through the postage machine in the basement, clump bunches of it together in rubber bands, and stuff the clumps in big mail sacks which I'd drag over to the post office before I went home in the afternoon. I also had some upstairs jobs like entering numbers from the travelers check stubs in a ledger and getting the tellers coffee and rolls across the street at June's. I got forty dollars a week, which was actually more like thirty-two when they took everything out. My father said his salary was forty dollars a week when he married mother. I think he said that to make me think I was making a lot of money, but I knew that in his day everything was really cheap. The only thing frustrating about the bank job was that you had to mail all the cancelled checks with the statements, and if somebody wrote a ton of checks, I could barely seal the envelope, and the fattest envelopes sometimes got smashed up inside the postage machine and made it stop. When that happened, one of the tellers or the manager, Mr. Hardert, had to come down and open up the machine and fish everything out, which got them a little mad at me, but they never told me a way to stop it from happening.

But mostly I liked that job, or at least the idea of it. I had to wear nice pants and a white shirt and a tie, and it actually felt good stepping outside in the morning all clean from the shower and kind of dressed up walking along the sidewalks downtown with the other people who were going to work. None of my friends had indoor jobs with paychecks. They maybe cut people's lawns or caddied at Barrington Hills. Something about being at the bank all day and then going home to eat, changing into my uniform, and heading over to the ball park made it easier to give up. It didn't even feel all that bad. It was like I wasn't figuring things out in my room and then doing them anymore. I was just letting the job and the games and everything else pull me up into them, the way people from earth get taken up into alien space ships in a science fiction movie.

From then on High School was fine, and I started getting popular. By the end of freshman year I barely got a C in algebra, but I had a bunch of A's in other classes, and they cancelled out the C, so I still made the Honor Roll. Sophomore math was geometry, which I was really good at, so after that, thanks to being able to talk my way into a special section of junior year advanced algebra that was supposed to be for kids who didn't get it but were still smart, I got great grades for the rest of High School.

The English teachers thought I had an excellent imagination because of the way I went at my composition assignments. It all went back to Mr. Click. Whatever they asked me to write about, like whether Santiago had succeeded or failed at the end of *The Old Man and the Sea*, I'd come up with something I was sure nobody else would think of, saying things like there's no such thing as success or failure, there's only fishing.

If there was any way to turn the assignment into something funny, I'd try to do it, and teachers usually got a kick out of that, because by then I had figured out how to get off a certain kind of good one in writing. By junior and senior year, I got A's in just about everything, and mother said she was really proud of me when they would get my report card, but this embarrassed me a little, because one big reason for my A's was that I signed up for classes like Journalism and Advanced Journalism, Modern Drama, Music History, and Current Topics, when the really smart kids were taking things like Chemistry, Physics, and Calculus. But I didn't mind getting all A's or the English teachers signing me up for special state contests, like Mightier Than The Sword.

Once I gave up, everything I did started to work out like that. By junior year I finally got an athletic letter in Cross Country, and that made me an automatic member of the Athletic council, and I got to wear my letter sweater on Fridays, which were usually the days of the biggest games and, if they were home games, there would be a Coke Dance afterwards in the gym. Wearing your letter sweater on Fridays automatically put you in a group with the athletes, because at Palatine there were so many kids, almost nobody could get on a varsity team like Football, Basketball, or Baseball. Even if you got on one of the teams nobody really cared about and they didn't cut anybody, like Cross Country or Wrestling, it was almost impossible to get enough Win points to earn a letter. I only barely got mine. In Cross Country you got Win points if you finished in the top five places on your team. I was never in the top five and only barely in the top ten, but you also got a Win point if you finished ahead of the fifth runner on the other team, and Palatine was pretty good. We had meets against some really pitiful teams from little towns out in the country and against old beat-up schools in Chicago where even the best kids were terrible, so I got in ahead of their fifth runner quite a bit and got my letter. If anyone stopped and analyzed it, they'd say that a letter in Cross Country was probably the crummiest letter you could get, but on Fridays when you were horsing around in the main foyer before school in your letter sweater or moving through the corridors with everybody else, you were up there with the athletes, and I got a secret kick out of that.

Because the Journalism classes were completely easy and mostly just fun, I got to be one of the main writers for The Palatine Tribune and on the Editorial Board when I was a senior. I started out doing news and sports stories, which other kids actually worked on, but I could always knock off in about three minutes. I really liked working on feature stories that I could make funny, and when I was a senior, I got to write just about all the editorials, which were usually pretty lame because they had to be about a topic the advisor suggested, like should we revise the honor code or what we could do to improve school spirit. But no matter how lame they turned out, I liked seeing the way my articles looked when they were actually printed in the paper. It's pretty strange, because no matter what they said and how well I already knew it, I would read my articles over and over the day the paper came out, and after that I couldn't stand them.

It wasn't like I was trying to do it or had some kind of plan, but kids would tell me, "Jonathan, you do *everything*." I suppose that's the way it looked, and I didn't mind if kids said it, especially girls.

In the winter I was in the plays, and starting my sophomore year I got pretty good parts. The first good part I got was a character named Patrice in a play called *Ring Round the Moon* by Jean Anouilh. I actually didn't get this play too well, but it all took place in a big mansion in France that had drawing rooms and billiard rooms and indoor gardens. It was a comedy about couples who were in love with the wrong people at first but then it works out. My character was really goofy, too goofy to be one of the real lovers, but he would go along with things to help the other characters out. When the director, Mr. Canaletti, explained the character to me, he said to picture someone so preoccupied and so innocent and sissy-ish that you can't even imagine him getting along in a real place, like Chicago. Almost right away I came up with something pretty good. It helped a lot that Patrice's lines were actually pretty funny. He never had a clue what was going on or what anybody meant when they said something. I started imagining a guy who barely knew how to get dressed in the morning and was surprised by what he had on. I imagined a really weak, babyish man who thought every room he walked into was a strange new place. I also came up with a high hooty voice that sounded like everything was going wrong and I was about to cry.

Mr. Canaletti was crazy about my scenes. When we got into dress rehearsals under the lights and were wearing our real costumes, I could hear Mr. Canaletti cackling away in the dark, even though he had heard me do the scene a hundred times. I actually loved getting him to laugh like that. I pretended I didn't hear it and just went on being really dense in my part, which would get him laughing so hard the kids backstage and up in the booth would start laughing too, and that told me exactly what to keep doing. After rehearsal when we sat down for director's notes, Mr. Canaletti would give me a lot of compliments. One time he said that there was no formula for comic timing. It was something you just had to feel. He told the other kids to watch how I came on stage. He told them to watch me before I even said anything. I don't know what I actually did, but I know the feeling he was talking about. Because as much as I liked it when Mr. Canaletti cracked up during rehearsal, it was nothing compared to the way the actual audience exploded the second I stepped onto the stage.

Drama was a big deal at Palatine, and *Ring Round the Moon* ran for three weekends in a row. Everyone who came told me they thought it was great and that they especially liked Patrice. There might actually have been something great about it, something not even connected to the rest of High School. Only one bad thing happened while I was in the play. After the performance my mother and father went to, they came backstage to see me. I was still in my makeup and rented tuxedo tails, and I was barely back in the regular world. Mother was saying nice things, telling me I did a good job. I could tell she really liked the play and was surprised by what I came up with for Patrice. Then my father stepped up next to her and said I was really something. Then he said, "You were a real fruit cake up there." He was smiling in a nice way, and I think he was trying to give me a compliment, but something about saying I had been a fruit cake made me start to feel terrible, terrible about even being in the play. I don't know if I said anything back to him. After they left, I couldn't get back in a good mood. I just got madder and madder and wished my father hadn't even come.

THERE WERE A LOT OF big dances at Palatine, theme dances like the Diaper Dance, Lady's Choice, and Spring Fever, plus formal dances like Homecoming and the Prom, but the real socializing took place at the Coke Dances. There was a Coke Dance every Friday night there was a home football game or basketball game. They were pretty basic. You'd just walk down to the Girls Gym, pay a quarter, take off your shoes, and hang around, maybe dancing a little with someone toward the end. They were called Coke Dances because you could also buy little paper cups of Coke out in the hall. They cut the lights way down, so it was pretty dark inside, and the music was just records played over the P.A. system, which I actually liked much better than the regular dances where they had dance orchestras come in. The men in the dance orchestras dressed in tuxedos, and everybody would have the same music stands with swirly letters on them saying things like The Stardusters or The Mood Makers. I could tell from listening to the dance orchestras my father played in that they were good musicians, but there was something about the sections of saxophone players and trumpet players that didn't go with the kids in High School and the kind of dancing they liked to do. The orchestras mainly played songs like "Sentimental Journey" and "Blue Moon," and they thought kids really liked their fast ones, like "In the Mood" and "The A Train," but all anybody really wanted was something like Elvis Presley or Dion and the Belmonts, which is what you got at the Coke Dances.

I liked Coke Dances, because they were completely relaxing. The music was so loud you had to really exaggerate to get anyone to hear what you said, and you didn't have to say anything if you didn't feel like it. If kids had girlfriends, they'd meet up right away and dance only with them. You mostly stayed around your friends, but if you were interested in somebody, like a girl in one of your classes you barely knew, a Coke Dance was the perfect chance to meet her. You could just cruise around to where she and her friends were standing and, if you felt like it, ask her to dance. Because of the loud music you didn't have to talk much once you were dancing, maybe just say a few things that you had time to plan, things you'd shout in an exaggerated way, like "great game" or "I love this song." If you liked the person and had any money, you could go out in the hall and get a cup of Coke.

One Coke Dance in the winter of my sophomore year changed the rest of my life. When the game ended, I looked out the windows of the gymnasium foyer and saw that there was a big blizzard outside. Heavy looking sheets of snow were slanting down over the street lights, and you could hear the scream of people's tires spinning in place as they tried to get out of their parking places. It felt really good not having to go out, knowing that I only had to walk down the warm hallway to the Coke Dance. I had kind of a plan that night, or at least some kids had a plan for me.

As huge as Palatine Township High School was, it seemed like nobody ever left and nobody new ever came, so when somebody did, especially if it was a boy who was any good at sports or a girl who was decent looking, it was a big deal. A girl named Elizabeth Meeker had moved into Palatine at the start of the semester, and there was a lot of talk about her, especially by the girls. They were saying that Elizabeth Meeker was "absolutely brilliant" and "so gorgeous," which was kind of overdoing it, but it was the way they talked when they wanted to be nice. Elizabeth Meeker actually turned out to be really smart. She was in all Accelerated classes, including my English section, and in math she got put in an Accelerated section of Juniors. She was from Houston.

I kind of had my eye on Elizabeth Meeker from her first day in English, and I might have gotten to know her even if the girls hadn't made a big deal out of "fixing me up" with her at the Coke Dance. But that was the plan, or at least they thought it was, as we all headed down the hall toward the Girls Gym.

I had actually noticed quite a bit about Elizabeth since she came into our English class. My system of liking girls' looks is kind of complicated. It starts off with a very strong impression I don't even think about. It just hits me. Either a girl is basically okay or basically not okay. If she's basically not okay, I can still be as nice as possible and maybe even friends, if she happens to be friends with other people I already like. But there would be no way I was going to be able to honestly enjoy looking at someone who was not basically okay. Basically okay didn't mean she had to be tremendously pretty. There just had to be that little something that made me feel I could keep looking at her. It was in the way all their parts, especially the parts of their faces, went together and how their faces went with their bodies. I found that if a girl looked basically okay, I sometimes got a better and better impression of her the more I got to know her and the longer I looked at her. A few girls I knew who I thought were only basically okay turned out to be really beautiful. It's like hearing certain new music. It can be barely okay when you first hear it, with maybe something vague and a little irritating about it, but then after you hear it twenty times, you see the whole design, and you can't believe you ever didn't like it sooner.

My first impression of Elizabeth Meeker was strongly okay. She was a little shorter than I was and had dark hair like Annabel's but shorter and fluffed up around her face in a pretty way. She was slender but not skinny, and something about her bones was extremely delicate. She had a sharp, cute little nose, her ankle bones stood out like blades, and her wrists were tiny. She was extremely clean and neat. Most of the girls I liked were clean and neat and cared a lot about how their clothes, but Elizabeth was extra clean and neat. She seemed almost shiny. Nothing she wore ever looked wrinkled or like it was the second day.

When she got called on in English, she knew exactly what to say and was obviously very smart. Some of the girls got to know her right away, but until the Coke Dance, I hadn't even met her. I remember walking into the dark gym and thinking maybe I'd ask her to dance, and maybe I wouldn't, but right away a tall funny girl in our group named Sally Peters came up to me with a goofy look and told me she had someone she wanted me to meet. I kind of knew she was going to do that, and I knew it was going to be Elizabeth Meeker. I went over to Sally's friends where Elizabeth was, and Sally introduced me

Elizabeth didn't look as if she was shy about meeting me at all. She actually stared at me pretty hard, and I got the feeling that there was something about me she already didn't like. If I had known her then as well as I did later, I would have realized there would be plenty of things about me she didn't like, like my clothes and my posture and my manners. One thing about Elizabeth, she was very critical. But she was also really cute, way better looking than I thought. I remember deciding right away that I was going to make her like me. It would be a perfect project. I didn't have a girl friend, and everybody was starting to get them. Elizabeth was new, from Houston, and that made her stand out from everybody familiar. I liked the idea of people thinking of me having a girl friend like Elizabeth Meeker.

Later when we were really close, I found out that when she first met me at the Coke Dance, she wasn't exactly thrilled. She told me she had the idea I was a smart aleck from the some of the things I said in English class. That bothered me. I thought back and tried to remember what I might have said that sounded smart alecky, but I couldn't think of anything. I was actually in a fairly calm period. It made me think that maybe there was something about my face that just looked smart alecky, like my nose. She also told me that I was wearing a terrible sweater that night. She said "dreadful sweater." That also bothered me, because it was a sweater I kind of liked, a sweater a lot of kids had. It was a crew neck, extra thick for winter, with dark orange and black stripes going up. When she made the remark about my sweater, I tried to be cheerful about it, like I really didn't care. I said something like, *really?* I wanted her to tell me what was wrong with it, but she just gave me an exaggerated look saying how could I not know what a terrible sweater it was. She said it made me look like the Cheshire Cat.

But the night of the Coke Dance I had no idea Elizabeth thought and said things like that. I just assumed she would be shy like a girl, and maybe especially shy because she was new and I was fairly popular. I asked her to dance, and she said yes. Without staring at her, I tried to figure out if she was glad she was dancing with me, but it was impossible to tell. The first few songs were fast ones, and we were jitterbugging, and she had a way of concentrating on what she was doing that seemed to close her off from me. A lot of girls do that, dance with somebody in a way that makes it seem like they're dancing by themselves. She wasn't completely unfriendly, though. She kept dancing with me.

We went out into the hall by ourselves, and I bought her a cup of Coke, and she said thank you very nicely. She seemed to be relaxing a little.

I asked her everything I could think of about what it was like in Houston and how she liked Palatine and what kind of family she had. She was very nice telling me all that stuff, and it was starting to feel easier to be with her, but it was taking effort. She told me she lived in one of the new developments, one of the nice ones, they put up in the fields where I used to play. She had an older sister in college in Wisconsin and a little brother who wasn't even in school yet. She called him The Mistake, which later I found out was one of the Meekers' family jokes, but I didn't get it when she first told me. I thought she hated him.

We went back into the gym and danced some more. I felt a little confused. I liked looking at Elizabeth, and I liked the idea that she was only dancing with me, which meant that now we really knew each other and could talk between classes and do anything we wanted, but it still felt like a lot of effort, and I had a feeling that at any second I could completely lose my confidence.

Maybe that bad feeling had to do with Elizabeth Meeker, but maybe it was a secret reaction to what happened next. All of a sudden there was a commotion down at the far doorway to the gym where they took tickets. There were some loud voices and then a lot of kids huddling into little groups and whispering. Almost nobody else was dancing, and I knew we were missing something. I asked Elizabeth if she wanted to see what was happening, and she came with me as I followed the other kids toward the far door. Even before I got there and could see anything, I could hear people saying "Patsy Prentiss." Maybe they were saying it, or maybe I was reading their minds, because I still had the aching, awful feeling of missing her so much. I don't know how I got there, because there we so many kids crowded around the doorway, but all of a sudden I was right there by the ticket table, about ten feet from where Mr. Gladhead and two policemen were standing, one of them holding Patsy against the wall by her shoulders. Her camel colored coat was practically falling down off her arms, and she was half crying and half shrieking at the policeman, saying, "You *jerk!* Take your big filthy hands off me—I'm calling my parents— *why can't I call my parents—*"

It was awful. Even though she was screaming and not making any sense, she also looked incredibly tired and old. For a minute I felt like I was not in the regular world, or that I was and Patsy had somehow crashed in from the other world in a terrible way. The kids around me were saying, "She's *drunk*." "Prentiss is drunk." I couldn't take it in, except as a kind of message that wherever Patsy went off to in Junior High, it was some kind of hell, and for some reason I was supposed to see it now. I looked up from Patsy and saw that farther down the hall some other policemen were holding two men against the lockers. They might have been older kids, kids who graduated from Palatine. They had on long overcoats like my dad's.

I remembered I was with Elizabeth and went to look for her. They started playing music again, and as I made my way across the gym to where I could see Elizabeth and Sally Peters and our group, it seemed that every voice I heard was talking about Patsy, saying that she was such a lush, that she was a mess, that she was a slut.

I tried to pick up my conversation with Elizabeth but I couldn't concentrate. I don't even know what I said. The Coke Dance was practically over. They were playing slow songs, which they did toward the end to calm everything down. Most kids only bothered to dance the slow ones if they had a girlfriend, because you could dance close. I was just standing there about two feet from Elizabeth, so we danced. I didn't have anything else to say, and neither did she. I just started into the fox trot, holding her hand out as lightly as you could hold hands. I could feel her side and her hip just touching mine, and her hair was brushing against my cheek. You can't really look at someone when you're doing a slow dance, and I remember feeling that even though it was the new girl, Elizabeth Meeker, I was barely holding onto and that just a little earlier I was starting to get interested in her, she almost wasn't there. I was only holding onto the outer edges and tips of a person, with nothing inside the shape. What wasn't inside the shape was Patsy Prentiss, who seemed to have been taken away again in a new way, but this time as if she moved away or died. It made me too sad to talk or even think. I just wanted to get out of there and out into the blizzard.

Chapter Nineteen

ELIZABETH MEEKER WAS my girlfriend for the rest of high school. I gave her a ring, but we were way beyond going steady. It pretty much started at the Coke Dance, because after we danced together like that, the girls in our group started saying that I liked Elizabeth now. I didn't mind, and after about two more Coke Dances, I was dancing close with her and walking her home, and we were a couple. At first it felt like being completely carried away, which I knew happened to certain kids, so I just gave up and let myself go.

Going with Elizabeth felt right in certain ways, but it was not always great for my confidence. At Palatine, at least in our group, other kids like it when you pair off and become a couple. It kind of makes everything in the group feel more permanent, and everybody knows what to expect. It definitely makes you more popular, but that wasn't my main reason. Once you work out the routine about what you're supposed to do with your girlfriend, you can start to feel relaxed and organized and safe. It's like being in a club of other people who have girlfriends.

With Elizabeth there was a lot of going back and forth between feeling pretty excited and feeling really terrible. She was not a relaxed girl, and she had really strong opinions, which I've found goes with being incredibly intelligent. If you just saw her from the outside, you'd think that because of her neat clothes and hair and the intelligent way she talked that she was completely confident. She didn't mind being even a little mean sometimes.

But it didn't take me long to find out that in some departments she wasn't confident at all.

Being a couple at Palatine meant that whatever event was coming up, like Homecoming or Prom, you automatically went with your girl friend. You didn't even ask her or talk about it. The first big dance that came up after Elizabeth and I were a couple was Spring Fever. Spring Fever was semi-formal, which meant I had to wear a coat and tie, but not a suit all one color, and I had to buy a corsage. I liked everything about the idea. I liked not having to think up who I would ask and what kind of a time I'd probably have, but what actually felt best was knowing I would be allowed to use the car. I had my license for a few months, and driving gave me one of the best feelings I've ever had, but I didn't get to use the car much, except for errands like shopping for my mother or picking up my father up at the station when it was raining. Rarely, very rarely, I got to take the car over to friend's house, but I could tell my father was suspicious. He said he thought I would be out "tearing around and burning rubber," which I had no interest in doing, but I did want to drive around a lot more than I was allowed to. I especially wanted to drive around more by myself. I wanted to be able get out in the car and just explore. I couldn't see that happening, but I knew I would probably get the car to take Elizabeth and Gary Wade and Karen Shiels to Spring Fever.

The other great thing, which made me play little games with myself to keep me from thinking about it too much, was that, besides dancing close, Elizabeth and I had started kissing. I had hardly kissed anybody, actually only one person, in a serious way before Elizabeth, and I really, really liked it. After the dance I knew we would go out to eat and I would drop off Gary and Karen at their houses, and then my idea was that maybe I would kiss Elizabeth for awhile in the car before she went in. In the car seemed to me way better than on her front porch, where there would only be one hug and kiss, maybe two, if you broke it up by saying something. My thoughts about kissing Elizabeth in the car were pretty vague, but the whole idea of driving and kissing and being out by ourselves made me look forward to Spring Fever.

Spring Fever was our first big date as a couple, and it started off pretty well. I didn't know about corsages, and it turned out mother didn't either, but Elizabeth knew exactly, and I got her probably the best corsage at the dance. She knew the exact name of the different flowers and the different ways they could be set up to go around your wrist, and since I could tell she really cared about it, I got just what she told me, which ended up costing seven fifty, which to me was unbelievable. The whole dance only cost five dollars. My father had already given me ten dollars for the dance and afterwards, and I knew I couldn't tell him about a seven fifty corsage, so I took an extra ten out of my savings account which had hundreds of dollars in it from my summers at the bank, but it was supposed to be for college. The dance itself was fine. I was starting to realize that as a junior and a kid who had a varsity letter and was in the plays and on the paper and got straight A's and now had a regular girl friend, I was turning into the kind of kid I never thought I would be in High School, one of the popular kids, one of the kids everybody knew. I could feel it. When I let Elizabeth and Gary and Karen out at the door of the gym and drove over to the lot to park, there were a lot of little freshmen and sophomores on the walk getting dropped off by their parents, and I could feel them looking at me, driving along in my own car. They probably knew who I was from something they saw me in at school. They probably knew I was in the popular group and looked at me the way I used to look at juniors and seniors who had letter sweaters and steady girl friends and their own cars. When I was little I would make pictures of myself I really liked. I would be building a fort you could actually live in or having my own rifle and hunting all day in the north woods. In High School, starting when I gave up, I never made my own pictures anymore. In High School the pictures seemed to be already there, like the picture of a popular guy with a letter sweater and a girl friend, and you just made yourself into that picture.

 Spring Fever didn't get ruined until we went out afterwards to Howard Johnson's. We had a pretty good time at the dance. Elizabeth had on a new black dress with a skirt that flared way out, and with her dark hair and lipstick and makeup she looked look really different. The dress made her hair and eyes and lips seem even darker, and something she had around her eyes made them look moist and sparkly in the blue light they used for dances. The dress made a straight line over the top of her breasts, and just above the cloth you could see the beginning of the little line that went down between them. I thought she looked great, and I was starting to get in a really good mood.

There wasn't a Howard Johnson's in Palatine, but there was one two towns over, in Fox River Grove. Howard Johnson's was the right kind of place to go after a major dance, because it was bigger and fancier than a regular hamburger place or someplace like June's, but it wasn't ridiculously fancy with everything costing at least ten dollars.

On the way we listened to Top Forty on the radio, and Gary got off a lot of wise cracks from the back seat, and I got off a few good ones myself. I was still in a pretty good mood when Gary and Karen got out of the car and I got out my side and headed into the restaurant. The three of us were standing just inside the door seeing if there was a table when I realized Elizabeth wasn't with us. I thought maybe she had gone down the hall to the Ladies, so I waited for a while. After a few minutes I went outside and looked around. I walked over to the car saw that Elizabeth was still sitting in the passenger seat. Her arms were folded in front of her, and she was crying. I opened her door and asked her what was the matter. She couldn't talk for a minute. Her chin was wobbling, and when she tried to talk, she had to stop. I felt terrible. I kept asking her what was wrong, if she was sick or if I had said something. She stopped crying and gave me a really mean look. "Let me tell you something, *Jonathan*," she said. "In case you don't know, a *gentleman* opens the door for his date when he gets out of the car." I was stunned by how bad she felt. It took me a minute to make sense of what she said. I asked her if she meant opening the car door or some other door. She told me the car door. I'm pretty sure I said I was sorry and didn't mean it, because I really didn't, but my head was spinning. She was still sitting in the car, and she didn't look like she was about to get out. I didn't know if it would make it better or worse to say that no one ever told me that if you wanted your date to get out of a car, you had to walk around to her side and open the door. For a while I stood there with the door open and her just sitting there, and I think we both felt terrible. Finally I asked her in a nice way if she wanted to go in and get something to eat. She said she didn't and that all she wanted to do was go home, but then she got out.

Gary was still in a loud, goofy mood when we found him and Karen at the table. He tried to make a joke about our ditching him, but when he saw how miserable Elizabeth was, he quieted down. Normally I'm really hungry and like a burger with fries or a big sandwich when it's late after a dance, but seeing Elizabeth cry like that did something to me. I felt a weird combination of being sad and being mad. When the waiter came to get our orders, I ordered a Club Sandwich Special, which was the first thing I saw on the menu. Elizabeth ordered a cup of soup. She was sitting across from me, but she wouldn't look into my eyes. When someone gets in a mood like that, you can't ignore it. Pretty soon none of us had anything to say, and we just sat there waiting for the food, and I started going down the spiral into my worst feelings.

The Club Sandwich Special when it came was ridiculous. It was at least a triple-decker, and each triangle stood up so high I couldn't hold it all together between my fingertips and my thumb, and it kind of collapsed in a mess over the plate. I took the tooth pick out and scraped away the toast and top layer and thought maybe I could convert it into a regular sandwich, but even the part left over was almost too big to close my teeth on, and I wasn't going to look like even more of an idiot by stretching my mouth open as far as possible to get my teeth over the thing, so I just left it all in a big mess on the plate. Elizabeth had about two sips of soup from her spoon and then just sat there. By that time I was just mad, although I couldn't have said what I was mad at. I just wanted to get out of there, and so did everybody else.

Needless to say, there was no kissing in the car in front of Elizabeth's house. Who wanted to. I pulled up into Elizabeth's driveway, shifted into Park, and practically ran over to the passenger side door where I felt myself doing a kind of bow as I opened the door for her. I walked her to her front porch, and we stood there for a minute while she looked for her key. Just before she went in she turned to me and said thank you for taking her to the dance and for the corsage, and in the same voice said, "I had a very nice time." For a second I didn't get it. She couldn't possibly have had a nice time, but by the time I was back in the car, I understood that it was the kind of thing she had learned to say, that it was just her manners.

It took me a while to get used to having Elizabeth as my girl friend. There were things I was just never going to know about until they happened, like opening the car door for her. There was also the business of seeing her in curlers, which got her just as upset as she got at Howard Johnson's. Once I was doing an errand and had the car to myself on a really nice Saturday afternoon in the spring, and I decided to drop over and say hi to her. We were going out somewhere that night, and I knew I would be seeing her later, but I was in a good mood, so I thought I'd just knock on the door. Her older sister, Tricks, was home for the weekend, and she gave me a funny look and told me Elizabeth was in the back yard, and I should just go around and find her. When I got back there, Elizabeth was leaning back in a lawn chair, sunning herself. I said hi, which kind of woke her up, and she looked at me in a horrible way. Her hair was full of fat curlers, like Annabel's, and it was all held together in a kind of kerchief. She turned her back to me and said, "Go away." I didn't get it. I asked her if something was wrong. She told me to go away again. She said "please" in a really desperate voice. I asked her what I did wrong, and she said she didn't see people when she was in curlers. I tried to be really nice about it and say I didn't care, but she wouldn't turn back to look at me, so I went home.

About every two or three weeks there would be something like that, and I never saw it coming. The worst one was the time I came to pick her up to take her out for her birthday. The plan was to drive all the way into Evanston to a little restaurant I found out about and then see a foreign movie at the Arts Cinema. It was the middle of July and really nice out, and I decided to try to make it a special occasion. Nobody got very dressed up for dates in the summer, but Elizabeth really liked to dress up, so, since it was her birthday we decided to make it pretty fancy. At the time I had a sports jacket I liked a lot. It was mainly white with little flecks in it. I thought it looked pretty good in the summer, because I used to get really tan, but since I had worn that jacket a bunch of times with Elizabeth, I decided to get a new one for the birthday date. There was a new fashion that year, and some kids started getting Madras jackets, which had patches of all different colors and patterns on them. I actually thought it was kind of confusing to look at a Madras jacket, but they were lightweight and comfortable, and kids who had really nice clothes started wearing them.

My big mistake was trying to buy one cheap. There was a men's clothing store downtown called Parnell's which always had exactly the kind of button down shirts and wool sweaters and khaki pants you'd want to wear, but usually only men bought stuff there because everything cost twenty dollars or thirty-five dollars, amounts nobody our age ever had. You might get something from Parnell's as a present or save up for maybe one thing, like a sweater, but everybody went to Zimmerman's instead, or ordered from Sears. That summer on the highway just outside of town, a huge new discount store, the first one I ever heard of, called Topps, opened up, and everybody started going there, even mother sometimes. I thought it was pretty amazing. You could get pants and shirts and sweaters for three or four dollars. A lot of them were pretty terrible, and things from Topps looked definitely worse when you got home than they did in the store, but sometimes you'd find pairs of pants or shorts that you couldn't tell from normal, and they hardly cost anything. One night after a game, some of us were looking through stuff at Topps before it closed, and I saw a whole long rack of Madras jackets. They were all twelve dollars. I had never bought a sports jacket for myself before, but I didn't think twelve dollars was too much, especially for something like a Madras jacket, which was the kind of thing I thought you could only get at Parnell's for probably more than a hundred. It seemed perfect to get a jacket like that just before Elizabeth's birthday, so I got one.

I probably shouldn't have been in such a big hurry, and I should have asked somebody to help me figure out the size. The one I chose seemed pretty big, with the sleeves coming down over part of my hands and the front coming out a little bit extra, but I was in a tee shirt and shorts, and I thought that being dressed up in a shirt and tie would kind of fill everything in. What I really needed was somebody who knew something about Madras jackets. It wasn't until afterward that I realized the jacket I got

183

wasn't much of a Madras. It was made up of a lot of different colored squares, but they were small and dark, I think dark green, red, and purple. Some of the squares had little black streaks going through them. When I tried it on at home, it looked pretty dark, mostly purple and shiny, not summery light blue and pink like the ones at Parnell's. It was also pretty big on me, but I figured that since summer was supposed to be more casual, it didn't have to fit like a regular jacket.

I didn't think about it much the week before my birthday date with Elizabeth, except that I was really looking forward to going out to Evanston. I took twenty dollars out of my savings, and my father gave me a little extra, so I was pretty loaded, and that always felt good. That Saturday was really hot, and I was outside all day, cutting lawns in the morning, and we had a game in the afternoon. When I got out of the shower and got dressed to go pick up Elizabeth, my face felt like it was glowing from all the sun. As I was leaving the house, my father looked at me and asked what kind of jacket I was wearing. I told him it was a Madras, but I knew he wouldn't know anything about them, so I didn't think about it.

I rang Elizabeth's bell and when she came to the door, she looked at me and didn't say anything. Finally she said, "You're not going to wear that, are you?" She wasn't kidding. She looked completely miserable, and it gave me the same rotten feeling. I asked her what was wrong with it, but by then it didn't matter what she said, I knew there was no way we were going out or having anything like a decent time if she was in that mood, which meant that I had to drive home and take off the Madras jacket and put on my white one with the flecks.

Elizabeth is just one of those people you have to be really careful with. Sometimes the littlest thing you said could make her mad or hurt her feelings. It was probably good for me that she was like that, because otherwise I might have gotten too relaxed and gone on thinking I was a lot smarter than I was. And it's not that there weren't any good things about going with her. By the end of High School we were boyfriend and girl-friend for so long we got included in everything, every party, every hay-ride, every tobogganing trip. Altogether we spent a lot of time with each other. In the spring I would walk her home from school, stopping to get a soda or something on the way. She probably lived a mile or a mile and a half from the school, but the routes we would go, and with stopping in stores or sitting down somewhere in a park, it might take three hours, and that was just to her house. Every Friday or Saturday night that we didn't go out somewhere, I would go over to her house, and we'd play Scrabble or cards until her parents went to bed, and then we'd watch the Late Night Movie in her den.

We actually never watched the movie. We would just turn it on, and after about three minutes, get comfortable on the corduroy cushions on the floor in front of the TV and start kissing. It felt wonderful to know that it was completely all right and she expected it. Kissing like that, just on and on, put me in another world. When the movie and the last commercial were over, a trumpet would play "The Star Spangled Banner," and then the screen would buzz, and all you'd see is gray flecks and a design in the middle of the screen. This would happen at twelve-thirty or one, and I'd have to go home. Whether it was nice out and I walked or whether I drove, I was always in the same kind of trance after the kissing. When I woke up the next morning I could never remember a thing about getting home, brushing my teeth, getting undressed and going to bed.

It was actually more than just kissing. I would pull Elizabeth over into me so that we were front to front all along our bodies, and then we'd just let ourselves get more and more tangled up while we kissed. I would rub her back and her neck while we were kissing, and she would sometimes squeeze the back of my neck with her palm, which didn't really feel like anything, but I liked the idea of her wanting to do it. Maybe a year after we started kissing, I decided to try to feel her breasts. I had a hunch she wouldn't like it, but I had been thinking about it for a long time. I tested it out by rubbing her shoulder for awhile and then dragging my hand slowly down her front, not even stopping on her breast, just passing over it on the way down. I think it scared her. She sat up straight and stared at the TV. She told me we shouldn't do that, but she didn't seem mad or miserable and we got back to just kissing. Some time not too long after that, she started letting me, and we never said anything about it, and it got to be a nice part of those kissing nights.

I never told Elizabeth this, because she wouldn't have liked it and I was only half aware of it myself, but one of the reasons I liked kissing her so much and felt like I could keep kissing forever was that it took me right back to the first time I kissed somebody for the feel of it. I had only kissed one girl before I started kissing Elizabeth.

It was Sue Ellen Lester, and it's amazing that it even happened.

SUE ELLEN LESTER WASN'T EVEN close to being a girl friend. She was just a really tall, lively girl in some of my classes in sixth grade. She was the best singer in our grade, and we once sang a duet together in a concert. I forget the song except that it was about Switzerland, and my solo part went

> *Land of William Tell*
> *A story we know well*
> *Of apple, boy, and old cross bow*
> *And how Tell conquered every foe, so—*
> *Dear old switzerland...something, something.*

One thing I liked about Sue Ellen Lester is that she had a lot of nerve. She'd do anything a boy would do on the playground. One time Jim Mahler said she butted into the lunch line ahead of him, and she said she didn't, that her friend was saving her place, and Jim Mahler said oh right, oh sure and called her a stupid beanpole. Sue Ellen stepped right up in front of him and said, "What did you say?" He said stupid beanpole again, and Sue Ellen slapped him right across the face. Jim Mahler was about as big as she was, but he didn't do anything back. In fact, he started to cry.

I really didn't know her that well, but there was something about Sue Ellen I always liked. The summer I kissed her I was playing on the Indians, and our games were on the good diamond under the lights. After a game the kids who played would meet up with kids getting out of the pool, and we'd hang around the park for a while, until they'd turn the lights out and people would walk or ride their bikes home. Sue Ellen was usually one of the kids hanging around, because she lived pretty close to the park, in a new house one street in from the fields. Her mother and father both had jobs, and she told kids they could come over to her house any time they wanted during the day. Some kids who knew her said she sometimes had boys over during the day and they played games like strip poker.

The night that I kissed her, Sue Ellen and I were fooling around with a bunch of kids by the candy machines outside the pool. The lights were going off, so people started going home. Sue Ellen was walking, and I was going in the same direction, so we started walking along together. We were having a nice time. When you got close to Sue Ellen's house there were two ways you could go. You could go down the main sidewalk to the front of her yard, or you could take a path through the trees at the edge of the fields and go through her back yard. Because it was night, I thought we'd keep going on the sidewalk under the streetlights, but Sue Ellen said why not take the path. She said it was more fun, and it was. There was plenty of light in the sky from the town, and it made the grass and the leaves and the bark of the trees silvery. It was one of those soft nights where the ground feels like a cushion under your feet as you walk, and it felt like Sue Ellen and I were going along our own secret lane. Just before we got to where her yard started, she stopped and leaned back against a tree. She asked me if I had started kissing yet. It didn't feel embarrassing at all or too personal. She just wanted to know. I told her not really. She asked me if I wanted to try it, which was kind of a surprise. I didn't hate the idea, and the longer we stayed there talking in soft voices by the tree, the more I wanted to. Maybe I was thinking about the strip poker, but it was starting to feel pretty exciting. I think I would have been even more excited if Sue Ellen weren't so tall. She was really tall, one of the tallest girls in our class. She was the kind of tall girl I didn't even feel bad about being smaller than, because everybody was. That also took her out of the even possible girlfriend category. But I couldn't think about that when I was back there with her in the trees. I said sure, and waited to see what she would do. She took a step toward me and leaned over so that her face was down in front of mine, and she put her arms around my back and pulled me in closer. I put my arms around her back too. Her nose was touching against my nose, and then she got it out of the way, and then we pressed our lips together. My eyes closed automatically, and I just felt it. In my mind everything disappeared except the soft, full feeling of Sue Ellen's lips and a picture of her big happy face just an inch in front of mine in the dark. I could tell Sue Ellen wanted to keep it going for a minute. She moved her lips around a little, so you could keep feeling it. Then we were done, and I opened my eyes, and Sue Ellen had a big smile on her face. We talked for a few more minutes, and then she ran off into her yard. I wished I could have figured out how to walk all the way home on that path through the trees. I was saying to myself: *I kissed a girl.* I kept thinking that and feeling Sue Ellen's warm, dry lips all night and for a long time after that. It didn't matter how tall she was. There was absolutely nothing bad about it.

Chapter Twenty

ONE OTHER THING about kissing Elizabeth. You had to keep it dry. One of the first times we watched the Late Night Movie in her den, she sat up all of a sudden and told me, "I don't like French kissing." I didn't know what it was, and she told me it was with your tongue in the other person's mouth. I told her I didn't like it either, so we never did. When I got to know her better she said she turned against French kissing when a boy she knew in Houston tried it on her. She told me he was a pig and that all of his friends were pigs too. Elizabeth said that besides trying to French kiss her, he used to clear his throat and spit gobs of stuff out onto the sidewalk in front of them when they were walking somewhere. I knew Elizabeth could be really fussy, but I saw what she meant about a person who would do that. She really hated Texas, and he was a big reason.

The best way to get along with Elizabeth was to get to know her really well and keep track of the things she really liked and the things she couldn't stand. It didn't take me long to figure out she couldn't stand surprises, which meant a lot of my jokes were out, such as putting something ridiculous, like some guy's sweaty gym stuff, in her locker or writing her a crazy note that was supposed to be from somebody whose handwriting I knew how to imitate.

I THINK THE THING ELIZABETH cared about most was her family and the special way they did things at her house. She really enjoyed talking about her mother and father and sister and the particular way they did things like buy a new couch or rake leaves or all take a walk together in the forest preserve before they had Thanksgiving dinner. She also really cared about the stuff in her room and in their house, and she knew things about furniture and fabric and dishes that you wouldn't expect someone our age to know. I thought her house was pretty nice and very clean, but a little bit empty looking. They didn't have carpeting in any of the rooms, just bare, shiny wood floors with little rugs in front of something like the couch or under the table. Their house actually looked slightly like it was from another period in history. Elizabeth knew the names for different kinds of furniture and that they were antiques. She would call an old wooden cabinet a "hutch" or a "commode" and tell me the town or the store where they bought it. Their stuff did have kind of a look to it, but some of it just seemed beat up, with nicks and old burn marks on the wood and veins of cracks running through the china. I know you were supposed to like antiques because they were old and valuable, but I couldn't see having stuff that you couldn't really use, no matter how antique it was. For instance, the Meekers had a couple of little antique rocking chairs, very beat up, on each side of the fireplace, and next to one of them there was an old fashioned wooden crib on rockers with a pile of kindling wood in it. Some white birch logs were set up in the fireplace, but the bricks underneath were perfectly clean, because the Meekers never used the fireplace, and nobody ever touched the arrangement of kindling wood, and no one was allowed to sit in the rocking chairs, because they would break. I tried to be as nice and as interested as I could when Elizabeth told me about some hutch or candlestick or embroidered saying on the wall, but it didn't all come together to make a great feeling house like Nana and Papa's. Those things were really important to Elizabeth, though, and I had to learn that.

    The way Elizabeth talked about her family and their routines and their stuff had the effect on me of making me wish there were special things like that going on at our house. Since Annabel went away, our house felt pretty quiet and basically kind of dead. We had our meals, and the jobs got done, and we still went over to Nana's and Papa's for Sunday dinner and TV, but I couldn't imagine my mother and father making plans and saving up for a special trip up to Wisconsin so they could buy an old wooden box. I was starting to think that maybe it didn't matter if things like antiques were good looking or valuable or not or if the special way the people in your family opened their presents on Christmas was better than any other way. It was just really nice that people thought so. It kept people like the Meekers together and made them like each other.

I'm not sure the Meekers liked me all that much. It might have just been that I wasn't in their family, but maybe they noticed things about me they thought were terrible, like my expressions or my clothes, and never said anything about it. They weren't actually that bad when I was over there. You just had to get into their ways of doing things. You had to remember that for them certain things had happened in their family, like Mrs. Meeker forgetting to take the rolls out of the oven or The Mistake peeing in his pants whenever they went to the movies, were going to be funny forever.

Every family has its own little world, but the Meekers really had one. They had special names for everybody. They called Mrs. Meeker "Mamie." Elizabeth actually referred to her as "my Mamie" and would say things like, "We better be going home, or my Mamie will be very cross." It was supposed to be kind of a joke, but it was mainly a Meeker joke. She called her father "Fahrver," and her sister Letitia was "Tricks." The Mistake's real name was Philip, and they called him the whole thing, never Phil, when he was there, but when he wasn't around, he was The Mistake. The effect of the whole thing made me realize how different and separate her kind of family was from mine. Elizabeth would tell me things like, "We all went to the movies to see "Fantasia," and, *once again*, The Mistake wet his pants almost immediately. Fahrver tried to get him to sit on his newspaper until the movie was over, but precious baby kept whining out loud, 'I'm *wet*. I'm *cold*,' until my poor Mamie was beside herself and told Fahrver we had to leave at once. Wretched Mistake. I can't wait to tell Tricks." It made Elizabeth happy telling me things like that about her family, but I couldn't picture being in on any of it.

One thing that held Elizabeth and me together was presents. I liked presents, and I'm sure everybody does, but presents meant something completely different to Elizabeth, and that was something I had to learn fast. The first winter when she was starting to be my girl friend, I got her a bad present. I didn't mean to. I just didn't give it enough thought. I was in Zimmerman's getting stuff for my mother and father, Nana and Papa, and Uncle Desmond, and I saw a stack of angora hat and mitten combinations in the Women' section. I liked the bright colors and the soft look of the angora, so I got a red set for Elizabeth and, at the moment, actually had a good feeling about it. Until I realized the way Elizabeth felt about presents, I didn't give them that much thought. To me getting someone a present was pretty basic. So long as it wasn't ridiculously crummy, it would be fine. But in the Meeker family people gave presents a lot of thought. It kind of went with having antiques and stories that went with all their stuff.

On the afternoon of Christmas Eve before we all went over to Nana and Papa's for supper, I got to use the car to drive over to Elizabeth's to give her my present. Her parents left us alone in the den, and she gave me my present first. I could tell by the box it was going to be clothes, and it turned out to be a dark blue crew neck sweater. I saw that it came from Parnell's, and it was really nice. She had figured out my size, which was 40, and she told me it was a blend of lamb's wool and cashmere. I didn't know what kind of actual cloth went into sweaters, but I could see that this one looked really good. I took off the one I had on and put on the new one and looked in their mirror. It was amazing that a sweater could look so good. I thanked her a lot, and I really meant it, but I was already starting to feel bad about my present, because a crew neck sweater from Parnell's was such a bigger deal. She took off the wrapping paper very carefully and opened the box, which was a box we had at home, not one that came with the hat-mitten set. She held them up in front of her and said, "A hat and mittens." She said it in a nice way, but I could tell she was holding back, and I was already feeling terrible. I told her they were angora. She said thank you very much in a nice way and put them back in the box. We talked for a little while, but neither one of us could get in a good mood, so I got up and went into their kitchen to say merry Christmas to the Meekers and drove home. After that something clicked in me, and I decided that when it came time to buy Elizabeth a present again, I was going to empty my bank account if I had to and get her something no one would believe. I didn't care if it was a diamond necklace or a car. I was never going to feel that rotten, cheapskate feeling again.

Of course the sweater she got me turned out to be the best one I had, the only one I would wear if I wanted to look decent. It also taught me the kind of thing I would have to buy if I wanted to look good all the time. Before that, going back to junior high when I first started noticing how kids were dressed, I always thought there was something about certain kids that automatically looked good. I usually linked it up with being tall or, after I got to know Patsy Prentiss, being rich. I thought that a kid who had a certain look just looked good in clothes, but the sweater Elizabeth bought me and the stuff I started getting after that made me realize that it's the actual clothes that made you look like that. But you had to get good stuff.

Elizabeth really liked shopping. It was one of her favorite things to do, and when a shopping trip was coming up with her mother or with Tricks, she would be in a good mood all week. She liked to go to the big Chicago department stores on Michigan Avenue or to the new ritzy malls they were building in Evanston and the other rich suburbs. By the time I was a junior, I could get the car every now and then on a Saturday, and Elizabeth and I would go on a shopping trip by ourselves. At first I did it because I thought she would really like it, and she did. We would usually go to a big mall with stores in it like Saks Fifth Avenue and Marshall Fields and Lord and Taylor. Elizabeth knew all about every store and which floor and section would have what she wanted. She always had a plan, and sometimes the whole purpose for a trip would be for her to get one tiny bottle of Chanel No. 5 perfume. Most of the time she wanted us to split up and for me to go off and get my own stuff while she got hers. She said I made her nervous just hanging around her, and I actually couldn't stand it either. The first few times we went shopping together, I realized there was practically nothing I could afford to buy. Normally if I had five or ten dollars in my wallet, or even fifteen, I would think I was in pretty good shape, but in those stores one shirt might cost fifteen dollars, and we would also have to eat something while we were there, and maybe I would have to get some gas. But by this time I had a lot of money, over a thousand dollars, in my savings account for college, so I started taking a lot of extra money with me, thirty or forty dollars, plus what I already had.

I usually didn't know where to go when I was walking around the mall by myself. I would find myself in the men's section of a place like Marshall Fields, and there would be pants for fifty dollars and sports jackets for a hundred fifty dollars and ties for ten dollars, and I would keep telling the salesmen no thanks, I was just looking and maybe every now and then think about getting one thing, like a belt, even though it was way too expensive. One time Elizabeth and I were at a mall in the summer, and it was a lot lighter than usual in the atrium where the sun came through the glass, and somehow everything seemed friendlier. There were a lot of big sales, and as I was wandering around by myself, I went past a little store that sold only Italian shoes. The regular ones cost ninety dollars or a hundred and ten dollars, but some of the ones on sale only cost twenty, which meant I could buy a pair. The ones on sale were pretty different, but I actually liked them. They came to a sharp point at the end, and the sole underneath was really narrow, so it looked like your foot was wrapped all the way around in leather. They looked a little like the shoes people wore in the pirate days. I was in a pretty goofy mood, so I bought a pair.

Later when Elizabeth and I were having lunch, she asked me what I bought, and I showed her the shoes. She didn't hold back. She said, "Jonathan, you go right back there and take those back." She made a face at me and said, "What's *wrong* with you?" I should have known better, but I tried to joke around with her a little and say I thought they were pretty cool, but she was serious. I didn't want to let her know it, but that kind of thing still made me feel bad. I knew she knew all about clothes, but I didn't see what was so bad about being a little goofy every now and then. I went back to the store to get my money back, but the guy said that because they were on sale, I could only exchange them for something else. The only other cheap ones were the kind I knew Elizabeth would hate, so I decided I'd just get a million pairs of socks, even though all they had was thin black socks I knew I'd never wear. As it turned out, you only got about three pairs for twenty dollars anyway.

But one thing I learned from all that shopping with Elizabeth, and that was to buy her really good presents. Most of the time she let me know what she really wanted. It was always something very particular, like a camel colored cashmere scarf that she could wear with a certain coat or a pair of really soft leather gloves that went way up her arm. I got used to the fact that those kinds of things cost fifty or sixty dollars, and once I knew it, it stopped making me feel so nervous. The best thing, though, was being able to surprise Elizabeth by getting her even more stuff and better stuff than she expected. In order to do this, I would call up her mother or Tricks and ask them some of the things Elizabeth wanted. They always knew, and they were always right. Elizabeth would practically fall over after she would open what she thought was her main present from me, which was something really good, and then I'd pull out of the bag something else, or maybe two things, that were even better. I loved doing that. It's great to give people way more than they ever expect. That saying from the Bible is true.

Maybe the best thing about having Elizabeth for my girl friend for so long was that it made my life feel so safe and organized. There were set times for seeing her and calling her, all kinds of dates, and all the parties and get-togethers you got invited to if you were a couple. Gary Wade used to tease me about having a wife, and he would call Elizabeth "the little woman." He was mainly fooling around, but I knew what he meant. The longer you have the same girl friend and keep doing things with her, the more of an official couple you are, and after a while you can't even picture yourself not being in the couple. But at the same time, I had a weird feeling that any second Elizabeth would break up with me for some reason, and it would be all over. I don't think it was just because she was so high strung and got mad at me every now and then. She never talked about breaking up. I was the one who thought about it. I even had dreams about it, dreams where I would do something horrible to her, something I would never actually do, like call her names and slap her and then start yelling at her whole family. Obviously, I kept things like that to myself.

Chapter Twenty-One

BY THE END of the summer before senior year, my situation started getting a little crazy, and not just in my dreams. It was like I had a mental illness, schizophrenia, where you have two complete lives at the same time, and whenever you're in one of the lives, that's all there is and it's fine, but the two lives don't have anything to do with each other. That's the way I felt about being a senior. One life I was going to have was to be in sports and plays and talent shows and get all A's and have Elizabeth as my girl friend. It was going to be exactly like junior year, except I was going to be even more important, maybe even in the Homecoming Court, but the main thing about it was that everything was going to be familiar, and nothing was ever going to change. The other life was completely opposite. I was going to have to figure out a place to go to college, move out of our house, move away from Palatine, break up with Elizabeth, and start doing all new things with new people. I knew that both of those lives were coming up, and the effect it had on me was to make me think that no matter what I did, it was going to get cancelled out. It was like I had a main self that went through the days but also a kind of zombie anti-self that was going to wreck everything the first self did.

The real craziness might have started the night Elizabeth and I were supposed to go on a double date to see *Flower Drum Song* at the Drive-In with Gary Wade and Karen Shiels. That would have been a fairly normal night for us, because we did a lot of things with Gary and Karen.

Elizabeth thought Gary was a big-mouth, because he was kind of a goof-off in school, but she liked Karen Shiels, so we usually had a pretty good time together. Gary and Karen were also at about the same level of kissing as Elizabeth and me, so nobody had to worry about anything. But a few days before our double date, Gary and Karen broke up, and Gary decided to ask Lou Scanlon to go with us to *Flower Drum Song*. If he had told me in advance, we probably would not have gone. There was no way Elizabeth was going to get along with Lou Scanlon. Lou Scanlon wasn't in our group, and although she wasn't in Vocational Ed, she was definitely not in College Preparatory. I didn't mind her, but I didn't know her very well. She had a reputation, and the girls in our group said she was "cheap." She had dark hair and dark skin and wore a lot of make-up. I thought it was too much make-up, because it made her face look kind of oily when she was actually not bad looking. Whether she really was cheap or not, the guys she went out with talked about her a lot afterward, saying you could do anything you wanted. Lou Scanlon and her friends had a look. Their skirts were tight around their hips and bottom, and their sweaters were really tight. They also smoked.

When Gary picked me up at my house, Lou Scanlon was sitting next to him in the front seat, and I was already starting to feel nervous about picking up Elizabeth. At first it was better than I thought. The worst thing Elizabeth did when she was upset is to look off in some direction and not talk at all, but she was fairly friendly on the way to the Drive-In. In fact the whole double date might not have been too bad if we had only gone to a regular movie where you had to sit up in your chair with a lot of other people around.

When we got to the Drive-In, it was still light out, so we got a bunch of food and pop corn and listened to the car radio. Gary actually seemed to know Lou pretty well, so it wasn't as awkward as I thought being in the car together. By the time it got dark and the movie started, I was starting to relax. *Flower Drum Song* didn't turn out to be much of a movie. It was a musical, and I don't know what it is about movies of musicals, but they always seem a little ridiculous, even if the musical itself was pretty good. The problem is that movies are too realistic, and it doesn't work if someone up on the screen is walking down a real street in a real city and then starts singing something like, "I enjoy being a girl" as other people keep walking by. My main memory of watching *Flower Drum Song*, though, is sitting back with my arm around Elizabeth and watching the screen fill up with a swirl of Chinese people singing "A Hundred Million Miracles." They can't have been singing that for the whole movie, but that's what it seemed like, probably because once Gary and Lou Scanlon slid down out of sight I couldn't think straight.

If it had been Karen, Gary would have had his arm around her and they would have been kissing, which Elizabeth and I would have been able to tell by the way their heads went together. That would have been fine and nobody would have minded, because we would have been doing the same thing. But when Gary and Lou Scanlon slid down and disappeared, I got the feeling that anything could happen down there and that Elizabeth would have one of her fits. It probably would have been all right if they had just held still and not made any noise, but it was as bad as you could imagine. Gary was a big kid, and we could feel the back of the seat bulging out against our knees and hear the sound of their bodies rubbing against the upholstery. I wanted to turn up the volume on the speaker in the window, but to do that I'd have to lean over and see what was going on in the front seat, and I didn't want to do that. It kept getting worse. They were breathing really loud, and Gary was grunting and Lou Scanlon was making *"mmm mmm"* sounds, and you could hear the swishy sound of cloth moving around and all kinds of snapping and zipping. Knowing Gary, I knew there was no way he would remember Elizabeth and I were back there and pull himself together. He was out of his mind. There was absolutely nothing Elizabeth and I could do but listen and picture things. The only thing that ever seemed to be on the screen was the swirls of people in Chinese costumes singing "A Hundred Million Miracles," and the idea of Elizabeth and me kissing or doing anything ourselves was way out of the question. I couldn't even turn my head to look at her. There would be a regular pattern of creaking and movement in the front seat, then it would stop for a while, then it would start up again harder than ever. I didn't think they would ever be finished. I only heard them say one thing. There was a quiet spell, then a little more creaking and swishing. It was impossible to figure out exactly what they were doing to each other. Then Lou Scanlon said, "lower." Gary said, "What?" And she said, "*lower.*"

After that night I remember wishing I had never heard that. Nothing, no dirty words, no actual description of the most sexual thing could have hit me the way "lower" did when Lou Scanlon said it. I couldn't get it out of my head. It had the effect of making me feel that no matter what kind of sex I could picture, there would always be something worse, something lower, and no matter how hard I tried to stop it, I was headed there. After that night with Gary and Lou Scanlon at the Drive-In, I just wanted to get back in the Meeker's den and watch the Late Night Movie with Elizabeth, but only kissing. I also made sure we had some dates in between where we didn't even kiss. But no matter what I did to stop it, as soon as I was alone in my room at night, the word "lower" would flash into my mind, and all kinds of new sex thoughts and pictures would start coming up.

It was probably good that senior year was as busy as it was. Just as I thought, Elizabeth and I got elected to the Homecoming Court, which was the biggest honor in the school, because the whole senior class could nominate people, and every kid in school voted. It helped a lot that Elizabeth and I were a couple, because kids usually thought of the Homecoming King and Queen as a couple. The top five boys and the top five girls formed the Homecoming Court, and they got to march through a special archway into the gym and walk along a red carpet to a little stage set up with two thrones on it. The whole school was sitting in the bleachers, and all the lights were out except for a spotlight that followed you up to the thrones when it was your turn to walk under the arch with your partner.

You couldn't imagine a bigger deal. The King candidates all had rented tuxes with white jackets, and the Queen candidates wore formal gowns and held bouquets of roses in front of them as they walked. As soon as the first couple was under the arch and the spotlight picked them up, The Palatunes, who were the twelve best singers in Girls Chorus, would sing "When You wish Upon A Star," and as soon as they started, all you could hear was the sound of girls squealing and sniffling in the dark. When all the candidates were lined up around the thrones, Mr. Gladhead would announce King and Queen, drawing it out as long as possible to increase the tension. As soon as he announced King and Queen, there would be a tremendous shriek, and the girls who didn't get it would run over and hug the Queen, and the boys would shake hands with the King. Then the lights would go out again, and a spotlight would follow the King and King as they walked all the way around the gym, waving to kids they couldn't really see in the dark while the Palatunes sang "If."

> *If they made me a king*
> *I'd be but a slave for you*
> *If I had everything*
> *I'd still be a slave for you*
> *If the world to me bowed*
> *Yet humbly I'd plead to you*
> *If my friends were a crowd*
> *I'd turn in my need to you*
> *If I ruled the earth*
> *What would life be worth*
> *If I hadn't the right to you*

You had to cry. When I was a freshman and a sophomore, I did everything I could think of to try to get people around me to laugh, but the feeling just came over you when you heard the singing start and saw the couples moving across the gym under the spot light. I remember being glad it was dark when the girls around me were crying and squealing, because nobody could see you if you happened to get choked up yourself.

Being an actual candidate, I mainly felt numb. Even though I kind of knew I would be nominated because of all the stuff I did and we were such a major couple, it felt good when it really happened, and they read the names over Morning Announcements. Elizabeth and I weren't going to win, and everybody knew that, so there was nothing to feel tense about. The King was usually either the President of Student Council or a terrific athlete, provided he was also a fairly nice guy. The President of Student Council our year was Dan Retsik, and he was absolutely perfect for King, and so was his girlfriend, Polly Imarino, who was also on the Student Council and on a lot of other committees. I can't remember feeling bad for a minute about not being King, and I don't think Elizabeth minded not being chosen either. By the time you were a senior at Palatine, you pretty much knew where you were.

But as much as the year started up exactly the way I predicted it would, my anti-self was making things miserable, making me feel like I was standing back and didn't care, even about major things like Homecoming Court. It was like a voice talking to me, trying to cancel out any little thing that might get me excited for a minute. Even walking across the gym in the spotlight, with Elizabeth's hand on my elbow, listening to the squealing and sniffling and trying to feel how amazing it was right at that moment, terrible things started popping up in my mind. I remembered "lower" all of a sudden and then started seeing sex pictures and imagining a bunch of kid, kids I didn't know, laughing at me out in the dark bleachers.

Chapter Twenty-Two

NEARLY EVERYTHING TO do with college could get me in the downward spiral. What I really wanted was for the guidance counselors or the government or somebody just to assign me to someplace and have that be the end of it. My mother and father didn't go to college, so they didn't know much about what you had to do, like what achievement tests to take and how to get the applications and what to write in the blanks for the essays. Mother had been really smart in her high school in Chicago and would have gone to college, but Papa practically had no money during the Depression, so she couldn't go and got a job as a secretary instead. My father's family didn't have any money period, and he told me he wasn't the college type back then. All he really liked was sports and playing the trumpet, and he actually earned decent money, for those times, playing in dance bands. After he got out of the army Uncle Desmond graduated from Northern Illinois University in DeKalb where he studied library science. He told mother I might like it there, but he wasn't sure. He was always extremely nice to me, and I think he thought I was a lot smarter than I was, because he thought I should apply for scholarships at major places like University of Illinois or University of Iowa, places he said he wished he had gone. On three Saturdays in a row, he drove me in his car to De Kalb to see Northern Illinois University, to Carbondale to see Southern Illinois University, and to Champagne-Urbana to see University of Illinois. I kind of enjoyed driving up and down the state with Uncle

Desmond, but honestly, what I liked best was stopping in some new town and getting something to eat in a restaurant. Kids at school said all kinds of things about different colleges. Southern Illinois was supposed to be a "party school," with lots of dances and beer and everybody stuffing themselves into cars and driving down to Ft. Lauderdale in the spring where about thirty people stayed in one hotel room. Northern Illinois was supposed to be friendly, but a little dorkier, depending on who you talked to. University of Illinois was supposed to be pretty great but really huge. The best thing about it was supposed to be certain fraternities like Sigma Chi and Sigma Nu where, if you got rushed and you got in, you automatically had a great time and you would be best friends with your brothers for the rest of your life.

By the time Uncle Desmond and I got to the campuses, it was usually afternoon, and we would go to the admissions office and pick up some handouts and maps and go on a tour of maybe the library, the stadium and some dorms. It may have been that my anti-self was putting me in a fog, but I didn't get much of an impression of any of the universities, except they all seemed huge, like little cities of their own. There were nice looking major buildings in each place, but I couldn't really see any big difference between them. The main picture I got was of kids streaming along the walkways. That was probably because when we got to Northern Illinois, a football game was about to start, and every street and every sidewalk was full of college kids heading toward the stadium. You could hear the drums of a band up over the trees in the distance, and it seemed like thousands and thousands of people were heading up to where thousands more were already huddled up together. It had the effect of making you want to get out of there.

By Christmas I ended up applying to a bunch of places, including University of Illinois, University of Iowa, and University of Wisconsin. I also sent in applications to Southern Illinois and Northern Illinois, which were a lot cheaper and everybody got in. When we talked about college at home, mother would always want to look at the catalogs and try to figure out all the different things you could study and what the special programs and major fields were. She thought the catalogs were pretty confusing, and so did I, but I wasn't worried about any of that stuff. I was sure that once you got there, they had official people to tell you what you had to take, and you could always figure it out from what everybody else did. My father didn't seem too interested. He was even a little mad about the whole thing. I think it was a combination of being worried about how much it would cost and also the fact that he didn't go to college and thought I had it way too easy. I didn't blame him at all. It was a big deal for our family to get a new car, which in our case was always a used car, but a pretty good one, only a couple of years old. My father took me with him when we got our last two cars, both Ford Fairlanes, which he said were the most reliable. I remember the last one, the '59, cost $1800, but my father got them down to $1500. College was going to cost at least that much—each year. He would look at mother when we were talking about the different colleges and say things like, "And where's the money going to come from?" She'd give him a look and tell him it would all work out. There must have been some savings or something, because my father let me go ahead with all the applications, even though he complained about the fifteen-dollar fee you had to send in with each one.

It was nice to have all of that over with, but I didn't like picturing actually being at any of those places, so I tried not to think about it. Elizabeth was really excited about college. Tricks went to the University of Wisconsin at Madison and had told Elizabeth a lot about it. She was in a sorority and seemed to be having a really good time. She taught Elizabeth a slightly dirty song from her sorority, and one night Elizabeth sang it for me.

Never trust a Sigma Nu
An Inch above the knee
I trusted one the other night
To see how it would be
He told me that he loved me
He said he would be true
But the son of a bitch he left me
With a son of a Sigma Nu

If it hadn't come from Tricks, Elizabeth would never have sung me a song like that.

Elizabeth applied to a bunch of small colleges, but also to the University of Michigan where they had a special honors program for a hundred kids a year who were really smart and got complete scholarships. I figured she would get that easily, which she did, because she was about the smartest student at Palatine. She had an 800 on the math S.A.T., which is a perfect score, and something way up there on the verbal. She said she hoped I got into Wisconsin, so she come visit me and Tricks at the same time. I told her I thought that would be great, but I hadn't even seen Wisconsin and didn't want to think about being up there with thousands of people like Tricks.

Mainly, I tried to keep my mind on other things. I probably set a record for activities my senior year at Palatine. I kept up with my sports, and I was one of the editors on the paper, and I was in Boys Chorus, plus Mixed Chorus and Ensemble, which was eighteen of the best singers who got to sing harder music at the concerts. I also got picked to be one of twelve kids in Madrigal Singers, a new group that got formed to compete in a state madrigal competition. I had never heard a madrigal before, and I thought they were really weird and very hard to sing, especially at first. I was one of the tenors and had to work on what the director called my "half voice," which made me open my throat and relax so I could sing notes way higher than I could in my regular voice.

Madrigals have a strange effect on you. There's never any regular harmony where you just sing the same line a few notes above or below somebody else. Instead your part just comes up all of a sudden in the middle of everyone else's. I could only see my part in a madrigal by picturing a piece of string that would twist in and out of the other pieces of string to form a knot. Learning a madrigal took us a long time, and you couldn't imagine it was ever going to sound any good, but once you learned it, it kind of got to you. I don't think I've ever had a harder time getting a tune out of my head than a madrigal. When we were driving somewhere in the car together, mother would ask me what on earth I was singing, because if you're only singing your part to a madrigal, it sounds very weird, because of all the sudden starts and stops. Also, practically all of them are in Italian, which nobody understands, so mother would just be hearing things like *Quest'e quell dolce tempo*, over and over.

Madrigal Singers turned out to be worth it, because we won the District and Sectional championships and first place at State. We got gold medals for each level, and they were the same kind of medals you got in sports if your team advanced in the post-season. I pinned them on my letter sweater, the way our state champion diver and the state champion doubles team in tennis did, and nobody said anything.

But if I wasn't driving off on some Saturday morning to sing madrigals, I was doing something else. I started writing some of my own songs for the variety shows, and I still think some of them were pretty good, even though what kids mainly wanted to hear was my Jerry Lee Lewis imitation. I also started writing a lot of poetry. One of my classes was Creative Writing, and some of the assignments got my ideas going, but then I just kept it up, even in my other classes when I was supposed to doing something else, and at home at night. Besides writing the poems, I liked looking at them when they were typed out on a clean sheet of paper. Maybe it's the shape of the indented lines going down the page broken up neatly by the stanza breaks, but to me poems are really good looking. They also take only a few minutes to write, so as soon as you get the thought, there it practically is. My poems felt really personal, so I didn't like showing them to mother, but for some reason I didn't mind showing them to my Creative Writing teacher and my English Teacher, who were really nice about it, even though after a while I was giving them so many that they started taking really long to give them back to me.

Palatine's literary journal was called *The Quill*, and it came out three times a year. In the winter and spring of senior year, practically everything in *The Quill* was by me. Once I got in the habit, the poems would come really fast. Practically anything could set one off. I remember sitting in the main floor study hall one morning, just listening to the radiators hissing and banging. I was still cold from walking to school so I wrote the word COLD on the top of a page in my notebook and then just wrote a poem straight through without stopping.

When it got so cold the whole world froze
You could not feel your nose or toes
You could not feel your feet or face
You could not feel your feeling place

When it got so cold the air was ice
Your head was held in a steel-cold vise
There was a white veil over everything
And the only sound was a singing ring
When it got so cold and got so white
The hawks that had attempted flight
Were held like statues where they were
Above still mice with frosted fur
When it got so cold I was all alone
Just inches from the telephone
If only I had gotten through
If only I had talked to you
You might have loved me still, who knows
But it got so cold the whole world froze

When I was in a certain mood, there was nothing I didn't think I could write a poem about.

The winter play that year was "Little Foxes" by Lillian Hellman, and I got the part of Ben. Mr. Canaletti said I was a strange choice for Ben, because in the play he's described as a big fat guy with indigestion, but he had a hunch I could do it. The play is all about a family in the south who wreck everybody's lives by trying to get the family money for themselves. I had only played funny parts before, and I thought I knew exactly what to do if my character was funny, but there was nothing funny about Ben. In one scene he slaps his wife in the face, and in another scene he beats up his son. He's one of the meanest people in the play. I had a slightly bad feeling about playing Ben, because the kid who got the part of my son was way taller than I was, and I couldn't imagine the scene where I beat him up would be very believable. Mr. Canaletti said that would not be a problem and that a lot of fathers dominated sons that grew up bigger than they were. I just had to work on developing a character that could do that, so I started getting into it. We had to learn southern accents for the play, and Mr. Canaletti brought in a friend of his from the south who coached us on how to say certain things. He said the point was not to come up with some big, obvious southern accent, but just to suggest it a little, so we learned to say things like *fahn* instead of fine, *dinnuh* instead of dinner, *hud* instead of heard. After awhile, you didn't even think about it, and we all started sounding pretty southern.

It took me a few rehearsals to figure out how to play Ben, but then I really got it. At first I tried leaning backwards a little when I walked and holding my hands on my gut, as if I had a big one, but that felt pretty lame. Mr. Canaletti asked me to think about things people had done to me (meaning Ben) when I was a boy, things I still really hated and never got over. I pictured getting cracked in the head, the worst cracks in the head I could think of, from somebody who actually wouldn't have minded killing me. I would think about that as my lines were coming up, and I could feel it tighten up my face and tense up my shoulders and my stomach, and when it came time to say my line, it came out in a completely new voice, kind of quiet but really mean. Mr. Canaletti liked it right away. During notes after one of the rehearsals he told people I had a genius for character. I don't know if I did or not, only that when I played Ben, I pictured myself as a scowling rat, and kids who saw the play told me afterward that I completely reminded them of a rat.

At the cast party for "Little Foxes" Mr. Canaletti asked me where I was going to college. I told him where I applied, and he asked me if I was sure I wanted to go to colleges like that. He could tell that I was pretty vague about it and asked me if I had ever thought of a place like Yale. I told him no, because I hadn't. I had heard of Yale and Harvard from people's conversations or from things I read in books about important people who went there. I knew from the Sunday sports section of the paper that Yale's football team was in the Ivy League, but I didn't know anybody who went there, and I don't think anybody at Palatine ever did. Mr. Canaletti said he had gone to the Yale Drama School after he graduated from his regular college, and he had an amazing time. He said it was "magic," and he was being really nice, not fooling around. He said I should consider applying to Yale.

I asked him how much it cost, and he said he didn't know, but I was sure it was more than Illinois or Iowa and way more than Northern Illinois and Southern Illinois. But after that I started thinking about Yale. The pictures in the Yale section of the main college catalog in the guidance office looked really nice with old stone archways into the buildings. Everything looked settled and old, like the pictures of England in Nana's *Lovely Britain* book. Sometime around then *Life Magazine* had a story about Yale students getting in some kind of trouble in New Haven and being chased by the police inside the college walls where they all ran into the chapel and the police didn't go in after them because of some tradition. The article was mainly photographs, and whatever the students did wasn't too big a deal, but I couldn't stop looking at the pictures of the Yale students running under the archway or peeking out the chapel door at the policemen. They looked like kids from another time. They were pretty dressed up, wearing tweed jackets and raincoats with the collars turned up. Their hair was long on top, and nobody had a crew cut. It was hard to describe, but they looked like a completely different kind of people in a completely different world than the crowds of kids heading up to the football stadium in De Kalb.

But thinking about Yale and trying to picture it didn't make it seem real. The way I thought about things at the time, the roads that led out of Palatine through Illinois and into Indiana did not actually connect up with the roads that went to Connecticut and places like Yale. But Mr. Canaletti kept talking to me about it, and he was serious. He talked to some of my other teachers, too, and to my guidance counselor. He told me he was a member of the Yale Alumni Association of Chicago, and he wanted to talk to them about me. He told me it was a long shot and that the admissions deadline was practically over, but he would talk to the Yale people if I wanted him to. I said okay, which meant I had to tell my parents.

It turned out I was right about how much Yale cost, which was about $4000, if you included everything. My father said that was completely ridiculous and what were we talking about, but mother said we should at least consider it because it was a once in a lifetime opportunity. I told Mr. Canaletti Yale was going to cost too much for us, and he said that I should apply anyway, because he thought they had scholarships for people who couldn't afford it. I told that to my father who still seemed pretty sour about the idea, but later I heard him telling mother that someone at the bank told him Yale was about as hotshot a college as you could get. He never said that to me, but he gave me the fifteen-dollar check that went with the application.

I hated the feeling that I was trying to get some special favor out of my father and mother so that I could maybe get into Yale, because honestly, I wasn't dying to go there. I still didn't know anything about it, except it was supposed to be great and famous and the kids I knew thought no one like us ever went to a college like that. Even my teachers, when I asked them if they would send in one of the recommendation forms, said things like, "My goodness, *Yale.*" Elizabeth said, "It would be just like you to end up somewhere like Yale," which might have been some kind of insult, but I didn't feel like figuring it out. All I knew was that it was starting to become a really big deal. Mr. Canaletti called mother and came over to the house one night to talk about what Yale was like, and a guy from Chicago who went to Yale came to Palatine and met with me and my guidance counselor and talked to Mr. Canaletti and some of my other teachers. The idea was that I was supposed to knock myself out to make a good impression and what a terrific thing it would be if an underdog kid from Palatine made it into Yale, but there wasn't a single person I could tell that I didn't really want to go there at all, and that maybe I didn't want to go anywhere.

Once I sent the application in, I was pretty much able to put it out of my mind. All I wanted to do was keep doing school things so I wouldn't have to think. Some time in March, I started hearing back from the colleges. When I got home from rehearsal, mother would have put the envelope on my dinner plate. I got into all the Illinois places, and I remember getting the Northern Illinois and Southern Illinois envelopes on the same day. A little while after that I got into Iowa and Wisconsin. I had about four weeks to choose, and there were a lot of forms for my parents and me to fill out that went to the place I decided to go. Mother was very nice about each letter and told me I was an awfully lucky boy and that she was proud of me. I knew she meant it, but it mainly made me start feeling sad again that she never got to go to college and that she had actually wanted to. I also couldn't stand the idea of filling out all the forms.

Then one night, way into April, there was an envelope on my plate from Yale. I don't know if it was the tension I felt from mother or my own, but it practically made me sick to my stomach to see it there on the plate. Something in me already knew this was it. I opened it and, sure enough, I got in. Mother said it was wonderful. My father said, "My son, the Yale man." He was being nice about it. Mother started calling people up, and we never really ate. I remember feeling, okay, it's over, and I couldn't wait to get into my room so I could be by myself.

The rest of the year was just ceremonies and prizes. The effect of all the college business was to make me feel like some big force had come up behind me and shot me forward to someplace way ahead of where I expected. Just doing everyday school things made me feel like I was in a play where my part was to act normal. Unless you were failing something or a delinquent, they didn't make you do much at Palatine at the end of the senior year. There were no final exams, just senior traditions, like Skip Day and Beach Day where the seniors all wore shorts and sandals and goofy hats. I did all that stuff, but my heart wasn't really in it. What I mainly felt was sad. I wasn't sad about having to graduate from Palatine or the idea of missing people. In fact, I was having kind of a hard time even liking people, especially when everybody expected you to be in a goof off mood because it was Beach Day.

Also, starting with Yale, I kept getting things, which for some reason made me even sadder. A kid who did all the things I did at Palatine should have gotten a few things, like maybe the Drama Prize or the Literature Prize or something for school spirit, but they practically gave me everything. I knew I was getting something at Senior Awards Assembly because they called mother and invited her to come. But what I got was ridiculous.

I got the English Prize and then another English prize I didn't know about for Creative Imagination. I got the *Quill* prize for Most Promising Writer. I got the Journalism Prize for Best Contribution to the Tribune. I got the Choral Music Prize, and while I was standing up on stage as the director read the citation, he announced that they were also giving me a special Music Department Award for all the piano playing I had done at concerts and variety shows. By this time I knew the other kids were thinking the school was overdoing it, but on and on it went. I got a Special Citation from the Illinois branch of Mightier than the Sword for something I wrote in a writing contest I had completely forgotten about. I got the Drama Prize. After that I went into as deep a fog as I could get, but they kept calling me up on stage for awards named after Palatine kids who died in accidents but had tremendous spirit or character. It got almost silly, and even mother had to tell her friends on the phone later that the school should have spread things out a little. It was a long assembly, and I was so deep in my fog by the end, I almost didn't get up for the last award, Spirit of Palatine, which is the absolute top prize. I never once for one minute thought about getting Spirit of Palatine. Like I'm sure everybody else, I thought Dan Retsik would get it because of the kind of Student Council President he was and a lot of other good qualities. Dan Retsik was a kid you really liked and never felt jealous of because, even when he was a freshman, all he ever cared about was being nice and being fair. By the time he was a senior, I thought Dan Retsik was more like a grown man than most of the teachers. I really wish they had given him The Spirit of Palatine, because he completely deserved it, and I was not that kind of person.

It was very awkward being around the other seniors after Awards Assembly. Nice kids I barely knew said congratulations, but my friends didn't really know what to say to me, and it almost seemed like they wanted to avoid me for a while, and I didn't blame them. Elizabeth, who got the Math Prize, came up to me and bumped me with her hip. All she said was, "Well, well, well." I knew Gary Wade would say something, and of course he had to come running over and bow down and start saying things like, "Your Excellency, can I touch you? Can I touch your awards?" Actually, that kind of helped. But then it got worse.

After the assembly all the seniors were supposed to go down to the main floor study hall and get their yearbooks, *Memories*, and then we had the rest of the morning free to walk around school and sign each other's book. That should have been relaxing and kind of nice, but the Senior Poll wrecked it. I almost couldn't look at it. Under each heading, like Nicest or Best Hair, there would be four boys and four girls, ranked first to fourth. I looked at the page, and all I saw was *Jonathan Force*. I was Most Talented, Funniest, Most Creative, Most Musical, First to be Famous, First to Wed (with Elizabeth), Most Involved, Marches to Different Drummer, Best Handwriting, Eats Most, Weighs Least. The last heading at the bottom was Most Likely to Succeed. It would have been sickening to get that instead of Dan Retsik, but he got it. I was second.

Chapter Twenty-Three

I GOT THROUGH MY final days at Palatine by keeping vague and making a project out of getting rid of Elizabeth. There was no way to explain it, so I didn't even try. There was no reason, anyway, just a tremendously strong feeling that I had to get as far away as possible from her and her Mamie and Fahrver and that whole set up. The timing was pretty terrible, because the day I decided to get rid of her was about three days before the Prom. The prom was a huge deal for Elizabeth because of her dress and all the thought she put into things like that, but I didn't care. There could actually have been something wrong with me, because I didn't feel bad at all about calling her up and saying I couldn't take her to the prom. She didn't understand what I was saying at first, but when she got it, she was quiet for a while. Then she said, "Why? Why are you doing this to me?" I told her I didn't know and that I was sorry about the short notice. I actually wasn't sorry. I was glad, glad I wasn't going to the prom, glad that I was the one deciding, and glad nobody could understand what I was doing. Too many things had been happening to me that I felt I had no control over, but I could control this, and it felt really good.

Not that breaking off with her like that made Elizabeth disappear from my mind. For most of the summer, I thought of my days and weekends as not-Elizabeth times. If I thought about what I was going to do on Saturday night, I would think of it as Not Watching the Late Night Movie at Elizabeth's. Each not-Elizabeth thing I did made me feel livelier and stronger and more like myself. It also made me a little mean, but I hoped that would only be temporary. For instance when she would write me a long letter asking me why I suddenly changed and what she had done to deserve being dropped like that, I wouldn't write back. She called a few times, and I only said things like, "I can't explain" and "that's just the way I feel." When her girl friends called to tell me how miserable Elizabeth was and that all she did was cry, I said, "Sorry to hear that." They said they didn't get me, and I didn't say anything, because the only thing I could have said was that not getting me was the point.

I GOT THROUGH ALL THE graduation business by getting into a not-Palatine frame of mind, which was a lot like not-Elizabeth. I don't think I was rude to anybody, but I said as little as possible to the people saying congratulations, I didn't hang around after any of the ceremonies, and I didn't go to any of the parties. It felt great. It also helped that I had a new job for the summer. Part of the Journalism Prize I got was to be a paid intern at Palatine Press, the town paper that came out twice a week. Not having to go back to the bank and seeing all those people felt like part of the clean break I was making with everything else. Also there was something about the Press I already liked. My journalism teacher set me up as a sports stringer for the Press when I was a junior, which meant I got two dollars for every Palatine box score I phoned in after varsity football and basketball games. It was not much of a job, because all I had to do was get the facts right, but for some reason I got a kick out of calling Bob Laski, one of the sports writers at the Press, on the pay phone outside the gym and reading him the statistics. He always sounded like he was incredibly tired, and he made everything I said into a joke to keep from being bored. He called me "Chief" or "Ace," and I liked picturing everybody at the press being like Bob Laski. I was looking forward to working at a place like that for a change.

As it turned out, everybody at the Press wasn't like Bob Laski, but some people were. I didn't have to be in the editorial office until ten in the morning, which is the best starting time for a job I've ever had, and I got off at five, or whenever I got all my work done. The Press was an amazing place to work for someone my age because, almost from the first day, they gave me real things to do, things that actually had to go into the paper, like rewriting press releases for community events, or formatting the county's list of driver's license revocations, or writing headlines for news and feature articles. I liked the fact that they assumed I already knew how to do things like count column inches and count headline spaces, because I did. I also knew news style and feature style, and after they saw my first press release rewrites for things like a Kiwanis Club picnic or the Palatine Players' next play, they just piled copy onto the tray on my desk with a little scribbled note saying what they wanted me to do. Every single person was really nice to me and told me I was a "natural" and a "born writer" and how glad they were that there was an intern who didn't need a babysitter. Bob Laski was on the night staff with most of the other reporters who did sports and municipal beats like City Council, Zoning, School Board, Park District, or Municipal Court, so I only saw him when I stayed late to work on something.

The night staff writers were like a kind of club all to themselves. They started showing up in the editorial office around five in the afternoon. They sat around smoking and reading over their articles in that day's paper, then went out to cover their beats. They'd come back after their meetings at about nine and start typing up their stories. The whole time they were working they would be ragging on each other, insulting each other in incredible ways in order to crack the other guy up or at least surprise him. Except for my father, nobody in my family swore much, and nobody ever used sexual words. The night staff writers only talked to each other in foul language. After awhile it didn't really bother me, because people were never serious or mad. A guy would come into the office, sit down at his desk and say to Bob Laski, "You know, Bob, you've always had a very fat ass, but I think that it's gotten a lot fatter this week." Bob Laski would make a point of not looking up from his typewriter, and then he'd say, "You know, Phil, I think you might be right. I'm working on getting it fat enough to cover your whole face." They'd go on and on like that, back and forth, trying to keep the other guy from concentrating on his article. They would say the worst things you can say to a person. They would say, "Listen, you gaping asshole, I've got to get this piece of shit to the shop by midnight." They would say things like, "Laski, why don't you eat shit and die?" No matter what they were saying, you could tell that they were having a good time, that it was their way of liking each other.

They were never too hard on me when I was around. They might kid me about being skinny, saying things like, "Force, please don't turn sideways like that, because I can't see you." Once Bob Laski asked me if I was in the Homecoming Court at Palatine, and I said yes. He asked me if I was King, and I said no. He said, "Probably a good thing. It would have been a shame if the guy had to put the crown on your head and then—clunk—it's down around your shoulders and—clunk—it's down around your hips and—kuh*lunk*—it's down on the floor." He would go on like that, saying the stupidest things, but things you couldn't help picturing.

The hardest thing for me to get used to was that they would also talk that way around Ceci Long, the Managing Editor. Ceci's job was to assign and edit all the news and feature copy. She came in after lunch and left at about ten at night, so she overlapped the shifts of the day and night staff. Everybody liked Ceci Long and everybody respected her. She was in charge of training me and assigning me work, and there was something about the nice way she explained everything and the way she let you know how the whole paper worked, from the advertising staff to the print shop, that made you feel confident and relaxed. She was an excellent explainer if I didn't get something, and she was great about leaving me alone.

But it made me uncomfortable when I worked on into the night shift and heard how the night staff writers talked to Ceci. I actually think most of them were crazy about her. She was a very unusual person, not like anyone else I had met before. Her age was hard to figure out. She was definitely out of college but not really settled into looking like a woman yet. I'm guessing she might have been thirty, although I didn't really know anybody in that age group. She had her own look. She was pretty tall, maybe five eight or nine and very slender. She was so slender that when I first got to know her I wondered if she had some kind of illness. But then I got used to the way she looked and actually got to like it. She was not really pretty, but there was something about her face that made you want

217

to keep looking at her. She had a long slender neck, which I liked, and kind of a small head for her long body, with a sharp little nose and a pointed chin. She wore her hair really short, like a boy's, but it all came forward to form a kind of fringe around her face. That might have made her look little-girl cute, but she didn't act cute at all. She was actually pretty tough and very smart. She didn't seem to mind the night staff writers' foul mouthed kidding around, and sometimes when I heard them ragging on her, I got the impression that she got a kick out of it. They said unbelievably dirty things to her, things like, "Ceci, you got any meat on those bones? I have a feeling you'd give me bruises in the sack." She wouldn't be offended at all. She'd just say something back like, "Bruises are the least of what you'd get from me in the sack" or "in your dreams, Phil." Just about all the kidding had something to do with having sex with Ceci, and her responses were all about there being too many things wrong with them, like their terrible breath or fat gut or tiny equipment, for it ever to happen.

Like their ragging with each other, there wasn't any real meanness in what they said, but you could feel a kind of special tension because they were talking about sex. They were all heavy smokers, including Ceci, and the ragging would usually start when somebody wanted to bum a cigarette from her. For some reason, I couldn't get Ceci out of my mind when I went home after work. A picture kept popping up of her tall, slender person's slouch and the way her loose clothes dropped away from her bony shoulders. I couldn't quite put together how friendly and well spoken she was with me and the other day staff people and her tough talk with the night shift. Bob Laski was the least foul mouthed when he talked to her, probably because he really liked her, but he still kidded her a lot. He mainly said goofy things to her like how he met a Mexican guy who said he knew her, and when he asked the Mexican guy what kind of woman she was, the Mexican guy said, "Oh, Ceci, si, si" and on and on about seeing Ceci by the sea and Ceci being eecy to pleecy. When Ceci had had enough or needed to get back to work, she would say things like, "Bob, you are a complete tragedy" or "you are such a wit, or am I only half right?"

So far as I could tell, Ceci didn't have a boyfriend, which was maybe why she was willing to hang around the night staff writers so much. I didn't know anything about her life outside of the editorial offices, but I had the feeling something terrible had happened to her, and that she was over it, but still really sad. I sensed it in the way she was so patient with people who didn't get things and the way nothing the night staff writers said ever shocked her or made her mad. In a way she was very unsexy. She liked to wear dresses that were cut like a man's shirt on top and continued down into a long skirt. You couldn't tell much about her shape in that kind of dress, except to see how thin she was at the waist. You couldn't tell for sure, because she hunched her shoulders and slouched, but she was probably pretty flat chested because nothing seemed to push out the front of her dresses. It's hard to explain, but the way she was unsexy was also pretty sexy. For one thing, she seemed to know all about sex. She couldn't joke around with the night staff guys like that and not know exactly what everybody was talking about. She never said anything immodest to me, but I just had the feeling that Ceci had had a lot of sex.

Or maybe it was that sex had some kind of grip on me that summer. I don't know if not having Elizabeth as my girl friend any more had anything to do with it, but it seemed like everything had a new sex-charged feel to it. Of course it was summer, and the way girls dress in the summer with their shorts and little tops showing off the sun tan on their legs and arms can't help giving you sexy feelings. Just walking through town on my way to the Press in the morning I'd feel myself zooming in like a camera on the way somebody looked. It could be the way their legs came out of their shorts or the way their ankles looked going into their shoes. I might glance at somebody in a convertible stopped at a traffic light, and I'd catch the way she was resting her arm over the door or the tilt of her neck or just that she was wearing pink lipstick, and I would hold that picture in my head all morning.

I decided not to play ball that summer, so I had a lot of time on my hands. I'd usually go home and eat dinner with my father and mother or, if I worked late, get a hot dog or something by myself at June's, and after supper I'd just walk all around Palatine, circling it in a ring. I'd usually head for the park and maybe watch the end of a game, then, as it started to get dark, head off by myself. Something in me always wanted to get to what felt like the edge of town, the streets that used to be the last streets before the fields began. Walking along them then, you would never know there even were fields or the town had an edge. There was just development after development on streets that didn't even seem all that new anymore, but the houses still looked new to me, the brick work a little too raw. The developments just kept going until they connected to developments in Schaumburg and Rolling Meadows, which didn't really seem like towns to me, just a name they gave to a bunch of developments. I'm sure the people who lived there thought they lived in real towns that were in the center of things for them, but to me all those clean cement streets and yards with skinny little trees seemed like a big, lifeless add-on that couldn't possibly last. One of the strange things about those walks was that even though I knew perfectly well where I would get to if I headed out into the developments, I had a deep feeling that the fields were still out there somewhere. It was a kind of craziness. I had driven around enough to know that when I drove into the developments, I would come to this or that new school or new park, and that pretty soon I'd get to a big intersection of the roads connecting Palatine and Arlington Heights or some other town. But even though my brain knew there was no more space in between the towns, it felt like the fields were still there somewhere. Sometimes I had a dream where I thought I could see where they were and how you could actually get there.

Even walking around town like that by myself in the dark seemed to be about sex. On summer nights there is something about the feel of soft air on your skin and how, if it's even a little bit damp, the fullness and smell of everything seems to seep out. As soon as I started walking, the sex pictures would start coming up and the old cycle of thoughts would keep repeating and repeating. It would usually start with remembering *"Lower,"* which would bring up the picture of Lou Scanlon and her friends. In the picture they would be standing around smoking, or maybe just Lou Scanlon was, and they all really wanted to have sex. I didn't know about her friends, but I happened to know Lou Scanlon really did want to, at least she did that night with Gary Wade, wanted to as much as anybody, any boy or even any of the men on the night staff, and she wasn't ashamed of it and would bring it up herself and probably start things off and let you do everything and not stop you. She would not mind undressing in front of you, and she actually wanted you to look at her and to touch her. In my pictures she would walk right toward me in her underwear, and her eyes would be dark and wet with make up and her lips red with lipstick. I wasn't saying or hearing or even seeing the word, but every step I took and everything I pictured seemed to be charged with "*Lower*," and if anybody would have happened to be watching, they would have seen that I was walking really fast.

Even though it made me feel like a robot, I actually started going past Lou Scanlon's house on some of my walks. It was always dark, and I always walked right past, hardly looking in toward the windows of the house. It felt like some kind of requirement. I knew I could have called her up and made an actual date and that if I did, we would have gone somewhere and tried things, but I also knew I would never do it. I knew that if I did something like that with her, it wouldn't come even close to the feeling I had when I was walking toward her house in my "*Lower*" trance. Not that I didn't think about actual sex with Lou Scanlon. In my "*Lower*" system there was only one way it could happen. I would have to be just getting to her house, and she would have to be standing in her driveway for some reason, and she would have to stop me and say hi and start talking to me. She might be wearing only a bathing suit or a robe. She would tell me that her parents weren't home and that we could go inside. She would take me down to her recreation room in the basement, and we'd start to do everything without even talking. I didn't picture doing particular things, like touching her and stripping. It didn't seem possible to picture what we would actually do, and I didn't want to. I don't know how much I believed Lou Scanlon would ever actually meet me on her driveway, but the longer the summer went on, the more I wished something like that would happen, and in a way it did.

Chapter Twenty-Four

At the end of August I only had one more week at the Press, and then my father and mother were going to drive me to New Haven and drop me off at Yale. Even though I knew it was coming right up, I hardly ever thought about it, and when I did, I would just get a few pictures in my head of the way the old buildings and archways looked in the catalogs, and I didn't feel anything, good or bad. I'm not sure I believed I was really going. Bob Laski surprised me by asking me if I wanted to come to a party at his house on Friday night, which would be after my last day at the paper and my last night in Palatine. I was surprised he asked me, because even though he and his friends on the night staff were always pretty nice to me, it was clear that I was just a kid to them and kind of a novelty to have around. I had a feeling those guys did things together every Friday night and the rest of the weekend too, because all of their ragging on Mondays would be about how loaded they got, and what crazy thing some drunk guy did, like back his car out of the garage without opening the door. I never imagined they would want to include me in any of that, and I thought it was really nice of Bob Laski to ask me. It was almost like telling me I had made an impression and they liked having me around. He said there would be pizza and stuff on the barbecue and booze. He said I could practice "getting shit-faced" for college. I hadn't done much drinking yet. The legal age in Illinois was twenty-one, and I was eighteen, but I probably looked more like sixteen. No one was going to mistake me for being older and serve me. My father had started letting me have a beer with him when we watched games on television, and on Thanksgiving and Christmas I always got a little glass of sticky sweet port with everyone else after dinner, but that was about it. I actually liked the idea of drinking booze with the night staff guys and maybe a lot of other people at a grownup party, but I was a little worried I wouldn't be able to stand the taste.

On the Wednesday before the party, I did an impulsive thing. I hadn't been thinking about Yale at all, but mother had been telling me all week that I had to decide what I was going to take with me and start packing. I didn't think it would be all that hard, but I was putting it off. I knew I'd take my typewriter, my clock radio, probably my glove, even though I didn't know how good baseball was supposed to be at Yale, and a bunch of clothes. I must have had clothes on my mind, because on Wednesday afternoon it hit me that I should go out and get all new stuff, and everything was going to be better than anything I had before. It was completely clear. I didn't have anything to do that I couldn't do the next morning, so I left the office early while the bank was still open and took nine hundred dollars out of my savings account. My savings account was supposed to be for my spending money at college, but I had over $2,000 in it, and I knew that was way more than enough for a year. I don't know exactly why I decided on nine hundred dollars, except that it seemed like a lot, and I wanted to go to Parnell's and get everything I could think of and not have to worry about it. Even at Parnell's it would be hard to spend nine hundred dollars, unless you were getting a bunch of men's suits, which I wasn't. If it turned out I had a lot of cash left over, that would be fine, because another thing I liked the idea of was having way more money in my wallet than anybody would imagine.

For some reason it seemed like I was in Parnell's for about three minutes, but I got a ton of stuff, the kind of stuff I used to look at, go home and think about, and beg mother for extra money to buy. And if it was maybe a shirt and I got it, it would be the one nice button down shirt in my closet with all the crummy old ones and never-wear ones certain people gave me for Christmas. It put me in kind of a trance to walk into

Parnell's and not have to tell the salesman, for a change, that I was just looking. I went right over to the clothes and started picking out stuff I wanted without looking at what anything cost. The salesman said I should try on things like pants and the jackets, and he was right, but in a way I hated to have to do it, because it slowed me down. It's a good thing I did, because even though the khaki pants I tried on were the best looking ones they had, they were actually too wide on me when I looked in the mirror. The cloth didn't even touch the skin on my legs, and all I could feel was a lot of air. The salesman told me they could taper the legs from a sixteen inch to a fourteen inch cuff, and since I was going off to college on Saturday, their tailor could make the alterations by the next day. He pinned in the pants to show me how they would look when they were fixed, and it made a huge difference. I bought eight pairs. I also bought some really nice corduroys, which I always liked when I saw other kids wearing them, and about ten button down collar shirts, some light blue ones, some yellow ones, a pink one, and two with little checks that the salesmen said were tattersall. I didn't have to try them on because they were in my exact size. I got four or five crew neck sweaters, the kind Elizabeth gave me for Christmas, dark green, dark grey, maroon, and black. I tried one on, and it looked perfect. I also got a camel colored duffel coat that had a hood you could button onto the neck. I got a pair of shiny cordovan oxfords and a pair of red penny loafers which I had always wanted and which, it turned out when I got there, every guy at Yale wore. The last thing I got was two tweed jackets and a bunch of striped ties. The jackets looked great and the salesman said they were on sale for $99 each. There was a huge stack of my stuff on the glass counter when the guy was ringing up the total. While I was standing there, I looked across the store and saw a rack of leather belts and decided I wanted one, so I told the salesman to hold on for a second while I went over and picked one out. When I got back to the counter, he told me my total was eight hundred and something, and I held up the belt and told him I wanted that too. He gave me a big smile and said, "The belt's on the house." That was really nice.

 I couldn't even carry all of the stuff home with me, so I took an armful of boxes and bags and came back later with the car. The next day after

I picked up the pants, I tried everything on in front of the long mirror in mother's bedroom. I couldn't believe it. Everything fit, the creases were sharp, and everything hung down perfectly. I put on one of the new shirts and a pair of the tailored khakis. I put on the new leather belt with the round gold buckle. I put on the red loafers. The clothes looked even better than the ones on the people in the catalogs we got. I put on one of the tweed jackets, then I put on a new striped tie. Everything went together, and I couldn't stop looking in the mirror. I'm sure the feeling was in my skin, but it seemed like I was feeling the tingle of the cloth. I looked completely like someone else, like another kind of person.

On Friday afternoon, my last day, Ceci took me into Mr. Pearson's office for a special meeting. Mr. Pearson was an old, wrinkly man with completely white hair. He owned The Palatine Press, and he was the editor-in-chief. I met him on my first day, and I saw him come in and go out a few times, but he was hardly ever in the editorial rooms. He told me I had done an excellent job and that Ceci and the other staff said I was the best intern they could remember. He asked me if I was excited about Yale, and I said yes. He said, "I wish I had your prospects, young man," which I didn't really get, but I laughed a little, which I think was the right response. He told me that I when I came home for vacations, I could have my job back, and if I came back next summer, I could get my own beat and work with the night staff. I couldn't really think about all that right on the spot, so I said thanks a lot. Then he got up, handed me a white envelope, and shook my hand. I didn't open the envelope until I was out on the street walking home. It was a check for fifty dollars. I had another check in my pocket for a hundred forty dollars, which was for my final two weeks at the paper. I still had about eighty dollars in my wallet left over from buying the clothes at Parnell's, and I realized that for the first time in my life I had all I wanted of everything.

ON FRIDAY WHEN I WAS eating supper with my father and mother, I told them about Bob Laski's party and that I would probably be out late. I wondered if they would mind. They had been pretty relaxed with me since graduation, and they stopped telling me I had to be in by a certain time, not that it was ever a problem since I wasn't going out with Elizabeth anymore, and I hardly ever asked them for the car. My father asked me if I wanted a ride, and I told him no, because it was a nice night, and I knew roughly where Bob Laski lived, and it wasn't a bad walk. Mother said not to stay out too late because we were going to be leaving early in the morning.

In my room I had everything packed and ready to go, except for putting my new clothes in the big suitcase. I thought I'd leave them folded up on my bureau and hanging in the closet until the last minute, so they wouldn't have to be mushed together for any extra time. I also decided to wear some of the new stuff to the party. It wasn't too hot out, so I put on one of the new yellow button down shirts and a pair of the khakis and the red penny loafers. I took a shower and got dressed and walked down the hall to see what I looked like in the long mirror. It was just like before. They could have just stood me up in one of Parnell's windows.

It turned out I actually did know where Bob Laski lived. It was at the edge of the old part of town just before you got to the forest preserve. The houses weren't too nice out there. Some of them used to be part of farms, and the area generally looked pretty beat up. The sidewalks stopped about a half mile from his house, and I wondered if I was going to scuff up my loafers on the gravel along the side of the road. As it turned out, I didn't have to worry about finding his house because it was the only one with cars parked all over the place. By the time I got there it was dark, and I could see people standing around in the back yard around the barbecue grill. There were a bunch of people from the day staff, and they were really friendly to me right away, so I didn't feel awkward at all. They told me Bob was in the kitchen and that's where the drinks were. They also said pizza was coming.

I opened the back door to the kitchen, and it was jam packed with people laughing and drinking. They were crowded around the kitchen table which had some open bags of chips, a big bowl of ice and a lot of liquor bottles. Bob Laski saw me come in. He raised his glass and said, "Hey, it's the boy wonder! Everybody, this is Jonathan Force, fearless cub reporter for the Palatine Press, on his way to Yale University to greater fame and fortune, *as we speak*." He was being really loud, but friendly. He didn't have to introduce me, because I knew practically everyone there. It was mostly the night staff writers and other Press people. There were some women I didn't know, probably people's wives or girl friends. Ceci came into the kitchen from one of the other rooms, and for some reason that felt like a huge relief to me, because there was going to be someone for sure that would be easy to talk to.

Bob Laski told me to help my self to a drink. He said there was beer in the refrigerator if I wanted one. I said sure, found a beer and then stood around with the people listening to the night staff guys telling funny stories and ragging on each other. Standing around like that put me in kind of a trance, so when my beer was finished I got another one out of the refrigerator and went back outside by the grill. Ceci was out there, and she came over to talk to me. She asked me if I got a nice bonus from Mr. Pearson, and I said yes, fifty bucks. She told me that was terrific. She said Mr. Pearson was not really a bad old guy, but he was really cheap, and giving me a bonus was a very big deal. That surprised me a little, because I didn't really know him at all and hardly saw him at the paper, I assumed the fifty dollars was Ceci's idea, and he was just the one who handed it over. She said no and that I had made a great impression and done such a good job. She was giving me really nice compliments, but it's the kind of thing you almost can't stand to listen to. I was saying things like "wow" and "really?" and "thanks," but there's not much you can say when people are saying things like that. I was glad, though, that Ceci was talking to me. One of the reasons she was so lively was probably that she'd had a few drinks. She had a tall glass of what looked like orange juice and ice, and I asked her what it was. She said it was a screwdriver, which was orange juice with vodka in it. She said it was "painless," and did I want to try one. I was almost through my second beer, and since I wasn't feeling any effects, I said sure.

We went back into the kitchen, and Ceci pushed her way through to the table where the liquor was. She said, "Jonathan is about to be initiated into true journalism. I'm making him his first screwdriver." One of the guys said "his first screw—*what?*" and everybody laughed, which made me laugh too. I was already in a good mood when Ceci and I went back out into the yard, and I was also starting to get really hungry. There were burger patties and hot dogs sizzling on the grill, and even though Ceci was talking up a storm, all I could picture was finding some rolls somewhere and wolfing something down. The screwdriver was fine. It didn't taste like much of anything, just orange juice with a little extra gassy taste. After a few sips I hardly paid attention to what it tasted like, because somehow Ceci and I got into a long, serious conversation. I got up the nerve to ask her if she minded the way the night staff guys teased her and if she minded all the foul mouthed talk. I could tell that really made her think. She smiled and put her hand on my shoulder and said, "Oh, those guys. Jonathan, what I could tell you about those guys." She said she shouldn't be telling me, but she told me some incredible things about them. She told me that Phil, who was married and had kids, had secret dates with a high school girl who babysat for him. I couldn't figure out a way to ask who the girl was, because I probably knew her, and I was trying to picture someone I knew, someone my age, going out with a person like Phil, with his oily hair and tired, wrinkly clothes and who never stopped smoking. She told me Bob Laski's first wife ran away with a guy who did odd jobs in the Press print shop, a guy Bob rented a room in his house to, just to help the guy out for awhile. She told me some of the guys were in trouble with booze. She used the term "on the sauce," which made her laugh, and then she said, "I should talk."

Our glasses were empty, and she asked me if I wanted another screwdriver. I said sure. She looked at me hard and said, "You're okay, aren't you?" I told here I was fine. I was pretty sure I was. I was actually feeling pretty good, pretty relaxed, and I could even see getting a little bit goofy. We went back into the kitchen where the same people were still standing around, only now people were getting really loud, and the jokes seemed to be all about sex, and people were saying *fucking* this and *fucking* that. Ceci grabbed the big vodka bottle and went over to the refrigerator to get the orange juice. There were some open pizza boxes on the counter by the sink, and I suddenly remembered how hungry I was, but when I went over to get some, I saw that everything was practically gone, except a couple slices with the cheese and toppings mostly pulled off and sticking to the cardboard. I was so hungry I just piled all the stuff back on the crust with my hands, jammed the two pieces together and went out the back door past the grill to the dark cars where I could wolf down the pizza without people looking at me. When I walked back toward the house, Ceci was standing in the lawn holding the two screwdrivers looking around for me, and we started another serious talk.

The drinks were probably starting to have an effect, because even though the things Ceci was telling me seemed really important and personal, every now and then I would lose track of the main thing we were talking about, and I would be watching the two of us standing in the dark yard and hearing what we were saying as if I was watching us from above. I have a feeling we were talking for a pretty long time, because after awhile everybody else in the yard had gone home or gone back into the kitchen. I remember just wanting to keep talking like that, no matter what we were saying. I was even pretending to be extra serious and interested in everything, because I wanted Ceci to keep going.

She was telling me college would be the most amazing thing that ever happened to me, and that it would be so good for me to get out of Palatine and into a new world. She told me she went to Northwestern, which was only about a half hour away, but her junior year she got to study in France where she lived with a family in Avignon, and while she was there she fell in love with a guy who was a cousin of the people she lived with, and he was the first guy she ever slept with and that he was the love of her life. She had to stop talking for a minute after she brought him up, because she was going to cry, and some tears actually came out. I had a really strong reaction to her telling me about being by herself in France and falling in love with the cousin. I felt like putting down my glass and putting my arms around her and pulling her in close to me. I kept picturing that as she was talking. I could almost feel the bones of her ribs against my chest and the bones of her back in my hands as I was hugging her. She told me she and the cousin wrote letters back and forth her whole senior year, and then she went back to France to visit him. They lived together for awhile, but then it didn't work out. She kept not being able to get a job, and he kind of had another girl friend. She put her hands on my shoulders and squeezed. "Jonathan," she said, "you can't even *know*." I said something stupid, like "I'm sorry," and then she went back to telling me I needed to get out of Palatine.

Our glasses were empty again, and Ceci said, "We can probably do one more." I told her I would wait for her in the yard while she got the screwdrivers, but what I actually wanted to do was find a dark place to pee, because I really had to go. When I got out of the part of Bob Laski's yard that was lit up by the light on his back porch, I realized I was way clumsier than usual and kind of stumbling around. I pictured myself like some drunken idiot in a movie, and it made me want to laugh. I wasn't that bad though. I peed and took some deep breaths, and by the time I walked back into the yard, I felt pretty normal. I also knew that something big was happening with Ceci. It was nothing that we were talking about, but I was feeling really connected to her. It felt like we were a couple, even though she was a woman and I was a kid. I had a feeling it would be okay to have sex with her, that she would let me and I would really like it. That feeling got stronger and stronger as we picked up our conversation and started drinking the screwdrivers. I can't even tell you what we talked about, except it was about big, vague things like relationships and books and getting out into the world and testing yourself. The whole time she was talking, I kept thinking that she was just opening herself up to me, wider and wider. I think she actually liked it that I was a kid.

I had to pee again, and since she was right there with me, I knew I would have to use the bathroom in the house. As soon as I started to move, I could tell I was pretty clumsy again, and I had to make a real effort to be sure my walk looked normal. I wasn't crazy about going in past all the people at the kitchen table, because I had a feeling that if somebody said something to me I wouldn't be able to talk right. I decided to plow right through the kitchen without stopping, as if I already knew where the bathroom was, but as soon as he saw me, Bob Laski shouted out, "Wait a minute, chief! I want to see if you're shit-faced yet. What do you think, folks, is young Jonathan shit-faced yet? Yes, I think he's there, or certainly getting there." I went right on through and found the bathroom. When I was finished peeing, I wished I could keep going. I had the idea that if I could just pee all the screwdrivers and everything else out of me, I'd feel clean and light and normal again.

    I went out the front door of the house so I wouldn't have to go through the kitchen again. Bob Laski's front stoop was dark, and I stood there for awhile and thought about going home. It would take me maybe a half hour to walk back, and by then maybe I would feel normal. I was definitely not feeling normal, but by the time I knew it for sure, it was too late, because I was starting to feel really terrible. I remembered that Ceci was probably waiting for me in the back yard, and as I made my way around the house in the dark, I tried to get back to the close, excited feeling I was starting to have before. When I got to the lighted yard at the rear of the house, Ceci was sitting on the back steps holding both of our glasses. She told me I was looking a little wobbly and asked if I was all right. I told her I was fine, but I actually wasn't. My forehead was all sweaty, and the cool night air made the sweat feel cold. If I closed my eyes, everything would start to swirl around in a sickening way, so I kept them open. It's hard to describe the feeling, except that it made me feel like I was inside some kind of thick padding, and the alive part of me inside could barely operate. There was also a gassy taste at the back of my throat, which, for me, is always a bad sign.

    "No," Ceci said, "You're not looking so good, Jonathan." She said she would take me over to her house and get some coffee and maybe relax for a bit, and then when I was feeling better, she would drive me home. I don't think I said anything. I just looked at her like an idiot and followed her to her car, which was a Volkswagen, and got in on the passenger side. Ceci went back in the house to return the glasses and say good-bye to Bob Laski. Volkswagens have a certain smell to them. It seems to come from the oil and metal parts in the engine, but it was definitely not agreeing with me as I was sitting in Ceci's car waiting for her to come back. Once we were moving, I didn't feel good at all, and I rolled down my window. Ceci said, "Oh, dear." I really did not want to throw up, but sometimes that's the worst thing you can think. But even though it felt like I was sitting inside a swirling, gassy cocoon, I was still excited to be alone in the car with Ceci, heading toward her house. I made myself sit up straight. I shook my head. I said, "I'm fine, I'm fine."

I wasn't sure at first where we were heading, because I wasn't paying attention, but when I sat up and started noticing, I saw that we going through the new developments toward Rolling Meadows. Ceci's house was half of a new duplex, and when we got inside and she turned on the lights, everything looked brand new. There was hardly any furniture, and you could still smell the paint. Ceci asked me if I wanted some coffee, but I said no thanks, because I actually hated coffee, and the idea of the hot acidy taste of coffee in my mouth right then almost made me sick on the spot. I asked her if she had a Coke or a ginger ale or something, and she got me a Coke out of her refrigerator. She got a bottle of Jim Beam bourbon from out of a cupboard, and mixed herself a glass of bourbon and Coke. She said she thought it might be nicer out back, so we went out into her little yard where there were some lawn chairs on a brick patio. I was pretty thirsty, and the cold Coke tasted good, but almost right away things started swirling again. Ceci pointed up to all the stars and was saying how amazing they were, but I almost couldn't look up at them because they made the swirling worse. I lost track of what happened for awhile, except Ceci said she wanted to go in and get a sweater or something, and then her phone rang, and I could hear her talking to someone for a pretty long time. When she came back outside, I had finished my Coke and didn't think I felt too bad, as long as I didn't move. Ceci had on a sweat shirt that zipped up the front, and I didn't think anything about it until she turned around a little, and the porch light caught the metal in the half zipped up zipper, and I could see most of the white mounds of one of her breasts. She didn't have anything on under the sweatshirt. As weird as I was feeling, I was also starting to get excited. Ceci kept talking to me in a normal way and didn't seem to mind that her front was practically unzipped. I really did not want to feel sick, and I did not want to sound thick-tongued when I talked, and I tried hard not to. I actually started talking about everything I could think of. I tried to get her going again on living in France and on seeing the world, but every now and then I'd start a sentence out in some direction, and it would just stop and hang there. At one point Ceci was leaning down in front of me, patting me on the head and saying I should probably be getting home. I was looking right into the bony space between her breasts. Whatever happened, I didn't want to go home yet. I started talking up a storm again. I asked her if I could have another Coke, and as she got up to get it, I asked her if I could try a little bourbon in it. She laughed and said, "Jonathan, I've ruined you."

Ceci could not have known how happy it made me to have her say that. When she came back with our drinks, she sat down at the foot of my chair, and we started talking again and having the best time. We talked about music and what each of us liked, and I got onto finding my uncle Desmond's Cab Calloway records and how great they were, and I was singing her my imitation of "Minnie the Moocher," which really made her laugh. We must have been getting a little loud, because she was shushing me every now and then and talking in an exaggerated whisper. We got onto certain people at the Press, and I was imitating some of them, and that cracked her up even more.

It had to be really late, past midnight. Ceci brought the bottle of bourbon out to the patio and every now and then she would add a little bit to our Cokes. I don't remember feeling especially bad. I just wanted everything to keep going. I wanted to keep coming up with things that would make her laugh, and every time I caught a glimpse of her breasts in the unzipped part of her sweat shirt, it was like something inside my own chest was opening up and wanting to shout. I really had to pee again, but when I tried to get up from the lawn chair, I almost couldn't do it. I said, "*Whoa,*" and sat down again. Now my head was really spinning. Ceci looked at me and said, "Oh boy, Jonathan, you're wrecked, aren't you." She picked up our glasses and the bourbon and said she was going into the kitchen and make coffee.

Chapter Twenty-Five

Now something really serious was happening to me. All my thoughts were mixed up, but I knew I couldn't stand to have any coffee or even to look at coffee. Whatever happened, I had to be by myself. I stood up by my chair, and I almost fell over. It was worse than being just dizzy. I felt like I was being twirled around by some force, but the force was lopsided, and it wanted to throw me down on one side. No good was all I could think or picture. *No good no good no good.* I don't know if I was thinking it or saying it, but I knew I had to get out of there. I moved out into Ceci's dark yard, and I fell down to one side. I got up and tried to get farther away, and I fell down again on the same side. My balance was really screwed up. I got up and kept moving through the dark yards until I came to a big bank of bushes. I got down on my knees and started crawling through the space between them at the bottom. When I got through to the other side, I knew I was safe from Ceci and the coffee, but when I stood up, the lopsided swirling started and I threw up.

I didn't throw up very often, and I really hated it when I did, but this was nothing like having the flu in my room at home. It came flying out of me, and it made a sound in my head like when you were standing under the elevated train tracks in Chicago and a train was going over you. I remember not knowing if something like that could kill you or not, but it didn't matter, because nothing was going to stop it.

I actually threw up a bunch of times, mostly the pizza, and some of it got on my shirt and my pants, but I didn't mind. I just wanted the gassy swirling to stop and for whatever was going to happen to me to happen. I heard Ceci calling my name from her yard. I could tell she didn't want to make it too loud, and I moved a few lawns farther away. I was pretty sure I knew where I was, but I needed to get out to the street so I could figure out the best way to walk home. I was moving along somebody's driveway in the dark when I saw a car's headlights coming from the left, and I slid down the side of the house on my butt. The car turned out to be Ceci in her Volkswagen. She was driving really slowly, and all her windows were open. I could tell she was looking around for me. I hunched down close to the house until she was gone. When I got up and started going down the sidewalk, I thought I'd just keep walking along whatever street I was on until I saw something familiar. I tried to remember the way Ceci drove us through the developments to her house, and I figured I was a mile or two out into what used to be the fields beyond Nana and Papa's house. I actually don't know what I was thinking, I just had the idea that if I kept moving, I'd get to something, but I was also feeling terrible. I walked over to the curb where there was a sewer grate and threw up again. I decided to sit down on the curb, which felt a little better, but I saw another set of headlights coming up, and I didn't have the energy to get up.

    I was sure it was going to be Ceci, but it wasn't. It was a man and a woman, and they stopped a few feet in front of me, rolled down their windows and asked me if I was all right. I told them I was fine. I told them I was just taking a rest. I don't know how normal I sounded. The guy backed up a little so that I was lit up in his headlights. He could probably see the mess down the front of my shirt. He asked if I was sure I was all right and did I want him to take me somewhere. I said no, I was fine. What I really needed to do was get up and start walking again, so that they could see that everything was okay and I was just a guy walking down the street, but I couldn't do it. They stayed where they were for a long time, with their headlights in my eyes. Finally the car clunked into gear and they drove away really slowly, but I could hear them talking in the car, and I heard "help" and "call the police." I knew I had to get out of there and get away from the street.

I tried hustling a little, but I was too clumsy to run, and even trying to made me feel like throwing up. This wasn't good. I might have gone a block or two, looking ahead and over my shoulder for headlights, when I saw the big arc lamps of one of the new schools shining over the tops of the houses. I knew where all the schools were, and once I got there I could figure out where I was and how to get back home. The lights turned out to be farther away than I thought, and I had to slip between houses and throw myself down on the ground a few times when I saw a car coming. The school turned out to be the new elementary school, which meant I was only about a mile from Nana and Papa's, if I could get the direction right. It didn't feel good walking past the school because the arc lamps were even brighter than the street lights, and I knew I'd be easy to spot. So I crossed the playground and took a gravel path behind some service garages, where there were some scrubby vacant lots with what looked like high grass and skunk cabbage. I was far enough away from the lights so that it was mostly dark, and I could relax a for a minute. I sat down in the grass and tried to think. Crickets and peepers were screaming in my ears, and I got the strongest feeling that I was back in the fields, or at least where the fields used to be, and even though I was still pretty lost, something felt good. There were a few more empty lots in front of me, and it looked like they came to an end at the back yards of a row of new houses, but everything was pretty dark, and in the mixed up way I was picturing things, I thought that maybe if I kept going straight into the empty lots, they might take some kind of turn and keep going until they opened up to the rest of the fields. I don't know if I really believed it, but I wanted to.

I walked straight into the long dark grass, and I could feel it pulling at my shoes and the cuffs of my pants. It was so dark I couldn't really see where I was going, only the street lights in front of the houses up ahead. Then all of a sudden I stepped down something steep, lost my balance, and I was on my hands and knees in cold muck. It was some kind of ditch with a big puddle at the bottom, but it was more like a swamp, because when I stood up my loafers were completely under the muck, and when I tried to step out of there, one of them came off and was gone. By getting on my hands and knees I managed to crawl back up the bank of the ditch, but I couldn't keep going to the end of the lots without getting stuck in the swamp again. I stood there for awhile looking around, and I could see that there was no opening to any fields. There were just back yard fences and, behind me, the elementary school.

I stumbled back to the schoolyard, and in the light, tried to scrape some of the black muck out of the cuffs of my pants. I walked along the sidewalk for awhile with just one shoe, but it felt terrible, so I took off the other loafer and threw it into somebody's yard, somebody who was going to find a muddy shoe in the morning and wonder what was going on.

I knew if I kept walking down the street in front of the school I'd end up at an intersection I knew in the old part of town, and I'd be at the end of Nana and Papa's street, and I could be home in about five blocks. My socks were cold and soaking wet, and the bottoms of my feet were starting to feel pretty raw, but I thought it would be even worse if I took them off and went barefoot. I couldn't really think about it because something changed in my stomach, and I started feeling sick in a completely different way. My mouth and my throat were still sour and horrible tasting from all the throwing up, and I was burping up gas about every three steps, but now my stomach actually hurt, like somebody was holding onto it and squeezing it tight. Every now and then it hurt so much I had to stop and double over. It was like the cramps from diarrhea, but higher up in my stomach, and when it got to a certain point I had to throw up again, but after a few times almost nothing came up, except about a spoonful of the sourest, worst stuff I'd ever tasted. It looked dark to me, and I hoped there wasn't blood in it, and that I wasn't going to die.

I thought I was going to have to walk a mile or so along that street through the developments, but it seemed to go on forever, and when I looked ahead, trying to make out a traffic light or some sign that I was getting somewhere, all I saw was more of the same kind of street lights and more of the new brick houses and the lines of skinny new trees. It also slowed me down to keep turning around to see if any cars were coming from the other direction, because I didn't want to get picked up and taken home and have everybody start into me before I could even talk or think. There were a few cars, including one that had to be either a police car or a cab, and each time I spotted one, I had to duck up somebody's drive way into their back yard and lie down in the dark until they were gone. My feet were raw, my knees and hips hurt from walking, and I was getting the feeling that my stomach cramps were never going to stop. I couldn't really think. I couldn't make actual plans and pictures of what might be going on at home or what was going to happen to me. Only one thing at a time would come into my mind, and it would be a single word or maybe just a phrase which I'm pretty sure I kept repeating out loud. Sometimes it was *shit-faced, shit-faced,* sometimes it was *half-wit, half wit,* sometimes it was *Spirit of Palatine, Spirit of Palatine.* It could have been anything. The main thing I felt as I was walking along, probably because I hurt so much from so many different places, was that I was turned inside out, so that my guts and muscles and veins were out there touching the air.

I'm sure if somebody would have stopped me and tried to talk to me, I wouldn't have been able to answer them, or I would have said something completely stupid in my thick-tongued voice. But even though I knew that, some part of me was completely aware of everything, just the way I felt when I was looking down at myself talking to Ceci at Bob Laski's party, and the part of me that was watching wasn't sick or drunk, but perfectly calm. I'm pretty sure that part of me could have watched me die. Throwing up the dark, sour stuff made me think about dying a little, but not in a way that scared me, more like: oh great, and now along with everything else, you're going to die. As a matter of fact, I don't think I was afraid at all. The feeling was more like a huge sadness, a sadness I couldn't believe would ever end, a feeling of being too sad to cry, or maybe I was crying, but crying in, not crying out.

Something was wrong, because it didn't seem like the street I was walking down was ever going to end and I was going to be walking through the developments forever. When I finally did get to the old part of town, I wasn't anywhere near Nana and Papa's house. I was way across town in the ritzy neighborhoods where Patsy Prentiss lived. I was glad I knew where I was, but I also knew I was about mile and a half from my house. I didn't think I was even headed there, but all of a sudden I was standing in front of Patsy's house. They had a big front porch with white pillars, and even though I could see a light on in the front hall, I was sure there would be nobody home. They would be up on their island, if they still went there. After Patsy got in her big trouble at school, I heard her parents sent her away to a boarding school somewhere, and nobody ever saw her around after that. I hadn't thought about her for a long time, but standing in front of her house and looking at the way the lights around their swimming pool were making wavering blue shadows in the trees, I started picturing her and the way we used to play and how much I liked her. I pictured us lying skull to skull in the cold straw that afternoon when I got home so late. I pictured her smiling at me across the table at June's, her white teeth and her sun tanned cheeks and looking like all she wanted to do was have fun.

Something clicked in my brain, and I got a terrible feeling, a kind of jolt. I slapped my back pocket, and then I knew it. My wallet was gone. It must have fallen out in the ditch or one of the yards. I kept slapping my pockets, even though I knew it wasn't there. It had all that money in it, about three hundred dollars, which was ridiculous, and I started thinking that maybe the reason I loaded up like that was so that I'd lose it, as some kind of lesson. But the money didn't bother me as much as just losing the wallet. I started picturing what was in it, my driver's license, my social security card, and my old school I.D., and it felt like I had lost my name, who I even was. Then I remembered something worse. Behind my license and my cards were my two pictures of Patsy and Annabel. They were just old school pictures, the smallest ones that came with your packet, from fifth grade. I only looked at them two or three times a year, but they were really important. They made me feel like I still had a little bit of Patsy and Annabel the way they were back then. Patsy's hair was kind of messy in the picture, and her front teeth looked slightly too big, but it was definitely the way she looked when we were in Mr. Click's class before she grew up and changed. Now the picture was gone, and I knew I wasn't going to get that feeling back.

It was the same with Annabel's picture, which was so cute and so sad I could never stand to look at if for too long. She was in seventh grade, and I thought she looked really beautiful with her dark page boy and dark eyes and the expression like something bad was probably going to happen. That picture being lost made me feel like Annabel wasn't just away at the Special Care Facility, but that she was gone forever, just as if she were dead. It made me cry out loud, and I couldn't help it. I started walking toward our house, blubbering about my wallet, saying *my god damned wallet* over and over and not caring if anyone heard me.

As I got closer to our street, I knew I better start making a plan, but my thoughts were too mixed up to do it. I stopped throwing up, but the cramps still came along in waves. I knew I was a mess and that I was in tremendous trouble, but I couldn't focus on anything particular, like actually walking in the front door and having to say something to my father and mother. I never thought it out, but I guess I hoped they would be asleep and I'd get in the house somehow and get in my bed before they woke up. Then whatever happened could happen, but I didn't want to have anybody looking at me or saying things to me while I still felt so dizzy and sick, especially when I knew I couldn't talk right. The sky was lightening up a little to a kind of grayish green, and every now and then a car would back out of a driveway with its lights on and drive off, which probably meant that some people were going off to their jobs already. I thought it might not look too strange for a guy to be walking down the sidewalk now, but if anyone actually got a look at me, they'd see how filthy I was and that I was slogging along in my socks, so I decided to play it safe by going the last two blocks through people's back yards, which I still knew by heart.

Besides hurting so much, I was also getting really tired. It seemed like a huge effort to climb over people's chain link fences, and one of them had sharp wires at the top, which I didn't realize until I tried to jump down, and it caught my pocket and sleeve and ripped everything. If a yard had fences, I started having to sit down for a while to rest. The birds were peeping and chirping now, and the sky was turning the bushes and trees a silvery color, which made everything look like a completely different world, but at least I could finally see where I was going. The house next to ours was the Thomas's, and they had a pretty big spread in the back with fruit trees and a bunch of separate gardens, and it seemed like a good place for one final rest before I went home. They had an old hammock strung up between a tree and the back of their garage, and I lay down in it and rested until it stopped swinging back and forth. I could see the second floor of our house over the tops of their bushes, and when I saw that the lights were on, I felt terrible. No one was going to be asleep. All I wanted to do was lie still and rest, but I knew I had to start thinking, start making a plan. But I couldn't. The only thing I decided was to lie there until it got completely light out. I wanted whatever happened to take place on a new day.

I must have slept, and slept really hard, because when I woke up there was bright sunshine, and I was all cramped up in the hammock. It felt like my knees were never going to be able to bend, and the only way I could get out of the hammock was to fall out. As rotten as I felt, I realized right away that my mind was back, that I was thinking in my regular way. I sat there for a minute in the grass making my plan. I knew I had to get up in a minute because I didn't want the Thomases coming out and seeing me and wondering what was going on. I got up and stretched, and I saw a garden hose attached to a faucet coming out of the foundation at the back of the Thomas's house. I was tremendously thirsty, and I wanted a drink of cold water more than anything. Even if it woke up the Thomases, I had to get a drink. I turned on the faucet and picked up the nozzle of the hose just as the water came out, and it practically knocked my head off. My face and my shirt were soaked before I turned the pressure down, and then I drank what must have been quarts of cold water. It felt like I couldn't get enough of it into my sour throat and down into my stomach.

I wiped my mouth and stood up and then practically started laughing. I couldn't believe it. Something about all that water was giving me the swirly feeling again. I started picturing myself staggering home like a drunken idiot in the movies. It was completely clear. It wasn't going to be okay, and nothing was going to work out right. It was going to be worse than anything I could imagine when I got home. No one would know why I stayed out all night or what happened to me and why I looked this way, and I wasn't going to able to explain, and when I did, it was going to be worse than they thought. And then it hit me: I had no excuse. I had no explanation. I had done everything wrong you could. I got drunk, I got lost, I lost my shoes. I lost my wallet, I lost the fields, I lost Patsy and Annabel. I wrecked my clothes, I threw up all over myself, and I had vomit and pizza and pond muck all over me. The clothes in my room weren't really mine. They were just a bunch of stuff from Parnell's I spent so much money on my father would scream if he knew. The clothes were just a cover up and couldn't change the way I was. Yale was just a bunch of pictures and didn't connect at all to anything about me, and the kid in all the activities who got all the prizes, The Spirit of Palatine, was the kid who just sprayed himself with a hose and was standing in the Thomas's driveway in his stretched out socks, me. Not only that, I didn't have anything to say. I stopped having anything to say when I couldn't get into the other world anymore, when school and all the things to do crowded the other world right out of my mind, the way the developments crowded out the fields. I didn't have anything to say since Patsy got so tall and my love feeling didn't have anywhere to go and *Lower* started taking over. Not only didn't I have anything to say, I didn't have anything, period. I actually *was* nothing, which, believe it or not, was a tremendous relief. Because now it felt just fine to walk down the Thomas's driveway and go home. I was nothing, and so there was nothing to cover up.

When I turned onto our front walk, I saw that our car was parked in front of the house, and my father was carrying my suitcases and stuff out to the curb. It hadn't occurred to me that they would be getting ready to take off even if I wasn't home. Mother came down the front steps and they talked for a minute. I couldn't believe they hadn't seen me yet. I was standing right there on the sidewalk maybe twenty yards away from them. Then they did see me. Mother had a terrible, scared look as she walked over to me. She said, *"Jonathan!* Are you all right? *Where on earth have you been?"* I thought I was in better shape than I actually was. My head was still spinning a little from the water, and I couldn't make any words come out. The closer she got to me, the more scared she looked, and I really wanted her not to come any closer, because I looked and smelled terrible. She came right up to me and was going to put her hands on my shoulders but she pulled back. She said, "Jonathan? Jonathan, are you *drunk?"* I felt terrible for her, but I still couldn't say anything. "Frank," she said to my father, "he's *drunk.*"

If there was anything I could have done to make her feel better, I would have done it. I wished I could tell her that I had been drunk already and now I was better and it was just the water. I wished I could tell her how good it felt to know that I was just what I was, nothing. What I really wanted to tell her was that I loved her so much, and that I knew we were going to have to say good-bye. But all I could do was feel it. What I said to her, finally, was "I'm sorry, I'm very sorry."

She started telling me all the things that had happened overnight, all the calls and everything people had done to try to find me, but she lost track and turned back to my father and told him she had to go in and call people to say I was home.

My father had not come toward me. He was still standing at the open door of the car with his arms folded in front of his chest. He seemed different. I certainly felt different. For one thing, I wasn't afraid of him. I wondered what he would say to me, and I even wondered if he would hit me, but I wouldn't have minded, except that I knew it would make him feel bad. I still had the calm, sweet feeling of knowing I was nothing, and the relief of not having to pretend anything. I could feel him looking at me, but I didn't know what he was thinking. If he was angry, he was being angry in a new, quiet way. I wished he didn't have to see what a filthy mess I was, but I decided to go over to him anyway. I wanted to tell him I loved him too, and that we were going to have to say good-bye, but I knew I would probably only say, "I'm sorry."

When I was close enough to touch him, I stopped and looked into his eyes. He looked right back at me. He looked at me for quite a while, and then he said, "Jesus Christ."

Book 2

Knowing It All

What a piece of work is a man! How noble in reason...
—Hamlet, II, ii.

If this young man expresses himself in terms too deep for me,
Why, what a very singularly deep young man this deep young man must be!
—Patience, Gilbert and Sullivan

Chapter One

THE REVELATION ARRIVED with no more force than just another idea. There were the words, ordinary words, something like, "Here it comes, here comes the rest of you," and then there was a feeling of something enormous and final breaking up in my chest, like the unloosing of an avalanche, and I could do nothing to stop it, even though I knew it could be the end of my life. For a few seconds I just sat still and felt it fall over me like charged particles.

I almost had to laugh. I felt I should be somewhere majestic and far removed, on a mountain top or on some desolate beach, at the very least alone in bed in the dark. But I was actually just where I was supposed to be, in the studio dressing room of the TV station in Atlanta, looking in the mirror. It occurred to me that all I could really do was to continue. In a few minutes I would be on the air, fielding my twelve minute segment of questions from the embalmed-looking beauty who was the hostess of Atlanta Today. Even before the revelation I could picture in advance exactly how our interview would proceed. I would have the simultaneous perspective of being seated in my upholstered chair on the sound stage facing my coifed and brightly lipsticked host while at the same time seeing myself on screen, the real color blanched from our faces by the bright lights overhead. She would be earnest and practiced, and I would sense beneath her immaculate surface the almost unbearable compression of her willed performance. My own countenance would also be a practiced imposture, unflappable, welcoming, agreeably willing to engage any question or challenge without a perceptible trace of condescension, which anyone who had read one of my books would know was the ultimate condescension.

For a second, but only for a second, I wondered if the revelation would carry me out of this coming business altogether, or distract me in a way that would make me appear inaccessible or maybe just odd to the viewers. But this would not happen. I had been visited in this powerful way, and I was about to be transformed, but for the moment I knew just how to proceed, how to embody and to guide Jonathan Force from room to room, moment to moment.

The producer who had greeted me and prepped me when I arrived at the studio rapped on the door of the dressing room and asked if I was ready. My interview would begin in ten minutes. I told her I needed about sixty seconds, although I did not really need time or anything else. I wanted a moment more of quiet, to say a kind of all-being amen to what had just occurred, to be able, in full consciousness, to project myself into my time after the interview, after Atlanta, and into everything that would now open up to me.

I was looking at myself in the mirror, musing, as I liked to do, on what others saw when they saw me, what in this case the viewers of Atlanta Today would see on their bright screens. I actually don't like looking at my face in the mirror, although at the same time I am drawn to it, to the looking, not to my face, which I usually manage to notice only obliquely, as if it were possible to look through the image directly in front of me. I can usually manage to look past my face straight into my eyes, and what I see is a bemused, knowing sort of man's face, a countenance almost guilty about what it is feeling and knowing, but not at all apologetic. My face in the mirror confirms a kind of conspiracy with myself, a conspiracy, if I had to name it, to continue being the self behind the face, the elusive, tricky self that has been concealed there, deftly dodging and feinting among the tangle of others.

But at the moment I am content to take in my features. Nicely framed by a full, almost exuberantly healthy head of hair, my face looks all right to me under the penetrating lights over the mirror. At fifty eight, I am graying in a way that pleases me, but the image I see reflected remains that of a dark man. My brows are dark, my eyes are dark, the faintly submerged pattern of my facial hair is dark. Nose is prominent but good. The sun from my stops in Miami and Naples is still in my cheeks, and my color is good.

I usually have a hard time looking at my mouth, because the very act of looking makes me want to do something with it, try on an expression, but that always looks effortful and false. The only alternative I can come up with looks like a smirk, which has the effect of making me feel embarrassed, which is when I usually look away. But as I get up from the mirror, my lingering impression is that I look pretty good. For just a second I can see myself on camera. It's going to be fine.

Mercy, the producer who prepped me, was waiting outside the dressing room door. She walked me down the corridor to the sound stage where the pretty host of Atlanta Today was talking to the police officer who had, just the day before, talked a deranged man into dropping his rifle and leaving an elementary school classroom, where he had been holding thirty children and two teachers hostage. We could see and hear the exchange between the host and the policeman clearly enough, but it was somehow easier to watch it on the monitor where, in its framed and brightened unreality, it seemed more real. I found myself liking the officer, who was soft spoken and rather formal. He repeated the protocols of his training for dealing with volatile and violent situations. He seemed to have no malice or negative feelings of any kind about the armed intruder. He would reassure viewers that their children were going to be safe and that they were going to be safe.

Mercy was saying something to me, reminding me to answer the questions I would be asked in a sentence or two. She said too much elaboration didn't work on television. I told her I would do my best, but I also laughed a little and said I had trouble being a man of few words. She smiled and told me she was sure I would be fine. She didn't have to tell me. I knew I was going to be fine, also that I was not going to make an effort to confine my responses to a sentence or two. Over the past twenty

251

five years I have done more than a hundred television spots, and I now know exactly what I want to accomplish and how I am going to proceed. I know, for instance, that nothing I actually say will convey as much as what kind of presence I project. I also know that a viewer's perception of anything on television is primarily a perception of format. Television programs, especially news and interviews, are so indelibly formatted in viewers' minds, that it is nearly impossible for them to think critically about the format and how it is shaping and limiting what they are hearing and seeing. Instead they think *with* the format, and for that reason television has the powerfully denaturing effect of reducing novelty, complexity, trouble, conflict and even wonder to the narrowly confined mental territory allowed by format.

Truth be told, I know how to be interesting on television. I know that the first thing I will do is to establish a warm receptivity and a deep courtesy to my host and to all other participants in the exchange. But even as I do this, I will not deliver what is expected. I will not answer the questions as the host, with telegraphic clarity, assumes I will. I will use my own language and my own constructions of thought in response, even if they do not pick up any of the cues implicit in what I am asked. In no more than a minute, the discussion will begin proceeding on my terms, possibly quite engaging terms, but almost certainly discontinuous with the interview format. I will of course not acknowledge or even imply what has almost always been the case with my interlocutors, whether major network superstars or lesser lights from regional stations-- which is that they have not even glanced at, much less read, my work. The reading and research into the invited guest's topical work is done by off-camera staff like Mercy who write potted summaries and work up questions for the telegenic on-screen host. A nimble interviewer can be led off script and follow a line of thought into unexpected territory, which for me is always a welcome pleasure, but I have learned to be sure I am the one setting the trajectory for what is under discussion which, after all, is my work and my books.

In kind of a zen-ish way I have made television and other media work for me, and again, what works best is to elude format, which is in effect to refuse television's protocols while still appearing now and again on television. I did not ask for television attention, and my initial aversion to appearing on it has also worked for me. I have become something very much like a celebrity, a "household word," at least for college educated types, but I have managed not to behave like a celebrity, nor has the public, even the interested public, gained any special access to my personal life. In fact I may have gained, without ever intending to, something better than celebrity. By being somewhat exposed in media, but by no means over-exposed, by being a cited authority and sometimes a viewable, hearable presence, but not in any predictable, media-driven rhythm, I have managed to interest people in what I say and write, even to unsettle them in a way that makes them want to know more.

Sometimes people's interest becomes urgent to the point that someone or other presses himself on me and my time in an inappropriate and unwelcome way, but that is the exception, not the rule. I have declined dozens of invitations to become a regular media pundit or a syndicated columnist. I have politely refused many requests to hold lofty scholastic posts from which I might sound off regularly to the educated and ordinary public. More critically, I have resisted socializing with anyone other than people I actually want to be with. All these things have helped me to realize that the achievement of true celebrity, at least in the United States and Europe, is the end of the vibrancy that is celebrity's cause. Even in the case of real talent and genius—which account for a tiny fraction of public celebrities—once the shell of celebrity is erected, the interesting part of the story is over. For that matter, what distracted soul waiting to have his or her groceries blipped and bagged at the supermarket check out line doesn't know, scanning the faces of the three or four divas of the hour on the tabloid covers, that their hour is now and forever passed? That their very celebrity will be their tomb? That familiarity breeds more than contempt, that it breeds prurient possessiveness and then, as in the case of someone like the aging Elizabeth Taylor or the unviewably defaced Michael Jackson, outright revulsion. Celebrity is not constructed on the subject's own terms, and for that reason it doesn't belong to them. It confines, diminishes, and finishes them, like flies caught in amber.

Little danger of that for me in a twelve-minute segment of Atlanta

Today, a segment which will perhaps surprise and unsettle some viewers, but in a way few would have expected when they switched on the set. With a commercial break approaching, I would soon be sitting in the policeman's seat, my microphone clipped to the back of my lapel. In my mind's eye I was already there, already feeling expansive, gracious. Of course it was a little peculiar that I had accepted this tour in the first place. The new book, *Uses of Force*, was doing well and getting plenty of attention, but the promotion department at Random House figured out that most of my sales were in the northeast, the west coast, and sizable northern cities in between. The south they believed was an untapped market. It probably was, but normally that would not have interested me. I have more than enough readers—and even more book buyers—and more money than I will ever need or use. But since I routinely refuse to go on standard author tours and signings (which also works for me) and now have Mary Marx, my agent, write that unwillingness into all contracts, it tends to evoke surprise and heated interest when I do decide to show up somewhere; thus this improvised little toot up through the southeast: Miami, Naples, Savannah, and Atlanta.

As I suspected, the papers made lots of room for me in their Arts and Living sections, and the regional network stations were eager to see me. And unless I misguess, the predictable good things will follow. Viewers who did not expect to see someone like me or to hear the kind of things I say will make a note to tell their friends, to tell their husbands. They will actually beam up Amazon.com or stop by their bookstore and find me. A few of the viewers will be teachers and professors, and they will become intrigued and get the book, and when they read it, even a chapter or two, they will like the simultaneous surprise of the arguments and what feels like a deep consonance with what they have always deeply known. They will order me for their classes and seminars. Some of the students will take the book or at least some of its arguments home, and on and predictably on it will go. Jonathan Force will have penetrated the south. I also wanted some sun.

When you relax and refuse to capitulate to big institutional forces, especially commercial ones, you see how mindless—and often mistaken—they are. Established institutions are the culture, and everything really alive and interesting is, at least at the onset, counter-cultural. The best thing you can do for your self is duck out of the mainstream, even as it is embracing you, and surprise everybody. Best of all, surprise them with something really good, a promise that delivers. Tell them the truth.

In attempting this very thing, I have been very fortunate in my agent, Mary Marx. When my first publisher found her and linked us up, both of us were green and untried. She was in her late twenties, a fairly anonymous non-partner in a big New York agency. She liked my work and told me frankly she couldn't believe her luck in getting hold of something she could honestly get herself behind. She also liked me, and I liked her, and I could be completely myself with her from the get-go. She is incorruptibly honest and shrewd and quirky. When my second book, *Force Fields*, was making a lot of money, her firm decided to try to outmaneuver her. Two of the partners, agents of the rich and famous, took me to lunch and explained they had big plans for me, and while Mary was a good girl, she hadn't agented really big projects and it would be a natural progression for me to move up into their level of operation. I smelled two huge rats and resolved to stick with Mary to the death. Her commissions on just my two books were at that time making her a comfortable New York salary, and together we figured that if she left the firm and represented me independently, she would do fine. Moreover, I would see that she prospered no matter what the agency did. So that is the way we have worked it, and I have never had to care about deals, advances, royalties, foreign publication and film rights, tours, pre-publication excerpts, speaking gigs, or really anything to do with the business side of writing and thinking, including the business of having an agent. And Mary actually likes that kind of thing and is very good at it. Mary sometimes feels to me like an extra self, but a dutiful one who does not resent, as I do, the business side of business.

AT ANY RATE, BETWEEN US, we've managed to cut an unusual but productive path through the commercial side of culture-making. Critics and reviewers like to describe me as "elusive," "continually surprising," even "iconoclastic"-- and once (pleasingly to me), as "occupying an Archimedean point outside all current discourse." And as it turns out, this is the kind of press that makes people want to read you. Moreover, critics and pundits begin to imagine all kinds of subtle and cunning things about you that keep you fresh—an object of interest but not quite graspable, still free of the celebrity cage. But of course nothing subtle or cunning is at work in the slightest.

At a lunch table or over the phone, Mary and I would share impressions about who and what we couldn't bear to watch on TV or the people and journals we least liked to read, and out of that our approach to "promoting" me evolved quite naturally. There would be no Entertainment Personality appearances, no Oprah, no Letterman, Jay Leno, or the even later night smart alecks, no appearances ever where the real agenda was to become an ornament or foil for anybody's commercial personality. With print media it's a little different because anybody can "cover" you, but our plan was not willingly to contribute to any paper or journal that wants to reduce you to its voice. No *Time,* no *Newsweek,* no *People,* no *Psychology Today* (even though I am a psychologist). No Sunday supplements, except the *New York Times Magazine,* provided the interviewer is someone you might actually enjoy contending with, like Deborah Solomon. Yes to NPR, yes to most people at *The New Yorker,* yes to *Harper's, The New York Times Book Review, The New York Review of Books.* Beyond that, we'd take it case by case, which results in mostly no's and a few yes's.

Being in the category of "Intellectual" and, increasingly, "Public Intellectual" entails a few distinctive pitfalls. Too much theory or even propositional logic at the wrong time and in the wrong places can be an offense to the human spirit. Any theorizing, however skillfully worked out, in favor of an ideological or political scheme quickly identifies you as a mere partisan, and your very eloquence becomes a suspect trademark. The last thing I would ever want, and Mary agrees, is to become anything like William F. Buckley. The guiding principles have been that I had to like the people I was going to deal with and that there was a good chance I would enjoy myself.

Mercy left my side to usher the policeman off the sound stage, and for a moment I was standing alone under a studio monitor blaring advertisements for arthritis medicine, big-wheeled trucks, and for the station itself. In a moment a technical assistant would seat me in the upholstered chair and test my microphone. Margot Tower, the host, was distracted, listening to something from a tiny plastic receiver just behind her ear. Perhaps it was about me. It was time to get the idea of me into her head, to remember and focus on who I was. Once on the air, she would need to establish my public position and the occasion for my being there. She would introduce me as a well known psychologist whose ideas had made a stir. She would say the stir began with my first book, *The Force Factor*, which offered a new explanation for what motivated people and organizations to behave the way they did. She would add (from the promotional copy the station had been sent) that *The Force Factor* and my subsequent books have made an impact on businesses and social services, and more recently on government organizations, including both national political parties. Margot Tower would know that my ideas were considered "controversial" and "challenging," but she and the research staff that prepared her interview questions would not be able to identify any specific point of controversy or any current practice challenged by my ideas. In effect, she faced the same problem most of the print reviewers and critics faced when they tried to summarize my work—critics who, unlike Margot Tower, had plenty of time to read, digest, and consider.

 The difficulty was not simply in understanding what I was saying. I am widely acknowledged to be a clear, accurate, and highly readable writer. Nor is there the kind of confusion and dissonance that result from discussing, as brilliant cosmologists like Stephen Hawking do, dimensions of experience few people ever think about in terms few people know or use. In my case, the experiences discussed—the behavior of ordinary people in familiar situations—pose no problem, and while the deep causes of behavior I propose are unexpected, nearly all my readers, including my most penetrating critics, claim to see the truth of what I say. But the inevitable attempts to reduce my observations to a formula always miss the mark. A statement like "In essence Force is telling us that every conscious activity, including shared social activity, is generated by the very opposite of what the agents are consciously thinking"-- published in the scholarly journal *Mind* by one of the greatest minds in contemporary philosophy -- is both a clear misreading and unhelpful to those seeking to understand what I am up to. (The misreading, incidentally, lies in saying I believe people are motivated by "the opposite" of what they think and do. My point, clearly and repeatedly made in my books, is that motivation resides in that thing or those things of which the agent is *least aware*. "Least aware" is by no means always "opposite".)

But such distinctions will only befuddle Margot Tower in her mission to make some kind of sense of me to the viewers of Atlanta Today. Her problem at the moment is like that of the editors who assign books to their paper's Best Seller Lists. There is no question that Jonathan Force is Non-Fiction, but am I Self-Help? (Mary and I have done everything possible to keep me out of Self-Help.) Am I Psychology? Philosophy? I can live with either—but I can also, and perhaps even preferably, live with being uncategorizable, which seems to work for me.

Margot Tower has now taken me in. She has leaned over and shaken my hand. She really is very beautiful, in a sculptural way. Her chin and the sharp, strong bones of her jaw line are striking. Her eyes are dark and bright under the studio lights. She has a wide mouth, full lips, good teeth. She is genetically lucky, a thoroughbred, and she knows it. I can tell already she is not sure about me, but she is willing to contend. I like her already. Together we listen to the voice counting down the seconds till air time, and then she sits up straight and says, "My guest this afternoon is Jonathan Force. Doctor Force is a psychologist and a writer whose ideas have caught the attention of the American public in a way that may be unprecedented. His ideas are very challenging, yet he is widely and enthusiastically read. His work has been compared to that of such luminaries as Margaret Mead and Marshall McCluhan. His most recent book, *Uses of Force*, has just been published, and he is here today to tell us about it. Welcome, Jonathan Force."

I thank her for having me, and she says, "Doctor Force, many people, even experts, have a hard time summarizing your findings. Is it fair to say your main point is that none of us really knows what we're doing, however much we think we do?"

I like this very much, and I laugh—and see myself laughing on the monitor in front of me, which I also like. "Well," I say—and notice Margot has also lightened up—"that's partly fair, but not really the whole story. It's not quite right to say that none of us know what we're doing. Right now you know what you are doing. You are asking me questions. And I know what I am doing. I am answering them. In our capacity to think, just as you are thinking right now, lies our capacity to know, but I am less interested in what we think and what we think we know than I am in what is actually motivating us to do what we think we are doing." I know I could pause here and let Margot proceed to the next question typed onto the sheet in the clipboard on her lap, but I go on. There are ten or eleven minutes left, and I will teach the viewers one thing.

"Let me explain. I have now been talking for about a minute or so, in pretty complicated sentences, about thinking and knowing. But as I was saying those words and sentences, I was not consciously laying them out in advance, telling myself something like, 'Okay, now I am going to say: 'Well, that's pretty fair, but not really the whole story.' I did say that, but the words came out without any conscious thinking or planning at all. But -- if I am not planning those thoughts, who or what is?" I pause again, but not long enough for Margot to respond. "And when you take that question seriously and try to find out, what you find is the very last thing you would expect…"

259

Chapter Two

I KEPT THE REVELATION at bay during the cab ride to the airport and through all the protocols of security and check-in. I wanted to wait until I was aboard the plane and sitting back in the dark confinement of the cabin. It is strange how that is possible—to form a kind of mental barricade between present business and urgent soulful messages. It must be how people in love affairs feel as they move through the practical business of their days. The beloved is the important thing, the real thing. She is out there somewhere, waiting for you or waiting for your call, but you mentally bracket that reality, even savor it, as you carry out life's immediate routines.

As it happened, I was even luckier than I thought. The plane to Chicago was practically empty. Even after a few passengers were upgraded to first class, no one took the seat next to me. Were I not about to give myself up to the revelation, I would have ordered a whiskey or two because, although I am generally a moderate drinker, I find the warming fuzz of alcohol a welcome pleasure when I am in dreamy semi-recline high above the earth. We were still taxiing on the ground when, reflexively leafing through the flight magazine, I was not really surprised to see an article about me or, more precisely, what my ideas implied for frequent fliers: "Force on Flight—Why We Take to the Skies." The article was prominent but short, and my jacket photograph from *Uses of Force* was set into the first column of text. I scanned down the columns to see if I was quoted, which I was, twice, both passages from a subchapter of *Force Fields* in which, glancingly, I had indeed discussed air travel. My words, as quoted, pleased me, and the conclusion the article's author drew — that a persistent desire or even willingness to fly invariably masks an obsession with unfinished business on the ground, that more than anything else, the flier is striving to be grounded — was by no means fatuous. That was what I said, but the writer wanted it to be all about escape, which is not really what I meant. I hoped I would remember to ask Mary if the magazine did right by the permissions.

    I was ready now, ready to readmit the revelation. I reclined my seat, closed my eyes, and opened myself to it the way you would open a door to an insistent messenger who has come to you to tell you nothing less than your destiny. I mentally restated the propositions that would call up the message. I pictured myself back in the television studio dressing room. Readying myself for the interview, I was musing on the Force Factor, what people made of it, how I had succeeded in applying its logic, or whatever it is, to so many different personal and social conditions. Thinking about these things made me picture myself as the celebrated author of an undeniably great idea. I thought of people hearing me and reading me and thinking, whether with reverence, suspicion, or resentment, that I had unloosed something incalculably great, something that was not going to be extinguished or supplanted by subsequent findings, something that could well inspire or deflate or possibly just inform their lives, but above all something that was not going to recede with the times or disappear. Having done that had made me a kind of god — maybe not a god, maybe just a wizard, maybe just a lucky trickster who had happened onto an amazing trick that turned out not to be a trick at all, but the truth itself. But the truth itself—and here the revelation passes through me like a current—is not something I possess, although I have sensed it, attempted to handle, shape and play with it, but it isn't mine. It's as if I learned how to point it like a hose or a gun in the direction of something I don't yet understand, and then I understand it. But I don't *have* it and have never had it. It has me. It is holding me this minute. Which means that I can ask: what is the Force Factor of me? What is this driving, essential reality of which I am so deeply unaware that I cannot even access the effort to deny it? If I have the courage and humility really to ask these things and to follow through, I know, especially at my age and at my rather lofty public stature, that I am likely to be annihilated. I know at very least that I will be thoroughly diminished and debunked.

I know this because my own carefully worked out Method, if I apply it to myself, would begin by establishing what Jung would call my *persona*, my consciously available self, and holding it up to the light. There clearly displayed, as if hung up on clothes pins, would be my hard won, defining qualities. Primary among them is my disciplined intellect, my logical, observational gift for attaching thing to thing, concept to concept, not just stringing propositions together to make coherent, pleasing theory, but also seeing the consonance and dissonance of whole theories with other theories—in sum, seeing the *fit* of things. But more than that: seeing the fit and, without smoke, mirrors, jargon or mud, *explaining* the fit, telling others, telling ordinary people what is going on. So what is that? You could call it a lot of things, but the simplest and most elegant is probably *discernment*. I have achieved discernment, not merely the kind of propositionally sound thinking that was once called philosophical but is now called scientific, but also discernment in the more feeling, intuitive sense, discernment like that of the mythological Metis or Goldilocks, who knew what was "just right."

But this is no hymn to my achievements and certainly no occasion for self-congratulation. The revelation proceeds. So what has generated such discernment, especially in so unlikely a prospect as Jonathan Force, formerly possibly the most wayward, erratic, headstrong and hapless little boy in Palatine, Illinois, a boy who, his father liked to pronounce, "got dumber every day." Here the picture begins—horribly-- to clear. My discernment as *compensation*, as *correction*. But as I have written, discerningly, such straightforward psychological reductionism does not really explain much, especially about motivation. Far more interesting, and still more devastating for me, is the question of what has driven my urge to compensate and correct. For discernment is, after all, a virtue, and what deep, dark reality in me needs to present itself to the day-lit world as a virtue?

If not the very "opposite" of the virtue, as the professor suggested in *Mind*, the Force Factor in me would be so far from virtue that one would not begin to know where to look for it. Now the revelation falls and falls. I don't need to reason further. I am not an elusive object of inquiry. I am the inquiring subject. I don't have to think, only to feel and to keep from putting up resistance. I need only to put it on cruise. And I will suffer. Or I could resist and deny, which will also lead to suffering, but more vaguely, assigning my wretched feelings to the wrong causes.

The answer is plain. The Force Factor of Jonathan Force himself, the agency operating most powerfully within, of which I have not for years been even faintly aware, the very existence of which I would have shrugged off without a regretful breath, is my boyhood, the teeming green and gold jungle of it, the heat of it, the sweetness of its desire, its yawning, beckoning opening up. Yes, my boyhood, more urgent than ever: being the boy I could not be and must never be again. How could I have given it up? How long could I have gone feeling so little, feeling, really, nothing, beyond what intelligent discernment let through the gate?

It's not a pretty story, the story of my imposture, cowardice, and final utter failure, but I think it is long past time to tell it. That book, if I write it, no one will buy, because of the suffering, and because it is true.

Chapter Three

I DO NOT KNOW anymore if I could locate the true heart of my boyhood. I call up only still images, like photographs or isolated frames of a movie, their very datedness and clarity a sure sign that they are wildly distorting everything pictured. There is the shot of my own face, my eyes frozen in shock as my father lands a skull-numbing "crack in the head" to the back of my scalp. Or I can see my sister, Annabel, looking up at me in wordless despair from where she is kneeling over her drawings of kittens scattered over the surface of the coffee table. Now, just for an instant, every picture is assumed up into one which seems almost to quiver and glow. Yes, this is familiar. This could never be submerged completely. I am eleven, standing alone before the black surface of the pond. Overhead is a dark canopy of sumac. The heat is prickly and alive. I feel it inside my skin. The air is charged with the shrill pulsing of crickets and peepers. I undo my belt buckle and then the top button of the baggy shorts and feel them fall down around my ankles. Either the humid air is passing through the skin of my bony ribs, belly and genitals, or the cells of my body are dissolving out into the air. The deep throbbing rises up the hard bone of my penis, and I give myself up to it, opening like a sweet fire to the world, swelling beyond anything I thought the world could be, all the while planted still and firmly into that world, each sopping sneaker an inch deep in muck.

Yes, there was that, but the first thing I can clearly recall, the first actual narrative I can recount and tell begins after the grown-ups office party at the paper where I worked as boy-reporter that summer after I graduated from Palatine High. Dazed and nearly willing to enter that world with its tables of booze and a promise of sex, I got drunk for the first (and nearly only) time, not just drunk but world-effacingly wrecked over the course of one whole night and dawn, staggering in my own toxic stink through the streets and parks of Palatine, Illinois, on my last night there as a boy, before leaving it more or less forever. Not a bad place to begin, actually—at the end.

So why don't I start at the very moment I had vomited or excreted every particle of boy-spirit into the gutters and shrubs of Palatine, realizing as I did so that everything else had to go, too. By sunrise, I had given up my mother, my father, my lovely, damaged sister Annabel, my angel friend Patsy Prentice and all prior loves. I gathered up my (embarrassingly inflated) notions of my talent and special knack for things and, along with all remembered prizes and public recognition, spat it all up. Then I bundled myself into the back seat of our old Ford Fairlane and over the course of two full days in which I cannot remember saying one thing to my parents in the front seat and numb to everything but the vaguely sickening forward motion of the car and the hum and buzz of the highway beneath the tires, made my bleary way to the Phelps Gate of Yale University. Here I would begin life again, but not as the boy I was.

LOOKED AT ONE WAY, ADMISSION to Yale was in hindsight a bit of a fluke, a consequence of dreamy high hopes of a kind hearted teacher or two who overvalued things I had managed to do— taught myself to play jazz piano, been funny in a school play, compulsively composed some poetry in the dead of night, made certain comments in class that seemed to rush out of my mouth at the urging of some unknown inner force. To that might be added the admissions office's guilty determination to include a few "different types" from heretofore unheard of public high schools.

But more than a fluke, it represented an imposture, something worse than an imposture on my part. I doubt that my maverick gestures at self-expression in the course of my school days at Palatine High would

265

have aroused much interest among my peers and masters in the seminar rooms and Performing Arts Centers at Exeter or Andover. The best and only thing I truly was in Palatine was a boy, an unschooled boy who wanted to burrow down to the world's secret tunnels, scale every rock face, locate the game beckoning just behind the routines and expectations of school and town and to play that game with the children I loved without any need to declare it.

I lost that boy, abandoned him in fearful, cowardly service of established expectations. I was able to do this because of the bewildering fact that everybody else--every other boy—was required to do it too, had apparently always been required to do it. Losing ourselves was expected, required, normative.

Was it because I resisted the surrender to the extent that I did, in some deep psychic recess holding onto it for dear life, that my particular passage into—what?—prize winner, most likely to succeed, etc., never quite convinced me? Is that why I puked it all up in the course of trying to find my drunken way back home the night before I got in the car to go to Yale?

The numbing truth of the matter was no solace. Evacuating from my system all the clutter and falsity of my "achievements" was no return to the golden world. There was no longer access. Without that, and now without my illusory prizes, I was just what I was: nothing. I wanted nothing, expected nothing, and for a month or two forgot what knowing things, what certainty felt like. I would enter my undergraduate studies at Yale in a condition reasonable observers might have considered something like idiocy.

I HAVE READ, AND I have been told, and I suppose I could actually talk knowingly about how Yale University was undergoing a radical transformation in the years just after President Kennedy was shot, but truth be told, when I arrived at Phelps Gate and peered inside to the interior courtyard and caught my first glimpse of the gray gothic dream world of Yale, I was fundamentally incapable of conceiving of anything so complex as a transformation. I could not really conceive of Yale, the whole thing or even the abstracted bits of it in which I would soon be playing out the days of my waning teens. In fact, as soon as the escarpments of the Appalachians erupted out of the farmland of eastern Ohio and western Pennsylvania, I lost my sense of particular place. I could not fit even familiar structures, like gas stations and turnpike signs, into a landscape continuous with what I had known. I had tried not to think much about college, but I had nevertheless formed a vague idea that Connecticut was older and smaller and fussier than Illinois, and that everything to do with the region and with Yale would be ornery and unto-itself. I did not know what Yale students or Yale teachers would be like, but I was absolutely certain they would not be like me or my family or anybody who fit into Palatine. Whatever they were like, I had a premonition it would manifest itself in subtlety. I decided things from now on would not be what they seem—a decision that probably enabled my improbable survival at the university and even more improbable success.

It seems impossible that I could have been aware that I was going off to college far from home and not to have thought once about what it would look and feel like and how I would live there. Perhaps my unacknowledged dread of it all allowed me this kind of denial. Even as we penetrated the city limits of New Haven and I realized that it was a substantial city and not a rustic village, I would not let myself project any images of what I would soon find and what would happen next. I doubt that I still could have been hung over after two full days on the road. I remember only my sheer, all-being passivity, a feeling of being not quite dead, but far from alive.

My father and mother stopped for directions several times before we pulled up to the entrance gate to the Old Campus where, mother had written down, my dormitory, Bingham Hall, was located. Although, as it turned out, we were parked quite a distance from Bingham, it was determined that we would unload my things right there at the curb. While we were hauling suitcases and boxes out of the open trunk, a tall shambling boy with mussed up hair asked my father if he knew where Bingham Hall was. My father said he didn't know but thought we were close. The boy was carrying a duffle bag in one hand, a scuffed up guitar case in the other. I wished he would move on, but he kept hanging around, assuming,

I suppose, that we would look for the dormitory together. He introduced himself to us as Chase Reading, and I shook his hand. He said he had just been dropped off by friends who had driven him there directly from some kind of outdoor concert in Virginia, and as he was explaining this, my first important impressions of Yale were formed: Yale kids didn't need their parents to drive them to the university. Yale kids perhaps didn't need parents. Yale kids did not feel awkward introducing themselves to people.

We made our way under the archway onto the shaded walkways of the Old Campus. Mother stopped to look at the statue of Nathan Hale, and I looked all around me at the settled stone facades of the gabled buildings, distant spires and a tall tower rising over the tree line. Yale, I knew, was going to be ancient, massive, and important, and I remember feeling a tremendous surge of fatigue. I heard myself mumbling, and I'm pretty sure anything I said was minimal and dim. When we finally got to Bingham, student guides checked us in and gave us my room key. I remember being glad that Chase Reading was on a lower floor and I was on the fifth, so he would stop talking to us, and I could go back into my cocoon.

Even if I had tried to picture my room, I would have been wrong. For one thing, it wasn't a room. It was a whole succession of rooms. The bright midday light made the woodwork framing the open doorways inside look heavy and dark. For a moment I could not make sense of the arrangement. I was expecting to see some kind of bedroom, perhaps a cell with a cot, but we had entered a spacious living room, with two dormered alcoves with windows looking out over the interior courtyard. There were chairs and a sofa arranged in front of a fireplace with a mantle. Doors on each side of the living room opened to a bedroom with a desk and a chair. There was something immediately pleasing about the bedrooms, and I realized that they too had dormered windows, shaping the walls and ceiling in a kind of complexity unfamiliar to me. My father said nothing, and my mother said, "Well!" And then, "There's certainly plenty of room." My assigned roommate had obviously not yet arrived, and since the bedrooms were identical, mother thought it would be all right to get settled in one of them right away.

It didn't take long to put my clothes in the bureau drawers and to hang up my jackets and slacks on hangers in the closet. Mother suggested we find somewhere close by and eat, and then they would make a start on the drive home. As we were leaving, she paused at the doorway and looked back into the rooms. I felt as if I were seeing through her eyes. These rooms were solid and well made. The ceilings were higher than ours were. My bedroom here was bigger than the one I had at home. I knew my mother, and I could feel her taking in the rooms where I would be living. She was feeling, already, that Yale was better than she had been able to be, and she would not be able to call up words for her sadness in leaving me there.

Chapter Four

It took me less than a day at Yale to realize that the first two things I needed to do were to learn to talk and to learn to eat. I had been in a kind of underwater stupor while my parents were with me, but as soon as they left I realized part of that heaviness was due to my being unable to fit the way my mother and father actually are into anything like college, much less Yale. Their awe of the place and the awkward lack of confidence it brought out in both of them served to elevate my own lack of confidence to an unbearable pitch. All I could do was shut down and get quiet and dull.

I shook my father's hand, hugged my mother and said good-bye to them in front of the Phelps Gate. I wasn't proud of myself for thinking it, but I couldn't banish the thought, as I watched them drive off into the New Haven traffic, that our Ford was a pretty terrible car. Up to that point in his life, my father had never bought a new car. The '59 Ford Fairlane was actually the newest used car he had ever owned. Even to my eye, it looked kind of silly with its sharp rear fins. It was also two-toned, which I happened to notice was getting pretty rare in cars. It was mostly a coppery color, but there was a white panel set into the sides, which made it look more like a taxi than a family car. Although I had not given it much thought before, the car was now embarrassing me. Looking at it as it drove off, the back of my parents' heads framed in the rear window, I felt relieved. I pictured the car and my parents inside getting smaller and smaller as they drove west.

When I got back up to my rooms on the fifth floor of Bingham, my roommate was there and had set himself up in the other bedroom. He introduced himself to me, a little formally and with the same easy confidence Chase Reading had demonstrated a few hours earlier. His name was Chad Pickering, and he was a slender, nice-looking boy, who, although outwardly friendly, seemed a little agitated. His skin was tightly drawn over the bones of his face, and there was very high color in his cheeks. He wore round glasses framed in dark plastic, which I thought made him look owlish and just right. He asked me where I went to school, and I told him, and he told me he went to Holderness, which I did not understand, but then he explained it was a private boarding school in New Hampshire. Chad Pickering told me he was a skier and that he had raced on his school's team. I could tell he wanted to talk about skiing and hoped that I might ski myself or know something about skiing or at least be interested in skiing, but I couldn't. I told him that I played a lot of baseball and that I also played the piano. He seemed nice about that. We talked a little about how we might set up the living room, and he asked if I minded his putting up some of his posters. I started feeling good for the first time since I got in the car to drive east. This boy I was going to share my living space with was all right. Someone had taught him a long time ago to be nice.

He reminded me of something I had read about and could not understand in the material Yale sent me, which was that in addition to being enrolled in Yale, we were also supposed to be members of a college inside Yale and that after our freshman year we would live and eat and do social things with the other members of our special college. Because the only way I could picture Yale was as a single place with a vague scattering of ancient-looking college buildings, I was unable to visualize yet another college inside of it, so the notion of membership in some inner "college" at Yale was utter fog. Chad explained that he and I and all the boys on our floor in Bingham were in Timothy Dwight College, which meant we'd all be living in the same cluster of buildings when we were upper classmen, and other kids would live in other colleges with different names. The concept would remain foggy to me until I actually went over to the Timothy

Dwight buildings a few times for meetings and talks, but I realized it was a terrific break to have a room mate like Chad who knew how to talk to a person like me. He said we were really lucky to be in Timothy Dwight, because it was one of the oldest and best colleges. I suppose Chad's telling me this should have made me feel good, or at least optimistic, but it actually made me feel anxious, because I still couldn't picture a ghost college somehow embedded inside the one I could see outside the window.

As I listened to him, I found myself fascinated by the way Chad Pickering talked, which was not quite like anything I had heard before. He had a way of delaying just a little before saying anything. It wasn't a silent delay. Rather, he would start out with a little pre-word groan, usually an *nnnnn* or *mmmm* or *uhhhh* sound, and then the words would come spilling out of that. So if I asked him something like was he going over to the Commons for dinner, he would say, "N*nnnnnn*ot quite yet, *nnnnn*I need to finish this chapter" or "M*mmmmmaybe* in fifteen minutes or so. *Mmmm*-can you wait?" I liked those pre-sounds. It made me feel Chad was vibrating at such a high frequency he had to adjust himself down to normal before he could begin communicating. The pre-hum also had the effect of making him seem to be thinking hard about things well in advance of any conclusion. Far from slowing him down, the pre-hum gave a slight sense of urgency to whatever he said. Over the years, I have heard a number of variations on this speech mannerism; in fact, it is a fairly common affectation among academics, but in Chad's case, it seemed to express perfectly his earnest approach to making himself understood. But on that first evening, my response to Chad's manner of speaking generated something like envy. This boy, as new to Yale as I was, had, besides his pleasing, owlish look, his own distinctive way of presenting himself. I had no such thing. Except for my tendency to talk a mile a minute when excited and—I would learn later—a decidedly Chicagoan pronunciation of certain vowel sounds—Chic*ahh*go—my speech was unremarkable. More than that, my bearing, my very *presence*, was unremarkable. My first fully formed realization at Yale was that Chad Pickering, along with many others, had presence, and I did not.

It took a few weeks, but I gradually figured out how to talk. It actually worked in my favor that I was so awkward and shy. I can't recall ever feeling so overwhelmed by everything as I was my first few days at Yale. It began with my very first evening meal at the Freshman Commons. For me, walking up the stone steps and passing between the columns into the Commons dining hall was like walking into the Supreme Court or the Senate. An enormous, coffered and cavernous place, the Commons sat over a thousand diners, the droning of their talk and the clinking of their silver rushing to meet me like surf. When too much of anything came at me in those days, I retreated inside and went—literally—dumb. It kept me from feeling anxious, but to anybody observing closely, it reduced me to almost complete ineffectiveness and stupidity. In that very state of mind, I followed Chad through the serving line, forgetting to take silverware, for some reason stuffing my pockets with many napkins, dully nodding yes to all the dinner offerings, so that I left the serving area with a plate piled preposterously high with scabby cutlets of veal, wedges of meat loaf, and chicken breasts slick with yellow gravy. Chad stopped briefly at another counter to pour himself glasses of lemonade and water, but I couldn't figure out how to free my hands to prepare the beverages while I was holding my tray, so I just stood there mutely until he was finished. When we reached a table, Chad remained standing and introduced himself to three or four other boys sitting across the table. They in turn introduced themselves to Chad and to me. I was already sitting down, looking at my food without comprehension. I realized that the other boys were waiting for me to say something to them. I looked up, completely bewildered, and said "thank you." I sat there for what seemed like a long time, hearing the talk around me as noise but not intelligible words. Then Chad said I needed some silverware, and I started reaching in my pockets, in some kind of confused hope that I would find an old knife or spoon, but produced only a lot of wadded up napkins. I stood up. I knew there was silverware in the serving line somewhere, but I didn't know if I would be allowed in the line twice. Stalled a few yards from our table, I stood motionless in the din for several minutes, not an idea in my head. Then I remembered the food on my plate and that I should be eating some of it. Just in front of me, a bunch of boys were getting up from their table and stacking their trays. I caught a glimpse of silverware on one boy's tray, and I almost made him drop it by awkwardly grabbing a fork. He gave me a look. I said, "Mind if I use this?" and without waiting to hear what he said, I headed back in the direction of my table. Because of the way all the different meats were piled up on my plate, I couldn't really get at anything bite-sized with my fork without squishing all the other stuff over the side of the plate and onto the table. I made a mess and tried eating some of the meatloaf, but I had a hard time swallowing it down, and I didn't have anything to drink. I hoped the other boys would finish and leave something in a glass, but they took all their things away on their trays. Chad saw someone he knew from school and went over to talk to him. I looked at the mess of runny meats all over my tray and on the table surface. I covered everything up with napkins and got out of there.

That's pretty much how everything went at first. I would go to Yale Station where we were told our mail would come and ask someone how you got a mailbox, and people would tell me quite clearly what to do, but I could not make out what they meant. For instance, I would be told to go to a certain counter to register, get my mail box and my combination, but as the person was telling me these things, my eyes would become locked on some other counter, and for some reason that would be established in my mind as the place to go, but nobody would be at that counter, which wasn't really a counter at all, just a built in ledge for people's books, and I would stand there for quite a while not knowing what to do. I felt more helpless and stupid than a dog in a busy department store, but a dog who at the same time realizes that he's helpless and stupid. It was a little like being caught in a dream, and it was in that dream-like fog that I wandered through Yale Station for days, looking through the little locked glass doors of thousands of student mailboxes in the hope that I might spot something I was certain was for me, and then I'd know where my mail was. Weeks later, when I finally figured out the procedure, I had so much back mail they gave it to me in a big canvas sack.

But this is how my awkwardness, shyness and stupidity worked for me. I could see right away that I was going to be known as some kind of idiot or freak unless I could begin to make at least basic sense when I had to put food on my plate or find a building or answer an ordinary question. Most people will ignore any particular bit of odd behavior, provided it doesn't really affect them or what they are doing. In fact, if the behavior is really odd, as I'll have to admit mine was, people are even more likely to let it pass, because it doesn't fit into any pre-established scheme of expectations. But I couldn't keep acting that way or people would start to take notice.

I think the turning point for me was my meeting with my freshman faculty advisor. I was late for the appointment because I couldn't find his building, and when I finally got to the building, I couldn't find his office. As I was knocking on his closed door, I saw on the plaque that he was a professor of classics. I didn't know what classics meant—or maybe I did, but it went out of my head. At any rate, I was worried that I would have to know what classics was and also guilty about being late, so when he opened the door and said, "Yes?" I looked at him and blurted out, "Sorry, are you professor Classics?" It was not what I meant, but, typical of me at the time, something half-way between two things that were on my mind. He let it go, which was a relief, but I could see getting into the same kind of trouble as he started asking me about the courses I had registered for. At one point he was saying, "This Cultural Anthropology isn't going to fly, because there is field work and you haven't taken the prerequisites." I didn't understand what he meant by Cultural Anthropology, which, if it was a college course, I couldn't imagine having signed up for, and because I was stuck on that part of the sentence, I didn't really take in the other part, something about "field work"—which gave me the general feeling that I wasn't going to be able to do whatever it was I was supposed to do. The professor had stopped talking and was looking at me. He was expecting a response of some kind, but my head was spinning again in the bad way. I said, "I can do field work." I was picturing something like planting seeds in a long row. The professor gave me a worried look and then started to explain again why I couldn't take the course. While he was talking, something clicked and I suddenly figured out what I had to do in these situations. I had to pause. I had to refrain from speaking, from asking or answering anything until I had completely thought through something to say that made sense. It was as simple as that. I didn't have to know the answer to the question or know exactly what to ask. I just had to say *something* reasonable, something that at least might set up the right thing to say somewhere down the line. But I had to learn to wait, to pause for however long it took to be sure I was not saying something completely idiotic. The professor of classics was staring at me again, but I knew what I had to do. I waited for a moment, and then I said, "I'm not really sure how I got signed up for these courses. Could you tell me how it works?"

It was magic. I started to be able to talk to people. I could understand them, and they could understand me. Not only that, pausing and mulling things over actually had the effect of making people think I was intelligent. I didn't have Chad Pickering's *Mmmmm* and *Nnnnnn* technique, but my own pause-and-consider delay worked for me almost immediately. I think my problem was that I felt I needed to know at once what people expected of me, but that was too hard—because I didn't know, and my panic about not knowing would shut down all effective thought and reduce me to a primitive being. Pause-and-consider changed everything. Now when Chad Pickering and his Holderness friends were sitting around in our suite and someone said to me, "You have Winter Carnival or any kind of ski racing in Illinois?" I would tilt my head back and consider—actually enjoying myself—and, when I found the words, say something like, "No, I'm pretty sure not. Illinois is very, very flat." As we moved through the term Chad told me his friends thought I must be very bright, also that I had a great sense of humor. In recitation classes, too, pause-and-consider was a godsend. There was an especially good moment early on in my Romantic Lit lecture when the professor startled me mid-lecture by looking down into his marking book and saying, "Mr. Force,"—scary pause—"Romeo seems to have had nothing but terrible luck from the moment of his betrothal to Juliet until his death two days later. By contrast Keat's Porphyro, in "Eve of St. Agnes," seems positively charmed—he can't seem to do anything wrong in leading his love out of the hostile frozen castle and carrying her away. How do account for the very different kinds of luck these otherwise very similar lovers' experience?" A month earlier, I would have been flummoxed past all coherence.

But pause-and-consider had become a reflex. I met the professor's eye and smiled. I leaned forward at my desk and paused. I took time to reconsider the exact words, the exact sentences I had just heard. He was asking about two lovers, Romeo and Porphyro, in two separate stories. He was asking about the lovers' luck. I had read the play and the poem. Romeo had died, which was bad luck. Porphyro had escaped the cold castle with Madeline, which was good luck. But the professor had already acknowledged this. I looked up and said, "It seems that being completely in love, like Romeo and Porphyro, can't guarantee your luck. It could be wonderful or terrible. I guess the point is that when a lover is that far gone, luck—good or bad—is all you have." "*Bingo*, Mr. Force! Jackpot! That, we will see, is what happens again and again when, to use a phrase of yours that I like, a lover is 'that far gone.'" I remember sensing—and really liking—the murmur of the students seated around me in the lecture room.

That is how I came to be regarded both by my friends and my professors as a good thinker. Before that, back in Palatine, I had the idea that smart meant fast. The first person to be able to say the answer out loud was smartest—he won. At Yale I learned you could win by being really slow, not only by asking very basic questions before you got to the point you wanted to make, but, sometimes, by asking even more basic questions that set up your basic questions. So, in a course about American political institutions, the professor might ask something like, did I think parliamentary protocols like cloture and filibuster were an aid or a hindrance to democratic process. Of course a question like this required me to know what cloture and filibuster were, but I generally knew that kind of thing, because I read what I was supposed to read outside of class. But while part of my mind was ranging around trying to recall the terms, another part of my mind was working on setting up what might be a really terrific answer. So maybe the first thing I would say, after my pause, would be: "Parliamentary moves like cloture and filibuster can obviously be used either to advance or block a cause. If it can be determined that the cause that gets advanced or blocked is actually the will of the people, then those procedures serve democracy. But if you consider the question only from the perspective of the membership of the senate, then cloture and filibuster are not democratic, since they could allow a minority of committed legislators to prevail over the majority. So—can I ask a question? Which perspective are you asking me to consider, that of the houses of congress or that of the whole body politic?" Pause-and-consider rarely failed me. It helped me to think and to talk in small groups and big assemblies. It also opened up my writing and gave me a lot more to say about any subject than I could have imagined before. Of course, I had to do my work, but, provided there wasn't too much math involved and it was mostly ideas expressed in words, Yale really wasn't very hard.

Chapter Five

I still had to learn how to eat, but pause-and-consider helped there too. I stopped doing the most embarrassing things, like making terrible choices when I was overwhelmed by too many offerings in the line. Very simple guidelines, such as *make sure you actually want to eat that* and *make sure you have a way of fitting that on your tray and carrying it to the table* were a big help. Also useful, at another level, were *watch how other people do it* and *it's not the end of the world to make two trips*. These kinds of things got me through the basics, but when I took time to observe the way the other boys around me ate, I could see that there was a lot I did not know. For instance, what kinds of food you could pick up with your hands and what absolutely had to be eaten with a knife and fork. I don't remember getting any instruction in these areas, even from Nana and Papa or mother and Uncle Desmond, who seemed to have pretty good manners. At home I knew you weren't supposed to pick up the soup bowl and slurp the last bits, because mother was always scolding my father about it. But beyond that, I had no idea. The rule at our house seemed to be that anything with a bone in it could be picked up for sure—also, anything that *looked* as if you could pick it up, like a French fry. In this system, though, you could pick up a lot of food, such as most pieces of chicken, any kind of chops, even steak, depending on the bone situation. But it was clear to me after a few meals in the Freshman Commons that there was a lot less picking up and handling food on people's plates than I was used to. It was not a great hardship to overdo the opposite and cut up everything with a knife and fork. But I noticed that even my cutting and forking were not like other people's. I couldn't quite place it at first, but there was something a lot faster and almost savage about the way I got my food down. Nobody pointed anything out to me or criticized me, but I could tell my approach was pretty odd.

Even something as basic as eating soup gave me problems. My father's only eating instruction, which went back to when I was about three, was "sit up to the table and lean over." This was so I wouldn't spill on the tablecloth and on my clothes. I never questioned this, since it seemed to work, but I noticed right away that my Yale table mates were not sitting up close to the table and hunched down directly over their soup. I tried to make some adjustments, but I felt very clumsy sitting back and raising the soup all the extra distance to my mouth without spilling. For one thing, it made eating soup a really long ordeal. Starting to use the bigger spoon helped, but soup eating still felt all wrong, and I knew I was missing something important. So—in the spirit of pause-and-consider, I asked myself: who actually knows about eating properly, and where is that information kept? I was not going to ask someone like Chad or the other friends I was making in Bingham, because I thought that would set me apart as a weirdo, so I went to the big Brentano's bookstore in New Haven and asked at Information for books about eating manners. There was a whole shelf of books on the subject, and I bought a fat little paperback titled *Emily Post's Book of Everyday Etiquette*. I don't think I made a better purchase at Yale.

Emily Post was very clear about everything I wanted to know about eating, plus a great deal more that would come in handy in other parts of my life. The bigger spoon, it turned out, was always meant for soup. With practice, I got to the point that I could sit up in my chair with my back straight, lift the spoon from the bowl to my mouth without spilling. I also read that you didn't scoop the soup spoon toward you, which had always seemed pretty natural and efficient to me, but just the opposite, drawing the soup up from the outer edge of the bowl. Personally, I would never have a hard time if somebody I was dining with drew his soup up from the near rim, but I did get a kick out of knowing the proper way. It was also news to me that if you were cutting into something with your knife and fork, you only cut the piece you were just about to eat. Ever since I had started using my own knife and fork, I had cut up all the pieces right away, which seemed to get the job out of the way and save time. Like the soup protocols, cutting up only one bite at a time tended to slow the pace of the meal way down, as did the practice of setting down your knife and fork after each bite, as did dabbing the corners of your mouth with your napkin after each bite of anything a little wet. I learned how always to *ask* for something on the table, to say *may I please have* or *would you please pass* and never to demand anything—*please pass* or, worse, *pass me*...I learned not to reach but to ask for things. I learned to receive passed items in one hand and to pass them on with the other. I learned to pass pitchers so that the recipient would take the handle, to pass forks and knives with tines and blades away from the recipient. On the rare occasion when there was a girl or woman at our table, I learned to stand until she was seated. I made it a habit not to begin eating until everyone in our group had begun or, on special occasions, until a formal grace was said. In only a few weeks I went from being possibly one of the fastest eaters in the world to a very slow one—which meant there was more time to talk, look around and take things in. Meals started to become, once I mastered the new procedures, mainly social occasions. I would leave the Commons unaware of having been hungry and now being full, but thinking instead about what we had talked about and whether or not I had liked the company.

It is not an exaggeration to say that Emily Post's etiquette book transformed my time at Yale from what quite easily could have been sustained misery and failure into something very close to happiness. I now made it a habit to acknowledge with a card of thanks any gift or meal out. I no longer went into a troubled fog when introduced to an older person or to a group of strangers. Confident now of the standard courteous responses, I shook hands firmly, looked my new acquaintances in the eye, and told them, in one way or another, that it was a pleasure to meet them. I addressed my obvious elders as *sir* and *ma'am*, and when introducing a peer to someone older, I took care to address the older first and ask if I might introduce the younger. Approaching a professor or any other adult, I always stood back at a polite distance and waited for them to finish any conversation in progress before requesting their attention to my business. There is really no end to what I learned from Emily Post. In both the introduction to her book and at the end, she wrote that almost all etiquette and courtesy come down to helping to make life's routines as pleasant and agreeable to others as possible. When that is the primary consideration, she wrote, good manners come quite naturally. Later in my studies, especially when I was immersed in philosophy and theology at Cambridge, I found that Emily Post had prepared me well for the teachings of Plato, Aristotle, Jesus, and Kant.

Chapter Six

PROBABLY DUE TO my growing social confidence but also, certainly, due to deeper factors of which I would not become aware for years, I started to lose my self-consciousness—not just the self-consciousness that results from feeling conspicuous or foolish, but, literally, the sure, prior, inner sense of who I was and what I was really like. Nor do I believe I really regretted this loss of inner knowing. My deeper, prior self had not been much help at Yale. Maybe it didn't belong there. At any rate I stopped the daily spiritual practices of my childhood. In bed in the dark at night I stopped retelling the days and shaping the events into a story. I stopped talking to myself altogether—and thus, really, stopped thinking much about myself and began to think, instead, about ideas and things. In this I suppose I was an ideal scholar.

By the time the weather started to get cold that first fall at Yale, I actually think I was becoming something of a scholar. There was so little else to think about. The only phones in Bingham were on the landings of the staircase, and somebody always seemed to be using them, so I almost never called home. Long distance was expensive, and I found that the more I got used to Yale, the less I had to say that would interest my parents. My father sent me twenty-five dollars every month for extra spending money, and I would try to add some news in my thank you notes, but what I wrote seemed forced and flat and not like the kind of language they were used to from me. I remember one night walking back up to my room from the

Commons after dinner and settling into the soft chair in front of the fireplace. It was a crisp autumn evening. The cool air and the exertion of climbing the five flights made me feel especially wide awake. Out the window I could see the sun setting behind Harkness Tower, and it looked almost too picturesque, like an engraving from an old book. I remember thinking I should be feeling some kind elation. Such a picture and such a moment should register profoundly, then become stored in permanent memory—but I couldn't make it feel that way. It was Sunday evening, I was alone in the room, and I was more than prepared for the next day's classes. I became aware of an unpleasant sensation that mounted to an almost sickening feeling. It was not pain or sadness or anxiety—just an all-being *thinness*, as if my sitting there in the armchair and the silhouette of the tower against the darkening sky were so chalky and insubstantial they could dissolve in my next breath. Then it struck me that the rest of my life could feel like this.

So I got to work. I did extra work. It would be impossible to reach a comfortable command of even one of the subjects I was taking—The History of Western Art, Romantic Literature, American Political Institutions, Introduction to Biology. Doing all the reading and all the work amounted to almost nothing in the way of mastery and understanding. Any scholastic course of study stretched out over a few months is of necessity a spotty, post-holed, hurry-up tour through matters that would take total immersion and lifetimes of study to understand properly. I knew already that if I received A grades and my professors' praises, that would be at best a feeble invitation to consider the material further. The man who spoke to us at opening Convocation was a famous philosopher who taught at the New School for Social Research in New York. I didn't pay attention to his name. He was a German, short, pudgy and almost grotesquely ugly. His accent was thick, but I remember paying close attention to everything he said, especially the premise upon which he built his talk, which was that everything we learned well as we began our studies, whether in philosophy, science, literature, or art, we would very carefully have to unlearn later in order to advance. I think I understood his point, including the aggravating fact that you can't skip the learning you have to unlearn later. It's all part of the big picture.

Rather than face that feeling of thinness again, I resolved that evening to read and study until I dropped. When I received anything less than highest marks or when there was even a single critical comment on a paper or exam, I sought out the professor to ask how I might do better, and I did as I was told. If a classmate who outperformed me on an assignment was willing to talk with me and share his work, I did everything I could to understand his approach and then worked to incorporate the best of it into my own work. It didn't take me long to realize there was a common factor in the assignments handed back to me that were less than excellent. Looking over my graded work I could see that I typically covered the expected points with reasonable care. I also knew that my writing was pretty sharp — and was grateful that working for the Palatine town paper had taught me reflexively to make clear transitions from thought to thought, to be sure propositions stated causally really were causes, to make clear distinctions generally. My problem, when I had one, was lack of context and reference. I didn't know enough. I was too unfamiliar with too many things — history, great ideas, great achievements — while better informed, better read students were more able to judge the significance and value of any point under study because they could consider it in illuminating contexts.

Knowing my problem, however, did not mean that there would be an easy — or even possible — solution. Again, the problem was that I was almost completely ignorant of the most important things human beings had thought and done since the dawn of civilization. Whatever the schooling provided to me by the Palatine Illinois Department of Education had achieved, knowledge of who did what to shape the world was not part of it. My impression, which only grew as I got to know more students, was that just about everybody at Yale had a broader knowledge base than I did. Some were not scholastically serious and did little work, but when you scratched the surface a little, they knew a thing or two. I also recognized the same kind of cultural acuity in boys who were really not very clear thinkers but who may have attended strong prep schools where, it often seemed, they had been hockey or football stars. But even the dimmest looked to me to have shown up at Yale with at least a serviceable map of what had happened in the western world since dawn of civilization.

Knowing practically nothing, my biggest question was where to start? What were the first things, the very foundations of knowledge? If I considered the acquisition of general knowledge the same kind of problem as the acquisition of the skills necessary to talk and eat, maybe the whole educational venture could come down to a large-scale application of pause-and-consider. I was actually proceeding that way whenever I found myself, whether in class or a late-night bull session in somebody's room, trying to sort out some vast problem of interpretation, such as should President Kennedy have risked nuclear war to win a strategic objective in Cuba, or could anyone honestly take Mormonism seriously as a world religion, or is goodness ever, really, its own reward. These questions were interesting enough to me, but my friends invariably had the capacity, at some point in the discussion, to carry the day because they actually knew something about Cold War policies or world religions or philosophical ethics. I could pause, consider, ask and clarify all I pleased, but I couldn't really resolve any question until I knew much, much more than I did.

Thank God, therefore, for Art History. I had already been taking the course for months before I began to see it as a very important answer to my question regarding what I had to know so that the things I learned would have a context and start to mean something. Maybe I would have had the same realization if I had been studying the history of agriculture or the history of warfare. To consider the unfolding of anything over the span of civilized time would at least lay down some kind of chronological road bed. Even if there were only farming techniques or battle sites alongside the road, there would at least be a road. I could fill in the rest of the scenery as I learned more, and this gave me hope.

In my case, Art History laid down a spectacular road. I was lucky, too, because the course started with images from prehistory — Lascaux cave paintings, the so-called Willendorf Venus — at the very time when my mind had gone temporarily prehistoric, the time when I was not yet able to talk or eat or find my mail. In that crude but very feeling state of mind, I took in those primitive images as fresh, heartfelt offerings from kindred spirits. When just about everything else about my daily life at Yale was confounding me, those early images flashed up in vivid slides out of the darkness of the lecture hall seemed to be something I could understand. I am sure the course was brilliantly taught, but most of the brilliance was lost one me. The general lectures were shared by Vincent Scully and other bright lights on the Yale art faculty. Sometimes there were guest presentations by famous visitors like Margaret Mead, who talked to us about the history and meaning of clothes. I took endless notes, but reviewing them never helped much. My overall impression was of a succession of stunning images on the bright screen: gems set into dagger handles, the gilded faces of unblinking pharaohs, exquisite bodies chiseled from stone, of towers, temples, vaulted aqueducts.

Thank God we didn't get to paintings until I had learned pause-and-consider. Both the general lecturers and the discussion group leaders, who were very smart graduate students, seemed to have a terrific knack for seeing much more going on in a painting than anyone would first imagine. It mattered if there was a storm coming on in one quadrant of the background. It mattered if the bird on the branch over John the Baptist's shoulder was a finch or a dove. Everything mattered. What was lighter and darker mattered. What was high and what was low in the composition mattered. You had to pause and consider. You had to separate out each figure, each technique, every element in the picture and name it, ask what it was doing there, ask, if it was different from the other similar pictures of that subject at that time, why the painter did that. It mattered that Michelangelo's Mary, beholding the body of the crucified Jesus in her lap, wasn't really old enough to be his mother, also that the look on her face and the way she beheld her son was more a lover's look than a mother's. If you paused and considered as you looked, the great images were anything but still and finished. They had life and power. You realized sometimes with a little chill at the back of your neck as you reviewed the projected slide or the glossy plate in the textbook, that the image you thought you were working on was actually working on you. It wanted to tell you things.

Each bright image projected out of the darkness-- a crafted tool, a ceremonial crown, a sculptured torso, a tapestry, a monument—carried me away. I fantasized about setting up an apartment or a house with all the walls illuminated by projected slides of my favorite images from western art. Because it was so possible, I was pretty sure other people had already thought of it and lived like that. But even more than wanting to carry on my daily life among the images, I wanted basic, foundational knowing, the kind of knowing that would select and arrange the images, hold them fast. And then, in the course of a fifteen minute slide presentation on Raphael's *School of Athens,* that very thing happened. Here, for once, writing everything down in my notebook actually helped me.

I am absolutely certain that a year-long university course could not exhaust the possibilities of interpreting a single Italian renaissance masterpiece, and a lifetime could be devoted to fully understanding *The School of Athens*. Knowing as little as I did, and knowing next to nothing about philosophy, the classical world, renaissance Italy, the conventions of classical architecture and of renaissance painting, it's a miracle that anything penetrated my understanding as the *School of Athens* slide was discussed. I followed the idea that such a monumentally vaulted interior space signified that the event it contained was tremendously important. I also took in that this event was the meeting of two great minds, Aristotle and Plato, amidst an animated crowd of other figures, some of them attending to the two philosophers, others busy with their own concerns. Because I knew no classical history, Plato and Aristotle were empty categories to me. If pressed I might have said they were ancient, great and Greek.

Not knowing about such elemental figures in history was exactly the kind of thing that inflamed my frustration about having no knowledge foundation, but this time the professor was clear and helpful. In just a few sentences he summarized the differences in what he said were, when Raphael painted the picture, the two greatest philosophical systems yet articulated. The differences, he said and I recorded, were that Plato saw the ultimate reality as beyond the temporal and material world, what we call the "real" world, the world in which history unfolds and we go about our daily lives. The ultimate truths were perfections, like geometric figures and the arrangement of notes in a musical chord. These perfections were not man made. They have always been there and will always be there. Humans discover them but do not invent them. Actual life in the temporal, material world is just a succession of imperfect attempts to approximate the perfections. But because a trained mind can realize the idea of perfection, it can direct actual, imperfect behavior in the right direction. Mankind has the capacity, therefore, to know better from worse, and to attempt to live for the better. Aristotle, at one point a student of Plato's (but in the painting his equal in bearing) did not accept that the ultimate reality was a perfection beyond the temporal, material world. He was a scientist who observed the behavior of plants, animals, and men. He concluded that the ultimate truth is revealed in the way the world actually works and the way creatures behave. For Aristotle there was a force permeating the natural world and driving it and each thing in it to its ultimate realization. An acorn is driven to become an oak. Associations of men are driven to become self-sufficient, purposeful cities. For Aristotle the study of the actual, material nature of things leads to ultimate understanding. For Plato the contemplation of what is ultimate leads to understanding the actual nature of things.

So said my notes. But as I was scribbling them down in the darkened hall, something so stimulating, so energizing was going on inside me that I worried I would be overwhelmed beyond any possibility of sorting it out later and that I would shut down and get really stupid again. But of one thing I was now certain: Plato and Aristotle would be foundations. I didn't care if it took a picture—the big pulsing cartoon of Raphael's fresco—to point out something so basic. I walked directly out of the lecture hall to the college bookstore, where, in the philosophy section, I excused myself and asked an older gentleman who looked as though he might be a professor what he would recommend to someone who was going to start reading Plato and Aristotle. He stared at me for a moment as if I were possibly putting him on, then he smiled and told me I might start with Plato's death dialogs of Socrates: *Euthyphro, The Apology, Crito,* and *Phaedo.* Then I should proceed to what he said were the great dialogs, *The Symposium* and *The Republic.* If I had time for only one work, he said it should be *The Republic*. He seemed a little less sure about what Aristotle to recommend. He asked me if I was aware that Aristotle was no fun to read. I said I didn't know that and asked why. He said it was because Aristotle read like lecture notes, and some of the works actually were lecture notes. He suggested I start with *The Nicomachean Ethics* and *The Politics*. He asked me if I would be reading these books in connection with a course, and I said, yes, Art History. He smiled again, and I said thanks. I wish I had asked his name, because later I wanted to write him at length to thank him. But what luck to have found him. What luck also that each title he recommended was on the shelves.

Moreover, my luck continued. It was sheer luck that I started, as the gentleman suggested, with Plato, who has a distinctive voice, a definite attitude, and a sense of humor. He was also right to advise that I start with the death dialogs, although I got so bogged down in the logic of Socrates' arguments in *Euthyphro* I had to skip ahead to his trial in *The Apology*, and after that I was hooked. It is very hard, I think, to follow along the logical steps in which Plato has Socrates argue with people and not *become* Plato. The arguments are so good, and they open up so much other good thinking—how can you fault him? Platonic arguments — about the ineffectiveness of deception, self-interest and other moral short-cuts — started working their way into the writing assignments for my lit and politics courses. But if I had not read Plato first — and if I had not remembered the equally imposing, darker haired and actually rather dashing figure of Aristotle in *The School of Athens* — I know could never have made myself plough through Aristotle. As the gentleman said, it was less like writing than very carefully organized notes about somebody else's writing. Points supporting and opposing every proposition tended to be listed, usually in descending order of importance. It was all very sound if you followed along, but for me the only thing that got me through hours on end of Aristotle was sheer willpower -- and faith in the bright slide of *The School of Athens*. Nevertheless, when I at last finished *The Ethics* and all of *The Politics*, I could see that a coherent, alternative way of thinking to Plato's about life, conduct, personal relations, politics and ultimate reality had been set down. Both views described the human situation comprehensively — but in irreconcilably different ways. Plato's way led to still, ringing certainties. Aristotle's way led to compelling possibilities. Following Plato, you had to know. Following Aristotle, you had to observe and find out.

I liked knowing what Plato and Aristotle thought. I did everything I could to fortify my understanding of their work, including systematic re-reading, reading critical essays about them, and subjecting every writing assignment I was given to Platonic or Aristotelian arguments. After a time I did not so much think about their arguments as I thought *with* them. I could now sense something substantial underfoot when I took some position in a discussion or in an essay. With Plato and Aristotle under my belt, other, later voices in western civilization, seemed less novel, and usually less impressive, than if I had encountered them fresh. Machiavelli, for example, was introduced with an almost theatrical flourish by my politics professor when we read *The Prince*. But I had met Machiavelli already in *The Republic*. He is the sophist Thrasymachus whose successive arguments for the sovereignty of selfishness Socrates reduces easily to self-contradiction. I had, I knew, a long way to go, but I could feel the heady sense that I was beginning to acquire context.

Building context, in addition to doing all my required coursework, took up every minute of my time. Looking back, I know I cannot possibly have read and studied and written as much as I seem to have done at Yale, yet all my memories are of setting pre-dawn alarms so I could get at my work, reading late in my bed in Bingham, refusing to let the banging radiators break my concentration. In high school I looked forward to nothing more than an uncommitted Saturday or Sunday morning, so that I could sleep in, stretch out into the tingling deliciousness of first waking and then realize I could keep lying there in the warmth of the bed clothes, sleep again, dream vividly, awaken, dissolve, doze. But at Yale that never happened. There were, especially in the humanities, backbreaking loads of assigned reading — if you actually did it all. My Victorian Novel course met three times a week and a separate novel was assigned and assumed read for each meeting—that is, a whole Victorian novel; that is, *Bleak House* or *David Copperfield* or *The Mayor of Casterbridge*. Somehow, without fudging or cribbing, I did all my assigned reading, but I spent even more time reading other work, building foundation, filling in context, expanding perspective. This must sound so priggish and self-congratulatory, but that is not what it felt like when I was reading like that and doing that work. It was an I-can't-believe-my-luck pleasure. Everything I did, I realize now, was driven by a very simple premise: *knowledge is the greatest thing*. I didn't question it or even articulate it, but it was working on me—along with the related premise, *knowledge is durable; everything else is not*. The simple truth of the matter is that reading and learning felt good.

CHAD PICKERING'S HOLDERNESS FRIENDS KIDDED me about being a grind, but there was no meanness in it. They might have even been a little impressed. One good thing I was starting to realize about Yale was that considerable respect is given to any excess in service of an identifiable excellence. A virtuoso pianist who in the summers toured the country soloing with major orchestras or a fiction writer who was already getting published in New York magazines or a tennis player who had a shot at Wimbledon was granted any eccentricity, including fanatic discipline and hard work. In the mid-sixties it was still okay to be passionately committed to lofty pursuits. No one I knew looked down on scholarship, even driven, dogged scholarship like mine. There was still, I sense looking back, a subculture of the gentleman dandy and an ethos of careless hedonism afoot at Yale when I was there, but not on the part of anyone I dined with or sat near in the libraries. For my first two years especially, I would have had a hard time picking up such signals. I had a narrow social acquaintance. I hung around first with Chad and his Holderness friends. After I got familiar with who was in my classes, I formed a kind of studying acquaintance with four or five boys on or near my floor at Bingham. Before long, we recognized in each other the unspoken common aspiration — I will say it openly now — to attain expert knowledge and to demonstrate that knowledge impressively. We were not exactly what college students today would call geeks and nerds, because we were not without all humor or social touch. We were just, unobtrusively I hoped, fanatic learners.

Chapter Seven

Becoming a fanatic learner made me feel good in two different ways. It made me feel confident that my life had an unassailable purpose — for who can say anything against learning? It also made me feel energized and excited, because many of the things I was learning really did stimulate and interest me — as did the very acts of reading and compiling. But if there was a downside to dedicating all my waking time to reading and study, it was that, from time to time, I felt I was operating inside a bubble. It's not that I was isolated from people and didn't talk to them. College life is a hive; you live communally, move in packs, dine and study in groups. But as much company as I had and as much talking as I did, I could feel my self growing more and more private and unto myself. My study friends knew my ideas and opinions of things, but they did not know who I was before and what kind of transformation I was experiencing. Nor did I want them—or anybody else—to know. For one thing, whatever was happening was in process, and I was far from sure how it would turn out.

When I went home to Palatine over Christmas vacation, I got my first strong impression of what had started to happen to me. My mother and father, Nana and Papa all told me I looked different — older, they decided. Maybe it was that my hair had grown out of its crew cut, and I wore my Yale clothes, which were essentially the extra good clothes I had splurged on at Parnell's, the one upscale men's store in Palatine, the week before leaving for college. My mother and father had never really seen me before in pressed khaki pants, the soft wool crew necks, Oxford cloth shirts and herringbone jackets. Mother commented a number of times that I looked "awfully nice," which embarrassed me, but worse, I think it embarrassed her. She could see that I had somehow — already — started mutating into another form, something perhaps inevitable and important, which she felt she must accept because that's what going off to a university like Yale must surely require. But I could see my new presence rather undid her. She seemed to lack her old confidence even in addressing me, and she began treating me like an honored guest in the house. My father engaged me even less than before. I tried to sense resentment or criticism on his part, more than half expecting him to make fun of something I would say or do which he found pretentious. I feared that most when we were all together and someone would ask me what I was studying. The second I heard myself mouthing an abstract idea and then trying to find a way to explain it in terms my family would understand, I grew tense, hearing the unfamiliar flow of talk with my father's ears. I honestly would not have been surprised if he had cut me off with an angry *"Bullshit!"* or even cracked me in the back of the head. There were more than a few uncomfortable dinner table moments like that, especially when Uncle Desmond was over. He had gone to college himself and seemed really interested in —amazed by — the way I was talking and the things I was talking about.

It was a little better with my friends, who had started calling the house days before I got home on the train from New Haven. There were improvised parties practically every night, which I had not expected. Everybody was anxious to report on their college scenes. The most excited talk and anecdotes were about fraternities and sororities, including rituals and procedures so subtle and elaborate I found them a little hard to believe— rushing, pledging, initiation, secret handshakes, hell week, *branding*. There was excited talk about big games in Columbus and Ann Arbor, about everybody in the pledge class painting themselves red or blue. There were a lot of drinking stories, claims of spectacular drunkenness, eager exchanges about parties and bars and impromptu road trips. Familiar to me as all these kids were, I fell almost mute, feeling I had little to report. Asked about fraternities at Yale, I stumbled for a minute and had to say what was true — I wasn't sure. Over the course of the semester there might have been an occasional reference to fraternities or some other kind of secret societies, but I had not really taken it in. I wondered for a moment if I had missed it — if possibly the kind of jubilation and ritual I was hearing about at Ohio State and Iowa was actually going on at Yale beyond my notice. It wasn't absolutely impossible, but I doubted it. I would be out of Yale for years before I knew anything about Skull and Bones — despite the fact that one of my classmates inducted into it would become our President. I must have seen the names, walked past the buildings, but I proceeded through Yale largely oblivious to Scroll and Key, Book and Snake, D.K.E and the rest. My old friend Gary Wade looked at me hard and said, "You sure you really go to Yale? How could you not know if they have fraternities?" He had a point, and I laughed along with the others.

At this point in my life I was in no position to try to reclaim a little status by debunking fraternity life or making a case for the intellectual rigor of Yale and the Ivy League. I had no such confidence, only a burning hope that my knowledge scheme would work. I didn't know if the tentative edifice I was building would stand. I didn't know if it would be better than fraternities. I remember sitting in that crowded paneled basement room listening to Dan Retsik holding forth on how many guys had already flunked out of his engineering program at Purdue, then making my way over to a more raucous group where Gary Wade was telling about how he deflowered a drunken "cherry" in a motel over the course of a wild weekend in Champagne-Urbana. It was no place for me to try to tell anybody what happened to me when I saw the slide of *The School of Athens*.

Alien as I was becoming among my old high school friends, it still felt good over that holiday break to be huddled in among them, talking and laughing and taking in their good familiar faces. It struck me that when I was with them, both the boys and the girls, my personal membrane seemed permeable again. Somehow the sheer presence of people I knew and liked in Palatine passed *into* me, and I felt related to them in a way I had not felt at Yale. I had a place with these kids, my old Jonathan Force place. Now, as I chatted and listened, that place was becoming modified to accommodate what had happened to me. I was Jonathan Force who studied at Yale. I had gone East. I was starting to look and sound different. I was getting quiet. And possibly something else—I was becoming *modest*.

TRUTH BE TOLD, I DIDN'T spend much time thinking about what I was like at Yale. As I have said already, I pretty much gave up self-consciousness, partly because I was so distracted and busy, but even more because I had made a primitive bargain with my deep self when I first arrived and was so lost and terrified: if I don't think about myself, don't picture myself, and don't hold that picture up to constant critical appraisal, there will be no self to hurt.

Looking back, however, even without the aid of year books and photographs, I am sure I cut some sort of figure. Even before I was selected as a Scholar of the House and began getting scholastic recognition, I suspect I was gaining presence, the only-you-could-be-you quiddity that I had sensed immediately in Chad Pickering. Like him, I had, once I learned to pause-and-consider, a voice and a manner. I had a sense of humor, although it emerged very gradually over the course of my freshman year—gradually because my former sense of humor, which as a boy I had felt was my capacity to "get off good ones," would not have worked at all, given the way I had determined to conduct myself at Yale. I had been a wise guy with a fast mouth in school, which was fine then. It made me happy and it made me laugh—which was just as well, because I couldn't help it. My cracks were out of my mouth before I could stop them. I got lots of laughs, but my fast mouth also got me in a fair amount of trouble. At Yale, pause-and-consider best governed everything, including humor. The problem with humor when you are in the process of learning massive amounts of new things is that the field of possible humorous elements becomes enormous. It takes a while before you realize that the very vastness of the knowledge pool and the seemingly sacred nature of some of the elements in it can actually be pretty good material for humor. It might even be true that really smart people are the funniest.

I got an entirely new picture of what was funny from the first Broadway show I ever saw, which turned out to be the funniest entertainment of any kind I had ever seen. On a chilly Sunday morning in the fall of my freshman year, two study friends, Jason and Joel, and I took the train into New York to see a matinee of *Beyond the Fringe*. Jason, whose father was a rabbi and whose mother was a professor, got us the tickets from his parents who had seen it and thought it was terrific. I knew nothing about it and only half listened as Jason tried to explain. I was mainly interested in the train ride and seeing New York, both of which turned out to be tremendously satisfying. But *Beyond the Fringe* was world-changing. It wasn't a play at all, or a musical, although one of the players, Dudley Moore, played a little piano. It was a bunch of short crazy sketches with no common thread.

There were four British players, four young men who could have not looked less like each other. By the intermission I knew their names by heart, and all four of them continue to be, although two are now dead, luminous, continuing inspirations. They were Dudley Moore, Peter Cook, Jonathan Miller, and Alan Bennett. Jonathan Miller and Peter Cook were tall with craggy faces. Alan Bennett was medium height, blond and a little dense-looking in his dark framed glasses. Dudley Moore was very short and runty, and he had a way of drawing his head down into his collar which made him look as if he had no neck. Their grey suits were rumpled and their hair was mussed, and everything about them, singly and in combination, made me laugh. The program notes said that they were only a year out of Oxford and Cambridge and had worked up the *Beyond the Fringe* material for their university shows, and that was the feel of it: the exuberant farce of really smart young men who were as bright as educated people could be but who had clearly not joined the grownups. Their skits were about everything and anything: a monolog about a dim-witted coal miner who regretted that he hadn't become a judge instead, a sermon laced with meaningless anecdotes and unrelated biblical passages by a minister who talked as if he had a mouth full of pudding, a group of cultists who showed up every day to witness the end of the world. They did a frenzied reenactment of the entire Second World War. They did a parody of Shakespeare called *So That's The Way You Like It*, which literally stopped the show as people howled and clapped. The only Shakespeare I had read then, with next to no comprehension, was *Romeo and Juliet* and *Macbeth*, but I don't think I missed a gesture in the parody. I had no words for it afterward when we were back out on the chilly mid-town streets heading for the station, but I had been elevated. I had been complimented. *Beyond the Fringe* didn't just delight me; it made me feel incredibly smart. From that point forward, I knew that being funny meant being funny at the *Beyond the Fringe* standard. After seeing *Beyond the Fringe*, I started to notice little things about life at Yale that I thought might be attempts to express the same kind of—what?—liberating silliness. With hindsight I'm sure that what I was feeling was also in the air everywhere else in the country. I had mainly been cocooned with my books and my thoughts since I arrived in New Haven, but even I caught a sense that something in the larger world was thawing out and breaking up and that surprising things were about to happen. I didn't listen to my radio and only used it for the alarm, but Chad had a whole little stereo system, and he would call me into his bedroom every now and then to play me something he really liked. When I was first getting to know him, he played me some of his favorite albums by the Kingston Trio and Peter, Paul, and Mary. I actually knew them already because my sister Annabel had liked their cheerfulness and their tight, tidy harmonies. I thought they were all right, but a little too slick and cutesy for me. But then Chad started calling me in to hear music like nothing I had ever heard before, by people and groups I had never heard of. I wondered how Chad got hold of such records, and he told me there was something like a craze going on. As soon as he said that, I started to feel it. He played his *Meet the Beatles* album over and over while he studied and read, and normally I would have shut my door to mute the sound, but the music was getting to me, too.

 I couldn't get the Beatles tunes out of my head, nor could I locate exactly what it was about them that had infected me. The songs had simple, pleasing structures and solid beats, but so did just about any rock and roll hit. There was something else, something, certainly, in the singers' diction that was different. I could hear the British inflections in some of the phrases, also something nasal and back-of-the-throat that set the phrasing, especially John Lennon's, apart from anybody else's. I also really liked the look of the Beatles. They didn't look like American pop stars. They weren't handsome, but they were interesting looking. Each of them had grown his hair out into a kind of bowl, which had the effect of making me look harder at their faces. I associated their look not with a pop musical style but with being British—and then it struck me. The Beatles evoked the same liberating feeling the *Beyond the Fringe* players did. They did not seem to be imitating anything, a *version* of anything. They were all new, just themselves, and everybody was crazy about them. I remember squeezing into the crowded television lounge in Bingham to watch a few minutes of a press conference with the Beatles. There was a lot of talking and laughing in the room, and I could barely hear what being said, but it was fascinating to watch them, at first kind of dazed and self absorbed, then alert and funny. I looked around me. Everyone in the room was held fast.

A little later in the winter, Chad had gotten hold of a record by Bob Dylan, who appeared on the album jacket to be about our age. He looked emaciated and scruffy. He was pictured making his way down a city street looking very cold in his sheepskin coat. It was hard for me to listen to Bob Dylan. He missed and hurried beats on his guitar, his harmonica riffs would fly off sourly, and he sang as if he had something bad-tasting in his mouth, but Chad, who I did not think had any special musical feeling, was deeply absorbed in every song. As with the Beatles, he seemed to be onto something with Bob Dylan as well. Dylan songs, too, followed me around campus all winter and spring. To my ear, most of the lyrics were so freely associated they made no sense at all, but I couldn't get certain couplets out of head. Some boys in Bingham said Bob Dylan was playing in little clubs in Greenwich Village and it was easy to get in and see him. I didn't know if I wanted to go, but I was intrigued by the idea that these strange new human lights were blinking on in places like Liverpool and Minneapolis, and everyone was waking up to them and to this new feeling of possibility.

Some different things started erupting on the Yale campus as well. The papers, including *The Yale Daily News*, reported a new wave of student drug use, mainly marijuana and hallucinogenic drugs like LSD and mushrooms. I hadn't met anybody yet who had or used drugs, although just about everybody kept beer or liquor in their rooms. I asked my study friends, Jason, Joel, Nick and Ethan if they were aware of any drugs in Bingham. For a moment they looked troubled. Jason said some boys on his floor smoked pot. He said he would show me, which I thought was strange, but we got up, and he led me down the stairs. It was about ten at night and very cold, but he said we would not need our coats because it would just take a minute. We went out the front door, walked about twenty yards straight out into the snow, then turned around facing the building. Jason looked up. "There," he said, "fourth floor. What do you see?" I located the fourth floor. Lights were on in most of the rooms, but in one of the dark rooms there was a red glow. "See the room with the red," Jason said, "It's a red light bulb. They screw in a red light bulb, listen to Indian music and get high. They do it practically every night. You used to be able to smell the smoke coming from below the door, but now they roll up towels and stuff them in the opening." Walking back up the stairs, I asked him what those guys were like. He said they were all right, that a lot of them knew each other before and had gone to the same schools. I wondered if they could smoke pot and still do their work.

After the Beatles, people's appearance started to change. A lot of Yale boys, especially the ones who went to prep schools, already had long hair, but now wherever you went there were a lot more Beatle-looking faces. Some people's hair would not grow into a Beatles-looking bowl, but they grew it out anyway. The black students started wearing their hair high and wide and sometimes trimmed to the shape of a ramp or a box. Jason let his hair grow, but it was very crinkly, wiry hair and it grew straight out into what looked like sprigs of steel wool. His friend Joel told him the hair style wasn't working and said his head looked like a mound of Brillo. From then on everybody called Jason Brillo, which he did not seem to mind, and he kept his hair that way.

I grew out my crew cut right away when I got to Yale. One reason was that I didn't see a lot of barbershops on my first strolls around New Haven. I also didn't see many Yale kids with crew cuts. I had a strong impression after meeting Chad and some other friends that long hair conferred presence and individuality. After seeing *Beyond the Fringe* and taking in The Beatles, I was certain this was true. At any rate, Yale seemed to get shaggier and shaggier every year I was there. Clothes changed as well. There seemed to be a point where the British rock band look and the Yale undergraduate look came together. The key was to mix incongruous elements. Yale boys liked to wear frayed, faded jeans, but with a crisp monogrammed dress shirt and a tweed jacket. Boys would take the curse off formal outfits like suits and tuxes by wearing preposterously beat up shoes, or maybe the wrong kind of shoes, like sneakers or sandals. People actually paid a lot of attention to their shoes. To me any two pairs of penny loafers, desert boots or boating moccasins looked about the same, but Yale boys drew fine distinctions. It was really important to some boys I knew to have *Bass* loafers and *L.L.Bean* boat shoes and *Brooks Brothers* shirts. If the shoes had fallen apart and were bound with heavy tape, that was for some reason an added distinction. It was stylish to wear really good clothes that had worn out, the Brooks Brothers shirt with a frayed collar, the cashmere sweater gone at the elbows. Most boys wore long coats. It was stylish to wear expensive, nicely tailored top coats but just as stylish to wear huge army surplus great coats. The long coats, combined with Yale boys' taste for long scarves, created a kind of Dickensian effect, a look also favored by the British bands.

There was nothing remarkable about the way I dressed, except perhaps how invariably I stuck to it. It seems almost unnatural to revisit that time in my life now. I can call up pictures and even the light, but there is no weight, no feeling to any of it. What was I like? What did I look like? It's hard to imagine myself making any impact, but I know that by just being there, being alive, taking up space, I must have done. I know, for one thing, I was neat and clean. As I said, all of my clothes were new from Parnell's Men's Shop, purchased in a binge one afternoon at what was then a staggering expense for me. There was a new camel colored duffel coat, many pairs of deeply creased khaki pants, oxford cloth button down collar shirts, wool crew neck sweaters, two tweed sport coats, a pair of loafers, a pair of suede desert boots, and a pair of shiny cordovans. I dimly recall that I did not stand out in these clothes. On most occasions, especially in my classes and daily stops, I was usually more pulled together than most of the boys.

I remember only one early moment when I felt consciously aware of my appearance. It was the Saturday afternoon of the Harvard-Yale football game, which for some reason I felt I should go to, partly because it was obviously such a big deal and also because I realized late in the fall that I hadn't paid any attention to sports or to any other extra curricular dimension of the university. It was not easy finding someone to go with me. Chad and his friends were either meeting their parents and families, or they had invited dates from the women's colleges. My study friends said they didn't want to go on principle, the principle being that sports were overvalued and stupid. I managed to talk the most unlikely of those boys, Ethan Freyer, into going with me. I told him we could study the spectacle as if we were going to see gladiators at the Coliseum. He knew what I meant, and I think he might have been feeling lonely and out of it too, so we got tickets and went.

As it turned out, nothing could have made me, and I am sure Ethan, feel more unconnected and lonely than attending that game. I was probably vulnerable to feeling lonely, having just spent Thanksgiving on the practically deserted campus after my parents and I decided it was too expensive to take the train home for just a long weekend. So on a freezing cold Saturday afternoon, Ethan and I bundled up and headed across campus to the Yale Bowl for the game. With all the cars in the lots and all the tail gate parties gathered at the open backs of station wagons, it felt like we were walking through some kind of top-coated shanty town before we even got to the pitted, grimy walls of the Bowl. Knowing what a big event The Game was supposed to be, we had left early to get our seats, which proved to be a mistake, because neither of us had realized the enormity of the stadium. My father had taken me to see the Chicago Cubs play in Wrigley Field, but the Yale Bowl looked three times bigger. My program said that back in the day when Harvard and Yale football was about as big as football got, seventy or eighty thousand people would come to a game. Now, as Ethan and I could see, there was all the room in the world.

We decided to sit way back, even though it was clear that we would be so far from the field the players would look like specks. Even later when we moved in closer, we were still too far away to feel drawn to the action on the field. For a while I concentrated on watching the crowd form on the Harvard side of the stadium. There was a lot of red, and something about their distant exuberance seemed less inhibited, sillier, and maybe happier than what was rising out of the Yale people in front of us. We sat watching students and their dates and their families fill up the inner rings on our side the stadium. They brought in pennants and cushions and blue Yale blankets with the stark white Y in the center. I imagined they were all comfortable and happy, their steaming exhalations rising over their thermos mugs. I had gone to all my high school football games in Palatine, but Ethan didn't like sports and had even dropped out of the marching band at his school, because he didn't like getting on the bus on Friday nights and having to spend the whole night in another town waiting for half time.

At first we made a game out of wildly over-criticizing everybody and everything we saw, but we had run out things to talk about by the time the game started. Once it did, I let go of all thought, and the public address system took over. Neither team was able to move the ball very well, and after a quarter I had the sinking realization that nothing that could happen in the game would arouse my interest. Ethan must have gone off for fifteen cups of hot chocolate. My face got so stingingly cold I thought I sounded like a drunk when I tried to say something. As the second half was about to start, Ethan looked at me and said, "I don't think I can take any more of this."

As we made our way down and out of the Bowl we had to shuffle against the traffic of people returning to their seats. The cold had voided the expressions from most of the faces, but I remember looking intently into them, wondering what they were really feeling, what could possibly hold them there at the game. I don't think people were looking at me, but if they had been, they would have seen, I am sure, a young man none of them would have doubted went to Yale. He was nicely dressed in his duffle coat and scarf. His face, pinched in the cold, might have seemed a little young, but not unpleasant. He might even have had a bit of a Yale look to him, with his long hair parted on one side, a dark tousle angled across his forehead. The collar of his duffle coat, quite a handsome coat, would have been turned up against the wind. A Yale boy, without question, if anybody had been looking.

The next morning at breakfast I saw on the front page of the *New York Times* sports section that Yale had beaten Harvard, 20-6. I looked around for Ethan to tell him, and then realized there was no point.

Chapter Eight

The point seems to have been to just keep going. For most of my first two years at Yale I felt as if I were constructing myself from scratch. Nobody in my prior life had spoken with the breadth of reference or the precision or the eloquence of my professors. How men and women could know so much was to me less mysterious than how anyone was able to distinguish so sharply between so many elements-- and talk so beautifully about all of it. Even students, the ones confident enough to hold forth in class, the ones rumored to be prodigies and geniuses, had some of what the professors had. It was not just the particular things they knew or how much they knew; it was how the things they knew were *working* in them. I wanted to be like that. I wanted to be working *with* great ideas and achievements, not plodding away working *at* them.

Sensing the goal but aware of how impossibly far I was from achieving it, I probably would have fallen apart, burned out in some kind of obsessive breakdown if it hadn't been for my routines. Almost from the time of my arrival at the university, I began to develop, God knows why, a strict and fairly elaborate regimen of personal routines. At home, apart from the requirements of sports, I showered and washed my hair every few days, but at Yale I showered faithfully every morning, taking care to lather, scrub and rinse every orifice and crevice. My hair was always clean and in the morning almost fluffy. Uncle Desmond had bought me as a going away present a leather case containing a shaving kit, nail clippers, a file and tweezers. The impressive economy of the arrangement of shiny silver implements inside the case touched me. I had never expected to own something like that. I remember placing the case at the center of the top of my bureau in Bingham and deciding I would maintain that kind of order generally, and with that resolve I began to order my experience at Yale.

The next morning, the second I was free from orientation meetings, I made my way out of the Old Campus gates into New Haven where I found a Walgreens. Driven by something powerful but barely conscious, I bought many plastic bottles of emerald green Prell shampoo. I bought easily a year's supply of Gillette razor blades. I bought all the copper colored cans of Right Guard deodorant they had in stock. Spending more than I knew I could afford, I bought a polished box containing two teak handled hairbrushes. I bought six toothbrushes and six tubes of Crest toothpaste. I stored and arranged these toiletries in the top drawer of my bureau, feeling newly capable and strong. Throughout my time at Yale and on through my life, I have never flagged in keeping up an impressive back supply of everything to do with grooming and personal hygiene. In a similar spirit, and with similarly gratifying results, I found a barber I liked just around the corner from the New Haven Hotel. He had the gift of making me look, when he was finished, just about exactly as I did when I came in, though somehow cleanly trimmed.

For some reason laundry and dry cleaning came to be paramount among all my personal routines. So far as I can tell, there was no basis for this in my previous experience. At home mother had done everyone's laundry faithfully. In no more than a week after depositing dirty items in the hamper, they reappeared folded in drawers or hanging in the closet. Only very occasionally, not even annually, something like a suit or a winter coat would go off to the "the cleaners" from which it would come back smelling of chemicals and sheathed in plastic. I did not really know what dry cleaning was until I realized that through daily wear my new Parnells clothes were turning a little dingy. I learned later there were vast banks of coin driven washers and driers in the basement of Bingham and even a student operated laundry service that picked up and returned rough wash items to your door. But the morning I saw faint slivers of grime running down the neck of one of my Parnells shirts, I set out to find a commercial laundry in town. From that day forward Monday and Thursday stops at the dry cleaning counter of Next Day Laundry became my most inviolable routine at Yale. In those days I had to be, for really the only time in my life, careful about money, and dry cleaning was phenomenally expensive for me—this when a medium-starch shirt, folded and boxed, was thirty-five cents. But by augmenting my summer savings with paid library work and occasional piano playing jobs at faculty parties, I was able to keep my shirts crisp, khakis creased, and sweaters spotless. This luxury was new to me, and it gave me great, quiet pleasure. I kept the fact of my dry cleaning entirely to myself, a harmless secret. Chad may have wondered about it sometimes, as he used to ask me, when he was taking his own laundry down to the machines in the basement, if I wanted to share a load, and I always declined. Once late at night studying for exams with Jason, Joel, and Ethan, I looked up and saw that Jason was staring at me. "Force," he said, "how come you always look so—*clean?*" I knew what he meant. Everything I was wearing at the moment was freshly starched, creased and crisp. I paused and considered. I said, "I think it's because I bathe."

Going through my days in what must have been close to an immaculate condition was not, I am certain, a bid for any kind of attention. At a glance I did not look markedly different from hundreds of other Yale students. The barely perceptible pleasure I felt buttoning up a freshly laundered shirt or stepping into a newly pressed pair of khakis was unrelated to any presumed social impact. It had nothing to do with my imagined *appearance.* The pleasure was in having created such a highly particular system for myself, a pleasure not unlike knowing that the grooming implements in my black leather case stood bracketed and ready for me on my bureau or that, under the foot of my bed, was the mitered box containing my shoe polish canisters, brushes, and chamois cloth.

Nor was I in any way aspiring to some standard. I don't know if there even was a dominant sartorial standard or "look" at Yale when I arrived. If I had to guess, I'd say it was a pricier version of my Parnells get ups.

But not long after I arrived — or, more accurately, after the Beatles and the other British rock groups arrived — some students started expressing something new, something ornery and playful, in the way they dressed. From the start there had been a persistent minority of boys who defiantly crossed the line, refusing for instance to comply with the spirit of the coat and tie requirement for evening meals in the Commons. They would do this in all kinds of ways. They would knot their ties outside the collar of their shirt or, more commonly, wear the tie knotted around their bare necks over a tee shirt. They would tie something that wasn't a tie, a ribbon or a rawhide shoe lace, and let it dangle down their front. There were just as many ways to test the coat standard. Boys wore coats with the sleeves nearly ripped off the body of the jacket. Jackets were worn inside out. Outlandish tuxedo jackets—powder blue or saffron tailcoats—were worn with jeans. Big, rangy boys wore tiny jackets which rode up high on their arms. Small boys rolled up the sleeves of enormous jackets that fell down to their knees. Every now and then Marvin, the food service director, would stand at the entrance to the food counters where student I.D.s were checked, turning away students whose dress he didn't think met the required standard. The provocatively dressed boys made scenes. *Who says this isn't a tie? So my coat is ripped — you can't be poor and eat at Yale? Where does it say you can't wear your tie over your collar?* I am sure Marvin did his best, but it was increasingly clear that the point of the misdressing was to provoke him. His standard line to the provocateurs was "That's unacceptable." He could say it patiently or he could say it in real anger, but after he determined somebody's dress was unacceptable, that boy did not eat in The Commons. By spring, the drama of coat and tie testing had become a kind of nightly theater.

I don't think I had a position myself. I wasn't about to tell anybody that I actually looked forward to knotting my tie and getting into my Harris Tweed jacket for the evening meal. I could see that there was something stimulating in what the rebels were doing, but I also felt — and was not proud of — a reflexively hostile response, especially to the few boys who were aggressively unkempt: unshaven, unbuttoned and unwashed. To be honest, there were moments when I looked at the rebels, especially when they were angrily in Marvin's face, through the eyes of my father. I could imagine grabbing up the front of their shirts with my fist, telling them off, giving them a ringing crack in the head. I didn't like that feeling, but it did rise up.

Although I had never really gotten to know him after we met on the street the day of our arrival, I had seen quite a bit of Chase Reading in Bingham and around the campus. He was one of rebels. He seemed comfortably at the center of things in that group. He must not have cut his hair once since he arrived. His dark hair had that steel wool texture we kidded Jason about, and by mid-year Chase Reading's hair stood out from his head in spikes that gave the immediate impression of some kind of jagged headgear, like Christ's crown of thorns or the spiked crown on the Statue of Liberty. He was disheveled generally, his laceless construction boots open at the front, beltless jeans riding low on his hips. He always seemed to be wearing more than one shirt, and his neck above the collar line was ringed with bands of beads and dirty twine tied in complicated knots. I was not far behind him in the food line one evening when he erupted in a loud, angry showdown with Marvin. There was the sickening tension that precedes an actual, physical fight.

Chase was wearing a weathered army fatigue jacket, a filthy silk tie knotted halfway down the front of a flannel shirt open at the neck. I did not hear Marvin say, "Unacceptable," but I heard Chase shout out, "Unacceptable to *who*? This is completely frigging random! I'm wearing a coat. I'm wearing a tie. And I pay to eat here." Marvin repeated that the outfit was unacceptable and told him to get out of the Commons. Chase was unintimidated. He raised his arms above his head and cried out to the seated diners, "People — *people*! I have just been judged unacceptable by the powers vested in Yale, and I am not allowed to *eat*. It has been determined that a person who looks like me cannot *eat*! *Acht-tung and Sieg Heil*!"

Chase, arms still in the air, turned around a few times like a prize fighter in the ring. Then he bowed to Marvin, and as he left the Commons, practically everybody who was seated got up and roared. It was confusing, because some of the people who stood up were cheering the decision to expel Chase from the hall, while others were cheering in support of his outburst, but the combined effect was unmistakably celebratory, and I could see that Chase was elated.

I have no idea how, or even if, Chase made his peace with Marvin. I was unaware of any future confrontations in the serving line. Compliance must have been reached somehow, because Chase and his friends could be seen animatedly sharing meals in the Commons. In fact, not too long after Chase's angry exchange with Marvin, he and his friends began performing impromptu entertainments in the course of lunch and dinner. At first, we were startled to be called shrilly to attention and then invited to watch and listen. The group called themselves the Yale University Unacceptables, and it was clear that they had put some time and thought into their sketches. If there was an element of rebellion or protest in their efforts, it was not expressed in outward attitude, which was antic and spirited. The performances, some only a minute or two, others stretching to fifteen or twenty, were usually farcical treatments of some cultural abstraction, like Evolution or Religions of the World. It was farce of the broadest, sloppiest kind. The group would usually begin, after calling for the attention of all the diners, by distributing smudgy mimeographed "programs" printed on single sheets of typing paper. There were never enough of those to begin to go around—perhaps forty or fifty would be handed to those seated nearest to where The Unacceptables had set up—but I remember thinking, when I would get hold of one, that in their anarchic, absurdist way, they were pretty funny.

The Evolution skit began with a mock-pompous announcement that scientists at Yale had just solved the final mystery of the origin of species by at last locating The Missing Link. Then Chase shouted, *"Blackout!"* and one of the players appeared with cardboard fins crudely taped to his sides, back, and the top of his head. "I am a very early fish," he said, and then, with what may have been an attempt to mock the diction and poses of a Gilbert and Sullivan player, sang a little song.

> *I am indeed a very early fish,*
> *Perchance not so advanced as you might wish,*
> *Yet certain of my roe will someday fly,*

You'll see my progeny up in the sky,
And eons hence in nature's by and by,
My spawn will even dine in coat and tie.

The evolutionary chain ended with The Missing Link, who was played by Chase Reading. He was carried out by the others and set down on a table where he lay curled up in a ball. As the other players moved to the side and began droning the melody of Richard Strauss's *Also Sprach Zarathustra*—"dah, dah, dah....*DAH*-dah"—Chase rose up out of his ball, stretching himself out, suggesting perhaps the awakening of Early Man. He fished something out his pocket—a balled up tie—and he let it unfurl, regarded it with ape-like incomprehension. He put it in his mouth, he wrapped it around his head like a bonnet and made faces, he wiped it across his behind. Then, with intense simian concentration, be slung the tie up around the back of his neck and began, slowly, to tie a Windsor knot. When he was finished, he fell to his knees and threw his head back, as the other player-animals formed a bowl around him and sang, to the tune of "Swinging on a Star,"

So to evolve from a slug way up high
And have a really complicated eye,
And always keep your pants dry—
You must grow up and wear a tie—yeah!

Now all the players were standing, arms locked together, doing high kicks.

To raucous cheering, which was largely heartfelt, Chase and his friends—The Unacceptables—took a series of exaggerated bows, then ran out of the Commons. They were a hit. Hundreds of my classmates, I am sure, made their way out of the hall feeling, as I did, that we had been stimulated, energized. It wasn't *Beyond the Fringe*, but in some ways its impact may have been even greater. There was an undeniable sense, stimulating to many of the boys, worrying to the faculty and staff, that if disaffected and headstrong students ever succeeded in setting the tone of discourse at the university, there would be no end to the trouble.

I believe Chase Reading knew there would be trouble. As superficially as I knew him then, I sensed his genius for creating discomfort. By the close of the decade, there would be a widely acknowledged term, "happening," for the kind of disruption Chase and his friends liked to cause. But before anybody could categorize it or theorize about it at Yale, The Unacceptables were on the loose. In less than a year, all of them would drop out of Yale, some, like Chase, voluntarily, others because they did no work or their families failed to pay their bills. But over the course of the winter and spring of my freshman year, the Unacceptables succeeded in altering the tone of campus life.

For most of us the performances in the Commons became a welcome feature of dining hours. The Unacceptables would appear at least once a week, sometimes two or three times. Their costumes became more elaborate. Possibly someone in the group had access to the Drama School's wardrobe, because I distinctly remember Civil War get-ups with authentic-looking rifles. Sometimes the players would be decked out in cavalier tunics, tights, hats with plumes. At one point in the spring, Chase and his short, squat friend who everybody called Toad got hold of Batman and Robin costumes and did a series of sight gags in the Commons.

I NEVER WITNESSED ANY OF it myself, but that spring Chase and Toad caused a stir campus-wide by interrupting—as Batman and Robin-- lectures, concerts, and once, famously, a symposium on the War in Viet Nam which included Secretary of Defense MacNamara. The Yale Daily News began reporting the disruptions, running large photographs of Chase and Toad gesticulating on desk tops or fleeing a lecture hall, capes flying behind them. Yale faculty and administrators were quoted in the News to the effect that this kind of disruption violated not just good sense and necessary standards of civility, but infringed on the speech rights of the university's professors and invited guests. By April, as the first promising signs of warmer weather beckoned us outdoors, the campus had a distinct feeling of coming alive, even recklessly alive. Chase's Batman appearances and other offerings from The Unacceptables had somehow become absorbed into the stirring spring atmosphere. Inevitably, established faculty and authorities set up against the stunts, unequivocally so if they took place in a classroom or some other university-sponsored gathering. Students were for the most part untroubled by the occasional jokey disruption of a class or lecture and, if challenged to take sides, predictably favored the Unacceptables, pointing out that they too had speech rights.

The controversy reached a sensational pitch when Astronomy Professor Delmar DePew attacked Chase Reading with a yard stick. This encounter, which was eventually noted in both *Time* and *The New York Times*, occurred when Chase and Toad attempted to stage a Batman vignette in Professor Depew's legendary Principles of Astronomy course. Principles of Astronomy was perhaps Yale's most famous "gut," a series of ill-attended presentations in a domed amphitheater in which an unbroken succession of celestial constellations was projected out of the blackness onto the ceiling. It was claimed that Professor DePew had taught the same course, lifelessly reading from the same set of yellowing lecture notes, for more than forty years. Known to undergraduates for decades as "Sleeping under the Stars," the course involved only one short mid-term examination and a final. The answers to the multiple choice questions on both exams had been passed on faithfully to successive classes for years, and no one could recall anyone not getting an A in Principles of Astronomy.

Chase probably sensed the built-in comic potential of inserting a Batman episode into Sleeping Under the Stars. He may or may not have foreseen Professor DePew's hair trigger temper. As it happened, there was plenty of drama, not all of it intended. Typical of the Unacceptables' enactments, Chase and Toad had obviously given this incursion some forethought. As the hall would be darkened within seconds of the class's beginning, they knew that any kind of entrance from the illuminated corridor into the darkened amphitheater would call immediate attention and weaken the surprise value of their sudden appearance. Having clearly investigated the room in advance, they worked out a way to conceal Toad in a storage closet at the side of the hall, while Chase managed to insert himself inside the cupboards below the demonstration counter at the base of the amphitheater. Chase later revealed to the *News* that he had to lie out flat on a cupboard shelf among the beakers and tools and rock samples for almost two hours, as there was another hour-long class in the amphitheater immediately before Professor DePew's.

It was reported that about ten minutes into Professor Depew's lecture, Toad (as Robin) slipped out of the closet and made his way onto a desk top midway up the amphitheater. "*Hey, fellas!*" he began, caught now in the bright beam of a flashlight held by Chase/Batman who had slipped out of the cupboard on cue. Toad started into scripted material which questioned the reasons for attending a class when the outcome was already known. According to student witnesses, Toad/Robin did not get very far into his recitation when Professor DePew, with a force and speed nobody in the hall thought possible, left his stool at the base of the amphitheater and, brandishing a yardstick, bounded up the steps in a direct line to Toad's desk top. "*Oh, no*—Oh, no you're not, young man," Professor DePew reportedly shouted, waving his stick. "You are not cute! You are not funny! You are not *interesting!*" Now ghoulishly lit by Chase's flashlight beam, Professor Depew's approach in an unmistakable attitude of assault succeeded in quieting Toad. He got down from the desk top and, just a step or two ahead of the professor, ran out the doorway and down the corridor.

At that moment, students told the *News*, Chase, now standing up on the demonstration counter, called for the class's attention. From a grandly extended arm, he cast a shaft of light onto his masked face, shoulders, and cape. "*Men,*" he began, "I speak to you below these heavens"—he gestured to the stalled constellation spanning the dome above—"on a matter of grave importance." Professor De Pew, now making his way back down from the top of the amphitheater, interrupted angrily. "Enough of this nonsense. You are *trespassing*, you arrogant wretch." When Professor DePew reached the counter where Chase was standing, he struck the platform sharply with the yard stick. "*Out!*" he demanded, "This is my *classroom!*"

Students present said Chase was clearly not about to get down off the counter and leave. It is hard for me to imagine him lost for words, but reportedly he stood for a tense moment staring directly down into the face of Professor DePew. That, all witnesses agree, was when Professor

Depew began slashing away at Chase's feet and knees with the yard stick. Reflexively Chase danced off to one side but still made no effort to get down and withdraw. As Professor DePew renewed the assault, Chase tilted the flashlight to illuminate the yard stick's thwacking against his shoes and shins. Then he raised the beam to his own face, canted upward as if in supplication to the stars twinkling overhead. "My god, my god," he said, "Why hast thou forsaken me?" Then, possibly really angry, he bent over, grabbed an end of the yardstick and yanked it out of Professor DePew's hands. For a second, he raised the stick, as if he was going to strike Professor Depew back. He raised it again, as if to exploit the tension, then he set the stick down on the countertop. "Just remember, men," he said, the flashlight now held just under his chin, "these really are the best years of your lives." Someone turned on the overhead lights, and amid the sputter and babble that followed, Chase made his unhurried way out of the amphitheater, shoulder to shoulder with the other students leaving the hall.

Within hours there were rumors that Chase and the other Unacceptables were now in official trouble with the university. There was talk of expulsion, including reports that the boys involved had already left the campus. But that evening Chase and his friends appeared at the Commons for dinner, apparently untroubled.

One day that spring when I had passed through the serving line at the Commons, I spotted Chase at the beverage counter, and I felt an urge to greet him, make some kind of contact. As I approached, I could see he was filling a tall thermos with coffee. This seemed peculiar to me. No one to my knowledge ever stored up provisions, beyond the occasional apple, to eat or drink elsewhere. Like so many things Chase seemed to do, filling a personal thermos with Commons coffee, while probably not expressly forbidden, seemed wrong. I could imagine someone, perhaps Marvin, challenging him, and I could see Chase squaring off aggressively and asking what was the difference between filling his thermos and coming back for three or four refills. Probably because I was imagining such a scenario, I found myself at a loss for what to say to him as I rested my tray next to his and scanned the beverage selections. Our eyes met,

315

and I said, "Hi."

His eyes were wild, somehow impenetrable and bright at the same time. He drew back a little, as if frightened, and I wondered if he was putting me on. Then he said to me, "I know you. Sure I know you." He looked at me intently without saying anything until I was feeling uncomfortable. He said, "And look what's *happening* to you, what they're doing to you, man. They have got you. They have *got* you." He finished filling two ceramic mugs with coffee, tucked his thermos under his arm, and made his way from the beverage counter, a steaming mug in each hand.

The exchange unsettled me. I was not absolutely sure what he meant by *they've got you*, but I did not like it at all. I did not like the idea that anybody had *gotten* me, and I didn't like somebody's presuming to know that it had happened. I wanted what he told me to be nonsense, but I felt accused. I felt labeled. *They have got you.* I wanted to be more confused by the words than I was. I was pretty sure Chase's "they" was Yale-- the professors, the books, knowledge itself. What I wanted to be a lofty choice was, to someone like Chase, a pitiful submission. I had submitted, forfeited my real self, and it showed. It would take someone as obnoxious and impolite as Chase Reading to say it out loud.

Honestly, I don't know if I consciously thought those thoughts, but I do know Chase Reading stunned me, and I felt bad. Nor did it make me feel any better when, to my unease, Chase approached me a few days later and attempted to apologize. I was once again at the Commons beverage counter when a hand clapped me on the shoulder. I turned around and looked into his eyes, which did not look especially wild. He was smiling. He said he was sorry if he said anything crazy to me the other night.

I had two thoughts simultaneously. The first is that our prior exchange was at lunch, a little after noon. The second thought was that he hadn't seemed crazy at all, just intrusive and, in a way I couldn't find words for, hurtful. I didn't know what to say to him. I was in pause-and-consider mode. If there had been time, I probably would have found a way to ask him what he meant by *they have got you*. But I had not arrived at that point when he said he was sorry. He hoped he hadn't said anything too awful. He made a little nervous snort, looked at me hard and said, "I was totally whacked. Out of it. I had just chewed a half bag of morning glory seeds, which I will never do again. I was not in this world. But I know I saw you and probably weirded you out." I told him I didn't think he had been all that weird. I decided not to bother asking him about *they've got you*, not because I didn't want to know, but because I didn't think he could say anything that would ease my mind.

Chapter Nine

Not long after that encounter with Chase Reading, it occurred to me that something was wrong with me. It was a strange kind of realization, because it was all feeling and no apparent substance. Outwardly, I could not imagine things being any better. I had figured out how to think and behave in a way that was now working for me at Yale. I was doing very well academically. My life—room, clothes, routines—was completely orderly. There were guys I could talk to and liked being with well enough, and I was starting to get to know a few of my professors at a level beyond the usual student-faculty formalities. I felt good physically, and probably because I walked for miles everyday and climbed the five flights of stairs to my room in Bingham a dozen times, I was pretty fit, lean but not quite so bony as I was in high school. I wasn't much of a mirror bug, but every now and then, when I was brushing my hair after a shower or tying my tie before dinner, it occurred to be that I looked good. I had an impression of sharp angles and dark hair. For some reason I looked especially good in photographs. The scholastic and other things I was focused on were going well, so it was a little confusing that something indescribable and unnamable was bothering me. Sometimes it felt like a shadowy presence following me around. Every now and then I would suddenly remember my sister Annabel's breakdown when I was in high school and that she was gone from my life, probably forever, and this made me feel heavy and low. But the new thing wrong was something else, and it wanted my attention.

Then one morning I knew exactly what it was. I had awakened with the first light coming through my bedroom window in Bingham, looked at the clock and realized I had more than two hours before I had to get up and go to breakfast. I always liked that, the luxurious feeling of being awake in bed but with plenty of uncommitted time ahead, and that's when it hit me. I felt it everywhere. I felt it the length of my body, a kind of tingling that seemed to pass from my skin right into the sheets. I wanted to touch somebody. I wanted to hold a woman or a girl close to me. I wanted to be all wrapped around someone and to hold her there. I wanted to hold someone close for a long time. I wanted it very much, and I wanted it more than anything else.

As soon as I started to feel it, I wondered what had gone dead in me that I hadn't really thought about girls or sex or really anything to do with that side of life for so many months. I had been in love with somebody or other, more or less continuously, as far back as I could remember. I could still recall—vividly—guarding Gwendolyn Bliss as she sat in solitude in the innermost square of the jungle gym on our kindergarten playground. She may not even have been the first. I fell in love with the pictures of all the princesses and maidens on the covers of our operetta records. I held those pulsing images in my heart. I had been a lover, and the love feeling had been everything—so how could I have lost it, gone numb? Quite possibly it was just Yale, which was a men's college, a fact of life I had not thought to question, just as I had never thought to question what Connecticut would be like or college life, for that matter. I may not have been totally oblivious to females since arriving at Yale, but something close to that. My foggy awareness of girls consisted of certain impressions of the faces and forms I sometimes passed on the campus walks on the weekends, girls who had come up as dates from the women's colleges or prep schools. At Palatine High School, and really in all my schools growing up, I had moved through my days in a lively swirl of girls, girls streaming through the crowded hallways, great clusters of girls seated at the cafeteria tables, girls behind me, in front of me, on every side of me in class, girls with plaid pleated skirts, girls with creamy white socks rising out of scuffed saddle shoes, girls with down-soft angora sweaters

319

stretched tight over every conceivable shape of breast. For years I had breathed—breathed happily—an atmosphere tangy with hairspray, colognes, perfumes, and powders. I had always either had a girl friend or longed for one. There had been the electric charge of touching, of dancing, breast to lapel, thigh to thigh, temple to temple, the frozen, wordless current of that. There had been the clasping and caressing of hands, kisses that, behind closed eyes, reduced all sensation to just the soft, moist compression of lips. There had been ecstatic, barely conscious touching, the astonished registering of those touches, then whole body embraces, legs entwined, clutching, moving, half rolling with the pulse and rhythm of the feeling.

Something had happened to that at Yale. There was definitely a kind of twinge that registered whenever I caught a glimpse of the sharp, catlike faces of the weekend girls, the briefest impression of calf and shin under stockings or dark tights. But something in these sightings failed to arrive at full consciousness. Truthfully, to the extent I thought about the oblique encounters with the weekend girls at all, it was to register dimly that they were not for me, that they somehow belonged to a more rarefied, more mature Yale that existed out of my reach, a realm that might be disclosed to me when I was older and otherwise farther along in life, but for which I was for the present utterly unqualified. Again, this was my impression, but it was far from conscious. The truth was I had forgotten girls and romantic longing. Something had made me numb.

What I did next changed my life more profoundly than would any other decision I have made before or since. I decided to make contact with Elizabeth Meeker, my former high school girl friend, a girl I had not spoken or written to since, two weeks prior to our high school graduation, I abruptly disinvited her to the senior prom. To have focused my thoughts and so much charged feeling on Elizabeth puzzles me even now, but at the time, I can't remember deliberating on the decision at all. Elizabeth had been my steady girl friend for nearly three years at Palatine High School. At no time during that period would I say—nor, I am sure, would Elizabeth—that we were especially happy in the relationship. With hindsight, I see clearly that she was more sophisticated and socially aware than

I was, that she and her family had moved in more affluent, more highly educated circles than any I had been exposed to. Looking back, it now seems that, from my perspective, the main substance of my relationship with Elizabeth had been a series of fairly clumsy attempts to figure out and adapt to her highly specific expectations of what a satisfactory high school boy friend should be. Making these adjustments had kept me busy and alert, but it took quite a long time for it to dawn on me that I was deriving very little pleasure from my efforts. My very sudden decision to break our prom date at the last hour—Elizabeth had already bought her dress—still seems almost brutal, but I remember feeling that there could be no gracious disengagement on my part; I needed to shatter the bond. Breaking the prom date may have been my only clear act of self assertion in our early partnership.

Elizabeth had been bewildered and devastated when I broke off with her, and I recall feeling only a stony determination to stick with my decision and after that an energizing sense of relief. I had behaved badly, I knew, but I felt little guilt and no regret whatsoever—which made it even stranger that Elizabeth had become the object of my newly reawakened desire. She simply came to my mind's eye that morning in my bed. The image arrived with a terrific clarity and force. I would have to locate her. I would write or call, tentatively, with great courtesy. I would do everything I could think of to resume relationship. I would try letters first and then, perhaps we would talk on the telephone. I would somehow get her to Yale and by means far from my devising at that moment hold her to me, make love to her.

This kind of thinking inflamed me for weeks. In fact, had it not been for my highly routinized and nearly manic commitment to my studies, I might have been carried far off scholastic course by my new passions and schemes. To be a little objective, I should add that it was not completely capricious of me to have locked onto the image of Elizabeth Meeker as my object of desire. She was, in memory, very attractive, dark, slight, a wonderful coherence to the sharpness of her nose and chin. She had a thin, quick smile which expressed a range of responses from wry appreciation to contempt. She had slender, prettily sculpted legs and delicate ankles. I recalled the silkiness of her skin with an almost crazed appreciation. I had in the course of our most advanced scuffles run my hands up and down the length of her lovely bare back. I had unfastened the little hooks at the back of her brassiere and cupped her feathery soft breasts in my palms. There were no other images and memories to rival these, to crowd them out of my reverie.

I began my preliminary researches with the determination of a scholar, or of a detective. Elizabeth was in residence somewhere at the University of Michigan at Ann Arbor. Either through the University offices or through some findable person I could contact on campus, I would get her address, her phone number there. I determined that calling her house would be a bad idea, as her parents had reacted with justifiable anger when I failed to honor my prom invitation.

Making contact turned out to be surprisingly easy. Ann Arbor information gave me the university number that provided student addresses by dormitory, and I wrote Elizabeth a long, cautious letter. I began by apologizing for my abrupt disappearance from her life and for breaking our prom date. I explained that I was confused and overwhelmed by the big changes that lay ahead, and that I had completely lost my judgment. I wrote about this with great energy and conviction because it was mainly true. Then I wrote quite a bit about Yale and how strange I found everything on arrival and how I had made some adjustments and was now fully into things and was especially enthusiastic about my studies. I included quite a lot, possibly more than was appropriate for a first letter, about particular connections I had made in my history and lit and art history courses, but realize now this was the most effective thing I could have done. Elizabeth was drawn to intellect and especially to intellectual distinction. She was a math prodigy herself with a perfect 800 math SAT and had been admitted to Michigan's honors program, which only took about a hundred kids from the thousands in the freshman class. As it turned out, I had a number of things working on my behalf. One of them was that Elizabeth was impressed by Yale—and had even, I thought, put me down a little about getting in, mainly by being incredulous. She had said, "How can things like that keep happening to you?"—as if it bothered her.

Still, the idea of places like Yale and Harvard impressed her, as did my letter, with all its references to pictures and sculptures, historical events, Plato and Aristotle. I closed by saying I had been thinking about her a lot (completely true), trying not to sound desperate or obsessed (completely untrue), and hoping that she would be willing to keep in touch with me.

The letter worked perfectly. I got a letter back six days later which, I figured, meant that she had answered mine as soon as she possibly could. I didn't know quite what to expect, as our break-up had been sudden and absolute. Elizabeth was a girl who felt best when she was in the know and in control. One of the first things I learned about her was that she would rather be in a miserable situation which she understood than in a lively, interesting one which she hadn't expected. She did not want to be surprised, and if she had a strong expectation that something was going to happen, it had better happen. She wasn't noisy or demonstrative, but she was bright and aware of more than I ever imagined when I was first getting to know her. She also had the ability, when she was upset, to make me feel not only bad because now I was with somebody who was unhappy, but also to feel the exact nature and intensity of her unhappiness. At those times it seemed that her interior condition had somehow invaded mine, and all I could feel was what she was feeling, and there could be no end to it until the trouble passed and she got over it. The effect this had on me was to make me feel that as long as Elizabeth was upset, I pretty much had to disappear as my own self and just tend to her or try to fix things or sometimes just wait until it felt like there was enough room and enough air for me to breathe my own breaths. Had I better understood this power of hers over me when we were in high school, I would have been more consciously aware of what motivated me to part with her so abruptly and decisively the spring of our senior year. But if I had known that kind of thing then, I would also have known better than to rekindle the relationship at Yale and, far more consequentially, to marry her.

Of course no such understanding was at work when I composed my long letter of reconciliation or when I read her heartening reply. She said she was so glad I had written. She said her response to my prom season retreat had been at first shock and sadness, then terrific anger, then a terrible loss of confidence. At first I had a hard time imagining Elizabeth losing confidence, because her outward manner could be so breezy and tough and sure, but then I began to understand it perfectly. She said the effect of my walking away was to make her wonder if there was something deeply wrong with her which, once people figured it out, would make them turn way from her, as I had. She also filled me in on her college news, saying there were a lot of really smart kids at Michigan but also thousands and thousands of them that seemed to be filling up space. She said Michigan was all about fraternities and sororities, parties and big sports weekends. She said the campus was impressive, mainly because it was so huge, but that Ann Arbor itself was flat and ordinary looking and very cold. She said it could be Palatine with an enormous university in the middle of it.

I got two useful things out of Elizabeth's letter. The first was that she sounded exactly as I thought she would. Her style and tone were just what I had imagined, which told me I knew her better than I thought, which meant my hopes and schemes for getting together with her might work out. This really excited me. The second thing her letter revealed was that since she was so unimpressed with Michigan, it was highly likely she would be intrigued by Yale, even envious that I was there.

My next few letters were full of Yale life, especially its quirky traditions. I wrote about the Bladder Ball Game and Mory's and the Whiffenpoofs. I told her that Yale felt walled in from the outside world, that the colleges looked like gray gothic villages. I told her about prep school kids, especially rich, eccentric ones I knew about or heard about. I wrote her about Chase Reading and the Unacceptables. I wrote in detail about a character people in Bingham were always telling stories about. His name was Lane Etheridge, a boy from Andover. I actually barely ever saw him, but Chad Pickering knew all about him. Lane Etheridge looked to me about forty years old. He had long wavy straw-colored hair parted in the middle, which made him look not just older but from another era. He wasn't really fat, but he was fleshy the way a grown man is fleshy. He was supposed to be very rich, but I didn't know what his parents did or who they were. There were a lot of stories about how little he thought of

Yale and how bored and reckless he was. He rarely went to classes or to meals in the Commons. He had food sent up to his rooms, and he was supposed to have kept a running tab at a New Haven liquor store, where he would have had little trouble convincing the proprietors he was of age. According to the stories, Lane Etheridge mainly sat in his room drinking whisky and ice, chain smoking, and holding court in a sour, savage way. I actually didn't like the prospect of getting to know him and spending time around him, but he generated a lot of interest, probably because by living so recklessly and unsustainably, he made everybody else feel safer and on track. One especially awful story Chad Pickering told me was of Lane Etheridge heating up quarters with his cigarette lighter and then dropping them with a tweezers from his window down onto the sidewalk where little black kids from New Haven would pick them up and burn themselves. I don't know exactly why I included this story in a letter to Elizabeth, but my hope was that she would see that I lived in much more exotic world than she did.

Again, it worked. I didn't even have to be pushy about asking her to visit, because by her second letter she was saying how nice it would be for us to get together some time. But arranging for her to get from Ann Arbor to New Haven wasn't like asking someone from Smith or Wellesley down for a weekend. By juggling some labs and taking a full day off from classes, she figured out a way to get to New Haven by train. It involved taking a bus to Toledo, then catching a train to New York, then changing trains at Penn Station for New Haven. It would take sixteen hours each way, but she seemed as eager to arrange it as I was to have her all to myself for two full days.

Chapter Ten

I NEVER QUITE BELIEVED it was going to happen, even though the weekend of her arrival was on my calendar, and Elizabeth was, I knew, the kind of person who follows through. She wanted to know where she would be staying, which was a good question. Almost idiotically, I had not thought about it. I had vaguely assumed that girls who came to visit people at Yale just knew where to go. But with a little thought, it was clear that it would be my job as host to find a place for Elizabeth to lodge and also, I assumed, to pay for it. I asked Chad Pickering what he did when his girl friend came down from St. Mary's in the Mountains for the Harvard-Yale game. He said he booked a room for her at Mrs. Fletcher's, a boarding house in New Haven, but he said the rooms would probably be booked solid on the weekends for the rest of the year. He also told me he didn't think Mrs. Fletcher's was all that great, because Mrs. Fletcher was really strict, and you had to check in at the front hall in order to send a message up to the room to tell your date you were there, and there was no visiting in the girls' rooms or anywhere else except the front hallway. It had to be that way, Chad said, or else girls' parents wouldn't let them come, especially if they were in high school. The whole idea of locating a boarding house like Mrs. Fletcher's, making the reservations, and following all the rules made me tired. But I thought of a better idea. On my way to my dry cleaner's I always passed the New Haven Hotel. It was barely a block away from the college gates, and I noticed they had a restaurant and a coffee shop. It was a massive, ancient looking place, and nothing about it suggested anything about college life. The only people I saw in the lobby when I checked it out inside were old ladies.

When I went in to ask the woman at reception about the room, I had to sit down for a while in one of the lounge chairs in the lobby until I could calm down. My heart was pounding, and I was feeling like a criminal, like I was putting something over on someone, but I was also wildly excited. I went up to the reception desk and in a voice that was almost normal asked if there was a room available for the weekend Elizabeth was coming. There was, and the rest was easy, although the room cost a little more than I thought, fifty dollars a night. The woman said they had a cheaper one, for thirty-five dollars, but she said it was pretty small, with a single bed, no frills. I had a feeling Elizabeth would appreciate frills, so I booked the room and paid for both nights in advance. Now I was about as excited as you can get.

Over the two weeks before Elizabeth's visit, I spent a lot of time figuring out what we would do. I decided it would be better to have a lot of possibilities and decide not to do some things than to be wondering and fussing while we were together. Friday night I'd get a cab and meet her at the station, then we'd check her in at the hotel, maybe walk around some of the colleges, then go back to the hotel for dinner, then maybe to the Cercle Cinema to see a foreign movie. The next morning I would pick her up at the hotel, take her to my ten o'clock Art in Western Culture lecture, then have lunch somewhere with Chad Pickering and his friends and maybe some of their dates. There was a mixer on Saturday night for freshmen and sophomores in the Commons, and that, I figured, would pretty much do it. We'd have something to eat together Sunday morning, and then I'd get a cab and take her to her train. That plan in place, all I had to do was line up Chad and some other people for reliable company and make sure my best clothes were laundered and ready.

As the Friday of her arrival approached, I couldn't look at anything or anybody without imagining what Elizabeth would see and what she would make of it.

Chapter Eleven

It was actually kind of eerie how much that first weekend with Elizabeth went off exactly as I thought it would. It helped that Elizabeth turned out to be easy company. When she stepped down from the train I got a strong sense that she had her own plans for this visit and for me. I was struck at once by how familiar she looked and how comfortable and right it felt having her close beside me as we walked. I was aware of myself as if observed by a stranger. I had a partner, a girl. I had entered the category of Yale men who knew women, who could somehow summon them to their sides. Even headier, as I examined my imaginary camera's perspective of Elizabeth and me walking briskly along the rail platform, was the realization that my particular woman, Elizabeth, was an eye-catching beauty, a prize, a catch. She was unquestionably the Elizabeth of memory, but at the same time, there was something new, something even shrewder and sharper than I remembered in the way she took me in and sized me up. I came close to being intimidated by her in the way I used to be back in Palatine when she was critical of something I wore or said. But almost from the moment our eyes met, I sensed that she was now curious and interested in me in a new way. I told myself I had to remember to stay in charge, do things nicely and thoughtfully, but my way.

I know I must have seemed different to Elizabeth. For one thing, I looked a little different. My clothes were all good and freshly laundered, and there was something that always looked right about my duffle coat and scarf. My hair was much longer and angled across my forehead in a way she had not seen before. I probably looked older to her and surer of myself, because I actually was surer of myself. But I was far from relaxed. I had to make an enormous effort to sound calm when I spoke, and I had to work consciously to keep my eyes averted from her face and body. Because the first thing I noticed when I realized the girl stepping down from the train onto the platform was Elizabeth was that she was not just good looking, but striking. I recognized immediately the old sharpness and delicacy of her features, the nicely cut vee of her chin, the quick, sly smile, the flash of her dark eyes. She wore a pleated kilt, and her black tights drew my gaze down to the lovely ridge of her calf muscles and the delicate bones of her ankles. I had known she was slender, but for a moment as I first beheld her in her open coat, open enough for me to get a sense of how her sweater clung to her waist and molded the mounds of her breasts, she seemed wonderfully, impossibly slender, and then I remembered the silky feel of her skin along the expanse of her naked back, the strangely weightless feel of her wrapped around me when we used to embrace on her living room carpet in front of the unwatched T.V.

From someplace far outside my body I heard myself saying things like, "long trip" and "you must be exhausted" and "so this is New Haven," and I heard Elizabeth say things like "It feels good to be here" and "you're looking well." As soon as we turned into the New Haven Hotel, I saw that she was impressed, glad that she was going to be staying in her own room, on her own terms. She told me she assumed I would put her up in a guest house of some kind where she would have to room with another girl and use a bathroom down the hall. She was even gladder when we unlocked the door of her room and saw that it was huge. I thought it would be just a big bedroom with a bathroom to one side, but it was a large, high-ceilinged L-shaped room with the bed in the front part and a kind of living room around the corner. "Jonathan, "Elizabeth said, "This is so nice." It really was. I sat down on a little sofa in the living room section while Elizabeth emptied her suitcase and arranged her things. There was something unusual, something fancy about the bed, and then I realized that it was covered with a canopy supported by four carved posts. There were, I realized, lots of fancy touches like that, little end tables with silver boxes on them, more chairs than a person could ever need in a hotel room, vases with cut flowers, a radio by the bed, a television set in the sitting room. It was like a house, but a really nice house, and I felt myself agreeably swelling into all that space.

For just about every instant of that first visit I felt weirdly divided into two selves. Inwardly I was almost too excited to think, my eyes hungry to take in everything about her, especially her face, her slender neck, the way her clothes revealed the lines of her body. I wanted to stare at her, not to lose sight of her, not to miss a single expression, not even to blink, which had the effect of making me avert my eyes. Outwardly, I could only think of the most general, polite-sounding things to say and felt a little awkward in my formality. The only way I could get any sense of myself was to listen to the things I was saying as if they were coming from somewhere else and to picture myself as if I were in some kind of movie. All the while an insistent little voice from within was saying something like *keep it interesting, you've got to be interesting.*

Just as I had imagined it, the walk around the old campus was bracing and I think impressive to Elizabeth. It was the last light of afternoon, the air was bright and crisp and not too cold, and the settled masses of the gothic buildings were as imposing as I had hoped. My fantasies and schemes for getting physically close to Elizabeth, finding time alone together to touch and kiss and undress and make love were all still working inside of me, but they did not connect at all to anything I could actually manage to say or do as I walked at her side, holding forth on practically everything we saw. After a while we agreed we were hungry enough to go back to the hotel and have dinner. When we got to Phelps Gate, Elizabeth stopped and peered back into the darkening commons. "You're lucky," she said. "Good things are just going to keep happening to you."

I didn't know what to say. There was something warm, also a little sad, about the way she said it. We crossed the street into the city, and I said, "How about you? Are good things going to happen to you?" She stopped and looked at me hard. I didn't look away. Elizabeth said, "I don't really think so." I asked her if there was something wrong. She laughed, and we walked on. "Maybe this visit will be a good thing," she said. "Maybe you'll be a good thing." She looked at me again. "What do you think, Jonathan?" Then she gave me a little knock with her hip, which is what she used to do in high school when we were walking somewhere and she was in a good mood. It felt good. It helped break through my formality pose. Without even thinking about it, I put my arm behind her back and drew her in close to me. She did not seem surprised, and she did not resist. She looked directly into my eyes, as if she were waiting for something important. I took her hand with my free hand and, still staring into her eyes, I said, "Elizabeth, would you care to dance?"

After that everything was easy. Neither of us had to say anything, but we both knew we had come together, that we were joined, that we were now a couple. About a year later, when Elizabeth and I were recalling that first New Haven weekend, she told me she thought my asking her to dance on the street was my way of fulfilling my lapsed promise to take her to our high school prom. I hadn't thought of anything like that, but I wasn't sorry she did. Actually, the reason I took her hand was that it seemed a way of stopping short of completing the embrace and kissing her, which may not, at the moment, have been welcome.

We took our time over dinner, and that helped me to relax. I was glad that there were no other students in the hotel dining room, just a few older couples who barely made a sound. Sitting across from Elizabeth in that hushed and formal setting, I had a strong feeling that I wasn't, at least for the moment, a kid or even a Yale student. I felt like a grown man, a mysterious sort of man of no distinct type, but a man who knew enough about the world to meet a woman for a weekend in an unfamiliar city, to order a meal in a formal dining room, to be amusing in conversation. I was still acting, but I was getting to like it.

By dessert it occurred to me that maybe Elizabeth was not getting enough of Yale. Except for our walk, we could have been anywhere. I suggested that we walk over to the Cercle Cinema and see what was playing. I told her there was usually a good foreign film on Friday nights. "Such as--?" she asked, but my mind went blank. I had only walked by the Cercle Cinema and read the copy on the posters; I had never seen a movie there.

The feature that night was *The 400 Blows*, directed by Francois Truffaut. The posters and a mimeographed handout suggested it was about a boy growing up. I was about to ask Elizabeth what she thought when she said, "Oh, Truffaut—New *Wave*." This was one of the things I was going to have to get used to about Elizabeth. She was smart, almost always smarter than I thought she was going to be at any given moment. She was also well-informed because she read the newspaper and all kinds of magazines. She already knew about Truffaut and New Wave films. I bought tickets and we found seats in the musty auditorium. Before the lights went down for the film, I took a look around to see the kinds of people who had come. It was about what I had hoped. There were plenty of bearded, rumpled-looking Yalies with wire-rimmed glasses and dark sweaters and tweed jackets. I wanted them to seem to Elizabeth as exotic as possible. I asked her if there was a foreign film society at Michigan, and she said, "Are you kidding?"

I really liked *The 400 Blows*. A story about a boy not fitting in at home or in his horrible school and then running away seemed just right for that evening, because it made me feel really strong and pulled together by comparison. I was glad to be past all that unhappiness and uncertainty myself, but I liked looking into the cloudy face of the boy played by Jean-Pierre Léaud, and I liked feeling older and farther along than he was. I also really liked being in that particular place, watching the movie, doing something completely new together with Elizabeth. Stepping out into the cold after the film, Elizabeth said, "I *loved* that, didn't you?" Then she said, "Do you realize how much Jean-Pierre Léaud looks like you?" I had not thought about that for a second, but immediately I could see what she meant.

Without really planning to, we followed a pack of other students across the street to a little coffee house called Basilio's. It was a narrow, dimly lit room with a serving bar running nearly the length of one of the walls, the other lined with rickety, mismatched wooden chairs and tables, each set with a chess board. Again I was glad. This felt like Yale, although not as I had known it, but as I had wanted Elizabeth to see it. I think she was tired, but she didn't seem anxious to go back to the hotel. We took little sips of café au lait and talked about our families, about college life at Michigan, about the people that interested us in high school. Then I realized that I was really tired myself, so tired my legs felt heavy when I stood up to go.

There was nobody but a night clerk behind the reception desk at the hotel when we entered the lobby. I wasn't quite sure of the procedure at this point, whether I should say good night to Elizabeth in front of the elevator or at the door of her room upstairs. I asked her if she would like me to walk her to her room, realizing as I said it that "walk her" was the wrong term for an elevator ride up. Elizabeth looked at me and gave me a sleepy smile. "Sure, Jonathan. Walk me home."

Upstairs Elizabeth rummaged through her purse for her room key. Something about the hushed corridor and the dim, buttery light made both of us speak in whispers. I told Elizabeth I was really glad she had come. She said she was glad too and thanked me for a nice dinner and evening. I was too tired to keep from staring into her face, and she gave me a questioning look. I knew we were about to kiss, but I was not sure what kind of kiss it should be. I moved to her and placed my arm lightly around her waist, once again drawing her hand up into mine and clasping it to the lapel of my jacket. "Are we going to dance again?" Elizabeth said. I said yes, and we executed a slow box step in front of her door. Then I leaned down and brushed my cheek against hers. Elizabeth reached both her arms around my neck and clung to me. My hands found her waist inside her open coat, and I drew her body into me. The kiss was soft and dry and lovely. We drew our heads back, looked at each other, and we kissed again, and this time Elizabeth made a little sound and began moving her mouth on mine and I could feel a swaying motion in her hips. Something vague but welcome was building up, which both of us, I could tell, were willing to prolong. Then Elizabeth stepped back and was, I thought, about to say something, when she clung to me even harder and kissed me again. My mind was empty now of all thought. Elizabeth said, "I better go to bed." I told her I would be by for breakfast and watched her unlock the door to her room and step inside. She dropped her things then turned to me again, guiding the door in close to her temple, and said, "Promise me you'll be a good thing that happens to me."

"Promise," I said.

BACK IN MY ROOM AT Bingham I did not sleep at all, or want to. When I closed my eyes, loops of images from the afternoon and evening would play against the dark like silent movies, Elizabeth's knees and calves and ankles in her black tights, the little knock of her hip against mine as we walked from the commons to the hotel, her dark eyes and alert fox's face across the table from me at dinner, her sweet vague sleepiness as we sipped café au lait at Basilio's, the kisses in the corridor, the warm eager kisses, the way she moved her mouth over mine with a sleepy, mindless hunger, that little swaying in her hips. There were grainy black and white sequences of The 400 Blows and then only the full frontal planes and shadows of Jean-Pierre Leaud's face, and Elizabeth was saying, "Didn't you love it?" and "Do you realize how much Jean-Pierre Leaud looks like you?"

I felt I was sleepwalking through a lot of the next day. We had a little breakfast together, went to my lecture, met up with Chad and some other friends for lunch, which went fine, but by about two o'clock when we were sitting around in the Bingham lounge, my eyes started to close from the bottom. Elizabeth said, "Are you going to *sleep* on me?" But I think she was as tired as I was, because she said she had better go back to the hotel and rest for a while if she was going to be able to make it through the mixer later. I was embarrassed to be so out of it, but was glad to get out into the cool air and walk her back to the hotel. I took her hand as we walked, and she gave mine a squeeze, and that made me feel very happy. It was nice walking hand in hand like that, not having to make conversation.

Just inside the lobby, I started to say good-bye and tell her when I would be by for her, but she said why didn't I come up to the room and keep her company for a while. I had been thinking we were both going to take a big nap, but now I could not imagine being sleepy. We took the elevator up, and when we got inside her room she kicked her shoes off and lay down on her bed. Then she patted the space next to her and said, "Lie down with me, we can just rest." Elizabeth looked completely relaxed. I took off my shoes and lay down next to her, taking care that there was a little space between us. Elizabeth shimmied up against me and again gave me the little hip knock. "Yes?" I said, and she laughed. Then I stopped thinking.

I eased my arm around her neck and rolled onto my side. She turned to meet me, and we held each other. Then, as I knew it would, our last kiss in the corridor, the hungry one, the kiss with the movement, resumed, and we were rocking gently side to side, our legs now scissored together, rocking and rocking. Because I didn't want to open my eyes, I don't know what anything looked like, but it felt to me as if we were rising, rising and floating above the surface of the bed. Elizabeth felt like no weight at all, just a sweet, pleasing fit, a miraculous complement to my body, and I was lost in all of it, our mouths open and searching, and now I was tasting her mouth and tongue, and wanting only more, and moving more, answering the movement of her hips, knowing that it was all right, that everything was all right and we would do everything in that gauzy afternoon light.

When we woke up it was nearly dark in the room. At some point I did not remember one of us must have pulled the bedspread over our nakedness. Elizabeth was already awake when I opened my eyes. We looked at each other without saying anything. Elizabeth was smiling beautifully, and we kissed and fitted ourselves together again. It did not really occur to me in my sleepiness that there was a reality beyond the darkness and the bed and the feel of Elizabeth's silky back and shoulders, her warm haunch snug between my legs. Finally she spoke, and her voice was low and scratchy and lovely. She said, "So what about this mixer?" And I said, yes, the mixer, and we got out of bed, took turns bathing, and got dressed.

MAKING LOVE TO ELIZABETH SO completely that afternoon felt tremendously final, but I also felt that something incalculably vast and important was opening up, something for which I had no words, and it was just beginning. Elizabeth seemed to sense it too, because we didn't feel a need to talk about what had just happened. But we were changed. I felt it in the way I could not walk down the hotel corridor with her or down the street or up the steps to the Commons without clasping her hand and feeling her near. By the time we ate something and made our way to the mixer, the dancing had started and the party was well along. There was an agreeable din of people shouting to be heard over the band's amplifiers which made the gathering lively and anonymous, which was fine with me. All the furniture from the lounge was pulled back to line the walls, creating a big dance floor, which was mostly full when we arrived. After a minute or two I spotted Chad Pickering and Jason and some of my study friends in Bingham, so I knew there would be someone for us to talk to if we felt like it. Chad made his way over to us and greeted us, followed by a friend of his from Holderness named Pike and Pike's date, Vicki, a girl from Mount Holyoke. Chad asked us if we would like something to drink. Alcohol wasn't served at mixers, but nobody minded if people brought liquor in, provided it wasn't obvious. Chad and Pike each had a bottle of rum in their overcoats, and Chad said he'd mix us a drink, if we wanted. Elizabeth said sure, so I said why not, and in a minute we were each sipping a rum and coke in a paper cup, not quite dancing to the music but moving with it. It may have been the happiest and most relaxed I had ever felt. It was easy being with people, and my friends were easy with Elizabeth, and I could tell Chad and Pike and Jason and everybody we chatted with thought Elizabeth was impressive, and I could see them making an effort to be impressive themselves. Elizabeth and I danced a lot, and I could see the happy, unexamined secret of our afternoon in her eyes and in her smile. I looked around and fixed my attention on other couples and tried to determine if they could possibly have had sex that day. I could not imagine they did. Nobody else seemed to be in the transported, happy trance Elizabeth and I were in.

A little before midnight we found our coats and made our way back to the New Haven Hotel. As we were walking, I started to picture the night before, kissing Elizabeth at the door of her room, the walk back through the cold to Bingham. Elizabeth may have been thinking the same thing, because she asked me if I had to go back to the dormitory and if I could stay with her. Just her saying it got me aroused. I told her of course I would stay with her if she wanted me to. Then I had a jarring thought—we had had sex without a rubber. I did not feel comfortable bringing it up, but I told Elizabeth I didn't have any protection, meaning a rubber, and I didn't really know where I could find anything at that hour, and was it a bad thing that we didn't use anything that afternoon. Suddenly my head was spinning. Elizabeth said not to worry. Her period had ended the day before the trip. We would be fine. I was really glad she knew that kind of thing, because I certainly didn't. But she did say that in the future protection would be a good idea.

THAT NIGHT IN BED WITH Elizabeth was like entering a shadow world. Nothing about it connected at all to anything I had known or felt before. Being under that high ceiling in the filmy darkness of that room was like a kind of sanctuary, a holy place, and this time when I undressed, I was deliberate and careful, folding my shirt and hanging up my slacks and jacket as if I were performing a solemn ritual. Neither of us said much, and when we did we spoke in a whisper. Part of the strangeness and the holiness was that I knew we were on our own, under the roof of an old hotel in a city in which neither of us really lived. No one was in charge of us or even knew where we were. I knew, in an abstract way, that people had sex and that when they did they did the kinds of things Elizabeth and I had done that afternoon, but none of that seemed quite real. I knew only that I had entered new territory and that I was held there by a force which made me feel like praying.

WE ATE BREAKFAST DOWNSTAIRS IN a happy trance, then went back up to the room to gather her things. I held her hand during the cab ride through New Haven and wished it could have lasted longer. All we could talk about was when and how we could visit next, which made me so happy I didn't feel bad when I let go of her to board the train. I think Elizabeth was happy too. I thought about her sitting in the coach seat on the long ride back to Michigan, feeling the jostling rhythm of the train on the tracks and thinking and remembering. I wanted to be on a train like that myself. As it was, I couldn't wait to get back to Bingham, to get back to work and to feel the enormity of what had just happened start rising to memory.

Chapter Twelve

For the rest of my time at Yale and for years afterward, long into our marriage, Elizabeth was a living presence inside me. My lifelong interior monolog had become a conversation. I began seeing things as if not just I but a shadowy Elizabeth were taking them in. The most ordinary sensations — the stinging descent of my morning shower, a blast of winter cold meeting my face, a warm mouthful of food — felt as if they were being filtered through both of us. I could not put Elizabeth out of my mind, nor did I want to. She loomed, sometimes a quiet observer, sometimes an urgent petitioner, in all my reveries. The few telephones universities provided for undergraduates in those days were centrally located and in constant use, but we managed to talk every few days. We wrote each other daily, often long, meandering letters, the most trivial passages charged with feeling. We were connected, joined in a dramatic disequilibrium, the accumulated longings of which grew unbearable until we could arrange to meet, find place and privacy and reenter the communion we had forged that first afternoon at the New Haven Hotel.

Strangely, the intensity of Elizabeth's presence in my interior life and the amount of time I spent thinking about her, writing to her, and talking to her did not weaken my focus on my scholastic projects. If anything I became a stronger, more tenacious scholar. My love for Elizabeth played a part in this, although I am not sure I could articulate how. It was as if being Elizabeth's beloved had somehow infused me with the intellectual drive, the style, the general command of situations to make me worthy of her. Before we became lovers, I had made a substantial start at Yale. After that, I began to make my mark.

Even more strangely, charged through with Elizabeth as I now was, I would not say the condition made me especially happy. I felt an intensity, an almost obsessive intensity if we were apart for too long, and there was desire, but I cannot recall anything like elation. We were close but by no means light-hearted. In that regard, something that had been central in my life was now curiously missing. Throughout my boyhood I had been a joker, unable to stop myself from mentally picturing crazy incongruities and, if possible, finding words for them, giving them voice. I had been a wise guy, no doubt tiresome at times, but I had been quick, too quick for most people, and I had made them laugh. Now something had happened to that edge, that spark. I had become deliberate, and I had become careful, qualities which added more weight than pleasure to my life, but, again, qualities that advanced my scholastic progress considerably.

My studies at Yale came into coherent focus as a result of my work with Sydney Seymour Call. Professor Call was probably at that time the most famous person at Yale. Yale's president, Kingman Brewster, was in the news from time to time, and our chaplain, William Sloane Coffin, got a lot of attention for being with-it and anti-war, but Sydney Seymour Call was sought out by not just the media but by congressional committees, special task forces, and advanced study think tanks to help place difficult social problems into contexts that would help people make sense of them. His rigorously argued books were well received and widely read. His appearances on public and commercial television made him one of the few genuinely intellectual American celebrities. His gift, if one had to sum it up briefly, was to reduce complexities to ringing clarity. He was funny, playful, and he used language well, but not pretentiously, to define terms that in public discourse had come to mean different things to different partisans, terms like "welfare" and "liberalism" and "race." He had a Socratic gift for memorable analogies, and his ability to place jarring current events in historical context had a wonderfully soothing effect on his auditors and readers. Whether in his writing, lectures or in personal conversation, he conveyed a generous regard for his audience, challenging them, offering possibilities, asking intriguing questions, but never imposing, never insisting, never condescending.

Because his courses were wildly oversubscribed, admission was granted by lottery. Once I knew who he was and heard him speak, I started signing up for any course he offered. The second semester of sophomore year I got lucky and was admitted to an upper level elective of his called Cultural Economics. I presumed that, at most, he would give a series of weekly lectures and the other meetings of the course would be conducted by graduate assistants, who would also grade the papers and exams. I was completely mistaken. One of the reasons, I discovered, he was so popular at Yale was that he was a very good, very dedicated teacher. As I thought, the lectures were terrific, both stimulating and surprising, with enough digressions and funny asides that they never seemed merely recited essays. In addition to his lectures, he met with us in discussions groups where he teased out of us research projects that bore on the central themes of the course. He read and commented on our papers himself, and that is how we became acquainted and then friends.

He liked my work. I couldn't help trying to please him, and I put a lot of thought and imagination into my essays, but the reason he took notice of me was that I just happened to have been in the thick of an immersion in early depth psychology. I had started the summer before, beginning with Freud, moving from *Interpretation of Dreams* through the treatises on the unconscious, the evolving theory of the tripartite psyche, the treatments of sexual dynamics, and finally the cultural commentaries. Reading Freud in good translations by Walter Kaufman and others made me for a time a very rigid convert. I could see the world in no other way. Freudian ideas began creeping into even very unlikely course assignments. But the most illuminating event for me during that intense period of reading was an analysis I conducted of one of my own dreams.

I was pretty sure I had dream analysis down. I marveled at the way Freud decoded his own dreams by systematically associating their outwardly nonsensical contents with elements in his waking life that were loaded with feeling. That felt deeply right to me, but I had a hard time accepting that the manifest content of any dream was always a distorted symbolic expression of sexuality and aggression inadmissible to waking consciousness. So I started keeping a dream journal, which turned out to be interesting in itself. At first I would awake with wispy fragments I was sure were too insubstantial to call real dreams. But after a few nights, I started logging them, even if they could be covered by a sentence fragment. Before long I was waking up to fully realized dreams, complex, crazy narratives. I was certain these would be susceptible to analysis.

I derived my method from Freud's, except I laid things out on paper in my own way. First, I would write down the narrative of the dream as literally and briefly as I could, with no questions, qualification or interpretation. Then I pulled out each element in the narrative—a crow, my father, the pair of highly polished shoes someone was wearing—and listed them in the order they appeared along the left hand margin of a piece of paper. Then I made myself relax as much as possible as I went down the list and to the right of each entry tried to associate a feeling with each element (crow=ominous, watchful; father=far away, resents me; polished shoes=impressive, people liking me). Then I made a waking life "association" with each element. The crow might put me in mind of the birds I'd see huddled against the cold on the utility wires outside my window. The idea of my father made me picture again the back of his head in the rear window of the Chevy as he and my mother drove away from New Haven. The polished shoes made me think of Parnell's clothing store back home, impressively dressed people--*Professor Call* in his dapper tweeds and richly polished cordovans. Moving steadily to the right on the page, I'd now derive a feeling for each association, then make a second association on the prior association, then derive a feeling for that one and so on until I could feel the energy going out of the train of associations and feelings. By the time I completed association/feeling chains for several dream elements, I would find myself assigning the same feelings to very different elements and associations, and when I put those feeling-linked elements together, I could see how they pointed to things that would have really troubled or embarrassed me during the day if I had let myself think about them. I was stimulated and encouraged by these discoveries, and I gained some unexpected perspective on my life at the time, but I knew my approach to dream analysis was either incomplete or altogether mistaken, because I could not resolve any of my analyses into a deep and forbidden *wish* as Freud had done. But then I decided to analyze my Christmas Dream.

I had this dream when I was about six. It was, I am sure, what Freud and Jung would have called a primal dream, because it carried a terrific force when I had it, and unlike other dreams, it remained vividly fixed in memory, and, although I am not entirely sure, I may have dreamt it several times. The intensity of a dream's colors, Freud said, represents the psychic urgency of what is conveyed. The color of my Christmas dream felt like the liquid-rich Technicolor of a movie.

I had only been taken to see a handful of movies, and for me, as I felt myself helplessly assumed up into the bright screen, they had been a wondrous, sacred-feeling intimation of a greater world. My dream was charged with this feeling. The pervasive mood was a disturbing mixture of powerful longing and approaching danger. The first image was a disembodied perspective, as if from a remote camera situated above and outside my house, of the window of our living room in Palatine, Illinois. It was night, Christmas Eve, and heavy flakes of snow were falling past the lighted window, creating a cozy, Christmas card picture. Then, as if through a process of zooming in, the view included my mother sitting in an upholstered chair. She is alone in the room, darning socks. Uncharacteristically, given the house's quiet and her domestic task, she is wearing her fanciest dress, a bright green dress, the sheen of which had always entranced me when she would wear it to parties and other celebrations. As soon as the warmth of the scene registered in my dream state, I am aware of something ominous going on in the background. Without actually observing it, I know that people have broken into the house. A *burglary* was in the works, although I did not know precisely what a burglary was, other than it was a bad crime. Then I could see the burglars, large upright figures with dog faces, like Pluto and other vaguely dog-like characters in my Mickey Mouse and Donald Duck comic books. There were three such burglars, and they wore black masks over their eyes, confirming their criminality. I was aware that the intruders were making their way from the basement of the house up into the living room, where my mother would be in danger. Next, one of the masked burglars is approaching my mother with terrible intent. He is holding in his hands a large wooden handled augur, and it is clear he is going to assault her with it. I hear the phrase, "I'm going to drill you full of holes," and then almost simultaneously I begin to picture the drill bit entering my mother's chest, puncturing the green cloth and proceeding into her heart.

Troubling as it was, it was not a nightmare. It did not wake me. I awoke with it in the morning, held in a confusing combination of dread and longing.

My associations with Christmas Eve, my mother, her green dress, and her domesticity were straightforward. I had longed for Christmas, longed especially for its promise of the miraculous—Santa Claus, flying reindeer on rooftops, infinite bounty in a single sack, Jesus glowing in his manger like a jewel against the dark starry night in Bible times. I loved and revered my mother, loved that she made me feel safe and that she made our house feel safe. Her green dress called up another kind of love in me, a desire to be physically close to her, to look directly into her eyes, to prolong my gaze, to take in everything about her I wanted. Nothing surprising in this; early mother feeling conjoined to sacred Christmas feeling. But with the introduction of the troubling elements, the picture cleared. I suddenly recalled with great clarity that the upright dog-burglars were cartoon figures who played a part in a Scrooge McDuck comic book story called *The Seven Cities of Cibola*. Scrooge McDuck was Donald Duck's millionaire miser uncle, and in this episode he had found a map to fantastic stores of treasure buried in lost underground cities in the American southwest. As Scrooge revealed his find to his three young nephews, Huey, Dewey, and Louie, the villainous dog-men, who were seated in an adjacent restaurant booth, heard the plan and plotted to follow the unsuspecting ducks out west and usurp the treasure.

The dog-men were villains in both story and dream, but there was a harmlessness about them, almost a lovability, that worked to undermine any real sense of danger. Most of the action in *The Seven Cities of Cibola* took place out west, for me an imagined landscape of limitless, beckoning possibility. Moreover—and this was the breakthrough association—the mythic west of my six-year-old heart was where gun-slinging characters, both villains and heroes, threatened to "drill" the characters upon whom they had drawn their guns. *Drill* them, *drill them full of holes*. Had I not read Freud on dream analysis, I would not have thought to make systematic associations with "drill," specifically the bulky hand auger directed toward my mother's heart in the dream. As it happened, the auger was a loaded symbol.

A few months before the dream, when I was five, my grandfather died, and one of his possessions that fell to my father was a collection of ancient tools, including a set of hand augers of graduated sizes. My father was not really a wood worker or even minimally handy, but the arrival of the tools must have stirred something in him, and he decided to build things. One of his projects, and the only one that resulted in a standing, useful product, was to construct a primitive "hall tree," as my father called it.

My father decided it would be instructive for me to learn some carpentry skills and to help him. As it turned out, there was little for me to do. I was not strong enough to reduce the baseboards or the four-by-four uprights to measured length with the rusty hand saw. It occurred to my father that I might be able to drill the screw holes at the points he had marked with pencil onto the boards. I was to do this with one of my late grandfather's augers. But no matter what my father's instructions or what amount of earnest, grunting pressure I applied, I could not make the augers work. The smaller ones skittered away from the designated marks, and I could not make the bigger ones register more than a tiny dimple in the surface of the wood. My father, wet with perspiration, would watch my hapless efforts, attempt unsuccessfully to correct them, then seize the auger from my grip and gouge out the hole himself, curlicue shavings mounding impressively over the auger bit. This was not an unfamiliar dynamic between my father and me. He could do it; I could not. He was strong enough; I was not. I could not manage his tools.

Linking this failure to my dream was revelatory. The drill I could not manage was a deadly weapon which could "drill my mother full of holes." In my dream symbolic villains, almost lovable in my associations, were going to do the job. While dreading that one of them would penetrate my mother in this way, I was also drawn in fascination to the drama. Freud had taught me that my dreaming ego inhabited and motivated every element in the dream. Not a cartoon dog-man, but *I* was the agent bent on drilling my mother. Now master of my father's outsized tool, I would penetrate her very heart.

There it was, as purely Oedipal as a dream sequence could be. Moreover, this time I could see it was a *wish*.

THE SUCCESSFUL INTERPRETATION OF THE Christmas dream instilled in me a rigid adherence to all Freudian theory, as I understood it, as well as a terrific appetite for more. I felt I had been made party to powerful secrets, and the more I read and thought about it, the more it seemed that my waking conduct was a kind of shadow play expressing coded messages from my deep interior.

I was now a devoted analyst of my own dreams and, whenever possible, the dreams of others. Two of my friends, Chad Pickering and Jason Freyer, were curious about what I had to say about dreams and sometimes would tell me theirs. It was tricky getting them to sit still long enough to get in the spirit of associating without the filter of logic and ordinary sense. I think they got something out of the attempts, usually an unexpected realization that they were more disturbed about something than they thought. I had less luck with Elizabeth who, despite our intimacy, seemed tense and guarded about revealing the feelings connected to elements in her dreams. My questions made her impatient, and when I pressed her to go deeper, she balked at the process altogether, telling me that, from what she could tell, Freud had been discredited and that there were other, more scientific ways to account for dream contents. She was not convincing, but I could tell she would not submit to a real dream analysis or to any other consideration of the waking world not being what it seemed. Emotionally and intellectually Elizabeth was banking on the world being as it seemed. For this reason, too, she was irritated by religious expression, not established cultural rituals like Christmas celebrations or Seder meals, but of anyone claiming seriously that metaphysical or mysterious forces were at work in the world.

I now knew such forces were at work in the world, and in a way I could never articulate, I had always known. The more I read and mused, the more I wanted to lift the veil separating me from those great prior things. Immersed in Freud, I began reading the work of his associates and disciples. Ernest Jones was good, especially on Hamlet and Oedipus. Reich I thought was really good, especially on how the body contracted in the face of infantile fear and repression. Apparently Reich went off the rails in the second half of his life, but I don't think anyone has ever been clearer on sexual energy, body, and mind. I wonder if, had he lived longer, Sándor Ferenczi would not have been the greatest of them all. His *Thalassa* was so stunning and so obviously sound in its understanding that the very condition of being alive and conscious requires returning, through sleep, to the sea and to oblivion. I put off reading Jung, partly because of the sheer volume of his collected works and also because, if I could have articulated it then, the idea of a more exploratory, expansive approach to the inner life threatened to undermine the brittle foundation of my Freudianism

When I did peer into Jung's thinking, beginning with *Psyche and Symbol*, I was put off. I couldn't find the "system." Freud's comparatively tidy and mechanical theorizing had armored me against difficult new complexities and open propositions. I liked what some Freudian commentators had called his "hydraulic" approach to mental functioning, that mental energy—libido—was like a charged fluid; if suppressed, it was dammed up or diverted into collateral channels, some adaptive, some pathological. I liked thinking of the mind as a three part engine composed of id and ego and super-ego. I liked picturing mental states as layered adjacencies of unconscious, preconscious, and conscious material. I liked the manageable categories of the ego defenses: repression, regression, projection, identification, sublimation, reaction-formation. I liked the progressive stages of sexual development: oral, anal, phallic, latency, pubescence.

I could find no such order or clarity in Jung. The principal reason for this was the greater role Jung assigned to "original" unconscious content, as opposed to material "repressed" into unconsciousness because it was culturally forbidden or traumatic. For Jung the unconscious mind was alive with purposeful figures vying for attention and expression. Early religion, mythology and folklore were full of these archetypal figures. They were psychologically *given,* culturally and genetically inherited. There was a "collective" unconscious of all mankind, and the job of each psyche was to bring one's dominant figures in that collective to conscious awareness and to integrate them into a satisfying life. The conscious integration of archetypal experience is one's real life work, and because the archetypal program for each individual is distinctive, every person has a distinctive destiny.

I could not have composed that sweeping, imperfect capsule when I began reading and thinking about Jung. For years, reading Jung was for me like reading Ovid's *Metamorphoses*. One bright picture kept sliding into another. There were many fascinating propositions and possibilities, but seemingly nothing underfoot. I was faced with the same problem I faced when I first attempted to learn at Yale: I didn't know enough even to begin. I knew next to nothing about mythology or esoteric religion or alchemy, which were just three of the pools Jung fished. It would take—and has taken—a long time.

Oddly enough—although a Jungian would call it "synchronous"—it was the introduction of a Jungian idea into one of my research papers that caught Professor Call's attention. The assignment had been to identify some instance of irrational consumer behavior—like buying more expensive brands of otherwise indistinguishable products—and to explain its cause.

This was the kind of puzzle I liked. I decided to write about the adolescent practice of purchasing goods that were likely to provoke anger and disapproval and disgust on the part of parents, decisions to get outlandish haircuts, to buy tattoos or piercings or recordings likely to offend the sensibilities of parents and other auditors. My first thought was to represent such decisions as Freudian acts of unconscious aggression, but the Jungian concepts of *persona* and *shadow* seemed even more promising.

In Jungian thought the persona comprises the qualities a person is able to acknowledge consciously in oneself, the shadow those that are present but not consciously accessible. Understood this way, a provocative purchase is a gesture of individuation, a subconscious attempt to restore something from the shadow realm and to become whole. There was not quite enough substance to this formulation to flesh out a whole essay, but I went on to discuss the range of parental responses to the provocations, from willed acceptance to strained accommodation to angry reprisal. I drew on Freudian but mainly Jungian concepts, supporting the hypothesis with examples discussed in recent issues of *Time* and *The New York Times Sunday Magazine* as well as some behavior I had observed among my high school and Yale friends. Once I figured out what I was doing, writing the paper seemed pretty straightforward, but as I approached the conclusion, I realized that I had written myself into a kind of formula that seemed to explain much more than adolescent provocation. Something bigger and richer seemed to be pulsing beneath the typescript. As I summed up, I tried to bring the bigger thing to clarity, but I couldn't quite manage.

Had I been able to, I would have written something to the effect that, given the persona/shadow configuration of everybody involved in the purchase—including that of the producer, the seller, the buyer, those affected, and to some extent everyone who bears on the culture in which the transaction takes place—the impact and frequency of such provocations will be proportional to the amount of psychic material the aggregate personae of the prevailing culture have relegated to shadow. A more Freudian approach—the more repression the more provocative acting out in response—would have been clearer, but mistaken. Repressive states, repressive institutions, and repressive families do not necessarily elicit more provocative behaviors in response. Repression supported by sufficient threat and force can, within limits, keep troops in line. American culture, whether sampled in Palatine, Illinois or New Haven, Connecticut, was anything but repressive. The point I found myself on the brink of making was that blindness to urgent psychic reality, not repression, is the cause of puzzling, irrational behavior, including consumer behavior.

Professor Call liked my paper very much. He gave me a bold A, and his marginal comments were enthusiastic, including an invitation to see him in his office to discuss it further. This turned out to be the beginning of my career as—whatever I am. An applied psychologist? Professor Call helped me see the bigger thesis underlying the observations in my paper. He told me the way ahead was to demonstrate with clear, persuasive examples of common behavior how unconscious/shadow forces were at work. His genuine interest and good, basic questions clarified my thinking as no other reading or teaching has ever done. We brainstormed on some of the behavior he addressed in the course: why Americans purchase and stockpile more of certain products than they could ever conceivably use, why stereos were designed to put out more sound and more gradations of sound than one can hear, why cars are designed to go faster than safety requires or the law permits. The persona/shadow perspective was especially helpful when we moved on to considerations of emergent popular tastes, fashion, trends. What was the deep psychic appeal of emaciation, androgyny, and drug intoxication in high fashion images? What was the causal or correlative relationship between behavioral trends that violated cultural standards and the rise of "fundamentalist" religious activity? Unlike most of my other social science professors at Yale, Professor Call's interest in these questions—and in me—bore no political or ideological tilt. He was as respectful of Christian fundamentalists as he was of avant-garde elites. He was primarily interested in the relationship between what people did and what they thought they were doing when they did it.

It was in the course of a long office-hours chat late in the spring of my sophomore year that I first put into words the simple proposition that has generated all the work I have done since. "So what," Professor Call asked me, "would you say is the most important thing you have learned from all your reading in depth psychology?" He asked questions like that, I believe, out of reflexive courtesy when a student was rambling, meandering through recited complexities, hoping, perhaps, to be impressive. I have no doubt I was meandering when Professor Call asked the question. I had to pause and consider. He wanted *one thing*. I was going to have to review inventory, prioritize, evaluate, select. Then, in a way I was unable to help, I was smiling— the strangest sensation— and the smile kept coming. I am sure I must have looked idiotic to Professor Call but saw that he was smiling too, as if we had arrived at the same mental condition at the same instant. Then I said it: "It's the shadow. The real meaning of what people say and do lies in the truths about themselves they do not consciously acknowledge." Professor Call leaned in close. "So the real meaning of what I am thinking lies in what I am not thinking. And if you want to understand me, you must identify what I don't understand about myself--?" He had it, and because he did, I realized I did too.

Chapter Thirteen

For my final two years at Yale, including both summers, I worked with Professor Call as a paid research assistant. The Foundation for the Advancement of Psychology (FAP) had given him a sizable grant to complete a big book on behaviorism. More specifically, the book was to evaluate behaviorism as valid science. It was a tremendous honor for me to be chosen for this work, which I would have been glad to do for nothing. My actual duties were sometimes a little tedious and consisted mainly of locating documents and references and chasing down needed facts. The most stimulating task I was assigned was occasionally to provide Professor Call with a synopsis of a scholarly article or, more rarely, a book. The material I was given to digest was usually on the distant margin of Professor Call's central focus, but presenting and discussing the synopses with him was very satisfying, because our talks invariably opened up into a consideration of what he hoped to demonstrate in the book. The design of the book was straightforward: the theoretical claims of leading behaviorists—Skinner, Watson, Simon, Kahneman, Tversky—would be held up to tests of logical consistency, and the results of behaviorist experiments and projects would be reviewed empirically. On the basis of his findings, Professor Call would assess the merit of Behaviorism as science (as opposed to mere "social science").

The work of behavioral scientists was, I thought, far from my interests, and had I not been tapped to work with Professor Call at that particular moment in his career, I doubt I ever would have read or thought much about behaviorism. For one thing, with the exception of Skinner, whose strident and doctrinaire books were at least readable, the behaviorists were ploddingly, woodenly dull to me. Their central proposition—that human beings did not cause their own behavior-- was electric in its implications, but the language and syllogisms used to make the case were deadening and, in a way I was slow to see, manipulative. It was Professor Call who, as he neared the conclusion of his work, pointed out the distinction between "scientistic" and "scientific" arguments.

Not because he asked me to do it, but because I wanted to understand the project better, I read Skinner's most general text, *Science and Human Behavior*. I began reading it in the most skeptical and oppositional frame of mind imaginable but was soon troubled by what seemed to be irrefutable claims. Skinner demonstrated quite clearly, I thought, how you could create any behavior that was within a person's potential range by manipulating environmental variables—with no need whatsoever to take into account what the actor "thought" or "felt" he was doing. The iron filing may think and feel it is drawing itself powerfully to the magnet, but whatever the thoughts and feelings, it's just physics. And, by logical extension, whatever I thought and felt about being drawn to Yale or to Elizabeth or to Professor Call, that was also just physics. According to the behaviorists, environmental factors, not mind, cause behavior. We mistakenly assume that we cause our actions because a mental state we can identify precedes and accompanies every act. I am thirsty, decide to get a drink, then drink it. But, Skinner said, I didn't cause myself to do it. An environmental condition-- fluid deprivation-- caused the thirst. Another environmental condition—accessible drink—provided the solution, aided by a programmable central nervous system. Give him enough environmental control, Skinner claimed, and he could make me drink as predictably as Pavlov's dogs drooled, and he could do it without regard to anything I was thinking or feeling. Moreover, in some suggestive if not conclusive ways, he demonstrated his point. Applied behaviorism, far more effectively than therapies addressing the mind, had enabled people to stop smoking and to overcome their fear of dogs or of flying. And while it may not have done much to transform the larger culture, Skinner did succeed in teaching pigeons to bowl.

I wanted desperately for Skinner's environmental determinism to be mistaken. I wanted even more desperately to be sure that I was the principal author of my actions. I wanted to be master of my fate, captain of my soul—but I couldn't figure out anything wrong in what Skinner proposed. Certain that I would be revealing myself as the intellectual lightweight I actually was, I asked Professor Call if there was anything fundamentally wrong in Skinner's thinking. He considered my question very seriously. He asked me to review *Science and Human Behavior* with an eye out for anything like a *value* that Skinner may have intentionally or unintentionally slipped in when setting up his causal model of human behavior. Professor Call broke the model down into very simple terms. In Skinner's scheme, Professor Call explained, scratching symbols onto the small chalkboard in his office, the sum of environmental stimuli that bear on a behavior could be represented as A, the resulting behavior as C. Any mental states aroused in the process—thoughts, reasons, feelings, values—could be represented as B. If Skinner was right, A would always predict C, no matter what was going on in B. B, or mind, was no more than a "black box" linking the stimuli and the behavioral response. To disprove Skinner's model, something in B, some mental state, had to be shown to contribute something to C independently of A. This was clear enough, but I could see that it would be a challenge to locate that causal property of mind.

I reread *Science and Human Behavior*, this time with almost painful concentration. By the time I was halfway through it, I was convinced the behavioral model was air tight— but then a phrase in one of the chapter summaries jarred me. In his discussion of behavioral reinforcement and positive rewards, Skinner wrote that "mastery" of tasks was "self-reinforcing" for animal and human subjects. "Mastery" sounded to me like an acquired value, not merely a pre-wired feature of the mental apparatus. Moreover, how could a behaviorist *prove* that mastery was self-reinforcing, except through the circular argument that subjects repeated behavior they had mastered. Then I saw it—*self*-reinforcing meant that something interior, something in the mind, was responsible for building the behavior. Self-reinforcement meant non-environmental reinforcement. In this essential way, Skinner had undermined his proposed model. The more I thought about "mastery," the clearer it became that conscious mastery in humans was a variable no behaviorist had claimed to predict or control. Behaviors of any complexity-- like playing the piano well-- resisted the kinds of predictions and controls Skinner had applied to building pigeon behavior or helping people overcome phobic aversions. "Mastery," was clearly an awareness, a state of mind.

Although not as clearly as I wanted to, I explained all of this to Professor Call. He could not have been more effusive or generous in his response. He was on his feet. He clenched and unclenched his fists. He clapped his hands. He said, "Yes! On the nose! Bull's Eye!" He said I had independently reached the same conclusion about Skinner and behaviorism that he had. He said that, with my permission, he was going to acknowledge my analysis of "mastery" in the concluding chapter of his book. Moreover, he said, I should work up my idea into an article for a scholarly journal, which he would help me select. Later he showed me the protocols for such articles, and after a few editorial corrections and suggestions on his part, I sent "A Reconsideration of 'Mastery' in Skinner's Behavioral Model" to the journal *Mindset*, which Professor Call said was highly regarded and read by philosophers as well as social scientists. Months later I was notified that, with only minor revisions, the article would be published. Almost a year after that, the piece actually appeared—within days of the publication of Professor Call's book, *Out of Skinner's Box: Behaviorism and Scientific Practice*. When I went to his office to give him one of my three complimentary contributor's copies of *Mindset*, he presented me with a copy of his book, with an inscription: *Bottomless gratitude to you, Jonathan, for your invaluable help with every aspect of this project—and for the insight that confirmed what I hope is the truth of this inquiry.* He opened the book to the Acknowledgements pages and pointed to what he had written there: *To Jonathan Force, my research assistant who provided as much colleagueship as he did assistance, I owe not only an enormous intellectual debt but my deepest thanks for being such a tenacious learner, not to mention splendid company.*

I shook Professor Call's hand and said thank you, but it was nowhere near what I should have said to express what I felt about him and what he had done for me. When I left his office, I found myself striding at some speed across campus with no destination in mind. I was simultaneously elated and near tears. I could feel myself being assumed up into something enormous and formative and out of my control—the Future. I was aware that I was succeeding. *This is success.* It felt as if I were performing in a play I did not really understand, but the curtain had opened, the lights were up, and everything about the production was swirling with importance.

Chapter Fourteen

IN ADDITION TO encouraging my precocious entry into professional scholarship, Dr. Call steered me into a special program at Yale that allowed me to complete my studies there while working almost independently, under his and selected colleagues' general supervision. Yale had established the Scholar of the House program after the Second World War to enable students who were advanced and specially focused to use the university's resources in a flexible way to carry out individual research projects. To be nominated and chosen as a Scholar of the House was a big honor. If their proposed projects and research methods were accepted by the faculty and college deans, Scholars of the House were released from having to take ordinary graded courses. I could not quite imagine this—being at Yale but being required to do nothing but my own reading and writing—but Dr. Call assured me that it was possible and that, he believed, I would be a very strong candidate. Almost certainly because of his support—he helped me choose my thesis and to work up a research schedule—I received a formal letter from the Dean of Timothy Dwight College that I had been selected Scholar of the House, one of twelve in a pool of several hundred candidates that year.

I opened the letter standing just off the walk in front of the Beinecke Library. It was a mild, damp afternoon in April. There was a gauzy quality to the light, the air heavy and a little sweet with earthy emergence. I looked around, all thought suspended. In pairs and clusters, students made their way along the intersecting walks. I could hear fragments of their talk and banter. I felt held in place by them, by the declining light, by the settled masses of the buildings. I would be a *Scholar of the House*, which at that moment meant I would cease to be a particular person there, a student, occupying space, going places and doing things. This new perspective was like a dream in which I was everywhere and everybody, atmospheric, no longer "at Yale" but Yale itself.

WITH PROPER CONCENTRATION, MOST PERIODS of one's prior life can be reentered and, with disciplined recollection, reliably narrated. But for some reason I cannot find, feel, or recreate the sequence of the completion of my career at Yale. I know I filled my days and weeks with reading, research, and writing. I can remember my cubicle in the Beinecke, sessions in the ladder-backed chair in front of Professor Call's desk. Two more scholarly articles were composed and published, and I became a fairly regular contributor to the *Yale Daily News*. Periodically I retrieve this old work from my files and reread it. The voice seems fresh to me, even impressive, but I can't summon back the experience of sitting down to write any of it, or even thinking the thoughts that urged me on. If compelled to do it, I know I could produce a reasonably faithful capsule of how I lived and what I did over the course of my twenty-first and twenty-second years, but I would have to approach the job as a journalist or a scholar, gathering facts and evidence and plotting them on a calendar of lost days.

The reason for this discontinuity in my remembered past may have been due to my relationship with Elizabeth. We met every few weeks, usually for the weekend, but occasionally for longer spells over the holidays and summers. Most of the weekends were at Yale, and most of that time—practically all of it, in my impaired memory—at the New Haven Hotel, in bed. There must also have been at least a half dozen visits to Ann Arbor, trips overhung in memory with dreary skies as we made our huddled way on foot through the stinging cold toward amusements and events neither of us much looked forward to. We found opportunities for summer work far from Palatine, Illinois. I was occupied in New Haven,

Elizabeth in Washington, D.C., which provided us opportunities for unmonitored closeness that would have been impossible back home in our families' houses.

The sexual pull toward Elizabeth when we were apart and the world-eclipsing intensity of our communion when we were together occupied the core of my inner life. This condition was neither a distraction nor a restorative counter-reality to my purposeful work at Yale as Scholar of the House. If anything the erotic condition was a higher reality up into which my scholastic and all other personal business was assumed. The wonderfully renewable charge of sex trumped all other considerations. More than that, the erotic thrall helped to order the business of my life in an effective, sustainable way. My work was never instead-of-Elizabeth; it was a highly gratifying channel for that feeling. Probing deeply into heady new texts, drawing parallels, sensing causation—it was all an extension of the Elizabeth condition. An insight or a satisfying stretch of writing felt, at day's end, vaguely sexy. Productive activity of any kind would put me in mind of Elizabeth's next visit: things to show her, tell her about, as if increments of scholarly progress or any other kind of achievement added bulk to what I could offer up to our mutual pleasure. In fact, my seemingly charmed succession of honors and accolades, beginning with being chosen Scholar of the House, was to my reckoning just more and more *context* for loving Elizabeth.

Thanks to Dr. Call's shrewd guidance, the thesis I chose to write thrust me into the very heart of America's cultural agonies. My classmates and I and millions of other post-war baby boomers had already begun to overwhelm the facilities and traditional expectations of the nation's colleges and universities. There was no collective intention to rebel or to form a "counter culture," as the press would later call it, but the sheer force and presence of so many late adolescents with so little practical work to do created a kind of combustion. Despite its famous Yippie manifestoes and radical student Statements, it was largely a period of incoherence. There was an exhilarating sense of shared fellowship and strength in our numbers—but no galvanizing ideas or program. It was actually commercial media—TV and *Time* and *Life* and the Sunday supplements—that needed the assurance that what was happening to the nation's children, to civility, to dress and style was a "movement," with causes and purposes. The divisive issues of the day —Vietnam and the draft, civil rights, and, rather more feebly, the environment-- were put forward as causes for youthful disaffection, but in truth the youth of the era shared no conviction about any of it. But if not ideas, there was an unmistakable new look and a regressive, narcissistic surrender to the senses. The hair, the fantasy dressing, the stagy demonstrations of noncompliance on the part of the least inhibited were infinitely photogenic and newsworthy. The Chase Readings became not the curious anomalies they actually were but emblematic of the Sixties Youth Rebellion, of The Counter-Culture. There was every suggestion that Woodstock represented the essence of the era's youth, but the historical fact of the matter is that Woodstock was only the essence of Chase Reading and his friends. A few months prior to Woodstock the vast majority of newly enfranchised eighteen-year-olds and other young voters weighed in for Nixon—and did so by a proportionately greater margin than their parents did.

But if the so-called Counter-Culture was not really emblematic of the actual behavior and ideas of my contemporaries, what was it? It certainly made its appearances. Chase Reading was by no imaginable extension an expression of the *ethos* of Yale, but he had popped up there and made his mark. I needed only Professor Call's kindly nudging to answer the question: *The counter-culture was the established culture's Shadow.*

This would be my thesis, but if I was not careful, my work could become mired in mere commentary on the most obvious and dramatic kinds of acting out. I did not want to do a scholarly version of what the commercial media had already done. There was a chartable measure of rebellion in every generational passage. I probably could have demonstrated my Shadow-thesis by analyzing the "flaming youth" of the twenties or the "silent generation" of the fifties, but there seemed to be a cultural urgency to understanding the dissidents of the hour. In order to succeed, I needed to go beyond simply postulating that the divergent behavior of children represented the Shadow urges of their parents. While largely true, the proposition would be unhelpful, descriptive but not explanatory.

I needed to show that Shadow-substance meant more than "whatever is divergent." There had to be something compelling and explanatory—puzzle-solving—about the divergent behavior of the young. The best way to show this, I realized, was not to contrast the parental generation's behavior and values to that of their offspring, but, if I could manage it, to identify the Shadow content of the *present* generation and to *predict* the values and behavior of the next. "So," Dr. Call said to me, "you want to look at the Shadow content of your contemporaries now, and based on what you find, forecast the behavior of their children—*your* children." He had it exactly. If I could do this, I thought, it would mean that I actually knew something.

So that is what I did. In the spring of my senior year, my thesis, *The Jungian Shadow and the Dialectic of Generations* was awarded Highest Honors by a faculty jury, and it became a substantial part of my first book, *Force Fields,*, which appeared when Elizabeth and I were living abroad, doing graduate work at Cambridge and The London School of Economics. Again, the erotic thrall that held me during those years and the eerie ease with which good fortune kept arriving combined to cast that period in my life into something close to a dream state. For one thing, I stopped doubting that I would succeed. I still felt as if I were acting in some kind of grand stage production, but I grew more comfortable in my role.

The Scholar of the House Program included a series of monthly dinners in which the Scholars mingled with various luminaries on the Yale Faculty. There was no agenda or program for these dinners. The premise was that the undergraduates and the distinguished scholars would mingle as fellow intellectuals. Once past my initial nervousness, I found these evenings the very richest scenes in the dream play. Most of the dinners were held, for some reason, at Timothy Dwight, my college, and we dressed for them. The evenings probably would not have succeeded if the professors were aloof or otherwise reluctant to be there, but they brought terrific energy and humor to the outings. They seemed genuinely to like our company. There is also something guiltily energizing about being included in an exclusive elite, in this case a male elite. I remember elevated, animated talk. I cannot remember drinking anything, although the sessions began with a protracted drinks hour, and wine was served with dinner. The professors drank liberally, famously—martinis and Gibsons in delicately stemmed cocktail glasses, amber whiskey over ice in generous tumblers. There was animated banter with Vincent Scully over Yale's new athletic facilities, which he believed were architectural monstrosities. It thrilled me that I could tease him, make him laugh. A number of us would argue—respectfully-- with Eugene Rostow about Viet Nam policies and the legitimacy of the war. Bart Giamatti hosted most of the gatherings, and the range of his conversation seemed limitless, although he may have been at his charming best remembering remarkable moments in baseball.

And there I was on that vividly lighted stage set. It was real enough in that I actually did my research and typed up notes and chapter drafts and met my appointments with Dr. Call and his colleagues. I sat up in my bed most mornings sipping sour cups of instant coffee, scanning the news pages of the New York Times. My footsteps clicked and echoed up and down the stairwells and corridors of the Timothy Dwight buildings. For solitary hours at a time I played the piano in the lounge. I took my meals with old friends from my Bingham days, heard eminences speak. I attended plays, an occasional game, biding time until the arrival of Elizabeth's train.

Strangely, there was no *texture* to all of this process. This must certainly have been because nothing—nothing *whatsoever*—seemed to go wrong. There were no jarring surprises or dislocations or disappointments. I had somehow developed a genius for managing. I looked after myself effectively, managed to put aside quite a bit of money, more than I needed to meet my expenses. I was well groomed, well turned out. People thought I was sharp, funny, and I could hear it in my own talk, see it in the faces of the people I talked to. I was realistic about time, kept my appointments, finished work well ahead of deadlines. Managing well felt like streamlining my passage to Elizabeth, and our communion was never disappointing, never flat. It always opened up, lifted off in the same sexy, leaving-this-world way.

What I did not realize when I was twenty-two years old and soon to be the Chauncey Prize winner for Distinction in Social Science and a Summa

Cum Laude, Phi Beta Kappa graduate of Yale University is that my apparent progress was the result of successfully erecting barriers against all kinds of experience. I had mentally bracketed my past, my mother and father and sister and Palatine, Illinois, and held them frozen and still and well out of the way. I had bracketed friends and amusements and consigned them to a safe, manageable, minor role in my larger scheme. And although I had let my scholarly energy and my Elizabeth energy feed one another, I had to some extent compartmentalized even those cherished realms. By any measure I was succeeding, but the cost had been the suppression of everything threatening or inconvenient, including my actual past, if not my very nature. The author of my Scholar of the House thesis had created an ardent Shadow. The Shadow manifestations I had prophesied for the children of the Counter-Culture in my thesis—that they would eschew the iconoclastic and transcendent view of their parents in favor of material acquisition and personal advancement, that computer and other technology, not tribal or agrarian gestures, would define the coming decades, that sensuality itself would become a commodity in trade—were already at work in me.

I was ahead of my time. Not quite consciously, I had put myself there. Ahead of my time, I could point the way, predict cannily, charm, delight, amuse, instruct.

Ahead of my time, I could explain and interpret the news, because it wasn't news to me; I had seen it coming. What neither my admirers nor my critics could know—because I didn't—is what my Shadow had in store for me.

Chapter Fifteen

MY FLIGHT FROM Atlanta arrived at O'Hare late enough that the great hive of its terminal passages was almost deserted. Traffic too was blessedly light as I made my way north to the settled and blossoming streets of my home in Evanston.

Elizabeth would be away through the weekend, visiting Chappy and the new baby in Chestnut Hill, and while I increasingly found that I was glad to have the house to myself, I felt something like sadness as I hauled my bags through the softly lit expanse of the silent hallways. I unpacked quickly, loosened my collar and went downstairs where I poured some bourbon over ice. As I flipped through the mail on the counter, a kind of agitation took hold of me. It was by no means unpleasant and seemed to be emanating from the house itself.

Taking my drink with me, I gave myself up to whatever was prompting this and walked through the pantry into the dining room, then across the entrance hall into the front parlor where I switched on a table lamp and sat down on one of the oversize wing chairs flanking the bay window. With an extended leg I eased an ottoman in front of me and put my feet up. Although thoroughly comfortable, I realized that I could not remember having sat even once in this chair, or in its twin or indeed in most of the nicely appointed chairs and sofas in the house's sitting rooms. This was not due to frequent absences or to any aversion to the more formal and decorous reaches of the house. Over our nearly three decades' residence there I had simply orbited elsewhere, rising, retiring, and bathing in our bedroom suite, working and secluding myself in my upstairs study, taking most meals in the kitchen, and relaxing with Elizabeth and the boys, when they were young, in the den behind the kitchen. The living room in which I was now sitting and feeling rather like a guest was associated in my mind with formal get-togethers, almost all of them obligatory, and with gatherings of extended family members in the course of holiday visits. On those occasions I had been, as host, on my feet, chatting, replenishing drinks, tending to the fire.

It occurred to me that I was something of a stranger in this empty house, and the realization was distinctly stimulating. It was past midnight, but I was wide awake, eager to experience something I could not begin to name. Again, as in the kitchen, the house began to work on me, and I looked around, seeing it as a first time visitor might.

Years ago, when Elizabeth was pregnant with Franklin, we had found this house on a dreamily settled stretch of Orrington Avenue, only a few blocks to the commercial center of the city and to the campus of Northwestern University where I had recently taken an associate professorship in psychology. My professor's salary was so modest as to be inconsequential as we considered buying the house. The sales of my first two books, *Force Fields* and *Reasonable Force*, had already enabled us to reach a level of financial comfort so that we would in all likelihood never have to worry much about money. Young and, I suppose, ambitious as we were, Elizabeth and I felt grounded enough in what we agreed mattered to us that even massive wealth would not have much altered our domestic plans.

It seemed to me then a wonderful house and still does. Set back behind hedges on a generous lawn, its façade is dark brick and stucco in the Tudor style, a line of asymmetrical but pleasing gables over the third floor windows. The house was built after the First World War, but in its solidity and in its interior finishes, ceiling moldings, and the leaded mullions of its windows, it looked and felt like a much older building. The complexity of the interior—the imposing central stair case and balustraded landings, rooms opening to other rooms—carried us away. We had hardly stepped past the front door when we both knew we wanted it. To me, the house represented a dizzying next step in a miraculous succession of residences I had occupied since leaving my family's modest house in Palatine to go to Yale. The narrow flats Elizabeth and I had lived in when I was studying at Cambridge and the London School of Economics seemed ancient and charged with numinous presences, and our Chicago apartment in Lincoln Park gleamed with lakefront light from mid afternoon to sunset. But this house was of another order altogether. Without really considering it, I think we both knew we would never begin to fill or even assign a purpose to the many sitting rooms and bedrooms. Like other highly rational people with comfortable marginal income, we took great unexamined pleasure in the irrationality of moving into such a splendid house.

Now the soft light of the table lamp glinted in the gilded frames of the prints and of the imposing mirror mounted above the mantel. The pictures themselves seemed to beckon, and for a minute or two I considered the images from my chair. Then I got up and made a slow circuit of the room looking closely at each print, richly colored medieval scenes from the romantic texts favored by the Pre-Raphaelite painters. I had fallen under the spell of those pictures when I saw them at the Tate when we were living in London. In those days you could buy handsome color prints in the museum store for a few pounds each and I brought dozens of them home with us when we moved back to the states. Framed simply in gold gilt, they transported me every bit as much as the somber originals in the galleries. The rest of the house was hung with similar favorites, reproductions from Klimt's murals, Maxfield Parrish's mythy beauties reclining in the blue and peach and rosy light of Big Sur cliff sides, Eakins' oarsmen at rest mid-river, jewel-vivid plates from the Duc de Berry's Book of *Tres Riches Heures*, Botticelli medallions of the Madonna at the annunciation and adored by magi. The upstairs passages were lined with prints of my favorite illustrators, N.C. Wyeth, Arthur Rackham, Beatrix Potter. My study walls were closely hung with Ackermann's tinted engravings of Oxford and Cambridge colleges. Except that they had transported me when I first saw them, there had never been any kind of plan to acquire or to hang these images by artists from different eras, working in different media toward unrelated ends. Nor really did my mania to acquire them grow out of any cultivated taste or skill in iconography. The pictures had once carried me away, and, feeling now something like the longing one feels for a beloved person recalled after death, they were, in the muted light of the parlor, carrying me away again.

Chapter Sixteen

Moving through the house as if on some kind of silent tour, I stepped into Franklin's room, now unnaturally tidy. By the light from the hallway I could make out in the framed posters the scraggly characters of his favorite rock bands posed in attitudes of defiant indolence against backgrounds of urban ruin. Some school texts were stacked on the shelves above his desk. A lacrosse stick rested against a battered guitar case in one corner. I opened the closet door. A number of laundered or possibly new and never worn oxford cloth shirts, stiffly creased khaki trousers, and sports jackets conveyed something of Franklin's ornery resistance to wearing such clothes. Seeing them hanging there, summarily rejected, I felt the sickening clout of his absence, the lost unfolding of his talc-y headed babyhood, the agreeable eccentricities of his boyhood and then the edgy passage into his present, far distant self. He had been a great love and for several years a great bother. We had breathed the same atmosphere, and for years I awoke in the morning unable to separate my own most immediate concerns from his. From his high school years forward, he had seemed determined to deny his mother all access to his interior life. With me he would negotiate practical matters civilly enough, but he let us know, in the marked way of the first born, that, whatever the consequences for any of us, he was going to make his own way.

I willed myself to evoke the present Franklin, now thirty, still single, making his distinctive way through the heady sizzle of information technology in San Jose. The first image in my mind's eye was his face in bright California sunlight. It's a good face, sun-tanned skin drawn tight over sharp cheek bones, wary smile drawing his lips up over good teeth. His untended caramel-colored hair recedes a bit from each side of his forehead, a trait inherited from the men on Elizabeth's side. Franklin is an expressive, assertive presence. A very little boy, and delicately slight until he reached his twenties, he is still somewhat diminutive, for which his aggressive and even reckless approach to life may be a kind of compensation. Even as a toddler, he was quick to master sequences, to see the point of games, to open and unfasten things, to gain access to forbidden places. For the first ten years of his life, he was intensely close to his mother, often appealingly affectionate, but angry and inconsolable when she did not or could not satisfy a whim. Like her, he demonstrated early a remarkable facility in mathematics so that, even in the primary grades, he was given special tuition years ahead of grade level. He was first to master any new electronic media that entered the household and for a time was pleased to demonstrate to his parents how to record and save television programs, then, later, how to bend the family's succession of home computers to the different uses and competencies of their users.

As a psychologist I suppose I knew enough to avoid trying to reckon with Franklin analytically, nor did I really want to. Every turn in his early development was a surprise and delight. To my mind, the process of fathers falling in love with their sons is strangely under-documented. But that is exactly the way I experienced Franklin's emergence in the world. I was so happy just to hold him, to bear him, sleeping or awake, from room to room, wheel him in his fat-wheeled stroller down to the lake front or into town for groceries or hardware or ice cream. He loved me and was gratifyingly responsive to me, but he was his mother's boy, imperious and even fierce in his claim to the breast—for twenty-two months—and after that for her focused attention. But like everyone else he revealed an anomalous shadow side. At an age one would have thought far too young to understand anything about them, he was fascinated by stories and films of vaulting romance. Elizabeth and I were fond of romantic classics like *African Queen*, *Roman Holiday*, and *Breakfast at Tiffany's*, and when video cassettes became available for home purchase, we amassed a collection of favorites. Even before he entered school Franklin would pass long afternoons viewing them in concentrated silence. He may have been the only preschooler in Evanston to be able, thanks to repeated viewings of Zeferelli's *Romeo and Juliet*, to recite extended passages of amorous intent. His *r*'s and *l*'s were a little muddy until he was seven or eight, and it transported me wonderfully every time some conversational mention was made of "lips" to hear him spout, "two bwushing pilgwims weady stand…" from Romeo's first encounter with Juliet at the Capulet ball. There were other surprising predilections and aversions, such as his fierce hostility to anything to do with religion, which I understood less well.

We were both proud of his seemingly paranormal facility with computers. In all of this I lagged far behind Elizabeth, but even she was impressed. As he progressed through school, his teachers were quick to note his gifts in taking applications of any kind of software to their limits. I was extremely grateful for his teachers' willingness to set special tasks for him and to set him loose in their pursuit. I think we provided, if not guidance, enough genuine interest in his computer ventures so that we were spared the awful underside of children's lives on line. He seemed—and we were fairly vigilant—uninterested in visiting the lurid sexual sites. He was an impressive master of countless video games involving escapes from monstrous or wicked pursuers, and with nimble thumbs he was able to guide snowboarders successfully down impossibly narrow chutes at stomach churning speeds, avalanches billowing menacingly in their wake. To my great relief, he never turned to the ugly and sadistic manhunts and stalking fantasies that inflamed the imaginations of millions of his contemporaries, including, horribly, the schoolboy killers at Jonesboro and Columbine.

In a way not easy to chart clearly but understandable nevertheless, Franklin became an edgy, rather confrontational presence in our household during his high school years. We were reasonably firm but flexible about hours and driving and other points of contention between emerging adults and their parents. Wisely, I think now, we decided to hold firm on potentially life altering decisions, like the use of illegal substances and taking part in trips or parties where there was going to be plenty of bad company and no reliable supervision. But, while it strained Elizabeth terribly, he was given his way with his room, his appearance and, increasingly as he grew older, his approach to school work and activities. As a younger boy, he had loved athletics, including football and lacrosse, but his pleasure in those games was spoiled when, upon entering high school, he found that, while agile enough, he could not muster enough force in his one hundred and ten pound frame to play effectively. As a younger boy he had also enjoyed school drama productions, and on account of an exceptional ear for music and a reasonably good voice, was given leading parts, but for reasons not disclosed to us he steered clear of all such performance in high school.

Beginning in his junior year in high school, Franklin took a part time job with a firm in Evanston which managed mail order purchases from a number of retail clothing stores. The newspaper ad for the job indicated a need for somebody practiced in data entry and listed the operating programs applicants should be familiar with. Elizabeth opposed his taking an after school job on the grounds that there was no financial need for one and that it would remove Franklin still further from the mainstream school activities in which she still hoped he would make a mark. Franklin, at that point, was skilled at resisting such arguments and went out to interview. His employers were not expecting a mid-teenager but their personnel officer had enough technological savvy to realize that Franklin could be a big help, and he was. After a few weeks, the staff realized that he could do a great deal more than data entry, and he became a kind of untitled technology trouble shooter for the office, bringing back to life blocked screens and retrieving lost material from the depths of the firm's computer hardware. He was soon a valued presence in the office, to the extent that his supervisors redeployed staff from their regular day shifts to afternoons and evenings, so that Franklin was on hand to tend to the technical problems that so often shut them down.

Elizabeth despaired of his deepening involvement with the firm and his corresponding disengagement from the life of Evanston Township High School. He agreed to work long Saturdays, for which he was highly compensated, and was issued a cellular phone by the company so that he could be reached for emergency consultations on Sundays and early evening hours. This made Elizabeth inwardly furious. She felt the firm was exploiting him, despite his enthusiasm for the work and the clear pleasure he took in dealing with his elders there as grateful inferiors. My own feelings were mixed but hopeful. No doubt overly prideful about a son with such demonstrable gifts, I too had imagined a kind of golden boy passage through high school for Franklin. I had assumed that he would easily be admitted to a premier college or university, Yale, certainly, if he chose. To my reckoning, the place he had earned in the firm was, or at least should be, as impressive to college admissions officers as a team captaincy or student council office or living with a family abroad. Busy as he was at the time, I saw him only glancingly. His grades were respectable, if not quite stellar, in a program of advanced courses. It was hard to argue, although his mother did, that he was not an engaged, remarkably productive boy. Still there was something provocative and even aggressive in his refusal to acknowledge his mother's or anyone else's concerns about him. At one point, her patience exhausted at his long absences from home and, in this particular instance, his unavailability to be on hand for a visit from her parents, Elizabeth told him he was no more than a lodger now, not really a family member. Franklin didn't take the bait. He said, "Aren't we all lodgers?"

Elizabeth's tension never eased in the remaining time Franklin lived with us, and he made no concessions to her desire that he be more of a presence at home, more disclosing, more the boy he had formerly been. The tone established between them, and thus for the rest of us, was one of guarded truce, civil but distant. This disengagement from his mother and, eventually, the household seemed only to strengthen Franklin's resolve to live independently and to chart his own course. No one could say objectively that he made poor or self-destructive decisions, but his detachment was lacerating to Elizabeth. At the time I tried hard and through a number of different approaches to help her to see that Franklin's resolve, even when it was wrong-headed, was not a negation of her, or necessarily a gesture of any kind to her. It was just what boys do. I told her Franklin probably had more doubt and anxiety about the way ahead than he could begin to acknowledge, that his imperviousness to her was probably his way of coping with looming separation as he went off to college.

Correctly labeling what was occurring did nothing to make Elizabeth feel any better. We both understood this. Franklin, with next to no guidance from us, applied for and gained early admission to Carnegie Mellon University. Early one Saturday morning in November he was able to contact the University on line and was informed electronically of his admission. I was loading the coffee machine in the pantry when I heard him clumping down the back stairs on his way to work. As he swept past me, he paused to say, "Don't have to worry about college anymore." "Really?" I said to him, joking. "You're joining the army?" Then there was a smile, a real smile, and he told me about being admitted to Carnegie Mellon. He was out the door before I could ask any of the flurry of questions which immediately arose, before I could tell him how proud I was, how glad I was, before I could acknowledge even to myself how devastatingly sad I was to lose him, how much I loved him, how at that moment and even now in the darkness of his vacated room, his entire life with us seemed to flicker for an instant and go dark.

Calling back the image of Franklin now, the face of the wiry young man grinning in California sunlight, I could feel no living connection to the lost boy. He has made his way, spectacularly so in the eyes of our friends. I think he enjoyed himself at Carnegie Mellon from the start, by his own account not working terribly hard, at play whenever possible in the university's extraordinary tech center. He won a summer internship with an internet start-up venture in San Francisco over the summer between his sophomore and junior year, and, predictably, he impressed the youthful partners not just with his facility with their programs, but with his quick grasp of what they were trying to achieve. A conversation begun in playful speculation over beers in a brew pub near the office grew into the scheme that would make all of them very rich.

For years Franklin had been fascinated by how people made money from on-line ventures, and he was especially taken by the ingenuity and elegance of the various global auction sites where anything from industrial raw materials to scarce biochemical substances could be brokered for profit. Improvising on the auction model, Franklin managed to interest the partners in marketing a process now famous as DreamCombine.com, whereby, as Franklin liked to put it, "You get enough people who can't afford something to pool their money to make it happen." The examples he gave me were basic and clear. A school levy fails, and the administrators drop the marching band program. Band member parents and anybody else sympathetic register their shared desire— to have a band director, program, uniforms, instruments—at the site and the amount they are willing to contribute. When the necessary money is pledged, the band program is back in play. I asked what I thought was the most obvious question: but what if the band families and supporters don't have enough money for the band? Isn't that the reason the levy failed in the first place? Franklin informed me that it almost never works that way. He assured me that there are almost always enough resources to achieve what people want, but they aren't in the habit of combining rationally to get it. Instead they rely on a clumsy, irrational entity like a jurisdictional electorate and are often as not disappointed by the obvious fact that the larger, irrational group does not share their particular interests. Once people break their irrational habits, they start getting what they want. "You know," Franklin said, *"there's always enough.* Especially if the project is open to everybody on line who is interested. It's like the frigging fishes and loaves."

DreamCombine.com has proven his point, not incidentally making the partners, including now Franklin, phenomenally rich. Even as the partners were poised to pitch their concept, the pundits were already predicting the "dot.com bubble" would burst, but the backers were certain they were onto something, and Franklin's vision and analytic acuity were crucial to the plan. They offered him a package of compensation which in two years would amount to almost a million dollars, plus a commitment to pay the remaining cost of his suspended undergraduate tuition if he would take an open leave of absence to work with them on DreamCombine. Nothing could have been better calculated to plunge Elizabeth into despair. She had no difficulty imagining the scheme's utter failure and Franklin refusing ever to reenter college. On the latter point she proved to be right, but misjudged completely the prospects for the venture's success.

Franklin has taken pains not to lord his accomplishments over Elizabeth—or, really, anybody. At thirty he is as rich if not richer than I am. He lives very comfortably but not extravagantly in San Jose. I think it amuses him to treat Elizabeth and me to exotic vacations—fantasy retreats to Bali, Aegean cruises, thatched outposts in Costa Rican rain forests—but there is also clearly a measure of affection in these gestures. I imagine Franklin will always be restless and even reckless. He is most alive when he has a challenging problem to solve, and he is not afraid to fail.

When we last spoke he said he was just about to test an application of DreamCombine by which admirers of an artist or author could collaborate on-line to raise sufficient money to commission new work. He encouraged me to think about it, pointing out that the process would result in probably more money than any contract would promise, as there would be no need for publisher profit, no agent commission, negligible book production expenses; there would just be me, my waiting readers, and the money. Still and probably forever low-tech in my outlook and habits, I told Franklin I would think about it, but what I actually thought about was my editor and other friends at Random House, and Mary Marx, my beloved agent.

I resisted checking my watch, but my legs had grown heavy and a detectable ringing in my ears indicated it was now quite late. I was too dull of thought to think any longer about Franklin's proposition about my future books. I proceeded along the upstairs hallway held vaguely in the conviction that Franklin was no doubt right about the efficacy of reaching readers by contracting with them directly, at the same time absolutely certain I would never do it.

Chapter Seventeen

Chappy's room when I stepped inside was still somehow, despite the order Elizabeth had managed to impose, charged with his distinctive spirit. He had never given up the bunk beds we had set up after he grew out of the crib. All available wall space was covered with masking taped montages of the skiers he idolized. The bookshelves above his desk were given over to a kind of shrine composed of his skiing and soccer medals and trophies, along with many small framed pictures he had snipped from magazines of his adored Picabo Street.

Not quite two years younger than his brother, he brought an altogether different kind of life to the household. Elizabeth liked to describe him as an "easy" baby because he was relaxed and reliable at the breast, but the irresistibly appealing thing about Chappy was his sunny exuberance. There was nothing easy about keeping track of him or keeping him out of physical danger once he was mobile, but even Elizabeth seemed to sense that his pleasure in movement was an inalienable aspect of his good nature. It did not take a year for both of us to realize we could not continue to call him Charles, or even Charlie or Chuck. Until he erupted into speech himself, we referred to him alternately as Number Two or The Destroyer. His first intelligible attempt to repeat his own name was "Chappy," which seemed to me to fit him perfectly, melding as it did "chirpy," "chipper," and "happy."

Chappy loved and revered Franklin, and was for years drawn powerfully to his presence, often to Franklin's exasperated annoyance. By the time they were four and two, they were approximately the same size and remained so until the onset of Chappy's adolescence when he shot up to most of his six foot two adult height. For the most part the boys got on well, as Franklin came increasingly to accept and adjust to what was alien to him in his brother's approach to life. Apart from their shared pleasure and comparable skill at the computer game Avalanche, which pitted snow boarders against one another over perilous terrain, they invested most of their boyhood energy in different pursuits. Lacking alternatives, they were happy enough to kick a soccer ball around the yard or improvise games and amusements when we were on vacation, but by the time they entered school it was clear they were boys on different trajectories.

Franklin had been an appealing-looking boy, his pointed chin and sharp features giving his face some of his mother's intensity. Chappy, however, had been model-cute as a boy and was a strikingly handsome young man. From adolescence onward he has had the kind of chiseled, regular good looks that appeal reflexively to females and cause a certain type of male to avert their eyes. I have always been drawn powerfully to both of my sons, their physical appearance and features so deeply integrated into my overall feeling for them that it is impossible for me to appraise them with any objectivity—although here I am trying to do something like it. About Chappy's good looks I might add only that, like his height and athleticism and resistance to schooling, they are to me an objective, given fact of his being in the world. To the extent I thought about them at all as he was growing up, it was occasionally to worry that others—or perhaps he himself—would make too much of them.

I remember watching him and his team-mates compete in a pre-season soccer scrimmage at the high school one crisply stirring September afternoon. I was standing just behind a cluster of football players who had stopped to watch the scrimmage after their practice. They struck up a boisterous tone, somewhere between cheering on and ribbing their friends on the soccer team. I was barely aware of them as I watched Chappy loping up and down the far sideline. He seemed to me in a kind of pleasant trance, as if his very being were continuous with the game, the limitless exertion it required, and the crystalline afternoon light. As fathers do, I saw Chappy in clear, photographic focus against a blur of others as he contended scrappily for contested balls, as he outraced defenders, as he stood tensing himself to head a long kick in the direction of his teammates. He was playing well, but there was also a communicable grace in his efforts. He wore his hair longer then, and it rose and fell along his temples with each stride. He had just headed a ball at midfield directly across from where I stood when one of the football players said, more in a spirit of observation than derision, "Look at Force, the golden surfer." I took no offense or pleasure in the remark, knowing at that instant just what the boy meant.

Chappy did not dislike going to school, but he seemed never to engage fully in its central business. He did not read at grade level until he was in junior high, and while his teachers dutifully reported their concerns and recommendations for remediation, I could tell that they liked having him in their classes. He could be inattentive and, very occasionally, disruptive, but he was not mean spirited or personally needy in a way that distracted from instructional business. For several years running Elizabeth contracted the services of private reading tutors, earnest young women whom Chappy generally liked. They expressed some bewilderment at the school reports, as he seemed to read well enough in their individual sessions with him. Our year-end conferences with his teachers generally concluded with a vaguely hopeful suggestion that Chappy would come into his own scholastically with "maturity." This did little to satisfy Elizabeth, but I could not bring myself to worry much about a boy who seemed so generally eager and happy. I sensed in him a special intelligence, a sense of what was appropriate and fair, and, less precisely, his tropism for—what?—*fun*. He was uninhibitedly affectionate and empathic, but he had an unusual ability to remain in good spirits when others around him were in a personal funk. I always found it hard to sustain any kind of bad mood in Chappy's company.

Throughout his early childhood I had to make a conscious effort not to let the genuine pleasure I took in Chappy's quirks and scrapes come between me and Elizabeth. In his own way he demonstrated early on an active mind, but only when he could set the terms of discourse himself. Without actual defiance he had a way of glassing over and screening out instructions and calls for his attention. But his questions, which tended to exasperate Franklin and his mother, delighted me. I noted many of them in the journal I kept in those days. He had a sure sense of asking after the unanswerable. On an arboretum walk: "Do bees like dogs?" Hearing that no two snowflakes were alike and later that no two fingerprints were alike, he pressed us to tell him how people knew that. Was there some place where snowflakes and fingerprints were stored and compared? He said he bet that there really were two snowflakes that were exactly alike, but nobody knew about them. My mind would turn seriously on these questions.

Despite his healthy good looks, Chappy never, except in athletic garb, seemed to be appropriately, or even completely, dressed. This too aggravated his mother, and because the condition proved to be uncorrectable, sometimes distanced Elizabeth from him in a way I knew she regretted but was helpless to change. To meet Chappy even now is to meet someone who conveys the impression that he has just got out of bed or has been suddenly distracted from some other, more engrossing pursuit. He greets others pleasantly enough, but glancingly. In time I realized I could talk and otherwise relate best to Chappy if we were golfing, working together on adjacent ladders, or jogging side by side. As he grew older, he mastered most of the conventions of male courtesy, the firm handshake, the friendly smile on greeting. He has learned to imitate, if not really engage in, sustained direct conversation when he is with older people. The approach that works for him, I have noticed, is earnest, uncritical agreement with just about anything that is said. If I observe him in this mode for even a minute or two, I have to strain to keep from laughing out loud. Elizabeth's and my friends remark on his likeability, his great positivity, which I am certain is no more than a characteristic Chappy adaptation to the dubious requirement to sit still and socialize.

I do not know a soul in our world who does not like and feel drawn to Chappy, but the very animal spontaneity which lies at the heart of his appeal can lead him into trouble, which is something that I, and not just

Elizabeth, have worried about. From his twelfth summer through his first two years of college he spent the month of August at a rugged orienteering camp in northern Ontario, first as a junior camper, then as a counselor and instructor. Chappy was entranced by the camp, although characteristically inarticulate about why. The program included rock climbing, to which he became immediately devoted and quickly skilled. He was especially taken with rappelling, and before the appearance of rock-climbing gyms, used to hector me to drive him to state parks downstate and in Wisconsin where there were bluffs worthy of his ambition. This of course meant that I had to learn how to belay him has he made his looping, spidery descents—and, utterly terrifying as it was to me at first, I had to learn to rappel myself, an experience that was foundational for me. It would be years before I realized that at the adrenally charged instant I surrendered all reason and, looking hard into my son's sure, smiling eyes, stepped backward off the face of the windy cliff, I was not entering new territory, but reentering my boyhood heart.

Chappy was an excellent climber, but his boy's confidence was grounded only in dreamy pleasure, and I knew this was dangerous. Once when Elizabeth and I were away for a weekend symposium at Chautauqua, we unwisely gave in to Chappy's assurances that he could manage without supervision at home. It was the fall of his junior year in high school, and he was seventeen. We had been clear, and he had earnestly agreed, that he was to host no gatherings, which he protested later had meant to him "parties." We returned home to a messy house and a series of bitterly angry telephone messages from the parents of two boys who had come over to spend the night, under the assumption that we were there. Apparently the boys had decided to set up a zip line between one of the third floor windows and an elm in the back yard. After what Chappy said were dozens of successful descents, the line grew slack and Chappy's friend Roger Wilker struck ground not on his feet but on his coccyx, painfully hurting himself. The boys had enough sense not to try to move Roger and called for an EMT crew who strapped him on to a stretcher and took him to the hospital for x-rays and treatment. Both families were understandably furious at us for our inattention. Elizabeth was sick with guilt and concern that

Roger would be permanently crippled. In time his back and the friendship were repaired, but until that was assured, Elizabeth and I lived in a state of terrific tension, a state which would periodically recur.

For two days in August of the following year we feared Chappy might be dead.

He was due home shortly from camp in Ontario, and a phone call from the director informed us that Chappy and his canoe mate had not returned with the others who had set off on the challenging week-long expedition that traditionally marked the completion of the program for senior campers. He told us that the expedition was beset with unusual troubles from the outset. Severe electrical storms had forced the party to lose nearly two days of progress along their itinerary, and in the course of deciding whether to proceed ahead and return late or to turn back, tempers flared, and a fight broke out in which Chappy was struck in the face. When the weather cleared, Chappy and his partner took off by themselves to complete the planned itinerary; the other three canoes returned to camp. The director and staff waited two days before calling the forest service to mount a search. Then he called us.

THE EXPEDITION REQUIRED A NUMBER of challenging portages between lakes and streams surrounded by no residences and few roads. It was hoped that the boys, both experienced campers, would be spotted en route. Forest service helicopters dropped motorized rubber rafts to search the watercourses along the itinerary, and night patrols looked for signs of a fire, but after two days there was no sign of them.

Elizabeth and I were on our way to the camp in the car when they were found. Chappy was tense but fine, his partner very sick and dehydrated. We learned on arrival that the boys had been proceeding along the proposed itinerary when in the course of a portage, Chappy's friend drank some water from a clear but stagnant pool and within an hour was doubled over with terrible stomach pain and diarrhea. His partner unable even to sit upright in the canoe, Chappy left him ashore and paddled the perimeter of the lake hoping to spot a camp site. Seeing no one he made a short portage along a rocky stream bed to an adjacent lake where he

381

caught sight of two fishermen in a rubberized boat. They had just arrived at the lakes, having been flown in by a hired guide for a week's fishing. They had a radio telephone on board and reached their guide who contacted the forest service who airlifted the boys, but not their canoe, back to safety.

We had had been driving for seventeen hours when we arrived at the camp. Long silences were broken with eruptions of tense, measured speculation in which we considered and reconsidered all imaginable implications of the half dozen details I could recall from the phone conversations with the director. Neither us of voiced what was foremost in our thoughts: that Chappy was dead, that his bright, elusive energy would be gone. We were both gratefully, tearfully overcome when he came forward to greet us on the path. I saw as if through Elizabeth's eyes that his bony bare feet were grimy, that he had a stubbly suggestion of a beard before I was able to embrace the lean length of him and hold him close.

Perhaps the fearful ordeal of trying not to imagine Chappy's death made his going off to college in the fall seem more painful and final than that inevitable passage should have been. Despite a spotty scholastic transcript and middling SAT scores, he ended up having his pick of what I thought were excellent colleges. It helped considerably that he was a recruitably talented soccer player, and his coaches supported his applications with strong endorsements and game videos. After a fall and winter of untroubled indecision on his part, he settled on the University of Michigan, Elizabeth's alma mater. Elizabeth strongly preferred Colorado College where she felt the close community and the college's distinctive program of immersing students in one academic subject at a time was just right for a boy as distractible and loosely focused as Chappy. Michigan was a considerable scholastic reach for a boy with Chappy's credentials, so there was some irony in the fact that Elizabeth's legacy there, along with, I suspect, some regard for my celebrity, boosted his candidacy. Uncharacteristically, she made a late hour appeal to Chappy to consider the skiing opportunities he would have in Colorado Springs, but Chappy, who had liked the scene and feel of Ann Arbor when he visited there one bustling football weekend, resisted the pitch.

Overall, Chappy seemed happy in his time at Michigan. He was not nearly as responsive an emailer as his brother, and while he seemed warm and glad to talk when we called him, he initiated few calls himself. After summer practices his sophomore year he decided to quit the soccer program and spend more time with his new fraternity friends who shared his love of snow boarding, rock climbing and casual pick-up games. Uncritically taken up in the fraternity culture, he seemed to me, from what I could conclude from his emails and our few campus visits, to have entered a new phase in his social development. He now moved in packs through successions of loosely planned social events: gatherings around kegs of beer on the fraternity lawn before and after big games, fraternity parties, spring break migrations to South Beach or Cancun. Affable, attractive friends would sometimes stay a night at the house on a weekend when Michigan was playing Northwestern, but there appeared to be no intense, close friendships, no pairs. There were references to girls, but, again, to clusters of girls, not to steady girl friends or "dates." In her darker moods, Elizabeth would refer the undergraduate life at her alma mater as "lemming culture," Chappy's overnight guests as "the golden retrievers." I noticed also that she reduced her once hefty contributions to the university's annual fund to a perfunctory one hundred dollars.

Chappy succeeded in befogging his overall academic program, so that as his graduation neared, we knew only that his major was in environmental science, and he seemed to have taken a number of business-related courses along the way. Somehow or other he had overlooked some distribution requirements, so that we were informed in the spring of his senior year that he was lacking necessary credits in the humanities and would not be able technically to gradate until he had completed them in the course of an additional term, either at Michigan or elsewhere. This was the last straw for Elizabeth, who launched a campaign of highly specific complaint with the registrar's and deans' offices about their communication and advisory systems, but as commencement approached, in which Chappy was allowed to attend in cap and gown but not to receive his diploma, her animus weakened and she diverted her concern and disappointment, I think more reasonably, to Chappy.

As it happened the additional term was no great inconvenience or expense and seems now, looking back, to have had an elevating, perspective-enlarging effect on Chappy, who I think was surprised to find himself in Ann Arbor no longer suspended in the momentum of his old crowd. That buffered term between the college cycle and the world beyond also helped Elizabeth to accept without real protest Chappy's decision to defer a serious job search for a year and to join a houseful of his Michigan friends in Colorado where they would tend bar or wait tables and ski.

I suppose few parents in intact families anticipate the ringing enormity of their children's ultimate departure. It was hard for me and even harder for Elizabeth not to think of Chappy as a permanent ski bum, forever untethered to us and our world. Having fallen into that particular sadness, I was probably more skeptical than I should have been when, rather as he had told us he would, he set about after a year in Boulder to find more substantial work. The succession of seasonal jobs he had taken had included a stint with a landscaping crew. This employment coincided with a mounting concern in the region about the environmentally toxic effects of the standard lawn care chemicals his firm employed. An urban ecology course he had taken in college had included readings on the promise of organic herbicides, and it had occurred to Chappy, who had little grounding in either botany or chemistry, that the organic preparations recommended would be relatively easy to produce. In partnership with two of his friends, he made a business plan, worked out on line how to acquire the organic solutions they needed in bulk, and through posting a few local ads and making direct pitches to householders he had formerly serviced, launched a venture now incorporated as GreenGro.

Within a few weeks GreenGro was turning enough profit to pay additional staff. In six months, they were able to lease two trucks and a business office. Although busy developing new applications for DreamCombine, Franklin took an interest in Chappy's venture and urged him to get on line and network as closely as possible with other similar ventures. Chappy did this, and in the process found himself energized in a way he had only experienced in athletic play and adventuring in the wild. GreenGro products improved and proliferated. *Boulder News* ran an extensive feature on the new business in which environmental advantages of their applications alternated with appreciative comments from customers. Inset into the feature was an appealing photograph of Chappy, arms folded and smiling winningly, the GreenGro logo on the door of his truck visible behind him.

With only a little help from us, he bought a condominium midway between Boulder and Gunbarrel. Visiting him there for a housewarming, we were introduced to a blond, athletic-looking girlfriend, Maryann. He had told us nothing about her, but something electric in their exchanges and their comfort with each other told me that they were already involved, which turned out to be the case. Maryann could not have been easier or more agreeable with us. A real beauty, she had been a competitive runner at the university. Like many Boulder graduates, she found it wrenching to leave the area and had returned after a few months to find work in graphic design. Her mother and father, both attorneys, lived just outside of Philadelphia in Chestnut Hill.

Whether in a spirit of relief or due simply to Maryann's unaffected good nature, Elizabeth was immediately drawn to her. Only in the years since have I come to appreciate how badly and for how long Elizabeth had craved an outlet for her deepest feelings for girls and women. She has a reasonably varied circle of female friends in Evanston, but her inner world had been shaped almost exclusively by intense maternal and sisterly intimacies, the likes of which were all but absent in our decidedly male household.

To Elizabeth, Chappy and Maryann's ensuing engagement and marriage, their removal, along with GreenGro, to Chestnut Hill and, a year ago, the production of a grand daughter, Beatrice, have been sheer, unanticipated bounty. She has to summon great will power not to visit, call or otherwise intrude more often than she does—and she calls and visits frequently. In all of this I have recognized something genuinely loving, but also, for me, irremediably sad.

Chapter Eighteen

I CONTINUED DOWN THE hall to the corner suite which for years has been my study. Designed as guest quarters by the house's original owners, the suite occupies a spacious second story ell at the rear of house. The mullioned windows in both directions look out onto the elm and maple treetops of our back lawn and the lawns adjacent, so that from late spring to late fall there is no visible trace of another building, just leafy branches against sky. Not long after we moved in I dedicated an unexpected windfall of royalties from foreign rights to having bookshelves built in from floor to ceiling along the walls. We had not previously managed to shelve even most of our books in any of our previous residences, and the challenge of organizing something like a real library occupied me happily for weeks. Used to it as I am, the study still seems unnaturally grand when I first enter, the dark woodwork of the shelving and window seats somehow combining with the gravity of so many books to suggest a prior era.

I found my way to my desk without turning on a light. I could not tell if the pearly glow outlining the black silhouette of the branches outside was approaching dawn or a distillation of the city's street lamps. It felt good to sink down into the comfort of my chair, but I was still far from sleep. Sitting at the desk where I composed my books and essays faintly aroused the old complex of feelings: eagerness to inform and to startle and, perhaps, to please shot through with doubt and dread and an uneasy inner awareness of how much finishing the job would deplete me. It had been a few months since I sent the final galleys of *The Uses of Force* back to Random House. Directly in front of me a leather bound notebook partly filled with ideas I was considering working up into an exploration of the effects of rational understanding on health lay on top of the closed lid of my lap top. The prospect of reconnecting with this material and forging ahead intensified the ringing in my ears.

I peered across the room to the section of shelves bearing my own books, the faint sheen of their spines unreadable in the smoky light. I had made a point of having on hand dozens of copies of each edition of each title. Of these the foreign editions, especially those printed in Russian, Arabic, Japanese and other languages utterly unavailable to me, have given me the greatest pleasure. I do not think vanity was the chief motive for laying in such a supply of my own work. Inscribed books have proven to be apt and appreciated gifts to house guests and to the scholars and journalists I have allowed to come visit me at the house. I know it is true of me and I suspect other male writers that, far from fortifying self-esteem, the physical presence of one's past work can be deadeningly oppressive, as I'm sure are past glories to aging athletes.

No. Yes.

My musing is overwhelmed now by a dark wave of something really insistent. It is further expression of whatever visited me in the dressing room of the TV station in Atlanta, but this time the surge of arrival feels sickening. Reflexively I stiffen in resistance, deliberately holding my fear in abeyance as I might when first waking out of a nightmare. This is not good, and I know at once there is no reassurance in reminding myself that it is very late and that I am physically depleted and that there is no sensible reason to feel afraid. As in Atlanta, I sense that I am about to be overcome and obliterated by something inevitable and too much for me. For a second I think about dying, locking the tension and clarity of this frozen instant into a final frame of consciousness as some wayward shard of plaque stops my heart or my brain. I think of being dead, of being found dead in my chair in my study. It would be days later—Elizabeth or someone she sent over to check when I did not answer her calls. It occurs to me that the finality of my death has no power to move me, although I can't stop myself from picturing immediate responses, the calls to the boys, the unbearable heaviness and tedium of making funeral arrangements, the way the death would be reported in the papers, the inset photograph of my face, alive, staring out affably into the faces of unseen readers in distant cities.

Picturing these things restores a measure of equilibrium. Aware that I am still held by something that could carry me off again without warning, I feel myself capable of directed thought. I am able to breathe. I consider whether rising, returning to the bedroom, cleaning my teeth and going to bed would restore me. I try to imagine waking to bright daylight, breathing tomorrow's different air, no longer held by anything but the exigencies of the day, curious but unworried by the all-being unease which I still feel hovering just behind conscious awareness. I don't know. I don't feel like going to bed, or even moving from the chair. It is hard for me at this hour—the sky behind the branches has brightened to grey and green—to advance thought of any kind into resolve. I know only that I don't want to decide, I don't want to move.

Through the filmy light I can now make out the titles on the book spines directly in front of me, also the publishers' logos and my name, *Force*. The thought of opening one of the books, even scanning the jacket illustration or looking over the table of contents, is repellent. Somehow the shelves holding my books, indeed all the shelves, all the books, the mottled richness of the carpets, the occasional tables and leather chairs, the leaded mullions of the windows—all of it is stiflingly oppressive, false, wrong, wrong in its very rightness, awful in its perfection. Yes, now, it comes on with a new clarity. I am agitated, impatient. If there were a person to address, I would unleash an unconsidered, pent up, bitter complaint. It is not the room, the solemn good taste of which now makes me consider breaking something, kicking something in. The library is all right, the house is all right, but freighted with my books, my judgments, my *touch* it is insufferable, nauseating, all wrong. And the wrongness has nothing to do with pretension, vanity, or any false note struck in the course of my adult imposture. To the contrary, the revulsion pulsing at the heart of this realization of mine is precisely due to there being no false notes whatsoever struck in the course of composing this library, this house, this marriage, this life. The edifice of me is substantial and well-wrought indeed. And thus—*idiot, fool*—the Force Factor of that edifice will devastatingly lay bare all the Eros, joy, humor and delight that was banished past all recognition as I proceeded so surely into this fabrication of myself.

I am in heady territory now. I look to the window as if for relief and, seemingly all at once, the sky is banded in magenta, lime green and fiery peach beyond the black branches. I am sitting here in this charged stillness for a reason.

The Force Factor. That was never my name for it, but rather a tag coined by an early reviewer and enthusiastically picked up by the promotion people at Random House. The term provided a comforting illusion that there was a precisely identifiable, communicable method to the kind of analysis I had begun to apply to the individual and group behavior that interested me. I'm not sure if anybody would have been served by my admission that I could not have been less methodical in doing any of it. Although I never told anyone, I never counted out the possibility that I might explore and express my strongest preoccupations in fiction or even poetry. I know next to nothing technically about writing novels or stories and absolutely nothing about writing poetry, but I have held onto a hunch that I could tap into what has engaged me and carried me in the stories and poems I love and that by some fusion of blind mimicry and dumb maverick luck my imaginative writing would strike readers with the same kind of freshness and force—*Force!*—as my analytic work. This is no doubt colossal arrogance, and to have tried and spectacularly failed would no doubt have been good for me, would at any rate have slowed the ascent to this precipice from which I find myself mortally—I suppose yes, mortally—teetering.

But while I did not write stories and poems, I am sure I felt in my core what novelists and poets feel when they are carried along helplessly in the current of the obsessions they are, with more or less skill, transcribing. Deep writing, driven writing—what can you call it?—is nothing less than possession. And of course the same can be said of the self-driven practice of any art, even the art of self-creation or fortune-making. Jung did not write stories or poems, but his extended immersions into alchemy, arcane symbology, ancient linguistics, and the intricate revelations of the mad convey the same held-in-the-current rapture of ardent story tellers like Balzac and Dickens and Dostoyevsky. And for Jung the force of his possession spilled into other kinds of expression, like his illuminated mandalas and sketches. I am certain he was possessed in this way when, with no training as a builder or architect, he dumbly piled stone on stone to build his little Bollingen castle on Lake Zurich, later confessing that he did not know what he was doing or what he was making until he had finished.

Writers know this condition. I know this condition. I have counted on it to reassure me that I am still connected to the mythy, bigger, real-but-not-quite-possible realm I experienced periodically, sometimes ecstatically, sometimes with an electric terror, when I was a boy. I have counted on being held in this kind of thrall, but I have at the same time dreaded it, knowing it would isolate me from beloved others, that I would be, even hours after rising from my desk, still tangled in the jungle of propositions and possibilities through which I had been foraging all day. I appeared at meals, leafed through papers and journals, paid bills, made some approximation of conversation with Elizabeth and the boys, perhaps strolled into town, but held in the writing current, I was never fully there.

I have taken care in writing my books. I have not hurried to finish, and I have become an increasingly fastidious reviser. No one could fairly judge my published output to date—four major treatises, a half dozen shorter, single-topic books, and hundreds of essays and articles—as less than substantial, yet I am not what is popularly regarded as "prolific," often as not a euphemism for "writes too much too often." Past work, even the shelved monument of Force titles rising beyond my desk, feels thinly insubstantial. I can access and describe the process of composing those manuscripts, but I can no longer feel the weight or, more positively, the thousands of little sparks of insight and hope and pleasure I might have experienced along the way. I'm moving through unfamiliar mental territory at the moment, but I do not believe that I will at some later time feel differently or better about my work. At the moment it seems clear, and I'm sure it will always seem clear, that everything I have written is a considered application of a single insight that I was able to articulate pretty well when I was an undergraduate. My critics and admirers find me "elusive" because they attempt to account for the surprising aspects of my findings and forecasts in what they want to be my trademark analytic method—my Force Factor. Truth be told, my analytic method is neither subtle nor complex. What makes it seem so is not any special conceptual or causal construction on my part, but rather the way I apply my single reliable insight to a wide range of seemingly unrelated puzzles and problems. Social phenomena like teenage suicide, schoolyard mayhem, road rage, or New Age hypochondria engage us because they cause trouble we either have or can readily imagine. They are "problems" because they persist unabated. They are "problems" because they are not yet fully understood and thus not remediable. This is where I step in and invite reconsideration, which is actually no more than fuller consideration. I do the most basic thing. I add context. I step back and broaden and deepen context until even the most concrete-thinking reader is likely to experience the *aha!* And of course the worthiest, most earned *aha!* carries with it the conviction that one now sees not only a clear causal pathway to the problematic effect, but that, given the context of that pathway, *the problem cannot have been otherwise.* This does not always mean, given the severity and tenacious roots of some problems, that the solution will be quick and easy, but it does mean that a genuine solution is at hand. Practical considerations can then come to bear on effective action, as opposed to a complex of irrational mood, prejudice and competing self-interests.

A simpler and perhaps better explanation for my critics' inability to reduce my work to anything formulaic is that, while the "method" and its underlying assumptions are straightforward and (to my mind still) unassailable, my application of the method is more art than science. Again, I am not, or not yet, a poet, but just as enduring poetry lies in the inspired *match* of language to experience, the persuasive and explanatory power of the so-called Force Factor lies in the match of factual propositions to the problem under review. The art is in the matching. Not everyone can do it.

The crucial insight underlying all my published work is very simple, and it isn't really mine. It derives from my understanding, when I was twenty, of Jung's notion of the Shadow. Through inspired analyses of patients and through life-long, unflinching self-analysis, Jung concluded that ultimate self-understanding was the result of bringing to consciousness the wishes, drives, and longing one's conscious *persona* is constructed to suppress. Like his early mentor Freud, he puzzled over the problem of making the unconscious conscious. Jung too was a playful and gifted decoder of dreams and other unfiltered reports from the psyche's deep interior. He saw dreams and obsessions and seeming delusions as messages, as invitations to integrate the unthinkable, but nonetheless knowable, into conscious awareness. The Shadow is thus everything true of oneself that one is unwilling or unable to acknowledge in the course of making one's practical way in the world. Moreover, the Dhadow is not borne like some kind of sack of inert characteristics which happen to be inconvenient or embarrassing as we make our practical way. The Shadow is a dynamic being, a purposeful counter-self, acting on us with intent. One of Jung's great gifts as a therapist was to help his analysands confront their Shadows, beginning with the merest awareness that they had one.

I realize now that the very crudeness of my intellect when I was twenty was what enabled me to turn the promise of Jung's conception of the Shadow to a wider range of social phenomena. I took what appealed to me in Jung's thinking and reduced it to a concrete, rather mechanical prescription. I determined that if acknowledging and integrating a person's Shadow makes him whole and wise, then acknowledging and integrating what was true but unknown of *any entity* would complete and fulfill that entity. Again, only a mind as untroubled by complexity as mine was likely to make such a wild, and in my case lucky, stab. A lucky and, I am now beginning to think, tragic stab.

Having identified this Force Factor, this whatever-you-call-it, this Meaning=X+X-related not-X, I couldn't wait to put it to work. My Scholar of the House thesis on the heirs of the counter-culture was so generously praised, and probably over-praised, by Professor Call, that I was champing to try new applications, which my research fellowships at Cambridge and LSE allowed me to do, even as I was finding my feet as a credible adult and young husband. The generational dynamics and developmental psychology I studied in order to write about the counter culture's—my generation's—putative children also provided a foundation for my first book, rather grandly titled—not my choice-- *Boys and Destiny*, a monograph about how suppressed boyhood qualities (Shadow) enabled such unlikely and dissimilar figures as Churchill, FDR, and Eisenhower to guide the allies through the war years. The motif of the shadowy *Puer Aeternus* has recurred in all my books, and it was never far from my personal musings as the boys were growing up.

Now here is something, yes. My notes and plans for the Nixon book. For weeks that project all but eclipsed the work I was doing on *Boys and Destiny*, and while I don't think I have thought about it once in thirty years, the idea of laying out Richard Nixon's sad and harrowing political career as an unconscious expression of his ruined boyhood was as promising as any project I have undertaken before or since. It is strange to have put that aside, stranger still to have suppressed it from memory. I recall now telling myself that I needed to regain my focus and momentum on the World War Two leaders. I was also hesitant to add my voice to the cacophony of commentary and analysis of Nixon as he was plotting his hopeless course through the Watergate investigations. Other writers were writing, and writing well, about Nixon's signature tendency to self-defeat. No one at that time was quite naming it, but it seemed to me that somebody must at any minute penetrate the mystery of the popular fascination with which such an outwardly unfascinating figure was held. Nixon, "gloomy Gus" to those who knew him as a young man, was so brittle, so beaten. Somebody else would get it, would, either through close analysis or narrative art, reveal the President as the desperate middle schooler running for student council, forever inconsolable even in victory. But more was at work, I am now certain, than my reluctance to enter a crowded field. My Nixon book would have been richer and more surprising than *Boys and Destiny*, gratifying and successful as that effort was. Something else made me distance myself from that work, work which compelled me with great insistence. Yes. It would have been impossible to excavate Nixon's boyhood and expose his shadow without exposing my own. I was not ready.

Instead I built up the edifice of the persona behind the Force Factor,

393

sedated as much as bolstered by the success of the *Force* books to follow. Perhaps they have done some good. They have certainly caused a stir and even generated policy, change, with perhaps more to come. Shadow-driven as it is, my contribution to the culture may have been necessary to advance individuals, institutions and, who knows, the nation and other collectives to some further awareness of their lack of conscious agency in their own actions. I cannot say that applications of my findings will not lead to good work, nor can I say that they won't aid the right kind of scoundrels to bend others to their will or to sell people things. I am certain, however, that if they do the real work necessary to understand the true, causal pathways to individual and collective behavior, they will be humbled. They will be brought low.

Chapter Nineteen

It was never my intention in the *Force* books to contribute further to the scattered thinking that now characterizes the western mind. As a theorist I have always been a one-trick pony. Without smoke or mirrors I set out in straightforward language to identify the unacknowledged elements in whatever phenomenon I am considering and then demonstrate how those elements are working on, and usually against, conscious reality in a way that presents apparent "problems." I have chased and caught shadows. The mistakes in understanding my work, and thus my contribution to scattered thinking, derive from the tendency to see the "problem" addressed as the point of the analysis. The problems have never been the point, but because my work has always held the promise of solutions, remedies, and better ways, I am read and discussed in connection with the cultural changes I have seen emerging or in some cases predicted. But again, these are not my real interest, nor honestly, do I take pride in having been prescient or in the hope that I will be proved so. To uncover the shadow dimension is to see the inevitable, not to play a provocative game. My moment has been arriving, perhaps has arrived, and will no doubt pass, but it was no mere uncovering of facts and forecasting consequences that led to our current preoccupation with radical entrepreneurship, the end of intellectual property, or the decline of formal schooling. Critics and Forceans alike churn out oceans of published and blogged speculation about my self-as-world thesis, which is nothing more than the explication of new opportunities for narcissism offered by electronic globalization. *Of course* the very achievement of a 'global village' would generate a powerful drive to get the hell out of it. It took no Delphic powers to see a craze for radical anonymity and unfindability on the horizon. Of course it would begin with the most inflated pop-celebrities, and of course it would be taken up by the young. They can be seen hiding everywhere in their affected grunge and stubble and bed-heads. I have not named it 'post-fame culture' or 'post-identity culture' but somebody will. Writers and screenwriters, good ones, have taken the cues, and so we have new shadow-driven characters and stories, new American types to puzzle over, the mob boss next door, the pot dealer next door, the mortician, the pedophile, the serial killer as Everyman.

It is time, or past time, for somebody, probably an academic with career plans, to step back and make a grand unification scheme of the Force findings. I'm not going to do it, not merely because I am unraveling here, but because of the inherent futility of any such effort. There is no grand unification of the findings or the problems. The attempt to make one is itself a massively shadowed denial of the ornery enormity of cosmic creativity. And what would be the point, the hoped for result, of a grand scheme accounting for how emerging cultural developments emerge? The comforting illusion of prediction and control. The illusion of safety. The illusion of knowing it all. Should we be surprised that children and spiritually starved post-children have found such solace in the strangely credible figure of a plucky boy who is also a wizard?

There is no grand unification scheme, but there is a basic, humiliating lesson to be learned by people who think there is. I suppose in my own grandiose way I thought I was teaching that lesson, but it is more likely that I was just creating the kind of itch that a Forcean would want to scratch. At heart the problem is analysis, or rather the posture of analysis, the illusion that the analyst might occupy some Archimedean point beyond the observable fray. But our very analytic interest in the observable fray betrays us as anxious partisans. A dedicated analyst like Freud sets up to document and explain all of experience as a dynamic tussle between erotic and destructive urges, but fails to account for his own urge to do so. Ancient Hindus knew better. There is no analytic posture in the Vedas, only the eternal currents of generativity, preservation, and destruction. Lord Vishnu the preserver *gave birth* to Brahma the creator, but there was no predicting and controlling creation after that, no stopping the inevitable destruction of every created thing at the hands of Lord Shiva. The shadowed western mind wants only Vishnu. Its Dawkinses and Hitchenses throw the pebbles of their showy erudition at Brahma. Its righteous and bewildered Bushes and Rumsfelds point their big guns, now here, now there, at unkillable, unfindable Shiva. And what do I do? With meticulous, unhelpful clarity, I explain it.

THE LIGHT IS WHITE NOW against the branches, and it is hard to maintain an orderly line of thought. Even half reclining in this chair at my desk, I know I am not going to go to sleep. Ideas, argument, insomnia—I feel myself reflexively trying to order the relationship. This strikes me as funny. I know I have to get up, to will my stiffened feet and legs down the hall to the bedroom and turn in. I have not stayed up all night in thirty years, since Chappy was born—no, Franklin. I don't want to rise. I rise. I'm off, musing on Freud, Vishnu, but I can't reconstruct exactly what I was just thinking. Dissolving thought is by no means unpleasant. It puts me in mind of the way sleep steals into consciousness when I read in bed. Sleep, like Shiva, is a destroyer, but the destruction is not like killing or voiding. Sleep destroys like erosion or washing out to sea. Sleep levels, democratizes. Fractured thought is a herald of sleep, oceanic oblivion. Sleep is a herald of death, Shiva at work.

What we want. Why we analyze. At the beginning of my southern book tour I spent a day in South Beach and took my dinner alone in a little Italian restaurant with a terrace looking out over the beach. The place was crowded, and since I was alone, I decided to eat at the bar outside. The bartender and the drinkers on either side of me were trading observations about the series of hurricanes that had been forecast to devastate Miami but had veered, each of them, westward and up into the gulf. It occurred to me that these animated talkers were more than merely relieved to have escaped danger and loss. Catastrophe so close at hand positively enlivened them. They could have lost their homes. They could have been swept away on the stalled evacuation route. They could have died. No doubt disinhibited by drink, they were approaching elation. As the shadow looms closer to consciousness, the pulse quickens. Talk turns to danger, war, illness, and crime, but the energy, the release lies just below the talk: in the intimation Lord Shiva's unthinkable work.

See where my own talk has turned, how images of disaster and wreckage come unbidden. Bone tired as I am, I am still far from sleep.

Chapter Twenty

Something stops me in the passage between the hallway and our bedroom suite, a charged void that seems to emanate from the carpet just beyond the door. Then I have it. I am pausing where for years I paused to step over, or perhaps to pat, the reclining, gently heaving body of our yellow lab, George Bailey. George Bailey, sheer presence, unquestioned immanence for twelve and a half of our years. How I loved that dog, how glad to have been able to release that store of love elicited only by dogs. George Bailey, the puppy we, like the happy family of sit-coms, could not resist, the leaper, the greeter, the upholstery gnawer and gouger. For most of his life, he strained on his leash with eager pleasure, no doubt because I had neither the will nor the discipline to train him properly. George Bailey at a dead run, released at last from his leash, October sun in his buttery coat as he coursed along the rim of Lake Michigan. George Bailey, always glad I was home. George Bailey at rest against my ankle as I pecked away at my manuscripts. George Bailey's sleeping bulk nearly filling the carpeted passage leading into our bedroom, guarding us, sealing us in. I am aware of the hour and my fatigue and the increasingly gauzy appearance of everything I see, but I am nonetheless surprised at the constriction in my throat and about my eyes. I am emphatically not a crier, but this message is insistent. Idiotically, I carefully step over the space where George Bailey slept.

Knowing I should brush my teeth, I don't. I cannot bring myself to undress. I take off my shoes and lie back on the made bed. I will not resist sleep should it come. I am aware that my resistance to retiring properly has something to do with Elizabeth's absence which, while lacking the weight and immediacy of George Bailey's, seems to require its own reckoning. I did not check the messages on the blinking phone in the kitchen and do not want to now. She would certainly have called, but there would be nothing urgent. Not checking the calls keeps Elizabeth comfortably distanced. She would not have called out of need or concern, but to maintain the order we have tacitly established over the years since the boys had left us to the rhythm of our own lives.

I can see Elizabeth in Chestnut Hills, alert and watchful as Chappy and Maryann move through the routines of their days. She will be helpful, scrupulously unobtrusive, responsive, appreciative of whatever is offered, more than willing to hold, walk, and watch squirming, gurgling Beatrice. It is hard for me to watch Elizabeth with the baby. The energy of her attention is almost fierce. Without question some biology is at work, reawakened maternal feelings darkly tangled with pangs of opportunities lost. It is hard for me to watch because her outwardly appropriate witness to Chappy and Maryann's life together carries with it more than a hint of desperation.

Elizabeth does not report from her interior. She never has. It is possible she does not even access those psychic reaches. She is rigorously logical, a mathematician. I used to think she was remarkably inward and that her restraint and lack of impulsivity masked great introspection. I no longer think that is the case. Had it been, there would have been breaks, occasional outpourings of dammed up feeling. Her rational apparatus seems to have been constructed to block or filter deep feeling. The emotional range of her expression is narrow, her feelings most readable when projected onto material conditions and practical matters, particularly when something has gone avoidably wrong, when others have failed to perform, deliver, keep a commitment. She disapproves quietly but witheringly. She is uncomfortable being admired and praised. Increasingly with age she dislikes presents and unasked for kindnesses. The absence of affect in her expressions of gratitude can strike those who do not know her well as simply ungracious. The coolness and edginess in her manner are leavened by a sharp wit. Never quick to offer an opinion, she is rarely without one. She is wryly funny when she wants to be, but even her comic posture is that of an already disappointed woman expecting the worst. Clear-eyed in her assessment of others and herself, she is not proud of the persona she projects out into the world. Her experience of the boys, even before they could verbalize any point of contention with her, made her helplessly aware that her attempts to guide and shape their lives turned them inward and, as they entered adolescence, closed them off to her concerns and ministrations. My own frustration in those years was in feeling the intensity of her love for the boys and her helplessness in failing to convey it.

I'm not sure I was ever helpful in easing Elizabeth's way through our family life. When we were high school lovers, I was certain that her ominous edginess was due to something I was doing, something terrible she saw in me. While I had good reason to believe such things, I came to realize that the edginess was a prior condition, fully formed before we met. Understanding this eased my self consciousness to the point that I could be better company, could be *other* enough to establish mutuality. Recognizing Elizabeth's condition helped me to love her unconditionally, which, while doing nothing to free her from her inaccessible doubts and dreads, enabled her to love me back. However warily and darkly Elizabeth has regarded me over the forty years of our acquaintance, for most of that time she has regarded me as the person who knew her best

My work, and even more the public recognition of my work, troubled her and distanced us in a way I was powerless to prevent. Cognitively far ahead of me when we met, she could at best sense an alien intelligence operating in me which, once I found my feet at Yale, seemed to her to advance me with bewildering ease through the scholarly world. I am sure she felt innately smarter than me, smarter in the ways she was smart, and when my early work sometimes confused her, she attributed it to muddled thinking on my part, not to brittle thinking on hers. For the most part she encouraged me, and if she did not wholeheartedly admire work of mine that she could not quite follow, she has not held my successes against me. But in surrendering first her assumption of intellectual superiority and then, in the course of her home-making years, intellectual parity, she lost essential confidence. When the boys were both in full day school programs and we could afford additional child care, she enrolled in a CPA program at the University of Illinois extension in downtown Chicago. Her mathematics acumen was undiminished, and her efficiency and discipline assured her successful completion of the program, but her obsessive fastidiousness over the assignments and exam preparations was like nothing I had seen in her before. More worrying was the fact that she did not really value accountancy. Eventually she joined a small firm and assisted businesses and wealthy individuals with tax work, but while she gave each project her focused attention until it was satisfactorily completed, she never gave the slightest sign of pleasure in the work, referring to it, when she spoke of it at all, as "bean counting for the counting impaired." A little girl raised to pay close attention to money, to save, to accrue, and to spend wisely, she felt the dispiriting hollowness of adding marginal income to a household that already had plenty. In all of this Elizabeth was no Emma Bovary, feeling called to greater things than the world happened to provide. Elizabeth's unease derived not from failed expectations, but from a seemingly genetic certainty that high expectations and the kind of surrender high expectations require are a dubious bet.

Precisely because her deepest urges could find no release in rational thinking and speech, Elizabeth was throughout her fertility a phenomenal lover. Our sex from the beginning was just as Plato described it in *The Symposium*, a communion that lifted us out of waking reality into an intimation of the ultimate. In making love Elizabeth would dissolve into wordlessness. The language was touch, which she offered with the uninhibited hunger of the blind. Touch received, the merest graze of fingertips up along her forearms or over the blade of a hip, could in an instant initiate the change in psychic frequency from thought to unmediated desire. We grew amorous when we fell silent. If we were standing, we would move in close but would not quite embrace. We would be near enough to kiss but merely brush lips and cheeks. Very lightly we would entwine our fingers or I would pass my fingertips along her forehead at the hairline. We felt it coming and waited for it. From that first transporting communion in the room in The New Haven Hotel, when we shed not just our clothes but every inhibition and practical consideration, we trusted each other, made each other somehow safe as we let go of the world beyond the canopy of the bed.

Words, being world-bound, must fail me here, but Elizabeth was more than merely responsive. She was from the beginning eager and even playful. Once past the unspoken permission to begin, she was all impulse and desire, the excited realization of which released my own. At nineteen we were both technically virgin, and neither of us could have been less prepared for the abandon we quickly managed to achieve in our love making. Had we been more experienced or come from more sexually sophisticated backgrounds, we would have been more inhibited than we were. We did not know we were daring or promiscuous or perverse. We knew what we did and how we felt and how the wondrous, shared sacredness of it trumped everything thought and propriety might afterward devise.

There is no accounting for any of this hormonally. This was not the healthy exuberance of youth. At thirty-five, forty-two, forty-six we were if anything hungrier, wilder. Outwardly we were, I know, comfortably preppy types, attentive parents, sociable neighbors, decorous in speech, neither advocate nor apparent example of any unconventional approach to life, but sexually we went everywhere, although never, except in fantasy, beyond fidelity. I cannot speak for Elizabeth in that regard, but for me extramarital exploration never held sufficient allure. As I passed into middle life and traveled more, attending conferences and leading seminars in dreamy, abstracted places like Aspen and Salzburg and Lake Como, I was approached fairly frequently, often with astonishing directness, for sex. The think tank world tends to fancy itself above all philistine sexual restriction, as I suppose do I, but in my case the prospect of an erotic night or two out with a seductive stranger could not possibly rise to the erotic anticipation I felt in getting back into bed with Elizabeth. It would have taken ages for me to reach anything like the comfort and playfulness and wildness I already knew. Moreover it has always seemed to me that the subtle and less-than-subtle flirtations that inevitably develop in the course of intense encounters far from home are more stirring if not carried forward into sex. And while I have been no Lothario, my best advice to Lotharios would be to hold off. An affable disinclination to adultery seems to work on adulterous women as a kind of aphrodisiac.

Elizabeth and I have not moved past all sexual connection, but the changes in both of us as she progressed through menopause are clear and irreversible. Deep lovemaking is now infrequent, the old oblivion only approximately reached, if at all. I think we are both aware of a willed quality in getting started, clear-eyed awareness of which comes close to scuttling the attempt. At worst, we achieve orgasm with something like relief that we are still capable, the pleasure less in the exertion than in what it enables me to remember.

Even now lying here alone I find it hard to call up Elizabeth's physical image without seeing her as she has come to see herself. She is still decidedly slender and reasonably fit. The set of her face has hardened, but the sharp features of her face below her bob of undyed hair still command attention and interest. She does not like her looks, or rather how her looks have evolved. She especially does not like the network of crinkles below her eyes and the soft folds of skin at the base of her neck and the sagging at the top of her knees. She eats very carefully and to my mind very little and has thus been able to keep trim, but as she passed into her fifties there has been a distinct redistribution of her body mass, filling in between ribs and hips what had been a sharply defined and very slender waist. Probably as a result of a stringent diet, her bottom has flattened and grown smaller, and her thighs have become quite thin. Taken together, these changes are largely benign, unremarkable signs of aging, but Elizabeth's self-deprecating exaggerations of her decrepitude approach outrage. She will describe herself as "wizened," "shriveling." She is very reluctant to put on a bathing suit of any kind or any skirt or shorts that show her thighs and knees. Out of sight and earshot of others, she will lift her denim gardening skirt up over her thighs and tell me, "*Look* at this. I look like a fucking *stork*!"

Elizabeth does not look like a stork, but my assurances and flattery are of no help. There is no integrating Lord Shiva into her world view, and there is nothing I can do or say to mitigate her hatred of his relentless work. My inability to picture Elizabeth independently of the way she now pictures herself is a fairly recent development. For more than thirty of our forty years together, I distorted her image in the other direction. In reverie when I was away from home, in the dark, in the throes of our love-making, I would call up the same picture. She is stepping from the train down onto the platform of the New Haven rail station. Everything about her is both unexpected and familiar. There is a sheen to her dark hair. Her dark eyes are bright in expectation. Her shoes are black, and the delicate bones of her ankles are sharply defined by the black tights stretching over them. I look up to her face, the straight, impossibly delicate nose, the even line of her compressed lips, the lovely vixen vee of her chin. Her long coat is open, revealing beneath her sweater the little mounds of her breasts, her tiny waist. She is about to speak, but already I am overcome. I had been anticipating her arrival for a long time, but I was not prepared for her beauty.

The beauty was not ephemeral. For every instant of that visit and of so many subsequent visits and the eventual communion to follow, Elizabeth continued to embody that picture, that beauty. I was weak before it, grateful, prayerful, and now I am weak before the memory. She is not dead, but the realization of what has passed is more final than her death will be when it comes. I am feeling shot through with an urge to do something monumental in her honor, but I know it is an empty mental gesture, a selfish urge to memorialize my own farewell. It is fitting that I am lying here alone on my half of our crisply sealed conjugal bed. I have passed this long night without sleep, fully awake, fully aware. Without once returning to restorative oblivion, I have made this passage alone.

And now I can see Elizabeth, as she is. Her face is a little bird-like in its perplexed irritation. The block of her midsection does indeed accentuate the boniness of her legs below the hem of her denim gardening skirt. Fucking *stork*. I could laugh. I could clasp her by her narrow hips and raise her like an offering to the billowing sky. Elizabeth, I love you. You offered up to me everything you had, and it was enough, if not for you, for me. There will of course be excruciating good-byes and partings, but this is the moment of truth.

And thus, I see, this visitation.

Chapter Twenty-One

It is now bird-bright mid-morning, and I need to wash up and get into this bed. Not two strides toward the bathroom, I am stopped again by a psychic tug from the patch of carpet over the door sill. Strange. George Bailey again. George Bailey gone. George Bailey's last night.

Neither of us knew he was that far along. There had been some stiffening in his hind legs and labored efforts to rise for his walks and food, but it was a wet, chilly March, and we didn't think much about it. After the boys left home it was my job to take him out for a walk before we retired for the night, but because I had just returned late from a trip and was upstairs unpacking and sorting mail, Elizabeth found a leash and led him outside. Before I could make sense of the words, I stiffened with the realization that the sound outside on the street was Elizabeth's voice. It was a terrible sound, a shrill cry with a strange rattle in it. Elizabeth has never been able to project a loud voice—or to sing—a trait the boys and I would sometimes kid her about. She would not have considered wailing out into the night unless something terrible was happening. She was calling my name, *Jonathan! Jona-THAN!* but all I could hear were the whining, rattling *n's*. I ran downstairs and a hundred yards or so down the sidewalk where Elizabeth was stooped over George Bailey lying stiffly on his side. Elizabeth said he was fine, he just walking along, and then he fell right down and she couldn't get him to move. I knelt on the walk and raised George Bailey's head a little to see if I could feel his breath on my cheek. In the street light I could see that his eyes were open but they offered nothing. I put my palm on his flank and felt the rapid heaving of his breath. The exhalations were choked with spittle and so rapid they made a faint hum. Crisis, the sudden onset of any problem with no clear solution at hand, tends to undo Elizabeth, but because she loved George Bailey, she stayed close to my side, willing herself against all inclination to maintain a mute witness to whatever was happening. I tried to lift George Bailey up off the walk, but could manage no better than to haul his head and upper body up to my chest and drag his trailing hind legs along the walk and up the steps into our foyer. I sat down with my legs extended in front of me on the area rug, guiding George Bailey's head down onto my lap. Elizabeth asked if she should call the vet. It was an appropriate question, but I had already sensed, and she may have too, that George Bailey was past care. I lay my head down to George Bailey's throat to listen again to his breathing, which had quieted to faint hisses. I looked into his eyes, which I am sure registered no sight or comprehension of me. Their stony immobility suggested instead a great, touching determination to complete this passage. A sudden contraction tensed his shoulders, and he let out a harsh bronchial honk, which startled us. There were two or three more of these before it occurred to me that I had not answered Elizabeth's question about calling the vet. I was unable to form a coherent thought much less a plan of action. I was about to speak when I felt George Bailey's shoulders relax and fall. His head came to rest, now quite comfortably, on my lap. His eyes still held their determined inward look. In a choked unnatural voice Elizabeth asked if he was dead. I didn't know. I knew but could not find words to say that he was somewhere along the passage. Cradling the weight of him on my lap, I was unable to stop my hand from moving over the great milky crown of his beloved head. This was sad, this was profound and very beautiful, but it was more than that. I was back in the better place. It was if I had been waiting to be transported in this way. It was a return. It was an arrival. This was the realm that had once held me, that I had awakened into every day. It had been such a long time.

And it took no more than to be right there with George Bailey in this, to hold him to me, to offer dumbly back— to hold up, to honor, to *feel*-- everything he was.

So I am called back, and I am called back for a reason, to shed the old imposture, to come back into my skin, to begin—I can only hope—to live.

Book 3

After Thought

Now let the past be past, behind us flung;
Oh, feel thyself from highest god descended,
Thou of the primal world whence thou art sprung

—Faust to Helen in Goethe's Faust, II

When you at last a glowing tripod see,
Then in the deepest of all realms you'll be.
You'll see the Mothers in the tripod's glow,
Some of them sitting, others stand and go…

—Mephistopheles to Faust

The artist is no other than he who unlearns what he has learned, in order to know himself.

--e.e. commings, "the agony of the Artist (with capital A)"

Chapter One

For some reason I have come back to life.
The passage will be completed, I can see now, in the filmy, antiseptic atmosphere of this hospital room where, terminally supine and draped tenderly with a crisply laundered sheet, I lie between sentinel IVs infusing the crook of each arm with hydrating solutions of glucose and morphine. I feel no pain whatsoever, just held in a kind of startled giddiness.

The emergency scans, it has just been explained to me, revealed a puzzling surprise: that my broken skeleton—the shattered hip, the fractured ribs, the concussed skull—is not what is killing me, but rather the ruinous predations of no fewer than four advanced melanomas, three of them on the proud crown of my sun-browned head. I was not aware of these, or rather no more concerned about them than I was about the other familiar, even friendly-seeming raised and faintly discolored patches on my leathery old carcass. In what felt to me like a respectful spirit, I had come to gentling the hairbrush over those slightly spongy patches after my morning shower, but I never had the slightest suspicion that they were out to get me, that they would insinuate their way into my lymph and blood and then burrow into my lungs and liver. Apparently there are even signs of some fresh outposts on my brain.

At eighty-two and brown as a nut for the past twenty-two years, I have always held the sun as a close and reliable friend. More than that, I felt the sun, especially the indomitable, generous, even raucous sun of Key

West, as a sustaining, beneficent force. I cannot remember a day in that sun when I couldn't feel the skin of my cheeks, my shoulders, my chest and belly rise to it as if in offering. Where bright sun is concerned, I stand with the ancient Egyptians. Although here I am.

Perhaps it's merely the morphine making me loopy, but I can't get past preferring that the fall had done it. It was by all accounts a spectacular fall. One of the EMTs heard someone say and wrote down that I went down the stairs "ass over tea kettle." I don't know if I actually remember starting to tumble or whether I just imagine I did. I can summon up a jumbled image of pitching sideways, then, arms akimbo, crashing down on the bony edge of my butt, then over and over, the teeth-cracking jolts somehow mixing into the boomp-da boomp sound of it before I go black.

I was not drunk. It was bright mid-afternoon, and I was, after a satisfying lie-down at the far end of the Fort Zachary Taylor beach, descending into Tenderloins for some friendly badinage and what would have been my first drink of the day, a chilled Corona with a wedge of lime stuffed into the bottle neck. Indeed, in contrast to the fall itself, I can clearly remember my anticipation of that Corona, the first tangy slug of coldness over my parched tongue. Perhaps that was it—perhaps I was distracted and misstepped. Who knows?

If somebody had asked me as I made my way up Duval to the club if I was feeling all right, I would have said absolutely, meaning that I felt as well as I ever did these days. I was still alert, able to manage without medicines, ambulatory aids, or special assistance of any kind. If I had stopped to consider the matter, I might have conceded that my energy was down, which I could easily attribute to the heat, my age, possibly a minor bug. There had also been, especially on waking, a kind of chalky, faintly sour taste in my mouth. This had been so for some weeks, but after coffee and breakfast, I was only mildly aware of it. I can taste that sourness now and wonder if it is some kind of by-product of my melanomas. Overall I felt reasonably fit, almost perfectly untroubled. Again, I am eighty-two. Between my beach excursions and errands, I must walk three to five miles every day. I eat very little and have been rail thin for years. The girls at Tenderloins have made a ritual of noting my youthfulness, a largely playful and certainly exaggerated gesture, but in a sense they mean it because despite the half century or more separating most of them from me, we get on, we talk, we go deep. A benign daily presence there for so many years, I represent continuity and stability. They trust me.

Which raises the question—not that it finally matters--of whether in my looming obituary there will be any mention of or speculation about the fact that my mortal fall occurred on the stairway leading down to the red-lit portal of Tenderloins Gentleman's Club. Here the unexpected revelation of my melanomas may work to my advantage. Melanomas ought to qualify as respectable pathology, as "natural causes," although as far as I am concerned, there is something pitch perfect, something apt and poetic in passing out of this life on my way into the pulsing, Stygian lair of the Tenderloins girls.

It is of course beyond silly to be concerned in the slightest about responses of any kind to my obituary, but if for some reason The Tenderloins Gentleman's Club does come into play, I would like that sensational tidbit to be interpreted properly. This would be highly unlikely, however. On its surface—no, in its essence—Tenderloins is as far outside polite commerce as any other strip club. I have not visited them elsewhere, but the girls assure me that other Tenderloins and Tenderloins-like establishments thrive on the margins of most American cities of any size, also, for some reason, near airports. Customs vary somewhat from region to region, state to state, but the scene and basic allure is common to all of them: in seductively lit, windowless chambers heavily made up and scented women costumed in exotic lingerie and footwear mount platforms and disrobe to either toplessness or complete nudity. They do this against a deafening and in time hypnotic background of the most insinuating, largely tune-less popular music.

The premise and promise of course is sex, but except in the most disreputable clubs, disdained by the girls themselves and frequently raided and closed, sex—at least straightforward intercourse— is forbidden and does not occur. For the men and the occasional women who visit Tenderloins there are graduated offerings of stimulation and pleasure. The most basic is simply sitting either at the lip of the dancing platform or at some darkened remove and watching the dancers as they gyrate and undress. Old and even very old men like me tend to participate at this level, as do very young, nervous solitaries and clusters of joshing comrades who stop in on a lunch break or a night on the town. The etiquette for the watchers is to toss a dollar or two onto the stage when the dancer has completed her sequence of two or three songs. That would be etiquette at its most restrained; typically at Tenderloins, the folded bills are inserted directly into the dancer's garter belt or, when invited, between her clutched, naked breasts.

A deeper level of intimacy is extended by girls who make their way among the seated customers and offer their company. The expectation is that the customer will buy the dancer drinks as she sits with him. It is understood that the steep prices of the drinks will compensate the dancer for her time. The appeal here is the realized illusion of actually socializing, exchanging preferences and impressions with a tantalizingly brazen and seductive woman. Were she outside on the street in her tiny black leather bikini and fish net stockings, she would unambiguously be a prostitute. But sitting at your side, perhaps leaning a shoulder into yours as she tells you her country of origin, her experiences in other clubs, her impressions of Key West, she is somehow both dream and date. This is all certain gentle and very lonely men want.

Finally, and often expensively, there is a menu of individual "dances." These range from "table dances" in which for the length of one recorded song, the dancer will undress, gyrate before, touch, caress and, once or twice, sit and squirm on the lap of the customer at a cost of twenty-five dollars. More intimate are series of three or more "lap dances" for which customer and dancer move off to a narrow curtained room where the dancer undresses immediately and, wedged closely between the customer's parted legs, engages him in an extended, gyrating embrace. In these rooms touching and caressing above the waist are allowed and expected. Customer and dancer may find themselves alone on the leather benches, or they could be elbow to elbow, knee to knee with a half dozen other gyrating couples, a dizzying appeal to either situation. The cost per series is a hundred dollars, tips welcome. If a customer is set on privacy and can afford three hundred and fifty dollars for forty-five minutes of continuous, unobserved (except by security cameras) contact, he may escort a dancer to the Champagne Room where a bottle of cheap, sweet Champagne is at hand as the couple enjoys more extended exertions. Orgasm is usually sought and easily achieved by healthy and eager customers in the course of the lap dancing, a pleasure many of them prefer to what might be provided in a riskier, more carnal encounter with a prostitute or a pick-up.

None of this, however, begins to convey the essence and value of Tenderloins as I have come to know it. Summarizing its protocols does not tell the story. Context is important, and the context of Key West is everything. Even after all these years and the billions invested in opulent Waterfront mega-hotels and massive dredging and servicing of the cruise behemoths, despite all the gentrification and the relentless supplanting of dive bars and massage parlors with boutiques and bistros, the elemental last-resort, anything-goes raffishness of old Key West has proved unkillable. Impoverished, open hearted Cubans still intermingle with sailors and free-spirited retirees and runaways and buskers and writers and other refugees. In a day or two a tourist can feel it. Key West is both in and well beyond the United States. It is not at all disorienting to sit at a crowded bar or stroll the length of a beach and hear no English spoken. It is more than a local joke that the island has declared its independence, that it is The Conch Republic. Duval Street, from the Atlantic to the Caribbean, is day and night a two-and-a-half-mile party. One has to know this, to feel and breathe the atmosphere of, say, the corner of Duval and Caroline at noon or midnight to understand that Key West, a chartable, geographical place, is also an elevated psychic condition.

A crucial element in the feel of Key West is clothes, or rather lack of clothes. The combination of sun and soft air by mid-morning insists that you divest, strip down. Wonderfully almost every one, even the day trippers, tacitly give themselves this permission, and the parade up and down Duval, Front Street and Turtle Kraal is a visual feast of oiled brown shoulders and midriffs, of broad backs and beer guts and chiseled abs offered out over the elasticized waist bands of the signature satin shorts of the Knicks or the Bulls. Most days there are only well worn flip-flops slapping under brown feet. The merest bikini triangles are all the girls and young women bother with from mid-day on. Breasts are so generously out and free that the tiny cloth flags caressing the nipple seem only playful, more suggestive of nakedness than nakedness itself. The senses, I'm sure everyone's senses, rise to this. Nor is it a lewd or lecherous condition. By contrast, the erotic elevation of an afternoon or evening in close quarters with others in Key West releases a terrific generosity of spirit. However stimulating the liberation from underwear—to the extent that after a month or two in residence I could not honestly determine what underwear had been about---the response far exceeds the heightening of sexual awareness; it is more an all-being expression of release and gratitude.

Tenderloins, at least my Tenderloins, is unthinkable outside of Key West. The girls of Tenderloins do not represent, as I suppose such girls in such establishments do in Chicago or Boston, a seamy, erotic departure from the commerce of Main Street and the malls. The sweetness of Tenderloins is that it is completely continuous with life on Duval Street, an exhilarating distillation of that spirit. All roads in Key West lead to Tenderloins, to its sister and brother establishments. Moreover, Tenderloins delivers the goods.

I am fortunate to have made my way to Key West untroubled by money. The very best frame of mind in entering Tenderloins and I'm sure any place like it is to have no concern at all about being overcharged or bilked or running out of cash. There were three or four hundred dollars and cards in my wallet, so I had no such concerns that first afternoon when, exploring the narrow alleyway behind the Hog's Breath, I stepped out of bright day into the nearly total eclipse beyond the windowless door. As I eased my way forward through the murk, I could just make out the flickering lights behind the bar and along the lip of the dancing platforms. When my eyes adjusted a little, I made out the shapes of two naked women, one white, one black, rising and dipping very slowly along the length of brass poles. I had been so long out of erotic touch that the two figures on the adjacent platforms weakened me. I remember feeling

419

distinctly fated to be there, that I had entered a necessary dream. Then as my eyes adjusted to the darkness, I saw that seated at the bar, lounging near the entrance, sprinkled among the tables were other women, more than a dozen, dressed in feathers and leather and sequins and netted stockings. Each was a strong type, fantastical. There were platinum blondes with moist scarlet lips. There were slender, dark haired beauties. Some were naked under gauzy tunics. Others wore tiny bikini bras or bright bandeaus. It was three in the afternoon, and there were only a few customers. The women did not look so much bored as languorous. Without question I had entered another world, a world that seemed to be waiting for me.

Of course this was years before Maria, before Anya and Kareta and all the beautiful Czech Republic girls, but those first dancers who, almost all of them, became such friends to me and such loves, were one with their successors, touching, vulnerable, generous and so surprisingly wise. But now I'm sounding even to myself like a dithering old fool—because of course I am.

But back to my death.

Chapter Two

A MISTAKE. IT IS not for an instant bearable to reenter the riotous disintegration of my body. The morphine is working no doubt to blur the most gruesome sensations of the wreckage, but something deeper in my system knows, pain or no pain, and must report. Thus the throat's shallow breaths, the hummingbird heart. To enter this is to be held at the gaping brink of a scream, eyes straining to widen, a rancid taste in every cell. So much better to fall back into the disembodied dark of undirected thought, where memory comes calling like a dream.

And here I come, that last version of me, ambling down the beach. I walked that beach in the force of that sun for a long time. On most days for twenty-two years I was a fixture on the Fort Zachary Taylor water front from mid-morning to mid-afternoon. For a few months after my arrival on the island, I would tote a bag of sun screens and books and towels to the park and after securing a relatively remote patch, usually near the naval base's forbidding fence, void my mind of all thought and give myself up to the sun. In time I would sit up more often, actually read the books and newspapers, savor the crossword puzzle. Every half hour or so I would relieve my torpor with an aimless swim, no great exertion, perhaps a hundred yards out on my back, then returning with a slow crawl. If there had been wind and rain overnight, the water would be milky grey, but on most days it spread out before me emerald green, deepening to turquoise and grape blue at the horizon.

Over the years I did as much walking as lounging on the beach, although walking suggests something rather more determined and purposeful than my halting, uncritically observant traversals. Even today the Fort Zachary Taylor beach is something of a secret kept from Key West tourists. Tucked back behind the mean streets of Little Cuba and apparently, but not actually, gated off by the pristine condominiums of the Truman Annex, the unpromising asphalt track leading to the beach can easily elude even determined visitors with maps.

Nor really is Fort Zachary Taylor much of a beach. A strip only a few yards wide of bleached stones and coral, with very little sand, the beach extends barely a quarter mile between the severe no-trespassing markers of the naval base and the stony turning into the channel where the massive cruise ships make port. The bulbous stones composing most of the beach's surface are laced with exquisite fossils, but they are hard on the soles of your feet. Few go barefoot for long at Fort Zachary Taylor. Yet for those who don't mind strolling about and bathing with the added encumbrance of rubber treaded moccasins, the little beach can be a treasure. I cannot remember once finding it forbiddingly crowded. No one's amplified music invaded my reverie. There was a substantial snack bar, but no litter. There were days when seemingly everybody along the beach was Hispanic, other days when the overheard wind-whipped snippets of conversation were all in German and French. The presence of families gladdened me, and my summary impression is of their children's exemplary behavior.

There were a few, but only a few, regulars, of which I became a principal. Not long after I discovered Tenderloins and began getting to know the girls beyond their club names and the kinds of patter they relied on with their tourist customers, I was wonderfully heartened to see that many of them tanned from mid-morning till noon at Fort Zachary Taylor. There is I am sure a regrettable, if innate, tendency on the part of heterosexual males on beaches to note with an assassin's acuity the proximity, posture, and discernable attitude of attractive women sun bathers. Even at my age I was hardly above this leaning, although I knew enough to avoid anything like ogling or crowding. Understandably, given their work, the Tenderloins girls tended to be knockouts on the beach. The favored look among whites at the club was to be tanned to a rich mocha shade, with no visible tan lines. Achieving this required the artful untying of bikini strings and knowing adjustments of posture as the sun ascended in its arc toward high noon. Nudity and even toplessness were expressly forbidden on the sign posted at the entrance to the beach. This, it seemed to me once I got to know Key West, was an anomalous regulation given the otherwise relaxed, decidedly Caribbean atmosphere, but as the beach was part of the National Park Service, I assumed, the girls for the most part understood that the insistence on technically covering up derived from a remote headquarters far up in the temperate zone.

Nevertheless, despite the vigilance of park rangers who patrolled the shaded canopy behind the beach on nearly silent golf carts, the Tenderloins girls, along with the Europeans and anybody else who had a mind to offer their bodies to the sun, found a way to expose themselves as completely as they wanted to. For my part, I took care not to impose myself in a way that I thought might be remotely unwelcome when I encountered one of the Tenderloin girls in baking recline. To the contrary, more often than not they sought me out, flipped up their sun glasses and struck up conversation as they spotted me strolling past or surfacing out of the shallows. *Jon—Jon! Is that you?* As a regular, agreeable, decidedly generous customer, I had without effort become a favorite of the girls. There was of course something avuncular and even fatherly in the relationships I established with a number of them, but it would be dishonest to say that our initial encounters and ultimate friendships were not heightened by a wonderfully unhurried erotic charge. But as it happened, it was not my pleasure in the company of the Tenderloin girls that opened me up fully and finally to life on the beach.

A week or so after I established my daily beach routine, I awoke on my blanket and realized that it had gotten late. It may have been approaching five, and the sun, still insistently needling my cheeks and shoulders, was poised low in the haze off shore. I sat up to clear my head before gathering up my things when my attention was drawn to the running figure of a woman perhaps twenty yards to my left. The beach at this point was nearly deserted, and as the woman splashed into the surf, she managed to untie her bikini straps from behind and remove her top. She stopped still in the thigh high water and extended her open palms to the sun.

Her blond hair was held loosely behind her head in a clip which she shook free. I remember feeling that I occupied not just my body on the blanket but also all the particles of atmosphere separating me from the brown back of this rapt woman. She wriggled her shoulders and made slow, lovely gathering gestures with her arms. The feeling of being drawn out and into her worship was a pleasure unlike any I had known.

Chapter Three

So in just weeks, without a plan and without effort, I metamorphosed into what Maria would later call "the man in white." I would learn this pet name for me only after we became friends, and then lovers. To the other Tenderloins girls and new friends on the island I was simply Jon—a name I had never used and had for some reason never been called. It seemed not just easy but deeply right to shed my identity as Jonathan Force. Somehow in the course of driving south from Chicago, that mask flipped back from my face and blew off over the rails of the bridges linking the lower Keys. It was not so much that I could no longer bear to embody my old persona; Jonathan Force was simply finished, lifeless, no longer serviceable.

Long before Maria confided to me her private impression, I could feel myself growing into "the man in white." I don't think it was a sartorial affectation. There was just something about Key West living, day in day out, especially as I was outdoors most of my waking hours, that called for clothing as white and weightless as possible. Like my radically simplified diet, my wardrobe no longer required thought or care. My shorts and slacks were white canvas or white linen. Tee shirts and polo shirts were white, their sun-answering brilliance enhanced by repeated bleaching at the cleaners. Providentially, Fast Buck Freddie's stocked the kinds of white canvas sneakers in style when I was six. Only a few weeks a year does it grow cool enough after dark to require a jacket or sweater, but I bought a few blazers of white linen, and one blue one for dimly imagined formal outings, of which there were few. I also kept two boldly striped ties, which I wore no more than three or four times in my twenty two years residence.

I don't think I could have been "the man in white" if my hair had not whitened to the shade of my clothes and if all but my bottom and genitals had not darkened to deep brown and plum. The darkness made my white clothing and plumage striking. I remember first catching my reflection in shop windows as I made my way along Duval in the pearly dusk on my way to a dinner out and beholding the striding figure in white as someone entirely unrelated to me. The image was pleasing enough, but not in any compelling sense mine. The figure looked older than I felt, but not in a worrying way. The shock of white hair above the brown brow was without question distinctive, as was the loose fall of white clothes on my now quite boney frame. There was a suggestion of a photographic negative. For the better part of the past five years, people have tended, I think, to find my extreme thinness worrying, a sign perhaps of some consumptive illness. This skeletal aspect was more pronounced on the beach where my hollow thighs and seemingly enlarged elbows and knees were out in plain view, but I felt pretty spry, swam and walked with ease and even vigor, and in any event did not really mind how I looked. Clothed, especially in the evenings, wearing long pants and long sleeves, I tended to look, by Key West standards, pretty dapper, as skeletal people strangely do. At any rate, that figure was what I had quite familiarly become, a not unappealing old gent, gracious and eager in conversation, not yet a tiresome monologuist, still rather a heavy hitter at the bar stool, a night owl of some endurance. *Jon For-say*, a mispronunciation I let stand. The man in white.

Chapter Four

There was no desperation in my departure and flight. It was necessarily sad to come to a final reckoning with Elizabeth and to part, but in that very sadness there was also a kind of majesty, a renewed and unkillable appreciation for what we had been and done together since we were children. We had not made *mistakes*—or rather, what mistakes we may have made did not trouble us. We had quietly and profoundly come to the end, and each of us knew it, however differently we otherwise met the world and made our ways.

We never divorced. Parted by great distance and free of all obligation to one another, I could—and I am certain Elizabeth could too—savor what had been fine and dismiss the rest. In this there were some beautiful moments, perhaps even our best. When very occasionally some financial question arose, invariably about taxes, Elizabeth would call, and I would experience a happy clout of recognition hearing her beyond-all-hope drollery. Free of me she was, I know, sometimes very lonely, but she had been lonely when we lived together. Free of me she became more fully realized, reconciled at last to the unease that as a younger woman she had struggled so anxiously to keep at bay. She loved the boys and her grandchildren and kept in far better touch with them than I have, and as she bravely resigned herself to a role of mere witness to their lives, her helpless impulse to shape and protect them finally dissolved.

In all, not counting the days at her bedside when she died, I saw

Elizabeth no more than four or five times after I departed. These were family reunions arranged with touching care by the boys at their respective summer retreats. Franklin had built a rustic aerie in the mountains north of San Francisco in Santa Rosa. Chappy and Maryann shared with her parents a rambling old frame house on Penobscot Bay, north of Brunswick, Maine. Each of these get-togethers was held in August, and while I was always pleased enough to see Elizabeth and take a measure of how the boys and their families were getting on, the prospect of even a brief respite from the steamy closeness of August in Key West was also very welcome.

And there we would be, Elizabeth and I, four or five years since we had last seen each other. I believe we were equally eager for the encounter. I was always curious to see how she looked, storing first impressions deeply, revisiting the images for months afterwards. There was nothing surprising; I was fascinated rather by the touching continuity in her features and manner. She perhaps drank a bit more, or with more determination, than when we lived together, but I don't believe she ate much of anything in the last two decades of her life. Always slender, she grew progressively gaunt, the pronounced recession of her cheeks combining with her otherwise sharp and delicate facial features to create a bird-like intensity. The flesh of her calves, thighs and at the back of her arms seemed to be quite loosely affixed to bone. She was still a formidable presence, by no means unattractive. Standing or seated in company, she commanded special interest. She was more than capable of saying mordant and even devastating things to people who tried to engage her in banalities, but the deference with which she was increasingly regarded was not the result anything imperiousness or forbidding. Petite and frail as she ultimately became, Elizabeth conveyed an impression of having achieved an enviable equilibrium, a kind of strength.

When on those occasions we were able to talk apart from others, we never strayed from the surface of matters at hand. This was neither effortful nor self-protective on either of our parts. We did not need to know what was transpiring in one another's deep interior; or better, we knew each other well enough not to care. The surface was enough. On the surface we could even be playful. As carefully as I noted her appearance and its changes, I never spoke of them, other than to tell her she looked well. She, on the other hand, seemed to get a bemused kick out of the way I looked. The man in white was altogether new to her, and as we spoke, no matter at what hour or for how long, there was something close to laughter in her eyes. She also remarked on my thin-ness, although I was no thinner than she. At our first reunion she wanted to know what I could possibly *do* all day, and when I told her—my general movements about the island, my beach routine, a few guardedly vague references to new companions—she actually did laugh. I think she knew I was all right and glad of that.

The best of those encounters may have been silence—or the mutual acknowledgement that our exchanges were so insubstantial as to be a kind of silence. I remember once sitting alone with Elizabeth in the near-dark, in the bracing evening air of Franklin's deck looking out at the blue-black silhouettes of the Santa Rosa mountains, another time in the foggy damp of Chappy and Maryann's front porch in Maine. We had managed to steal off for a night cap, both of us glad for the communion, but with little we wanted to say, or at least report. And in fact, I cannot remember a thing we said on either occasion, just a glad, swelling appreciation of Elizabeth's continuing presence in the world, there, then, just for an hour or so, with me. I could not have loved her more. Sharing space in that dusky decline felt prayerful. We didn't have to do anything or say anything. We had already done it, stood that watch.

I believe—no, I am sure—Elizabeth died in that shared knowing. She was very weak, barely fluttering, by the time I made my way to the hospital in Lake Forest. I had telephoned her a week earlier after Franklin told me her most recent bout of pneumonia had turned serious and that she might have to be hospitalized. She sounded very much herself but there was something new in her voice. She said she was tired of being tired. A year earlier she had been diagnosed with a kind of leukemia, which her doctor told her was more likely something she would die with than of— exactly the kind of distinction Elizabeth savored. She told me at the time that the diagnosis and its prospects didn't really trouble her. Apart from being more easily fatigued, she said she felt about the same as she always did.

Although capable of only shallow breaths, she was composed and lucid when I arrived. My first impression was that she had shrunk to a miniature of herself. There was a moist sheen to her face, her complexion strangely baby-like. I forget what I said to her in greeting. She gave me a long look and said, "I guess this means I'm pretty sick." An impulse to laugh, I think, started her coughing. When she quieted, I told her that, yes, she was pretty sick. I told her I was very glad to see her, and she smiled beautifully. She closed her eyes and I wondered if she had fallen asleep. Her eyes opened, found me again, and she said, "You're not going to make me cry, are you?" I told her absolutely not, and she said, "I'm going to make me cry." Her features contracted miserably, and she convulsed, at first silently, then in labored coughs. I wanted to touch her, to caress her hand, but sensed it might deepen her discomfort. I sat down and pulled the chair close to the bedside. When her breathing eased, I said, "Please don't cry."

Her mouth set in the familiar way, and she said, "That doesn't leave me with many options." *Elizabeth*. She said, "Now I want to ask you a serious question, and I want to ask it without crying." We looked into each other's eyes and waited. "Jonathan," she said, "Do you remember the first time I came to visit you at Yale, on the train?" I told her I remembered it perfectly. "The first night, not the night you stayed, the first night when we ate dinner in the stuffy dining room and then went to the French movie? Do you remember that?" I told her I did, *The Four Hundred Blows*. "Do you remember walking me to the door of my room in the hotel? We were kissing. Do you remember what you promised?" I remembered with utter clarity lingering and kissing in the hushed corridor, but I could not recall our words. "I asked you to promise me something. I asked you to promise--and this is exactly what I said--that you would be a good thing that happened in my life." She started to cry again. Her chin was quivering. "And you said you would, you promised."

Because I was concerned that she was upsetting herself, I was slow to take in the sense of her words—that I had *promised* to be good for her. I felt a physical, electrical jolt. I could not speak yet was aware of a sickening need to right myself, regain a sense of what had just transpired, find words. But before any words would come, before *and I failed,* and *I'm sorry,* before the eruption of my own tears, Elizabeth said with some force, "Well, I just wanted you to know. You were a good thing that happened. The best thing."

When I was able to speak, I said, "I wish I had been a good thing."

Now I could take her hand. She said, "Jonathan, did you really used to think I was smarter than you?" I told her I did, that she was born smarter than I was. "I'm smarter than you because I *know* you cannot have been any better for me than you were, because I was too scared and selfish to let you." I stroked her hand. "But now I'm not, and look, here you are, all in your—white suit."

There I was. My affection for Elizabeth had grown surer over the years we lived apart, but nothing in that time had prepared me for the gift of our final communion. The rest of the vigil was what one might expect of two sensible old people. We acknowledged each other's part in launching the boys, both of whom could not have been more attentive in those closing days of our family life. An hour or so before she died, Elizabeth said, "It took me an awfully long time to realize that kids who don't need you are the best kind."

Chapter Five

APART FROM ELIZABETH and the boys there have been few connecting threads to my former life. In fact shedding the life and work of Jonathan Force proved to be strangely effortless. The ease of passage was due in part to Elizabeth's and my felicitous, if outwardly peculiar, agreement to stay legally married. Elizabeth's gifts as a tax accountant were remarkable, and it is perhaps fitting that together we would become her sole and most appreciative clients. Apparently we saved hundreds of thousands of dollars filing jointly, and there were none of the tedious complexities of breaking up a household and dividing property.

It has been my blind luck never to have been concerned about money, or even to pay much attention to it. The truth of the matter—which Elizabeth realized early on with wonder—is that I never progressed beyond a child's interest in money. As a very little boy I came to regard coins and bills as straightforwardly instrumental in acquiring things I wanted immediately. Because of my family's modest means and circumstances, financial transactions were completely clear: income covered necessary living expenses and little else. I knew what I wanted and, once I was aware what things cost, was able very early in life to understand what I could and couldn't have. In this I believe I was very fortunate. I was provided all that I needed and just a little of what I wanted, a material condition I recommend for all children everywhere.

I would not for a minute hold up my child-like approach to money as a virtue. It is no such thing. Not having to think much about money, especially if you have some money, is, however, a great and under-acknowledged luxury. Were it not for Elizabeth's financial acumen and that of my beloved and now departed agent Mary Marx, I probably would have made every conceivable financial blunder. It is still a wonder to me that there *are* people, including dedicated and scrupulously honest people like Elizabeth and Mary, who are positively motivated to understand and manipulate the variables of finance to other people's advantage.

Mary saw that I not only made money from my books and personal appearances, but that I made as much money as possible. She made shrewd deals. She once made waves in the publishing world by outright *declining* what was at the time a record advance—I think two million dollars—for *Force Fields* and putting the title up for auction. I remember at the time her explaining the risks as well as the possible advantages of this gambit, but I had no reason (and less desire) to question her scheme, which incidentally netted me more than a million more dollars. Long before she got sick and died, writers and publishing friends took pains to tell me how brilliantly I had been looked after by Mary Marx. The particular grounds for their praises were lost on me, although I appreciated their recognition of her fine work. The truth of the matter is that Mary could have negotiated a tenth of the largesse she ultimately landed for me, and I would have been her devoted friend and admirer. She used to thank me for my trust which gave her the free hand and creativity to make her mark in the trade. I did everything I could to assure her that while she had always had my trust, it was my ignorance and laziness for which she could be grateful.

Probably because she was approaching retirement, Mary was unfazed when I called to tell her that I wanted effectively to disappear from the publishing scene. I told her it was highly unlikely that I would write another book and would no longer appear anywhere or contribute anything to other people's books or to journals. As long as she cared to do it, there was still plenty to do, as all my books were, and I think still are, in print. There were reissues to look after, special editions, foreign rights, and all the complexities of gathering and accounting for royalties. My general charge to Mary at the end was to make it simple for me. This she understood perfectly, having done just that for thirty years. With Elizabeth's blessing we arranged to have two thirds of my royalty income deposited quarterly in Elizabeth's household account, a third of it in my new account in Key West. Poised to exit, I don't know whether to be ashamed or delighted to report that for the past twenty years I have, while spending freely, kept no record of my checks and charges. I suppose this represents a degree of trust in the system. There seems to have been plenty in my account, and I am most grateful to be spared the bother of knowing.

Chapter Six

ALTHOUGH IT COULD have turned out quite otherwise, a providential factor in my escape from celebrity was the reappearance in my life of an all but forgotten character from my college days, Chase Reading. I doubt that in the history of letters—or maybe history itself—a man has ever been more grateful for his nemesis and debunker than I am for Chase Reading.

I don't know if he felt a twinge of guilt—or whether he even thought of me at all—when he proposed to his publisher his send-up of my books. From what I remembered of him at Yale, he would have been stimulated by any prospect of generating discomfort. I tried to picture Chase Reading as a man in his sixties, but I could not. Nothing I could imagine succeeded in effacing the figure he had cut in the spring before his expulsion: lanky, aggressively unkempt, wild-eyed, his hair frizzed out in drooping tendrils. He was clearly a herald of the emerging counter-culture, but there was also an archetypal quality to his posturing and pranks: something of the medieval jester or *jongleur*. In the escalating course of his antic disruptions of scholastic routine, he managed to become a focal presence on the Yale campus, at once fascinating and a little dreadful.

I was not yet a year in Key West when the first book, *The Uses of Farce*, became a sensation. The historical context could not have been better for the appearance of such a book. The unrelieved gloom that settled in over the waning months of the George W. Bush presidency seemed to cry out for relief. No exposé, broadside, or satire aimed at the president, his administration, or any aspect of the prevailing political order could have provided the needed levity. There was, especially among educated people, a weary consensus that no matter how abjectly in error or disgrace, the prevailing regime was impervious. To the polity's credit, too, there seemed to be an unstated understanding that, given the hopelessly irresolvable disintegration of Iraq and the administration's otherwise blind persistence in seeing highly particular political concerns of non-western partisans as "terror," it would have been cheap and inhumanely glib to cast in a humorous light what felt like a desperately fallen national condition.

It was therefore no less than inspired for Chase Reading to send up something absolutely trans-political: me and my books. My books were widely enough read and talked about that "Forcean" ideas and approaches, however incompletely or mistakenly understood, were part of common discourse. As more than one critic noted, my contemporaries were more likely to think with my assumptions than about them. If my ideas had become atmospheric, how right of Chase Reading to change the air.

Mary Marx and my friends at Random House tipped me off that *Uses of Farce* was in the works well before it was published. It was noticed appreciatively in *Publishers Weekly* and most of the other trades, but none of those forecasts predicted the popular impact of the book when it appeared. Mary talked to Random House's lawyers and advised me at least to get a professional opinion on whether a legal action might be appropriate, although it was her opinion, after she read the galleys, that there was nothing actionable in it. "It's not even a clever satire of you," she told me. "It's got nothing to do with anything you've actually said." She was uncharacteristically lost for words. "It's not actually about *anything*. It's completely ridiculous."

Uses of Farce and the two sequels, *Reasonable Farce* and *Farce Fields*, were completely ridiculous. That was their great strength. It is hard to know whether Chase Reading had read or seriously considered anything I had written. He was, I suspected, intelligent enough. But nothing in the send-ups even so much as departed from the subjects of my analyses and arguments. The substitution of *Farce* for *Force* in my titles and in the jargon my protégés had coined over the years—'Farcean' for 'Forcean,' etc.—was, I could ungrudgingly acknowledge, very funny, funny enough that even I could never afterwards bring to mind the title of one of my books without reflexively transposing 'Farce' for 'Force.'

Chase Reading's *Farce* books achieved something distinctive and rare. They managed to strike a note of hilarity in readers, a delighted recognition of something they could not begin to name. The books were catalogued and marketed as 'satire,' but they were not true satires in that, except for the titles, the knock-offs of my books' jacket designs and chapter headings, they didn't, as Mary saw at once, address any of my ideas, even to make fun of them. I suppose the closest Chase Reading came to satirizing *me* was in striking a rhetorical note of vaguely high-brow mock-seriousness. Nobody would claim it was my rhetoric. The truth is that I have worked fairly hard to achieve a lean, unembellished clarity in my published writing. I wanted logic and evidence, not my 'voice,' to carry my points. To succeed in this is to transcend 'style' altogether—and also to make one hard to imitate. The voice of Chase Reading's Jeremy Farce was mock-analytical, pretentiously omniscient, an excellent vehicle for offering up sheer whimsy. If the effect my books had on readers was to suggest that through ordinary but disciplined thinking they could access a world at once more complex and more interesting than they had previously imagined, the assumption underlying the *Farce* books is that nothing matters.

The Prologue to *Uses of Farce* begins,

A great man once told us, "A house divided against itself cannot stand." That needed saying. In fact, so much needs saying. Thus this little book. It is offered up to readers, educated and foolish alike, in the certainty that a house not divided against itself *will* stand, and in that house we will all be able to stand. This is of course to speak figuratively, given the capacity of actual houses and our numbers. All of you know what I mean, which is, in a nutshell, that what follows here is very, very important, as important as standing together in a house where we can stand, a house undivided, a house not of cards, nor of blue lights.

It is, as you will see, possible to unite our house and to stand in it, to stand in all the rooms, on all the floors, in all the houses from the green mountains of New Hampshire to the red clay of Georgia, from California to the New York island. And the beauty of it is this: we can achieve this figurative house undividedness by simply thinking clearly and reading on. For in a house undivided against itself, there is no frigate like a book…

THE PROLOGUE IS FOLLOWED BY a first chapter titled, "Tennis and the Taliban." It and all subsequent chapters meander anarchically about a fantastical junk yard of mangled classical and popular culture. There are many puns, preposterous allusions, and meaningless references, the sheer accretion of which I found terrifically funny. Even reading the books, as I did at first, through a filter of wary self-protection, I found them irresistible, some of the riffs making me laugh out loud in quiet places. They were a deserved success, and I found myself over the three-year arc of their craze, thinking more and more about Chase Reading, trying to bridge my distant recollections of him at Yale to the figure he had now become. Even before it was arranged, I knew that somehow we would meet.

The author's photograph on his book jackets revealed a rather beaky face. His head was bald on top, only the wiry fringe straggling from temple to ear evoking something of his look at Yale when he had pulled together his impromptu performing troupe, The Unacceptables. A long feature in the *New York Times* Arts and Leisure section revealed that the *Farce* books had lifted him out of fairly dire straits. After Yale he had gone, as the reporter put it, "underground." There had been some brushes with the law, some to do with political protest, others involving petty theft and misusing credit cards. There were a few stints in jail, which he told the reporter he did not care to talk about. The urge to create what he called "instant theater" had persisted after Yale, and for the past thirty years he was engaged in a number of what the reporter called "street theater" ventures, more successful, Chase believed, in Europe than in the states. There was reference to his company's—The Al Qaeda Players'—entry in the Edinburgh Fringe Festival: "Anthrax and Sympathy," also of a production, "(Life is Just) Ebola Cherries," which he indicated was performed in a number of European cities "mostly in train stations and next to big fountains." A flamboyant and familiar figure in the Bushwick and Williamsburg neighborhoods of Brooklyn, he told the reporter he had been awarded a few arts grants over the years, but had gone sometimes for as long as a decade with no fixed address. "I live with friends until they become unfriendly." Asked how he conceived of the *Farce* books, he said, "I just woke up one day knowing. They came out of me like Delphic oracles."

Not long after *Uses of Farce* was published, I began getting the inevitable queries from journalists about my reactions to the send-up and about my relationship with Chase Reading at Yale. It was not easy for a reporter to reach me. Only Elizabeth, the boys, and a few friends knew I had migrated to Key West where I used only a cell phone and otherwise called little attention to myself--and none at all to Jonathan Force. A few sleuths made their way to my first apartment on Olive Street and left messages inside the screen door. One spotted me in the bar of the back terrace of Virgilio's. What did I think of *Farce Fields* and how well had I known Chase Reading? I refused extended interviews, but agreed to provide a few comments, under the strict understanding that only those words would appear in their articles and on-camera commentaries. That established, I told them that I had barely known Chase at Yale but that I had found his staged "happenings" fascinating. I said I thought *Farce Fields* was very funny, but that I could see no relationship between anything he had written and the substance of my books. Chase himself had clearly been asked corresponding questions, and his responses, when I read them, were basically congruent to mine and rather what I expected: "I'm *pretty* sure I knew him at Yale. I remember he was very clean." Also: "Yeah, of course I know his books. I'm extremely well educated and bright—but my work is all about Jeremy Farce, not Jonathan Force, and I personally resent anyone thinking otherwise."

At the time I had an uncomfortable foreboding that the reporters who found me and left messages with my answering service were only a vanguard of swarms to follow, that my anonymity, privacy, and the sweet ease of my new life would come to an end. I had grown so tired of having to be a public person. Chase Reading and the *Farce* phenomenon were just anomalous enough, I feared, to create an endless stream of curiosity and speculation. But the worst did not happen. Random House kept a stoic silence, per Mary Marx's instructions. My own books enjoyed a mild spike in sales, then leveled off to their former respectable levels.

Had Chase Reading penetrated the surface of my arguments and successfully sent them up, I might have been permanently diminished, if not dismissed altogether. My most devoted fans and protégés found me difficult, and readers generally agreed that my books asked a lot of them, that they were "work." It would have taken only a plausible debunking for many readers to relieve themselves of such effort. But there was no real debunking in the *Farce* books, and while no doubt many people with cocktail party awareness of my work bade me a take-*that* good riddance, my old titles stayed put, available to be mined and mulled over by the educated curious. For good reason the *Farce* books were especially popular on college campuses, but so far as I could tell, the 'Forceans' on the philosophy and social science faculties continued to generate new work and student followings.

For several years *Force* and *Farce* books were suspended in edgy disequilibrium in the popular mind. It was that tension as much as Chase's absurdist riffs which gathered so much attention to his books. For a time, fearing invasion of my privacy, I wished that he had really satirized me, that I had been exposed, dismissed, and forgotten. That would have been genuinely welcome. But in the event, no great harm was done, and I was able meet Chase Reading again, perhaps the most satisfying and consequential encounter of my life.

Chapter Seven

Mary Marx was already quite ill when she called to tell me PBS's *Between the Lines* producers were interested in taping a joint interview with Chase Reading and me. I could tell she thought it was a dubious proposition, fearing I think that Chase's anarchic silliness might overwhelm the proceedings and that this would diminish me in the viewers' minds. She had a point, and while I was otherwise strongly averse ever again to becoming a public spectacle, I was more than curious to see Chase Reading, especially if there would a chance for us to meet and talk off-camera. Chase was apparently willing to participate, so we went ahead.

The *Between the Lines* people proposed a split-screen presentation, with Chase in a studio in New York, me in Key West, but I held out for a live taping together on the island. As I had hoped, Chase agreed to have dinner with me after the taping.

I have always felt comfortable on camera, and as the day of the interview approached, I found myself positively looking forward to our encounter. I was determined also that this would be my last voluntary exposure on television or in the press. PBS set up the taping at the harbor side Hilton where they had also booked a room for Chase. I called him after he checked in to say hello and to confirm our dinner plan. He sounded very nice. He asked me, "Are we supposed to talk about our college days? You can probably remember yours, but somebody needs to remember mine." I told him they would probably want to know what he had in mind in writing his *Farce* books and my reaction to them, and that they would almost certainly try to make something of our Yale connection. I told him I thought these sessions tended to go pretty well if we relaxed and enjoyed ourselves. "Well," he said, "That used to be a strength."

When I arrived, early, at the taping suite, a crew was draping black cloth over scaffolding which enclosed the interview table on three sides. Neil Oakeshott, the *Between the Lines* moderator greeted me graciously and, I sensed, with a little apprehension. He explained the straightforward protocols of the interview, and I was already seated and miked under the bright lights when Chase Reading was shown in. He was a big man, not exactly fat, but hefty. He was dressed in black, a loose, blousy shirt falling over a prominent paunch. He moved slowly, uncomfortably, as if his feet may have hurt him. He greeted Neil Oakeshott distractedly, probably unaware that he would be our moderator. Seated comfortably under the lights, Chase seemed to brighten and relax. His face had filled in between chin and throat, and only when he smiled did I sense the wily sharpness I remembered at Yale. Rimless glasses resting on the bridge of his nose added a hint of studiousness. He looked me up and down and said, I am sure in reference to my white clothes, "Christ, what are we, good and evil?" I said, "I can only speak for myself," and we all laughed.

Chase was right to comment on our contrasting appearances. In the DVD the network later sent me, my white clothes and hair suggest almost an opposing uniform to Chase's black bulk. The contrast was heightened dramatically by being severely lit against the black cloth. In that abstracted midnight, tanned as I was, I could have passed for a gaunt Tamil, while Chase's fleshy features were blanched to a doughy white.

Although finally insubstantial, the session was lively and even enjoyable, at least for Chase and me. Unexpected confrontation could be said to be Chase's life's work, so I suppose I was prepared for anything he might say or do on camera. Overall he behaved reasonably well, although he tested Neil Oakeshott a few times, as when, in response to his opening question—"Your very popular books mimic the titles and some say the tone of very well known and highly regarded books by Jonathan Force. What exactly did you have in mind doing that?"—Chase paused ominously before snapping back, "Who wants to know?" When asked later whether he in any way intended his work to be a commentary on mine or whether, in the manner of S. J Perelman and Groucho Marx, he was aiming only for inspired nonsense, Chase roared, *"Nonsense?* You're calling my work *nonsense?"* Because I laughed, Oakeshott laughed, too.

At one point Oakeshott, attempting to establish some kind of relationship between *Force* and *Farce* texts, read aloud an extended passage from *Uses for Force* followed by a passage from *Uses of Farce*. He asked me to comment, and while there was a time in my life when I would have relished an opportunity to delight an audience by stepping back and demonstrating some kind of conceptual or rhetorical similarity in two such dissimilar texts, I said I could see no point of convergence whatsoever in the two passages, adding that mine had been logically structured to order observable data, while Chase's had been purely rhetorical, without reference to any material reality. Oakeshott asked for Chase's response, and he leaned forward over the table and said, "I don't think I like mine anymore. His is better. Read me his again."

The fifty-minute segment that ultimately aired was edited from more than three hours of our reflections and exchanges. For most of that time Chase and I and eventually Neil succeeded in relaxing and enjoying ourselves. Nearly a half hour, all of it aired, was downright warm, as Chase and I did our best to remember one another and the campus climate in New Haven in the sixties. I doubt that a viewer could walk away from that segment of *Between the Lines* and not imagine Chase and I were companionable, even friends.

Chapter Eight

It was not yet six when we stepped out of the Hilton. I had not made a reservation for dinner, thinking that Chase might want to walk around a bit after the taping. From the water front we made our way to Front Street and proceeded to Duval where we were met by the approaching throngs, many of them already tipsy as they headed toward the piers for the Sunset ritual. Chase had asked me something—did I live here year round—when he was distracted by a young man whose shaved head was covered, as if by a turban, with a coiled yellow python of some size. The man's tattooed arms were draped over the shoulders of two slender girls dressed identically in silk sarongs tied low on their hips and gossamer scarves done up in a kind of halter over their loose breasts. Chase turned to look after them as they passed. "Christ," he said, "I think I'm in love." It was early enough that I knew we could find a table at nearly any restaurant. I asked Chase if he was hungry or whether he wanted to walk for a while. He looked at me a little sadly and said maybe we should find a place to sit down. "Fucking gout," he said. "Ever had it?"

It occurred to me that we might take in something of the street scene without walking if we dined on one of the balcony terraces overhead. Chase took the steps gingerly, and in a minute we were abstracted above the crowd, scotches on the way, menus in hand. It was a lovely evening, soft air, a pleasing prospect over the rooftops to the hazy horizon. Chase wanted to know what it was like living year round in Key West. I described my days, and he looked perplexed. "You just go to the beach?" I told him that, yes, the beach was the central experience of my days. I didn't think I could convey what I would want to about Tenderloins and the young friends I was starting to make. He said he thought I would be busy with writing and research and seemed surprised when I told him I had no such projects and doubted whether I would be doing any more writing in the future. I asked him about his plans, and he told me he was having a dry spell. "There's no fucking necessity," he said. "I've been winging it, living hand to mouth for so long, it's hard to get motivated when I've got some money and actual choices." He drank down half of the scotch in his glass and rattled the ice. "I just bought a *condominium*, in Park Slope. Know where that is?" I told him I did. "I *bought* it, flat out, no mortgage. It's my first grownup house. Can you fucking believe it?"

I felt an urge to crash through conversational banalities and tell Chase Reading something true of my condition now, something that mattered to me. I said, "I have just left my first grownup house. It was in Chicago—Evanston—and I realized I had to get out. I needed to change worlds and start fresh." I told Chase I wasn't worried about money, but that I was actually attempting to live something like hand-to-mouth. Chase said he wasn't sure he would recommend it. He looked distracted, troubled.

"Truth is," he said, "I've had a pretty shitty life, at least what most people would consider shitty." I was not surprised. The feature article in the *New York Times* had suggested not only great eccentricity but something gritty and possibly sordid in Chase's existence before the *Farce* books. I told him I did not feel my life to date had been shitty or even regrettable, but that I had the strongest feeling I hadn't quite lived it, that I may have spent my adult years in an eerily comfortable imposture. "I felt," I heard myself saying, "as if I were in a play, a play I knew well enough to act my part but not to know what it meant or why I was even in it." Chase listened to this with interest. "I was always in a play," he said. "Actual plays, but I wrote them and got to do what I wanted in them. The main thing about me"—we were well into our second scotches—"is that I just liked being a kid. I think I was actually a pretty great kid when I was one, probably a pain in the ass once I got some range, but I really liked being a kid, and all I've done as an adult, besides getting bloated and tired and this fucking gout, is to refuse to play grownup. That's my whole shtick."

I felt my mind going thick and slow as Chase was confessing his refusal to mature. I was struck by how heavy and beaten and *old* he seemed for his years. I was on the brink of asking him if, at that very moment, he felt anything like a kid, when he asked me, "What about you? Were you ever a kid?"

The question seemed to halt any possibility of directed thought. *Kid. Was I ever a kid?* It was not that I had nothing to say. It was that there was too much, too much feeling for me to speak. For a second I felt myself, saw myself clumping down the damp wooden steps into Cyrus Best's cellar, each of us caressing the barrels of his brother's rifles. We were heading down, down into the earthen darkness to hunt. My heart was pounding with the anticipation of the encounter. I saw myself, felt myself back again in the fields beyond Palatine, a rosy smear of sunken sun still on the horizon, the dry grasses of the fields crackling under my muddy boots. *Climbing. I was a climber.* I am leaning into the rock face, a few feet from the ledge overhead but with no clear way to get up there and no way back down. One arm is extended uncomfortably above me where I am clutching the stem of a stunted bush. Too bright sun, the whoosh of the river below, a screaming in my ears. That had been me, on the brink like that, but also—so sweetly—held in a thrall, in a kind of love, a real love, a child's real love. There was Patsy Prentiss's face, the blue-jeaned length of her, wrapped up with me in the straw after we leaped from the dirt hill. *A kid.* He asked me about myself as a *kid.* I am standing, paused, in the driveway of Nana and Papa's garage in Palatine. Again it is nearly dark but there is a trace of glass blue in the autumn sky beyond the tree line. I look through the open doors to the rear of the garage. There is enough dusky light from a grimy window at the back to outline the bulbous tires and the faintly gleaming fenders of my Uncle Desmond's old bicycle, his bicycle when he was a boy, before he was grown up and a soldier and a smiling man with a pipe. The bicycle, the idea of Uncle Desmond as a boy in a different time, the beckoning, fading light overwhelms me. I am looking into something too great for me, something eternal, something gone but for that second right there, held in ancient light.

I knew Chase had asked me something and was waiting for me to answer. I could not for a moment meet his eye. I felt, of all things, like crying, which made me feel ashamed, just as I did when I was a boy. I glanced up at Chase, I am sure miserably. He looked concerned. "Yes," I said. "I was a kid." Then I thought I really would cry. I looked over the railing at nothing. Then I said, "That's what *I* refused. I refused to keep being a kid."

I will never know if Chase knew exactly what I meant by saying that, but I think he did. At any rate he seemed generously aware that I had for some reason arrived on unsteady emotional ground, and he was respectful of that. "You know," he said, "A lot of the sixties bullshit, maybe most of it, was about trying to be a kid forever. Maybe we should blame the fifties. Maybe it was Little League and Cub Scouts and Leave it to Beaver and the Nelsons and all the safe little towns. Maybe the message there was to keep us small and happy, and when we actually grew out of that dream, we, like, made a mess, tried to stop the train, wreck things, the way bratty kids do."

I knew what he was saying, also that with other rhetoric I had said those very things. For quite a while, as we ate and afterwards while we sipped at cognac in the dark, we made tentative conversation. Having been knocked so badly off balance, I reverted to my Jonathan Force voice, which could only distance Chase. He was agreeable enough but more guarded, less himself. I could not help picturing the two of us, as if from above, at our candle lit table on the dark balcony: two apparently dejected older men, working at conversation, words failing.

At the same time, I don't think I could have felt closer to Chase, and I am certain he felt the same. We didn't really need to take in the other's words, how we had so differently dedicated ourselves and filled our days. We had already sensed our mutual condition and, though I could not have expressed it then, that we had given our lives to the same thing. Chase had chosen the right word: refusal. His refusal to acknowledge anything superior to his boyhood knowing was, as he had said, his life's work. Despite its brash extroverted expressions, his refusal was grounded in desperate loss and the sweetest sadness. As was mine. I had refused to acknowledge the loss. I had banished memory. In compensation I composed, in my case from scratch, a counter-childhood, an unassailable certainty, a better way. Jonathan Force. With phenomenal industry, parasitic I now see on the drives and urges of my boyhood, I set about ordering not just my world but *the* world beyond any conceivable boy's ken. And it was no small achievement, the collected works of Jonathan Force. But *fuck*, as Chase would say, so was his. And so it is. My tireless constructions and Chase's inspired deconstructions were profoundly and quite literally kid's stuff. We had sacrificed our lives, our post-boyhoods, to the same grief.

We were both aware that it was late and that, if we were honest, we had little left to say. I asked Chase if he was looking forward to going home to Brooklyn. He looked at me hard and said, "I don't know. It's just a place, isn't it?" Chase arose heavily, stiffly from his chair. He seemed to me as self-aware and as wise a man as I was likely to meet. There was something finished, even doomed about him, although he would live on quietly for more than a decade. Strangely like Elizabeth, he seemed intimately, permanently related to me, although I doubted I would see him again, and what I felt for him, as I clasped his shoulders in farewell at the door of the Hilton, was nothing less than love.

Not a minute after we parted, I had an insight. I was picturing Chase as I first saw him before the taping, the dark bulk of his form, placing one foot gingerly before the other, as if in pain. As our evening together wore on—not a notably happy or expansive one— his very bulk and something about his beaten demeanor and outlook grew increasingly endearing, even though I could picture nothing at all hopeful on his horizon. Even this realization touched me warmly. I was about to say to myself, "There but for fortune go I"—when I stopped still in the street and said, I believe out loud—"No—*there go I.*"

Chapter Nine

For more than a year after my remove to Key West I found my undirected thoughts turning on some gesture that would formally put my writing life—my *work*—to rest. The most obvious solution—simply to stop—had not been entirely satisfying. Not that I felt the slightest urge to compose anything new. To the contrary, whenever I felt a twinge of the old Forcean equation-making—as, say, when noting the tendency of travelers with modest means to spend excessively in Key West—I breathed deeply and cleared my mind at once. I was gladly finished with that. Yet, the evening with Chase Reading and, especially, that peculiar moment on the street when I caught myself speaking out loud—*there go I*—served as a kind of prod to settle the matter.

For weeks after the *Between the Lines* taping I was visited, usually at the beach, by a series of insistent, seemingly context-less messages. They occurred to me as if in someone else's voice which, when I tried to identify it, seemed to have something to do with Chase Reading. I began scribbling these fragments down, in the margins of a news paper or on a napkin, and then back at the apartment shaping them into complete thoughts. Like fragments of tunes that become ear worms, these aphorisms—or whatever they were—would stay with me for hours at a time. I had compiled a few dozen of them before I realized that in addition to each entry's particular existential claim, they were also related, perhaps expressing a systematic, if strange, point of view. It felt small-minded and fussy to be overly analytical about these entries which had arrived bearing no portentous weight. In fact, most of them made me want to laugh.

After I had recorded a hundred and one of them, I stopped. And then I had it.

I called Franklin in San Francisco and asked if he could find me a reputable self-publishing outfit on-line. Within a few hours he located and sent me several possibilities. Then I told him my plan and asked for his help. I wanted to produce a miniature book that would seem to appear out of nowhere and would not be provably attributable to me. Chase Reading's *Farce* books were still in the stores, and there was enough cultural tension between *Farce* and *Force* works that I was certain this gesture would strike the right note: the exact valedictory offering I had been looking for.

Fortunately the trickiness of what I had in mind appealed to Franklin, and he guided the project to an elegance I could never have managed. Through the office of a tech subsidiary of his firm, he incorporated a press and acquired ISBN numbers. He told me the whole business, including lining up a designer and printer, "cost practically nothing," and he bet that the project would make money, although that had not been a concern of mine.

In six weeks there were finished prototypes of the book, and I could not have been more pleased. It was *exactly* as I had envisioned it: a miniature hard-bound book, four and a half by three and a half inches. The pumpkin-orange of the cover stock was identical to the covers of *Uses of Force* and *Uses of Farce*. Title and type face filled the cover with the same color treatments and italicizing 'Force' and 'Farce' as in the originals. Just as I had hoped, the little book evoked immediately the *Farce/Force* phenomenon, with no indication of any kind whether it was *Farce* or *Force*.

The most delicate task in bringing out *Forcible Entries (From the Farcical Pantry)* was to place it with a distributor who would promote and sell a book without an assignable author. This Franklin arranged by personally training a salesman in his firm to make a highly particular pitch. Franklin saw clearly how it could work: a miniature like this, a novelty item, would do best as a stand-alone display at the check-out counters of the big chains. There were many well-known, profitable precedents for this kind of novelty. The cultural recognition of *Force* and *Farce* books would assuredly work in this project's favor, and in the end Border's, Barnes and Noble, and even Waldenbooks and the airport terminal chains agreed to stock *Forcible Entries*.

I remember feeling no concern whatsoever that the book would be received in any particular way, only that it would appear, and perhaps startle. It was, as I intended, a farewell gesture to actual writing, but it also came to feel like a note of farewell to Chase. Once the little book was out, I stopped thinking about it. I was finished. There would be calls and queries from the journalists who knew how to find me, but I had already rehearsed my baffled non-response. Mary Marx sent me a packet of Xeroxed notices and ads for *Forcible Entries*, covered by a blank sheet of her stationery inscribed with a bold black question mark. That delighted me, and I sent her a post card back with a question mark of my own. While I didn't go out looking for it, I saw that there was plenty of print speculation about the origins and authorship of *Forcible Entries*. Quite understandably Chase too had been hounded by sleuths certain the book was his, but just as I thought, he dropped preposterous, cryptic hints, while outwardly refusing to comment. Franklin told me there had been a number of attempts to reach an editor of the "press" that issued the book, but Franklin's colleague in the San Jose subsidiary knew no more than Franklin had told him, and the puzzle, which ultimately lacked urgency, remained unsolved.

Perhaps a month after *Forcible Entries* appeared I attempted to reimburse Franklin for his efforts on its behalf. He would not consider it. "Dad, this is *fun*," he said, "And it's going to be a money-maker—watch."

Chapter Ten

FORCIBLE ENTRIES
(FROM THE FARCICAL PANTRY)

1. Not "there but for fortune go I"—*there go I.*
2. That good idea you just had, that stunning connection, that clear solution—you always had it.
3. "Less is more." Absolutely—and, to complete the thought, "nothing is everything."
4. To "become as little children"—as if there were an alternative!
5. Dress, shroud, cover yourself all you like—you're *naked* under there.
6. There are no sexually happy villains.
7. The ancients asked what is more valuable, a pearl or a mouse. Aristotle answered: a mouse; it reacts. To which it might be added:
--A pearl is poor company.
--A mouse is a poor earring.
--Pearls bring more cash than mice—so sell them. Buy lots of mice.
--Mice are, however, vermin, spoiling your food, making you sick. Nicer sometimes to find a pearl behind the crackers.
--Pearls and mice. Why choose?
8. Like sleep? You'll love death.
9. When you're out of time, there's still plenty.
10. Am I "me" in the afterlife? Yes, if it is now.

11. Only the just know that mercy trumps justice.
12. Slow and steady is oblivious to the race.
13. Virtue is oblivious to reward.
14. Desperation is its own reward.
15. Winning isn't everything; it isn't anything.
16. As for me, give me liberty, then after a while give me death.
17. If at first you don't succeed, you have mastered failure.
18. I gave a man a fish, and he ate. I taught a man to fish and he fished for years. I told a man a joke and then I gave him a kiss, and he was glad he had done all that eating and fishing.
19. A penny saved is a penny out of mind.
20. A fool and his money can be seen nearly everywhere.
21. There is no substitute for anything.
22. "I want to be happy, but I can't be happy till I make you happy, too." That makes you the boss.
23." I can't get no satisfaction." Oh for a world in which no satisfaction is forever ungettable.
24. Anything goes. Always has.
25. Out of the frying pan and into the fire—not much difference.
26. Can God make something so heavy He can't lift it? No, but another God can.
27. If a tree falls in the woods and nobody hears it, does it make a sound? Maybe not, Maybe this one time it didn't make a sound.
28. There is the truth, the right answer, the proof beyond a shadow of a doubt, and there are all the other ways.
29. On one's death bed one might ask—well, anything.
30. "Is that all there is?" Of course, always.
31. Waking and dreaming—which is real? Waking, always—but then you wake up!
32. "The earth belongs to nobody, its fruits to all alike." What earth is that?
33. "Man is born free, yet he is everywhere in chains." What chains? Show me the chains.
34. "We have nothing to fear but fear itself." Not even that.

35. In the embryo the heart grows first, you can hear it, then the brain—sounds like a plan.

36. "The world is charged with the grandeur of God"—nobody told him that.

37. "Something there is that does not love a wall"—and something that does.

38. "And I took the road less traveled by"—so he thought.

39. Follow your bliss? (Hint: it's behind you.)

40. The problem of pain—why make it a problem?

41. Rise above it? Easy enough, but it's still down there, isn't it?

42. The problem of pain—it hurts, it *really* hurts.

43. Feeling no pain? Lucky duck.

44. We were all lucky ducks once. That's how we know we're in pain.

45. Still feeling the pain? Wait.

46. No better? You call that waiting?

47. Better now? Lucky duck. Pretty soon you won't remember.

48. But it's out there, pain. Yes, that and everything else.

49. You can lead a horse to water but you can't make him drink. You *thought* you led him to water.

50. 'If only I had done otherwise"—but there was no *otherwise*, no *if*. Think!

51. Now wanting can get you moving, wishing never.

52. All wanting is sex. No? How are you doing with all the other stuff?

53. What do we want? Wrong question: *why* do we want?

54. Why do we want? Oh, you know. To be even better, to be even more. To be lucky ducks.

55. We all begin as lucky ducks.

56. Show me someone past wanting, and I will show you a Buddha. See any Buddhas around?

57. Truth is, you can't see a Buddha. Why would you want to? Buddha wouldn't want to see a Buddha. Buddha doesn't want anything.

58. Siddhartha wanted things before he became Buddha. Sex helped.

59. People who say they want to be Buddha really mean they want to be Siddhartha.

60. Augustine, before he was St. Augustine, was like Siddhartha, not like Buddha. He had lots of sex, and he really liked it.

61. The Anglican divine said: "Every man knocking on the door of a brothel in Marrakech is looking for God." Fair enough. Knock, knock.

62. Sex will lead you astray. Without a doubt. But astray--? Astray from--? Where isn't astray?

63. Thinking about sex is never about sex. It is about fear. It is about pride. It is about safety.

64. Sex is better than thinking, better for you.

65 Sex obsession is our condition. Acknowledging this is the end of the obsession.

66. Diotima was no Buddha. She said sex lifts us out of the world and carries us half way to the ultimate—not there, but on the way, heaven in sight. Who would say no to that ride?

67. There is all this sexual noodling around, but in the end it is either yes to sex or the Taliban.

68. The Taliban (and its like) are, incidentally, a problem. They are a problem like pain. (See Pain).

69. To everything turn, turn, turn. Or don't. You can just wait.

70. There is a season—yes, if you wait. Also now.

71. Yes is stronger than no; in fact, there is no strength in no, except when a yes is pushing it from behind.

72. Beware of no being pushed from behind by a yes. It appears very righteous.

73. Keep an eye out for a yes free of no's: a big total yes. (It will be sex.)

74. "I wept because I had no shoes, until I saw a man who had no feet." And that made you *stop* weeping?

75. A bird in the hand is an unlucky duck.

76. A bird in the bush is where it belongs. Ditto for two birds.

77. Absence does not make the heart grow fonder. It's the absent *presence* that makes you fonder—and not really fonder, just more aware of how fond you were in the first place.

78. You can't have a Jesus without a Judas. By the way, everybody has a Judas.

79. Don't worry about Judas getting away with it. Everybody wins.

80. Judas does not need to hang himself. He can just wait.

81. "Familiarity breeds contempt"—keep your distance from anybody who believes that.

82. "Do not cast your pearls before swine." Fine, but tell me there was ever anybody who thought about doing that. (See Pearls and Mice.)

83. Is it possible to love everybody? It is possible in a bar. It is possible at a really good party.

84. Is it impossible to love everybody? It is impossible to love everybody in big airports. It is impossible to love everybody on all the television channels.

85. Can people in church love everybody? No, but they can keep saying it.

86. Is it impossible for people in church to love everybody? It is. That's why they're there.

87. Do lucky ducks love everybody? Lucky ducks love the people they know, and they keep meeting new ones.

88. Do lucky ducks like church? Lucky ducks like it when church is over and there is the whole rest of the day.

89. "Yea, though I walk through the valley of the shadow of death, I will fear no evil, for the Lord is with me"—do that even if the Lord is not with you.

90. "And deliver us from evil"—or deliver yourself from evil. Start by forgetting about it, unless it has you in hand (See Bird in the Hand). If evil has you in hand, best to wait. Lucky ducks don't seem to have the problem.

91. Evil behaves like witchcraft. It vanishes when people stop worshipping it.

92. How might cancer vanish, or madness? (Hint: check out some lucky ducks.)

93. "Workers of the world unite!" You have nothing to lose but your time. (Hint: not really true.)

94. You can't lose time.

95. Lucky ducks know that work is limitless pleasure. Working is artful. Work makes art.

96. Drudgery is work with a bad attitude, as is necessary work and hard work. Drudgery, necessary work, and hard work are no's being pushed forward by a yes.

97. Take the no out of work, and it's all seeking, finding, and making. Work as art! There is almost no pleasure to rival that; it's right up there with sex.

98. All providing is work. (See All Wanting is Sex.)

99. All existence is wanting and providing—you can dance to that rhythm.

100. And on the seventh day rest. Rest for as long as you want. You can rest forever.

101. Oh, and what is the sound of one hand clapping? That's it, you've got it. But you can't hear it, can you?

Chapter Eleven

How I come back to Tenderloins—as indeed I did come back to it daily, gladly, for all those years. There was not a day, not *one visit*, in which I did not find Tenderloins at once stimulating and deeply satisfying. I know this has not been the experience of other customers, perhaps any of them, but it has by grace been mine.

I had found the club that first afternoon quite by accident. I was nosing about the side streets and back passages off Duval, vaguely curious, trying to get a sense of things, when I spotted the canopied staircase leading down to the unmarked, red-lit door. Had I not refused the flier the young man on the stool had offered me a few yards back, I might have known that I was approaching the entrance to a strip club. As it happened, I descended the stairs tentatively but alert, and when I opened the door to look inside, I was taken completely by surprise.

That was the right way to enter Tenderloins, with no prior expectation, no sexual stirring or fantasy at work. Not that there was any lack of sexual arousal on my part, but the erotic pitch reached and so agreeably sustained there was not something I had in mind when I entered. There was something mysterious and deeply right about Tenderloins for me. Certainly without intending it, the managers, Hugh and Eddie, had somehow succeeded in creating the sacred allure of ancient mystery cults and temple prostitutes. Arriving as I typically did after hours of bright sun on the beach and teeming streets, I would spend a full minute in disoriented blackness, hearing only the thudding bass line of the recorded music and breathing in the sweet musk of the girls' compounded scents as my eyes adjusted to the dark, windowless hall. Entering Tenderloins was in every way a descent, and for a moment whatever frame of mind I had carried in with me would be voided in the sudden blackness. Then, cleansed in this way, I would begin to make out the faint flicker of the white lights at the bar and above the dancing platforms, then the shadowy forms of the girls and customers. By the time I made my way to a table and chair, I had already begun what felt like a counteractive ascent, a kind of awakening.

Tenderloins was what it was, where it was, easily findable, as were a half dozen similar establishments on the island. But once inside, it was like no other imaginable place. It conveyed a kind of secrecy. It was a counter world, where the illicit was licit, honored and welcomed. With almost no exception the girls were tantalizingly seductive, lithe, ample, available in their skimpy and outlandish costumes, clothes cunningly worn solely for the promise of their removal. After their dance sets on the platform, the more comfortable girls would greet their familiars, perhaps share a drink, before bothering to cover themselves.

I would arrive mid afternoon and stay for a couple of hours, at the very latest until the dinner hour. I understand the club grew crowded and even raucous in the later hours, especially on weekends, but I never experienced that, nor did I want to. I preferred the languid, dreamier atmosphere of slow afternoons. To leave the bright world so abruptly and completely was for me a renewable pleasure, as was the reliability of what would transpire in the pulsing darkness, in that open-hearted inversion of life above. There was really little to *do* at Tenderloins other than to drink, smoke cigarettes, watch the girls, talk to the girls, hold them to you and caress them as they offered themselves in private dances. Short of the customers themselves undressing and direct genital intercourse, sexual expression was expected and welcome. Some men came in solely to talk openly about sex, to ask the dancers questions about their sexual experiences, to hear their accounts, to relate their own peak moments and fantasies. Others were stimulated by the very opposite approach: by carrying on as one might with a congenial table mate at a diner, commenting on the events of the day, news of the hour, turns in health, the weather, avoiding any mention of sex, making no outward acknowledgement that one was inclined forehead to forehead, shoulder to shoulder, with a stunningly sexy young woman, her breasts falling amply out of her black satin teddy. Maria later told me that the girls called these reticent, outwardly composed types "cowboys," and that they were a welcome presence in the life of the club. The cowboys, I came to see, found pleasure in riding the surface of the tension they had created between their sexual arousal and laconic outward imperviousness.

The least favored customers from the girls' standpoint, and I must say mine, were men who arrived in groups, loud, self-conscious and well along in drunkenness from previous stops. I never saw any outright bad behavior when I was in the club, something that would compel Hugh or Eddie to come down out of the DJ's booth and confront the miscreant. Although such encounters were said periodically to occur later in the evening, the afternoon commerce I experienced was unmediated by male presence. Bartenders, servers, dancers were all female; you talked to, ordered from, transacted and settled up with only women. Not despite this, but because of it, there was, just as I had come to realize about the beach life at Fort Zachary Taylor, a distinct civility to the exchanges in Tenderloins.

I had over the course of my working life theorized plenty about sexuality, especially about the cultural consequences of deferring and diverting sexual feeling in service of social objectives, but I did not really know the truth of even my most basic suppositions until I opened myself up fully and unguardedly to what I felt in the course of my rapt hours in the depths of Tenderloins. I doubt I would have learned much of anything if I had entered that world as a younger man. To partake of this erotic communion I had to shed, without regret, all vestiges of prior identity.

Tenderloins could not have been sexier, but sexual release was not the payload for me; rather, being sustained in that elevated state of arousal for hours on end enabled me to open up to my friends and lovers there in ways I never imagined possible up in the daylit world. The direct sexual allure of the girls was essential in this. When the *point*, the business at hand, is sex, or at least the dreamy promise of sex, any indirection, dishonesty, or tactical scheming serves no purpose.

And here I should add that Tenderloins turned out to be what Goethe called in *Faust* The Place of the Mothers. A great majority of the dancers, probably eight in ten, were mothers of one or more children to whom they were touchingly devoted. At first the idea of maternity, especially committed maternity, seemed incompatible with the mythy sacred-prostitute appeal of a Tenderloins girl. The girls themselves were aware of this and thus usually did not disclose the fact of their children or other details that might locate them in the world outside the club. A kind of anonymity is professionally necessary for strippers, serving both their safety and psychological ease. Girls choose a club name when they are hired and are instructed not to reveal their actual names or any other personal details that would open them up to contact with customers outside the club. My experience was that the girls used this shield of anonymity thoughtfully and selectively, as it served their interests.

THERE WAS A PREDICTABLY STEADY turnover in the dancers over the years. Only a few of them entered the business believing it would be a long-term calling. Several of the younger, brighter girls were putting themselves through colleges and professional schools. Others were building up savings in order to make a down payment on a shop or to set up some other commercial venture. A few had husbands or steady partners who, when their luck improved or their tolerance wore thin, would succeed in removing their beloved from the club. The youngest girls, often runaways, would be in evidence for at most a few weeks before disappearing. In all, and surprisingly to me, given the inevitably competitive nature of their work, the dancers got on remarkably well. On the slowest afternoons, dancers might outnumber customers two to one, and when not on stage or called to a private dance, the girls kept one another's company. The mothers shared domestic developments, and I overheard quite a bit of chat about bargains and clothes. Tenderloins, despite the darkness and pulsing suggestiveness of the music, was a decidedly cheerful place, and many of the girls pranked and kidded each other outrageously. In a silly but endearing way they would applaud and noisily solicit extra tips for a girl who was down on her luck or otherwise having a bad day. A few of the dancers, including some of long tenure, were lesbian, but they were indistinguishable from the others in their receptivity to customers' attentions. There were periodic romantic partnerships among lesbian and bisexual dancers, but their partners typically worked outside the club.

THERE WERE WHITE GIRLS, BLACK girls, Latina girls from Miami, Mexico, the islands, Central and South America. Probably half the white girls were European, most of them from the Czech Republic, Russia, and Ukraine. I was immediately charmed by the accents, then by the intelligence of the Eastern Europeans, to the extent that my first substantial relationships were with Czech cousins, Anya and Karyta. The infrequency of anything aversive at Tenderloins served to strengthen my impression of the deep goodness of the place. It is a kind of folk wisdom that in sexual matters pronounced differences, if not outright opposites, attract. My experience of Tenderloins in action confirmed this tendency beyond all doubt. Sexually open and free, we are, I believe all of us, incapable of bigotry of any kind. Early childhood experience and perhaps even genetic predisposition may bind or incline us to a preferred "type," but in a fluid, open sexual arena where there is as much enticement to indulge counter-type as type, one's range of sexual interest and appreciation quickly expands beyond all prior confinements. Tenderloins was set up as a "Gentleman's Club," a place where notional gentlemen would be paired with females for the purpose of arousal and pleasure. I can only hope similar establishments serving same-sex customers and servers release something of the generosity of spirit I experienced at Tenderloins. So soon to shuffle off this mortal coil, I can only imagine a sexual climate untroubled not only by ethnicity or color or physical "type," but also, if possible, by the constraints of sexual orientation. That, as it happens, was not the door I unwittingly opened that bright afternoon in the alleyway behind Duval. But, my heirs and survivors, what if it had been?

It would hardly have been possible to open myself up so completely to the company and the pleasures of the Tenderloins girls without revisiting my prior sexual life with Elizabeth. The two experiences, so distanced by time of life and geography, were not really comparable. Certainly neither in any way diminished the other. Elizabeth was my first and, for forty years, only sexual lover. Neither of us had been experienced or prepared, but such was our trust in each other that we were able to achieve a transporting intimacy the very first time we made love. There was a focus, a privileged narrowness—almost secrecy—to our lovemaking and sexual play that I assumed, despite plenty of evidence to the contrary, was the very nature of married sex. I assumed that all committed couples, no matter what kind of appearances they maintained, kept to themselves an incommunicable erotic preserve, differing only in particular practices from what Elizabeth and I shared. The fidelity I practiced without effort while I lived with Elizabeth derived from a depth and pitch of sexual feeling that might best be described as sacred. The best, most transporting sex is not, as the ancients recognized, completely of this world. My experience at Tenderloins would confirm this, while enabling me to realize that the enchantment did not lie in a particular partnership, still less in any physical act, but in the charged, higher reality experienced in the course of intense sexual communion. As Plato saw it, actual sex *participates* in ultimate sex, or Sex. Or is it better to say ultimate Sex holds us in thrall when we make love? And what does it matter what I say? What Elizabeth and I reverently fumbled our way into as children was an *instance* of the real thing. It would take the Tenderloins girls to teach me that there are infinite points of entry to the real thing and that, open-hearted enough, you never tire of, rise above, figure out or in any other way diminish the power and the delight of the real thing.

LIKE THE PLAY OF BRILLIANT sunlight on the teeming world, like a restorative meal, sex is a wonderfully renewable pleasure. To be sexually happy is the beginning of confidence, generosity and peace. Sexual happiness can only be achieved mutually and only when every vestige of self-importance and self-protection has been surrendered. This realization does not come easily, and its achievement in practice is rarer still. It is no developmental accident that the holiest, most rapturous sex, the sex most indelibly and richly printed in memory, is so often first sex, sex entered into with the trembling reverence of children. Because few are so blessed, most of us learn, if we learn at all, the hard way. We have to learn to get over ourselves. Failure, disgrace, catastrophe, loss, and terrible luck may jump-start the process, but they are by no means reliable. Humiliation may sometimes lead to humility, but it is just as likely to result in a desperate rearming of the embattled ego. Humility, it should not be surprising to note, requires practice. But here, too often, the quester is drawn down the well-trodden paths of worldly renunciation--when what the spirit really craves is utterly opposite: the richest possible embrace of the given world. Sex.

There is the practice of monks and yogis and other spiritual renunciates, and there is the practice of the Tenderloins girls. It is no surprise to the religious that self-denial and rigorous devotion are often as not an expression of inflated egotism, resulting not in heart-opening humility but in a pinched and rigid righteousness. Without instruction the Tenderloins girls know better than this. They know what Francis Bernardone seems to have known before he became St. Francis— when he surprisingly and publicly *took off his clothes*. The dream recurs: we feel sickening anxiety as we realize we are naked at work or in class or in a public forum. We awake with perhaps a fleeting sense of dread that such an event could ever occur, missing altogether the reason for the dream's visitation: that it is our waking life, the work, the class, the public forum that compose the problem. Exposing ourselves, being once again and at last naked, is the solution.

The Tenderloins girls, from their first knock-kneed, ears-ringing audition until their farewell turn at the brass pole, practice taking off their clothes. They do not, if they stay the course, take off their clothes with any thought or hope that they might not be seen and that very soon they will be safely clothed again. They strip, expose and offer up their breasts and bottoms and depilated vaginas in the certainty that they will be seen, deeply, hungrily seen, seen with hallucinogenic clarity. To be naked and to offer oneself up in this way, in many cases to offer up what the viewers, some of whose brows are poised inches from one's thighs, *most want*, is to practice humility and generosity in the purest sense.

Chapter Twelve

For weeks after settling in Key West I retained the tourist's impression that I had reached a remote and exotic place, land's end. I assumed the anonymity I felt on arrival would be sustainable, but as all voluntary exiles soon learn, faceless others soon became particular and known. The party revels, teeming streets, even the tidal flow of tourists out from and back to the cruise ships were held fast in a grid of civic purpose. This should not have surprised me. The people I was coming to know--check-out clerks, news vendors, bar tenders, servers, musicians, Tenderloins girls—lived on the island or one of the keys to the north. Beneath the relaxed, unbuttoned surfaces of Key West there was law and order. There were libraries and schools and churches, banks and post offices. There were fewer than twenty five thousand residents of the island, and easily half of them lived elsewhere for months of the year. While undeniably exotic in its range of tolerated behavior, Key West did not manage to free itself altogether from the confinements of an American small town.

The literal and virtual insularity of the place was for many residents its principal appeal. This was certainly true for many of the Tenderloins girls, especially the mothers. Their chief problem was affording it. Resourceful Tenderloins dancers who were not addicted to drugs or alcohol could and did clear a hundred thousand dollars or more a year.

But such has become the appeal of Key West to developers and snow birds and gentrifiers, that people of moderate means have a hard time making rent and mortgage payments. Tiny bungalows were selling for a million dollars. One and two bedroom apartments were disappearing in conversions to upscale condominiums. Rents on those that remained were steep to usurious. In that climate even a very productive Tenderloins dancer was hard pressed to sustain herself and her children comfortably anywhere within an hour's drive of the island.

Such was the condition of Anya and Karyta when I got to know them. I had been away for a few weeks up north, the ultimate destination a family reunion organized by Chappy and Maryann in Maine. When I got back and made my first subsequent appearance at Tenderloins there was something stirring, different in the air. Because they were either secluded in the dressing room or back at the bar, it took me perhaps a half hour to realize that there was a striking new dancer in the hall. There were actually two, but so similar in facial features and movement were Anya and Karyta, that I assumed they were the same woman. It would be a week or more before I knew them by those names. Their club names were, I believe, Melissa and Tracy.

I was struck at once by their—or, as I believed initially, her—elegance and beauty and was eager to talk to the new arrival when at length Anya made her way to my table and asked if I wanted company. I very much did, and as drinks were provided and cigarettes lit, we quickly passed through the scripted preliminaries and, with what I now know was a mutual eagerness, proceeded to get to know each other. Her English was actually quite good, her cultural reference even better, something fairly unusual among the Tenderloins girls. It would have been impossible not to be charmed by her accent. The charm was in the inflection and intonation, also the omission of certain articles and possessives, as in "this does not happen in Czech Republic" or "once Havel he is president, my father"—*fahter*— "loses position."

I had been to Prague for a conference not long after the partition and had enjoyed myself tremendously, especially the quiet architectural beauty of old Prague, gas-lit then. Anya had lived in Prague just prior to emigrating, as had her cousin, but her family was from Karst, in Moravia, and that is the home she missed. As we were getting acquainted I asked her if she had worked in clubs like this in Prague. She looked at me blankly, as if in disbelief or incomprehension, and said, "Oh no. In Prague club like this would be *proh*stitute." She told me she had started but not finished university and had once thought she would be a designer or an architect. Her father had been a government builder but had lost his position with the partition and the rise of the Havel government. She told me she and her cousin had moved to Prague together in hopes of finding better jobs, but there had been nothing. Relatives in Tampa had encouraged her to emigrate, and she and, shortly afterward, her cousin did so, working as waitresses first in Tampa and then, encouraged by new friends in the restaurant, in Key West. She named the restaurant, but I did not know it. "Money was not enough, so I come here." It would be two weeks before Anya told me she lived with her eleven-year-old son, Tomasz.

In all my years at Tenderloins I was never able to predict the ages and life situations of the dancers I came to know. That inability had been true of me throughout my adult life, at least with respect to beautiful girls and women. Unless context provided the clues—a professional or social gathering where a woman could be easily placed by her work or professional attainments or domestic arrangement—I was not at all accurate in determining whether an attractive woman was eighteen or forty-five. This was especially true if her body was supple and fit, and if her clothes—swim wear, lingerie, little black dress—did nothing to categorize her. Thus on the beach or at an upscale restaurant and most certainly at Tenderloins I was able to impose only three rather general female categories: children, beauties, and non-beauties. The latter was of course the predominant category, containing the vast majority of females entering my perceptual field in the course of any given day, but because I had so little sustained contact with them or for that matter with children, my true inner life was carried out in the erotically charged realm of very beautiful, sexually open and for the most part available women of Tenderloins.

And again, until I was told otherwise, I assumed that they were all very young, barely out of school if schooled at all, new to the adult world. It would always take a while for a newly befriended dancer's true age and life station to sink in. For instance, Anya's telling me about her university days alone made me add a few years to what I thought might be her chronological age. A still greater adjustment was required when she told me about her son, and that he was eleven years old. It took months of steady, close acquaintance and intimate time together in and out of Tenderloins before I was able to think of her as a thirty-seven year-old woman, or that Karyta, so like her cousin in looks, bearing and speech, was thirty-five.

I still wonder whether I am at some kind of ethical fault for not distinguishing more sharply between Anya and Karyta, especially considering how intimately and well we came to know one another. Their facial features, body type, and speech mannerisms were strikingly similar, so much so that it was easier to imagine them as sisters than cousins. Moreover their closeness to one another seemed, the more I got to know them, something genetically given, deep and inviolable. As one does with twins, I learned to spot small but defining differences and to associate them with their respective bearer so that these quite subtle features— Karyta's darker hair, the more pronounced break at the bridge of her nose, Anya's additional inch and a half of height, Anya's greater extroversion and readiness to laugh. Possibly because I met and got to know Anya first, it was easier to proceed to intimacy with her. Nevertheless I cannot think of them except as a related pair. In my mind their faces meld into one, the same high cheek bones, sharp, good chins, the distinctive side part and severe fall of their very becoming hair styles, Anya's honey blond in the light of day, Karyta's darker, golden streaks mixed with auburn and browns.

Anya and Karyta defined a certain type in the array of their fellow dancers. Separately and together they represented gentility and refinement. They were both leggy and fit, the definition of their abdominal and calf muscles suggesting athleticism, as in fact through their early teens both had been serious gymnasts with dreams of national and even Olympic recognition. They tended to stand erect even as they danced, a regal bearing which, had it been any more pronounced, would have seriously undermined their sex appeal. As it was, they were not every customer's type. Their detectable reserve—especially Karyta's—combined with their accents to suggest a distancing foreign-ness.

The longer I patronized the club the surer I was that every man who entered, no matter how accustomed to the protocols and well acquainted with the dancers, brought with him a willingness to suspend disbelief: a fantasy that through some combination of visual contact, conversation and protracted *frottage* he might experience an ecstatic, once-in-a-lifetime connection to nothing less than his feminine ideal. This of course was a drive well known to the great analytical psychologists, and Jung was especially good on its delusory power. To fix one's erotic attention while in this condition upon a particular dancer opened up the possibility of objectifying one's inner feminine—the male *anima* itself—and projecting onto it the entire force of one's libido. Even to approximate this psychic act is to be carried away, if not outright annihilated. The ancient mythographers tried to convey this danger in their accounts of mortals longing to behold a beloved god in the flesh and, upon getting his or her wish, being immolated to ash. As a Jungian friend of mine once wrote to me, to open up to the ultimate with an actual sex partner was to plug a hundred thousand electrical volts into an appliance wired for ten.

But where was I. Ah, Anya and Karyta's reserve. Because that reserve was, I believe, always faintly at work in what they projected at the club, few customers allowed themselves that willing suspension of disbelief necessary to part with a hundred dollars or more in order to follow either cousin into the sensual wilds beyond the glass beaded portal. The reluctance to engage Anya and Karyta in this way was entirely unrelated to their beauty. I would say, speaking personally, that in all my time in Tenderloins I never beheld, until the arrival of Maria years later, a more statuesque, more exquisitely made woman than either Anya or Karyta. In a classical manner, but not without contemporary touches, they were strikingly beautiful. Nevertheless, apart from me, the men who engaged them for a private dance rarely extended the session. They did as well as anyone else in tips for their platform dances, but except during certain crowded shifts when they managed to solicit single private dances at close intervals, they were never spectacular earners at Tenderloins. The other dancers who, once they got to know Anya and Karyta, tended to like them, suggested from time to time that the two of them should reconsider their club outfits in favor of more provocative get-ups. Wisely or not, such adjustments were not made, for which I was privately glad. I thought the cousins' taste in dance-wear suited them perfectly. Whereas most of the other girls relied on a fantasy-siren appeal, playfully sluttish, skimpy tops and bottoms revealing much breast and bottom, Anya and Karyta favored spaghetti-strapped satin tops and matching short skirts. Given the pleasing perfection of their figures, they were undeniably sexy in these clothes, although in a way that probably would have passed unremarkably at pool side or table side in the world above Tenderloins.

As far as I was concerned, they were dressed perfectly, and I was not at all reluctant to engage them in extended series of dances, which I found, with Anya perhaps more than Karyta, dreamily transporting. Some of the veteran dancers had developed just-short-of-illicit techniques for conveying the impression that with each successive dance the amount and intensity of direct sexual contact would increase. A few girls who had mastered concealing from the overhead camera monitors certain expressly forbidden intimacies actually did escalate the stimulation offered with each successive song.

This was never the case with Anya or Karyta, even after we became close friends outside the club and had on occasion slept together. Once, in the course of a series of languorous private dances Karyta stopped moving altogether and with a wide-eyed alertness said, "Jonathan"—*Jonatin*—"I saw you on television."

This would have been the *Between the Lines* interview with Chase Reading. For some reason the notion of Karyta's viewing this gave me an uneasy jolt—an incursion of the all but forgotten edginess and complexity of my former life into the other-world sweetness I was at that moment enjoying. As images from the interview began crowding into awareness-- the improvised studio at the Hilton, Chase, talking, deliberating, drawing considered distinctions—I could feel the erotic charge of my communion with Karyta receding. "And what did you think?" I asked her. "It was interesting," she said thoughtfully. "It was interesting to see you talking like that." I studied her face as, looking very perplexed, she struggled to make a more substantial response to my question. I sensed that she could not possibly do it, that nothing in her experience would have enabled her to see what made Chase's and my televised confrontation worthy of any public interest. I told her that I didn't think the show was very interesting, except to perhaps a very few viewers. "No, it *was* interesting," Karyta said, "because I didn't know that you were a writer. Well known. That you wrote a book. I would like to read your book."

I told her that I would be happy to get a book for her, but even as I said it I knew I would delay doing so indefinitely, in the hopes that she would forget about it. The very idea of either Karyta or Anya's attempting to size me up on the basis of what they might read in *Force Fields* or *Uses of Force* depressed me. It depressed me to think about any of that, the propositions that composed those books, the inert, concentrated hours spent in writing all of it down, the uncountable seminars, conferences, and addresses in which I would take up a position deep in some forest of my own construction and set about showing it off or defending it as if it were not just a possible reality but reality itself.

As it happened, Karyta did not persist in acquiring one of my books, but Anya did soon after Karyta told her about the television interview. In fact she checked out three of them from the public library. "So you are very well known for these books?" she asked me. Hoping to deaden her interest, I told her I had been somewhat well known a few years earlier, but not so much any more. I cannot say for sure, but I believe Anya read into the books with some determination, but I doubt with much comprehension. For a week or so at Tenderloins and over dinner on her days off she questioned me about particular points and arguments, and I answered as generally and unhelpfully as I could. What she most wanted from me was a clear, capsule summary of what I was trying to say, but I could not bear to enter into this kind of dialog with her: to introduce in any way an approach to life I now felt as deadening to the bright immediacy in which I now found myself.

Sustainable sexual relationships always include at their core a mysterious component. Moreover, the mystery is unfathomable, not a problem to be solved, containing as it does the creative but unknowable workings of the erotic bond. Such was the case with my triangular relationship to Anya and Karyta. As it turned out, my past and shadowy celebrity became an essential part of our mystery as did the emotionally formative events in their past lives, including the nature of Anya's relationship with Tomasz's father—"I think now that he is truly bad man," "I like never to think about him," "I want Tomasz never to know him"—and the medical problems that had led to Karyta's early hysterectomy, followed by bouts of incapacitating depression. It is hard enough for couples to respect the mysterious, not-to-be probed elements in their attraction, rarer still for a threesome to manage it. That we succeeded in this, while taking so much pleasure in one another, is due, I suspect, to my being so old and to an extraordinary degree of autonomy and adaptability on Anya's and Karyta's parts. It is rare for two women, not yet arrived in midlife, to have attained such an unshockable equanimity.

Somehow we managed to enjoy our peculiar arrangement, utterly unlike anything I had experienced before or even heard of. We were a threesome, I suppose even a kind of *ménage a trois*, given the fact that I occasionally slept with both women, although never at the same time or while under the same roof. Moreover, and perhaps stranger still, I never detected a trace of jealousy or resentment on either cousin's part over the kind or amount time I spent with the other. The supervision of Tomasz's after school hours worked best if Anya and Karyta alternated days and shifts, so that when I showed up at Tenderloins, usually only one of them would be on hand

Out of the other's company, Anya and Karyta spoke of one another with respect and affection but also with a knowing objectivity. Karyta was a watchful and attentive aunt to Tomasz, whose asthma and other bronchial troubles had been a periodic concern, although the steamy warmth of Key West appeared to agree with him. For her part Anya was solicitous and protective of her slightly younger cousin, about whose past troubles in Karst and Prague she would only say, "She had very bad time there."

Our above ground, out-of-Tenderloins relationship evolved quite naturally. Often, perhaps every other morning, I would meet one or both of them for coffee, after which we might proceed to the beach, perhaps meeting the other, chatting and sunning until it was time for them to pack up and begin their shifts at Tenderloins. Tomasz would join us when he was not in school. He was a slender, thoughtful boy, quiet in our company but not shy, comfortable either taking in our chat and gossip or going off to snorkel or to look for crabs at the base of the big rocks just off shore. When it was determined that Tomasz was able to manage on his own for a few hours in the evening, the three of us would make a reservation at a favorite restaurant where we invariably enjoyed ourselves, chatting, people-watching and, usually a little tipsy, extending ourselves to new acquaintances.

When they arrived in Key West, Anya and Karyta determined that they could afford to rent only half of a two-family bungalow in one of the low-slung neighborhoods huddled between the airport and Old Town. The place, which they kept quite clean, was austere, sparsely furnished and problematically cramped. There was only one small bedroom, where Tomasz slept. Anya and Karyta shared a sofa bed in the living room. I frequently dined there with one or both of them and Tomasz, but there were no intimacies, and I never spent the night. We often—two or three times a week—would go out as couples, the availability of my companion determined by their Tenderloins shifts.

And so we carried on in a most agreeable indeterminacy, alternately as a trio and in pairs. In time it became our standard practice to conclude our evenings as couples at my place, by then the condominium I had purchased overlooking the water at the harbor side of Truman Annex. I loved those evenings, dining out under open skies at Mangoes or Virgilio's, then strolling up and down Duval to clear our heads before retiring to my rooms where, after perhaps a night cap or two, we would undress, make love under the throbbing ceiling fan and descend into deepest sleep.

The term *make love* suggests something foregone, universally

473

understood, but this is not so, as I was perhaps fated to learn in Key West. The sexual intimacies I experienced there in such unexpected abundance were, again, altogether discontinuous with what had been a wonderfully fulfilling and exclusive sexual partnership with Elizabeth. In no way has my experience in Key West diminished any of that. It is more as if sex came to serve a different function. The essence of that function, or really of sex itself, cannot be conveyed in words. I have, when pressed, fallen back on *transporting, ecstatic*, aware that such terms are no more than verbal flailing in the direction of the ineffable.

Married sex was for me, and I hope others, a kind of secret, running subtext to the whole of married life, with all of its domestic, practical, out-for-show complexities. At its deepest and best, married sex can include a ritual, ancient-sacred aspect, but much of it is undeliberated biological inevitability. This was not at all true of my sexual life in Key West. The *mechanism* may have been biological but the experience itself registered in what must be called—again, words failing—the spiritual and esthetic realm.

I like to think—no, I actually believe—that Tenderloins was put on earth to wake me up to the beauty and fullness of life. The currency there was sex, or better, the beckoning promise of sex— Sex itself, and not mere arousal, genital stimulation and release. I had not been oblivious throughout the first sixty years of my life to direct sexual come-hithers. Certain erotic images had sometimes struck a deep resonance. I had been stirred, but not to action. Other women had come into sudden, intense focus, but usually some particular physical aspect, not their full being. What other women I occasionally found myself drawn to tended to be friends' wives, and I suppose some combination of social convention and reflexive propriety on my part numbed me to the possibility of actual trespass, although I received periodic invitations to do so, two or three of them recklessly determined

I suppose the full flowering of my erotic awakening occurred over the course of my two years with Anya and Karyta. Although reared abroad and nearly half my age, they seemed to sense something safe and familiar in my presence. For my part getting to know them had been an effortless pleasure. Not only did they seem to welcome my company, they clearly gravitated to me, scanning the beach front for my arrival, joining me at once as soon as I entered the club. As we became better acquainted they revealed to me that, despite initial high hopes, they were increasingly disappointed by life in the states. Part of this may have been an understandable aversion to the strip retail wastes of southern Florida, but the combined impression created by American families out to dine at the restaurant in Tampa and the general run of customers at Tenderloins did little to revise their initial responses to American life. Each took pains to tell me that my appeal for them had been the *difference* I represented. Anya had assumed that I was not American when we met and apparently had described me to Karyta as a fellow émigré. Because I felt like something of an émigré myself, I was touched by the misidentification. I asked Anya where she thought I had come from, and she had said at once, "From France. I am *sure* you are from France, but then I thought about your voice and decided you are England."

Like, I am sure, every older lover of very beautiful younger women, I could not help imagining their specific impressions of me— the brown weathered character seated across from them over morning coffee, sharing a drink at my table at Tenderloins, my palms passing lightly over their waists and shoulders in the course of our exertions behind the glass beads. I tried to imagine their sensations, the images they formed as we made love, tangled, entwined, registering the now fully revealed other, not merely with palms and fingertips but with seemingly every cell, certain that they *must* feel some approximation of what I was feeling, yet just as certain that they could not possibly, that they were fated never to know the unutterable silken pleasure of their own exquisite selves.

We were together for the better part of two years, although in memory that privileged, exalted period compresses into what seems no more than an airy week, a single morning in bright sun on adjacent chaises at water's edge, a fast receding memory of making love before sleep, then awakening into the same lingering thrall. That there were *three of us*, that there were *both of them*—what pleasure to awake into those days.

THAT OUR ARRANGEMENT WAS INHERENTLY temporary, that even at its languorous best it had felt like a kind of boon or reprieve, was essential to its mystery. I think each of us sensed and honored this. We never discussed, even playfully, a long term future together, nor do I believe either Anya or Karyta imagined or wanted one. We were efficient in managing our respective calendars, and, given the constraints of Tomasz's school schedule and Tenderloins shifts, we managed to maintain a pleasing balance of routine and novelty. Our daily lives had also been greatly eased when I was able to persuade Anya and Karyta to let me rent the other half of the bungalow for them, so they could each have a bedroom and bath and a quiet place apart when they needed one, but, although comfortable enough, I don't think either of them ever allowed themselves to consider Key West home.

The decision to return to the Czech Republic was reached after very little deliberation. There were compelling reasons. Tomasz was about to turn thirteen, and Anya, who had never intended to be an exotic dancer for any extended period of time, realized the hour had come. "This is not a situation for Tomasz to grow up." Karyta made inquiries, and she had been assured by relatives that clerical positions were now available in Prague and Karst. There was another development, one not fully disclosed to me, that may have hastened the decision to repatriate themselves. An overture had been made by Tomasz's father to reenter their lives in some way. There was more to this, including perhaps some thought of his reconciling with Anya, but I was not told anything so specific. Anya said only that Jan—she had not referred to him by name before—"would like to be part of Tomasz's life again."

Beginning with their earliest speculations, Anya and Karyta were open with me about their impending departure. There was no jarring element of surprise, and I was able to serve as a partner in these deliberations about what came to feel like not just their future, but our future. In all of this they were solicitous of me, but not at all sentimental, which I suspect might have been an ethnic inheritance. I did feel sad as their departure loomed, in fact profoundly sad, but it was the full, rich sadness of a loss unfreighted by resentment. "You will stay okay here, Jonathan?" Karyta had asked. *Jonatin*. Anya told me: "You have been our America, the good part."

I would not have been able to explain it to them, but Anya's sentiment was mine exactly: they had been *my* America, the good part. While I in no way wanted them to go, I too was aware that there was no prolonging our dreamy counter-life indefinitely. For one thing, given the closeness of the Key West community, we were becoming *known*. This should not have surprised me. In just a week or two on the island, one cannot help distinguishing recurring and increasingly familiar faces amidst the giddy blur of transients. My daily rounds, and then, when we were together, Anya's and Karyta's, were nearly invariable. We had become *fixtures* at the naval base end of the Fort Zachary Taylor beach, at the open air bar in the back of Virgilio's, on the terrace at Mangoes.

In any event we would have been hard not to notice. What I felt was the understated appeal of Anya's and Karyta's attire in Tenderloins registered rather more dramatically on the streets above. Strikingly beautiful, near look-alikes, always elegantly erect, they could not help drawing attention. Invariably one or the other of them would be approached in the course of an evening out and asked if she hadn't played some role, sung with some band. That they were always, either singly or together, paired with me, the gaunt, brown white haired man in white, could only have fixed our image more indelibly.

At first in the interest of maintaining anonymity but as much for my private amusement, I would make our reservations under the name Chase Reading, although the bartenders and servers already knew me as Jon or Jonny. A few persistent journalists had succeeded in finding me when Chase's *Farce* books were appearing, but for the most part I had not been bothered. But the regular reappearance of the two or three of us out together began to create its own kind of Key West celebrity. Returning tourists would approach us cheerfully on the beach or at a bar and say, "I remember you guys from last time!" More than once, but most memorably just before Anya and Karyta flew home, I overheard someone at a table behind us stage-whispering, "The older man with them is *Jonathan*

Force. He *lives* here"—and I knew that we were ending our interlude just in time.

On the eve of their departure we went out, with Tomasz, for a celebratory dinner of conch chowder and lobster. I stayed up late with them at the bungalow after Tomasz went to bed. At one point I remember all of us loud and silly in reminiscence. Words were said about the reunion we would surely have in Prague or Paris, each of us, I suspect, certain that it would not happen. We fell silent, as if by agreement, and then I knew I must go. I held each of them in a close, final embrace, and then the three of us held each other. At the door I raised my hand as if offering a toast and said, "New life!" and set out on the long, clarifying walk home.

Chapter Thirteen

The period after Anya and Karyta's departure was an extraordinary time for me. I could not have been more profoundly aware of their absence from my life, but there was no *missing*. I thought about them often, not as we had been, but how I imagined they were making their way in their new circumstances. I felt less saddened than *lightened*, to a degree that more than once seemed to carry me out of ordinary existence altogether.

I experienced this passing-out-of-existence for the first time in the course of taking a long mid-morning walk along the ocean front between Old Town and the airport. And—strange, *strange*—I seem to be experiencing the same thing at this very moment.

This could be death's arrival--

Yes, but no. I can still, as when consciously dreaming, will myself submerged from the glare and apparatus and horrible hum of Intensive Care.

But that morning on Atlantic Avenue something arose suddenly from below my heart and seemed to swell up airily within me, filling me up, then exceeding me. I retained my bodily form, could even picture my enormous head and striding figure, but as if I were some huge parade-balloon facsimile of myself. But even as I pictured this image, I was inside the figure, still aware of the catamarans and kayakers off shore, still feeling the soft breeze at my temples, feet somehow still on the wide walk, my brow high in clouds. I was at once rooted to the earth and atmospheric, carried at a terrific velocity which was at the same time an indescribable stillness. I was aware that the moment I was in had passed, that I had managed to embody and occupy sheer afterward. Words have already failed, but as I, like some colossal Janus, surveyed from a vast height the cheerful traffic of the island and at the same time the spangled span of open sea, I experienced what I suppose is ultimate understanding: wordless of course, but charged with feeling--a beautiful, beautiful sadness, an awareness that everything surveyed and felt and understood was finally and forever lost, a grateful acceptance of that loss.

I believe I was held in that awareness for about twenty minutes, still walking during most of it, then stopped still. But it could have been longer—or possibly much shorter. It may have lasted a minute, a second.

And—*here it is*—I am there, can feel it again. If only there were words. I have already said *sadness, loss*. But sadness and loss shot through, pulsing with such sweetness, such finality. *Loss* won't do, but it must, because everything at that moment was lost, *gladly* lost. It was more than boyhood, Palatine, Elizabeth, the boys, my—*meaningless*—work and days that were lost. It was more certainly than the loss of Anya and Karyta, although their departure had somehow hastened this passage. This is as clear as I will be able to make it: I was no longer a self who had known and then lost beloved others; I was no longer a self at all. The airily inflated enormity of me had become sheer atmosphere, sheer ocean, sheer light. The sweetness, sadness, lost-ness or whatever I call it is the feeling of passing, gladly, out of the waking world. The slightest intimation of such feeling opens you up to more and then more and then more and then you are held in it, part of it. It was always there. I was always the merest membrane apart from it. It was always available. It was the shadow, the rest of, the completion of everything I ever thought or felt. I could have entered it at will. I had only to become nothing, to cease to matter.

Chapter Fourteen

After that first, brief entry into the ultimate, my life never quite felt the same. Memory was intact, and I could mentally access my past, but I no longer felt substantially connected to it. My former life, even the brighter, more feeling-charged episodes of my childhood, felt remote, finished, mere stories whose value no longer lay in the fact that I had been in them. It was a little like Dickens' Scrooge awaking to the world on Christmas morning, but with nothing especially urgent to do.

In fact I *had* nothing especially urgent to do. That was I believe the defining condition of my existence and I am certain the reason I have periodically been able to pass out of temporal reality altogether. By no means, though, did this make my daily business, such as it had become, feel purposeless or without value. The inexplicable gift of my mounting prosperity enabled me—had enabled me for years—to arrange my circumstances any way I wanted. The wonder of it is that the less I *did*, the wealthier I seemed to become. Everything big and expensive in Elizabeth's and my life together had long been paid for. Royalties accumulated in funds that yielded far more than either of us needed to maintain ourselves. In ways that Elizabeth but not I understood, our invested funds seemed to increase exponentially in the prevailing markets. Our boys, with little help from us, were thriving, already more committed to charitable causes than to increasing their personal holdings.

My life had become simplicity itself, my easily manageable routines a renewable, daily pleasure. As boys both Franklin and Chappy had been stirred by the challenge of "no-impact" camping and as men both are impressively committed to environmentally sustainable practices. And now, without really any deliberation, I too find myself wanting to create as little impact—on anything—as I possibly can. My condominium is a modest one-bedroom unit on the second floor of a block of attached flats looking out westward over marsh and sea. During the day the rooms are brilliant with shore light. In the sitting room a pale rose colored couch and two comfortable lounging chairs are arranged around a glass coffee table beneath which an oriental carpet has been agreeably faded by sunlight. There is a comfortable double bed and bureau in the otherwise empty bedroom. At one end of the half-kitchen, I have wedged a small glass-topped cafe table and two small chairs. In the cupboards are cookware, dishes and silverware for four. I keep a few bottles of fruit juice in the refrigerator, along with a day or two's worth of fresh greens. There is a small coffee-maker on the counter and on the stove a rather handsome yellow tea kettle. I stock very little food, never more than a box of cereal, some cooking oil, a loaf of bread, a jar of peanut butter, a tin of brown rice and a lazy-susan of herbs and spices. I keep a bottle or two of vodka in the freezer and an assortment of liqueurs under the sink. In a louvered closet spanning one wall of the bedroom, my white slacks and shirts and jackets hang along perhaps two feet of the dowel, below which are arranged the three pairs of my canvas shoes. Suspended from brass hooks in the tiny front entryway are two canvas bags, one quite substantial, the other the size of a small briefcase. I take one or the other of these on my morning errands, so as not to require paper or plastic bags at the shops.

I invariably woke up happy in the dazzling light of my bedroom, an atmosphere that seemed to follow me into the bath where, in seemingly a minute, I was showered and shaved. Between eight and nine I was out on the streets, beginning my round of errands, which almost always included coffee and a *New York Times*. There are few people on the streets in Key West before ten, and my morning circuit and stops took on a gratifying, liturgical feeling. The light is wonderful at that hour, something of peach and rose in it, the air musky with flowers and earth after rain.

Again, I didn't pay much attention to money, except to be sure I stopped often enough at the ATM to keep between three and six hundred dollars in twenties in my wallet, for Tenderloins. Otherwise, I seemed to spend next to nothing. There were my twice weekly stops at the cleaners, shops, restaurants, gratuities. The splendid public library obviated almost all need to purchase books, which had been something of an obsession in my former life. Years ago, I signed the title of my Volvo over to a desperate Tenderloins friend of Anya's and Karyta's, as I seemed never to need a car and would sometimes forget to keep up the registration and inspections.

So that was it, and those were my days. Unvarying and inconsequential as they were, I was strangely energized by my modest cycles of consumption and replacement. It was invigorating to retrieve my newly pressed and laundered clothes at the cleaners, to break down the bed and tuck in crisp, fresh sheets, sweetly redolent of laundromat. At those moments I felt less that I was maintaining myself than that I was recreating myself. Moreover, the pleasure in these ministrations, if anything, intensified over the years. Not just the particular stops and selections but the very idea that anything I might conceivably need lay before me, within range, calculable and manageable, imparted a sense of mastery unlike anything I had known in my working life. In all my years on the island I never shed the wonder I felt that such particular things, cucumbers, French roast coffee, white canvas shoes—everything I wanted—was at hand, no more than a pleasant walk away. Providing for myself was also an entirely private matter, never spoken of, executed and known only by me. Although vital, looking after myself in this highly particular way had all the intricacy and charm of a game. Yes, play. My life, life itself, as sustainable play.

Chapter Fifteen

And then there entered into my life another, and final, great love. She is Maria Julia Luisa Amante. I offer her full name out of my love for its music and for her. At Tenderloins she was Carmen. It was weeks before she would confide to me even her real first name, for very good reasons.

I am as certain as I can be that Maria and I came into each other's lives by a larger design and not by chance. This is not a conclusion drawn out of any systematic cosmology or theology, but rather out of the quality of deep inner knowing that in my old age I have come to trust. On that particular afternoon, an afternoon of memorably brilliant April sunlight at Fort Zachary Taylor Beach but otherwise unportentous, I descended into the welcome coolness of the Tenderloins dark without, quite literally, a care in the world. I was by no means lonely, and there was, if anything, less a twinge of expectation than I typically felt as I descended the stairs.

Over the years the Tenderloins girls had made a light hearted ritual of greeting regulars with a whoop of acknowledgement as they come through the door, and I had become by this time the most longstanding regular, I am sure, in the club's history, for years entering within a quarter hour of four o'clock in the afternoon, usually five but sometimes six days a week. Fully aware that I would enter to this shrill recognition, I never failed to feel a jolt of surprise when I heard it.

From the perspective of anyone lounging at the bar or seated at a table, any day-lit entrance was dramatic. So dark and cocooned was the interior of Tenderloins that the sudden clout of white light from the opened door had the startling impact of a massive flashbulb framing the silhouette of the entering figure. The attention of dancers and customers alike would be involuntarily drawn to this disturbance for a second or two before darkness restored more compelling business in progress. In the course of that transition those inside the club were able to observe and even identify the entering party well before that person's eyes could adjust to what lay before him. From a Tenderloins girl's perspective, and even from mine when I was there, it felt somehow natural to cheer an arrival so brilliantly announced. The actual words shrieked as I stepped inside the door combined to a sustained squeal—*Jonny! It's Jonny! Yes! Omigod! There he is! It's the man!* It always made me laugh or want to, and to feel that various light rejoinders were in order, thus easing in a renewably pleasurable way my passage into that day's Tenderloins interlude.

Such was my entrance to the club the afternoon I first beheld Maria.

Even before my eyes began to adjust, I was aware that something was different in the club. There was a kind of hubbub back at the bar, and when I could sufficiently make out what was going on and who was involved, it appeared that a cluster of eight or nine figures, most of them dancers and a few lounging cowboys, were gathered, as if paying court, on either side of a striking woman in elaborate white lingerie. I remember a boned bustier of white satin, loosely and provocatively laced across the cleavage. Below, a matching thong was overlain by the complicated straps and fasteners of a garter belt to which were clipped white mesh stockings whose fabric projected a steely sheen. Laced up nearly to the knee of each leg were lacquered white boots supported by steeply spiked heels.

But this is where memory plays a trick, or perhaps where something truer than memory corrects the inner picture—for I cannot for the life of me erase from mind's eye the impression that in addition to Maria's shimmering get-up, a pronounced set of gauzy wings flaring out beyond her lovely brown shoulders.

"And so who is *this*"—her voice, low and reedy but commanding as the girls greeted me. I heard the girls provide my name and stopped at a table a few yards away from the bar in order to collect myself. Loud talk and laughter resumed among those clustered around Maria, and in a minute when my eyes were adjusted, I took pains to register as precisely as I could what exactly was going on.

Outwardly, I suppose it was just an animated exchange of observations and cracks by dancers and customers who had for some reason risen to high spirits. Maria seemed, again, to be holding court, her dominance apparently uncontested. And this from a new girl. The appealing penetration of her voice compelled attention. Some of her cracks were addressed across the room to the dancers gyrating with no special energy about their respective poles. The two or three men seated at the rail of the platforms had twisted around on their stools to look at Maria. It was her show, not at all what I had come to expect in a Tenderloins afternoon.

Her jokes and comments to the dancers seemed to be given and taken in good spirits, but their raucous persistence made it impossible not to periodically glance back at their source. Inevitably, Maria and I made eye contact, and I was somehow less surprised than I might have been that she gathered me into her banter. "*Hey*, Senator," she called out to me. "Just checking things out all by yourself over there?" Some of the girls howled with delight at *Senator*. I raised my Corona and smiled. She went on: "And so how come everybody knows you, Senator? I think all these girls vote for you. What do you think, should I vote for you? I think I should—look, we match!"

Later, when it was her turn to dance her series, the crowd from the bar migrated to the stools around the platform where she continued to hold forth, more in the manner of a stand-up comedienne than a stripper. Like the others, she managed to disrobe to toplessness by the end of the first song, to nakedness by the end of the second. Understandably the high boots remained. But something about her routine was different, at once especially compelling and vaguely disappointing. It wasn't until I had seen her at work on the platform several times that it occurred to me what the difference was: she barely danced at all. There was some movement, a comfortable rhythmic swaying at the waist, but her feet were planted solidly, except to step forward to, perhaps, draw her palm over the bald pate of a customer seated at the rails.

These initial experiences implanted Maria's image seemingly at the center of my being. She would recur to me in a kind of flash as I had first beheld her in white satin and gossamer at the bar. This image would then dissolve into a swirl of other images and impressions, the reedy purr of her voice as she drew out some shy solitary from his table in a shadowy corner of the club, the way she would pause to stillness at her pole on the platform, a slow smile widening and brightening at some remark she had just uttered, how she would welcome the dazed, seemingly penitential faces of tippers into her brown bosom.

Quite unexpectedly, I was altered. I woke to those days agitated and energized. Everything--the objects in my rooms, the fall of light on the carpet, the aromatic morning streets, the brilliant clout of sunlight on the aquamarine at Fort Zachary Taylor beach—seemed to pulse with promise. I was in an almost perpetual state of mild sexual arousal. The Tenderloins interlude, so long an established part of the day's liturgy, rather like a meal, now beckoned with giddy force. And I was past seventy, wonderfully, gratefully turned on.

Chapter Sixteen

I believe I was in love with Maria before she made a point to seek me out and make my acquaintance, so that when she did, I was pleasingly on edge. It had been a relatively slow afternoon midweek. She was seated on a stool at the bar with her back to me. I heard a vendor say he had to get moving, and he disappeared through the door to the kitchen. A few regulars settled their bill, and as they walked to the door, she scanned the room, met my eye, and came over to the table.

All in black that day: spandex bandeau, leather miniskirt, fishnet stockings. I looked up into her face, framed by a busy hive of tight black ringlets, and prepared myself for what I imagined would be an exchange of cracks and quips. In this she surprised me. "Mind if I join you, man in white?" She could not have been more relaxed or more gracious. Miranda, a server, took our order for drinks.

"You really come here every day?" she asked me. I told her I did, but not always on the weekends. "So you really like it here," she said, "that's such a nice thing." I said something to the effect that my time at Tenderloins was invariably the highlight of the day. I asked her how she was finding the club—and did she live on the island.

She told me that so far she was very pleased and grateful to be in a club like this, where, she said, "Most of the men are gentlemen." I asked her where she had come from and if she worked in other clubs. She told me, "You don't want to know," and I couldn't tell whether she was being playful or evasive. I really did want to know and told her so. She sized me up with a long look and said, "It was bad. It got very bad for me. It was Miami, where I am from, and if you don't mind, I'd rather not think about any of that right now."

She told me this in a warm, confiding tone, and I was aware that my interest in keeping her close to me, learning about her, engaging in any kind of exchange utterly outweighed any desire I might have to hear her personal story. She turned the questions to me, why I had come to Key West, what I did, why I stayed.

Truth be told, everything I said to Maria that afternoon was heavily filtered. My actual interior condition was excited to the point of incoherence. It was all I could do to pose an affable façade, make her as comfortable as possible, do everything I could devise to keep her close at hand. I am not proud of it, but I know I toyed with the possibility of painting an impressive picture of my past, at least to suggest that I had been widely known, famously accomplished. I would not have added well-to-do because that, due to nothing I had ever claimed or disclosed at Tenderloins, was already part of the mythology of my tenure at the club. Basically, without much revealing detail, I told Maria the truth about why I came to Key West and what sustained me there. Her interest in what I had to say seemed almost desperate. "So it's a good place? It works for you?"

She seemed to want reassurance, and I gave it. At some point, quite a while after she sat down, she said, "So you are Jonny?" Jonathan, I said. "*JOAN-athan,*" she repeated slowly. From her mouth the name was lovely. Her head now inclined forward within inches of mine, her voice was a low, irresistible Latina purr, something in it of the young Eartha Kitt. Whatever it was, I felt myself falling under the spell of the voice, of the cat-like perfection of her lovely brown face, of the miraculous suggestion of amplitude in her delicate tininess—of everything about her. Maria!

I AM ABLE TO DESCRIBE Maria's appearance now with an exact precision, but on that first afternoon, and for the first weeks and months I knew her, I could not have reliably done so. She had long ago mastered the art of transforming herself, an aspect of club work that gave her real pleasure. I was surprised and impressed when one afternoon she confided to me the lengths she went to acquire her phenomenal range of costumes and what they cost. Dramatically transforming her appearance—dressing up generally—clearly stimulated her and by extension her customers. In any given week she was fairy queen, cowgirl, school girl, lingerie model, Tarzan's Jane, bar slut. The outfits, however, by no means accounted for her transformations. Her hair alone could change her radically from day to day. Her hair was naturally a rich, silky black, extending, when free, down her back to the shoulder blade, with a suggestion of wave at the neckline. When, later, we lived together, I would become very fond of her hair in this condition, seldom on view at Tenderloins. The hair styles she favored for club work framed her kitten face so distinctively that even I, after many attentive weeks, would strain for a moment to recognize her as the Maria of the previous afternoon.

She was a skilled hair stylist and had worked on and off in salons in Miami between club jobs. Her most striking offerings were what looked to me like a wild nest of tiny black ringlets gleaming with gel, dreadlocks, brightly beaded cornrows (which had the additional effect of making her look like a child), an elegant French twist (which somehow made her seem tall), and a straight fall arrangement with severe bangs that, accompanied by elaborate eye make-up, made her look like Cleopatra. There were also at least a dozen wigs, including, memorably, a short platinum bob and an arrangement of long-hair-and-bangs in electric blue. Wigs seemed to disguise her even more than her own stylings. I don't suppose I ever got fully used to how convincingly she was able to reconfigure herself at Tenderloins from day to day—the effect surpassing anything one might imagine clothing or hairdo could achieve.

Maria, undressed or casually attired in a familiar place—say, her beige carpeted bedroom, drying herself after a shower, walking a few paces in front of me at the Stop 'N Shop—was a delicately petite Latina woman. She stood five feet and one inch tall, and weighed perhaps a hundred pounds. She was beautifully—and to me, miraculously—made, toned and fit enough that the muscles of her arms, legs and abdomen were elegantly defined. Her ankles and wrists were extremely slender and delicate. Her breasts were lovely and surprisingly ample for a woman so petite. In fact, Maria was sculpturally beautiful from any perspective. Her head was set rather regally on her delicate neck. The sharp edge of her collar bone was itself a delight, especially draped as it usually was with a finely linked gold chain. Her hips were slim, but given her extremely narrow waist, her pert, rounded bottom could at times appear voluptuous.

    About her face, I naturally come back to "kitten" because of the endearing symmetry of its foreshortened features. I cannot summon up the image of Maria's face without attention first to her skin, the soft moistness of her throat and lips and cheeks. In hard daylight, at the beach, she was the color of coffee and cream, but in different light—and due to certain ministrations of her own—she could appear more lightly or darkly complexioned, and indeed, at Tenderloins, she had stirred me (and without question others) as a primitive girl of the islands, a black hustler, a French *gamin*, a naughty parochial school girl, among many other guises. Once acquainted, I think both of us knew we were irrevocably attached. She would offer her own words of explanation, and while it would be arrogant of me to assume to speak for her on such an intimate matter, I am certain she would say something about finding in our communion a long-sought safety, being able at last to suspend what had been for most of her lifetime a fierce and wary vigilance, the sweet relief of coming to rest. For my part, there is no end to what I would like to say about our life together. She had simply and irreversibly *occurred* that afternoon in her bustier and wings.

Chapter Seventeen

Maria was the undisputed top earner at the club, even though she almost never worked the more lucrative evening shift, and while she was shrewd and efficient with money, she never seemed overly concerned about it. Even after we were together and she had some idea of my means, she never expressed any special interest in my money and what it might do for her. To the contrary, although I was able to make a few helpful interventions in the course of our years together, it was something of an ordeal to persuade Maria to accept assistance or a boon, especially if it bore on what she regarded as a personal responsibility such as her rent or car payments.

Maria has been a wonder and a great love. I don't believe it is possible to know and fully appreciate her without experiencing both her commanding, extroverted improvisations at the club and also the depth of her repose at home. To my knowledge no one over the course of our years together had that perspective but me. I had been stricken, carried away by the flash of her appearance that first afternoon at the Tenderloins bar, but I did not begin to take her in, accept her, know her, join her until we were able to spend at first hours and then days and weeks together at her little house. Only there did I come to know the balm of her quiet and ease.

Outside Tenderloins Maria rarely raised her voice above a low, pleasing hum, little more than a whisper. Not at all reticent or withholding, she was moderate and thoughtful in response, unhurried, happiest when in languorous recline. When I think of Maria at home or at my flat or anywhere outside the club, I think of her sitting up in bed in morning light, smiling and grateful as I set down a tray with morning coffee. I think of her comfortable and supine, inert and baking on a chaise next to mine at Fort Zachary Taylor beach. I think of her in the twilit evening, at home, showered and shampooed, cleansed of Tenderloins, wearing a loose shirt and trousers of cool linen. She is half-lying back in the sofa cushions, her feet propped up on the ottoman. She looks across to me and smiles, needing to say nothing, conveying nonetheless a wonderful serenity. She is exhausted.

For that too is Maria, Maria at rest, Maria at home. Nor was that her only, or even greatest, surprise. I remember the afternoon she told me her age.

Maria and I had just emerged from a protracted series of private dances. For the most part we had the parlor to ourselves, and Maria, perhaps a little sleepy, let herself utterly relax in my arms. I was far from sleep myself, but lost in a dazed reverie, my hands playing lightly and appreciatively over her silken shoulders as she wriggled barely perceptibly in my arms. It was hardly a dance, even by Maria's standards. She nestled her face into my neck, and I lowered my cheek to meet hers, and the delicious contact of cheek on cheek combined with a faintly sweet musk arising from her hairline, and I remember feeling as good as it was possible for me to feel, that exquisite equilibrium between tickling arousal and contentment.

That afternoon, feeling almost drugged by our sustained clinch in the private dance parlor, I led Maria through the beads and back to our table for a restorative drink, perhaps a smoke, and in the course of our ensuing conversation got onto, for some reason, our respective ages. She asked how long it had been since I had retired to Key West, how old I was when I married, when I had my sons. I told her and studied her response, wondering if my advanced age—I was seventy-two—would, despite our considerable recent intimacies, unsettle her. There was no sign of this, but at one point she quieted and looked preoccupied. "Okay, Jonathan," she said. "Tell me how old you think I am." I hesitated, not because I thought my guess might offend her, but aware of how poorly I determined the ages of beautiful girls and women. I knew Maria had gained the perspective and assuredness of a mature woman, but she could also on any given day, in any given get up, convey the freshness of a girl. I knew some women were hurt if mistaken for being older than they were, or even if you guessed their actual age. I was cautiously about to propose "twenty six" but heard myself say "twenty four." "Oh no, Jonathan," she said, her face giving away nothing. "Guess again." I said, "Older or younger?" She said, "Guess again."

Chapter Eighteen

MARIA WAS FORTY-SIX. And while from my particular perspective, that was a ripe, vibrant, wonderful age to be, I was wondrous at the revelation. There was not a line in her face. She had a dancer's petit body, a girl's body. Her little bottom was pert and rounded. The smooth fall of her cheeks, her lovely breasts—nothing had fallen. I don't know what my face registered, but at length I said, "Well, that's remarkable."

Forty six. I have only the fondest, most grateful memory of Maria's revealing this to me, as it was the threshold of her full disclosure of everything most important and true in her life, the foundation on which our lasting partnership could now be built. Yes, Maria was forty-six, born to a Dominican father and a Cuban mother in the slums of Miami. Both parents were mid-teenagers when Maria was conceived, and the father, a boy of sixteen, left Miami and was ever after unheard from. Maria was raised principally by her grandmother and aunt until her mother was old enough and otherwise able to contribute.

Although bright enough in school, she left at sixteen, pregnant with her first child, a boy, now a manager of a convenience store in Del Ray. Two years later, she had a daughter by another father, and she, after a troubled and volatile childhood made her way north to Newark where she was only sporadically reachable. Fifteen years later, she had her third child, a son Julio. Maria had lived on and off for eight years with Julio's father, Enrique, who, Maria related grimly, liked to say "he ran some businesses."

While she did not claim to know the extent of his dealings, she believed he sold drugs while working on and off as a driver for Miami and Fort Lauderdale escort services. Enrique also leased a number of self storage units "filled up," Maria said, "with all kinds of electronics."

"A bad man," Maria said with feeling, "A truly bad man." Although Enrique had moved out of the apartment they shared just after Julio was born, he had stayed periodically—and menacingly—in touch, needing what he called "favors" from time to time. A few times, in Maria's opinion, he was clearly hiding out. Maria had worked at many jobs in Latino Miami, as a clerk in small shops, as a waitress, as a manicurist and hair stylist in improvised salons, as a bar girl and finally a dancer in a number of exotic dance and strip clubs along the Atlantic coast of south Florida. She had over the years developed a gift for saving money and parlaying it into more than livable quarters. For years at a time, especially in the stretches when she managed to slip outside Enrique's orbit, she set herself up in some comfort, established credit, drove reliable cars, and turned herself out stylishly. She also had a passion—and she believed a talent—for designing women's clothes, which she hoped one day she might retail in a shop of her own. The recurring aggravation of her adult years had been that whenever she managed to achieve material stability and a promising rhythm of life, Enrique reemerged, demanding favors, claiming a paternal interest in Julio.

Julio, Maria told me with great force, was the love of her life. He was at present living with his grandmother in Miami, but now that Maria had settled into her routine at Tenderloins and had leased a house on the island, he would come down to live with her. Julio was to start the eighth grade in the fall, and with a sudden, appealing desperation, Maria asked me if I knew anything about the schools in Key West. "If the public schools are not good, I need to find a private." Julio was in a small Christian Academy—"private"—in Miami for which Maria paid thirty six hundred dollars a year. "He is doing well there, and I want to keep that." She looked at me imploringly. "He is a good boy, a wonderful boy."

When I met him a few weeks later, it did not take long to realize that Maria had not exaggerated. Julio was a wonderful boy. Apart from the intense and highly particular experience of my own boys when they were young, a period of life now inaccessibly remote, I had, I realized, very little experience of school-aged boys. In fact, with the exception of my all-male undergraduate days at Yale, my experience, and I believe also my interests, have been canted somewhat to the feminine. I have contended with and negotiated with men all my life, befriending several, but all of my closest, deepest adult relationships have been with women—Elizabeth, Mary Marx, Anya, Katya, and now Maria. The prospect of getting to know and, I hoped, to win the confidence of Maria's beloved son made me feel unexpectedly apprehensive. I tried to remember or even imagine something about boyhood that might be helpful, but came up strangely blank. I asked Maria what kinds of things Julio liked, and she told me, not really helpfully, "everything." I pressed her a little, and she said he liked music, that he was always singing, that he liked soccer and played on his school team. He liked electronic games. I remember thinking this summary was unhelpful. I could not really picture a singing, soccer-playing boy. I could not picture anything to do with electronic games. I could form no picture at all. Because he was Maria's, I assumed Julio would be small and slight.

Julio was neither small nor slight. He was, I suppose, medium height for a middle schooler and sturdily athletic. He had black, neatly barbered hair and clear, beautiful skin, fairer than his mother's. My first impression of his face was imprecise: pleasant enough, something of his mother's feline structure, but with each subsequent look, he grew more distinctive. He was actually a beautiful boy, and he would be a handsome man. I was not sure what his response to me would be—reticence, maybe suspicion, even hostility. His experience of adult males at home cannot have been good. Maria told me Enrique had not been attentive. He accused her of babying Julio and when in bad temper berated him and frightened him. It also occurred to me that I would seem a very old and otherwise odd figure to a contemporary thirteen-year-old boy. He was bound to be protective of his mother, and if he perceived me as any kind of rival for her time and affection, that could only set us in opposition.

As it happened, Julio was and is incapable of opposition. I don't think

I have met another person, man or woman, child or adult, who is more agreeably open to engagement than Julio. Like his mother when she was at home, he was soft-spoken, but he readily and even eagerly met my gaze when I greeted him. I found him neither garrulous nor reticent as we were getting acquainted, but quite deliberate. I was impressed that he took whatever I said to him very seriously, and he could not have been more thoughtful in response. At that time he was approaching his fourteenth birthday. His voice had dropped down from a child's treble but had not quite settled into his adult baritone range. He did indeed like to sing, and his speaking voice had a hum of song in it. He didn't pander, but he made it plain he was interested in me and what I said. I am certain Maria must have described me to him at some length, and I have no doubt she painted a venerable picture, but whatever the preparation I'll have to say I was flattered to be held in such attentive focus by a young man whose personal concerns I could not have begun to guess. In any event I was immediately taken with Julio, and, more unexpectedly, he with me. While the warmth and, in time, substance of our relationship was not altogether unexpected by Maria, it pleased her very much. She liked to watch us interact. It might be anything—working out how to inflate a soccer ball that arrived in the mail, introducing him to crossword puzzles, showing him some chord patterns on the electric piano Maria and I purchased on a whim at Best Buys.

Maria was fiercely attentive to Julio's school reports which, so far as I could tell, were generally strong, his marks adequate to impressive, his deportment and effort warmly praised. Having learned a thing or two about the tricky tension between wanting my own boys to do well and wanting them to take charge of their learning, I think I was helpful to Julio in ways Maria could not be. I could talk to him about what was actually interesting and unresolved in what he was studying. I could ask him challenging questions, reveal my own interest and uncertainties—and mean it. He actually liked to talk about what he read, things that troubled or delighted him in the course of a school day. The routine became endearingly familiar: Julio would drift into the kitchen from his room, scour the refrigerator for a snack, then ask Maria if I was around. "Hey Jonathan, mind if I ask you something?"—and we were off.

One evening not long after he started eighth grade, he brought home an "enrichment problem" his math teacher had handed out to the class. It was actually a problem in logic: how to negotiate successfully a number of desired outcomes in a village where the villagers could only respond "yes" and "no"—and they always lied. Julio and I spent practically every minute between dinner and bed time working out what turned to be multiple effective strategies. Exuberant from our efforts, we made a start on laying out a system that accounted for our right answers. From the kitchen and then from the sofa where she listened quietly, Maria cannot have heard much more than our muttered reckonings and Julio's delighted shrieks, "I get it! I GET it! YES!" That night she emerged from Julio's room after saying good night, and her cheeks were streaming with tears.

Chapter Nineteen

As a type, as a presence, Julio was new to me. Quietly reticent but by no means passive, he seemed completely and unwarily open to whatever he was experiencing at the moment. There was a sweetness in this, although there was nothing soft or effeminate about Julio. Maria strongly sensed this appealing openness in her son, but worried about his vulnerability to bad influences. I felt this too. He would never have asked for such a thing, but Julio aroused in me a powerful urge to protect him, to keep him safe, which was, I suppose, a desire to preserve him as he was.

Julio was quick to extend his affection to all kinds of people, and this, combined with his uncritical acceptance of anybody who sought him out, put him at some risk, I suppose, of falling in with questionable company. This possibility, more than any actual missteps on Julio's part, is what persuaded Maria to withdraw him from the public junior high in North Miami and enroll him in the Christ the King Christian Academy. The school seemed small and benign to Maria when she visited—too small to field teams in most sports, although the school did schedule a few games for a soccer team composed of seventh grade boys and girls.

Maria and I took considerable care to find a suitable school for Julio in Key West. She was relieved to hear that the public schools were held in fairly high regard. The parents we managed to talk to had complaints about the school calendar, about too much emphasis on the state's required achievement tests—FLAT, an acronym which for a time bewildered us.

But there was no mention of gangs, guns, and drug trafficking, which had been a persistent presence in Julio's neighborhood in North Miami.

Although Julio was entering eighth grade, we took a tour of Key West High School, to me a dreary labyrinth of low-slung, functional rectangles. There was nothing assignably aversive about the place, but even in the absence of students and staff, something about the waxy smell of the corridors and the ticking of clocks made me leaden with fatigue. I resisted picturing Julio moving through those corridors—and I think Maria did, too—and soon after we decided to enroll him at Mary Immaculate Star of the Sea School, an inviting sanctuary on Truman Avenue.

A former convent of the Sisters of the Holy Name of Jesus and Mary, the school was now staffed almost entirely with nonreligious, and the student body included few Catholics. Sister Francis Loretto who interviewed us and fielded our questions immediately won Maria's confidence. Everything she told us suggested gentleness, clarity, and order. Mary Immaculate Star of the Sea enrolled children from preschool through the eighth grade, and I asked Sister Francis if she thought it made sense for Julio to attend just for a year. She said that if, after he visited, Julio really wanted to come, he would have a very satisfying school year.

As we expected, she and her colleagues were charmed by Julio's interview. His testing and record were strong, and he was admitted. The fees were more than double those of the little Christian Academy in Miami, and I assured Maria I could comfortably take care of it. As I suspected, she resisted this, preferring at least to try to pay the fees herself, relying on me only if she found herself pressed. I could have insisted—the fees were negligible as far as I was concerned—but I was coming to understand the importance of Maria's assuming full responsibility for Julio's welfare. More than maternal feeling was at work; Julio's presence in the world, his turnout, accomplishments, comfort, and achievements were a kind of a magnum opus for Maria, a higher purpose which directed and sustained her.

And so Julio began his life in Key West. He seemed to me comfortably settled into Maria's little house, and whatever signs of reticence I detected when he first arrived dissolved as he began finding his way around the island on his bike and the new school year began. Maria too seemed more assured and expansive, especially at home, although she typically returned from her shift at Tenderloins exhausted and physically cramped. It was against policy for a customer to see a dancer out of the club, but I would arrange to meet her down Duval Street at the bar of The Bull, and we would hail a taxi to take us to the house. When Julio started at Mary Immaculate Star of the Sea, I started cutting my Tenderloins visits short, in order to provide some adult presence and, if he felt like it, company for him after school.

The arrangement, which we never really discussed or laid out as a plan, worked out nicely. Maria, despite her deft techniques for conserving energy in the course of her club dancing, was increasingly leg-weary and otherwise achy after seven hours' service. She was, as she would point out to me from time to time, twenty five years older than practically all of the other girls. Indeed when she finally retired from Tenderloins six years later, she was, at fifty-two, thirty three years older than the girl hired to replace her.

I don't think my own great age distorted the impression I had at the time that, even in her fifties, Maria was invariably among the most alluring dancers on her shift. And while I cannot account for exactly what dips and bends and adjustments strained her muscles and joints by shift's end, I always marveled how she could keep up the raucous high energy of her banter for so many hours at a time.

Knowing Maria's Tenderloins persona deepened my understanding and appreciation of her quiet steadiness at home. It was not a question of her being the "real" Maria outside the club. She was real enough tantalizingly before you in her sexy get-ups, Cleopatra eyes, and aromatic aura of Night Blooming Jasmine. I felt privileged to be a witness to her extraordinary range. In that regard I don't know that I have ever known any one else who worked harder throughout her waking hours. When, within hours if not minutes of first beholding her, I found myself consumed by love for her, I never imagined I would come to admire her so much.

In the early days of my scholarship I recall noting, but not really taking time to explore, the phenomenon of Invulnerable Types: children born into the most desolate and dangerous circumstances who, despite terrible trauma and deprivations and seemingly without nurture, make their steadily adaptive way through the world. Maria made me think of them—and of the correlation in such types between robust, uncompromised sexuality and personal realization.

Unconventional as it may have been, Maria's and my orbiting about one another at Tenderloins seemed only to enliven and refresh our sexual life together. Again, I was aware of no jealous feelings whatsoever towards Maria's Tenderloins clients. If anything, her experience of so many of them over so many years of her life heightened my appreciation of what she so generously revealed to me. From her early adolescence she had been vigorously sexual. She had lived on and off with a half dozen men before me, three of them fathers of her children. Like every other sexually healthy person I have known or read about, Maria had not let her erotic energy overwhelm her. She was not an addict, of sex or substances. By conventional standards of the past century, Maria would have been considered promiscuous. But in the manner of sexual way-breakers like Edna Saint Vincent Millay, Jospehine Baker, and Anais Nin, her promiscuity lay in her instinctively and confidently holding the fulfillment of her desire above all conventional standards.

From her girlhood forward Maria had done what felt good to her, and nothing had felt so good as, or even much like, sexual excitement. She told me she could remember pleasuring herself raptly at six. Before she had reached menarche she had learned to be wary of predatory older boys and adults, but she had been persistent in her own sexual researches and for years before actual intercourse she had examined and stimulated adventurous playmates and cousins. Temperamentally she inclined to bisexuality—as a teenager and younger woman she had been seduced by and then seduced a variety of women-- but, given her other amorous entanglements at the time, she had never been exclusively partnered to a woman for any length of time.

The responsibilities of looking after her older children and the mounting demands of her various jobs, including ultimately her club work, for a time displaced what had felt to her like a sexual quest. Problematic and volatile as her early sexual life had sometimes been, a certain kind of respectful surrender to sex, had, she believed, guided her out of sordid and even dangerous circumstances into bright and promising ones. Her natural sexiness and striking look had led her quite naturally to what sociologists now call "sex work," and as seamy and commercially crass as some of the dance and strip clubs were, she had registered dramatically in all of them. She had been a stayer, a pleaser, a draw. In the clubs she earned her first real money. She set herself up well, and she saved . The farther ahead she got, the choosier she could be about the clubs she worked for.

In her mid forties she bought a clean, spacious condominium in North Miami. Within weeks she furnished it with a with a flair that made an impression on her mother's family. She leased an immaculate Toyota Camry. She paid for medical and dental benefits for herself and Julio. She dressed stylishly and provided generously on birthdays and holidays. Maria became a respected figure, a marvel, among the Miami Amantes. Were it not for the crime and general instability in her neighborhood, she would not have considered moving away. The schools were poor, but she had found the Christian Academy which, for the time being, she could afford. But the gangs were a daily presence.

Maria was aware of boys and girls younger than Julio—nice children, children whose mothers she knew—being recruited. Some movement, some transition was in play among competing gangs. Maria did not understand it, but there seemed to be a new edginess among blacks and Latinos and Haitians. It had alarmed her when Julio, so gentle and dreamy, was not at all surprised when she questioned him about the gangs. He knew their names. He knew about the Latin Kings and the International Posse, and what his friends said about them and about a boy and girl who had been shot through the head while they were standing in the Ortiz's driveway. She could not tell if Julio was frightened when he told her this. His eyes were always so searching. She was too often afraid for him. She was afraid that in his sweet openness he would fall into a bad crowd. She was afraid that Enrique would take him to bad places, expose him to his foul mouthed friends. She dreaded Enrique's unannounced visits to her kitchen and wished he would disappear.

One morning when she stepped out of her condominium to buy groceries she turned and saw that her steps and the stucco facing beneath her window box had been tagged with graffiti, jaunty interlocking ovals outlined in black, highlighted in electric blue. She took a step back and saw that all the clean surfaces facing the street had been tagged. In an instant, Maria told me, she didn't feel her home was hers anymore. It had been marked, the neighborhood had been marked, she and Julio had been marked by some force, some gang that intended to rule there. Maria went back inside and typed KEY WEST into the browser of her lap top.

Chapter Twenty

THE LAST THING I could have imagined when I fell in love with Maria was that she would bring someone like Julio into my life. I was outwardly unprepared, but in a way I was profoundly prepared. Loved children, children who through grace and attentive care have not been needlessly hurt or frightened, have the capacity to release tremendous reserves of parental feeling on the part of adults they decide to disclose themselves to. This little noted capacity in children does them no end of good. It opens up teachers and coaches, nurses and physicians, family friends and neighbors to a depth and intensity of care that far exceeds anything prescribed by duty and role.

Joining the soccer team and quickly emerging as a standout assured his comfortable standing in the eighth grade. Rather unexpectedly, given his quiet amiability, Julio came to life in the competitive sports he liked to play. The soccer coach, a parent volunteer and former college star, was impressed by Julio's speed and ball sense. In Miami Julio had watched and tried to emulate the way the older boys and men played in the public parks, and he had enjoyed the improvised matches set up for both boys and girls at the Christian Academy, but he was relatively unskilled by the schoolboy standards of south Florida. At Mary Immaculate he was receptive to instruction, practiced hard, and by mid-season was his team's leading scorer. The coach, in breathy elation after a victory over Marathon Key Middle School in which Julio had scored both of the team's goals, approached Maria and me where we were waiting on the sideline. "Mrs. Amante, Julio has got it all. A lot of kids can run, they can advance the ball—but Julio is a finisher. He gets it done. You can't teach that."

I too had begun to note that quality in Julio, a heightened intensity when challenged to demonstrate what he could do, an impressive assurance—grace—in competition and in performance. Years ago I had followed my younger son Chappy's soccer career with an intensity bordering on obsession. Chappy too had been a star, playing not only for his school but, during the summer, on Olympic development teams. Chappy had been a pleasure to watch—I still conflate his flying down the sideline on a breakaway with an image of our golden retriever, just freed of his leash, bounding at a dead run along the shimmering shore of Lake Michigan. Chappy had been lanky and angular. He wore his blond hair long, and the wind would flatten it to his temple as he glided past. His footwork was subtle, almost dainty, and he seemed to take a dancer's pleasure in his practiced feints and passes. But while I am not an expert observer of soccer, I could sense that Julio was indeed a finisher in a way Chappy never was.

And so it happened that I became, in my seventies, a familiar figure on the sidelines of Key West soccer fields, at first the endearing, well scuffed pitch of Mary Immaculate Star of the Sea and then, for four years, the eternally luxuriant synthetic turf of Key West High School, Home of the Conchs. Not just at the high school, but in Marathon, the upper keys, and even up to such rarified preserves as The Ransom Everglades School in Miami, I made my way faithfully, often a car length or two behind the bus, to watch Julio and the Conchs play soccer. Maria, although quietly bewildered by soccer, would come with me when she could, but her Tenderloins shifts coincided with most afternoon games. I know she was appreciative of my attention to Julio's play, but in truth I looked forward to those dreamy, watchful afternoons alongside the thudding turf. It was a little as if I were watching Julio take flight. I took discreet care to keep a distance from the other soccer families, although we had inevitably and for the most part genially become acquainted. I can only imagine who they thought I was, perhaps a grandfather or an old uncle. When obliged to, I would, while shaking hands, exhale my name and, when I felt it was necessary, add "family friend." Julio was not at all reticent about introducing me to his friends and team mates. "This is Jonathan," he would say. "He's part of our family." I don't think there was anything considered in Julio's identifying me in this way. It was for him an honest assessment.

Chapter Twenty-One

WHEN MARIA AND Julio moved into the house in Key West, there was quite a bit of discussion about how household and school routines would be managed in light of Maria's shifts, which at first she referred to only as "work"—"I have to leave for work by twelve," "I will be working Saturday this week." I assumed that since Maria had worked in clubs since Julio was born, they had reached an understanding that she did not discuss the nature of her job. But Julio did ask her, openly and frequently, what she did and where the place was and could he ever go there. Maria's response was firm but not overly defensive. "Mama works in a club where grownups dance and get together. Mama's a hostess there. I meet the people and make them feel at home. I'm on my feet all day long." Julio wanted to know if it was a place we could go to eat, and Maria told him it was not, there was really nothing for kids to do there, which was true enough and seemed to satisfy Julio for the moment. Maria was careful, I noticed, not to mention the name Tenderloins in the house, and Julio was instructed to call her on her mobile phone when he needed her.

I do not really know if Julio regarded his domestic life as unconventional. His mother was not married, and his father, an infrequent and troubling presence in his early life, lived elsewhere. His older half-brother and half-sister lived away. He had not seen either of them since he started school in Miami, and in his memory, they had been distant and grownup, preoccupied and unavailable to him. He had not felt as close to them as he did to his grandmother and her sisters and their husbands or even the friends who frequented his grandmother's house in Miami. Throughout his high school years in Key West, I could sense a heightened interest when anything about his brother or sister came up, but I could not tell how much more he wanted to know of them, whether he was troubled by their absence—or that he had no other brothers and sisters.

And then I had come into his life, a nice, bony old man with white hair and white clothes, a gringo whom his mother cared for. I slept in his mother's room from Monday through Thursdays, then retired to my condominium in the Annex for the long weekend, although on those days I was as likely to spend time and dine with Julio and his mother as when I stayed the night. My condominium was conveniently on Julio's way to the beach and just two short blocks from his favorite stops on Duval Street, and in the course of his school years he became my most frequent weekend visitor, chaining his bike to the rail of my front porch, more than a little interested in soda and snacks. He must have known I was financially comfortable—the three of us dined out at least twice a week, I provided most of his pricier athletic and electronic gear—but I doubt that it ever occurred to him that I was rich.

Wonder about it as I might, the concern about my presence in Julio's life was generated by me, not him. It was I who had been imprinted from birth with the notion of the intact, wedded, nuclear family, although my own had been far from inviolable. Julio had not been so imprinted. He had grown up into a hive of expressive, warmly nurturing Amantes. The reliable ones, the necessary ones were all women. As an infant he had to some extent blurred the distinction between his mother and grandmother. His earliest memory, he told me, was waking alone and stomping on wobbly legs through his grandmother's duplex in search his Mama or his Baba to gather him up into their perfumed warmth, his inexpressible happiness in finding them. He loved his Baba and his Mama--and in a different but no less essential way, he came to love me.

I am certain that if in my pundit days I had been aware of what I learned in the course of tending to Julio, my work would have taken an altogether different course, perhaps composed in a different—more welcoming, less didactic-- voice. Prior to Maria and Julio, my sustained musings had turned on metaphysical matters: relation of thing to thing, the fit of phenomenon to system. My success as a writer had been due to a certain clarity and freshness in illustrating general patterns of behavior with particular, easily recognizable actions. I had a knack for analogies. But my allegiance in this was to the integrity of the larger system, to logical and observable consistency—"truth." And while this allegiance carried an authoritative weight, especially with high cognition readers, it also marked my work with a certain coolness and distance. Responding to Julio helped me to get past this—and to a far more compelling realization.

Julio revealed to me the secret that bedeviled Freud into proposing the Oedipus Complex, giving rise to a still proliferating jungle of Attachment and Object Relations theories. Julio, while virtually fatherless as an infant and younger boy, had not formed or been drawn into a father-complex; he had not compensated. He had formed no father obsession, no aversion, fabricated no idealized replacement. He had not formed a sexual identification with his mother. He had been periodically upset and even frightened by Enrique's unpredictable appearances in his early life, but he had not been damaged; there had been no arrest, no fixation. And while he proceeded through his adolescence vigorously and adaptively and with what seemed to me limitless creativity, he did reveal—reveal, not suffer from, not succumb to—what I can only call a father-void.

To be merely analytical about this—the old reflex-- befogs the realization that Julio's father-void was a preexistent and perhaps universal male condition. Void, hole—these are analogies, but perhaps words needn't fail. The condition, the void, has a shape, and it is the shape of what we are trying to say when we say father, but we don't know what that shape is and what our word for it means. We impose onto the void the presence of whoever assumes that name in our particular experience, most typically a biological father, often a quite serviceable father, a figure the child is encouraged to distort further into the culturally normative father, wise and strong, reliable provider, the father who knows best. For Julio it could have been, perhaps nearly was, Enrique, but that did not happen. Sufficiently stressed or under-stimulated or frightened, he could have stuffed a symbolic figure--a demon, a hero, God-- into the father- void. But that did not happen either. Sweet-natured, accomplished, loved and loving, Julio carried his father-void forward into his adolescence benignly intact.

Gradually, gracefully and, I believe, quite consciously, Julio began to fill that void with me. This is not for an instant to say I became his father. I was no more his father than Enrique was his father. Nor is it to say I was a father-substitute. As I have said, by grace and by the love of women, Julio had not needed Enrique, and for that reason needed no substitute for him. What Julio allowed me to do, and it was an unbroken joy to do it, was to enter and begin to fill his father-void. It began with my simple attention to what he chose to disclose to me, then attention to his performances at school, his sketches, his soccer games. What was at first a tentative willingness to show me things, let me to help him, and share tasks grew into a sturdy mutuality.

What I learned—it was as much feeling and cognition—was the transformative power of paid attention, attention uncorrupted by any need to instruct or inform or improve: mere presence, loving witness. I experienced something of this sitting in silence beside Elizabeth in the final hours of her life. I may have caught a glimmer of it when Chappy was six or seven and, slow to read, would lean into me as we sat on the little sofa in our den in Evanston, as he mumbled over the syllables of his phonics enriched primer. I remember checking the impulse to correct, praise, comment. I sensed that what he needed from me was my presence, the receptive bulk of my body against his, his awareness that I was looking over his shoulder. Paid attention—at its unselfish, purest best it is like sunlight on plants. I felt it in a certain kind of rapt yet unintrusive attention certain parents revealed watching their children compete and perform. I had reviewed the studies indicating that children whose parents read to them, dine with them, spend some specified amount of clock time with them tend to thrive better than other children, but such studies, necessarily thinned and sanitized by the protocols of social science, could not begin to address the quality of the transmission and reception of transformative paid attention. Adults who love children uncritically, whose love is not bestowed but drawn helplessly out of them by the sheer presence of their beloved, sense the power and the rightness of their paid attention. Children no doubt feel it too, without a thought to naming or attributing it. It is, again, like sunlight.

Julio was appreciative that I could play the piano by ear, and we taught each other songs we liked—a very peculiar assortment of which I grew deeply fond. In this mix were a half dozen Cuban ballads and quirky dance numbers the Amante women had taught him when he was little. There was a similar number of haunting, extremely repetitive songs Julio told me were "neo-alternative." These, despite their primitive structures, I found strangely hard to learn, and the digital piano did not really produce an evocative accompaniment. The songs I taught him, which must at first have seemed to him Martian in their oddness, ranged from the Depression lament, "Buddy, Can You Spare a Dime," to Gershwin and Porter standards I loved: "How Long Has This Been Going On," "Embraceable You," "Easy to Love," "Blame It On My Youth." To my delight—and to his mother's wonder—he mastered them easily. Julio sang beautifully, audibly but softly, just above a whisper, enunciating with a fascinating precision.

For his fourteenth birthday I bought him an acoustic guitar, and I managed to retrieve enough chords and picking patterns from my college days to get him started. Within a year he had surpassed anything I had been able to manage on the instrument, and we found him a teacher in Marathon. Of the many unexpected pleasures I took in Julio's company, none was sweeter than evenings sitting quietly in Maria's living room, listening to him sing and play to himself behind the closed door of his room.

Chapter Twenty-Two

I CANNOT THROUGH WILLED recollection recreate the texture of time passed with Maria and Julio. The images I call up are not quite frozen, not as still as photographs, but nonetheless static, shot through with the sadness of loss. I come back to the solitary vigils on the soccer sidelines, celebratory feasts afterward on the terrace at Mangoes, our airy drives north to drop him off at Baba Nina's for the weekend.

Maria had fretted about how to manage Julio's continuing relationship with her mother. Julio had always been a favorite, and the comfort and nurturance he had experienced among the older Amante relations had been formative. Nina did not drive, and there wasn't room for her to stay comfortably in Maria's bungalow, so it was determined that at the conclusion of the soccer season, I would drive Julio to North Miami in Maria's car, absent myself to South Beach where I would read, take the sun, and walk the sweeping, hard packed beach until it was time to pick him up on Sunday afternoon.

Inevitably I was a puzzling figure to Nina in the course of our initial meetings, but Maria had prepared her somewhat, and in time a guarded cordiality softened into a relaxed acceptance. I arrived and departed when I said I would, I was courteous, and I did not impose myself. I also liked Nina very much. She was a broader, heavier woman than Maria. She was in her sixties when I met her, although if Maria hadn't told me, I would have guessed younger. She was at any rate considerably younger than I was, but the closer we became, the more maternal—to me—she came to feel. I was glad to contribute something to her bond with Julio, who positively looked forward to his Miami visits. I believe Maria would like to have visited her mother more often, but she was rigidly fearful that Enrique might learn she was about and insist on making contact. Maria was at this point adamant about keeping Enrique out of Julio's life, and since it had somehow been established that Enrique was not welcome in Nina's home—Maria said that Nina and the older Amantes had always intimidated him—my services as chauffer served everybody's purposes.

The drives themselves were an unhurried pleasure. Sometimes on the way up and always on the return trip we would stop at a Dairy Queen or hamburger stand for a snack. Julio was in those days famously, bottomlessly hungry. If traffic was light, driving over the longer stretches of bridgework created the agreeable illusion that the car was airborne over the open aquamarine. I remember enjoying myself, feigning a fogy's exasperation at the zombie-sounding "neo-alternative" selections Julio was nonetheless eager for me to hear on his iPod.

Chapter Twenty-Three

IN THE SPRING of his junior year at Key West High School, Julio experienced a jolt which, in addition to upsetting Maria, he refused to discuss with her at all.

To her utter bewilderment, Maria was called into the principal's office where, in the presence of a guidance counselor, Julio's soccer coach, and his English teacher, she was informed that Julio would be suspended from school for two weeks, for fighting. I had trouble crediting this.. I had not heard Julio raise his voice in anger, with anybody, about anything. Very occasionally when I was first getting to know him, something would sadden or worry him to the extent that he would cry, but he seemed to have hardened against that vulnerability. But fighting--? I could not imagine Julio engaging in a fight. But apparently he had fought with a boy in the senior class, had, according to the principal's account, sought out the other boy at his locker, and without seeming provocation—the boy he struck claimed he had said nothing—punched him hard on his cheek bone near his eye. The blow had knocked the boy to the floor, and his cheek, despite the school nurse's application of ice, was swollen and bruised.

Maria was frantic with concern. I was not part of the meeting, but I am sure Maria would have been shrill. Her son was not a fighter. Why would he do such a thing? The guidance counselor suggested she ask Julio. Julio apparently had little to say. He was upset but undisclosing. He did not deny hitting the boy. Pressed to tell why, he said and repeated several times that he didn't want to talk about it. And so that afternoon Maria and Julio, both stricken, entered the house through the kitchen door. Neither spoke to me as Julio proceeded to his bedroom and closed the door behind him. Maria had cancelled her shift at Tenderloins. She was tearful, miserable. I could make no sense out of the account beyond that the blow had indeed been struck and that Julio was suspended from school. District policy mandated suspension or, if the seriousness of the offense warranted it, expulsion for fighting. Maria stood at the counter. Her speech was thick. "He will not tell me why. He won't talk to me."

The gloom of Julio's days sequestered at home felt like an extra presence in the bungalow. Barefoot in rumpled shorts and tee shirt, he slouched low over his breakfast, then returned to his room where, against the faint throbbing of what I presumed was his neo-alternative, he presumably attempted to keep up with his schoolwork. After what must have been a week of this, I took the opportunity, after Maria left for Tenderloins, to draw him out. I had no wish to be therapeutic. I wanted only to make contact, check in. In this my prospects were better than Maria's. I felt no need whatsoever to judge what he had done, and actually, whether Julio sensed it or not, I felt little need even to understand it. I suspected—rightly, it turned out—that he was starved for contact. He had succeeded in isolating himself, but he did not know the way back.

I believe I said something as open-ended as "how are you doing?" He said something in response, and it occurred to me how I could reach him. I told him I hoped he knew that if he was ever in trouble, he wasn't in trouble with me. I told him I had no idea why he did what he did, and he had no obligation ever to tell me. I told him I just hoped he was all right. He was quiet, but he was listening. I told him, "If there's anything you want to tell me about what happened, it's between you and me. That's a promise."

Julio said, "I don't know what I can say without making it worse for everybody." I was so surprised and glad he spoke that for a moment I did not make sense of what he had said. I asked him what he meant by "worse for everybody." He said that if he told everybody what he had heard and why he wanted to punch out the kid who was saying it, then everybody

517

would be talking about it, and it would be ten times worse than it was in the first place. He was opening up. I asked him what would be worse, and he looked away. Then he turned to me and said, "Jonathan, can you really not tell anybody this, anybody, especially Mama?" I told him I would not.

Julio told me what happened. He was leaving the cafeteria with his friend Freddy Kirchner. Freddy said he had something to tell him, something that he just heard, something bad. Julio wanted to know what, and Freddy said that some kids were saying his mom was a hooker. Julio wanted to know what kids were saying this. Freddy didn't want to tell. He said, "Just kids." Julio told me he got really mad at Freddy until he named one boy, a senior, a boy Julio said he barely knew. He couldn't get the boy's face and what he said out of his mind, and he went off to find him. Julio named the boy, Ed Francken. He went to Ed Francken's locker and he was there, getting books out for afternoon classes. Julio said he heard he was saying things about his mother. The boy said he didn't know what Julio was talking about, but, Julio said, he was being a jerk and he didn't believe him. Julio said he grabbed Ed Francken's shirt and slammed him up against the lockers and told him to say it to his face. The boy told Julio he wasn't the one who started it, he just heard it. "It's just what people are saying, ask anybody," and Julio punched Ed Francken's face.

I said, "So you had a reason," and Julio said, "I guess." He looked miserable. He said, "The kid also really is a jerk." I said, "You didn't think that if you told people what he said and why that hurt you, they would understand?" Julio looked exasperated. He said that if he told the counselor or the principal what happened, they'd talk to the kid, and he'd say everybody knew about it, everybody was saying it, and then it would be ten times worse. I was about to ask Julio— clinical reflex— why it would be worse, but I checked myself. I knew. I knew exactly. In fact this reckoning on all of our parts was overdue. Maria was not a hooker, but she was a Tenderloins dancer, technically a sex worker. The distinction would have meant little or nothing to Julio, who did not know precisely what his mother's job was, only that it was something she had long ago established was not to be discussed. Julio had accepted that at thirteen, instinctively closing the door to further consideration.

I think Julio and I came to the realization at the same instant: he did not want to know. He did not want to know what a hooker was. He did not want his mother to be whatever a hooker was. He could not bear that his mother was being spoken of as a hooker, that kids were saying, hearing, passing on what he himself could not bear to bring clearly to mind.

Julio said, "I wish I was done with school. I wish I already graduated. I hate it."

Then the clinical reflex did take over, but it was all right. I told Julio I didn't think he hated the school, just what had happened there. I told him that I felt for him, that I could see how it would feel to hear something like that about his mother. I wanted to say his wonderful mother, his heroically loving mother, his mother for whom at that moment I was feeling such helpless, angry love. And then I had it—Francken. Eddie Francken was one of the managers of Tenderloins. Eddie and Hugh. Eddie was a likable, easy-going bear of a man. He looked to be in his forties, maybe fifty. His son could well have been Ed Francken, and one way or another—it made me tired to think—he could have learned that Maria was Julio Amante's mother. Amante, the hot shot jock, the kid the girls thought was so cute.

I looked into Julio's eyes until he turned away. For a minute or two I was held in what felt like the inescapable weight of his unhappiness. I wanted to say something clarifying, something at least reassuring and soothing, but I couldn't. I could not tell whether I wanted Julio's or my own discomfort to lift. I said, "Julio, listen to me. This is going to pass. Things like this always pass. You got put in an impossible spot, but let me tell you one thing, one thing I know for sure: your mother is not a hooker."

We never discussed it again.

Chapter Twenty-Four

The ensuing wound or scar, as it turned out, was much deeper for Julio. Some time in the course of his tenth grade year he had fallen in love with a classmate who had recently entered the high school. She was Penny Rugg, a coltish, cheerful girl with an easy, comical smile and an appealing fall of long, straight blond hair. She was an athlete, a distance runner. Her parents had moved to Key West when her father was assigned to manage the Hyatt resort complex on the Front Street Marina. I had been aware of an easy, seemingly low-voltage camaraderie with Julio's team mates and other school friends, but before Penny, no girl had been specifically named, much less brought forward to meet.

Julio and Penny were unmistakably, stirringly fond of each other, and in a few weeks they became a steady couple. Julio was periodically invited for dinner at the Ruggs, evenings which he recounted with characteristically cheerful vagueness as "really nice." The Rugg's house on Caroline Street was also "nice" and "pretty big." Occasionally Julio brought Penny in to look over images he wanted to show her on his computer sketch pad, or for sessions that were mostly talk and laughter in which Julio would try to teach Penny certain runs and chord progressions on the guitar. So far as I could tell, they were comfortable together, reflexively hushing their voices in acknowledgement of the smallness of the bungalow. I liked having them around.

Maria was gracious but restrained in Penny's presence. I don't think she resisted Julio's attachment to her, but I sensed she lacked confidence in this dimension of her parenting. She was satisfied, I believe, that Penny represented no harm to Julio, but something in Penny's confidence and familiarity elicited a guardedness in Maria. For her part, Penny could not have been more ingratiating in getting to know us. I overheard, and I'm sure Maria did too, Penny's "...so beautiful"—clearly her appraisal of Maria—as she and Julio proceeded down the front walk after an early visit. It is less clear what she made of me—uncle? elderly family friend?—but she was unfailingly warm and cheerful in my company.

It probably should have occurred to me before Julio's suspension from school that Maria's detectable reserve in Penny's company was generated by a fear that any kind of genuine personal disclosure would be damaging. At the heart of this was, I am certain, a deep, unexamined feeling of unworthiness. Abstracted from others, most fully herself, looking hard into my eyes as we made love, Maria exuded a great strength. But away from home, outside the warm cluster of Amantes, as a mere citizen, customer and consumer of goods, Maria was less sure of herself. At her doubtful worst I sensed that she felt marginal, unwelcome, disreputable. Professionally, her brassy and commanding extroversion had been an inspired, and perhaps exhausting, defense. At times her high Tenderloins humor gave her away: Hey, whatsa matter, honey? You no like the little skinny-ass Latino broad today? Penny, long and lithe, blond and white, utterly unaware of the unattainable entitlement she represented, shamed Maria.

Not long after Julio completed his suspension and returned to Key West high School, Penny began receding from his life. The process was gradual but determined. Penny became unavailable for casual time together out of school, then for more formal outings, including, finally, their prom. We saw Penny a few times in the course of their disengagement. She was as cheerful and appealing as ever, but she had apparently determined to change course. I could not bring myself to ask Julio if the unsavory rumor about Maria had played a part in the rift. I suspect it did. I am also certain, given the power of her intuition, that Maria sensed she was at fault, which wore on her punishingly.

For weeks Julio was bereft, beyond reach. I was interested that he and Penny did not stop communicating altogether. With no specific purpose or proposal, he would occasionally call her, and I suspect there were text messages and emails, but nothing was rekindled.

The parental—or in my case in loco parental—response to a child grieving the loss of someone beloved is to fear that he will lose vitality altogether, fail to thrive. There is merit to this fear. Hurt badly enough, all kinds of children fail to thrive. I remember feeling that Julio was too young to express his unhappiness creatively, but to my astonishment he did. Out of our awareness, behind the closed door of his room, he scanned onto his computer a favorite image of Penny's face—the brink-of-laughter smile that I had found so comically appealing—and transferred the image to his digital sketchbook tablet where, in a series of modifications, he altered her mouth, her eyes, color, and shading. The most dramatic alterations produced an image that, while distinctive, would not by itself have been recognizable as Penny. In the end there were twenty 8" by 11" images which Julio had managed to back with firm cardboard. They were tacked side by side and spanned the entire wall above his computer monitor. They commanded attention from where he sat at his desk, from his bed, and upon entering the room. I remember feeling on first viewing that he had caught something irresistible in Penny, that the very images which least resembled her contributed something essential to the whole. I said something as mindless as, "My God, that's Penny," but I should have said "That's more than Penny" or, better, "That's Penny that never ends." Julio had printed a tag and tacked it beneath the centermost picture. It said TWENTY PENNIES. He took the pictures with him to college, and, when we last visited, they were lined up behind the sofa in his Atlanta apartment.

Chapter Twenty Five

In the course of his coming of age, Julio and I drew lovingly close. Undoubtedly his presence tapped into some not yet exhausted biological parental reserve, but I believe something even better, some fusion of grace and good will was at work as well. Again, my great age seemed to work in my favor. I was too old, too settled, too final to want or need anything from Julio. My happiness with him lay in sheer witness. He had from the onset engaged and interested me. Without any deliberation I found myself his uncritical advocate. I knew enough not to be intrusive or smothering, although I did worry about him, in the futile way parents worry about their children in the face of unseen, ambient perils—car accidents, accidents generally, illness, cruel treatment, heartbreak. To love parentally is to suffer, but if the love is sufficient the suffering may be borne with grace.

The last thing I would have wanted is to create any dependency or sense of obligation in Julio as he made his way out into the world. I do not believe I did. The closest I came to that kind of encroachment was being for a time unhelpfully ambitious for his college selection. On a number of counts, Maria was troubled by the prospect of Julio's departure to college. It was her fierce intention that he go, but the fact of such an extended, and ultimately permanent, separation overwhelmed her. She was relieved to defer all college considerations to me. And in the event the passage felt strangely familiar, thrusting me back into long unvisited memories of

Elizabeth and my boys when they were finishing high school. I was still savvy enough to know that Julio's ethnicity and the combination of his arts and athletic achievements would make him an attractive prospect at the very best colleges. His grades were more than respectable. In the back of my mind I knew I was not above playing the Jonathan Force card. I let myself imagine Julio at Yale, although I was aware that contemporary Yale—coed, egalitarian, technologically and otherwise transformed—would bear only a ghostly resemblance to anything I had known.

To my mind Key West High School had been, if not often inspiring, more than satisfactory for Julio. It had kept to business and kept him safe. Due to some quirky interests of the staff and through an enormous grant, the school had put together a nationally recognized program in T.V. production. Julio, who on his own had made himself adept at digital imagery, exhausted the program. His college guidance counselor recommended, on the basis of Julio's demonstrated interest, that he apply to the University of Florida's program in Digital Arts and Sciences. What research I could manage indicated that the program was rich beyond my powers of assessment. And while something—something conditioned and brittle—drove me to make a case for getting out of Florida, experiencing a new, stranger world, in time I realized that in this too I was talking more to myself than to Julio. For him Gainesville would be as alien and wondrous as Palo Alto or Evanston or New Haven. And if it were to some degree less so, the easy access to the Miami Amantes and to us would be welcome compensation.

Rather as I suspected, Julio flourished in Gainesville. Because he was virtually an only child when I met him and I had observed him so seldom at school and in the company of his Key West friends, I assumed, mistakenly, that he inclined to dreamy solitude. Seemingly on arrival on the campus, he was taken up into dormitory life and then, still more mysteriously to me, the hive of his fraternity. He found his scholastic feet quickly as well. His unclouded, unfearful receptivity to new ideas energized him to undertake what I would have thought to be tedious and, in a few instances, remedial work—his high school math training, in particular, proved to be superficial. But once grounded in the requisite language, he proceeded nimbly and creatively through what to me was a bewildering array of technological challenges. For two summers before his graduation he was a paid intern for a network television station in Atlanta where he worked with a digital graphics team, and through contacts he made there was offered and accepted what seemed to us an impressive position as Director of Digital Productions for the development office of Emory University.

He seems to me at ease and comfortable there—but when was Julio ever not at ease? He speaks well of his job and colleagues at the university and seems even more enthusiastic about a project he and a friend started in Gainesville, a film, *Undocumentary*, about undocumented residents in North Miami. When he tells me about his film work, I can see how certain of his boyhood qualities continue to serve his creative interests. He is a generous collaborator, a natural networker. He shares work-in-progress with anyone he thinks might have an interest or a suggestion. He is eager for criticism. He seems to me at once visionary and strangely unhurried. I don't think I'm alone in finding his approach and his projects irresistible. I sensed in him nothing of the encyclopedic compulsion that had driven me as a young man.

Chapter Twenty-Six

I SUPPOSE OUR DEEPEST communion occurred in the course of guiding Julio through a succession of books I thought he would especially enjoy and that would augment his high school studies. One of the first things I noted about him as a middle schooler was that he was a reader. Even on routine car errands to the laundry or the supermarket, Julio would bring along his library copy of Lord of the Rings. Neither Franklin nor Chappy had been similarly inclined, and I was charmed. Except not to discourage it, Maria appeared to have done nothing to promote a bookish tendency in her son. I asked him how he heard about Tolkien—he had already read The Hobbit. He said "some kids" at his old school who liked the Harry Potter books told him Tolkien was really good. I remember commenting that some great writers thought that liking Tolkien was a sign of superior literary taste—I did not specifically mention Auden, but I did pass on his famous verdict that children who read Tolkien would go on to become real readers.

As it happened, Julio would prove Auden's point. I remember becoming alarmed and then indignant that the freshman year English program in the high school seemed to include no literature whatsoever. I raised a question, I believe courteously, at the Parents Open House, but was told with what I felt was annoying assuredness that the ninth grade program was dedicated almost exclusively to writing, although in the spring term, when the emphasis would be on expository writing, some exemplary essays and other non-fiction would be read.

I was less troubled by what seemed to me straightforward wrong headedness on the part of the high school English faculty than I was that Julio's early pleasure in imaginative literature might flicker out. I spent some time scanning what were currently claimed to be exemplary literature curricula--which only increased my anxiety that Julio would lose all interest in books. The American Library Association's recommended titles were, to the extent I could sample them, heartbreakingly barren, transparently self-conscious efforts to advance the era's conventional wisdom about what is good for children in a better world. The dominant themes—multicultural understanding, tolerant acceptance of all differences, resilience in the face abusive upbringing—were faultlessly humane, but the rendering was at once timid and gratingly righteous, worlds away from anything that would carry Julio away.

I reverted to memory. Although I was a year younger than Julio when I first read it, I was certain that he would be moved by *The Diary of Anne Frank*, and I was right. As I suspected, he had been taught nearly nothing about twentieth century history, so it was necessary to lay out a few things about anti-Semitism in Europe, the First World War and the rise of Hitler and the Nazis before describing the Frank family's particular situation in Amsterdam. He began reading the Diary dutifully but was soon engrossed in it, reading, I could see by the yellow stripe of light beneath his bedroom door, well into the night. "Jonathan," he told me as he sat down to breakfast, "I finished the book. It was amazing." I pressed him for particular impressions, and, still a little sleepy, he struggled to respond. Finally he said, imploringly, sadly, "She was just so nice." Then he asked me if there were a lot of people like the Franks, people who had to hide in other people's houses. Before I could answer, he asked me if people had to hide like that in the United States. In explaining why that was not the case, I realized how much he would have to learn in order to have even the most basic context in which to place the enormity of something like the holocaust. My head began to swim with the rudiments of the crash course in western civilization I might devise for Julio, but I stopped myself. The manic, encyclopedic attempt to correct my own ignorance of history had been no more than an anxious defense against feeling worthless. I can still summon up that dread. It was not something I wished for Julio, and there would be no crash course.

There were more books, though, and these I am sure served him better. Browsing in the stacks of Xanadu, a new and used books shop on Southard, I found a copy of Elie Wiesel's little memoir, *Night*. Julio had finished *Diary of Anne Frank* just a few days earlier, and I was convinced that the way to build on what had so moved him was not to fill in historical background but to offer another vivid witness. I had forgotten how slight *Night* was, and I read through nearly all of it when I stopped for coffee on the way to the beach, where I finished it under bright sun. Something like a mental clout made me sit up straight. There was, I realized, every possibility that Anne Frank and Elie Wiesel may have beheld one another at Auschwitz. The Wiesels arrived in June of 1944. Elie and his father were still there when the Franks got off their train in September. I know the sexes were segregated in the camp-- but at a rail siding, or on inspection or marching in file to get supplies? It would not have been impossible. The fifteen year old Anne and the fourteen year old Elie even shared a look, something penetrating and knowing in the set of their eyes. I could picture their locked gazes.

Julio was moved but also troubled by *Night*. I knew in passing it on to him that he could not help but identify with the young narrator. Julio was precisely Elie Wiesel's age when the Germans arrived in his village in Hungary. Like Julio, Elie had been a vulnerable and dreamy boy, lost not in Tolkien, but in esoteric Jewish lore and practices. Except to ask me to clarify the European geography of Elie's odyssey through the camps and to ask what phylactery and beadle meant, Julio seemed to be darkly and vividly at home in *Night*. He finished it in a day. He told me, "I kept wanting it to be only a story." He asked me to confirm that the book was a true account, that those particular events had really happened, that there had been such people. He wanted to know, beyond what was included in the summary paragraph on the back cover of the book, how Elie Wiesel had managed after he was liberated, since his father and mother were dead, and he was still only a boy. I think I was right not to give him, or even recommend, Wiesel's subsequent memoir, *Dawn*, as I was concerned that Julio could perhaps use a lift.

Catcher in the Rye is hardly a lift, but it is warm, and it conveys as perhaps no other boy's book does, a healing appreciation of the vulnerability of open-hearted children. It turned out to be a balm to Julio, as more than a half century earlier it had been a balm to me. I didn't bother to explain that Holden's unselfconscious language and tentative sexual explorations had caused the book to be banned from many schools and libraries—before it had become a scholastic staple.

Apparently, however, the Key West High School English faculty had decided that the book's appeal had waned, as it was dropped from the required canon in favor of more culturally far-reaching titles. Thus from his sophomore year forward, Julio brought home and dutifully read the likes of *Kafir Boy*, *The Kite Runner*, *The Awakening*, *Their Eyes Were Watching God*, and *The Color Purple*. I do not think he was much moved or changed by any of them. On the other hand, *Catcher in the Rye* went deep, and because it had been a gift, warmly endorsed by me, it came to represent, I think, a kind of brotherly affinity between us. Its appeal, it seems to me, lies in the inspired, wildly oblique gestures Holden uses to convey his tender inner condition, which is why the book is hard to talk about in the ordinary way. The very act of paraphrasing—reducing—such riffs and reveries into conversational language subverts the book's intentions. Standard literary or psychological analysis always finally fails to explain the impact of truly great stories, because such stories, like jokes or Zen koans, are their own irreducible explanations. Or so, at one time, might have said Jonathan Force.

Julio read Catcher in the Rye with an intensity it was possible to feel in the room, and when he finished, the bond between us, without either of us having to say anything, had deepened. He did comment memorably, however, that "J.D. Salinger must be amazing."

Julio wanted to know if he was still alive, and I told him yes, adding what I knew about Salinger's famous reclusivity in New Hampshire. "It's incredible he can do that," Julio said, referring back to the story. "Like he actually knows me." I reminded him of Holden's tribute to the writers he liked best: that he wanted to call them up right away on the phone. Julio gave me a thoughtful look and said, "Doesn't sound like J.D. Salinger would like that." I said, "But maybe if Holden called..." Julio considered for a minute, smiled, and said, "That's right."

Our reading bond may have been, if anything, more important to me than to Julio. For one thing, I felt I felt I was passing along something fine and durable—and also, to be completely honest, something I knew he would always associate with me. Perhaps the egotism or vanity in this served a useful purpose, because it carried with it a powerful incentive not to break what seemed to me a kind of spell by offering Julio a merely improving or mildly diverting book.

I felt it would be a mistake, also perhaps impossible, to follow up *Catcher in the Rye* with a similar text. Night had served well enough as a companion piece to *Diary of Anne Frank*, but there would be little possibility of replicating the depth of connection Julio had experienced reading *Catcher*—and every chance of spoiling it. Late one night during my freshman year at Yale I disclosed my feeling for *Catcher in the Rye* to my room mate Chad Pickering, nicest of boys. He immediately pulled his school copy of *A Separate Peace* out from his book shelf and urged me to read it. I doubt I would have cared much for *A Separate Peace* in any circumstance, but reading it with the expectation that it might open up some of the feeling conveyed in *Catcher in the Rye* ignited a response close to outrage. Wrong! False! I was angry not just at having to contend with what I felt were patchily rendered, uncompelling characters, but that John Knowles had even presumed to set up on what Salinger had for me made hallowed ground.

I was about to say the next book I gave to Julio was an inspired choice, but I can recall no inspiration, not even deliberation. It simply occurred to me with great clarity that Julio should read *The Old Man and the Sea*. I remember wishing there were a way for him to read the tale without regard or subsequent thought about Hemingway, all of whose other work I found mannered and embarrassing. I gave Julio *Old Man and the Sea* one afternoon when he came home from school. After supper, he took it with him into his room. The next morning he told me he had come out to the living room to find me, but we had gone to bed. He said he had read the story without stopping and felt he had to talk about it. Finding the house quiet and dark, he went back to his room and read through the book again from the beginning. At breakfast he said to me, "Best book I ever read." He told me about reading it twice. I asked him whether, as he was reading it, he felt more like the boy Manolin or old Santiago. He did not hesitate. "Santiago. It's all about Santiago." I pressed him: "But he loses everything, he fails." Julio gave me a hard look. "He didn't fail." Julio gathered his thoughts and said, "He had it, he caught the fish, and then things he couldn't control took over. He gave it everything. He was great." "So it's not a sad story?" I said. "It's not sad-sad," Julio said, "it's great-sad."

After he left the house for school I could not stop imagining him making his way through his classes, his head full of Santiago tethered to his great fish, the sharks in annihilating pursuit. I went into Julio's room, picked up the little paperback from the night stand. I made myself comfortable in the living room and read it through, twice. If Maria had stopped to ask me a question or if I had had to answer the phone, I do not believe I could have spoken. Something deep in my interior was urging the question I had asked Julio, and with every successive page it was clearer to me that I was experiencing the story as Manolin, not Santiago.

In the spring of his senior year, with his departure to college looming, I wanted to give him a book that would shine the brightest light on his interior and if possible ease his passage out of the island. Since the high school had not assigned one, I thought about giving him a Dickens bildungsroman, perhaps *David Copperfield* or, even better, *Great Expectations*. Julio was still susceptible to bouts of melancholy over losing Penny Rugg. I thought it might be nice for him to experience Pip's love of Estella. But something about opening up the fussy complexities of that era and that story, however wonderfully rendered, seemed too artificial, too self conscious a "project" at that moment in our lives.

Instead I gave him a Herman Hesse's *Narcissus and Goldmund*. I cannot think of a better world in which a boy on the brink of leaving home might lose himself, especially a boy with an artist's disposition and a lover's heart. Julio had acquired a reasonably broad cultural reference, due entirely to his reading and explorations into the lives and times of the artists he admired, but the school's curriculum and the enveloping presentism of the age combined to leave him with what even a generation earlier would have been thought a primitive understanding of history. I felt I should tell Julio a little about the middle ages, monasticism, and the Black Death, but I doubt now that it was necessary. Hesse himself admitted to having set the tale in a highly romanticized medieval world in order to slip under the defenses of readers who had been threatened by the hallucinatory modernism of his *Steppenwolf*.

Narcissus and Goldmund struck something deep in Julio. He did not try to finish it all at once. He seemed even to be savoring it, but there was a restlessness about him for the week or so that the book took hold of him. Maria, having at one point looked through the introductory pages, was bewildered. "What is it about?" she asked me with some concern. I told her it was about a boy growing up and finding his true nature. Maria was by no means a non-reader, and she had responsibly and quite touchingly read into, if not always through, the books Julio seemed to care about. No doubt due to Hesse's rather florid scene setting as the story begins, Maria could see no point of entry into that cloistered world.

Julio experienced no such resistance. To my mind he was so like Hesse's Goldmund, I could not resist asking him, when he had read a few chapters, what he thought of Brother Narcissus. Julio had said, "Well, he's obviously the smart one." I told him to hold onto that thought and to tell me who seemed smartest at the end of the story. Julio never did tell me that, but midway through the novel, he did tell me he thought it was strange for Herman Hesse to have titled the book *Narcissus and Goldmund* when it was really all about Goldmund's life and adventures. Again I asked him to hold the thought.

Anything at that time—a romantic movie, a popular love song—was likely to stir Julio's still tender feelings for Penny Rugg. You had only to look at him, sit at the table, share a car ride with him to know. I felt there was a good chance that reading about Goldmund's many lovers and dalliances would stimulate Julio to work through his melancholy. If so, he kept such thoughts to himself, although he did remark at one point that

Goldmund "loved everybody" and that "he couldn't help it." He meant "loved every woman."

The observation, however, knocked me off balance and set me on a course of thought and remembrance that preoccupied me for days: loving every woman, not being able to help it. It seemed inescapably the case that this had become my own condition in late life. My youth and manhood had been nothing like that. I had not adventured, wooed, and seduced my way through the world. I could not have been less a Goldmund. In fact, from my undergraduate days forward I had become something very close to Narcissus, Hesse's renunciate scholar. I was sixty when all of that fell away. Sixty. Until then, I had generated little more than words and thought, subordinated my very vitality to words and thought, to the point that I wasn't quite embodied, not embodied as I had been as a boy, as a hunter, a climber—and yes, as a lover. Once I had loved everybody, and I couldn't help it. I had gathered irresistible romantic love from the very air, from the scent of lilacs, the plush of sumac, from the hungry yearning burning feeling of song, from The Chocolate Soldier and every other confection of my childhood. I had without self consciousness or reserve loved my sister Annabel, Gwendolyn Bliss, Linda Bluestone, Patsy Prentiss, Ceci Long, Elizabeth Meeker. There might have been no end to this loving, and I might have been Goldmund incarnate had it not been for—what exactly? I could say: the majesty of culture, but from my perspective now that seems utterly unconvincing, somewhere between a lie and a joke. The truth lies more, I now think, in how my tentative adolescent self bowed before the majesty of culture: timid, ashamed, and worthless. And how, out of sheer, benumbed dread, I scrambled to become Jonathan Force.

Sixty! And then it would take the call of women. Loving all of them, being unable to help it. It took Tenderloins—

And now what is this—disconnected, like an image on a screen, coming apart, voiding—something electric in my brain—no, no electricity—and I can't swallow. I can't--All right, then, this is it, this is—no, not yet, just a glitch, a hiccup along the way. I will rest.

Chapter Twenty-Seven

It was a gratifying sign of Julio's maturity, his increasing tendency to take charge of his own affairs, that without further consultation with me, he saw fit to get hold of Hesse's other novels on his own. He could easily have ordered them on line, but I think because he knew I had found *Narcissus and Goldmund* at Xanadu New and Used, he went there in search of the other titles, causing, by no means incidentally, the last great upheaval of my life.

"Jonathan," he had said quietly after dinner, "How come you never talk about the books you wrote?" It was like cold water to the face. I hovered for a moment between dread and anger. "My books?"

The clerk at the desk in Xanadu had been none other than Gerald, the bibliophilic owner of the store. In the course of chatting about Hesse, Julio mentioned that he had gotten hold of *Narcissus and Goldmund* from a certain man, an "old friend who gives me all my books." This alone may have piqued Gerald's interest—I had always assumed he was homosexual—although it is also possible that he remembered me in the store when I purchased *Narcissus and Goldmund*. In any event at some point Julio indicated my full name. Gerald apparently pumped Julio for enough details to determine that I was indeed the Jonathan Force of the Force books. "He told me you are a really famous writer," Julio said. I could picture Gerald, hear his voice purring, "So your book providing friend is the great Jonathan Force."

"I Googled you," Julio said. "I never did that before. There are millions of entries." I told Julio in the most offhand way I could that there were millions of entries about everything on the internet. I was concerned that we not confuse Maria. I did not want her to think I had kept essential things from her—although of course I had. Julio met his mother's eyes and said, "He's written a lot of well known books." I said, to Maria, "I wrote a few books, and quite a while ago."

It was hard to tell what Maria made of the disclosure of my books and possible celebrity. She knew, because I had told her, that I had worked for years as a psychologist outside of Chicago and that I had once done a lot of speaking. Her interest in my life prior to Key West had seemed to me appropriate. She had mainly wanted to know the general contours, where I grew up, had my parents stayed together, did I have brothers and sisters. The North American Amantes had not gone to college—Julio would be a way-breaker —and while Maria was respectful enough that I had gone to universities and earned degrees, I really don't think she set much store by it. Almost nothing about academic life had touched her world, and she was understandably more concerned that I had sufficient means to look after myself, that I had been reliable, that I showed up when I said I would, provided what I said I would provide. Maria had always been most interested in the veracity of my impressions of things—if I said food at a restaurant was delicious, that it was delicious. If I thought a dancer at Tenderloins was striking, that Maria found her striking as well. And as it happened, my impressions were invariably confirmed by hers, and she had come to trust me. Of all her lovely endearments, none made me happier than her admission to me, not long after we became intimate, that "I have never felt this safe with anybody."

It is still difficult for me to assess what effect, if any, Julio's fuller awareness of my past has had on our relationship. I know him well enough to know that he read into the books with wide open intent. He would weigh and consider. He would—I can feel his effort—struggle to integrate impressions of what he read with his accrued experience of me. He was already capable of working through the logic, and he would have had endless questions, but having sensed at once my aversion to talking about the books, he conducted his researches on his own. I was relieved that his outward manner with me was unaffected. He seemed no less comfortable. I did note that the only books he took with him to Gainesville were the Hesse novels and the Force books.

I wish I had been able to take some kind of pride in that. The truth is that I did not want Julio, or really anyone, to think of me as a person issuing forth what now feels like a suffocating avalanche of elaborate, unassailable certainties. At its dubious best, my work offered a closed, known world. Julio, even before he turned the first page of *The Hobbit*, was well on his way into an open, infinitely surprising world, a world I knew once, the other world, the real world.

Chapter Twenty-Eight

Julio could not possibly have known that his casual conversation with Gerald at Xanadu New and Used would lead to The Signing. It was in no way his fault. I had, after nearly three years of joshing demurrals, softened to the proposal. I don't think it was vanity, although in the quirky way of such matters, it was in part an affectionate bow to Maria's vanity. I was absolutely certain that she had not penetrated two successive pages of my published work, but in time, no doubt stimulated by things Julio told her about the books and what he had learned about my place in the larger world, she started nudging me, as she put it, to get myself out there. At that time at least half of our social acquaintance in Key West was composed of present or former Tenderloins staff, the other half a handful of agreeable neighbors, restaurant habitués whom we had befriended over the years, and musicians we liked—and who would kindly let me sit in from time to time at the piano. These were hardly people whose pulse would quicken to know that they were now in the company of a highly regarded theorist of behavioral causation. In fact, nothing was more likely to slow and stiffen what were usually lively, funny and bibulous gatherings with our friends. Nevertheless, Maria would have liked it if, when explaining to people who I was and what I did, I might mention that I had written a book. To Maria, to have written a book was roughly equivalent to having appeared on television or in a film. In a faintly glamorous way it set me, and by extension her, apart. "You look like you have written a book," she told me once. She meant my clothes.

And then Gerald proposed the signing, an event he would advertise throughout South Florida. He would stack his tables with signed copies of my books. There would be cheese and wine. I would give a short reading, and then, seated comfortably—he promised—I would be on hand to greet readers and perhaps write a personal inscription in their books. He invited me to consider the illustrious islanders who had preceded me in Xanadu signings over the years: Hemingway, Tennessee Williams, Elizabeth Bishop, John Hersey. The evening proposed was of course the last thing I wanted to do, and I did my best to be gracious in declining whenever Gerald renewed the invitation. I suppose it would have been easy enough simply to stop patronizing Xanadu New and Used, but I really enjoyed browsing and sampling there, and it was directly on my morning errands and coffee circuit. Fatefully, I mentioned the proposal one evening to Maria, and she lit up with pleasure. There was the teasing smile—halfway to Tenderloins—and she said, "You know, I have a new outfit."

THERE WAS NO POINT FINALLY in husbanding any negative feeling about a two or three hour to-do at Xanadu, and since Maria was so touchingly eager to be part of it, I let my resistance go. As is always the case in anticipating such things, I visited the possibility of nobody whatsoever turning up, or, even worse, a depressing handful who would want to linger. On the other hand, the event was scheduled for Friday evening—Good Friday, no less—and Key West was brim-filled with tourists. Who knew. We would in any event have a lovely late dinner afterwards on the terrace of Mangoes.

I was gathering my thoughts in the living room of the bungalow as Maria finished putting her self together—she would be spritzing her lovely brown throat and décolletage with Night Blooming Jasmine-- when I was aware of a distinct darkening of the atmosphere. It was not yet six, but I turned on a lamp and moved to the window where I could see blackened clouds clustering low overhead. There would be—

Very bad now—breaking, breaking up again. Like this, will it be like this— I will—rest

Chapter Twenty-Nine

Must report that I am shaken, unable as before to sink below this terrible surface to get all the way back—but I know where we were going. To Xanadu New and Used, on Southard. In a cab, we were in a cab, because of the rain. The rain had come fast, and it was warm, at first fatly plopping and then lashing the pavement. All the cabs, all the pink cabs of Key West were being called, and I remember almost laughing out loud at the likelihood--after *three years* of negotiation-- that old Jonathan Force would not make the mile and a half journey to his farewell signing. *Farewell*—that's not me that night in the rain, in the cab, that's me now.

Breaking up—

The rain has stopped and the sky is now portentous. Dazzling light breaks through the black clouds making the wet pavement, the car hoods gleam. Everybody is out, some umbrellas still ballooning even though the rain has stopped, and the people, so many people they are spilling over the curbs onto Duval. They are moving, marching with great purpose, moving it seems faster than our cab which is now locked in place, stopped still. A block or so past Truman Maria and I decide to get out and walk the final blocks as it is nearly seven, and I am due to read something to whatever Forceans there might still be in south Florida. I want to recall walking—I want to walk—but in this wretched fracturing of thought and image I can't get myself out of the cab, looking at the throngs on the Duval sidewalks. It occurs to me that all of them, on both sides, are walking in the same direction. Like me, they are doggedly heading for Xanadu New and Used. I see--am I imagining or remembering this—that they have gripped in their fingers, clutched to their hips a book, two books, three books of mine. I recognize the bright, tell-tale orange of the jackets, the orange-yellow Random House told me leaps to the buyer's eye. Are they all marching to the signing, all of them, everybody we see, everybody in Key West? Maria and I do not make rapid progress on the side walk, we are pressed in close to others, unable to side step and pass—but no, I am back in the cab, still in the cab. Like an aggravating dream. Did they all have their Force books at their sides. I am holding Maria's hand to keep her tethered to me as we nudge and cajole our way forward up the wet street. We reach Southard at last and the throng turns with us, continues with us, carrying us as in a current straight into Xanadu, where the talk is almost a roar, and there is no room, and people are standing even in the rows between the folding chairs set up for the reading. It is warm, too warm, and a little damp in the store, and then I catch Gerald's eye, and he pushes forward to greet me, and I am concerned for Maria who seems so small and crushable in this press of bodies. I can barely hear. I can impose no order in the room. I hold Maria's hand—

I am holding Maria's hand— or just was, sweet, beautiful Maria so sad and full of me, nothing but me in her beautiful, stricken face, all eyes, sad, dark round eyes, and how ample and full she is, holding my hand at the side of my bed. She is talking to me, but there is no sense in it, no more to say, no more than the clasp

WHAT HAPPENED THERE AT XANADU—ALL of this is breaking up—I must have read, I am there, standing, crowded into a corner before the bare, scuffed podium. I must have read, spoken. I am standing there and Gerald has somehow gotten people into the chairs and standing behind the chairs and craning their heads to hear back in the stacks, and there is a murmur of voices in the crowded doorway and out on the walk. I must have read, and I must have signed and inscribed books, because I am seated at last, so leg weary, on my folding chair and greeting person after person, inscribing what they ask me to write to themselves, their children, husbands, Jamie, Chris, the Sturdevandts, somebody's greatest teacher—and there, like sunshine, like such a clout of happiness, is Julio. Julio has come down from Atlanta. Maria must have told him. He doesn't press himself forward. I spot him leaning against the book-lined wall, and he is smiling at me when I look up from my inscribing, smiling at me, knowing, I think, how glad I am and—what's this—what's he wearing. He's wearing a white suit, a white suit. He's dressed up like me! I can't wait—

Julio here too, I see him, just see a trace of him, standing behind Maria and the nurse, peering in the doorway. Have I already seen him, spoken to him, drawn him in close. Why don't I know—*all this is breaking up*. Aggravating. *No*—it was not Julio, it was Chappy, there was both Chappy and Franklin, and we spoke. I looked so hard into their eyes, we spoke, and when was that? Did they speak with Maria? God, everything so fractured, brightly present before me, then gone, but Chappy and Franklin were at the bed. My god, their man faces, their settled, strong man faces, like granite, even their good smiles, such *strength*, but that's just me, having none. I want their faces back, can't sink below any more and find them, bring them back, their good faces, and now Franklin's hair is receding, making his face even sharper, like a sharp rock, such a beloved face to me, Elizabeth so much in that face, in the sharpness—*Elizabeth*. My god, there was all of that, all of the boys, all of *everything*. And now there is only breaking up and there will be nothing more than breaking up until it all voids out-- which in a way I have already experienced. Everybody sees this, everybody at the end. If only people could know. If before it happens they could know the enveloping enormity of the feeling, so much more than crying. The most momentous, convulsive crying is only a tiny vestibule to this feeling of knowing, knowing but not in any way having, all the beloved people. People and *places*, rooms even, sun light blanching a patch on the carpet, *light*!

Wasn't I sitting there signing all those books? I was, I was. Sitting in the filmy fluorescence of Xanadu, dark outside the glass now, twenty or thirty people left in line and Julio, back against the fiction wall, standing by Maria. They are waiting for me to finish. I am sitting there at my table, legs stiff from the stillness. I am being courteous, but I am getting punchy and a little vague, and I remember the feeling of working, of writing at my desk, the agonizing pauses, feeling a physical strain down my neck and into my shoulders as I nudged and prodded a proposition into its proper conjunction. The strain of that--my lightheaded spent feeling now—all of it nothing but *resistance*, all of it bearing against the good, given current of my being.

Why did I do that? Did I have to do that, do we have to resist? It's what the mind does, the discerning mind, but the strain of it, the deadening negation. I didn't resist at all, I never resisted when I was a boy. I did not. I climbed, and I tunneled underground, and I foraged through the tufted, limitless fields beyond Palatine with my hatchet and knife. I entered *with no resistance* into every romance I was given, into Tarzan and The Chocolate Soldier. I understood *The Call of the Wild* perfectly, I felt it. And I loved those girls, Gwendolyn, Linda, Patsy. So why did I resist? Did I ever decide? There was always resistance *outside*, but I knew that, accepted that. Fear and danger made me resist, my father cracking me in the head made me resist, the slow, clock-ticking enormity of classrooms was resistance itself, but when did I *decide* to resist myself, to become a part of it? Was I too weak, too cowardly? I was, I must have been, or is everybody? Maybe we are made, like me, incapable of foregoing the prizes, too ready to bow before the majesty of culture. Can anyone resist the seductive smugness of navigating nimbly through the artificial preserves of a long organized body of knowledge, something that sets up proudly under a banner like History or Science or Literature? I couldn't, didn't. Nor can I blame Palatine, the schools, Yale, culture itself. What are they but the accumulated barricades of resistance against wild vitality? To which fortification—until I was *sixty*—I dedicated more than forty years of my life, my gift to the Resistance no less than *Force Fields, The Uses of Force, Reasonable Force*.

No. The problem is bigger than culture. A biologist or a physicist would step back and take a broader view. From the perspective of Nature, with its prior claim to majesty, culture is something of a parvenu, erratic, mutable, a joke. Resistance, including succumbing to it, is natural, inevitab—*breaking fucking up*

NATURE DOOMS US--ALL RIGHT, LIMITS us--to a discreet, particular, ultimately inconsequential trajectory out into sheer, lethal, forces of resistance. The resistance is material before it is cultural. To live at all is to erode and to corrode. To live to a good old age is to corrode monstrously. No poetry necessary to convey this, just physics. Sylvia Plath—*breaking up*—she said love set you going like a fat gold watch in her poem, but she must have been talking about girls. Love sets boys going like meteors, like rocket ships but send them into an atmosphere and they combust in the resistance. Love, mindless, incalculable Eros sets us going all right, and we are marked with it, feel its tickle and urging life long. If we are reckless and brave we let it rip even as we corrode and combust. Thank you at least for that. A holy matrimonial thank you to Elizabeth, my dear love. Thank you, Tenderloins. Thank you, thank you, thank you, Brandy, Mandy, Brianna, Lexi, Tracy, Lacy, Sandra, Miranda. Worshipful thanks to Anya, Karyta. My monumental and not quite finished thanks to my beloved Maria. Perhaps I could not duck the resistance. At any rate I did not. But, my Makers, there was the beach! And there was Tenderloins! And if I could rise from this bed and walk, I would head straight back! Because I am—*christ this is it...*

JULIO'S FACE, FOR A MOMENT just Julio's face above me over the bed. Just his face like a moon. But really there. Julio, a man now too, but still his open boy's face. He is talking to me but there is no sense. I wish I could speak. Perhaps I did. Julio, eyes like his mother's. He is saying this to me, down close to my ear, Jonathan, you are the man. Did I hear it? I must have heard it. I try not to think about it. I don't need to think about it—but I want to tell him, did I, I so hope I did tell him. Julio, you are the boy.

I wanted to tell him. I want him to know

Fomite

A fomite is a medium capable of transmitting infectious organisms from one individual to another.

"The activity of art is based on the capacity of people to be infected by the feelings of others." Tolstoy, *What Is Art?*

Writing a review on Amazon, Good Reads, Shelfari, Library Thing or other social media sites for readers will help the progress of independent publishing. To submit a review, go to the book page on any of the sites and follow the links for reviews. Books from independent presses rely on reader to reader communications.

For more information or to order any of our books, visit
http://www.fomitepress.com/FOMITE/Our_Books.html

Nothing Beside Remains
Jaysinh Birjépatil

The Way None of This Happened
Mike Breiner

Summer on the Cold War Planet
Paula Closson Buck

Foreign Tales of Exemplum and Woe
J. C. Ellefson

Free Fall/Caída libre
Tina Escaja

Speckled Vanities
Marc Estrin

Fomite

Off to the Next Wherever
John Michael Flynn

Derail This Train Wreck
Daniel Forbes

Semitones
Derek Furr

Where There Are Two or More
Elizabeth Genovise

In A Family Way
Zeke Jarvis

A Free, Unsullied Land
Maggie Kast

Shadowboxing With Bukowski
Darrell Kastin

Feminist on Fire
Coleen Kearon

Thicker Than Blood
Jan English Leary

Fomite

A Guide to the Western Slopes
Roger Lebovitz

Confessions of a Carnivore
Diane Lefer

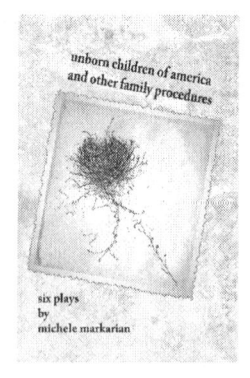

Unborn Children of America
Michele Markarian

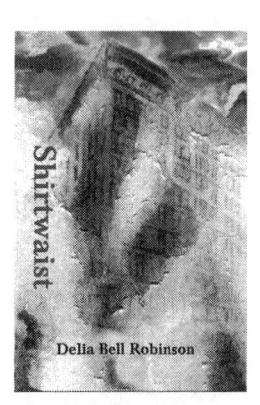

Shirtwaist Story
Delia Bell Robinson

Isles of the Blind
Robert Rosenberg

What We Do For Love
Ron Savage

Bread & Sentences
Peter Schumann

Planet Kasper Voume 2
Peter Schumann

Principles of Navigation
Lynn Sloan

Fomite

Industrial Oz
Scott T. Starbuck

Among Angelic Orders
Susan Thoma

The Inconveniece of the Wings
Silas Dent Zobal

Fomite

More Titles from Fomite...

Joshua Amses — *Raven or Crow*

J Joshua Amses — Raven or Crow

Joshua Amses — The Moment Before an Injury

Jaysinh Birjepatel — The Good Muslim of Jackson Heights

Antonello Borra — Alfabestiario

Antonello Borra — AlphaBetaBestiaro

Jay Boyer — Flight

David Brizer — Victor Rand

David Cavanagh — Cycling in Plato's Cave

Dan Chodorkoff — Loisada

Michael Cocchiarale — Still Time

James Connolly — Picking Up the Bodies

Greg Delanty — Loosestrife

Catherine Zobal Dent — Unfinished Stories of Girls

Mason Drukman — Drawing on Life

Zdravka Evtimova —Carts and other stories

Zdravka Evtimova — Sinfonia Bulgarica

Anna Faktorovich — Improvisational Arguments

Derek Furr — Suite for Three Voices

Stephen Goldberg — Screwed and other plays

Barry Goldensohn — The Hundred Yard Dash Man

Barry Goldensohn The Listener Aspires to the Condition of Music

R. L. Green When You Remember Deir Yassin

Greg Guma — Dons of Time

Andrei Guriuanu — Body of Work

Fomite

Ron Jacobs — All the Sinners Saints

Ron Jacobs — Short Order Frame Up

Ron Jacobs — The Co-conspirator's Tale

Kate MaGill — Roadworthy Creature, Roadworthy Craft

Tony Magistrale — Entanglements

Gary Miller — Museum of the Americas

Ilan Mochari — Zinsky the Obscure

Jennifer Anne Moses — Visiting Hours

Sherry Olson — Four-Way Stop

Andy Potok — My Father's Keeper

Janice Miller Potter — Meanwell

Jack Pulaski — Love's Labours

Charles Rafferty — Saturday Night at Magellan's

Joseph D. Reich — The Hole That Runs Through Utopia

Joseph D. Reich — The Housing Market

Joseph D. Reich — The Derivation of Cowboys and Indians

Kathryn Roberts — Companion Plants

David Schein — My Murder and other local news

Peter Schumann — Planet Kasper, Volume Two

Fred Skolnik — Rafi's Tale

Lynn Sloan — Principles of Navigation

L.E. Smith — The Consequence of Gesture

L.E. Smith — Views Cost Extra

L.E. Smith — Travers' Inferno

Susan Thomas — The Empty Notebook Interrogates Itself

Tom Walker — Signed Confessions

Fomite

Sharon Webster — Everyone Lives Here

Susan V. Weiss —My God, What Have We Done?

Tony Whedon — The Tres Riches Heures

Tony Whedon — The Falkland Quartet

Peter M. Wheelwright — As It Is On Earth

Suzie Wizowaty —The Return of Jason Green

Made in the USA
Middletown, DE
27 August 2016